HALLDÓR LAXNESS

World Light

Halldór Laxness was born near Reykjavík, Iceland, in 1902. His first novel was published when he was seventeen. The undisputed master of contemporary Icelandic fiction, and one of the outstanding novelists of the century, he has written more than sixty books, including novels, short stories, essays, poems, plays, and memoirs. In 1955 he was awarded the Nobel Prize for Literature. He died in 1998.

INTERNATIONAL

Also by HALLDÓR LAXNESS

Independent People
Paradise Reclaimed

WORLD LIGHT

HALLDÓR LAXNESS

*Translated from the Icelandic
by Magnus Magnusson*

Introduction by Sven Birkerts

VINTAGE INTERNATIONAL

VINTAGE BOOKS

A DIVISION OF RANDOM HOUSE, INC.

NEW YORK

FIRST VINTAGE INTERNATIONAL EDITION, OCTOBER 2002

Library of Congress Cataloging-in-Publication Data
Halldór Laxness, 1902–1998
World light/Halldór Laxness; translated from the Icelandic
by Magnus Magnusson.
[Heimsljós. English]
p. cm.
ISBN: 0-375-72757-4
PT7511.L3 H413 2002
839'.6934—dc21
2002024994

Book design by Mia Risberg

www.vintagebooks.com

Printed in the United States of America
10 9 8 7 6 5 4 3 2 1

INTRODUCTION TO HALLDÓR LAXNESS'S

World Light

BY SVEN BIRKERTS

The first, and possibly main, thing to be said about Halldór Laxness's *World Light* is that it is a surpassingly strange novel. Strange as in exalting, eye-opening, and sense-refreshing. But certainly strange. The book fits on none of the usual grids. It cannot be assimilated to the categories of psychological novel, or social, or historical, or philosophical, or, quite, spiritual; certainly it has elements of all. Neither is it an old style *Bildungsroman,* though in its presentation of a life in fairly distinct "stages," it owes some debt to that form. It does not create a strong dramatic arc, avoiding most strategies whereby tensions are gathered toward resolution, creating instead its own unique terms and procedures. Nor does it have as its core preoccupation the exploration of human relationships. And though it features as its protagonist an individual with a strong visionary aptitude, it does not ascend, except in isolated—wonderful—bursts, into the realms of higher seeing; it remains quite closely tethered to the inhospitable ground surface of its Icelandic setting. *World Light,* more than almost any novel I can think of, declares itself *sui generis,* summoning readers with its call to independence.

Moving in on the novel from a distance, we can first try to place it in the context of the author's career. Halldór Laxness, the undisputed giant of Icelandic letters, was born Halldór Kiljan Guthdjónsson in Reykjavík in 1902, and began to publish early—a privately printed love story, *Child of Nature,* appearing when he was just seventeen, followed in short order by stories, a novel, a treatise on Catholicism, a collection of essays, and poems, all before his thirtieth year. In the decade of his thirties, Laxness would produce his monumental saga, *Independent People* (1934–35), various stories and essays, a play, and then, in 1937, first issued in four separate volumes, *World Light.* Dozens of works of all descriptions followed decade after decade, including *The Fish Can Sing,* representing the more directly lyrical turn of his late career, which was published in 1957, two years after the author was awarded the Nobel Prize in Literature. Many of these works have not been translated into English and remain inaccessible to this reader. But the point is obvious: *World Light,* like any of Laxness's works we may wish to single out, is but a boulder in a rockslide, one small part of what might be seen as a compulsive lifelong quest to fix a world to the page.

Yet for all that, there is nothing that feels rushed or *ad hoc* or partial about the novel. It possesses an almost glacial mass and solidity, and unfolds in an atmosphere of such pre-electronic stasis that the present-day reader may feel she has been removed to a counterworld, a place of the imagination where everything happens differently, where scarcely any news of modernity has reached. How odd it feels when we encounter, as we do, once or twice, references to the telephone or to airplanes, reminders that the world of the novel might be more or less contemporaneous with novels by Virginia Woolf or D.H. Lawrence.

Laxness's narrative of the hardscrabble and ultimately (at least from the outside) tragic life of Ólafur Kárason is based, at least in part, on events and episodes from the life of one Magnus Hjaltason Magnússon, an Icelandic folk poet (1873–1916), including Magnússon's abandonment by his mother, his long childhood illness as well as the extreme deprivations he endured, his tormented marriage to a grasping, manipulative epileptic woman, and his prison sentence for the sexual violation of a fourteen-year-old girl. But if the Magnússon story activated Laxness's imagination and gave him a scaffold of sorts, his mission was less to re-create the life than to use the solitudes and encounters of that life to help him body forth a whole culture, the world of tough-luck villages and remote farmsteads, and to play variations upon some of his favored themes, like the isolation of the creative imagination, the deep-rooted struggles between the forces of labor and capital, and the all-transforming power of the spiritual encounter.

The four books of *World Light* can be seen to represent the four essential stages, or passages, in the life of Ólafur Kárason, taking him from the damaging indignities of his boyhood in the rural isolation of the oddly named Fótur-undir-Fótarfæti, into the isolation and romantic and poetic questing of his young manhood in the village of Sviðinsvík; through the demoralizing entrapment of marriage and the abrasions of political and moral struggle in the conflict between union-activists and owners that transforms village life for a long period; bringing us finally to his public disgrace, trial, and imprisonment, all of which destroy the frail structures of his life and pave the way for his tragic romantic transfiguration. But while movement from our first introduction to our last sighting—the poet walking out to his certain death on the vast glacier—can hardly be called happy or fulfilling, the paradoxical triumph of the novel is that the reader nevertheless feels throughout the ennobling and redeeming force of the spirit.

This redemption is manifest for Ólafur—and the reader—both as a sense of mystical union, experienced over and over through the poet's encounters with the beauty of the physical world *and* in his periodic seizures of creative inspiration. And this last points to what is probably the greatest liberty Laxness has taken with his source material. For folk poet Magnússon was by all accounts regarded as a second-rate versifier, hardly a vessel for the Northern Muse. But whatever the objective quality of Ólafur's verses—the cited examples don't make the case for greatness—the visitations he experiences have a Rilkean intensity and integrity. The author, so fond of mocking his characters, protagonist included, is dead earnest in depicting the shuddering inrush of inspiration. It renders all of Ólafur's real-life travails temporarily moot.

* * *

World Light opens with great vividness and compression. The boy Ólafur, who will come to seem to us as solitary as any character in literature, the works of Beckett included, is seen standing by himself on the shore of the bay of Ljósavík. Within a few pages we have grasped both his situation and his character. A dreamer, drawn to the distant promise of books as well as to the immediate solace of his natural surrounding, Ólafur is ridiculed and ritually abused by the rudely unreflective members of his adoptive family. His mother, who is still alive, had him sent away from her in a sack while he was still a baby. He has been taken in less out of kindness than in the vain hope that he will grow up to be a useful worker on the homestead. Life at Fótur-undir-Fótarfæti is bitter, at near-subsistence level—"sometimes the evening meal was only pickled tripe and milk"(5)—and Ólafur, frail as he is, can do little to pull his weight. He lives in corners and crannies, hiding from the blows of his two thuggish "brothers," his inconspicuousness belying the fierce intensity of his inwardness, which battens onto whatever scraps it can—cautionary stories told by his stepmother, the few books and pamphlets he comes across. From these paltry influences arises his ambition: "Often the boy was overwhelmed by an uncontrollable yearning to write down in a hundred books everything he saw, despite what anyone said—two hundred books as thick as the *Book of Sermons,* whole Bibles, whole chests of books"(7).

Then there is the matter of his spiritual susceptibility. Not yet nine, he is described as having mystical encounters worthy of one of the Desert Fathers: "He would be standing down by the bay, perhaps, in the early days of spring, or up on the headland to the west of the bay where there was a mound with a rich green tussock on top. . . . Then suddenly he felt he saw God's image open before him. He felt the deity reveal itself in Nature in an inexpressible music, the sonic revelation of the deity; and before he knew it he himself had become a trembling voice in a celestial chorus of glory"(10). At times Ólafur seems to be a splinter of the extraordinary wedged into a world driven forward by the most limiting natural exigencies.

Humiliated by his family, divided within himself by their conflicting claims on him, brought to the breaking point by the tension between his inward sense of things and the unyielding crudity of his circumstance, Ólafur collapses into his long infirmity—the nature of his illness is never clear, not to the family or the reader—taking to his little bed under the eaves. Here, mostly ignored, reviled from a distance, he retreats into a kind of waking coma, a condition of extreme life deprivation interrupted only by the arrival, for a time, of an old man named Jósep, with whom he discusses the glories of poetry and the Icelandic sagas before the old man dies, and the sporadic visits from Magnína, the poignantly obese daughter of the house, who surreptitiously reads to Ólafur from the one precious book in the house, *The Felsenburg Stories.*

Laxness, so generously lyrical in scenes of spiritual encounter, can also render the near-absolute stasis of Ólafur's confinement: "This boy had counted the floorboards and the joints and the planks in the clinker-built ceiling more than a thousand times . . . He knew every single knot in the ceiling and the floor, and every single nail, and how the rust from the nails had stained the wood" (71). We can scarcely believe that anything will ever change. But always, when the limits of the tolerable have been reached and exceeded, comes rescue: "Then suddenly Magnína came up the stairs, brought out a worn book from under her apron, and sat down on the edge of his bed" (71).

The subtle art of the first section is to persuade us of Ólafur's absolute estrangement and to prepare the ground for the various strange transformations that will follow in succeeding sections. Soon enough the family will give up on the useless invalid, whose illness is regarded as sheer laziness by the vicious brothers, and he will be sent away to burden others.

The first book closes with several fateful encounters, a phrase which is to be taken quite literally, for Ólafur's life, like the lives of characters in myth and legend, is in a sense nothing *but* a sequence of fateful encounters.

At one point, not long before his departure, the family celebrates the wedding of Jónas, one of the brothers. The house is full of guests. Ólafur, abed as ever, listening to the noises downstairs, suddenly discovers that there is a young woman in the room with him. This is Jarþrúður from Gil, who for some reason—poor health, it appears—is avoiding the festivities. Her exhausted indistinctness is vivid. Ólafur "had to examine her carefully to make sure she had any appearance at all. Youth had faded from her cheeks and her eyes were brownish and moist like seaweed . . ." (90–91) But Jarþrúður seems to be a young woman of some sensibility, and as they converse, she somehow manages to extract from Ólafur the promise that he will one day marry her, a promise that will become one of the terrible manacles of his later life.

Then, one day soon after, the mysterious "escort" Reimar comes to

take the young man away. The destination is unclear. Indeed, departure is thrust upon Ólafur like some arbitrary stroke of fate. The boy is
so weak that he has to be carted away over the mountains and through
the rocky valleys on a stretcher. But Reimar, who will play a crucial
messenger role at novel's end, has a plan. He brings him to Þórunn of
Kambar, a beautiful, provocative priestess figure who lives with her sisters at an isolated farmstead. There, with incantations and the laying on
of hands, Þórunn miraculously restores Ólafur to health, gives him
back to the world, though that world will prove for long years to be
but the shambles of an isolated fishing village.

The second book begins with Ólafur's arrival in Sviðinsvík, where his
visionary inwardness will suffer the complex assaults of new circumstance. The young poet, destitute, necessarily reliant on the proverbial
kindness of strangers, is pulled inexorably into the intensities of village
life, first through his contact with Vegmey, yet another of the mysterious young women who appear in the pages of the novel as if by spontaneous generation, then with the various rivalrous town officials—the
partish officer, the Privy-Councillor, and Pétur Þríhross, manager of
the Regeneration Company, a peculiar mercantile operation that
seems to have the whole village clutched in its economic tentacles.

Through the offices of the energetically self-involved Þríhross,
Ólafur comes to squat in a dilapidated abandoned manor house called
the Palace of the Summerlands, to which he repairs when he is not for-
aging for food, composing poems for village occasions, or wandering
about the countryside, often as not thinking of Vegmey. The soul of
the poet is compelled by beauty and the fierce longing for love. Looking at Vegmey, he has seen "that hot, wordless dreamland which is
sometimes in a girl's eyes when she looks at a man" (142).

The second book, drawing a broad and often satirical portrait
of village life, is episodically constructed around Ólafur's various
encounters and involvements. If his interactions with Pétur Þríhross
expose him to the machinating intelligence of the merchant entrepre-
neur, then his later friendship with Örn Úlfar exposes him to the most
extreme political idealism. Örn may be a socialist dreamer, but he is
also an activist bent upon breaking the monopolistic hold that the

Regeneration Company has over the village. He wants to help his fellow villagers establish a union that will guarantee them equitable wages. While Örn is Ólafur's opposite—a man of action and engagement—the two men share an emotional zealousness in the service of a larger vision of life.

More kindred in obvious ways is the poetess, a laborer's wife who takes Ólafur in and feeds him when he needs care, and who, far more importantly, encourages him in his poetic pursuits: "The poetess gave him paper and exercise books, and then he would sit up late, sometimes all night, writing with all his might as if the end of the world could overwhelm them at any moment and everything depended on getting enough words down on paper before the sun, the moon and the stars were wiped out" (192).

Events in this second book take an overtly comic turn when Þórunn of Kambor, who had been the one to restore Ólafur to health, is brought in by the manager to conduct a séance, one radical consequence of which is the decision of the town's Psychic Research Society to disinter the bones of Satan and Musa, a long-dead murderer and adultress, to have them reburied, an initiative meant to mark a symbolic new beginning for the village. The intensity of debate among the locals inscribes as nothing else could the credulous insularity of village life.

That this new beginning should coincide with the arrival of one Júel J. Júel, a scheming confederate of the manager's—the man with the marvelous broad-brimmed hat—is, we suspect, a slyly effective commentary by Laxness on what Marx characterized as the witchcraft of economics. Príhross, who would bring the marvels of modern capitalism to the village, is also the guiding spirit of the Psychic Research Society. To raise money for their plan to capitalize the Regeneration Company, Júel and Príhross, like any good mafiosi, insure the Palace at Summerlands for a huge sum of money and then arrange to have it burned to the ground, leaving Ólafur once again homeless. Very shortly thereafter—such is the pattern of "coincidence" in the poet's life—he receives a letter from Jarþrúður, who he has not seen since the long-ago night of Jónas's wedding, and who now insists that he honor the promise he made to one day marry her. Ólafur, as ever, capitulates before the power of the word. With this paired turn of events Laxness has everything in place for the third book.

The title of this third book, "The House of the Poet," can be interpreted both literally and figuratively. Literally it designates the next phase of Ólafur's tormented pilgrimage. Some time after the destruction of the Palace of the Summerlands—insurance money from which has now rejuvenated the Regeneration Company, boosting Pétur Þríhross in his monopolistic ambitions—we find Ólafur and Jarþrúður living in their own little shack, called "The Heights." Things have changed. While Jarþrúður is still his "intended," they have a child, Margrét, a sickly little girl much beloved by Ólafur. The passing of five years has brought the poet responsibilities, and with these a much more complicated relation to his soul's vocation. Writes Laxness, modulating as he does so effectively from the idiom of daily life to a rich prophetic cadence: "If it ever happened that the poet felt a little obstinate and complacent, perhaps even touched with a certain arrogance at being a poet, such feelings vanished the moment his intended started to cry—not to mention if the little girl started crying as well. It was hard to say which was strongest in the poet's soul—the desire to please or the fear of hurting. When happiness came to this poet in his solitary moments, he was free and did not have a house. When he saw before him their tear-stained faces, he suddenly had a house. To be alone, that is to be a poet. To be involved in the unhappiness of others, that is to have a house" (326–327).

But the pull of poetry, the spirit, what Ólafur calls "the Voice," remains powerful, declaring its own imperatives: "Every time he was allowed to go out, and not on some routine errand connected with his livelihood or his home, it was as if he were being given the world for a little while. However small a digression it was from his everyday routine, the Voice began to echo at once. It was the same Voice as of old. The difference was that when he was a child he thought he knew what it was, and that he understood it, and he gave it a name; but the older and wiser he became, the more difficult he found it to say what it was, or to understand it, except that he felt it called him away from other people and the responsibilities of life to the place where it alone reigned" (336–337).

Again, Laxness sets into stark opposition the claims of the world and the claims of the spirit. The world, for Ólafur, is both the domestic—his suffocating, sorrowful bond to Jarþrúður and his genuine love for Margrét, who will soon be taken by illness—and the public, the societal. In these next pages the conflict between union forces and property—socialism and capitalism, if you will—will come to a head, first with the stand-off between the Þríhross's organization, the so-called Society of True Iceland (its nationalist chauvinism obviously, but not exclusively, a phenomenon of the Thirties) and the Laborers, who are cast by their adversaries as nonpatriotic agitators. Though Ólafur struggles to stay uninvolved, he is pressured from both sides—by his friend Örn as well as by Jarþrúður, who has thrown in her lot with the Society.

While there are escalating protests and threats of work stoppage, the full-out battle never quite materializes—scandal at a distance destroys the financial structure of the Society and the workers ultimately get their most basic demands met. Orchestrating the conflict in its local terms, moving between straight-on and satirical scenes of agitation and encounter, Laxness has given the forces at large in Europe and America their particular Icelandic refraction.

Laxness had himself turned to socialism during a two-year stay in America in the late 1920s, which not surprisingly put him at odds with many sectors of his society, and this third book puts on display the two very different strains of his writing sensibility. The passionate rhetoric of Örn carries no sarcastic undertones: "He who doesn't choose justice isn't human. I have little fondness for that pity which the coward calls love . . . What is love? If a loving person sees someone's eye being gouged out, he howls as if his own eye were being gouged out. On the other hand he isn't moved at all if he sees powerful liars utterly rob a whole people of their sight and thereby their good sense as well" (408).

But there is a deep division in this author, for he asks us to heed the unmistakable passion of Ólafur, too. When he is roused to speech at a public meeting, he declares that "whoever is a poet and a scholar loves the world more than all others do, even though he has never owned a share in a boat, yes, and not even managed to be classed as a quarry-man. The fact is that it is much more difficult to be a poet and write poetry about the world than it is to be a man and live out in the world. You hump rocks for next to no pay and have lost your livelihood to thieves, but the poet is the emotion of the world, and it is in the poet that all men suffer" (301). Is this a contradiction or is there a strange fusion of the transpersonal, a deep compatibility between the views of the political idealist and those of the martyr poet?

If Laxness lets the political struggle resolve the tumult of con- crete circumstance—a nod to the determining power of concrete cir- cumstances and Marxian materialism—his working through of the opposition between the world and the spirit is a good deal more ambiguous and suggestive.

This latter conflict is given its final and most wrenching twist in "The Beauty of the Heavens," the last book of *World Light*. As the section opens, Ólafur and Jarþrúður have relocated to the remote community of Bervík. They are now married. Ólafur's last-ditch effort to dissolve the unhappy relationship and send Jarþrúður away has failed and he has con- cluded that for better or worse—mostly worse—they are fated to be together. He now tries to salvage a life for himself by working as a district schoolmaster. But it is this very engagement that leads to his undoing. Staying the night at the home of one of his pupils, Ólafur ends up getting into the girl's bed, and in short order his indiscretion is discovered. He is accused of sexual assault, tried, convicted, and sent away to the capital city, Reykjavík, to serve out a prison sentence. The most unworldly of men—here is a true Dostoevskian touch—finally has his face pushed down into the vile muck of the world. He is guilty and he must pay, and there is not a vestige of uplift to be found.

But Laxness, ever maneuvering his oppositions and tensions, has in fact set the poet up for his tragic apotheosis. If the crime was carnal— the result of his desperate yearning for womanly solace, even if in the bed of a precocious adolescent—the final release will be overwhelm- ingly spiritual. Spiritual *and* romantic, I should say. In his last days of confinement, when he has done plumbing abjection, coming to know and befriend some of the vilest of his country's citizens, he has a prophetic dream in which his admired poet Sigurður Breiðfjörd appears before him in a golden chariot: "And he spoke four words. He spoke one mysterious name. This name echoed through that myth-like dream, and in a flash it was woven with letters of fire across the soul's heaven: 'Her name is Bera'" (559).

Soon after, when Ólafur is preparing to board the ship that will return him to his village, he sees a young woman waiting in the crowd, and is instantly smitten. He recognizes the hand of his fate. Laxness's description captures, yet again, the poet's fundamental innocence and unworldliness, not to mention his susceptibility to beauty: "She was wearing a light coat, bareheaded, with quite a large suitcase by her side. What attracted his attention before anything else was the youthful freshness of her skin, the unbelievable wholesomeness of her coloring; yet she was closer to being pale than ruddy. Although something in the skin was related to the creaminess of summer growth, she was nonetheless closer to the plants, especially those which bear so tender a flower that the lightest touch leaves a mark. To protect her, Nature had covered her with a sort of magic helmet of invisibility . . ." (564). Making her acquaintance, Ólafur insists that her name is Bera, though she denies it.

Ólafur's spiritual longing has become tyrannical in him. Nothing will sway him from the conviction that this girl is his destiny. What is remarkable is that she seems willing enough to accept the intensity of his attentions:

"Don't you think it funny that we should be alone here in a strange place?" he asked.

"No," she replied. "What about you?"

"In reality we have never existed until this moment," he said.

"I don't understand you," she said.

"You and I were somewhere else before, certainly; but not We," he said. "Nor the place, either. Today the world was born."

"Now you're trying to frighten me again," she said, but looked at him and smiled a little, so that he would not think she was angry (574).

Their shipboard relationship, erotically charged but Platonic—if this is not a contradiction—is magical. Knowing that they must soon part, Ólafur nonetheless draws closer and closer to what feels to him like the purpose of his life. Meeting the girl on the deck one night, he realizes:

"With one glance the eyes of beauty, wiser than all books, could wipe away all the anxiety, guilt and remorse of a whole lifetime. She had come to see him in the secrecy of this night to rehabilitate him, to give him the right to live a new life where beauty would reign alone" (583).

But of course a love like this cannot survive. The two part, as they must. And when he returns to Bervík, heartsick with longing, Ólafur tries to resume his old life as best he can. He is consumed by longing for his Bera. Then one day he hears from his old messenger friend, Reimar, now a traveling postman, that his beloved is dead. He refuses the information: It cannot be.

The last two chapters of the book take us out of the known world, the world that has caused Ólafur so much confusion and suffering, and in two great lurches lifts us free. Chapter 24 presents without commentary a fourteen-line poem, Ólafur's deep response to the news he has received. Denying the ultimate reality of death, he writes:

> *And though the hands that freed me now are dust*
> *And death's cold handshake holds them in its grip,*
>
> *It doesn't harm my song; my memory of thee*
> *Has taken root forever in my mind,*
> *Of tenderness and love and mercy kind,*
> *Just as you were when first you came to me;* (595)

Typical romantic sentiments, one might say, expressions of the common conceit that love is deathless and memory prevails over the eroding action of circumstance. But the short final chapter brings together the poet's artistic faith and his deepest resolve, the resolve which turns sentiment into the most profound resolution. Ólafur, having followed the peculiarly twisting path of his fate, can now set forth to embrace his death. He sets off on an undefined journey across the great glacier that has loomed over his home; in a short while he has left the familiar coordinates of the old world behind:

"Over the ocean, black clouds started gathering. He continued on, onto the glacier, towards the dawn, from ridge to ridge, in deep, new-fallen snow, paying no heed to the storms that might pursue him. As a child he had stood by the seashore at Ljósavík and watched the waves soughing in and out, but now he was heading away from the sea. 'Think of me when you are in glorious sunshine.' Soon the day of resurrection will shine on the bright paths where she awaits her poet.

"And beauty shall reign alone." (598)

Somehow the term "suicide" does not do justice to Ólafur's last decision. Suicide is an act of vengeance against the self. When Gerald Crich walked away into the snowfields in Lawrence's *Women In Love,* that was suicide, a willed cutting the self away from life, an expression of utter despair. Ólafur's end asks to be viewed poetically, as a continuation, a plunge taken, in full confidence, toward what he believes is a higher realization. The terms are elusive. The closing passage speaks of "resurrection," but not in a Christian sense so much as an ultimate romantic apotheosis, the eternal union of lover and beloved. It also invokes beauty as the highest of all ideals—beauty as the perfect material manifestation of spirit. And this is fitting, for from the earliest days, back when he was a boy just coming into consciousness, Ólafur has found in beauty the poet's truest intimation: that there is a purpose behind the screen of appearances; that the world is intended, not arbitrary. The recognition of the power of beauty made Ólafur a poet, and now—we very much want to believe—beauty will become his place of rescue. The world light of the title is the light that shines through from elsewhere, and Ólafur's last leap is toward trusting it absolutely.

TRANSLATOR'S NOTE: PRONUNCIATION

The modern Icelandic alphabet has thirty-two letters, compared with twenty-six in modern English. There are two extra consonants (ð and þ), and an additional diphthong (æ). Readers may find a note on the pronunciations of specifically Icelandic letters helpful:

ð (Ð), known as "eth" or "crossed d," is pronounced like the (voiced) *th* in *breathe*.
þ (Þ), known as "thorn," is pronounced like the (unvoiced) *th* in *breaths*.
æ is pronounced like the *i* in *life*.

The pronunciation of the vowels is conditioned by the accents:

á like the *ow* in *owl*
é like the *ye* in *yet*
í like the *ee* in *seen*
ó like *o* in *note*
ö like the *eu* in French *fleur*
ú like the *oo* in *soon*
ý like the *ee* in *seen*
au like the *œi* in French *œil*
ei, ey, like the *ay* in *tray*

Please note asterisks (*) within the text indicate an explanatory note to be found on pages 599–606.

BOOK ONE

THE REVELATION
OF THE DEITY

I

He was standing on the foreshore below the farm with the oyster catchers and purple sandpipers, watching the waves soughing in and out. He was probably shirking. He was a foster child, and therefore the life in his heart was a separate life, a different blood, without relationship to the others. He was not part of anything, he was on the outside, and there was often an emptiness around him. And long ago he had begun to yearn for some indefinable solace. This narrow bay with its small blue shells and the waves gently rippling in over the sand, with the cliffs on one side and a green headland on the other—this was his friend. It was called Ljósavík.

Did he have no one, then? Was no one kind to him except this little bay? No, no one was kind to him. But on the other hand, no one was downright unkind to him, not so that he had to fear for his life. That did not come until later. When he was teased, the teasing was mostly in fun; the difficulty was in knowing how to take it. When he was thrashed, the thrashing arose from necessity; it was Justice. But there were many things which did not concern him, thank goodness. For instance the elder brother, Jónas, who owned several sheep and a share in a fishing boat, once threw a basin of water over his mother, Kamarilla, as she was going down the stairs one evening. That was nothing to be concerned about. But when the younger brother, Júst, who was also a sheep-farmer and boat-owner, amused himself by

3

picking him up by the ears because it was such fun finding out how much pain the dear little chap could stand, that *did* concern him, unfortunately.

In springtime the brothers dug holes through the overhanging banks of the river farther up the valley and guddled for trout; then they threw the living fish at the boy toddling unsuspectingly nearby and shouted, "It bites!" That made him frightened, and the brothers found that great fun. In the evening they put one of these fiendish trout in an old wooden bucket right beside his bed. He thought the devil himself was in that pail. That night when he tried to sneak downstairs in mortal terror to take refuge with his foster mother, they cried, "The trout will jump out of the pail and bite you!"

"They're just making it up," said the housekeeper, Karítas, the mother of the farm girl, Kristjána.

Then the boy did not know whom to believe. You see, he could not be sure about anything these two women told him. They had very protruding eyes. Once he forgot himself when he had been sent to fetch a pony; he had been thinking about God and watching two birds paddling around on the foreshore. Needless to say he was thrashed for shirking. But while his foster mother was bringing out the birch from under her pillow, the widow Karítas felt constrained to say, "Serves him right, the lazy little so-and-so!" And young Kristjána added, "Yes, he's always shirking!"

But when he was thrashed he was never smacked very hard, only just a little because God's justice is inescapable: God punishes all those who shirk. When the thrashing was over, he pulled up his trousers and wiped away his tears and sniffed. His foster mother went downstairs to see to the evening meal. Then the widow Karítas came over and patted his cheek and said, "Pooh, God doesn't care at all, you poor wretch—as if He had time to bother about that!" Young Kristjána groped inside her bodice and brought out a warm piece of half-melted brown-sugar candy she had pilfered from the larder that morning: "Crunch it up quickly and swallow it down at once, and I'll kill you if you tell anyone!" That was how kind and good and affectionate they could be because they had seen him being thrashed;

and when they were kind to him, he did not think their eyes protruded much after all. They were never very unkind to him when there was no one else present.

Magnína, the daughter of the house, taught him to read from a tattered old spelling book they had there. She loomed over him like a mound and pointed at the letters with a knitting needle. She cuffed him on the ear if he got the same letter wrong thrice, but never hard and never in anger, almost absentmindedly, and it did not worry him. She was stout and solid and blue in the face, and the dog sneezed whenever he sniffed at her. She wore two pairs of enormously thick stockings because her feet were always cold; the outer stockings were always hanging down and the inner stockings were sometimes hanging down, too. She never teased him for fun and never told lies about him to get him into trouble; she never picked on him when she was in a bad temper, and she never wished him down into the bad place. But she never came to his rescue when he was being teased or when he was being beaten without just cause; she never took his side when lies were told about him, and she was never cheerful.

On the other hand there were times when she would do him a kindness quite without thinking. There was boiled salt fish for the midday meal, and in the evening there was hash and pickled tripe with pieces of sheep's lung thrown in; sometimes the evening meal was only pickled tripe and milk. But the days were very long and the sea and the sky were gray and dull, and it was snowing on the mountain on the other side of the fjord, and she would be alone in the loft with the boy, and it seemed as if life would never end and never get any better. Then she would slip down to the larder and find herself a slice of rolled tripe or a piece of pickled brisket or some pickled lamb fries. The boy slavered on to the spelling book and she cuffed him on the ear and told him to stop spitting on the book. Then she would give him a piece of the brisket, right out of the blue, without any show of affection, as if nothing could be more natural. And his mouth and his throat and his whole body would feel wonderful for a while.

When he was eight years old he had read the book of *Icelandic Folktales,* and Bishop Peter's *Short Stories,* and St. Luke's Gospel, which made him cry because Jesus was so alone in the world. On the other hand he could never get used to thinking of Vídalín's *Book of Sermons** as a book at all. He had a great longing to read more but there were no other books there except one, *The Felsenburg Stories,** which Magnína had inherited from her father. No one else was allowed to read that book; it was a secret book. He had a great longing to read *The Felsenburg Stories* and all the books in the world— except the *Book of Sermons.*

"If you mention *The Felsenburg Stories* once again, I'll thrash you!" said Magnína.

Early on, he had come to suspect that in books in general, but especially in *The Felsenburg Stories,* was to be found that indefinable solace he yearned for but could not name. Magnína wrote out the alphabet for him, but only once; she had no time for more because it took her so long to form each letter. In any case there was no paper, and even when there was, no one was allowed to waste it. He would furtively scratch letters with a stick on bare patches of earth or in the snow, but he was forbidden to do that and was told he was writing himself to the devil. So he had to write on his soul.

Kamarilla, the housewife, was the implacable enemy of literature. When it became apparent that the boy had an unnatural desire to pore over letters, she told him the cautionary story of G. Grímsson of Grunnavík.* He did not call himself "Guðmundur Grímsson" as other people would; he used only an initial and added a place-name, to imitate the gentry. It was a dreadful story. G. Grímsson of Grunnavík was a good-for-nothing poet and wrote a hundred books. He was a bad man. When he was young he would not get married, but had thirty children instead. He hated people, and wrote about them. He had written a host of books about innocent people who had never done him any harm.

"No one would have anything to do with a person like that, except the ugly crones he brought upon himself in his old age. In their old age, people get what they bring upon themselves. That's what comes of thinking about books. Yes, I knew him well in his time, that Guðmundur, always poring over his books, never tried to earn a living for himself or for others. He was a terrible scoundrel. I was just a snotty little girl at the time. He lived all by himself in a hovel on the other side of the mountains, beside another fjord, and God punished him with a leaky roof and various other things. That showed him how much good it did him. He sat in an oilskin in the living room and the rain dripped onto his bald head because he wouldn't earn a living for himself and for others, drop after drop trickling down his neck because he was always poring over his books. God was punishing him. But his heart was hardened and knew no humility, and he went on writing a hundred books by the feeble glimmer of an oil lamp, two hundred books. And when he dies it's obvious enough where he'll go, because God doesn't like having books written about people; only God has the right to judge people. Besides which, God himself has written the Bible, which contains everything that needs to be written. Those who think about other books sit alone and destitute by a guttering light in their old age, and fiends and devils afflict them."

But the story had quite the opposite effect to what was intended. Instead of acting on the boy as an edifying parable, it beckoned him irresistibly to something forbidden and alluring; his imagination dwelt on books with redoubled eagerness after hearing about the punishment of this lonely sage and his hundred books. Often the boy was overwhelmed by an uncontrollable yearning to write down in a hundred books everything he saw, despite what anyone said— two hundred books as thick as the *Book of Sermons,* whole Bibles, whole chests full of books.

His name was Ólafur Kárason, usually shortened to Óli or Lafi. He was standing by the bay. There were oyster catchers and purple sandpipers there, too, which scampered a few steps up the beach before the incoming wave whose foam swirled around their slender legs as it broke and soughed back again. He always wore the cast-off clothing of the brothers, who were big men. The seat of his trousers reached down to the backs of his knees and each trouser leg was rolled up at least ten times; the arms of his jersey reached a long way beyond his fingers, and he was always having to roll up the sleeves. He had a green felt hat which had been a Sunday-best hat in its youth before the rats got at it; it came well down over his ears, and the brim rested on his shoulders. He decided to call himself "Ó. Kárason of Ljósavík." He addressed himself by this name, and talked a lot to himself. "Ó. Kárason of Ljósavík, there you stand!" he said. Yes, there he stood.

His foster mother was rummaging in the lumber box one day for something she had lost, with the boy behind her, when out of the rubbish came the remains of a tattered old book.

"Can I have it?" asked Ó. Kárason of Ljósavík.

"Certainly not!" said Kamarilla. "The very idea!"

But even so he managed to get hold of the book without his foster mother's knowledge, and he stuck it under his jersey and kept it at his breast, close to his heart. He tried to read it in secret, but it was printed in Gothic lettering and the title page was missing. Every time he thought he was beginning to understand the book someone would come along and he would have to hide it hastily under his jersey again; he was often very close to being caught. What could there be in his book? He kept his own book against his own heart, and did not know what was in it. He was determined to keep it until he grew up. But then pages began to drop out of it here and there, and it became more and more difficult to read the longer he kept it hidden next to his bare skin. It was as if the book had been dipped into a pot of fat.

There was often an itch at his heart because of the book, but that did not matter. It was a secret to own such a book; it was really a kind of refuge, even though he had no idea what was in the book. He was sure it was a good book, and it is fun having a secret if it is not anything wicked—one has plenty to think about all day, and one dreams about it at night.

But on the first day of summer the secret was discovered. Kamarilla the housewife made him change his underclothes after the winter; this ceremony took place up in the loft in the middle of the day, and he was taken unawares by it. He peeled off his clothes one by one, and his heart beat furiously; finally he took off his shirt. There was no way of hiding the book any longer. It fell to the floor.

"My goodness me!" said his foster mother. "God have mercy on me; what the devil's the child got under his shirt? Magnína, come and see this dreadful sight!"

The boy stood before them, stark naked and anguished, while the two women examined the book carefully.

"Who gave you this book?"

"I sort of just f-found it."

"Yes, it's just as I thought. Not enough to be going around with a book, but a stolen one at that! Magnína, put this devilish thing in the fire at once!"

He started crying then. This was the first great sorrow of his life he could remember. He was sure he had not cried so bitterly since he was sent away from his mother in a sack one winter's day, long before memory began. Admittedly he had never understood the book, but that did not matter. What mattered was that this was his secret, his dream, his refuge; in short, it was his book. He wept as only children weep when they suffer injustice at the hands of those stronger than themselves. It is the most bitter weeping in the world. That was what happened to his book; it was taken from him and burned. And he was left standing naked and without a book on the first day of summer.

— **2** —

Other children had fathers and mothers and honored them, and they prospered and lived to a ripe old age; but he was often bitter towards his father and mother and dishonored them in his heart. His mother had cuckolded his father, and his father had betrayed his mother, and both of them had betrayed the boy. The only consolation was that he had a Father in heaven. And yet—it would have been better to have a father on earth.

All winter and far into spring there were readings about his Father in heaven, from devotional homilies each evening and from the *Book of Sermons* on Sundays. His foster mother would assume a solemn, frozen expression and begin to read; she read in a chant that slackened at every pause, rather like a melody ending on a falling note; up and down, up and down, over and over again, until eventually the lesson came to an end. These readings had nothing to do with everyday life, and at other times, indeed, no one on the farm seemed to have any love for God or expect anything of Him except Ó. Kárason of Ljósavík. The brothers sprawled back during the lesson and sometimes kicked one another and cursed one another between their teeth, as each thought the other was in the way; the women stared wide-eyed into the blue as if all this great talk about God struck no answering chord in them. But then the foster mother's sight began to fail, and little Óli was barely ten years old when he was given the task of reading the lesson on less important occasions. "What a lot of damned rubbish the brat talks!" the brothers would say during the reading, as if the boy himself were responsible for what the man in the *Book of Sermons* had written. On the other hand it was true that he never achieved his foster mother's peculiar chant, far less the special expression on her face. But at least he understood God, and there was no one in that house who understood God except him. And though the devotional homilies were tedious and the *Book of Sermons* much worse, it did not matter, because Ó. Kárason of Ljósavík, you see, appreciated God not according to any devotional homily or *Book of Sermons,* not according to any gospel or doctrine, but in another and much more remarkable way.

He was not quite nine years old, in fact, when he first began to have spiritual experiences. He would be standing down by the bay, perhaps, in the early days of spring, or up on the headland to the west of the bay where there was a mound with a rich green tussock on top, or perhaps up on the hill above the homefield when the grass was high and ready for mowing. Then suddenly he felt he saw God's image open before him. He felt the deity reveal itself in Nature in an inexpressible music, the sonic revelation of the deity; and before he knew it he himself had become a trembling voice in a celestial chorus of glory. His soul seemed to be rising out of his body like frothing milk brimming over the edge of a basin; it was as if his soul were flowing into an unfathomable ocean of higher life, beyond words, beyond all perception, his body suffused by some surging light that was beyond all light. Sighing, he became aware of his own insignificance in the midst of this infinite chorus of glory and radiance; his whole consciousness dissolved into one sacred, tearful yearning to be allowed to be one with the Highest and be no longer any part of himself. He lay for a long time on the sand or on the grass, and wept tears of deep and fervent happiness, face to face with the inexpressible. "God, God, God!" he cried, trembling with love and reverence, and kissed the ground and dug his fingers into the turf. The feeling of well-being stayed with him after he began to come round; he went on lying there; he lay in a tranquil trance and felt that never again could there be any shadows in his life, that all adversity was merely chaff, that nothing could matter any more, that everything was good. He had perceived the One. His Father in heaven had taken him to His heart by the farthest northern seas.

No one in the house had any suspicion that the boy was in direct communication with the deity, nor would anyone in the house have understood it. Everyone in the house went on listening to God's Word out of a book. He alone knew that even if these people listened to God's Word for a thousand years they would never understand God, and anyway it would probably never occur to God to take them to His heart. The boy read aloud from the *Book of Sermons,* and the people stared vacantly and scratched themselves and dozed and suspected nothing. They thought he knew no more about God than they themselves did.

It was the practice there to load him with far more work than he was fit for. During the winter when he was ten years old, he had to carry all the water for the house and the barn. He was slightly built and delicate, pale, with large blue eyes and a reddish tinge to his hair. He very seldom had enough to eat, but he lacked the courage to steal from the larder like Kristjána, the farm girl, who could do as she pleased because she had a mother and had started making eyes at the brothers, besides. Ó. Kárason of Ljósavík was extremely honest, because he had no one on his side in anything. Often he was not served until the others had finished and gone out, just because he was alone in the world. And as anyone who has ever been a child knows, it is a great ordeal to have to wait until the others have finished and not be allowed to say anything, either; he was not allowed to say anything because he had no one. But sometimes it happened that Magnína, the daughter of the house, would give him her leftovers when everyone else had gone out, and sometimes there was a tasty morsel left in her bowl, although no one had noticed how it had got there. In general, the members of the family did most of their eating, in secret, between meals.

Carrying water: after the first two buckets the boy would be very tired, but that was just the beginning. He carried and carried. He had to fill two large barrels and also carry two buckets for the rams. Before long he would begin to stagger, and his knees and arms would tremble with exhaustion. Often the weather was bad; snow and sleet and storm. The wind tore at the buckets; sometimes it was as if he were going to take off completely, buckets and all. But he did not take off. He put the buckets down while the gust roared past. He tried to tie his green hat tighter under his chin with frozen fingers that were numb from the bucket handles. He asked God to give him supernatural strength, but God was too busy to respond. Onwards, onwards! Twenty more trips to go. The water splashed from the buckets over his feet, all the way up to his knees; he was soaking wet, and there was a frost. He slipped on the icy path, and the water spilled out of both buckets; it spilled underneath him and over him. He began to cry, but he was only crying for himself; nobody paid any attention to what happened to him. He felt that the world was avenging itself on him for something he had never done, perhaps just for the fact that his mother had had an extra child, or that his father had run away from his mother. Then one of the brothers would appear between the barn and the house and shout, "Having a nap, then?" So he would stand up soaking wet in the frost and start to adjust his green hat which had been knocked askew when he fell. And thus each day he was taxed beyond his strength. Every morning he woke up with dread in his heart and nausea in his throat; the divinely merciful hand of sleep was withdrawn, and the day faced him with new water-carrying, new storms, new hunger, weariness, exhaustion, chivvying, cursing, blows, kicks, thrashings. His whole life in childhood was one endless ordeal, like those fairy tales in which men fight with giants and dragons and devils.

Sometimes he was momentarily seized by a realization, like some deeper insight into existence, that he had a mother; he would stop suddenly, in midbreath perhaps, as this realization pierced him so sharply that he felt faint. He had an overwhelming urge to throw away whatever he was holding and take to his heels, away, away, over mountains and moors, fjords and valleys, through towns and parishes, until he found her. But his feet were fettered. He had to content himself with leaning against God's bosom. And when least expected, Magnína might give him a piece of flatbread with butter on it. Sometimes when he was toiling outside and she was sitting inside in the warmth of the living room, all fat and comfortable, he would make up his mind to go to her sometime and lean against her bosom and weep. But when he was alone with her in the loft he lost all desire to do so. He doubted then whether she had a human bosom. She really had no body at all, you see, much less an actual figure; she was merely a trunk. There was a smell off her. She was like a wall of treble thickness. He gazed at her and wondered to himself, Can it possibly be that deep, deep inside all that there lurks a soul?

During the season, one or both of the brothers went to the fishing at the nearest fishing-village and lived away from home. It was the only time of year that there were no sulks and tempers on the farm; the brothers were always spiteful to one another, because each of them wanted to be in sole charge. No one ever knew who was master on the farm; people came and went, the hired hands for the haymaking or for the spring work, but no one knew who was the master. Brother Júst thought that Jónas, who was older, did not have the brains to run a farm, and Jónas thought that Júst was not old enough to run a farm. Each countermanded the other's orders. They did not often come to blows in real earnest in front of other people, but they often made threats and looked daggers at one another; it would have done no harm if the Christian ideal of brotherly love had been a little stronger. The housewife herself was evasive when asked to intervene; she was a widow, and the estate was still undivided. The hired hands often walked out. The housekeeper, Karítas, and her daughter were the only ones who had the knack of dealing with both masters without trouble.

One winter's morning in his eleventh year the boy was sent to drive the horses out to the pastures. The dog came up behind one of the horses and sank his teeth into its fetlock. The horse took fright and kicked out; the boy was standing just behind, and the hoof caught him a terrible blow on the forehead just above the temple and knocked him unconscious. Someone from another farm happened to pass by and found the boy lying stunned on the ice and thought him dead and carried him home; but he was alive, not dead, worse luck, and came round again. But he was dazed for a long time, his mind in a fog, with terrible headaches and loss of appetite and weakness. He lay in bed for a long time, and no one was particularly unpleasant to him for a while. For more than a whole week the brothers did not curse him to hell, and his foster mother called him her poor little scamp. One day Magnína handed him a piece of buttered flatbread between meals, as if it were a matter of course, and sat down beside him and read to him out of a book she had borrowed from somewhere. It was poetry and he did not understand it, but that did not matter; what was more important was that he now realized what sort of a person this bulky, self-contained girl really was.

But after a while the same old attitudes reasserted themselves, and people began to express openly their opinions of that pauper who lay there stuffing himself and imagining he was ill while other people had to slave for him. The housewife, Kamarilla, wrote to the boy's father in some distant town and demanded increased maintenance for him. Then the boy began to get up and about again and started carrying water once more. He often had unbearable headaches, but no one listened to any nonsense about illness any more. Spring was coming and there was plenty of work to do, mucking out the sheep shed, carting manure to the homefield and spreading it. He scarcely ever had an opportunity to make contact with the deity.

Then Magnína had a birthday, and Ó. Kárason of Ljósavík was determined to reward her for having been so good to him that winter. He composed a poem about her. He took an old ditty as a model and tried to compose something using rhymes and kennings. These were two of the lines in the poem:

> *Brightest star of paradise,*
> *Eden's purest sapling.*

He was so elated when he had composed the poem that he felt there was nothing in heaven or earth he could not do. He was convinced that in the poem there lay hidden some deep poetic meaning, even though on the surface, perhaps, it was difficult to understand. He approached Magnína with thudding heart as she stood in the field with her dung rake, and asked her hastily and without looking up if she would like to hear a birthday poem—and gasped it out. She stopped raking and looked at him in amazement.

"Say it again," she said.

He recited it again. She sniffed, turned away, and started raking again. No, she did not even thank him for it. He was about to go.

"Listen," she said. "Let me hear it once again."

He recited it once more.

"I think you're off your head," she said. "Who's 'Eden's purest sapling'? Is that me?"

It was quite obvious that she did not understand poetry. She was treble thickness after all. Probably she had only been reading for her own amusement during the winter when she had read to him. Probably she had only given him the remains of her buttered flatbread because she could not finish it herself.

"I really ought to thrash you!" she said. "Pretending to be composing poetry, and you don't even know what it means yourself! Who knows you haven't cast some evil spell on me?"

He started to cry, and said, "You mustn't tell my foster mother about it."

"Fie on you!" she said.

He was crimson with shame and felt he could never look anyone in the face again for the rest of his life. Yes, he should have known all along what kind of person she really was—you only had to look at her standing there in the field with her head scarf down behind her ears, purple in the cheeks and sweating, with her skirts hitched up and her stockings down, and the dog sneezing whenever he went near her. How on earth had it ever occurred to him to call her Eden's purest sapling?

By nighttime they had all heard the poem. And they all set about the poet, each in his own way.

"What a little brat, started on the smut already!" said the brothers.

"Yes, and blaspheming, too!" said the housekeeper, Karítas. "They start early enough, these unfortunates!"

"He's only pretending he composed it," said the girl, Kristjána. "He's obviously heard it somewhere and stolen it."

"If I ever hear of your using filthy doggerel here in my house again, you're for the birch; that's for sure!" said his foster mother. "And now you'll have no meat for supper for a week, just to teach you that all poets are damned good-for-nothings and criminals, except for the late Pastor Hallgrímur Pétursson."*

Only Magnína said nothing; she was quite content to have learned the poem and got all this started.

Later that evening young Kristjána went down to do the milking. Dusk was falling. The boy was sitting almost invisible beside the stairway, hunched over his bowl of gruel, as she walked past him. His foster mother was sitting farther in, at her window, knitting. But as Kristjána was going past him on her way down the stairs, she stopped on the top step and bent over him.

"Listen, Lafi, would you compose a little poem about me?" she whispered to him confidentially.

He made no reply.

"Will you?" she said. "Just one?"

He crouched lower over his gruel and kept silent with all his might.

"Just one tiny one?" she wheedled, and bent right down to him as if she were going to go down his throat; her eyes were very protruding.

"Shut up!" he said, and started to cry.

At that she drew herself up again and said aloud, so that his foster mother could easily hear: "What a damned little wretch, the brat, nothing but smut and blaspheming already, and stealing poems from other people and pretending to have composed them himself, and to a grown-up woman at that! He'll turn out well, I must say! Yes, they start early enough, these criminals!"

— 3 —

And so the years went by without any change in the established ratio between the orphan's age and the labor expected of him. In summer he was roused at five o'clock in the morning with the adults and was kept at work for as long as able-bodied men. He said he had terrible headaches—but there is no limit to the querulous excuses that idlers can dream up. The brothers gave him contradictory orders in turn; the one threatened to kill him if he did not do something, the other said that the dear little chap knew what to expect if he did; and young Kristjána laughed. Then they called one another liar, thief, and wencher. Kristjána laughed and laughed and was against them both and for them both. Sometimes it ended with their coming to blows instead of killing Ó. Kárason of Ljósavík; and then all was quiet for a while.

In winter his morning call to go out to the barn was reckoned by the Seven Stars. He used to spend most of the morning pottering about in the barn. You see, he could not stand cow dung and did not dare to let it touch him anywhere, not even the rags he wore, and he was always thinking up new and different methods of keeping clean—which only delayed him even more. For instance, he invented a method of hauling out the dung in an old bucket by means of strings he fixed to the roof, whereby the bucket of dung was hoisted up to the rafters; but either it got stuck there because of some mysterious fault in the contraption and he would have to apply great ingenuity to get it down again, or else the string would break and the

bucket would come hurtling down onto the floor, or splash over
some innocent cow or over the inventor himself. His working methods in the barn were called "dawdling" and "idling" and "loafing" and
various other names.

It happened less and less frequently now that Magnína, the daughter of the house, would give him a slice of rolled tripe or pickled
brisket, not to mention buttered flatbread, because he was no longer
a child. A big girl can do this or that for a child, and perhaps a little
for a grown man, too, but a half-grown brat of a boy deserved no better than to make do with skimmed milk, hash and bits of pickled
sheep's lung, not to mention excellent boiled fish, just like any other
outsider. And his foster mother, Kamarilla, had almost stopped
thrashing him after he was thirteen, which showed that she, too, no
longer cared about him. He often wished that she would thrash him
a little, as in the old days, and then be a little kind to him afterwards.
He would have died of loneliness and other things if the divine
Omnipotence had not called him whenever It had the chance and
invited him to become one with the radiant glory of heaven and
earth. He tried whenever the opportunity occurred to obey this call
and allow his soul to become one with a higher world beyond this
world. He did not compose poetry openly now—his first experience
at that had taught him a lesson; he resolved not to compose poetry
openly until he was grown up and living among good and high-
minded men, who he imagined must exist somewhere. But that did
not stop him composing poetry; he composed just for himself now.
Sometimes he scratched out a whole verse on the ice. He committed
to memory every scrap of poetry he heard, and absorbed everything
to do with knowledge, and was determined to write it all down in
books later on—you see, he had the idea that there were too few
books in the world, and that somewhere in the world there were
people waiting impatiently, hungry for more books to be written.

Soon the time came for him to be confirmed, and he was given the
catechism and told to learn it. He was placed at the table under the
window upstairs and the book was put in front of him. His foster
mother sat on the other side of the table and kept a close watch on
him; she made sure that he looked neither to right nor left, neither up

nor down, but absolutely straight at the text. If he tried to stretch his neck a little for relief or to shake away his headache when he felt faint, that was called "letting his eyes rove in all directions," or "gaping into the blue like an idiot," or else "Just look at him goggling away like that—he's useless at everything he turns his hand or mind to!"

The God of the catechism was not the God of ecstasy and revelation; this was the old acquaintance from the *Book of Sermons,* and the boy had difficulty in understanding Him and caring for Him. Magnína was given the task of supervising his lessons. The text had to be learned by heart: there was a danger that some vital part of God would be lost if one missed a single word. Nor could one ask any questions about God, because God had no time for idle chatter: "I am your God," He says. "What more do you want?"

Among other things, the catechism said: "Ill treatment of animals bears witness to a cruel and godless heart."

The boy recited, "A hundred and eleven treatment of animals bears witness to a cruel and godless heart."

"Carry on," she said. "What next?"

"Shouldn't it be 'the hundred and eleventh treatment of animals'?" he asked.

"Yes," said Magnína, "the hundred and eleventh treatment of animals; you've done that bit. Go on."

"What is the hundred and eleventh treatment of animals?" he asked.

"What?" she said. "Haven't you been told over and over again that you mustn't ask questions about godly matters? Only simpletons do that. The hundred and eleventh treatment of animals—now then, go on."

Nevertheless she thought there was something a bit dubious about this; she frowned and began to peer at the book and was not quite satisfied, but paid no attention when he carried on reciting; she even interrupted him.

"The hundred and eleventh treatment is obviously cruel and godless treatment," she said. "You should have known that without being told."

"What kind of treatment is that?" he asked.

"I'm not obliged to tell you that," she said. "Go on."

He went on reciting, and recited for a long time, but she paid no attention to what he was saying; finally she interrupted him again.

"The hundred and eleventh treatment of animals is, for instance, forgetting to feed the dog," she said.

The church stood farther out, down the fjord, and in the spring the children attended at the pastor's from both directions, out from the valley and in from the headland.

The boy often had pains in the stomach, in addition to the headaches; he was pale and dull-witted, and when people around him were talking, he did not know what they were talking about. There were other children as stupid as he was, and those who were quick on the uptake often laughed out loud at those who were slow; it was like a stab, quick and searing. Those who were quick-witted formed a group and understood one another; those who were pale and dull-witted and ill and slow did not form a group and did not understand one another. Some were big and strong and ruddy faced and knew a lot and talked a lot; he did not know how to talk. When they laughed, it frightened him. He did not know how to play games and could not perform any tricks; they could perform tricks. When he was alone he felt he could do everything they could do, and more besides; but when he was with others, everything was befogged for him. It was never clear around him except when he was alone.

He was examined in the passage about the ill treatment of animals.

"The hundred and eleventh treatment of animals bears witness to a cruel and godless heart," he said.

"Eh?" said the pastor. "What's that?"

"It's forgetting to feed the dog," he replied.

The pastor laughed, and then all the children began to laugh as well. They went on laughing for the rest of the period, spasms of giggling that seemingly could not be suppressed, and he sat through this humiliation, dripping with sweat and scarlet with shame, in a white fog. What were all the birchings of childhood compared to this? Finally he began to cry. This startled the other children, and some of them stopped laughing. The pastor came over to him and patted his cheek, and said it could happen to anyone to give a wrong answer about God's Word; it did not matter at all, he himself often did not know how to answer questions about God's Word.

It was now late in the afternoon, and the children were allowed to go home. When they went outside, some of them came over to him to be nice to him, wanting to make up for having laughed at him; others came to question him further about the hundred and eleventh treatment of animals. He tied his handkerchief round his catechism, put on his cap without answering, and took to his heels homewards. They went on laughing and ran after him and jeered at him, because it is such fun to tease those who are peculiar and alone. The crowd overtook him on the gravel plain to the east of the parsonage. No, they could not leave him alone; they had to pester him, in fun or in earnest, because he was so funny and had misunderstood the Christian faith. He sat down on a stone and held on tightly to his catechism in the handkerchief.

Then a voice said, "You should be ashamed of yourselves, children, for not leaving him alone. What harm has he done you? Go on home and leave him in peace."

Soon they had all drifted away, up the valley. He stood up and shuffled along behind them, alone. Then he noticed that there were two girls from the confirmation class walking in front of him. They were walking arm in arm and going very slowly, and he wished they would walk faster because on no account did he want to catch up with them. Finally they stopped, looked back, and waited for him. He saw only one of them. It was Guðrún from Grænhóll; it was she who had chased the other children away when they were pestering him. He came closer to them and did not dare to look up, but he could feel her looking at him.

"It didn't matter at all," she said.

"Eh?" he said.

"I mean when you gave the wrong answer; lots of people make mistakes," she said. "And it doesn't matter at all."

She lived a little farther up the fjord, and she was nearly home. So there were people in the world after all who wanted to help others for no reason at all except the goodness of their hearts! He could not say anything; but it was as if his grief had melted away at the kindness in her eyes.

"Where does your father live?" she asked.

"I don't know," he answered.

"And haven't you got a mother, either?" she asked.

"Yes," he said.

"Where is she?"

He nearly started to cry all over again, because she was asking him about that. He still could not believe that anyone should actually care whether he, a foster child at Fótur-undir-Fótarfæti, had a mother and a father. But when she saw that he was going to cry again, she said hastily, "If you'd like to come home with me to Græn-hóll, I'll ask Mummy to make you some coffee."

He was extremely grateful to her, but was too shy to accept right away; and he was not supposed to linger on the way home.

"I know it's terrible to be an orphan," she said, "but Lauga and I want you to be happy. Isn't that true, Lauga? Don't we want him to be happy?"

"Yes," said the other girl.

"We'll always take your side whenever the other children start teasing you. Won't we, Lauga?"

"Yes," said Lauga.

"Just you tell us if someone's teasing you," she said. "I'll soon deal with those boys, whichever of them it is."

Soon afterwards they shook hands with him and said good-bye and turned off the path and walked up by the river; their farms were right at the roots of the mountain. She forgot to repeat the invitation to coffee. He gazed after her as she walked away, tall and fair, bare-headed and rosy-cheeked, with a firm stride like a grown-up girl's. She did not look back at him. They walked farther and farther up by the river. In his mind's eye from then on she was always associated with running water, and he threw himself down on the riverbank and cried out to God. "God, God, God!" he said. For a long time he never thought about any other human being. In the parsonage or in church he was aware of no one else; other people were nothing but smoke. He felt it every time she moved, even though he had his back to her. He saw her skipping across a little stream in midafternoon: she—and the clear running water of spring at the start of the growing-season—and sunshine.

On another occasion they were all playing on the riverbank, all the children, with the towering mountains on one side and the fjord on the other. It was evening. Guðrún was hot and flushed and just like a grown-up girl, and she had undone her top button, and the river flowed past, broad and calm. Her blonde braids had been tossed forward over her breast and one of them had become loosened, and her eyes sparkled. Then someone from one of the farms called out to the children that it was time to come in. He walked home alone and cried out to God. It was no doubt true; he was just the dregs of humanity and living under the yoke of slavery, a foster child who had no one and who misunderstood the Christian faith to an important extent. But all the same, let them beat him and scold him; God had revealed much to him. No one had ever perceived such immense visions as he had seen. Guðrún of Grænhóll! Then they were confirmed. Some of them did not see one another again for twenty or thirty years; some never met again. She never spoke to him except on that one occasion.

— **4** —

One day in February a snowstorm blew up. It was low tide, and the sheep were out on the nesses and the skerries of the isthmus, and the boy was sent out to bring them in. It was not the first time he had got soaked running through the seaweed, nor was it the first time that the bitter winter cold had sliced through his threadbare woolen jacket. But on this occasion the storm was exceptionally severe, and it was freezing very hard. He had had a cold all winter and at times had been unable to speak for hoarseness. When he came in out of the snowstorm that evening, he was ill. At least, he said he was ill. He complained of pains in his back, and said he was sweating and shivering by turns.

"It's growing-pains," said his foster mother, Kamarilla.

"There's no end to what our sweet little friend can dream up," said the younger brother, Júst.

That night the boy said he was drenched in sweat and had a stitch and could not get his breath, and he cried aloud to God.

"It's lovely to hear our sweet little friend singing in the middle of the night," said Júst.

Next morning when the brothers rose, the elder brother said that this was the latest method of avoiding going to the barn and touching cow dung. "Out of bed, you little devil!" he said. "You're no more ill than I am!"

But the foster mother, Kamarilla, put her hand on his forehead and found it very hot. She thought it best to let the poor wretch stay in bed that morning.

So he lay there hovering between life and death, and time passed—or rather, time ceased to pass. Day and night, weekdays and Sundays, no longer succeeded one another in the order laid down by the calendar issued by the Icelandic National Society; there was no longer any distinction between one and two. The narrow became broad and the long became short of its own accord and without natural cause; there was no relationship between things. The fever pushed life and all consciousness on to another plane where all measures of time were wiped out, where one did not know what one was nor what one had been nor what one would become, nor what would come next; one was a compound of the greatest dissimilarities of existence, one was God, one was eternity, one was a glowing spark or a strange rhythm, one was the stream or the river or a girl, one was a bay down by the sea and there was a bird, one was the part of the homefield wall that faced the mountain. Events were always incredibly varied, one novelty after another, without rule or logic.

Occasionally he was washed up on the shores of reality, but only for a short spell at a time; he just had time to wonder at how quiet and uneventful everything was in reality. He could not understand how people could live a whole lifetime in this dreary sphere of consciousness called reality, where one thing corresponds to another and night separates the days and everything happens according to the laws of nature, and this is such and such, and that follows this. But fortunately he soon drifted back into the realm of improbability where no one knew what followed which, where nothing corresponded to anything, where everything was possible, particularly the incredible and the incomprehensible. Before he knew it, his being had once again become a welter of hallucination and consolation and lightning flashes and God and release from reality and from human strife and human reason, from life and from death.

But then he opened his eyes one day and it was all over. It was just like waking up in the normal way, the day was like any other day, and there was a tiny patch of sunshine on the sloping ceiling above him. Magnína had her back to him and was bending over a basin, washing herself and combing her hair, and her outer stockings reached only up to her knees—there were no garters on them and that was why they had slipped down. He thought of sitting up as usual, but he was now so weak that he could not even move an arm. It took an incredible effort even to move one finger; it was best not to move at all, best just to look at that friendly little sunbeam on the ceiling! But he felt he had to say something. He remembered dimly that something had happened but he did not properly know what he ought to say, and he really could not be bothered thinking about it. He was so tired and this was so pleasant. What was it that had happened? It was best to wait. And he waited. At long last Magnína finished washing herself; surely she would turn around now? Then she turned around. She was only halfway through the second braid. She looked at him and saw that his eyes were open.

"Are you awake?" she asked, and went on braiding her hair.

"Yes," he whispered.

"Have you recovered then?" she said, and put one strand of the braid into her mouth while she combed out the other.

"Yes," he said.

He wanted to ask something but could not find the right question; so he said nothing for fear of asking a wrong one.

"It's God's mercy you didn't die on our hands," she said.

"What?" he said. "Am I not going to die?"

"No," she replied.

"I thought I was," he said apologetically—he had asked the wrong question after all, and he was sorry.

"We were quite sure you were going to die, but now I can see it in your eyes that you're alive," said the girl.

He said no more and did not mind not having died. Actually he was a little disappointed, even though that patch of sunshine was on the ceiling; the world of perception was unbelievably poor compared with the world of hallucination.

"Perhaps you'd like a cup of milk?" asked Magnína. "It's awful to see how skinny you've become."

She brought him some warm fresh milk and bent over him and raised his head from the pillow; the smell that gushed up from inside her dress was the same smell as before. Yes, he was sorry he had not died.

Then he began to get better. His recovery was very slow, certainly; he could not eat much and he dozed a lot, but when he was awake his senses were all there. He was on his way to life again, to stay here for a little longer, the same lonely orphan as before, in the same place on earth, out by the farthest seas. There was peace around him for a time while he was getting better; no one threatened to beat him. When he looked at the sunbeam on the ceiling above him, he was sometimes seized by an unnatural optimism: "Blessed sun!" he thought to himself, and felt that life was worth living, and was thankful to God for having created the sun to shine upon mankind. The days were rapidly getting longer. He sat up in bed and gazed enraptured at the sunbeams of life. Once again the old harmonies began to stir in his soul, the sounds he knew from his boyhood, the harp of the universe. He stared into the blue for a long time, he was for a time quite oblivious to his surroundings, his soul took part in this divine concert in enthralled gratitude, beyond words; for a moment he felt that he was living the very love of God, everything was perfect and good. He did not come to until Magnína had called his name three times.

"Are you having an attack?" she asked.

"No," he replied.

He lay down and pulled the tattered cover up over his eyes. A few days went by, and the revelation of the deity continued to echo in his soul when he was alone with the sunbeam on the ceiling. He was given pure fresh milk, sometimes even buttered flatbread. No one said "Go there!" or "Do that!" in bad weather, each countermanding the other's orders, or "There won't be a bone left unbroken in your body if you shirk!" He was hoping and praying that he would not recover too quickly.

But not all the days were days of sunshine, far from it. There were also sunless days, no divine music, no rapture, no consoling memory, no redeeming hope, only a colorless everyday perception, a dreary consciousness of self which dreaded most of all the prospect of eternal life, a dumb yearning like a leaden ache for something which could save him from the terrible immortality of the soul that stretched before him.

He had long since finished reading the few books in the house, and there was no longer anything new in them—except for *The Felsenburg Stories,* which he had not dared to mention for many years for fear of being thrashed. This book was kept deep in Magnína's clothes chest, and he could count the number of times he had been allowed to look at its outer covers, never inside it. It was a secret book; he had heard Kamarilla scolding her daughter for keeping the light burning, reading it at night.

"I do so want to read a book," he said.

"There aren't any books here," Magnína said. "Not that kind of books. Not for reading."

"What about *The Felsenburg Stories?*" he asked, in the hope that she would not thrash someone who was ill in bed and past the age of confirmation, besides.

At that she became solemn and put her head to one side and pressed her lips together and looked severely down at her darning.

"*The Felsenburg Stories,*" she said. "Let me just tell you that that's not light reading. It's a Christian book."

"That doesn't matter," he said.

"It doesn't matter? Of course it matters. It's a book about human life in the world. It could lead you into sin at your age."

"I've been confirmed," he said.

"Yes, any idiot can be confirmed," she retorted. "But do you think it brings a great understanding of Jesus in human life? I don't know what sins I might have committed if I had read such a book before I began to understand. When you're older, perhaps."

But even so she came with *The Felsenburg Stories* the following day, in midafternoon, when no one else was in the loft. The expectation in his eyes was like an ocean. She almost smiled for a moment at the sight of those huge, yearning eyes; then she sat down on the edge of his bed and opened the book. No, he was not allowed to handle the book. It was obvious from its thickness that it was an extremely Christian book, and yet there was about it a quality that filled the heart with disquiet and made one feel on tenterhooks.

"'I, Eberhard Julius, first saw the light of this world in the year 1706, during the great eclipse which filled my father, who was a wealthy merchant, and other people, with great fear.'"

There were footsteps downstairs and she suddenly stopped reading without going any farther. She had the kind of face that has fat cheeks and impersonal eyes that make very little effort to think and very little effort to dare, and there is some hidden master in the soul who slams the door and forestalls any decision when it comes to the bit, so that apathy settles over the flesh once again, humdrum and hopeless.

"God help me, I must be out of my mind!" she said, and shut the book and looked at the covers for a moment in panic, as if it were a book of witchcraft; then she thrust it hastily under her apron and went away.

Next day when he mentioned the book again, she became angry.

"Hold your tongue or I'll tell my mother on you!" she said.

He did not know what he had done, but he had no doubt it was something wicked, and he was afraid. But soon he had other matters to think about. His foster mother, Kamarilla, handed him his rags the next day, all newly washed and the stockings darned; when he fainted she laid a cold cloth on his brow and helped him to his feet. The brothers had gone to the fishing; there could be no more lying in bed now. A few days later they began to rouse him to go out to the barn. The water-carrying started again, and the water splashed over his feet. There were the usual storms at Easter. Kristjána and Karítas told his foster mother that he was always shirking; but sometimes Kristjána secretly gave him a morsel of brown-sugar candy warm from her bosom.

Magnína said nothing—for a long time.

— 5 —

Winter was almost over. The brothers were away from home all week, and so the boy was not subjected to the usual beatings and abuse. But sometimes they came home on Saturday nights, particularly if the weather were bad, and then they were usually drunk; so the boy preferred to linger in the barn as long as he possibly could, watering the cows over and over again. On Sunday mornings the brothers had a long lie, each in his own bed on either side of the loft, and talked together in an obscene language of their own from under the bedclothes. They laughed a lot, and their laughter seemed to come from deep down in their throats, or even deeper. Kristjána often had occasion to slip up to the loft during these morning devotions. When she walked between the beds, the brothers always stuck their legs out from under the bedclothes to try to trip her up; she always let out piercing shrieks as if she were in dire peril. The brothers enjoyed this hugely, but if the boy were nearby and saw and heard what was going on, he could not help taking the girl's side in his mind, even though she was so seldom on his side. But though the girl shrieked, she was not too afraid to have a go at their legs in turn, and either she won or lost and then slipped downstairs again crimson in the face; but it was not long before she had found urgent cause to go back up to the loft again.

One Sunday morning, as so often before, the younger brother,

Júst, stuck his leg up under her skirts and she let out a loud shriek, and her skirts went up past her knees.

But this time the elder brother, Jónas, said, "What the devil are you doing with your leg up her skirts?"

"Take it easy, brother," said Júst.

"You've no right to put your leg up her skirts, I tell you! Remove it at once!"

Young Kristjána went on shrieking at intervals, until the elder brother, Jónas, got out of bed, fastened his underpants, and rescued her. And then the fight started. The brothers did not fight very often, but when they did, it was in grim earnest. They fought just as they were when they jumped out of bed, rather scantily clad. The girl retreated halfway down the stairs and gaped at the battle and clapped her hands every time one of them seemed about to get the better of the other, squealing with delight and alarm rather like a wild mare. But she moved farther and farther down the stairs the lower the breeches slipped down the brothers' buttocks; her eyes became wilder and wilder, and now instead of screaming she gasped. Finally she had disappeared down the hatchway entirely except for her eyes.

The boy, Ólafur Kárason, had been sitting at the far end of the loft, swallowing his pickled tripe after his morning work in the barn. But when he realized that the fighting was in deadly earnest, he stopped looking at what was going on, for fear that he might somehow be involved in the struggle and punished. He sat in the corner of his bed, quivering with neutrality, and concentrated on his food with all his might.

Finally the younger brother, Júst, lay on the floor and could not get up again, with the elder brother, Jónas, on top of him, his backside in the air.

"I could do with a knife for this damned skirt-lifter," the elder brother hissed between his teeth, not forgetting to mention the rather special use to which he wanted to put the knife under these particular circumstances.

Ó. Kárason drew his legs in and shrank into a huddle, and forgot to chew his black-pudding or to close his eyes. And just at that moment, Jónas commanded, "Ólafur, get me that knife under the rafters there, or I'll kill you!"

The boy had no time for any moral or other reflections. The reflex of obedience overwhelmed everything else. With a convulsive start he pushed away his bowl, reached up, and drew the knife out from under the rafters. It was a butcher knife.

But as he was handing Jónas the butcher knife the maiden Kristjána, who had almost disappeared down the hatchway a short time ago, suddenly leapt back into the loft again, this time with real terror in her face as if she had fully understood, despite her youth, the questionable side of the particular operation that the elder brother felt himself constrained to perform upon his younger brother. With the maiden's understanding of this central point, the Judgment of Solomon was given. The tears welled up in her eyes. She threw herself down on her knees in front of the brothers and put her arms around the neck of the victor.

"Dearest darling Jónas," she begged, "I beseech you by all that is most sacred, do it to me instead!"

At that, Jónas released his younger brother, dropped the butcher knife on the floor, fastened his underpants, took the girl into bed and embraced her, and drew the bedclothes up over them.

What would now have been more natural and obvious than for the younger brother, Júst, to pick up the knife from the floor and turn with single-minded purpose on his brother and the girl in the bed? But no, that is not what he did. Certainly, he stood up and reached for the knife, but he paid no attention to what was going on in the bed. Instead he turned toward Ólafur Kárason of Ljósavík. He took his time; he hitched his trousers up with great care, and then walked with magnificent restraint to the far end of the loft, and stopped in front of the boy.

"And now we'll just chop your head off, my friend," he said, in that warm, loving tone that people use when they have an enemy at their mercy.

The ice-cold anguish of death pierced through Ólafur Kárason of Ljósavík: first through his spine, then through all his nerves, into all his limbs and out to his fingertips, for now he knew that his last moment had come and that he would never again be able to stand at his bay and look at the waves breaking as they came in. Almighty God had forsaken him—that is all one gets for being neutral. Brother Júst took hold of him calmly with one hand, laid his head on the edge of the bed, and made ready to cut his throat there and then.

But by God's grace, just as these momentous events were about to take place, the foster mother Kamarilla appeared in the loft, seized her son by the shoulder, wrenched the knife from him and put it carefully away in its place under the rafters, then dragged the eiderdown off the elder brother's bed and hauled the maiden out. The girl hastily smoothed her skirts down with one hand and covered her face with the other as she fled weeping down the stairs. The foster mother had a few well-chosen words to say about the younger generation, and ordered her sons to get up. Then she called the whole household together, brought out the *Book of Sermons,* and read the lesson. Then they all sat down to their meal.

6

Oh, how bitter it was to be young and full of yearning for God and all that was good, to know that God's image was revealed all around you, and yet never to have time to enjoy it—to have to endure, instead, constant tyranny and distress and frightful ailments in the chest, back, stomach, and head! While he was in this darkness of despair of human life, he learned that his mother had recently established herself as a seamstress in Aðalfjörður; and in some people's eyes it was regarded as a sign of no little arrogance for an uneducated woman to set herself up as a seamstress in the largest market town in the province, when other people had to be content with earning a living in the usual way. Hitherto it had never been thought to bring good fortune to have ideas above one's station.

In his heart the boy had often felt very bitter toward his mother for having sent him away in a sack in the middle of winter, to be brought up among strangers; indeed he had heard, more than ten years after he had been parted from her, that he had cried so hard that everyone thought he was going to burst; a northeasterly gale had been blowing. How could his mother have brought herself to send him away in a northeasterly gale, considering how much he must have loved her! A long, long time afterwards, when he began to think about it, he had vowed in revenge never to go back to her, whatever distress he might be in. But later, when he had once spent an entire day helping the brothers cut roofing-turf, he had been so sick with terror of the big, sharp turf-cutters they were wielding that he resolved to go back to her, unconditionally. He forgot that his mother had sent him away and imagined to himself that she lived in a timbered house with a door on one side and a window on each side of the door, and a high roof, and a chimney. He could even see the room, and in it a divan, yes, and window curtains just as in the pastor's house, and a picture on the wall, what is more, and most certainly a calendar. And he was with her.

He had come across mountains and deserts. She welcomed him with open arms, smiling, and embraced him hard and wept because she had sent him away in a sack in winter, and said that he was to stay with her forever. He forgave her, and wept. It was so lovely to be with her again. Yes, in the darkness as he was falling asleep, the way to her was smooth and easy to find, and the distance was hardly more than a stone's throw. But when he woke up in the morning and went outside, the air was gray and dank as usual, bereft of any enchantment or stimulation; all distances had suddenly become real once again; the mountain had sheer cliffs and sharp ridges. Other mountains rose on either side of the fjord. The way to his mother lay over many mountains, high moorlands, deep dales, and skerried fjords.

In the summer the brothers quarreled incessantly about the running of the farm, although no one apart from themselves could see any essential difference between their methods. But their greatest bone of contention was over the right to play around with Kristjána before they took a nap after the midday meal in the fields. The girl was quite willing to resolve this stubborn problem by letting each of them have one of her thighs on which to rest his head during the mid-day break. But neither of them would accept this simple solution.

As summer declined, the evenings began to darken and the birds fell silent; and that secret promise which characterizes the sky of early summer, those light, white clouds which sometimes piled up over the blue mountaintops in untidy heaps, soft and fresh as newly curdled milk—where were they now? The rain clouds of late summer spread over the whole sky, gray and heavy. The time for bringing the sheep down from the mountains was approaching, and there was still a lot of hay lying out in the meadows. Then came a dry spell, but it lasted only for two days; on the evening of the second day the storm clouds started gathering, and the rain was imminent again. Gather the hay! Gather the hay! The brothers were going berserk. On such evenings, people who work in the hayfields are like men possessed, striving to bring in the hay before it is too late. Dusk was beginning to fall.

Somehow or other it had been agreed that Jónas should truss hay with the hired hand, and Júst with Kristjána. But as the evening grew darker, the elder brother, Jónas, called out to Ólafur Kárason to go over to where Júst and Kristjána were working and help them with the rakings.

The younger brother heard this order from a distance, but instead of answering his brother directly, he went over to the boy and asked his dear little friend to go up the hill for him and fetch some horses, so that the hay could be taken home before it started to rain.

The boy stood there in the meadow with his masters, one on either side of him; the one told him to stay, the other told him to go, with rain threatening and not a moment to be wasted.

"You'll stay down here in the meadow, wretch," said Jónas.

"You'll go up the hill, friend," said Júst.

Kristjána came closer, and laughed.

Now, Jónas was certainly the older and stronger of the two, and it had been proved that when it came to a fight in earnest he could get the better of his younger brother; so according to the rule of force, it was better to obey Jónas. But on the other hand, Júst was considered the cleverer of the two, and for that reason it was difficult to predict what measures he might resort to if he were worsted; he could say "My friend" with a smile, and cut your throat. If you valued your life at all, it was safer to obey Júst, even though he were in the wrong.

"Up the hill, my friend," said Júst sweetly, and came a step closer to the boy.

"You'll stay down here!" bellowed Jónas, and he, too, came a step closer.

"Do as I tell you," whispered Júst.

"Do as I tell you!" roared Jónas.

It had now reached the point where young Kristjána was beginning to enjoy herself; she clapped her hands and shrieked. The hired hands, too, looked over their shoulders for a moment, even though it was now absolutely vital to carry on working. In no time at all the brothers' struggle for the boy's soul had reached the stage where each felt his honor was at stake.

Even though the boy had felt like running away only a moment ago, he now could not move a muscle or a limb and stayed where he was. He stood stock-still. But though he stood still, he was not doing so to disobey Júst's orders or to obey Jónas's command; he stood still because the terror in his heart was stronger than all other forces, internal or external. He was paralyzed. It was as if the blood had congealed in his veins. He felt as if a whole eternity had passed, even though the whole business, from beginning to end, had lasted for no more than a few seconds. He could never remember clearly what actually happened—one never tries to recall such moments afterwards. He only saw the fists being raised.

— 7 —

Some hideous memories and still more hideous forebodings drifted through his consciousness as he came round. It was nighttime, and an oil lamp glimmered faintly; rain drummed against the window. He heard himself groaning as if it were a stranger far away. Then the girl bent over him, and suddenly he realized what it was she smelled of—it was verdigris. But when she tried to raise him up and give him a drink of cold water, he began to see terrible faces in front of him: savage dogs, bloodshot eyes, fangs. They were going to tear him to pieces and kill him. Then they tore him to pieces and killed him.

He came round like that, time and again, and lost consciousness at once. At last he managed to remember who he was and where he was: the farm was Fótur-undir-Fótarfæti, the loft was such-and-such a size, Magnína was Magnína, and so on. In short, this was the world. But unfortunately he had once again forgotten what it was she smelled of.

If the pains in his head ever happened to ease for a spell, it was only to give place to other ailments in his body—a stitch in his side, gripes, pains in the back; he never had a moment of well-being. But the womenfolk on the whole did their best for him, and Magnína once even gave him hot scones. The two men in command, Jónas and Júst, left him in peace for most of the time, because he would be dying soon anyway. Instead of having to toil for eighteen hours a day, he now lay brooding over the cross he had to bear. Whenever the pains gave him any respite, he tried to compose a poem or some verses, mostly of a religious nature, but sometimes in the style of the old ditties that everyone knew. Otherwise he just lay there, the very embodiment of human helplessness, and stared up at the sloping ceiling.

But as the autumn passed, people's respect for his afflictions began to dwindle; their Christian attitude gradually gave way to talk of "the parish" in his presence. He was given to understand that the parish council at Sviðinsvík had been informed that he had taken to his bed and that they would have to start paying maintenance for him.

During those dreary autumn days when the only prospect facing the crossbearer was to be on the parish for life, he found consolation in remembering Guðrún of Grænhóll in the green glory of spring, standing like a vision beside a broad, calm river, with the top button of her cardigan undone; and he was determined to compose a poem about her so that the unborn generations should never forget her. He searched for a model in all the poetry he knew, and tried out various different verse forms, but thought her too exalted for any of them, either psalms or ballads. In the end he came to the conclusion that she belonged in folktales; and when he at last discovered this, he was able to compose something in a style worthy of her, and he scrawled his poem on a scrap of paper that evening.

> *An evening rare beyond compare,*
>   *The river glistened;*
> *And standing there a maiden fair,*
>   *Her dress at the top unfastened.*
> *Let mine be thine, and live with me forever;*
> *Mankind's sorrows will afflict thee never.*
>
> *Her fresh young gaze and winsome ways*
>   *Charmed each meeting;*
> *With kindly phrase to him she pays*
>   *A tender greeting.*
> *Let mine be thine, and live with me forever;*
> *Mankind's sorrows shall afflict thee never.*
>
> *Her shining eyes and fond replies*
>   *Will leave him never,*
> *Until he dies and buried lies*
>   *Alone forever.*
> *Let mine be thine, and live with me forever;*
> *Mankind's sorrows shall afflict thee never.*

Next day he could not find the poem anywhere, even though he was sure he had put it under his pillow the night before. But when the younger members of the family were eating their breakfast in the loft, through the bedclothes he sensed from their conversation that some grave misfortune had befallen the house.

"Yes, they're a charming lot, these wretches who lie groaning in their beds at the expense of impoverished far-off parishes. And I'd be extremely interested to learn who the wench was in this valley who's supposed to have unbuttoned her dress in front of him."

"If you ask me, Jónas, I think that all smut and lecherous talk is beneath me and therefore no concern of mine," said Magnína. "I think the most sensible thing to do in a case like this is to heed the old saying that 'pauper's talk means nothing.'"

"Her dress unfastened at the top! I've never heard such filthy talk in a poem about an innocent woman in all my born days," said the elder brother. "All I can say is that it's a mercy her clothes weren't unfastened lower down as well, whoever she was!"

"If you're going to carry on talking like that over this God-given food, I'm going down to the kitchen to call my mother," said Magnína.

"Well, as far as I'm concerned, and I'm the oldest and most experienced man in the family, I say that if there's going to be any more of this open obscenity here in this house, then it's going to be me who's in charge of the birch from now on. I don't care what anyone else says."

The younger brother, Júst, who had taken no part in this conversation so far, now had this to say:

"Let me tell you a little story which I know you will think very peculiar, even though it's absolutely true. I got it from a reliable man from the west who was my shipmate last winter, and he was told it by an old woman who remembered very clearly when it happened. There was once a parish pauper at Saeból, in Aðalvík, and would you believe it—he, too, began to use obscene and blasphemous talk openly in the house that gave him board and lodging. He started composing doggerel of a kind that even if I knew it by heart it would never even occur to me to let it soil my mouth. And what ploy do you imagine the people of Saeból thought up to get rid of him? They sold our little friend for bait to a foreign fishing-smack, to tell you the honest truth. And the fishermen tied our little friend alive to the mast and hacked tiny little bits off him as required. No, there was certainly no question of killing people on that boat! But it's said that for six days his screams carried all the way to land while they were fishing on the offshore bank there; on the seventh day, however, no more was heard, and it's said that they had caught enough fish and put out to sea. It was thought in the west that the last thing they cut from him was his heart. Yes, that's how they dealt with their parish paupers in the western fjords if they didn't behave themselves properly!"

The patient lay screaming the whole afternoon, and Magnína felt obliged to sit beside him and give him cold water to drink after her brothers had gone out; his sufferings so affected her that she could not give full vent to the loathing and disgust at his obscene doggerel that shocked and bruised all her finer sensibilities.

"I can't see anything for it but to write a description of your illness and send it to the doctor," she said that evening.

"Couldn't that be a bit dangerous?" he asked between groans.

"Dangerous?" she said. "To get oneself cured? What a ridiculous idea!"

"I mean, if the cure should be too quick," he said.

"Too quick?"

"Yes, and cause a relapse. It's bound to take a long, long time for someone in my wretched state of health to get fully cured."

But a few days later she was sitting in the loft, and the boy was crying out with pain again. He groaned loud and long, but she was getting used to it now and could not be bothered doing anything about it. Finally he said, "Yes, I think I'll just have to ask you to write out a description of the illness, as you were suggesting."

But Magnína was not quite so enthusiastic about writing anything now. It was not until several days later that she brought herself to it and came up with pen and paper. She sat down at the window and stared vacantly out into the blue, tilted her head sideways in resignation, and heaved a deep sigh. She appeared to be in real distress over it, and he almost felt a little sorry for her.

"I simply don't know what to write," she said.

"Just write that I'm ill," he said.

"It's not so easy to write that sort of thing," she said, and pondered again for a long time. "Where do you feel it?"

"In my whole body," he said, "but especially in the head, chest, back, and belly. You can safely say that I'm not too bad in the arms and legs. But you'd better say that the worst pains are in the head, and that it's as if something in my head were broken."

"How do you think I can write when you speak so quickly? And if you're going to suggest that someone in our house, where everyone's so good to you, has broken your skull, then I might as well tell you that it's no part of our job to write out a description of that kind."

"No, I had no intention of doing that, Magnína. How can you believe anything so wicked of me? Here in this house where everyone's so good to me! I just meant that my head feels as if my brain had begun to grow out into one ear. But if you don't want any mention of the head, we can just take the chest and those parts."

"I could always mention the head, I suppose," she said drily, "but I don't want to make all that much of it. I can say that the brain has started to grow out into the ear at one place, because that's like anything else which comes from inside and therefore can't give rise to any misunderstanding. But even so I think it would be best for all concerned if we confine ourselves to the chest."

"Yes, you can feel for yourself how my breastbone is sticking out," he said.

She felt his chest and noticed at once that the breastbone was sticking out a lot.

"In fact it feels as if there must be a cyst under the breastbone," he said. "I wouldn't be surprised if everything there has congealed into a malignant tumor—cyst, liver, lungs, and pericardium. At any rate the cyst's in a dreadful place. But as far as the lungs themselves are concerned, it's no exaggeration to say that one can hear the rattling of the tubercles from far away."

When the chest ailments had been recorded as accurately as possible, it was the turn of the belly complaints; that was another long and complicated story.

The preparation of the whole catalogue took the best part of the day; then it was sent to the doctor at Sviðinsvík at the first opportunity, with a request to send medicine as soon as possible.

The doctor at Sviðinsvík sent back word that for illnesses of this kind there were no effective medicines in the accepted sense of the word. He said that to cure illnesses of this kind there was nothing for it but to consume a whole pharmacopoeia costing up to two thousand krónur—and who could afford that in these difficult times? The doctor said he had never heard of anyone, man or woman, as ill as this boy was. If he had to give his honest opinion, he reckoned there was no hope for him at all; more than anything else, he would like to do an autopsy on him, he said.

— 8 —

That winter, when Ólafur Kárason had become bedridden for good and the parish was paying maintenance for him, they started looking around for an extra hand to see to the barn and carry water and tend the sheep on the foreshore. So one day at the end of October an old pauper was brought to the farm; he, too, was alone in the world, and his name was Jósep. He had red-rimmed eyes and a thin nose, with a white beard rimming his chin and white hair that covered his ears; his clothes were made of canvas, and they shone like a mirror, particularly at the knees and elbows. He had also some personal possessions which he carried in a kerchief; they made a small, flat bundle. He put this bundle on his knee when he sat down, and he trembled a little. He had greeted everyone, but contrary to custom no one had asked him what the news was. He was given some pickled tripe in a bowl, and he put his package under his thigh while he ate. His hands shook all the time.

Had he no luggage?

"I'm wearing two pairs of socks," he said apologetically.

Did he not have an overcoat?

"Oh, I don't really need an overcoat," he answered politely. "My clothes are wind- and water-proof; I've had them for more than ten years and they're still as good as new."

"I don't call that having clothes," said the housewife, Kamarilla. "I thought I deserved better of the parish officer than to have his paupers sent to me naked."

"It's not his fault, no one can help that—these are my clothes and no one has to wear them except me."

He seemed inclined to the opinion that in accordance with some special higher decree it had been ordained that these canvas clothes were the only clothes he was to have; in other words, that He who ruled the world seemed to have shown him some special consideration in this respect.

He was now told to go and fetch some water. The barn was needing water and the kitchen barrel was almost empty; it was best to get a move on; it was getting late. He stood up with the characteristic movements of the rheumatic, not quite straight in the back or the knees. He held his package awkwardly in his gnarled hands and shot a sideways glance at the invalid, as if asking a question.

"What's in the handkerchief?" asked Kamarilla.

"Oh, it's nothing, really," he said.

"I'll look after it for you," said Kamarilla.

"Oh, there's no need, thank you," he said, and finally stuck the package inside his jacket.

He was extremely taciturn, and so fastidious that there was never a speck of dirt to be seen on him. When he came in that evening he sat down on the bed opposite the invalid's bed and picked pieces of moss out of his socks and shredded them between his trembling fingers. He was very decrepit. He was given wool to wind, so that he should not sit idle-handed; but he was not very adept at winding wool, and his balls of yarn became rather tangled. No one told him to take off his wet clothes. He said nothing. Then it was bedtime. He took his package out of his jacket and put it carefully under his pillow. He looked at the invalid, and the invalid looked at him, but they did not exchange a word. It was not the custom in that house to bid one another good-night. Soon Kamarilla put the light out.

The first time they talked together was on a Sunday morning just before breakfast. They were alone in the loft. Then the old man said, as if he were talking to himself, and without looking at the boy: "Oh, you're not having a very cheerful childhood, somehow, poor soul."

"No," said Ólafur Kárason. "I'm like any other of our Lord's cross-bearers; most of the time there's little respite for me."

"I know all about it," said the old man. "I, too, was in bad health when I was a youngster."

"So you understand ill health, then?" asked the boy.

"Usually you get a little better for a time, if you don't die young," answered the old man. "It's best to die young."

"I'm ready to die when God calls me," said the boy.

"It's not at all certain that He will call you," said Jósep. "I, too, was ready to go at your age, but it's as if He prefers not to take those who are ready to go. It's as if the others are more vulnerable."

They were both silent for a while, and the old man leaned forward in his seat and shredded pieces of moss he had picked from his socks.

"I have the feeling that something must have happened to you sometime, Jósep," said the boy.

"No," said Jósep, and looked at the boy suspiciously. "Not that I know of. I can't really imagine what it is that should have happened to me."

"No, it just occurred to me," said the boy.

There was a brief pause.

"Maybe you're a bit lacking, poor fellow," the old man then said.

"Eh?"

"I mean, whether you're perhaps lacking something where the soul is concerned—you can't read, perhaps, or something like that?"

"What makes you think that?"

"Oh, it just occurred to me because of the question you asked: you were asking whether something had happened to me."

"The pastor reckoned I could read," said the boy. "And I'm quite certain that if I had a book, I'd get better much more quickly."

"Oh, there's nothing certain about that," said the old man. "A book isn't everything. It requires understanding to read a book."

"I have a little understanding," said the boy. "And whenever I have respite from the pain, I think a lot about poetry and that sort of thing."

"Yes," said the old man, "you think about a lot of things when you're ill, and that's because you don't know what you ought to be thinking. Have you begun to understand kennings* yet?"

"I can hardly say that," said the boy, "except for the very simplest ones, such as 'ring-bearer.'"*

"Yes, that's a very trivial kenning," said Jósep. "But what do you say about 'Fjalar's stream's bird'?"*

His worn, weather-beaten face brightened momentarily at the kenning; it was something that came from within, a shadow of a smile.

"I've never heard such a remarkable kenning in my life," said the boy in amazement.

"Then what do you say about 'Hárbarður's mead-horn's liquor'*— if I remember rightly, these are both from Pastor Snorri of Húsafell."

The boy was completely dumbfounded.

"Then I shall teach you a whole stanza by Pastor Snorri," said the old man, "so that you will have something to think about for the next week.

> *"'Fjölnir's cream I make to flow*
> *From Rögnir's bowl to Boðn's churn;*
> *Friggja's fine churn-pump turns the cream*
> *To Billingur's butter for Suttungur's cook.'"**

They broke off their conversation when the rest of the household came into the loft. But Ólafur Kárason was elated at having had the good fortune to make the acquaintance of a man who understood poetic kennings. He resolved to waste no opportunity for learning, now that he had the chance at last. But they were seldom alone, and higher things were frowned upon in that house, because from time immemorial the Icelandic people have had to struggle against men who called themselves poets and would not work for their living. Besides, the old man was inclined to hoard his knowledge and was reluctant to give the explanations of the kennings. Perhaps he had paid dearly for this little learning of his. And perhaps he had also some secret reason for being suspicious; perhaps he had suffered some minor disappointment in life, even if nothing had actually happened to him. He was also afraid of being laughed at, like all old people, and he had difficulty in finding any reason why anyone should want to turn to him in all sincerity. It took him a long time to be convinced that the boy's hunger for learning was not some concealed plot to pull his leg.

But finally he took his package from under his jacket and asked the boy to look after it for him during the day. In the evening he took it back again and kept it under his pillow during the night. Ó. Kárason of Ljósavík had never been anyone's confidant before—and now he had suddenly become a sort of bank vault. It was little wonder that he looked upon it as an important task to be entrusted thus with the total wealth of a seventy-year-old man every day.

In his handkerchief were a few tattered books; they contained manuscript copies of ballads, written in a remarkably beautiful Gothic hand, and every page had drawings in the margins. He handed the boy one book at a time, but would not let him handle them for very long.

"These were written out by Guðmundur Grímsson of Grunnavík," he said solemnly, and ran the edge of his hand over the books, as if he were smoothing out imaginary wrinkles.

In addition there was a large collection of poetry he had copied out himself, remarkable poems and verses of considerable intricacy which he had been collecting all his life; but the book had been filled up some years earlier. He had also scribbled into this book a few ditties and stanzas he had composed himself; for the truth was that he had had an inclination toward becoming a poet in his younger years, and of course had had to go on the parish. Certainly he had never dreamed of calling himself a poet proper, but on the other hand he had made the acquaintance of poets in his day—whether God had sent him poverty as a punishment for that or not. Anyway, he had no regrets about having made the acquaintance of poets. Some men became rich and had fine progeny and retired with dignity in their old age—but they had never made the acquaintance of poets. What was their life worth?

"I have seen all my seven children die; the earth took some, the sea took the others; some were fully grown, some died in childhood. And I have lost their mother, and all my closest relatives, and I myself had to give up my farm and go on the parish after living in the same croft for forty years—but what does that matter? I had Guðmundur Grímsson of Grunnavík for a friend. At any time I was ready to lead my only cow out of the barn and take it to him if he needed it, even if it meant depriving my own children of their sustenance. If I had the chance of living my whole life over again and having all my seven children alive, but doing without the friendship of Guðmundur Grímsson of Grunnavík, I would not accept it. Guðmundur Grímsson of Grunnavík is a master and a sage. He is undoubtedly the greatest living master and sage in Scandinavia. He has written more than two hundred books, including the history of three counties, the biographies of pastors and sheriffs, a seven-volume history of great events of the past, scores of genealogies, several ballads, a hundred and fifty short stories, a book of folktales, a history of the Chinese, and other learned works, as well as four thousand poems, not forgetting his great educational treatise on the vernacular language of the Gascons in ancient times. It was compiled from some tattered old manuscripts he found in an old woman's cottage up north in Kvifjáryndisdalur when he was a youngster, and it has taken him all his life to master this language. The sheriff was shown his treatise, and he sent it to a world-famous professor in Denmark, and it's thought that he will get a prize for it sometime, perhaps a gold medal; he has already got five krónur from the sheriff for it."

When Ó. Kárason of Ljósavík had become acquainted with Jósep's stock of literature and had found the key to it, his poetic directions changed radically. For a time he had leaned strongly toward the psalm form because his fate was in the hands of God, but more particularly because it was easier for those who were not all that well versed in kennings. But though he had always considered it absolutely vital, when his sufferings were greatest, to compose poems about the mercy of God and the duty of the afflicted to bear their cross patiently, nevertheless he had, deep down, remained convinced that nothing could truly be called poetry if it did not use kennings. Now to his great surprise he suddenly discovered that ballads not only contained kennings, but also that their heroes overcame their enemies not by humility but by fighting them to the bitter end. This made him rack his brains furiously. No, he did not believe he was in any condition to fight; he was bound to God through his illness and his misery; he lived his life in the shadow of another world. But nonetheless he admired the ballads; with their heroes, princesses, battles and sea journeys they signified for him a world he was prevented from enjoying—this world. He pulled the eiderdown over his head.

— 9 —

All at once the memory of Guðrún of Grænhóll rose like a sun over his mind. She was on the bank of a clear-water stream early in the spring. She was flushed with walking. He had the feeling that it was early morning, or rather late at night at midsummer when nothing is real, when hill and heath dissolve into a blue unreality, when matter itself becomes almost translucent in this mystical clarity which is neither night nor day; the awareness which is confronted by this sublime wakefulness is neither sleep nor waking. And in the middle of this landscape the girl appeared like some shimmering illusion; her hair shone; he saw her lips moving; he heard the sound of her voice. With a start he sat up in bed—was it possible that anything like that could happen? Did she exist?

He lay there all day, drunk with happiness, thinking about this sight, this vision. But little by little his ecstasy faded. By nightfall he was sad and depressed; the world's sorrows engulfed him again; he felt that he would never be able to throw off this burden—and besides, he had unbearable headaches. That night he could not sleep because the paralyzing anguish of life was clawing at his heart; he could no longer entice any consoling vision into his consciousness; he felt that God was punishing him for something terrible he had done. Once again he was gripped by that crushing dread of the soul's immortality, and besought the Lord to extinguish his life forever.

When all was said and done, the unemotional days were the happiest, the days of healthy, natural boredom when sleep did not flee away in the evenings but came as a friend and brought day to a close. On those days he would seize with the curiosity of the idle upon every trivial thing that happened within range of his vision.

He followed closely the cat's every movement from the moment it began to wash itself, reaching with its paw behind its ear, until it finished washing itself and lay down and went to sleep. He followed the sunbeam which crept slowly up from the floor, across his bed, and all the way up to the sloping ceiling; by then it was six o'clock; the evening ray was very red. Any human speech he heard enchanted him, or at least made him strain his ears to listen; he felt that everything concerned him, he wanted to know everything. Every word he caught gave him food for thought. Many things he had never paid any heed to when he was healthy now aroused his interest and exercised his mind; he listened eagerly for news of any kind, so hungry was his perception, so desperately did his mind crave to be fed.

These were the doldrums of the soul. Magnína moved sluggishly about the loft for most of the day, and in the evening, when it began to grow dark, it was as if the darkness developed around her and then spread out from her, little by little, to the rest of the room. She did not talk to him, but he watched her moving around or being still, and he was aware of her smell. She often had knitting in her hands; never anything downright coarse because she was the daughter of the house, but never anything very fine even though she was the daughter of the house. He often tried to look her in the face, but there was never any joy in her face, nor any sorrow either. There was just obstinate peevishness, often accompanied by a little mumbling; then she would exhale noisily a little and then sniff a little. It was as if she were alternately inhaling and exhaling that smell of hers. If he talked to her without being asked, she would take that as a sign that he was better. He did not talk to her.

Summer was on the way and everyone was out-of-doors except his foster mother, who did the cooking and seldom came upstairs to the loft except for a short nap at noon. The midsummer days were very still. He heard the faint murmur of summer birdsong through closed windows; it was impossible to open a window there. Whenever he felt quite safe he would try, despite unbearable suffering, to creep out of bed and over to the window and look out over the calm fjord and the mountain beyond it, mirrored in the water. There was a glitter of white birds' wings over Ljósavík, a flock of terns. He was amazed at how tranquil and sublime the life of midsummer was, how calm and dignified its movements were. He imagined that eternal bliss, if it existed at all, would be like this—just like this midsummer. Then summer was over, and the evenings drew in again.

As autumn passed, the old man was often in a difficult mood. He would sulkily brush the splashes of mud off his clothes or angrily shred the pieces of moss he picked from his socks, and mumble inaudibly into his beard, and the brothers jeered at him as they wolfed their supper at the other end of the loft. The trouble was that just about this time the old man had stopped obeying orders and had started doing things his own way, especially when he was given contradictory orders from opposite sides. One day in October there was a furious rainstorm, as often happens in autumn, the clouds black in the sky and mud everywhere. The boy Ólafur Kárason lay staring up at the sloping ceiling in a trance of monotony; perhaps he was also thinking that on such an autumn day of glowering skies, drenching rain and endless mud, no one should be pitied for being on the outside of earthly life. Then suddenly, in the middle of the day, the old man came up the stairs, soaking wet and without his cap. But the really unusual thing about him at that moment—this fastidious man who was always cleaning his canvas clothes, who would not even tolerate a bit of moss on his socks—was that he was covered with mud on one side, all the way up to the cheek. There was mud also on those silver-white locks which were his ornament and badge of dignity. And he was weeping.

No one who has heard an old man weeping can ever forget it, and Ó. Kárason of Ljósavík, who only a moment ago had been standing on the outside of earthly life, suddenly found himself in the middle of it. He listened appalled to this broken, feeble sobbing. He had always imagined that old men could not weep, but from that moment on he knew the opposite: that no one can weep more bitterly; that the weeping of old men is the only true weeping. He propped himself up on one elbow to look.

"What's wrong, Jósep?" he asked finally.

The old man answered through his sobs (he still had not recovered sufficiently to clean up his clothes): "I was struck," he said. "I was pushed."

A younger child would have said of other children, "They hit me; they pushed me," and would have named names. But after having been a luckless poet, after having lived forty years on a croft and lost seven children to the earth or to the sea, he only said, "I was struck; I was pushed." He did not accuse anyone. The power that governed his life was impersonal.

Yes, he had been struck down into the mud in front of the barn, this fastidious man, this elderly poet. The boy pulled the bedclothes up over his head and trembled a little. He at once realized in his heart that he did not possess the kind of strength required to console an old man. One can commit misdeeds against a child and justify them in the eyes of oneself and God and the world, for life itself justifies everything and reconciles youth to everything; but nothing can make up for all the wrongs that have been committed against old people in Iceland. When the boy looked out from under the bedclothes again the old man had gone; he had only come to fetch his kerchief.

That evening the boy heard the old man's departure being discussed up in the loft. He heard the brothers over and over again petulantly mentioning the nether regions. The housewife, Kamarilla, said that they might just as well have led out their best cow and drowned her in the deepest part of the ocean as drive away the only person on the farm who brought any appreciable amount of money into the house. Magnína was furious and snorted and sniffed in turn, until she said aloud that there would have been a lot more sense in driving away some people who were less useful guests in the larder than the old man had been. *Some* people, she said. The conversation quickly reached the level which was customary in that place.

Next morning the mountains were white all the way down to the sea; a bitterly cold storm was blowing, with heavy snow showers. That day the parish officer came on a visit. He brought Jósep with him, mounted on a pony he was leading by a halter. The old man had taken refuge with the parish officer the night before and asked to be transferred to another farm; but the parish officer unfortunately could not possibly think of any better place than the one where he had already been deposited. He invited his elderly visitor to stay overnight, then set him on a horse the following morning and led him to this proper place. The housewife, Kamarilla, had a drop of brennivín.* The parish officer needed capable men for his boat that winter. Magnína had a wash and combed her hair, in order to wait upon the visitor. There were cheerful sounds of welcome from the room below.

But the old man dragged himself upstairs to the loft and lay down on his bed. He had arrived at the parish officer's house the previous day hot from his flight; but there was little warmth in the blankets of the authorities, and he had caught a chill. If anyone thought it odd that the parish officer should have led the old man's horse on a halter, it was simply because the old man had been trembling so violently that he was unable to hold the reins himself. The widow Karítas had to be summoned to help him off with his canvas clothes. Then he pulled the bedclothes up and turned his face to the wall.

Old people are very little trouble when they are ill. They die without any fuss. In reality there is no creature on earth so alone as an old man. There is no point in fussing around old men who are ill, or trying to help them; and in this respect old men are like animals—they die as helpless as animals. This man, this fastidious old man who owned a few books in a kerchief and seven children in the earth or in the sea, and who had wanted to be a poet—how lonely and helpless he was when he died! Nothing at all was done for him in the last days of his life. And yet his death was considered a loss, for no other creature on that farm provided as much money as he had done; he had provided more than a hundred krónur a year in hard cash.

Some people might think that everything happened in storybook fashion, and that the old man died at once; but that was not what happened at all. He did not die at once, but lingered on for many days, even though he did not quote poetry and intricate kennings very much, under the circumstances. But how incredibly still he lay during those days before he died! And how incredibly little was done for him during those days before he died! Nothing at all, except that Ó. Kárason of Ljósavík propped himself up in bed every now and again and had a look at him.

Once or twice the old man, too, tried to sit up in bed and say something in his delirium. Usually he would be asking whether Guðmundur Grímsson of Grunnavík would not care to read aloud a small section of his *History of the Chinese* or else a brief obituary, because the weather was so good.

"Wouldn't you like a sip of cold water, Jósep?" asked Ó. Kárason of Ljósavík.

A long time later, the old man tried to lift his head again and said, "Listen, Guðmundur, I can look after the barn for you so that you don't have to interrupt your work on the *History of the Seven Sages.*"

"You should be thinking about your late wife and children, dear, instead of talking about that devil Guðmundur who never tried to earn a living for himself or others," said the housewife, Kamarilla.

But the old man probably reckoned that the people the housewife had mentioned could take care of themselves. He was with Guðmundur now, and he fell back against the pillow.

Soon it was Sunday. Old Jósep had lain with scarcely a movement for two days without saying anything worthy of note. Kamarilla brought out the *Book of Sermons* and read the Sunday lesson. "And it came to pass that Jesus said unto his disciples. . . ." Then the lesson came to an end. But when the reading was over and the last psalm had been sung, old Jósep made one more attempt to sit up in bed. His expression now was that of the dying, transfigured and bright, for the sun of another world was rising for him; his tongue, which had been fettered in his mouth for the last few days, was freed again, and his blurred speech was clear and coherent once more.

"Guðmundur Grímsson of Grunnavík is a great poet," he said. That was all he said. These were his last words. Soon he was dead. Kamarilla the housewife stood beside the bed and watched the man dying. He had said his last words. "Yes," said Kamarilla, "we shall all have to say our last words some day." She closed his eyes at once. The weather outside was fine; there was no rain. She wiped one eye with the corner of her apron, for appearance's sake.

So now Ó. Kárason of Ljósavík had death as a companion in the next bed. There would come moments when this young invalid would have a horror of death, but now he was impressed at how quiet a visitor he was, how natural and straightforward. In reality it seemed as if nothing had actually occurred, it had all happened so politely. Old Jósep's last words continued to echo through the boy's mind: Guðmundur Grímsson of Grunnavík. So distinguished was this visitor, Death, that when he approached, people involuntarily blurted out the name they held dearest. For the rest of his life the boy could see in his mind's eye the old man dying and Kamarilla standing by his bedside, and the name Guðmundur Grímsson of Grunnavík, so hated and so loved, sounding in the air around them. Such has been the conflict over Icelandic poets since time immemorial: some people damned them all their lives, others died with their names on their lips.

But that night the boy could not sleep. It was autumn, and he could hear the storm raging outside. In the bed opposite him lay a corpse. Yes, in his childhood that man, too, had heard the Revelation of the Deity. His whole mind had been directed toward one single harmony. When he was a child, he had lain in a green hollow in springtime and called out to The One. He had been ill, but later he had got better—for a time. Then he had built himself a cottage and had begotten seven children by his wife, but they all had vanished into the earth or the sea before he went on the parish again. No, nothing had ever happened to him; anyone who imagined that something had happened to him must be a bit lacking. Guðmundur Grímsson of Grunnavík had been his life. Now he was a corpse. What—*who* was a corpse?

The boy sat bolt upright in bed, terror-stricken, in the middle of the night, because he thought someone was whispering, "Ólafur Kárason of Ljósavík is a corpse." In other words he felt that it was he himself who lay dead at last, on the bed opposite, after this purposeless life of his, with all its dreams unfulfilled. It was so real, so vivid, that he felt compelled to deny it aloud: "My God, my God, no, no, no!" he cried aloud, over and over again in the middle of the night. Someone at the other end of the room stirred in his sleep, and the boy cowered down under the bedclothes with his heart beating furiously. He called upon God hundreds of times because he thought it so terrible to have been struck and pushed into the mud in his old age and to be dead at last without having become a poet. Gradually he became less agitated.

No, he was not dead. "I shall get well," he said to himself. "I *shall*. Some day. Arise," he thought. "Become a great poet." He tried to forget this autumn night, looking forward instead to the day when he would arise. One morning he would wake up early. That morning he would suddenly have recovered his health. He would get dressed as if the past were over, and walk carefree out into the spring. There would be this strong, tranquil clarity over land and sea, this glossy sheen on the ocean, velvet-smooth clouds off the coast, the uninterrupted sound of birdsong, a thrush up on the hillside. The flowers would be blossoming in the homefield. And no one would be up and about except him, so unsullied was this morning; no one had set foot in the dew of this morning, no one; no one had seen this morning except him. Glorious vistas opened their arms to him alone; and he walked smiling towards the beauty of this day.

Yes, one spring morning he would wake up early.

_____ **10** _____

Some people from another district who had got themselves ferried over the fjord brought a letter and a small parcel for the moribund soul who lay yearning in the corner under the sloping ceiling. "My dear son . . ." It was a letter from his father, writing to him from a distant fjord. So after all it was his father who remembered him even though he had once deserted his mother. His father told him to be of good heart. Unfortunately, his father said, he could not come to see him, but he said he was asking God to be with him. His father said he was in great difficulties himself, from poverty and ill health, and that he was in receipt of parish support himself, but he said that God was with him. That was why he was thinking about his son. On the other hand his mother was now an important person at Aðalfjörður and did not remember him at all, and the boy was angry with his mother and wished he could have some other mother, sometime; it could still make him weep to think that his very own mother should have sent him away in a sack in the middle of winter.

In the parcel there were three books. One was a book of poems by his father, called *New Poetics*, a little book, all in ballad form. There were poems about skippers, congratulatory odes to merchants and pastors, verses on tobacco and the weather, as well as a narrative poem about a remarkable and unusual drunken brawl that took place in Aðalfjörður some years back in which one man lost his front teeth, and so on. The second book was the *Núma Ballads* by Sigurður Breiðfjörð, printed in the old Gothic lettering.* And finally there was a notebook with a hundred blank pages, a penholder, three pen nibs, and a little bottle of ink.

At first glance, the writing materials were to him the most precious of these gifts. With them he was at last given the long-desired opportunity of becoming an intellectual and making his words immortal. Thereafter, when he himself was dead, he imagined that his poems would be published in some mysterious way, and the nation would read them for comfort in adversity, as it had read the poems of other poets before him; it was his highest wish that his poems could help those as unfortunate as himself to have patience to endure. They would say, "He has bequeathed to us sublime psalms with kennings, so that we could find the spirit." Perhaps even his mother would then begin to feel fond of him, although it would be too late then.

It was not until he began leafing through the *Núma Ballads* that he began to feel doubt about the value of his own unwritten books. Acquaintaince with Sigurður Breiðfjörð's poetry brought a new dawn of experience, brighter than any that had been before. The artificial vocabulary of the kennings in the *Ordeals of Jóhánna* and the other masterpieces by Pastor Snorri of Húsafell, which the late Jósep had liked best, at once seemed poverty-stricken and dreary now, compared with Sigurður Breiðfjörð's pure Eddaic style and his clearly comprehensible subject matter, and above all that enchanting gift of expression that roused in the heart an incurable awareness of beauty and sorrow. Previously he had thought that all poets were glorious and that all poetry was of equal worth provided that it dealt chiefly with heroic exploits, or especially with Jesus Christ's feats of redemption, in either a sufficiently intricate or a sufficiently religious way. "The motherland where men were born"—now he discovered in a flash that there were differences between poets. And wherein did this difference lie? Mainly in the fact that other poets seemed to have only the vaguest notion about the way that leads to the heart, whereas Sigurður Breiðfjörð followed this mysterious path quite instinctively— but without leaving behind him any signposts for other poets to follow; yes, he found his way into every heart and touched it with beauty and sorrow.

When there was no one else in the loft, the boy would sit up hastily, bring out the *Núma Ballads*, from under his pillow, and swallow a few verses, forgetting for the moment all his sufferings. If he heard someone on the stairs, he would hastily thrust the book under the pillow and lie back again. But the lovely lines did not fade in his mind even though someone arrived; they continued to echo and seethe there. Toward the end of winter he knew all the poems by heart, and Sigurður Breiðfjörð reigned supreme over his soul and was his refuge in all his sufferings. And so it came about that on the first sunny days of February the poet himself stepped down from the little sunbeam on the ceiling, as if from a heavenly golden chariot, rosy-cheeked and blue-eyed, and laid his gentle master's hand on the pain-racked head of Ólafur Kárason of Ljósavík and said, "You are the light of the world." It was one of those dreams that make the dreamer a happy man, ready to bear with a happy heart anything that might happen to him. Tirelessly the boy thought about the poet and his golden chariot whenever he was in distress; such can be the therapeutic effect of one single dream. One day in the dark of winter, in the middle of this dreary world which was so hostile to a sensitive heart, the great poet himself had come to him in his golden chariot and had baptized him into the light:

Beaten, bruised, in fetters bound,
In darkness when in bed I lie,
To me o'er the sunlit sound
Comes Sigurður Breiðfjörð from the sky.

In his eyes a smile I see
Gleam from his chariot of gold,
The smile which once, from sorrow free,
I sang to my love of old.

In the darkness of the barn at night
I hear his voice, I see his eyes;
He summons me toward the light,
The golden chambers of the skies.

—— **II** ——

When the parish pauper started writing out his own poetry in a book on Sundays, it was hardly surprising that the members of the family began to look at him askance.

"He's healthy enough for that sort of rubbish, the damned malingerer," said the elder brother, Jónas.

"Oh, you never know, perhaps our little friend's book might just happen to get torn to pieces one day," said Júst.

But when they looked at him writing, their irritation was mingled with fear, as when a dog eyes a cat. Sometimes the boy felt that the dread with which the written word filled them was even stronger than the hatred they felt for mankind. And now, as ill luck would have it, a scrap of paper with the poem about Sigurður Breiðfjörð on it was blown by a draft down the stairs and fell into the family's hands.

"Never in my whole life have I ever seen or heard such filth!" said the housewife, Kamarilla. "Nor did I ever dream that I had reared such a viper at my breast, who dares to accuse us of beating him and maltreating him and says he is made to sleep in the barn—yes, and

other lies of this sort that I and the rest of us here will be quick to
refute with witnesses and oaths if it's your intention to let other
people see these scraps of paper. But what you say about us is as
nothing to the way you blaspheme about God, and you'd better
know now, if you didn't know it before, that I shall not suffer blasphemy to go unpunished in my house which the Lord has blessed for
so long. And I must say that never in my whole life have I heard such
depraved ideas in a young rascal, uttering the name of Sigurður
Breiðfjörð in the same breath as that of our Father, for if there was
ever a drunkard and lecher and dishonest rogue in Iceland it was
him—not content with being sentenced to twenty-seven strokes of
the birch for lechery, he even sold his own wife to a Dane in the Vest-
mannaeyjar Islands for a dog! And how did he end up? Little wonder
that he himself died like a dog in Reykjavík and was buried there like
a dog, unnoticed and unmourned."

Ólafur Kárason, on the other hand, was convinced that this shock-
ing tale was told not so much to let the truth be known as from
a desire to make the listener a better person, for he had his own
unshakable religious experience as proof that Sigurður Breiðfjörð
had come to him in a golden chariot from the heavens. But what distressed him far more, not unnaturally, was the fact that he was given
nothing to eat that evening. Instead, Magnína found cause to make
several visits to the loft, where she huffed and snorted as if there were
a bad smell in the room, and cursed the abomination and lechery
that went on among some people and particularly among weaklings
and wretches who could not even go to the privy without help. And
when he eventually plucked up courage and remarked that someone
had forgotten to bring him his supper that evening, she said, "You
can just let your sweetheart in the golden chariot bring you your supper. Why should I bother myself with that? I see nothing to smile
about."

Later that evening the brothers came in and ate in front of him,
smacking their lips enthusiastically, and sucking at their teeth long
after they had finished their meal.

"What should one do, exactly, with a lewd blasphemer like this?"

said the elder brother. "To Hell with having such a creature in one's own home."

"Oh, I should think the best thing is to take our dear friend into the darkness of the barn," said the younger brother sweetly.

For three days no one spoke to him except for gibes in the third person—"Strange how people who are beaten and bruised and bound in fetters don't just stand up and go where they would be better treated." "Extraordinary that someone can be brought up among Christian people and never learn a sense of shame." "Incomprehensible morality some wretches have, composing filthy lampoons about their benefactors—not content with composing harmless nonsense and rubbish, but mixing in obscenity and heresy with it."

His supper was withheld from him altogether in the hope that such measures would teach him to write poetry that would commend itself to Christian folk; everyone avoided him as if he were a leper, and in the evenings no one came into the loft and no light was lit, just to help him to realize how wicked he was and to let him experience literally what it was like to lie in darkness; and so he lay there alone and helpless in the darkness, ravenously hungry, racked with unbearable headaches and trembling with agony of soul.

Then the elder brother, Jónas, came up to the loft one evening, lit a small lamp, rummaged behind his bed, brought out his shaving tackle, and began to hone his razor. The boy was seized by ice-cold terror, because whenever he heard a knife being sharpened he always feared the worst. But on this occasion Jónas was not planning to cut anybody's throat, but only to have a shave. This was only small consolation, however, because the boy knew from experience that shaving, for these brothers, was always performed with the utmost ferocity and accompanied by the most foul language reminiscent of bloodbaths and cattle-slaughtering, if not of downright crime. He could never feel himself to be safe while this butchery was going on anywhere near him; it was as if a great weight were lifted from him when the champion finally sheathed his greedy weapon again. He devoutly hoped that Jónas would slouch off when he had finished shaving; he made himself as inconspicuous as possible, pulled the bedclothes over his head, and pretended to be asleep. There was no one else in the loft. But Jónas showed no signs of slouching off; he went on preening himself in front of the mirror, pulling his face into various horrible grimaces, and cursing and swearing under his breath. Finally he put the mirror back on the shelf—but he did not go out. He began to peer toward the boy at the far end of the loft, clearing his throat and spitting in his direction, as if he were addressing him. Finally he came slouching over to him, right to his bedside. The boy smelled everything that was happening through a corner of his blanket. Now Jónas was right beside the bed. He laid his terrible paw on his shoulder, and for a moment the boy was convinced he was holding an open knife in his other hand, and he let out a scream.

"What are you yelling for?" said Jónas. "I don't see anything to yell about."

"Dear, dear Jónas," he implored tearfully. "Let me live. Don't hurt me, I'm so terribly ill. In God's name."

"I'll be damned, always composing obscenities and blasphemies."

"I'll never do it again, dearest Jónas," said the poet. "But it seems to relieve my pains when I think about literature."

"It's all the same to me," said Jónas. "The parish pays, not me. And I've never beaten you. Or are you daring to suggest that I've ever beaten you?"

"No, no, God in Heaven above knows that you've never beaten me, Jónas."

"No—at least, never very much."

"Never at all, dear Jónas."

"At least I never knocked you out."

"I call Jesus to witness that you've never beaten me, Jónas," said the boy.

"Well, then," said Jónas. "So why can't you keep your bloody mouth shut instead of composing filthy lampoons about all of us here and accusing us and telling lies about us maltreating you? We who treat you so well that there is no one else in the whole parish who lives in such luxury as you?"

"Would you like me to compose a eulogy in your honor, Jónas?" asked the poet.

"Listen, aren't you just a bloody doggerel merchant?" asked Jónas.

"Yes," said the poet. "But when a man is both spiritually and physically ill, one becomes a poet involuntarily; you simply can't help it."

"Yes, you're just a useless wretch like all the others."

Now there was a short pause in the conversation, until to the boy's astonishment Jónas asked directly: "Have you ever in your whole life heard a more rubbishy bit of poetry than this?

> *"'Your love I never sought to buy*
> *With words as precious tokens.*
> *Your heart knew what in mine did lie—*
> *In silence love was spoken.'"*

The boy recognized at once the verse from Sigurður Breiðfjörð's *Núma Ballads* but did not dare to express an opinion, for he understood that Jónas was against the poem.

"Can't you open your trap to answer, or do you want me to give you a hiding? If you don't say at once whether it's good or bad I'll soon show you what you'll get for it."

"It's good," the boy whispered in a trembling voice.

"No, to Hell with that, I'm not going to let myself be treated like this in my own house! It would serve you right if I gave you such a hiding that there wouldn't be a bone left unbroken in your body—to say that this wretched doggerel and obscenity about an honorable girl who is no damned concern of yours is good poetry, when it's by that lecher and good-for-nothing Júst, what's more, who'll never be master of this household!"

"But that poem," said the boy. "It's by Sigurður Breiðfjörð; I saw it in print in the *Núma Ballads*."

Jónas stopped cursing for a moment and his face became completely expressionless, as if the news had paralyzed him; and finally he said dully, "No, you're lying."

"As I live, it's the truth," said the boy.

"Never in all my born days have I heard anything so filthy! To think that a wretched swine like that should be called one's own brother—stealing poetry from a man lying dead in his grave in order to buy his way into her favor! You see, she promised to sleep with the one who first composed a poem about her. And that's the difference between us brothers, I'm honest but he's a thief, and if it isn't breaking the law to steal poetry from a dead man, then I don't know what stealing is; and stealing's not the right word for it either. It's grave robbing, and what a bloody fool I've been, I could just as easily have done it myself."

When Jónas had reproached himself for his folly for a while, he pulled a plug of tobacco out of his pocket, bit off a piece, and then offered the plug to the boy. "I order you to take a bite," he said, and the boy did not dare to refuse.

"Listen," he then whispered, his mouth bulging with tobacco, and leaned over the invalid. "Listen, have you ever tried your hand at composing a proposal to a woman?"

Ólafur Kárason was covered in confusion and answered inaudibly.

"No, I suppose it's too much to expect you to have the brains for that," said Jónas. "Obviously you're impotent, like all invalids. But it can be hellishly difficult, even though you're as fully virile as I am, to put together a poem to a woman and get it to rhyme properly—even when she's more or less offered to sleep with you. To get it to rhyme properly, man, that's the hardest thing about poetry, even when you're going mad with frustration, even though you start the moment you get up and try all day and lie awake far into the night. I would rather pay my worst enemy twenty-five *aurar* than have to toil at that myself."

"I'd be more than happy to compose a little poem to her for you, if you like, Jónas," said the poet. "And it won't cost you a thing, either. That's the least I owe you for having been so good to me always."

"I insist on paying," said Jónas. "I'm an honest man. I'm no grave robber. At the very least I shall order Magnína to give you some food at once tomorrow morning, like any other person outside the family. But if you put any obscenity into it I'll kill you; make it so that it's easy to understand, and remember to work her name into the poem, and mine too, Jónas Bjarnason, sheep-farmer and boat-owner at Fótur-undir-Fótarfæti here in this parish, so that she can see that I composed the poem to her myself, and that my poem wasn't stolen from a dead man in his grave like my brother Júst's poem, do you hear me?"

"What's the girl's name, if I may ask?" said the poet.

"What's that got to do with you, you fool? It's me who's composing the poem, not you. It's me who's the poet, in fact, not the devil Júst, and I command you to put into the poem that Júst is both a reactionary, a thief, a traitor, and a rebel against me and his mother, and that he will never succeed in having charge of this farm. And put into the poem that he would soon ruin this farm completely with his extravagance and improvidence if he was ever allowed to run it. And she'll soon be for it if she lets my brother Júst take her, lock, stock, and barrel, before his mother's very eyes, as she did last night, and all for a poem he stole from a dead man; and for God's sake don't forget to put it into the poem that she's a bloody mare who's been playing merry hell from morning to night ever since she came of age and never given a clean-living fellow a moment's peace, always biting and kicking; and that my brother Júst is a year and a half younger than I am, and that I'm the rightful head of this household, and that she can have plenty of figs from me, and brennivín as well, but never to excess up in the hayloft until she's as tight as a tick, as she was with Júst, who will undoubtedly end up on the parish; and tell her that she'll only have herself to blame if she lets him drag her into destitution, and you can be as coarse as you like to her and say that I'll kill her stone dead, so help me—do you hear me?"

When Jónas was gone, Ólafur Kárason composed in the darkness this "Poem to the Dearly Beloved":

> *I know a girl who far outshines all others,*
> *A lively filly in a herd of mothers;*
> *With lovely eyes and legs so neat,*
> *She neighs and bites and kicks her feet,*
> *Oh, maiden sweet!*
> > *Sweet buds of Christian love will flower*
> > *Around her bower.*

They've all been trying hard, I know, to win her,
But none has managed yet, I think, to pin her;
Until she found a man to keep,
A boat-owner who handles sheep,
Both wise and deep.
  Sweet buds of Christian love will flower
  Around her bower.

He'll give her brennivín in moderation,
Sweets and figs and fruit from every nation;
If she doesn't lose her charm,
He will give her Fótur, his farm,
And his strong arm.
  Sweet buds of Christian love will flower
  Around her bower.

Next morning the pauper was given food to eat, like other people.

—— **12** ——

Shortly after New Year the brothers abandoned their battlefield at
home and left for distant fishing stations. There was not much talk
about their departure beforehand; their mother saw to their gear
herself, and then they were gone, leaving behind the womenfolk
and the poet. The older women and Kristjána shared the work in
the barn and feeding the livestock; Magnína did the cooking for the
household; and the poet lay under the sloping ceiling and waited for
the sunbeam. But when Magnína was left alone in the house, she
often sat upstairs in the loft on her mother's soft bed and stared at
the frostwork on the window and yawned and sniffed and counted
how many pairs of stockings she had, and perhaps changed her stockings or put an extra pair on. She was usually chewing or munch-
ing something. Some days she would wash her face, and behind
the ears as well. Then she would pull her feet up on to the bed and

lie down on her side and fall asleep; perhaps she had left a pot on the stove, and she would wake up at the smell of burning which wafted up from the kitchen into the loft; the porridge would be scorched.

Often when she was preening herself in the loft at midday, the boy wondered whether he should dare speak to her to pass the time. He yearned so much for the company of a living soul. Most of all he longed to talk about the Light and the Spirit. He looked at her furtively, sidelong, and tried to size her up from the point of view of Light and Spirit. He asked himself, Could there be a secret chord lurking somewhere deep in that dark flesh?

After the brothers had gone she made a habit of coming up to the loft at bedtime and sitting at her mother's bedside; they talked together in undertones, but the invalid was curious and sharp-eared like all those who are on the outside of the world. On Magnína's side the conversation to begin with was all more or less harmless criticisms of some people, she was never entirely satisfied with some people, probably because she was not satisfied enough with herself.

But one night the tune changed. Something had happened; the boy caught a hint of some long-drawn-out tale of crime, with big, fat, heavy sighs and frequent invocations to Jesus above Who knew it was all true. The mother tried to make little of it for a long time, but in the end she fell silent, so cogent was the evidence. Then Magnína said, "Didn't I tell you in the autumn that this would happen if you let that hussy stay?"

The mother said nothing.

"Didn't I perhaps warn you about those whore's eyes of hers?"

And when the mother still made no reply, the daughter grew impatient and said loudly, "You just say nothing!"

"I don't see that it's any use saying very much," said the mother.

"I can believe that!" said Magnína. "There's nothing much said to some people. Some people can do anything they like. It's a different story for other people. Decent people are never allowed to call their lives their own all their born days. Decent people have to live and die like haltered beasts."

"Which of the boys could it have been?" said Kamarilla thought-fully.

"Which? As if it was only one or the other? No, if it had only been one of them I wouldn't be saying anything. But since when have whores like that been content until they have reduced everything in trousers around them down to their own level? My God in heaven, what have I done to deserve this!"

"Oh, it's just the way life goes, Magnína dear," her mother said. "We just have to take that sort of thing with understanding."

"All right, then," said Magnína, "if that's the way life goes, then it's best to let this immorality remain here. But one thing's certain, I'm going away from here."

"I don't like driving these two poor wretches away, mother and daughter, with the fishing season just started and no man on the farm, apart from the parish pauper over there in the corner."

"Yes, I know, that's you all over, you gather round you evil-minded harlots and useless parish paupers, but your own children whom you have taught to live a decent Christian life you drive from home, out into the snow in the middle of winter. But to get a decent man on the farm, a clean-living man who's good with animals and does his work honestly and leaves other people in peace—that's something you can't understand. And I'm sure no one bothers to feel sorry for me, my brothers' own sister, having to cook and serve food to this creature who has degraded them both, yes, and on top of that to have to listen to my own mother finding excuses for her, a harlot, pregnant by any male who comes along, in the middle of the high-way so to speak, while other people are made to pine away like some sort of outlaws in their own family home."

Magnína had now begun to sniff abnormally often; soon she had started to cry, and the boy heard her wailing over and over again between her sobs, "Yes, I'm just like any other poor, lonely wretch." He did not dare on any account to sit up in bed and look, but he had a great desire to see how this big, bulky girl went about the business of weeping. At her weeping he felt his heart beat faster; he was strangely sensitive to weeping, and for some mysterious reason he felt affection for those who wept, especially those who wept because they were alone. He felt that all those who were alone were kin to himself, and now he had suddenly begun to feel fond of the daughter, Magnína. It is a remarkable experience when someone we do not love is suddenly revealed in a new light. He had actually never known this girl, and now he knew her. Never understood her, and now he understood her. All of a sudden he realized that they shared the same road, two lonely people; and at the same time he realized that it was not just hardship, loss of parents, poetry, the parish, and a cross to bear that made the individual lonely, but also thighs that were too fat, sugar, rolled tripe, pickled lamb fries, brisket, mother-love, hope of an inheritance, and happiness.

Human beings, in point of fact, are lonely by nature, and one should feel sorry for them and love them and mourn with them. It is certain that people would understand one another better and love one another more if they would admit to one another how lonely they were, how sad they were in their tormented, anxious longings and feeble hopes. Magnína could also find consolation in the spirit, that good refuge for the wretched, the ones who were alone but lacked the courage to be so.

— **13** —

She sat in the loft next morning, unwashed and uncombed, and stared at the frostwork of winter, dejected, a little red-eyed, as if she had slept badly; yet she did not yawn, but moved her lips a little every now and again, as if she were speaking. The gray cat came over with arched back and tail on high and rubbed itself, purring, against her leg; she gave a start because she did not realize what it was—but it was only that damned cat.

"Be off with you, you pest!" she said.

The cat was taken aback and looked at the girl, peering, and rubbed itself against a leg of the bed. The girl stamped on the floor. Startled, the cat leapt right up onto the bed beside her. By now Magnína was angry. She was rather short-tempered that day, bless her, and did not want to have any living creature near her; she picked up the cat by the scruff of the neck and put it down the stairway. Then she sat down again, and the boy saw the back of her head once more and those fat shoulders as she sat there.

"It is hard to be alone."

He scarcely realized what he was saying before it was over and done with and the words were out. It was like jumping off the edge of a high cliff in a dream; one does not know where one is going to land. Where was he going to land now? There was a long silence and he felt that he was still hovering in the air. Finally she looked round and said, rather brusquely, "What's that?" That was all.

"I was saying that it's hard to be alone," he said, and heaved a deep sigh.

"Oh, I don't suppose that those who have nothing to do except lie in bed all day and let others slave for them have much to say on that subject," said Magnína.

"Oh, no one does that for fun, Magnína dear," he replied. "Some people don't need to envy others anything."

"'Some people'"—she turned right round and looked straight at him; this was the language she understood.

"Some people think that some people aren't as ill as they pretend to be," she said. "But obviously that doesn't concern us so long as we get paid for your keep."

"It's awful," he said, nearly in tears, "to be the slave of mankind because of poverty, and even more awful to be ill in soul and body and never to know a happy day. Yes, Magnína. And yet it's worst of all to be misunderstood by the nation."

"Misunderstood by the nation?" she said. "You? A child?"

"I'm not so much of a child that I haven't got a soul; Jesus the Savior knows that and it will be proved on the Day of Judgment," he said.

"How old are you now?" she asked.

"I'm seventeen."

"That's right, you're over seventeen now," she said, and had started actually talking to him. She went on with a sigh, "Yes, it's awful to be young. But what's that compared to soon becoming old!"

"Nonsense, you're not very old, Magnína," he said consolingly. "There are lots of people as old as you. And older."

"No one knows how old I am except I myself," she said. "I'm so terribly old now. And if everything were carefully examined, I'm undoubtedly just as much in bad health as you are, yes, even worse than you are, what's more, although I never let on about it. No, the doctor doesn't exist who understands me, or has ever understood me, or ever will understand me. No."

"Yes, but what does it matter if a person is in bad health when he is among his own! To have no one—that is really to be in bad health. Magnína, I have no one."

"Do I have someone then, perhaps?" she asked. "Whom do you think I have? No, I've never had anyone. I don't call it having some-one just because one perhaps has the right to board and lodging. You get board and lodging, too."

When it came to the point, she did not understand him; he could hear it from the way she suddenly sniffed.

"You don't understand me," he said.

"I simply don't understand what people are thinking about when they start grumbling," she said. "I don't grumble."

She went downstairs, and he really did not know whether she was good or bad; the stairs creaked, but the smell of her remained behind in the loft. She came back to the loft again with the cat in her arms and a lump of brown sugar, and she gave him a generous piece and said as she handed it to him, "We mustn't waste the sugar like this."

When all was said and done she had understood him—a little; and in her own way.

— 14 —

Next morning she was alone in the loft once again; but she was not at all dejected now, just in her usual mood. She was examining stock-ings. No one had more patience over stockings than Magnína, whether she was knitting them or darning them; but she had no time at all for garters, and her stockings were always slipping down her legs. Nothing was said. Every now and again she sniffed, and he measured the interval between each sniff by counting from one up to, at the highest tally, five hundred and seventy-three. Finally she laid the stockings aside and began to stare into the blue. Once or twice he had the impression that she was on the point of looking in his direction.

"Were you talking about something yesterday, Ólafur?" she asked at last.

"No," he answered. "It was nothing, really."

"Yes," she said. "You were certainly talking about something."

"No," he said. "I was only talking about how ill I was. But it doesn't matter."

"If I remember correctly, you were talking about how alone you were in the world, and that you had no one to care for you."

"It doesn't matter," he said.

"That's odd," she said. "And why have you stopped asking me to read you *The Felsenburg Stories* as you used to?"

"You didn't want to," he said, but his heart almost missed a beat when he heard the book mentioned again. There had been a time when he believed that in that book was enshrined the indefinable solace that everyone begins to yearn for at an early age. He had long since banished from his mind all hope about this book. But how quick the heart is to become attentive when it hears an old and forgotten hope whispered anew: was he, at last, to be allowed it?

"You said I wasn't allowed it," he said.

"I never said you weren't allowed it," she said. "You should tell the truth. We always tell the truth in this house. I only said you were too young, then. You lacked the fear of God and the worldly experience to understand such a book."

"Am I to be allowed it now?" he asked, and could scarcely hide his delight.

"That's not what I said," she replied. "At least not today. And not tomorrow. And not the next day. And perhaps never. I don't imagine it would do you much good, considering how ill you are. But I'll think about it a bit when it's nearer spring and the days get longer."

This boy had counted the floorboards and the joints and the

planks in the clinker-built ceiling more than a thousand times, and imagined to himself that the boards were alternately black and white. He knew every single knot in the ceiling and the floor, and every single nail, and how the rust from the nails had stained the wood. He knew intimately every detail of all the counterpanes and bedclothes in the loft; in his sufferings he had counted every square and every stripe on them. Few prospects are as horrible as the immortality of the soul; as a concept it seems to be the height of cruelty. He had lain like that, day after day, month after month, a Christian person with nothing to look forward to, not even death, because according to Christian belief this, the final consolation, does not exist. Times without number he had listened with excited curiosity to the arrival of even the most humble visitors, in the hope of hearing just the slightest hint of what the soul yearned for—the truth, that long-desired consolation, the most important news of all. And now, suddenly, there was something else. This book that he had always yearned for was now in prospect. He kept an anxious watch on the daylight next morning, in the hope that the little Nordic sunbeam of the world would reach the sloping ceiling a little sooner that day. It was almost ten o'clock and not a sign of a sunbeam on the ceiling, and the hoarfrost was still blue on the window. He had a very severe headache and had begun to fear once more that life was unending. Then suddenly Magnína came up the stairs, brought out a worn book from under her apron, and sat down on the edge of his bed.

"I had better let you hear the beginning," she said.

He longed to be able to hug the book and kiss it and shed sweet tears over it, but when she saw him stretch out his arms she said it was her own book which she had got from her late father, and that she alone decided who could touch her book. "It might get torn, no one knows how to handle it in the right way except me, it's that sort of book, and what's more, you should be grateful that I want to read aloud to you from my own book."

"Yes, Magnína," he said, moved. "Thanks be to God."

And so the solemn opening words of this classic Christian novel began:

" 'I, Everhard Julius, first saw the light of this world in the year 1706, during the great eclipse. . . .' "

At these words the boy was suddenly seized by a strange mixture of mysticism and sanctity, because for some reason they reminded him of the opening words of Holy Writ. It was just that there was something mysterious and religious, if not downright revelatory, about seeing the light of the world for the first time precisely on the particular day when the light of the world was completely invisible to both God and man; the Lord must have had something special in mind when he let this man be born. If only she would now carry on and not close her book after this solemn opening, as she had done once before!

She carried on.

But though the book was first and foremost a Christian book, and a devotional book, and in style and content just like something out of the Bible, it was not long before the boy realized that it also had certain characteristics which one never finds in devotional books, or only very seldom, even though they are what one most longs for. It was precisely this characteristic which emerged at once, quite unmistakeably, in the letter from Captain Wolfgang to Eberhard Julius asking this God-fearing child of the eclipse to meet him in Hamburg; it was apparent during Eberhard's search for Wolfgang; but it really came into its own when the story turned to the well-mannered adventures, the exemplary, teetotal and Lutheran travels of this right-thinking captain in the distant, coffee-rich continents of the southern hemisphere. In short, Ólafur Kárason of Ljósavík found himself for the first time in the enchanting atmosphere of romantic fiction; nor was it long before he was introduced in generous measure to the abundantly attractive demeanor of young ladies, which is nowhere so well known nor so conscientiously recorded as in that particular literary genre. When Captain Wolfgang was peeping through the leaves of an arbor at the Cape of Good Hope and looking at the girl who was dancing there, and no less when he had sat down beside her and engaged her in spiritual, candid and truth-seeking conversation, the orphan boy with the romantic imagination who cowered in his bed there under a sloping ceiling by the farthest northern seas could not help being touched by a funny feeling. It was a momentous inward experience.

" 'You say you find me pleasing,' said the lady, 'and yet you do not even kiss me once, even though you are alone with me here and need have nothing to fear.' "

At these words Captain Wolfgang made so bold as to kiss her, to which she responded with ten or twelve kisses of her own. This dancing lady was in reality a princess from Java; a sixty-year-old, aristocratic governor had brought her out here, and kept her in the charge of an old crone. But the old crone was as righteous and fair-minded as the governor seemed to be lacking in these virtues, and she could not refrain from telling Captain Wolfgang what a great sin it was to deprive this poor innocent child of the company of men.

Ólafur Kárason listened, fascinated, to Magnína's affected and reverent Bible-reading tones, and though the observation about the sinful lack of male company this poor child had to endure evoked notions in him that were too obscure to be called fully sympathetic understanding, he was nevertheless overwhelmed by indignation and sorrow over the treatment which this dancing girl had to suffer at the hands of the sixty-year-old governor, as well as by a sincere desire that she might have around her only gentle poetic men who never did a fine girl any harm but applied themselves instead to composing well-wrought verses about her or even whole spiritual poems.

Ólafur Kárason's respect for everything noble in woman's nature, and for the magic of literary art in general, was not impaired when the dancing girl without more ado handed Captain Wolfgang a bulging purse of gold the next day as a reward for the kisses. There can be few things more delightful than to be given a generous measure of gold coins by a beautiful young maiden in payment for a few innocent kisses in an arbor, and nothing which could entrance a young poet's fancy more. When Captain Wolfgang had pocketed the money, the dancing girl rejoiced over his modesty and bestowed on him the most tender caresses, and swore by the holy Christian faith and by her own god Thoume that she was consumed by burning love for this high-minded sea captain. But at this point in the story the captain seemed strangely irresolute, for as he himself recounted: " 'I was more than a little taken aback when I realized that I was in love with a heathen woman.'"

How was Captain Wolfgang to conduct himself in this dilemma? Fortunately these anxieties vanished quickly like dew in the morning sun, "'when I discovered after further inquiry that she desperately wanted to become a Christian.'"

Next day Magnína came back with the book, sat down beside the invalid without a word, and began to read; and this blissful and enchanting story continued, in which a clean and true love for the Lutheran faith was constantly matched by an edifying and unaffected disgust for the abominable depravity which characterizes the wicked men of this world.

The story now turned to Wolfgang's noble-minded and extremely solemn adventure with the daughter of the governor of Hispaniola. This girl was named Donna Salome, and was seventeen or eighteen years old. Their romance was not quite so engagingly attractive, certainly, as the earlier one in the arbor at the Cape of Good Hope, but it was if anything even more Christian and even more edifying; that is to say, it was attended by an even more truly religious gravity, and this gravity manifested itself chiefly in the fact that Wolfgang married Donna openly and definitely, and their marriage was in every respect unblemished and incorruptible, even though it was perhaps impossible to deny that Donna Salome had originally inclined towards the Catholic faith. But alas, Donna Salome died in childbirth, sweetly and spiritually, nine months after the wedding; and although it was a bitter loss, Wolfgang was left with one consolation in his life, namely that Donna Salome, a few weeks before her death, had "had conversations with the pastor about religion, and the principles of the Lutheran faith had taken root in her heart."

— 15 —

It had seldom or never happened before, but now it happened frequently: he would open his eyes in the morning in joyful anticipation of the coming day. He waited impatiently for the people to leave the house to attend to their various tasks. At last they would all be gone. Magnína appeared in the loft, brought out her book from under her apron, sat down beside him and started to read. She said nothing by way of preamble, and when she had finished reading she went away without a word. Sometimes she would stop reading suddenly if she thought she heard sounds of movement downstairs, and she would glance down in alarm, but her ears had deceived her. She never once looked in his direction while she read. She read everything with the same devotional intonation, whether it was about the depravity of Lemelie or the virtues of Concordia; it all had the same pious, mystical effect on her. He often had the feeling, however, that she was reading first and foremost for herself; it never occurred to her to ask whether he found the book enjoyable, indeed she always seemed to be a little bad-tempered, and often he wondered what wrong he could have done her; it was as if some unfriendly force were compelling her to read for him against her will. Previously she had sometimes addressed him of her own accord, but since she started reading to him she had never spoken to him. Sometimes, during the reading, she would forget how time was passing; there would be movement downstairs, the women would be back from the barn and she had forgotten to see to the meal. She would stop in midsentence, thrust the book under her apron, and disappear. Who would have believed that this girl could react so quickly?

There was a man named van Leuven, a most excellent man. His wife was the splendid Concordia whom the whole nation knows because she was not only beautiful but also endowed with all the virtues which can adorn a woman, and her name will never be forgotten as long as there is life on earth. On a sea voyage with this exemplary couple was the promising young man Albert Julius. They were shipwrecked on a desert island called Felsenburg. The fourth person who survived the shipwreck was the scoundrel Lemelie. This villian seized the first opportunity of doing away with the estimable van Leuven with a view to gaining Concordia's love. A few days after the murder, however, this Lemelie luckily had the misfortune to

impale himself on a bayonet held by the promising young man Albert
Julius, and that was the end of Lemelie. Before he died, however, he
had the consideration to confess his sins to the widow Concordia
and Albert Julius, and to cut a long story short there were few sins in
that catalogue which were milder than rape, incest, and infanticide.
But when the story reached the point where Lemelie had burned his
two illegitimate children "in a crucible," Magnína stopped reading.
She laid the book down in her lap and stared straight ahead in some
perplexity. Ólafur Kárason was also somewhat perplexed. He was
convinced that she was filled with horror at the depravity that exists
in the world, and he felt he had to say something to comfort her so
that she would not take it too much to heart.

"Magnína dear," he said gently, "don't you think this could have
been a little exaggerated?"

But once again he had miscalculated completely, as he had done
before.

"Do you think I'm reading you some damned lie?" she said, and
looked at him angrily.

"No, I didn't mean it that way," he said. "I only meant that some
people think that some things might be a little exaggerated even
though they're written in books."

"No, you certainly don't deserve to have someone read to you out
of one's own book; indeed I should have known all along that those
wretches who go in for composing obscene verses in their childhood,
and carry on doing it from then on, wouldn't benefit very much from
having someone read to them from a remarkable and true Lutheran
book which describes the wickedness of men as they really are!"

She slammed the book shut, thrust it under her apron, stood up
and stalked over to the stairs. "It's just like these wretches to be
unable to bear to hear the truth about themselves," she muttered as
she was going down the stairs, but loud enough to ensure that he
could hear it.

He suffered greatly from remorse of conscience for the rest of the
day; he was all the men in the world in one, you see, and all the sins
of this unhappy sex from time immemorial afflicted him at once in a

mysterious way and robbed him of his peace of mind. He slept very badly that night, and felt that some terrible punishment was looming over him. So it was little wonder that he was relieved next morning when Magnína came up to the loft and started reading to him from the book, the book she had given him all too clearly to understand he was unworthy of hearing. The horrible confessions of Lemelie continued, but this time she did not let it affect her; but when she had been reading for a while, she interjected this warning:

"I'm going to tell you once and for all that if you're going to interrupt me when I'm reading from this book, it will be the last time I read to you. This book is against sin, and it's my own book, and I won't have a single word said while I'm reading from it."

Bathed in sweat and with palpitating heart, the boy listened while the confessions of Lemelie continued, and did not dare to say a word. Then Lemelie died. And now Albert Julius and the widow Concordia were alone on the desert island of Felsenburg.

The love which demands nothing but beauty itself and lives in selfless worship, as when he beheld Guðrún of Grænhóll standing before him in the landscape—that is the love that no disappointment can ever conquer, perhaps not even death itself (if that existed). This was the love that the story described in the chapter about young Albert and the beautiful, virtuous widow. In this love story it was as if he heard anew the origins of his own soul after a long silence, that ethereal music of divine revelation which is so rare in literature but which Nature alone preserves, if you know how to listen. He listened.

Albert Julius lived for a long time in selfless adoration of that beautiful lady of all the virtues. He contemplated her beauty and nobility, and his heart was deeply moved, but without saying a single word, however much he wanted to. But one day, when he thought that Concordia was elsewhere, he could not resist taking the widow's lovely infant daughter in his arms, kissing her many times, and addressing her distractedly with these words:

"'Oh, you darling little angel! How I wish you were fifteen years old already! Merciful God, give me the strength to stifle completely the natural instincts for marriage that are innate in all men! You know my heart, and You know that my love has nothing to do with lechery.'"

But Concordia herself was hiding somewhere in the background and heard everything that Albert had said to her darling infant daughter. And next day the young man received a letter from Concordia, dated January 8, 1648, which went as follows:

"'Dearest friend: I heard nearly everything you said to my daughter at the North Rock yesterday. Your wish is natural and reasonable and in accordance with the laws of God and man; I am a widow who has suffered much, but I know that all fortune and misfortune come from God. But even though I am thereby free again and beholden to no one, I could scarcely have brought myself ever to marry again had not my heart been moved by your pure and ardent love, and had not your honorable behavior prompted me to offer myself to you as your wife. So now it lies within your discretion whether tomorrow morning, the day of your birthday, you want to unite the two of us in matrimony (there being no pastor here) after we have prayed to God and His holy angels to be with us, and then live together as lawful Christian man and wife. I know that you are such an upright, honorable, and sincere man that you will not consider it a sign of promiscuity if I offer myself to you like this.'"

And finally: "'Take then unto yourself your dearly beloved, the widow of the late van Leuven, for your own wife, and live in the most joyful matrimony with her from now onwards; may God always be with us. When you have read this letter you will find me, feeling rather shy, down by the dam. Concordia van Leuven.'"

Magnína's voice never reflected her emotions; it did not soften at all at the reading of this touching letter. On the other hand she stopped reading when she reached the end of the letter. She sat for a long time in silence. Ólafur Kárason, too, was silent. Only the silent music of admiration echoed in the room. Finally the girl closed the book, sighed, and said, "Yes, that could happen there. Provided it's far enough away. And long enough ago."

He was eager to comfort her and said, "I'm quite sure, Magnína, that true love can dwell in every Christian heart, even nowadays, if one is fortunate."

"No, it isn't possible here," she said, like a person answering in his sleep when you hold his little finger, and went on staring into the blue without moving. "There are so many people around. Everyone believes ill of everyone else. But two people alone on a desert island where there are no other people around, that's a different matter entirely. It's as if that's what God intended in the beginning when He created two people and left them by themselves."

But nothing could cast a shadow over the literary happiness of this moment in the boy's soul; it was a new day, and goodness was no longer infinitely distant as so often before. Guðrún of Grænhóll, he thought—she was like a brilliantly colored cloud at sunrise on a spring morning, an unreal vision on the banks of a running stream: what youth, beauty, and courage; it was not real, in fact, and even if it had been real it was only half true, and perhaps not at all true, even, nothing but an apparition and a revelation. And when would he ever become man enough to pursue and catch an apparition and a revelation? The only woman on whom he could build his hope was the mature Concordia of reality, van Leuven's widow, who would look at him with maternal compassion, who would make the final decision for him where his courage faltered, ready and willing to acknowledge his virtues and to care for him. "I believe," he whispered at last, "that life's Concordia will be victorious sometime in my life."

He started up from his trance at his own words, and noticed that a long time must have passed in silence; Magnína still sat slumped on the edge of his bed, fat in the back and flabby, the book limp on her lap. But what amazed him most were the tears that trickled down her cheeks like a strange leak from somewhere, uninterrupted and without any sobbing. For a long time he watched her weeping and wondered what was causing it. Was it just ordinary water that flowed in the ordinary way? Or did it come from some inward emotion? Did she understand the spirit? Did they perhaps understand one another after all? Had their souls at last met in admiration for that true art which places honorable courtship uppermost of all human values, Christian marriage excepted?

She went on weeping like that for a long time, as if in some kind of comfortable, effortless madness. Finally she stood up without any fuss, smoothed her apron modestly down over her hips, and was gone. Later that day she came up with a piece of buttered flatbread and gave it to him; it was the first time she had given him a tidbit since he was little. Yes, that is how literature can melt the frozen springs of affection in the human heart. He was grateful to God that it had pleased Him at last to open the heart of this stout girl to spiritual things.

—— **16** ——

Then it was Holy Week with its long devotional readings, spring cleaning and westerly storms, and there was no mention of literature, in general nothing that touched the heart, only the story of the Passion. The girl who had given him a little piece of flatbread because they both had begun to understand spiritual matters now paid no attention to him at all for days on end, as if he did not exist. He had stopped knowing what to think.

Easter morning was a clear day with hoarfrost, and the women were looking forward to going to church and hurried through the work in the barn. But there was only one riding horse available, and the question was who should ride it, the mother or the daughter—because they were both too fat to walk. It was decided in the end that the mother should ride to church, for she had many things to see to as a farm-owner and few opportunities to meet people. So everyone went off to church except Magnína, who stayed behind at home with the Lord's crossbearer. She said she had always been disregarded all her born days; everyone had their hopes fulfilled in this life except her. No one had ever asked her what she herself wanted, no one tried to understand that she might enjoy meeting Christian folk, too, no less than others did, even though it was only during church feasts. In fact she did not understand why she owned any Sunday-best clothes; her Sunday-best was allowed to rot at the bottom of her clothes chest while some people who did not deserve to have Sunday-best at all got the opportunity of wearing them. Yes, she said she really could spit on some people, and their morality was such that they would be in grave difficulties if they had to answer the pastor about this or that concerning the condition they were in, while decent people did not even have the opportunity of going to God's House on the blessed Easter Sunday of Our Savior. She sat at the window, dejected, after the others had left, and sniffed, and made no attempt to tidy herself up, did not even have a wash on the blessed Easter Sunday of Our Savior; she had never been of any account among people.

"Well," she said at last, breaking the silence when she had been pottering there for a long time. "I suppose I'd better fight my way through the lesson, seeing it's the day it is."

"Yes, do that, Magnína," said the boy, delighted that she was going to do something, or at least had said something.

"Do that?" she echoed haughtily, and looked at him. "I could give orders myself if I were obeyed."

"I didn't mean to give you orders, Magnína," he said. "I only said it was only right and proper to read the lesson in Jesus' name on Easter Day itself."

"In Jesus' name?" she repeated. "Well I never! Is this creature now using the Lord's name, too! Not that I'm going to, but it would be no more than you deserve if I were to read the lesson over you; it's anyway the only thing one can do with such chronic wretches who will never thrive."

He did not dare to say anything more about the reading after that, because he did not know whether he ought to talk about it as a blessing or a punishment in order to be somehow in agreement with Magnína; so he said piteously, "If only one soul in the world would be good to me and show me a little affection, even for only one day a year, I'm sure I wouldn't take long to get better."

"Yes, I'm sure of that—to have everyone waiting on you hand and foot; that's the only thing that's wrong with you!"

"I yearn so much to find God in people," said the poet. "That's the only thing I yearn for. I'm sure that if I found that, I would be fully cured that same day."

"Well, I'd better bring out the *Book of Sermons*," she said, wanting to break off this spiritual and emotional conversation as quickly as possible when she felt him getting the upper hand. "Since you insist," she added.

She waddled off and came back after a long time with a book. But it was not the *Book of Sermons* she had brought as threatened; it was *The Felsenburg Stories*. In her other hand she was carrying a piece of flatbread with newly churned fresh-smelling butter on it, and a lump of brown-sugar candy. She put them down in front of him and said, "This certainly ought to make you better; someone's being good to you now, as far as I can see."

His eyes filled with tears and he could not refrain from telling her straight out, in a tearful voice, that he had known for a long time that she was the only person in that house who could forgive those who were in distress, and that was precisely what spirituality was about; and he began to nibble his way through the flatbread.

She scratched herself a little here and there and sat down on the edge of the bed and began to leaf through the book, and while she was trying to find the place he looked at her from the side and studied the fat on her back; the swelling began at the vertebrae of her neck and spread like a shield over her shoulders and down over her upper arms, and right down to her broad rump, so that her waist was actually just a notional line; and she sniffed, and it seemed that she was never going to find the place in the book where she had stopped. And then she found it.

"Yes, following her directions he had found her, feeling rather shy, down by the dam, that's where we had got to."

And with that the love story of Albert and Concordia was really over. Soon they were married and began to have children, which unfortunately is so often the sad ending to love stories; time passed and there was really no romance in life any more, only the tedious tranquillity of marriage without excitement or curiosity, the dull routine of making a comfortable living with nothing to nourish the imagination.

The kind of problem which appealed to the reader's attention did not arise again until the children grew up, when the question became urgent—how were these decent and well-brought-up youngsters to be provided with marriage partners to prevent them "committing incest by marrying one another when the sexual urge overwhelmed their reason and virtue," as the book expressed it with its candid Christian lack of tolerance towards sin and the Devil.

But one fine day at about the time that the children were all of marriageable age, by good fortune another shipwreck occurred and new castaways were washed ashore on the island, including two excellent sisters from Middelborg in Zeeland, who promptly married the sons of Albert and Concordia. But it is no wonder that people should now ask, how was this Christian tale to be continued, since marriage was at once the climax of the story and the ultimate aim of morality? But luckily it turned out that the young maidens had been engaged in a fierce struggle with the Devil as he manifested himself in man's unmarried state, and outside of that state nothing worth relating seems to happen in Christendom. The cause and origin of these events was that some philanderers had lured these sisters on board a ship, in concert with their godless brother, on the pretext that a decent and decorous party was being held there; but instead of escorting the young ladies home after the party, they got well and truly drunk during the evening, weighed anchor, put to sea with the ladies on board, and headed for the Banthamis and Molucca Islands. Apart from the philanderers, there were on board this ship two mysterious French damsels, well-spoken girls of pleasing appearance, although experience was later to show their real characters. The two sisters soon found that the social courtesies dwindled the farther they sailed, and to cut a long story short, that very first night the philanderers drank themselves into a state of such insenate intoxication that they tried to take carnal advantage of the sisters there and then. The sisters defended themselves with bread knives, and the outcome of this first encounter was that the philanderers found it prudent to retire to their own bunks.

But virtue's struggle with the unmarried state that prevailed on that ship was by no means at an end thereby, far from it. It was only just starting. As the days passed, more and more of the ship's distinguished passengers found occasion to reveal publicly their inner beings, including the two beautiful and well-spoken French girls and an exceptionally handsome French gentleman. "'We sisters eventually let ourselves be persuaded to go down to the saloon. But horror of horrors, never had I seen anything like it!—that handsome French gentleman was sitting stark naked between those two depraved harlots, and in such a disgusting attitude, that we screamed aloud and covered our eyes and took refuge in a corner.'"

At this point a shudder ran through Magnína and she had to stop reading. She stood up and closed the stair-hatch carefully because of the draft, then searched for another pair of stockings in some agitation, found them, and put them on as well. She made no comment, and did not look at the boy. Then she sat down again on the edge of the bed and started to read once more. She read for a long time about the instructive and exemplary battle waged by these high-minded German sisters to preserve their maidenhood in this company of French-natured people who, when they were out of sight of land, seemed to hold chastity of no account and marriage even less; and the pupils of the listener's eyes went on dilating, the sweat broke out on his forehead, his veins swelled, and his heart trembled.

"'At last the lechery of these debauched villains could no longer be cooled in any way but was inflamed into a dreadful blaze of lust; and one night three rogues suddenly burst in on us with the obvious intention of trying to rape us. But each of us always had an open pocketknife lying ready under our pillows. . . .'"

The shuddering that now overwhelmed Magnína seemed as if it would never end; soon she was quivering, not like a leaf but like a mountain; she stared straight ahead with the vacant, foolish expression which characterizes people when they are shivering, and tried to bite on her teeth as hard as she could, which only made them chatter all the more.

"Are you feeling cold, Magnína?" said the boy. "I don't know what it can be, but I'm feeling cold too."

"I simply can't understand it," said the girl. "I've read it often enough to myself. But it's so terrible to read about godless people to others. I simply can't understand how I could bring myself to do it for any living soul. May Jesus God in Heaven never let anything like this ever happen to anyone. I couldn't bear it!"

In a shaking voice which kept on cracking, and through chattering teeth, she made one further desperate attempt:

" 'But this shameful comedy was suddenly transformed into bloody tragedy; for as soon as we could get our breaths and could use our knives which we were secretly holding in our hands, we thrust them, both at the same time, into those accursed lechers, so that our clothing was quite drenched with their blood.' "

But then she could go no further. The book fell shut and sank into her lap and slipped all the way down to the floor. "Dear God, I've actually read that aloud, I thought that was something I could never do aloud for any living soul. I must be out of my mind. Let me come into the warmth beside you for a little so that I don't catch pneumonia."

She did not waste any time, but slipped off her shoes, lifted the bedclothes, and was in bed beside him, and the whole bed groaned as if every plank would break; she was like an army in herself and there was scarcely any room left over for him, and though she only lay half on top of him he felt as if a whole nation were lying on him. She was almost sobbing for breath, as if she were drowning. He felt sorry for her, and hoped and prayed that she would stop shivering and recover. She lay there twitching, this big, heavy person, and every now and again she flowed over him in huge billows, like surf.

But when he touched her he found that she was bare above the knee, and then he realized at last that all those stockings had nothing to hold them up—poor girl, no wonder those broad thighs of hers were always cold. But the more he tried to squeeze up against the wall, the closer she pressed against him. There was no escaping her, she was everywhere around him, her smell filled his senses, one of his cheeks was wet from her lips. In reality it was just like the world itself which is everywhere about you and even inside you; he was no longer aware of her as the individual, Magnína, but in some way as his atmosphere and reality, and he himself was actually only a small part of her, as a fish is part of the sea, suddenly he was living her in the same unconditional way in which a fish lives the sea, nothing was more straightforward, this was the natural life. He had loved Guðrún of Grænhóll and Concordia of Felsenburg before, in daydreams when he was alone in the loft; that was the love that begins in the soul and gradually spreads outwards, it had never been essentially natural; this time the love started in the body and spread inwards, so that in a flash he thought this bulky girl to be everything the soul yearned for, everything he had had to miss in life, the world itself—at last he was no longer alone. But after all it was just like any other flash of lightning which touches the soul in the midst of melancholy; it was gone again, and she was all around him once more like a wall of treble thickness and threatened to suffocate him, her smell was stronger than ever before, she hurt him and he winced, and she rose up on one elbow, her face gleaming with sweat and her hair disheveled, and looked at him angrily and said, "What's this, then?"

"I can't help it," he said miserably, then turned towards the wall and pulled the bedclothes over his face.

"I suppose it was obvious," she said. "I should have known. A useless wretch and weakling and pauper like you!"

She got out of bed and snorted; she was no longer shivering; she was hot and bedraggled.

"Luckily I haven't made much of a habit of going to bed with men until now, and I'm still innocent of men. And I hope to God I always will be."

"It wasn't my fault," said the boy from under the bedclothes.

"No, I suppose it was all my fault that I felt faint and had to lie down for a little! Was it perhaps my fault that you couldn't leave me in peace? No, I should have known, one is never left in peace by these male wretches, no matter how useless they are. But let me just tell you this, that if you ever touch me again, I shall tell my mother."

"I couldn't help it," he protested, almost in tears. "I didn't mean it. It wasn't my fault."

"I only wish that all miserable wretches were buried thirty feet underground, who can't even leave a girl in peace on a Savior's Easter Sunday itself," she said, then bit her lip, grimaced, and snorted.

She struggled to put her shoes on, picked up her book off the floor and vanished down the stairs; that evening and the next day she was ill.

— **17** —

When all was said and done, Magnína did not understand the spirit after all—or rather, she misunderstood it to an essential extent. She did not read world literature in order to allow the soul to hover freely in those higher spheres which an invalid parish pauper held to be the ultimate degree of perfection in life, but only to soothe or to arouse one heavy, malodorous body. He knew quite well she could not help it. She had not given herself that body, it was others who had done that; it was, in fact, an alien body which she would willingly have got rid of if she could, and he was not angry with her, either—only sad at life. Both Christianity and literature were primarily physical needs which could only find fulfillment in organs situated below the midriff. How could he, this slender parish pauper, ever become a Christian and a poet in the eyes of someone so fat? She had never despised him so much as she did after this Easter. Whenever she passed through the loft, she could not help showing her contempt for the wretch who lay there stuffing himself and pretending to be ill, year after year, making innocent people in another parish slave for his upkeep while upright, truth-loving and well-born people had to wait on him hand and foot. Every Christian person with any self-respect was bound to class such wretches with thieves, liars and scum—and in any case they would end up in prison sooner or later, thank God.

This was the sort of diatribe he had to listen to, racked with headaches as he was, in his unquenchable yearning to escape from himself and his own worthlessness—so hard-hearted was this Magnína who had risen from his bed on the Easter Sunday of Our Savior, determined never to read to him from her book again. And sometimes when he lay sleepless at night, trembling with anguish about himself

and about life itself, he would ask, "Isn't it true, then, that God created men and will redeem them?"

Yes, it is hard to be a poet by the farthest northern seas.

At dusk one evening when he was feeling very low, he suddenly
heard someone whispering beside his bed; he had not heard anyone
coming, and it startled him.

"It's only me. I was only going to give you a piece of sugar. It's for
that other thing, you remember. Everything's all right now."

"It can't be right for you to give me so much sugar, Kristjána," said
the poet. "And I don't deserve it anyway."

"Yes," she said, "it's absolutely right, because soon I'll own all the
sugar in this family, and old Magna will have to ask me for it. You
see, I got a letter from him today, and we'll be getting married soon.
Thank you a thousand times for the poem and let me kiss you for it.
I've never heard such a beautiful poem in all my life, but I didn't
want to thank you for it until I knew whether or not he was in
earnest. And now he's in earnest and I'm quite certain that you're the
best poet in this parish. I don't care in the least if they all say you're a
deranged bloody wretch; I say it's all a lie because you composed the
poem."

"Thank you, Kristjána dear, I've always known that you were a
generous girl and spiritually minded," said the poet.

"Listen, did you honestly mean it; do you think I'm really as
pretty as it says in the poem?"

She was bending right down over him and speaking very intimately, she was so close to him, moreover, that he himself felt that
nothing in the poem had been exaggerated, and he vowed and swore
that he thought her just as pretty as it said in the poem.

"Let me kiss you," she said, and kissed him a little. "You see, I'm
quite sure that if you hadn't been poor and everyone bad to you, you
could have learned to dance and have the makings of a fine gentleman; you've got the sort of blue eyes and lovely hair and you're so
pale and clean and only slightly freckled, but that doesn't matter and
I'll never forget you all my life."

Then she kissed him once again, and their mouths tasted sweet.

"I can always feel within myself if a poem is well composed or not, and the moment I heard it I made up my mind to accept Jónas; and anyway that damned Júst was never really serious about proposing to me, and now the sugar won't be spared, I can tell you, and now old Magna's going to catch it. And even though Jónas is crazy he's ten thousand times a better man than Júst, and I've never really loved Júst very much, and it serves him right that he isn't getting me, because he didn't propose to me soon enough."

She stuffed the poet's mouth cramful of sugar so that he could not speak, but it did not matter—it was she who was talking; this was her day.

"So when we're married," she said, "we'll take you in and you can stay with us as long as you like and lie in bed all day, and it won't even occur to me to take a single penny for you from the parish; and you'll have plenty of paper and plenty of books from me, and when my husband Jónas isn't at home you'll be my sweetheart, because I've always known that you're the only person who understands me. Yes, and even if it costs me my own life I'll repay you for your beautiful poem, as God and Jesus Christ are my witnesses."

In reality it was he who had conquered in this long-drawn-out and tangled love story in that house; in his very hopelessness and worthlessness he had achieved the distinction that his poem had managed to sway the right heart. It was a great encouragement, and he felt he could live on this success for a long time. When all was said and done, there was still justice in the world and a healthy common sense in life. And though Magnína insisted to her mother that Júst was the father of the child and should consider himself lucky to have escaped, it did not affect the matter at all; the main thing was that Ólafur's poem had won a total victory and swayed the heart, which is the proper party in affairs of this kind, whoever might have fathered the child. Perhaps she had taken up with Júst because of the poem stolen from the *Núma Ballads*; but it was Jónas who got her finally and married her in a Christian way on the strength of an original poem by Ólafur Kárason of Ljósavík.

18

They married at the height of spring, and the birds were singing. Guests arrived from far and wide, the farmyard and the house were crowded, there were dogs barking in the homefield and out in the meadows. Everywhere there was talking, in the living room, in the passages, and on the paved doorstep, and women blessing this and that and everything. People also came crowding up to the loft where the parish pauper lay, and one man asked whether he would not like to sniff some tobacco, and he took a pinch of snuff and sneezed. One fat woman came and said, almost in tears, that God laid the sorest burdens on those He loved, and Ólafur Kárason was almost in tears himself because he felt that this woman understood him; but then she vanished when word came that the wedding was about to begin, and everyone went down into the living room. In reality no one had meant anything by talking to the parish pauper, none of them cared at all, no one even thought of carrying him downstairs to let him see the wedding like other folk; he was not allowed to see the wedding that he himself had brought about with his poetic talent—such is the lot of poets. He heard only the distant murmur of the singing; the fjord outside the window was blue in the sunshine with green slopes on the other side, and the birds flew past the window again and again, and he could not help thinking with bitterness of Kristjána who had said she was ready to lay down her life for him but had now forgotten him and did not have him carried downstairs, and was going away to live in another district.

But when all was said and done he was not alone after all; almost as soon as the murmur of the psalm began, he heard someone weeping. He had thought he was alone in the loft, but perhaps one is never alone, perhaps one is never so distressed that there is not someone else weeping at one's side, visible or invisible.

It was a woman. She was sitting motionless across the room from him when the people downstairs began to sing, and he had not noticed her; and even now when he noticed her, he had to examine her carefully to make sure she had any actual appearance at all. Youth had faded from her cheeks and her eyes were brownish and moist like seaweed, and they began to weep soon during the first verse of the psalm, probably because whatever happened here on earth touched her or because life was so important to her—to anyone who weeps, life has some importance. She was wearing a tasselled cap, but her hair was unkempt, and she had on an old pleated skirt but not the formal costume bodice, much less a silken bow; instead she wore an old cardigan, but the patch on the left elbow was neat, and she had a new shawl over her shoulders which was obviously her Sunday-best. On the other hand she had no handkerchief with which to dry her eyes when she wept, but had to cry into her best blue apron, and it was obvious at once that she was one of those people whom God particularly loves; she went on weeping. By the time the last verse had ended she had finished crying; the pastor began the prayer, and the birds flew past the window as if out of curiosity. She looked at them flying past, and went on staring at the window for a long time; and a long time after they had flown by she said almost inaudibly to herself, "Poor blessed birds."

"What's your name?" he asked in a low voice.

She was flushed with weeping and looked younger. But she did not dare look at him because she was ashamed of having shown that she was so sensitive to what happened in the world and cared so much about life that she had started weeping. After a little while, however, she told him her name and where she lived—Jarþrúður, from Gil—and also that she had been in poor health since she was young, but that God had always been good to her.

"Then we are both Our Lord's crossbearers," he said gratefully.

"Yes, but you're said to be so brave always," she said. "You're an example to everyone in distress. But what am I? I'm nothing but sin."

She was almost in tears again because of her conviction that she was one of the greatest female sinners of our time. "I'm sure that there is no one in the whole world who is so laden with sins as I am."

"Be of good heart, Jarþrúður dear," he said. "I can see in you that you are one of those people whom God loves most particularly."

"Do you think so?" she asked, and looked at him with those large, distant, seaweed-moist eyes glowing with gratitude. "Oh, it does one so much good to listen to you talking to one, because everyone says you're a national poet, like our late Hallgrímur Pétursson, who had leprosy. Now I'm sure I'll feel well for many days. Even though I'm the worst person in the land, I've always known that Jesus is good. And forgive me for having begun to talk to you and defiled this blessed holy hour."

"No one can forbid us to talk together about God under any circumstances," said the poet. "Perhaps we'll never have a chance of talking together again."

"No, don't say that," she said, and was nearly in tears again. "Say something instead that I can keep in my heart every night. You're such a great poet."

"Whether or not this is the last time we can talk together," he said, and he felt a divine power swelling in him with every word, "one thing is certain—that Providence lets those who are in distress come together at the last and have something to talk about as a result. It may well be that they aren't allowed to see each other except the once, just the one day, before they die. The loveliest flowers on earth don't blossom for more than one day, either. I think it's something if a person is allowed to flower, even though it's only for one day in his or her life. How many others there are to whom God gave no sensitivity and who therefore were never unhappy and never talked together, so that their lives never flowered for even one single day!"

"Yes," she whispered, "now let His wise, almighty hand extinguish my life forever!"

"For two years I've never raised my head from this pillow," he said, even though this was not strictly true.

"Yes, but you're so young," she said. "The Lord can easily raise you up when least expected. You've no idea what He might have in mind for you in the future. But I—how old I am! I'm ashamed to say it. I'm so terribly, terribly old! I could be your mother."

"I am seventeen," he said.

She lifted her apron to her face again and sobbed, "I, too, was once seventeen." She peeped out from behind the corner of her apron and would not believe it. "No, I can't understand at all how you can possibly talk to someone as old as me, no, don't look at me, and don't look at my clothes either because I have no clothes, my mistress just lent me this old pleated skirt that belonged to her late mother-in-law."

"I'm not looking at your clothes, Jarþrúður," said the poet. "I'm looking into your eyes."

She took her apron away from her eyes and gazed at him for a long time with a foolish look of amazement; but when she had stopped being surprised and had begun to believe that this was all true, she became frightened and asked in agitation, "But if you recover your health, then you'd never talk to me again, would you?"

He said, "Only those who are alone and those who are distressed understand the spirit, and you are the first person who has understood me."

And thus they carried on their sage and pious conversation as long as the wedding ceremony lasted; about the spirit; and Jesus; and those in distress, and how God loves them above all others; and she knew various things he had never heard, and had read the whole of the psalmbook backwards and forwards for more than twenty-five years; the psalmbook was not only her sole possession here on earth, but also her sole consolation and hope, not just the book of books but almost the most precious thing in all creation. When she was feeling most distressed she laid God's psalmbook on her weak and grief-stricken breast; it soothed the pains of body and soul. "Yes, soon they will all be gone," she said, and smiled foolishly.

But just then the pastor's sermon came to an end, and during the second psalm she became so grateful and enraptured that she said she felt she had become his real mother now; and she sat down on the edge of his bed and did not cry at all during the second psalm, and said that all her life she had wanted so much to have a child and had begged Jesus with burning tears to grant her wish, but from now on she did not want to have any other child than Ólafur Kárason.

He said that if she came here another time when there was peace and quiet he would let her hear everything he had written; for the time being he only showed her the outside of his book of poems and she was allowed to hold it briefly in her gnarled hands—some of her fingers were buckled into the palms from holding knitting needles. She examined both sides of the book, then stared in silent admiration at the poet himself, and he confided to her that he was really called Ólafur Kárason of Ljósavík; and at that she started sobbing again and shook her head in despair, and said she did not believe she could be the mother of such a great man; and he comforted her and said, "Yes, of course you can."

"I shall pray to God every day all summer, morning and night, to strengthen your spirit and make you recover." But then she was overcome with grief again and said, "But if you get better you will just show your book to some other woman"—and with that she gave up all hope.

But he swore, aloud and in silence, that he would never show his book to any other woman; she was the only person in the world who understood him, the only person in the world who could appreciate the spirit properly. From now on he was going to look upon her as his mother, not least since his own mother had established herself as an independent seamstress in a famous market town and had never once sent her greetings to him, whatever distress he was in, but had sent him away in a sack in the middle of winter. Such are the moments of bliss that only those in distress can experience; and then the wedding was over.

—— 19 ——

Guðrún of Grænhóll had moved with her parents out of the parish to another and much better district, and he knew he would never see her again. Magnína, who had given him buttered flatbread and read to him from *The Felsenburg Stories* for a time, had long since stopped reading to him; he was never allowed to know the ending of these exciting tales from that distant island—and, believe it or not, he never again wanted to find out. On the contrary, every time the thought of that book came into his mind he was seized with fear and guilt. And young Kristjána, who had come to him one night to thank him for the poem and had invited him to stay with her when she was married, and had promised to do everything for him, even lay down her life for him—when she had left the farm as a married woman she had even forgotten to say good-bye to him. It looked as if his life would never brighten again. The days passed with incessant sufferings of soul and body, unendurable headaches caused by old blows from beasts and men, terrible pains in his chest and endless indigestion; in addition there were the sleepless nights of despair with their remorseless balance sheets of his wretched life, and the one question repeated like a constant refrain, "Where will it all end for me?"

Often he felt he could scarcely survive many more days now, and then he would turn in the midst of his pain to his book of poems, to add just one little poem yet before he died; for what caused him most sorrow was how few poems he would leave behind him to gladden other people after his death. Often he felt in the middle of the poem that he had not the strength to finish it, that he would die before he could finish it, and he besought the Lord with all his heart to eke out his life just to the end of this one brief poem; and he promised the Lord that when it was finished he would die content and never ask Him again. Often he was amazed that he had not died long ago, considering all his troubles, and he asked aloud, "Is there no limit, then, to human suffering?"

There were now new people he did not know on the farm; no one paid any attention to him, they were all busy with their own tasks, and strangers' hands dished out his gruel to him at mealtimes. If he tried to crawl out of bed to the window to look at the green homefield and the blue sea, he fainted. It was safest to lie still. He gazed up at the sloping ceiling and thought of the time when he was little and God had been revealed to him in a glory of harmony; but the faculties of childhood, too, were now gone.

Had everyone, then, turned his back on this destitute human being under the sloping ceiling? Had everyone forgotten this living corpse? Was there no heart anywhere that could bestow on him the one grace of heaven and earth—one word of love? Yes, that heart did exist.

One day he received a parcel from the district on the other side of the mountains. It was a small, rectangular package, and it was addressed to: Ólafur Kárason of Ljósavík, Esq., Poet, at Fótur-undir-Fótarfæti.

No one on the farm recognized this Poet of Ljósavík, for he had confided the secret of his name to no one else. But someone recollected dimly that a wretch of a poet was lying on a pallet up in the corner of the loft, and the parcel was eventually delivered. It contained the tattered remains of a psalmbook. It was the sort of psalmbook that an uncommonly sinful person had used every day of her life for consolation and had torn asunder with her eyes in the hope that something even more wonderful might lie hidden behind the lines—but probably without ever finding the Lord. Unfortunately there was no accompanying letter, because she herself could not write—some kind person had addressed the parcel for her; but it was the best she could do, she had sent him the only security in the world a sinful person possessed, and it is not everyone who gives such a gift.

Was it not strange that he should so nearly have forgotten her, this one soul who had understood him completely? How could he have been on the point of despair when he had a friend like that? He was ashamed of his ingratitude to the Creator, to have thought himself to be alone when there was a living heart on the other side of the mountains who loved him and had given him its all. He was convinced that her love would never fail, because she was in poor health and on the parish like himself; she was known as Jarþrúður the Epileptic.

He wrote her a letter on all the paper he had left. He said that her pure friendship, as revealed in the gift of the psalmbook, was what would give him the strength to bear life's burdens and afflictions in the future. He said that seldom had he been so engulfed in ultimate darkness as in these past weeks since the wedding took place. Summer was beginning for other people, he alone was forbidden to enjoy it; but now it no longer mattered to him whether he missed this summer and all future summers on earth; her gift was like a gently healing hand, and he was now ready to bear mankind's cross patiently to the end of the road. He asked whether he could from now on look upon her as his sweetheart? Certainly, he said, he could not offer her anything in return except his love, but he was sure that if he knew he was allowed to love her, and that she would give him her heart in return, the time would come when they would both be fully recovered in health, because God is love, and love heals everything and conquers everything, and in time, perhaps, they could set up a little home together in a comfortable croft not far from a market town.

In reality, he said, he looked upon them as being already married in a mystical and supernatural way, that God himself had married them in spirit and in truth the other day; their whole acquaintanceship was bound up with one particular wedding; and in affirmation of this he was sending her the following poem, to the same psalm tune as the wedding hymn that had brought their hearts together:

> *How cold and wretched and sad it is*
> *In ultimate darkness, with yearning laden;*
> *For none here knows what spirit is,*
> *And none understands you, Christian maiden.*
> *My lady crowned,*
> *Closed is the Sound;*
> *Wanting I'm found,*
> *And lie here bound*
> *In death's deep grave,*
> *In death's deep grave.*
>
> *Oh, Iceland's Concordia, pure and clear,*
> *Divine star of the spirit's morrow—*
> *My soul is with you, far or near,*
> *From heights of joy to depths of sorrow;*
> *Your soul takes flight,*
> *A lamp to light*
> *The dark of night;*
> *Your life shines bright*
> *In heaven's halls,*
> *In heaven's halls.*

He addressed the letter and sealed it and asked for it to be entrusted to anyone who was going across the mountains, and his soul rejoiced after having written the letter; it is the best medicine of all to know oneself in contact with a loving heart. That night he had pleasant dreams and thought of his sweetheart when he lay awake between slumbers; and when he woke up in the morning she was the first thought that came to his mind.

Now, whatever the reason for it, this young man had got the idea that letters were inviolate, whoever might have written them and whatever their destination. But in this, as in so many other things, he was grievously mistaken. The following day the foster mother, Kamar- illa, came up to the loft with his letter in her hand, and he could see that it had been torn open.

"Writing letters, I see!" she said.

"Just the one," he said.

"And you a parish pauper!"

"But I thought I had a soul even though I'm on the parish," he said, and gasped.

"I've no wish to have souls of that kind here in my house," said Kamarilla. "And this will be the last letter you ever write here in my house. Since you mean to start proposing marriage to women who lie on the ground foaming at the mouth, and since on top of that you have behaved indecently towards my own daughter on Easter Sun- day itself when everyone else had gone to church, and since you won't stop composing disgraceful and obscene verses full of insults against us who run this household, then I'm going to tell you once and for all that we here in this house have no wish to nurture such a snake at our breast any longer. Besides, I'm sick and tired of punish- ing you with starvation for all your libels, obscenities and blas- phemies—it's been shown over and over again that it doesn't have the slightest effect anyway. But since you're planning to introduce open debauchery into my house, not to mention comparing me and my house to the ultimate darkness, and were going to send this letter to another district, then I'm calling a halt here and now: I refuse to take any further responsibility for you, either on behalf of the church authorities or the parish of Sviðinsvík!"

And with these words she tore his letter into little pieces before his eyes and threw the scraps down the stair-hatch. A moment later she was gone.

He was alone. Never had he been cut so deeply or so mercilessly to the very quick of his consciousness. His most intimate, most sacred manifestations of life had been denounced as crimes; the most vulnerable flowers of his heart had been torn up by the roots and held up to view as poisonous, loathsome weeds. It took him a long time to realize that so much injustice actually could exist in the world, to convince himself how totally defenseless he was, how infinitely far from possessing anything with even the remotest resemblance to any form of protection or shield. But when it eventually became clear to him, he began to cry.

He had not cried since he was a little boy, and now he no longer recognized the sound of his own weeping. It had become deep and hoarse, something alien had got into it, so that he became afraid of his own weeping as if it were some unknown strange monster. He was also amazed at how much it hurt his throat when he wept. He did not remember feeling sore in the throat when he had wept in his childhood. Little by little he stopped crying.

He lay silent for a long time, motionless, exhausted, bereft of his last hope. Once again the immortality of the soul loomed over his mind's eye in all its appalling cruelty, and the hope of absolute death became once again the only imaginable consolation for his soul. Finally the headaches came to his rescue and made him forget.

And so the afternoon passed, and then it was evening. He opened his eyes and woke from his sleep. He was lucky to have been able to sleep. What a wonderful mediator this brother of death was! The boy who had gone to sleep in pain now woke up in gratitude. There was no longer darkness in his soul. The evening sunbeam lay across his bed, and the moment he opened his eyes he felt he was no longer alone. This was not just a vague notion; it was an unshakable conviction. This sunbeam had dimension and shape, he could handle it like any other object; yes, it was that golden carriage of old, it had come back. Deep in the ultimate darkness of despair, when all avenues are closed, when you are bereft of final hope, separated from the only heart that ever loved you—then the carriage comes. And from it steps the invisible friend, the friend whom no power in the universe can separate from us as long as we have the ability to bear the suffer-

ings of human life and meet the injustice of the world; because it is
he, this invisible friend, who helps one to bear the sufferings of
human life, to meet the injustice of the world. Once it had been the
sonic revelation of the deity, later it had been Sigurður Breiðfjörð;
now he no longer asked its name or nature. It was enough to feel his
presence, to know that it was he, the invisible friend.

The boy felt now that no injustice could ever be victorious in his
life in the future. He would never forget this presence, and even
though he might never live to see another happy day, he was now
more than ever determined to make his life an unbroken echo of
what he had perceived when he was young, and to teach other men
in poetry what he had learned in sorrow.

It was certainly true—this boy had perhaps become a little disappointed in people, he had instinctively believed that people were
more perfect than they actually are; in childhood one cannot help
believing this. Certainly his fellow men had turned their backs on
him and deserted him, and one could also say with some truth that
they had been the cause of his ill health in body and spirit, indeed of
all his misfortunes in general. But he was not angry with them for
that, he did not hate them, he did not find their inclinations base nor
their desires disgusting, far from it. He felt no rancor towards anyone.
He respected everyone, without reason, and wanted instinctively to
please everyone; moreover, he was grateful to God for all the wonderful people he had got to know in his lifetime, right from the time
when memory began until this day. And if the same people who had
turned their backs on him and despised him yesterday had come to
him again today, he would have had just as much faith in them as
before. He would have felt they understood him and understood the
spirit even though they did no more than sit down for a moment on
the edge of his bed. Whosoever has met the invisible friend can never
again see any evil in people, and even though they took everything
from him, every smallest pleasure, every faintest hope, it would make
no difference—he would nonetheless do everything he could to enrich
them, to increase their happiness, to strengthen their hopes, to beautify their lives. They could call his words smut and blasphemy, they
could call the things closest to his heart crimes and debauchery, they

could starve him, they could drive him from this house, ill and help-less—he would nonetheless continue ceaselessly to dedicate to these people everything most precious in himself. Yes, it is a painful lot to be a poet and to love both God and man by the farthest northern seas! He who has chosen that lot for himself will never achieve any success, any reward now or later, any fulfillment in life, any happy days, any moments of consolation or rest. On the other hand, the invisible friend will help him to bear the sufferings of mankind and protect him from ever being overcome by injustice.

—— **20** ——

A June morning—seldom had the blessed summer sun shone with more brilliance on that bleak northern coast. He had known for a long time that one spring morning he would wake up early, and yet no day took him so much by surprise as this one.

He had had an inkling the previous evening that an overnight vis-itor had arrived; he had heard his cheerful laughter from down below, and even heard the joyless people of that household joining in. But it was not until dawn the next morning that Kamarilla told Ólafur Kárason why the visitor had come; he had been sent by the parish council at Sviðinsvík to fetch him. "And let me now put some clothes on you, you poor scamp."

He did not say anything and could not even think, either. All he could feel was his foster mother trying to put some socks on him. But when people tried to help him to his feet and make him stand upright, he fainted. When he came round again his escort, Reimar, was standing over him; Reimar greeted him with a kiss and a hand-shake, and examined him with that critical, appraising look with which experienced carriers examine fragile goods that have to be handled with care, and laughed.

"It'll be no trouble at all to shift him!" said Reimar, in order to cre-ate a mood of optimism and confidence about the undertaking.

He was a genial, ruddy-complexioned man, with watery eyes and an easy manner. He had two horses with him, and the younger brother, Júst, helped him to lash together a stretcher. The route lay over high moorland. The sun shone sweetly on the blue bay and the fresh green homefield and the buttercups on the grassy slope in front of the farmhouse; swarms of birds eddied over the skerries and the isthmus.

When the boy had been dressed in a weird assortment of clothes which had been collected here and there, he was carried outside and tied to the stretcher on a bed of strips of dried turf, with a bag of hay as a pillow and a coarse blanket on top of him. He was quite sure he would be dead within the hour; he was incapable of appreciating as he should the eternal blue heaven above him, and was only grieved that he had not had time to say good-bye to the old knots in his sloping ceiling.

"We're off to see the world lo then!" said Reimar, when the boy had been firmly lashed to the stretcher, and laughed.

The whole family was out in the farmyard to say good-bye to the parish pauper. The foster mother, Kamarilla, handed him a piece of sugar candy—the first and last time she ever gave him anything in the way of sweets; then she lifted her apron to her eye and wiped away a genuine tear. Finally she reached up to him on the stretcher and kissed him, and at the same time asked God and the Holy Ghost to bless forever this crossbearer of the Lord; he felt her tears sliding down his cheek, and they tickled.

"Good-bye," said Magnína, and gave him a fat, limp handshake, sniffed, and turned away. Then she turned to him again and wished him a good journey. She was holding something peculiar under her apron.

"Well, my dear chap," said brother Júst, who now not only owned many sheep and a part-share in a fishing boat but had also become a farmer in his own right with undisputed control over everything that concerned this household on land and sea. "If you ever get better you will always be cordially welcome back here again, for instance at the haymaking or as a winter hand, because now there's no one here to order you to stay down in the meadow when you should be going up the hill! And you know from experience, my friend, that our treatment of people here at Fotúr has never been thought worse than else-where."

Reimar kissed all the people good-bye and led the horses along the path towards the road. The stretcher started creaking and groaning at once. Then Magnína called out and asked Reimar to wait for a moment, she wanted to adjust the boy's blanket; she came and adjusted it, and at the same time she brought out from under her apron a book wrapped in a kerchief, and slipped it under his blanket.

"It's only *The Felsenburg Stories*," she said. "I don't enjoy them any more. You can have them. You enjoy stories so much."

"Thank you, Magnína dear," he said.

"It's nothing," she said.

She walked a few steps beside the stretcher when Reimar led the horses off again. She looked down at the path and said, "I thought I deserved a letter from you just as much as some people did. And a poem at the end."

She could not keep up with the horses any longer because she was so heavy. She was left standing in the middle of the path, holding a corner of her apron in her hands and gazing after their parish pauper.

—— **21** ——

The route lay past the head of the fjord and from there up onto the mountains; the path zigzagged dizzily up the pass. All around them was the summer, a sky-blue gladness on the world all the way out over the farthest ocean; there was a glitter on the silver-white breasts of birds down by the shore, and the little mountain flowers beside the path, and the moss and the boulders; the dew was drying, smoke was beginning to rise from the farms, there were buttercups in the home-field, ewes with their lambs. An Icelandic spring morning—it was just this kind of supreme happiness that the boy had lived in his yearning dreams during the long winter nights of death; but surrounded now by all this bliss he was far from enjoying it to the full. He was extremely frightened. He thought the stretcher would topple off the horse at every bend in the path, and below lay the ravine, so deep that the river at the bottom looked like a tiny brook and the sheep on its banks no larger than toys. The creaking of the stretcher and the belly-rumbling of the newlyfed horses sounded in his ears like the fury of the elements; two years under the sloping ceiling had made him unaccustomed to sound and movement, and the slightest obstacle on the path was a dire peril. And besides, there were ravens hovering high overhead, ready to tear his eyes out. He was quite convinced he would pass away before they reached the top of the mountain.

On the other hand, Reimar did not seem to have the slightest inkling about his companion's death throes, for he kept up a cheerful chatter to no one in particular all the way up the mountainside, when he was not urging on the horses. He had heard, you see, that the patient had a natural bent for poetry, and when the stretcher was pitching worse than ever he recited some verses about worldly pleasures, about warm flatbread, fat women, cold buttermilk, and riding horses, and asked the invalid whether he had heard that one. And by the time they had reached the brow of the mountain he had recited so much enchanting poetry that Ólafur Kárason had forgotten his imminent death and had stopped noticing the creaking of the stretcher.

"You're not a poet yourself, are you, Reimar?" he asked finally.

"Oh, I don't suppose there are many other poets more often on people's lips, my friend," said the poet Reimar. "Just ask the womenfolk of Sviðinsvík! I can admit to four whole ballad cycles by your leave, my friend—the Ballad of Memrok and Kalibab, the Ballad of Nagel and Apagitta, the Ballad of Queen Engilrad of Samsey, and the Ballad of Rokkefor and Kamenber—quite apart from all the modern poetry, like for example more than twenty marriage odes, fifty elegies (for which I never charge less than seventy-five *aurar* apiece), nearly two hundred love poems to girls and young men (in other people's names), and that's not counting all my own poetry which I composed from the heart, such as for example about adulteries in Sviðinsvík, accidents, being without tobacco, drinking sessions, and that sort of thing. Last but not least, I permit myself to mention lesser versifyings, my friend, for example verses about horses, sea journeys, and worldly pleasures; lampoons, obscene verses, children's ditties, riddling rhymes, acrostics, and spontaneous compositions. Yes, I think I could say I've ridden the Muse pretty hard, my friend!"

Ólafur Kárason had not heard so much poetry for years on end, under the sloping ceiling, as he now heard on the mountainside from midmorning till midafternoon. If Reimar were asked to give the first verse of the Ballad of Memrok and Kalibab, he had no objection to carrying on until he had finished the Ballad of Rokkefor and Kamenber, and this even with the wind full in his face all the time. In a pause between ballads the younger poet took the opportunity of asking, "Don't you find it exceedingly difficult to be a poet, Reimar?"

Reimar did not know how to answer this question; it took him completely aback, and he was nonplussed by it.

"Difficult? Me? To be a poet? Just ask the womenfolk about that, my friend, whether our Reimar finds it difficult to be a poet! It was only yesterday that I rode into the yard of one of the better farms hereabouts, and the daughter of the house was standing outside, smiling, and without more ado I addressed her with a double-rhymed, quatro-syllabic verse that just came to me as I bent down from the saddle to greet her. No, it's not difficult to be a poet, my friend, it's a pleasure to be a poet. It's a question of talent, you see."

"What do you think is needed to be a good poet?" the boy asked.

"Needed?" he echoed, and laughed. "Just ask the womenfolk that!"

But later he began to give it some further thought all the same; this side of the matter had in reality never occurred to him before.

"There are really only two things needed," he said when he had thought enough about it, "and that is to alliterate and to rhyme. That's the beginning and the end of all poetic art. The man who follows that rule will always be able to compose something for someone. But the man who doesn't follow it will never be able to compose anything for anyone. To speak impromptu—anyone can do that. But to rhyme—only poets can do that. That's the talent, if I may say so, you see. The more elaborate the better. Of course, acrostics can become a bit repetitive, I don't deny that, and there aren't many girls in the younger generation who can appreciate that sort of thing, but there's no doubt about it that one can never have too much internal rhyme. And then of course it doesn't do any harm to be able to use

kennings correctly; but I have a firm rule never to use too many kennings. I only use kennings for three things—women, men, and ships;
on the whole there's no need for any more kennings than that in Iceland nowadays."

"But what do you say, Reimar, if the poet wants to turn his
thoughts to the soul and to spiritual matters?"

"Spiritual matters? The soul?" said Reimar the poet. "Do you
mean elegies for the dead and suchlike?"

"No, I mean the spirit," said the young poet, "the soul."

"What's all this talk about the soul, boy? The soul, that's the pastor's business, the girls don't want to hear about anything like that.
And you'll soon find out, my friend, that those who make a habit of
talking about the soul always mean something entirely different deep
down; they just don't dare to say it aloud. In good old Icelandic the
soul just means a bag,* let me tell you, my friend, and I reckon that
those who talk most about the soul would like it very much better if
you put something into their bag, my friend. That's the way I look at
it, anyway."

With that, Ólafur Kárason of Ljósavík stopped asking questions;
he thought of the revelation of the deity, of Sigurður Breiðfjörð and
the invisible friend, and he doubted whether Reimar was as much a
man of the spirit as he was famous as a poet.

—— **22** ——

By now they were well on their way across the plateau of the mountains. The farms had all disappeared, all the valleys were levelled
out, the fjords buried in the mountains; and the mountains had
merged into one another, only their tops swelling one behind the
other like undulating lowlands—and far away on the other horizon,
the sea. The air up there was like the two-thousand-krónur pharmacopoeia one had always longed for but never been able to afford, at
once cooling and exhilarating; it sent intoxicating waves through the
boy's body, he was no longer frightened. The sloping ceiling under

which he had cowered for two years and from where he had been resurrected a few hours ago was now like any other past event which did
not concern him at all; he was no longer the most wretched creature
on earth. On the contrary he was a living participant in the ethereal
joy of the mountains; he was no longer afraid of anything, not even
the immortality of the soul.

"Here's the county boundary, and now we'll eat."

The poet Reimar led the horses off the path into a hollow, to the
side of a little mountain stream. He released the boy from the
stretcher and laid him down on the moss, and the boy lay there on
the moss and gazed up at the azure sky of eternity which had now
become his friend again at last.

Reimar opened his knapsack with a contented look of expectation
on his face, and their senses were filled with the aroma of bread and
fish and cold coffee. The older poet handed the younger one a generous strip of dried fish, and as he did so he said, "Listen, it's just
occurred to me, shouldn't we just use this opportunity and get you
cured on the way?"

"Oh, that's easier said than done, Reimar, curing me," said the
young poet.

"There's plenty of butter in the jar here," said Reimar.

"The illness I have is one that even doctors don't understand at all."

"Here's a fine, fat piece of flank, dammit, it couldn't have been better if it had come off old Magnína herself; yes, they must have been
in high old spirits at getting rid of us this morning, these women at
Fótur!"

"Oh, it's not surprising, poor things," said the boy. "I've been a
terrible burden to that household all these years."

They both ate heartily, but the horses snorted down by the stream
and did not like the grazing. High above them a black-backed gull
called menacingly, and that was the only sound in the unpeopled
stillness of the mountain moorlands. When they had eaten their fill,
Reimar offered his charge a pinch of snuff, but Ólafur declined and
said it gave him a headache. Reimar wiped his clasp knife clean on
his trousers and put it into his pocket.

"No, it's no great problem, curing one little illness nowadays, I can tell you, my friend," he said.

The invalid said then that it was not just a question of suffering from only one illness. There were many illnesses, all intertwined with one another. His skull had been broken three times, by both men and beasts. His brain was growing out into the ear at one place, and this was accompanied by the most uncontrollable headaches. In addition, his breast-bone was sticking out and there was a cyst under it, and everything had congealed into a malignant tumor—cyst, liver and pericardium. In addition to that, he had various stomach ailments and could scarcely say he had digested a single bit of food these last two years.

"That's quite a mouthful," said the poet Reimar.

The young poet went on and said that the district doctor had never in his whole life known of anyone so ill, and really knew of no means of dealing with so many illnesses in any one person, except perhaps by cutting him up.

"Well, I'll be damned!" said Reimar. "You were lucky he didn't get his hands on your carcass. He's such a butcher and misanthrope that he never attends any patients unless he's allowed to cut them up into little pieces; and I myself have seen him with my very own eyes flaying a woman alive!

"But now," he went on, "I'll tell you a very different story, my friend. On the other side of the mountains there's another fjord, not a dreary fjord like the fjord to the east but a pleasant fjord. It's fine country there, and remarkable people. On some of the farms there are the Hidden People—no, there's no point in looking at me like that, I can't help it, and why the devil shouldn't Hidden People exist anyway? I've never known the Hidden People to do folk any harm—quite the contrary, in fact. But whether Hidden People exist or not, I don't know of any dale or fjord in these parts which is better for women than the one to the west of these mountains we're on at present. Or have you never heard of the cures at Kambar?"

The boy had to admit with shame that he had never heard about anything which had happened to the west of these mountains.

"Well, I never! Says he's ill and has a soul and I don't know what else, and hasn't heard of Þórunn of Kambar, the only person in this province who dispatches cancer and peritonitis, fiends and devils, as easily as I crumple up this fishskin and toss it onto those boulders there! How does she do it? Well, you don't know very much, my friend, I must say! The way she does it, let me tell you, is that one evening last autumn when the nights had begun to draw in, she was out walking beyond the homefield when she made contact with an elf-man beneath the crags, let me tell you, my friend. Yes, and you don't need to go all red in the face at that, it wasn't the sort of relationship which all sorts of riffraff and rogues imagine is the only relationship possible between people in this world and the next.

"No, this elf was an excellent fellow and a genius in word and deed, a very different sort from me and the likes of me, I can tell you, my friend. In fact it was the elf doctor, Friðrik. Since then she has met him every day, all winter and all spring, and received from him the most infallible medical advice. Some say he learned his elf medicine in his time at the Black School in Paris, and even that he's a spirit, but I don't really believe that. All I know is that through her, people are cured, and they're cured by something, whatever it might be. According to what Þórunn herself says, he's not entirely unlike the French captain who often came to the fjords here when she was a child, and was said to have got on very well indeed with a lot of people; but she says that Friðrik is all for Christianity, so that her mother thinks he's perhaps Jesus Christ, but I won't go any further into that, my friend."

The more they talked about the Kambar girls, the more Reimar had to say in their praise and favor, but most of all about Þórunn and her doctor. Reimar had written to this girl no fewer than six marriage proposals in verse on behalf of respectable men of substance in different parts of the district—"And they weren't all just talk, my friend, though I say it myself—strictly between ourselves, of course, seeing that I'm a married man with six children in Sviðinsvík. But Þórunn rejected all six of them, and I can vouch for that about some of them, because I myself composed her refusals to them, and there was no question of always choosing the most refined words, I can tell you, my friend; indeed I know of one man who has been completely deranged for three years because of her. Yes, she's a glorious woman, is Þórunn!"

He guaranteed the boy a total cure from Þórunn's Friðrik, a long and happy life, children, and descendants. But the boy was a little alarmed at the prospect of coming into the presence of so glorious a person, and felt he was too wretched and insignificant to deserve anything like that. And in addition, some religious scruples now asserted themselves. You see, deep down he was extremely apprehensive about becoming involved with supernatural forces west of these mountains. He knew the forces which reigned east of the mountains, where he had been brought up; people there had believed chiefly in God and Jesus, two related forces, both of which were thoroughly familiar to him from the *Book of Sermons,* the psalmbook, and so on. West of the mountains there reigned obviously different supernatural beings, powers he had not, unfortunately, had an opportunity of getting to know. And somehow or other, since Reimar had dispatched the spirit like a sheep with the staggers earlier that day, this spiritual young man no longer dared to rely blindly on man's infallibility. At least he had to ask himself the question in all seriousness—whether it would be right to give up all hope of that reliable supernatural power with which he had been brought up on the east of the mountains, in exchange for the uncertain supernatural powers on the west side. Was it likely that God and Jesus would accept it in patience and silence if he were now to turn to Friðrik and Þórunn? This boy, you see, did not want to offend anybody.

At this county boundary he was once again seized by that paralyzing terror that had reigned in his breast for so long before he became ill, but which had never filled his consciousness to a greater degree, perhaps, than during those last two years when he lay helpless under the sloping ceiling: the uncertainty as to which of those two forces that battled for control of the farm he should obey, Jónas or Júst; how he should choose between those two extremely present gods when the one said "Go!" and the other "Stay!"; the one "Down here in the meadow!" and the other "Up the hill!" What punishment would Júst mete out to him if he obeyed Jónas, or Jónas, if he obeyed

Júst? Which of them was right and which wrong, which good and which bad?

It also occurred to him now whether the elf doctor, Friðrik, might be the devil himself, so that each step he took towards such a creature could affect the salvation of his soul. But he did not dare to discuss such matters with a man who was so insensitive to everything spiritual as Reimar was. When all was said and done, however, there was no one to say that these newly discovered supernatural powers west of the mountains might not be stronger than the familiar powers to the east. In reality one never knows what supernatural power will conquer in the end, so it probably is more sensible to believe in them all, or at least to show them all the same politeness, in the hope that one or the other of them will prevail in the end and will reward neutrality and courtesy. And on these grounds the boy agreed in a whisper to put his fate in the hands of Friðrik and Þórunn, in the hope that it was God's will that he should be cured in Jesus' name. It was actually uniting east and west, meadow and hill, and wiping out all county boundaries—and he hoped that with such an inoffensive declaration he would not offend anyone.

On the other hand, Reimar answered this by saying that God had no will and did not care about anything and had no attitudes about anything, and that is just why He was God, because otherwise how could He be God, the way things were happening abroad these days?— if any God existed at all, which he said even the most renowned foreign scholars were still unable to prove. "No, there's no point in looking at me like that, my friend; I can't help it, it's not my fault, and as far as I'm concerned God can exist if He likes for all I care. But whether there is a God or not, the main thing is to will something yourself, and if you will something, you must use your brains to think up the dodges needed to bring about whatever it is you want; that's intelligence, you see. And now I'll lash you to this stretcher for the last time, because tomorrow you'll be running about in the fields like a calf on a spring morning. No, it's no problem to cure one damned illness nowadays, I can tell you, my friend. And now let's have a party with the Kambar girls tonight!"

—— 23 ——

The evening shadows were getting very long when they were at the foot of the mountain on the west side; around midnight they were in a narrow valley girt by towering mountains, with crofts and their homefields scattered here and there. The farm of Kambar stood under the crags down by the sea.

"That's the landing the Kambar girls sail from when they go to the dances at Sviðinsvík. Yes, and no question of studying the weather when they're going anywhere; they don't give a damn if the sea's a bit rough, my friend. Yes, they're certainly freedom-heroines, these girls!"

When they neared the farm, Reimar left the bridle path and set course straight for the farmhouse, so delighted was he at the prospect: "Just go direct, my friend," he cried, and drove the horses pell-mell over hummocks and through impassable bogs where they sank up to their bellies, while the stretcher threatened to break apart.

The little homefield round the farm was crowded with ewes and their lambs, no attempt had been made to keep them out; but four fierce dogs sprang down from the wall of the house and raced towards the visitors with extraordinary vehemence. Two dilapidated wooden gables faced towards the sea, but otherwise the farmhouse was just a shapeless pile. A woman in dun-colored rags came out on to the paving as if by accident, shaded her eyes with her hand and saw the visitors approaching over the bog, and shouted in through the open door; a second appeared, and a third. They stood in the yard for a moment, plain and colorless, and then disappeared into the house and closed the door behind them.

"They've seen us," said Reimar confidentially, and winked at the invalid.

When they reached the farmhouse the yard was empty and the door locked, while the dogs went on raging round them like mad things. Reimar led the horses right up to the front window and knocked on the door. There was no reply. He went on knocking for a while, and when the knocking had no effect he tried shouting a greeting through the window, and when that too proved of no avail he climbed up onto the roof and shouted down the chimney, but that made no difference either; the house was dead. This went on for a long time. The house was in a state of seige. Reimar showed not the slightest sign of giving up. At long last they caught a glimpse of the farmer's eye peering out through the half-opened door. He asked what the hell all this hammering was about, who was out there making such a row?

"Just a couple of fellows," said Reimar.

The farmer came halfway out through the door, with one hand on the latch and holding up his trousers with the other. He had been in bed, and he greeted Reimar with only moderate cordiality; but Reimar leapt at him and embraced him and kissed him and blessed him with a torrent of fine words.

"What the devil have you got on these pack horses?" asked the farmer. "Is it timber?"

"It's a patient," said Reimar.

"I've been in bad health all my life, but no one ever put me on a stretcher and forced me on other folk," said the farmer.

"Yes, but this one has nothing left to do but give up the ghost, by your leave, my friend."

"What the devil, what's wrong with him then?"

"Oh, every damned thing's wrong with him, I can tell you, both in body and in soul."

"No, I've had enough of this," said the farmer. "I'm absolutely sick and tired of it. There's no profit in it at all, and to tell you the honest truth I think it's best to let that brute of a doctor hack them to pieces."

Then he caught sight of the boy and said sympathetically, "Oh, it's only a wretch of a boy. Who's responsible for him?"

"I've brought him over for someone in Sviðinsvík. Actually he belongs to the parish, and it just sort of occurred to me on my way past whether Friðrik would care to have a look at him."

"I don't know anything about any damned Friðrik," said the farmer, and refused to countenance it at all. "I've told the girl again and again to stop meddling in things that don't concern her at all; it always leads to an evil end. The house has been full of raving lunatics most of the winter. And what do I get out of it? Nothing but distraints and legal actions."

"If Þórunn wanted to attend to him, it would be well worthwhile for the parish to compensate her—although unfortunately I don't have the authority to promise anything like that. People like this are a real burden, and it's anything but fun for the parish."

"How long has he been bedridden?"

"Four years."

"Four years? No, now you're lying. Isn't he just mad, then?"

The farmer came right out of the house now to have a look at this long-suffering person and gave him his hand, although none too cordially. "As I was saying, I can't offer you any hospitality here. The wife's not right in the head and there's nothing for visitors to sleep on, and my own insides aren't feeling too good; so it's better not to hold you up any longer."

The farmer kept shivering; he jerked his shoulders and scratched himself here and there, looked up at the sky, and yawned.

"What d'you think the weather will do?" asked Reimar.

"Oh, someone would have said sometime or other that it would do something," said the farmer. "But luckily it won't do anything. Except that everything is going to Hell, bit by bit."

But Reimar had no intention of giving up, and tried to spin out the conversation as much as he could and turn every reflection to more optimistic conclusions, and was always having a peep at the windows, while the young poet waited on the stretcher, ravenously hungry, aching all over and racked with headaches, having abandoned all hope that any miracle would happen there, and the horses hungry and restless after traveling for twenty hours.

"Yes, that's the way it is, my lad," said the farmer, with ever more inserts and additions the longer his tale of woe went on. "I obviously don't do it for fun, turning people away who come here on stretchers in the middle of the night—but what can I do? Have I done anything to deserve to be a free hospital for the whole nation? I say free, because though the occasional person might slip a króna or two to Þórunn or hand the old woman a pound of butter, what's that? It's like pissing into your own shoe. No, it's all going the same way, the sheep dying, no grass in the homefield, the cow had to have the bull yet again last Saturday, not a fin out of the sea, a distraint yesterday, I'm liable to prosecution and legal action from the authorities, the old woman ill, Þórunn up to her eyes in miracles, and I myself refused a bit of tobacco on account by the high-ups in Sviðinsvík. I ask you—is it any sort of life?"

— 24 —

But just when the conversation between farmer and visitor had reached this chapter of the jeremiad, the door was suddenly thrown wide open, and on the doorstep there appeared three lovely young ladies, all attired in the most brightly hued dresses. Smiling radiantly they came up to the great poet and greeted him affectionately, bade him be welcome, and invited him to come in and make himself at home; the farmer himself had completely vanished from the scene, as if the ground had swallowed him up. Never had Ólafur Kárason of Ljósavík imagined that three such refined ladies could emerge from such an unprepossessing house. One was clad in red, the second in blue, the third in green. They lent the beautiful spring afterglow a particularly festive air as they stepped forward in greeting, and in their cheerful smiles there lurked no trace of inner tension. To be sure, the young patient on the stretcher was incapable of distinguishing between their individual appearances. They affected his senses like some overwhelming abundance of blossoming womanhood, at once impersonal and formless, almost liquid; it was like looking at the sun—one cannot see the individual rays. But the poet Reimar— now there was a man who knew how to respond to such courtesies! He let go the reins of his horse, turned towards these comely ladies, embraced them vigorously, and kissed them one after the other, and this ceremony was accompanied by many and varied blessings, sighs, invocations to God and girlish shrieks.

"Dear Jesus!" they said when they began to get their breath back. "You haven't got a dead man with you, have you?"

"No," said Reimar, "he isn't dead, but he's damn far gone, poor creature. Someone asked me to bring him west over the mountains. You see, he's been bedridden at the parish's expense for nearly eight years, but recently he got the confounded idea of proposing marriage to some woman, I tell you, my friends; so the people felt unable to take any further responsibility for him on behalf of the church authorities and reported it to the parish council. Apart from that, he's a lad of intelligence. Þórunn dear, how d'you feel about this? There's often been need but now there's necessity, as the saying goes, to rid the parish of a heavy burden."

"Come in, dear, do!" said one.

"Stay the night, dear, do!" said the second.

"Yes, and do be entertaining, dear!" said the third.

But the boy thought he heard one of them add carelessly, as if it did not matter at all: "It won't take long to cure one patient, heavens above!"

"But I'd much rather leave the horses outside the homefield, when the grass is so nearly ready for mowing," said Reimar.

"Pooh!" they said, and laughed. "Just leave the damned old hacks in the homefield, man. Everything grazes in the homefield anyway; Daddy can jolly well drive them out tomorrow morning. And now in with the corpse; yes, he shall certainly be resurrected, that one! And now there shall be pancakes baked at Kambar!"

The horses were let loose in the homefield, and the patient was carried into the house. He was laid down on a bench. It was a room painted blue, with a picture of the King of Britain, God Bless This House, the Virgin Mary with the heart exposed, and a porcelain dog. The girls bent down over him, one after another, and examined him politely, but not thoroughly, and touched his hair lightly because it had a reddish tinge and was so soft.

They kept up a cheerful conversation with Reimar for a time, amusing stories about various people and their love affairs or drinking bouts, and they recited the latest verses about them from Sviðinsvík. Reimar was blue in the face with laughing. Ólafur Kárason had never imagined that such hilarity could exist here on earth.

"That's enough now. Out you go, girls, and take Reimar with you to where he likes best to be!"

Suddenly everything was very quiet and still, and the patient was left alone in that blue room with Þórunn of Kambar, the Virgin Mary, the King of Britain and the handsome porcelain dog. She stood at the window gazing out at the unreal landscape of the spring night and had suddenly become serious. He felt that she saw him and only him all the time, even though she was looking in the opposite direction. She said nothing. He was so uncanny that there was no one like him in that parish nor in Sviðinsvík; yes, there are all kinds of incredible people in Iceland. His trousers were so patched and darned that they seemed to have been handed down from one generation of parish paupers to another for more than two hundred years. He had on a discarded duffel jacket with a shawl under it, and a coarse cold-weather scarf wound round his neck. There was a weird contrast between this coarse clothing and the man who wore it; it was quite clear that it was not his own personality, but the thinking and feelings of others, which was expressed in what he was wearing. He himself was delicate and radiant, like a tender plant; every line of his body suggested a personal life, every movement an expression, every proportion a grace; his skin was smooth and bright, so that one felt it would leave marks and stains if one touched him; the structure of his features was neat and regular, his reddish hair flowed in large locks over his cheeks and ears, and by virtue of that pleasing color the eyes shone doubly blue, deep and sincere, grave, questioning.

She went on gazing out the window. Nothing was said. When at last she looked at him, he felt there was resentment in her glance, but the longer she regarded him the more her expression softened. He smiled back at her, unreservedly, gratefully, candidly, like a child. In that sudden smile his whole soul was revealed to her, the way a whole landscape is revealed in one flash of lightning at night, and one knows precisely where one is.

"So you have come to me."

"Yes," he whispered.

"Why?" she asked.

"To be cured by you."

"Do you believe that I can cure you?"

"Yes."

"I alone?"

"No."

"Who else?"

"Friðrik."

"Do you believe it with all your heart?"

"Yes."

"And with all your soul?"

"Yes."

"And with all your body?"

"Yes—insofar as the body can believe."

"Then why didn't you come to me before?"

"I didn't know about it until today, up on the mountains, when Reimar told me."

"Oh, was it he who told you about it!" she replied, and was not very impressed. "I should know well enough what he believes in, the damned rascal! Never believe anything Reimar tells you about me. Will you promise me that?"

"Yes," whispered the patient.

"Now you know what to believe," she said. "And what not to believe."

Her voice had two different registers, which made it more attractive than any voice, just like a spring plant that has its roots in the dirty soil and a single blossom which opens to the clean air. In her presence he felt most distinctly that all the truths east of the mountains had become invalid and that new truths had taken their place. She had glowing eyes in which red or green fires glinted briefly, depending on how the light fell on them, but when you looked more closely you saw they were neither red nor green; they were more like white-hot iron by daylight. The expression of her mouth, the smile—that was something quite impersonal and yet very special, something one recognizes in other people and animals and oneself without it concerning anyone; it came and went in a flash, fleetingly.

Soon she stopped talking to him and began thinking about something else, and hummed the "Giants' Dance," absentmindedly; she was staring out of the window again and was thinking about something far away. In this way she was obviously at one with the spirit that inhabits two worlds. But when she had finished gazing out the window and had stopped humming absentmindedly, she remembered him again and gave him a fleeting smile and came over to him and squeezed his hand as a sign that she was back.

"We must have maturity," she said, as if in direct continuation of the "Giants' Dance"—"spiritual maturity. What is spiritual maturity? It is to be receptive to those currents that are all around us from good and willing friends. We must love one another like invisible beings in space. God is love. You must pray for Iceland."

"Yes," he said.

"All the air around is full of currents," she said. "You must believe that."

"Yes."

"One thing is essential. Do you know what it is?"

"No."

"It is to find the right current; the current of love; the current of spiritual maturity; the current of perfection that roots out everything base and earthly and physical. It is that eternal current of love which created the solar system and holds the firmament together so that it doesn't fall apart. I see light."

Then she started looking out of the window again, out into the night, forgetting herself as she had done before and absently humming the "Giants' Dance" again; then she came to, once more, looking at him, laughed in a deep voice and asked, "Is it true that you were proposing to a woman? Fie on you, that's wicked."

He blushed furiously at this question, but she got no other reply, because his tongue lay paralyzed in his mouth. She touched that red hair of his and asked, "How old are you?"

"I'm past seventeen."

"I don't care. It's wicked nonetheless. We must have spiritual maturity in order to make contact with the right currents. We must work for the victory of goodness. We must sacrifice everything to beautify the soul. We must pray. We must see light. Listen, what else did Reimar tell you about me on the mountains today?"

"He said you had had six letters of proposal from men."

"He's lying in his teeth, the damned ram!—a parish pauper himself many times over, with a wife and children in Sviðinsvík, apart from all the illegitimate brats. It was he himself who wrote all the letters to me on his own behalf, but that won't get him very far, even though he's so liberal-minded and can cobble the odd verse together; it would take a greater poet than that to lift the skirts of little Þórunn of Kambar!"

Then she sang another snatch of the "Giants' Dance," out of the blue, and added, "Besides which, I'm going south soon with Friðrik and buying a house."

She gazed out at the spring in a trance and went on talking to him out of the trance and humming snatches of the "Giants' Dance" between sentences. "I get money from people all over the country, who are dying. They just write me letters and ask me to send Friðrik, describing the plan of their house in detail and telling me exactly where their bed is so that Friðrik won't lose his way in a strange house; and they send me piles of money, bank notes, man, silver, even gold, what's more. Will you come to my house in the south?" And once again she touched his hair.

"I thank you with all my heart," he said, and only wished she would go on singing, talking and sitting. Yes, it was wonderful to live like that, just listening and holding hands and letting her touch his hair and feeling the right current, and seeing the house in the south reflected in her eyes. He had never felt such a sense of release in the presence of any other person.

"Do you know why I'm touching your hair?" she asked.

"No," he said.

"It's because there is gold dust in your hair," she said.

"Gold dust?" he asked in amazement, very red in the face, and she colored a little at seeing him blush, and almost laughed, and said:

"Shall I tell you the story about the gold dust and the flower?"

"Yes," he whispered.

"It was last winter, at Christmas, some three months after Friðrik had performed his first miracle through me. There was a woman in the north of Iceland, a wealthy woman and a very fine person, and she was so ill that there was nothing left for her but to die. She suffered from some strange and frightful disease and had been bedridden for many years and had sought help from all the most famous doctors, and all the most important doctors in the land had examined her and no one knew what was wrong with her. Every conceivable medicine from innumerable pharmacies had been tried, and still the blessed woman got worse and worse, and finally the doctors gave her up for lost and no less a person than the Medical Officer of Health for Iceland, moreover, gave her a signed certificate to the effect that she had just three months to live and not a day more. And now she had only a month left to live—just try to put yourself in her place, just one single month. It was then that she got to hear about me, Þórunn of Kambar, and my friend Friðrik the doctor. She reckoned since she had tried all the others she might as well try us too—we couldn't do worse than kill her, anyway. So she set about having a letter written, giving a detailed description of the house where she lived, and what's more an excellent description of the district where the farm was, along with a drawing of all the highest mountains in the vicinity to make quite sure that Friðrik wouldn't get lost and would find the right valley. I'm afraid I've forgotten the description, but it was a lovely district, one of those big, important districts in the north where people are so cultured and so well-to-do. And on her farm was a modern house, with pipes for clean water and other pipes for dirty water, so there wasn't any need to wear yourself out fetching water, I can tell you, to say nothing of these damned bloody slops! Yes, and a modern kitchen range.

"But what do you think was enclosed in the letter? A bank note, man, yes, two enormous bank notes, what's more, as true as I sit here. So you can bet your life I wasn't slow in going to see my Friðrik and describing to him the farm and the district where she lived, and that she slept upstairs in a big room and the door was at the far end to the right, if I remember correctly, and there was a dormer window on the west side if he preferred to enter through the roof. So of course Friðrik asked me to send his greetings, and fixed a night on which he would visit her, and gave instructions that the doors were to be left unlocked and the window off the catch. And naturally it didn't take long for Friðrik to see what was wrong with the woman: she had both cancer and consumption. But because both these illnesses were so advanced that there was no possibility of curing them separately, Friðrik said he saw no alternative but to make a difficult current-experiment on the woman with a view to shifting the consumption into the cancer in the hope that the cancer would die of consumption. And this cure he performed on the eve of the twenty-eighth of December last, at half-past three after midnight. No one knows what took place, except that the woman says she woke up all of a sudden at a strange current that went through her whole body, and within a short time she had begun to shiver all over. And she felt again and again that something strange was being done to her internally, but she couldn't see who was doing it. You see, no one is allowed to see Friðrik except me, myself, but I can tell you, because it's you, that he has black eyes and a cap and a dark moustache turned up at the ends, and always wears a blue cheviot suit and polished shoes, yes, and a thousand-krónur diamond ring on his forefinger. The woman remembers nothing more of what happened, except that she thinks she must have fallen asleep from it all.

"But on the morning of the twenty-eighth of December, when people got up to make coffee, there was one of those really fierce snowstorms you get in the north and a biting, searing frost—note that. But the doomed woman—what had happened to her? She was sitting up in bed resting on one elbow, perfectly well, with a blissful smile on her lips and a lovely, fragrant, newly opened spring flower in her hand, and the crown of the flower was sprinkled with gold dust."

Þórunn of Kambar closed her eyes, put her head back, raised her clasped hands to her breast, and repeated in a whisper, "And the crown of the flower was sprinkled with gold dust."

She sat like that for a while, in silent ecstasy, with eyes closed and hands clasped at her breast; at last she opened her eyes again, looked at him, and said, "My friend, wait for just a moment, I'm going out now to talk to him."

He lay there alone in the room, opposite that handsome porcelain dog, his life in the balance, being weighed by secret forces, with a marvelous smell of baking and sounds of cheerful laughter from the kitchen.

She came back after a moment. She was carrying a tray laden with hot pancakes and a pint bottle with only some dregs of medicine in the bottom, but no coffee or milk. She laid the tray on the table with great ceremony, looked at the boy with her ambiguous, crystalline smile that was like the refraction of light in a prism, and said confidentially, "You have nothing more to fear; your stretcher can stay here. He doesn't think it's necessary to come himself, but says you are to take this medicine. And he gave me a current for you."

She took the big medicine bottle, tilted it carefully and poured a trickle into a teaspoon, counting the drops exactly; the bottle had a gummed label on which was printed in large capital letters the words BORACIC ACID SOLUTION. Then she walked over to him, smiling, and gave him the medicine.

"Lie back now for a little, while it's taking effect," she said. "Then I'll give you the current."

He had scarcely got the medicine down before the effects began to make themselves felt. The medicine gave him some previously unknown strength which went through his body in waves and streamed from the innermost recesses of his heart to the outermost nerves of his skin and filled his soul with a strange new joy; and besides, the girl was now sitting beside him with eyes closed and head thrown back, and had placed the tips of her fingers on his temples. With every breath he felt lighter and lighter; an unknown power was possessing his earthly substance and irradiating it.

"Do you feel the current?" whispered Þórunn of Kambar, and her fingers had begun to tremble on his temples. "Look, now it's coming! Don't you feel yourself trembling, too?"

He distinctly felt the current from her trembling fingers, and this current went on growing until her whole body had begun to tremble and she no longer had control of her hands. Soon the trembling affected the boy's body, too, and within a short time they were both shaking from head to toe, like a leaf in a hurricane, and there was some magnetic force between them so that for a time it seemed as if they would never be able to free themselves from one another, and the boy's mind became more and more dulled and threatened to dissolve completely in this meaningless vibration.

When he came to again, the current had stopped, the trembling was gone, and she was standing in front of him calling his name in fear; but luckily he was not dead, he had just fainted for a moment. She moistened his brow with a drop or two of that excellent medicine.

"There we are," she said. "It's finished now. Help yourself to some pancakes."

Never in his whole life had he tasted anything which even remotely compared with the deliciousness of these pancakes, and indeed he never tasted anything for the rest of his life that could compare with them. One after another he gulped down these matchless apogees of the baker's art, while Þórunn of Kambar sat beside him and looked on, and ran her hand every now and again over his red-tinged hair which reminded her of the flower with the gold dust. Then the pancakes were all eaten, and she reached out her hand to him and said:

"Now let us walk into the spring night."

She put her arm under his, and they stood up and walked out of the house, side by side; out through the passage; out into the yard; out into the homefield.

The night was a transparent veil, just like her own eyes, bluish and cool; there were calm clouds glowing in the east, placid ewes in the homefield, the dogs asleep, the lowland dissolved in mist which hugged the slopes of the mountain and reached all the way up to the crags, a flat calm on the white fjord, terns. They stood like that in the homefield, amid the wise sheep, gazing, almost dissolving, and practically no reality left, only the trance-like state of the spring night, far from sleep, beyond waking; a world; consciousness.

He had laid his face against her shoulder.

"God," he whispered, because now he heard again the revelation of the deity. "I am not worthy of this!"

She ran her hand caressingly over his golden locks.

"God," he groaned. "Yes, I have always known!"

He felt he was now standing after long wanderings at the well of life itself, and would have nothing to fear, ever, for all eternity.

— 25 —

Next morning they were given cold pancakes by the old woman, while the daughters slept. They gave the farmer the stretcher towards their board and lodging and rode away.

It was the same enchanting weather. When there are two fine-weather mornings in succession in Iceland, it is as if all the cares of life have vanished for good. The air was saturated with the fragrance of land and sea. There was a ceaseless murmur of love song in the calling of the seabirds. In the sunshine there was a tranquil, maternal, oblivious delight. It was as if the luxuriant hay of the homefield and the more humble grass of the bogs would never again be able to wither. The sea was so still and mirror-smooth that it was impossible for such a sea ever to become turbulent again from now on. The clear-blue, loving sky looked as if it could never again become the arena of pitiless storms.

They did not ride hard, but let the horses jog along at their own pace; they were pack horses and had been borrowed from somewhere out by the fjord. Reimar was not as exuberant as he had been the previous day, and was mostly silent; and what surprised the boy was that after all his enthusiasm yesterday he should today turn out to be quite unmoved by the instant spiritual boracic cures and the miracles wrought by currents and vibrations. They rode along the seashore and there were hosts of terns, and this unspiritual poet was no more impressed by the supernatural than if a tern had landed some droppings on his head.

It was a very different matter with the boy. His thoughts could not stop dwelling on the blissful memory of the night, when he had rested his head against the breast of this supernatural maiden and had drunk from it the life-giving strength of the Hidden People. He chose her as his life and truth, his well of health and resurrection. To know her was the same kind of joy as to flower, to part from her was as beautiful as an incurable sorrow.

But incredibly enough he simply could not recall the image of her to mind, this magically blissful spring morning after that unreal night. Even her hands had not stayed in his memory, however rich in miracles they were. Her image was a blurred apparition, a transient refraction of light in a transparent vessel on a clear blue night in spring, while the landscape all around was dissolving.

"Why is it," he asked, "that I find it impossible to remember what the girls at Kambar look like?"

"As if it matters a damn what the damned wenches look like!" said Reimar the poet. "The eldest has been publicly disgraced and has a two-year-old brat, the middle one's a nymphomaniac, and the third is just a common or garden witch if I'm to tell you the absolute truth, my friend; yes, and has been involved with six that I know of, and that's the least of it."

Ólafur Kárason gaped at his escort like an idiot, opened his mouth, and then closed it again.

"Believe me, I know our Þórunn of Kambar!" Reimar continued. "Witches like her can go riding on their broomsticks all night as far as I'm concerned; I'm not after them."

But luckily Ólafur Kárason remembered the promise he had made to Þórunn of Kambar that night, to believe nothing that Reimar might say about her, and therefore the radiant, shimmering, crystalline memory of the girl which he treasured in his mind could not fade.

No, no, no. Nothing could cast a shadow on the gladness of this day.

But what was most wonderful of all was that he now felt he would be a genius and would one day enrich unborn generations with immortal masterpieces, like Sigurður Breiðfjörð. From now on he would never need to beseech God to stretch out his life for the length of one poem; now he was completely well and at the same time capable of composing a whole ballad cycle at a single sitting for the nation which waited for continuing epic events in literature, yes, even of writing the history of a whole district, if it came to that, from the Age of Settlement to the present day.

But Reimar the poet, who had a wife and six children in Sviðinsvík, was in no hurry today; he laboriously followed every wind and bend

of the path—he called it just jogging along harmlessly—and wanted
to stop at as many farms as possible and take the opportunity of talking to decent people. But the younger poet was a little vexed that the
older poet should not think it worth relating anywhere they went
that he was escorting a man who had experienced a miracle the night
before, and did not even mention their visit to Kambar except to say
they had stayed overnight farther up the fjord.

"And now we ought to look in at old Guðmundur's shack and ask
to see the medal," he said.

The dilapidated door of Guðmundur Grímsson of Grunnavík's
cottage faced down towards the stony shore, but above it was carved
in Gothic capital lettering the name of the dwelling of the gods—
GIMLI. Three brown old tatterdemalions with caps pulled down to
their noses asked whom they wanted an elegy composed for, and said
that the time had come to sing the parish council at Sviðinsvík down
to Hell. Reimar now became witty and said that unfortunately he did
not have a dead man with him, but a man who had newly been raised
from the dead, and asked if he could come in; but the old crones
would not allow it without the master's permission since no one was
dead and there was no prospect of profit from the visitors. But they
promised to ask, and one by one disappeared from the yard. The
travelers remained outside by the wall of the cottage and looked up at
the precipitous mountain with the sheer cliff-walls looming over the
house, no fewer than twenty layers of rock ledges rearing, one above
the other, and the low-lying land between mountain and sea just a
notional flatness that had no substance in reality.

"It's quite astonishing that the snow avalanches haven't swept this
wretched little shack far out to sea long ago," said Reimar, "or that
the rocks that come raining down from the cliff ledges the whole
time haven't crushed it to smithereens. And look down there at the
shore; see how the surf has worn these huge boulders smooth, right
on the threshold of the cottage. Yet he has sat here peacefully with his
tattered old books and his writing desk for fifty years."

But Ólafur Kárason of Ljósavík did not think it at all astonishing
that this little house should still stand, because he who yesterday had

been cured in a supernatural way of an incurable illness was convinced that the gods whose dwelling was carved above the door gave special protection to Icelandic literature, and one fine day, when their time came, would redeem the whole world.

Guðmundur Grímsson of Grunnavík sat in his house surrounded by many walls of books; his helmet-like face with bushy eyebrows, huge cheekbones, eagle nose and doggedly set mouth reared above the stacks of books as awesome as if the sheer cliff-walls of the mountains which towered over the farthest sea in the world had been personalized in this human countenance. Most of the books were from the past, some bound in skin-clad wooden boards with brass clasps, some wrapped in dressed hide and tied with thongs or string, others locked away in sealskin-covered chests. When the visitors asked his permission to look at his books, he replied that no one could look at his books: Iceland's ages were embalmed in them, one cannot look at something like that; it takes a long life, eighty years at least, to live oneself into Iceland's literature, even if it is only to be able to realize how little it is possible to know of it and how much less one can understand.

Since he would not allow them to look at his books, Reimar asked whether he would show them the gold medal he got from abroad, and tell them the story of it.

Guðmundur Grímsson explained that he had written two hundred and thirty books. He said he had never received any recognition here in Iceland, which arose firstly from the fact that he was against the modern culture and secondly from the fact that he had never written a single syllable in pursuit of his own fame but only for his own pleasure and to rescue from oblivion much learned historical and literary material. But once, just for fun, he had written a textbook of the Gascon language as it had been spoken in the Pyrenees about two hundred years ago; he prepared this book from the journals of an old pastor who had given shelter for a whole winter to some survivors of a Gascon shipwreck in the century before last. The sheriff had bought this book from him and later sent it to Copenhagen, and from there it had been sent to France, where it had been published, and one world-famous professor in that country had writ-

ten a doctoral thesis on it, and the French Academy had then decorated Guðmundur Grímsson of Grunnavík with a gold medal to
honor his achievement. In this way he had rescued the cultural her-
itage of a foreign country in his spare time, without really having
intended to do anything with it. He unbuttoned his oilskin and put
his hand inside his shirt and drew out a medal; on one side was a picture of the goddess of wisdom, Minerva, in whom they believe in
France, on the other side an inscription in Latin. Ólafur Kárason had
often heard people talking about gold, he had dreamed about gold
and, what is more, often mentioned it in his poetry; but this was the
first time he had ever actually seen gold. Its luster made his eyes blur
with joy and struck him dumb with enchantment. He had never
imagined that gold was so beautiful; he wished that this moment
would never end—and then it ended. The old man put the medal
back into his shirt without having let go of it, and buttoned up his
oilskin with his bluish hands. The boy thought he was growing taller
and taller with every breath.

Guðmundur Grímsson of Grunnavík had reached the age when
new acquaintances brought him nothing any more. He had long
since grown tired of talking about his books to new people; they were
only a repetition of a thousand other people he had known before,
and most of them talked in the same way about the books which
were his life for a thousand years. It could well be that in his young
days he had been the most human of men—nothing was more likely,
in fact. No one could know which of his friends he perhaps remembered when the drops dripped from the roof at night, drop after
drop. Now he had long since ceased to be a man; he was the sage of
the ages, the writer, whom no threat from the elements could force to
lay aside his book and his quill pen; this massive face which was the
unconquerable face of Iceland. And at this moment Ólafur Kárason
felt it had been worthwhile to endure everything in order to have had
the good fortune to see this face. Illness of body and soul, hunger,
beatings, calumnies, false accusations, misunderstandings, lies, deceit—
they all meant nothing. When the visitors walked out into the open
air again the boy was so weak and trembling that Reimar thought he

had become ill again. But he was not ill; it was only that he had just seen the greatest living master and sage in Scandinavia.

"Now we'll return the hacks to where they belong," said Reimar, "and then we'll get ourselves ferried over to Sviðinsvík."

The afterglow of sunset lay on the green turf of the place from which they set sail that evening, and on the cliffs and the dead-calm sea. There were two strangers at the oars, and Reimar steered, while Ólafur Kárason sat in the stern. And with that their handsome-prowed boat set out.

The boy looked at the splendid rays of the sunset on the white creamy water, feeling as brave and optimistic as Iceland's first settler in the morning of time, without experience, new. It was a broad fjord and the shore on the other side was far away. He felt he had died and had awoken to eternal life, and was sailing to the unknown land on the other side. The sun had set; white mist rose from the valleys and nestled against the green slopes of the mountains. It was as if the land were dissolving in one dizzying, elf-like night-vision without reality. The solid and the liquid became one, the sky stepped down and the earth up, an unreal aura of some incredibly distant future or past was over everything, another time over the world. Even the men in front of him in the boat were dissolving into the blue and gold harmonies of color; their rhythmic movements at the oars obeyed the laws of another sphere, a higher seamanship. Then the land disappeared altogether into the mist except for glimpses of the highest cliffs of the mountains away, away up, like a world of trolls we have left behind and which does not concern us any more.

Little by little they approached the shore on the other side. One began to see the gleam of the palaces of the unknown land down by the sea. He stared for a long time at these palaces glittering through the light mist before he dared to believe his own eyes. But finally he could not doubt it any longer—these palaces were all of pure gold. There shone from them the same luster as from the old scholar's medal. Enraptured, the young poet gazed at the afterglow gleaming on all that gold behind the white, loving mists of the spring night.

And so the boat glided onward, toward the unknown.

BOOK TWO

THE PALACE
OF THE SUMMERLAND

When the poet woke up in the morning, an old man was standing over him with a stick in his hand, trying to beat him.

"I won't have sheep in my homefield!" the old man was mumbling, over and over again. But he no longer had much strength, and his blows were fairly harmless.

It was a panelled living room with a sloping ceiling. There was a small cooking stove against one of the side walls; farther in there was a sort of low partition protruding into the middle of the floor, rather like a stall in a barn.

"My homefield!" raged the old man, and went on tapping the boy with the stick.

Only half-awake, the boy did not remember that he had been cured in a supernatural way and was now perfectly healthy, thanks to a miracle; he thought he was still sorely afflicted by several fatal internal ailments, and he replied in his old plaintive tone that he did not feel strong enough to get up because of his prolonged sufferings.

On the other side of the living room a naked man was sitting on his bed; he was ruddy-faced and plump, with jowls down to his shoulders. He slobbered out of one corner of his mouth and said "Vavva-vavva," over and over again.

"Give me your hand and let me greet you," said the boy, and tried to shake hands with the old man in the hope that he would stop belaboring him and enter into more amicable relations. But the old man was devoid of all tenderness and compassion, and was beyond all such superfluous courtesies.

"It's my homefield! My homefield! The Privy Councillor* and I were the same age; it's not true he stole butter; I won't have sheep in my homefield, drive them out of my homefield at once!" he said, and was in no mood to shake hands with anyone, either in greeting or reconciliation.

He had a little jutting beard, and one eye closed and one eye open; in the open eye there lurked some weird fervor which the boy did not fully understand. His right hand was withered. At long last he wearied of his efforts to rouse the boy, shuffled over to his own bed and sat down.

The boy wanted to ingratiate himself with the household and promote a Christian frame of mind in the community, and he did not lose heart even though he had failed with the old man; he said Good-morning and bowed politely towards the fat naked man who was sitting there on the bed opposite like some overgrown infant, squinting at the newcomer without altering his rather monotonous conversational topic of "Vavva-vavva." But when the visitor bade him good-morning, he was so surprised that he stopped saying "Vavva-vavva."

"Good-morning," said the boy again, raising his voice to show he was in earnest. There was silence for a while, until the fat naked man could not contain himself any longer and started to giggle with peculiar throaty noises.

"That's Jón Einarsson the heathen," explained the old man. "Don't pay any attention to him; he doesn't know how to cross himself. Get up at once, because there are sheep in my homefield!"

The sloping ceiling was black with damp, with patches of white mildew here and there like splashes of whey. The air in the house was foul. "I'll try to get up," said the boy, and began to try to get up. But he had grown so much taller in the last two years that he did not realize how much room and time each movement took; he had grown unaccustomed to moving at all, and had forgotten how to put his clothes on. The old man kept harping on about his homefield being full of sheep.

At last the boy managed to get up. He looked out of the window. There was a road, and on the other side of the road there was a little cottage with a turf roof and timbered walls and an open door and a girl leaning against the doorpost, and other little cottages here and there, and little homefields, and a large homefield that stretched far up the mountainside.

"Which is your homefield?" asked the boy.

"I own all the homefields; they're all mine, the Upper homefield, too; no one has any right to have sheep in my homefield," said the old man. "I was confirmed with the Privy Councillor!"

"Eh?" said the boy.

"Homefields!" said the old man. "My homefields!"

"Vavva-vavva," said the heathen, talking loudly now and trying to assert himself in the conversation.

"But there aren't any sheep in the homefield," said the boy.

"I'll complain to the sheriff!" said the old man.

"Yes, but there aren't any sheep," said the boy, raising his voice. "You perhaps think there are sheep, but there aren't any sheep. There are buttercups. There are acres of buttercups."

"Drive them out, quick!" said the old man. "The Privy Councillor and I!"

"They're buttercups!" yelled the boy, now convinced that the old man was not only blind but deaf as well.

"Vavva-vavva!" bawled the heathen, who was also getting excited now and wanted to get worked up over this like the others.

But just as it was becoming obvious that these people had the greater difficulty in understanding one another the more they talked together, something unforeseen occurred and they had to break off the conversation. From behind them came a hoarse and hissing howl, like that of some nameless animal, so that the newcomer to the company, Ólafur Kárason, gave a start and was scared. When he turned to look, he saw a face peering round the side of the partition, pallid and drawn, with black hair, black eyes, and black teeth. The face went on peering into the living room for a while with irrational malevolence and uttering those awful cries, each more terrible than the last.

"Don't pay any attention to her; she's a monster," said the old man; he was determined to keep on discussing his homefields.

But the boy could not tear his eyes away from this ghastly apparition which came creeping out from behind the partition; first came a shoulder, then the doubled-up torso of a woman, until eventually a half-naked creature had crawled out onto the floor, all in a heap. The boy felt sure it was heading in his direction.

But Ólafur Kárason was not the only one to be frightened; the heathen had stopped giggling and working himself up, and had lain down on the bed and begun to wail piteously. The old man was the only one who was not taken aback; while Ólafur Kárason thought it best to crawl back into bed again, the old man got to his feet and brandished his stick at this crouched, four-legged human creature. Happy the one who never set foot in that house!

The old man's first puny blow had just landed on the monster when the door opened and in came an old woman with a small face and sunken cheeks, and a thin nose peeping out from under her knitted cap; she was carrying a red codling.

"Poor wretches," she piped, like the soughing of the wind, and yet with a certain kindness, as when one is talking to hens. She put the codling down and went over to the creature and said, "Poor dear"; she certainly did not think of hitting her, but shooed her gently back behind the partition and helped to bed her down again. As soon as she had done this, the heathen got his courage back and sat up in bed and resumed his simple conversation at the point where he had broken off. The old man's warrior zeal also abated gradually; he sat down with his stick, and squinted at everything and nothing with that weird peering eye of his, full of senile malice. Ólafur Kárason got out of bed again.

Then the old woman said to him, "Are you out of bed, too, my poor wretch? Have you taken leave of your senses?"

The boy pointed to the old man and said he had ordered him to drive the sheep from the homefield, but there was nothing in the homefield except buttercups.

"He's got an obsession about it," said the old woman. "Don't pay any attention to it. Go back to bed and tuck yourself well in."

But this young man no longer wanted to lie down and tuck himself in; he had had quite enough of that. Certainly, God had struck him down for a time, but at the same time had granted him the special privilege of allowing him to lie on a sickbed at Fótur-undir-Fótarfæti for a mere two years; yes, it had been a fine and blissful life, even magnificent and splendid now and again. At Fótur-undir-Fótarfæti, people had been just like ordinary people. But here, in this nameless house, even a dead man would have risen up in indignation and walked out

"I am in good health," said Ólafur Kárason of Ljósavík.

"No," piped the old woman, "you're ill, and very ill at that. The parish council doesn't make mistakes like that."

"I swear it!" said the boy. "I was cured in a supernatural way; there was a miracle. It was the elf doctor, Friðrik."

"Yes, the devil was also given power to heal the sick in the beginning," said the old woman, "but what's that kind of healing worth? Go back to bed at once and tuck yourself in, for you're bound to have a relapse anyway before you know it. I'll be bringing you all a drop of warm water in a cup soon, my poor little wretches."

"But I can stand upright," the boy insisted, his voice shrill from vehemence and with almost a sob in his throat; and the old woman watched the way he got to his feet and stood upright, and obviously had difficulty in believing her own eyes.

"No," she said finally, "I simply don't understand the parish council any more. Or the nation as a whole."

"I can't help that," said the boy apologetically. "No one lies ill in bed longer than the Almighty decides."

She went on looking despairingly at the way the boy managed to stand upright. Then she began to tend the fire.

"It's now three days since my best-loved wretch, bless him, was carried from that bed you slept in last night," she said in a cold, God-fearing and solemn tone of voice, like wind soughing through an open fish shed, "and what a very difficult patient he was! So it's no wonder I was beginning to hope to God that I would now get an easier patient, something like my dear heathen, and preferably the sort of patient who would survive me, because in the end one can get so tired of seeing them all die off. And then the parish council sends me a perfectly healthy man!"

"Oh, it's not really the parish council's fault," said the boy, with his tireless urge to excuse those who had done no wrong or had been wrongly blamed for something; but it was no use. Words and excuses had no effect in this place; the old woman could not forgive the parish council. On the other hand she tried to bear it stoically and said, "I'm not complaining. I have my children whom God has given me around me here, even though the parish council sends me a perfectly healthy man. Those who are in distress are my children. I have always been a fortunate person."

"I own the whole estate!" protested the old man angrily, and waved his left fist in the air.

"Yes, yes, Gísli dear," said the old woman kindly. "You own the whole estate." Then she added in explanation to the boy, "This is old Gísli the landowner, you see."

"Does he then also own the big homefields below the mountain here?" said the boy.

"I'm the same age as the Privy Councillor!" said Gísli the landowner. "I own the Upper homefields, too."

"Yes, dear," said the old woman. "The Upper homefields, too. Why shouldn't you own everything like anyone else, since no one owns anything any more!"

"Does no one own anything any more, then?" asked the poet.

"No. No one owns anything any more. The whole basis of our existence has disappeared completely here. When our Privy Councillor went away, everything went. The Regeneration Company, that's death."

The longer the conversation went on, the more new and unknown factors were introduced. "Forgive me for asking, but I've been ill in bed for so long, you see, even though I'm fully recovered now, and I was told so little, that's why there's so much I don't understand. What is the Privy Councillor? And why did the Privy Councillor go away? And what is the Regeneration Company? And what's the difference between the two?"

"The difference?" said the old woman, amazed at such ignorance. "I suppose you might say it's the difference between a thick felt hat and a bare bald head! What's the Regeneration Company? It's Pétur Þríhross Pálsson, to say nothing worse. But the Privy Councillor? Now that was a man, yes, a true man, what's more! Next to the Lord himself he was our life, and in his day no one had to live on seaweed and water; and besides, there were young and cheerful and able-bodied people here on the estate then. He provided everyone with food and housing and work, and he minted money himself; yes, everyone here had enough money in his time; yes, and he even imported honey to the township for a time; but the most fortunate ones, perhaps, were those who were allowed to drown in his ships, luckier at least than the ones who survived. Why did the Privy Councillor go away, you ask? The Privy Councillor went away when he had made enough money, of course, because naturally he had no obligations to anyone here, and besides the fish had all vanished. But it's all the same where the Privy Councillor is, God will guide the Privy Councillor wherever he goes, and reward the Privy Councillor, and forgive me."

"I don't see how there could have been much well-being to speak of, since it was better to be drowned," said the boy after careful thought.

"I won't have rats in my cutter!" said Gísli the landowner.

But the old woman said the poet was being stupid, and stubbornly insisted that it was a blessing to be drowned. "It is a sweet death, drowning," she maintained. "And those who are allowed to lose their dear ones to the sea may thank God compared with those who have to watch their young ones wasting away on dry land, like my daughter who has to watch her children withering away from consumption. I have lost my three sons to the sea, stalwart men and Vikings every one, and yet I was never one of those who said that the Privy Councillor's ships were leakier than any other ships afloat, and to the best of my knowledge the cutter *Júliana* had been taken over by the Regeneration Company, which was supposed to keep everything afloat, when she sank with my son-in-law, Jón, who left a

widow and seven children. No, I certainly haven't been more unfortunate than many other women here in the village, far from it; everything has turned out well for me. God has given me three patients
and sometimes four in place of what I have lost; but you I can't keep,
since you can put your clothes on without help, because it's not the
responsibility of the parish to keep anyone alive except those who are
bedridden or at the very least paralyzed down one side."

"I thank you with all my heart," said the poet, taking a sip of his
water, and finding it difficult to conceal his joy at being allowed to
leave. Whatever the woman said, however much she praised Providence, deep within himself he heard only the one voice which cried
out in panic, "Away, away!" He took his bundle from under the pillow and offered the old woman his hand. But when he had said
good-bye to her, he had not the courage to shake hands with the rest
of the household. Away, away from these faces! Away from this fetid
air! Away! Some sights would make even the most hideous deity
seem improbable, let alone the more beautiful gods. They can usurp
a man's soul and dominate his consciousness with dreadful tyranny
all his life; their monstrous faces peer forth incessantly, even in the
midst of the most beautiful visions; they go on forever corrupting
even the loveliest thoughts with bitter gall, oh, away! In his flight he
bumped into the walls and the doorpost, like a man trying to escape
in a dream.

— 2 —

He was standing in the open. He had got his freedom, certainly, but
freedom is not an aim in itself, and he had no idea where to go; the
question was, what ways were open to him? Gradually his heartbeat
steadied after his flight, but he remained standing in the roadway
with his bundle under his arm, staring into the blue.

Then he heard someone saying from the other side of the road,
"Who are you?" It was the girl standing in the doorway; she was still
leaning against one of the doorposts, with her toes braced against the
other.

He did not know what to say: who was he, indeed? It was an open question; certainly, he had been something once—a corner of a living room, a sloping ceiling, a ray of sunshine, a poem by Sigurður Breiðfjörð—but now? He did not know; no one knew.

"My name is Ólafur Kárason," he said, so as not to look a complete fool, but very uncertainly, and had a twinge of conscience at once because he felt he had no right to say "I" nor any other word of that land. To add "of Ljósavík" would have been to make himself a laughingstock before God and man; it did not even occur to him.

"Where are you from?" she asked.

"I'm told I was born in this parish," he said. "But actually I'm from Fótur-undir-Fótarfæti."

"Hahaha!" said the girl. "Fotarfótur! I've never heard anything like it in my life! Hahaha, hahaha!"

"I've been an invalid," he said, in the hope that she would stop laughing. She stopped laughing.

"Have you come here for treatment?" she asked.

"No," he said, "I was brought here."

He did not dare to confide in such a laughter-prone girl the story of the miracle at Kambar. What is a miracle, after all? The old woman in the house behind him had connected it with the devil; but when he looked at this cheerful and natural young girl standing in her doorway, it suddenly occurred to him that a miracle was at once both ridiculous and humiliating, and he blushed scarlet.

"Were you brought here?" she asked. "Who brought you? Are you on the parish, perhaps?"

"Yes," he said, hanging his head. "Unfortunately."

He was very ashamed of having to admit such a thing to a fine young girl, but she did not hold it against him, far from it. She was quite ready to reassure him: "Everyone will be on the parish soon, hahaha!" she said. "How many brothers and sisters have you got?"

"I don't know," he said.

"Hahaha, doesn't even know how many brothers and sisters he's got!" she said. "I've got nine, and some have got far more, yes, and no mother, either. Have you got a mother?"

"Yes," he said, with assurance.

"My mother's dead," said the girl. "She died last year, hahaha!"

The boy did not quite know how to take this unexpected announcement of death; perhaps he should have told the truth, that he did not really have a mother either; but the girl was much more quick-witted than he and instantly asked him another question; she was a very agreeable girl and quite certainly a nice person.

"What's that you've got under your arm?" she asked.

"It's my things," he said.

"Is it shoes?"

"No," he said. "I haven't got any shoes except these thin shoes I'm wearing just now."

"I haven't got any shoes either," she said, and kicked her legs in the air one after the other to show what dilapidated shoes she was wearing, and it was certainly true, her shoes were old and cracked although they had originally been made in Denmark. But her calves were young and rounded, the knees large and strong, and he had never seen so far up a girl's legs before. And despite the bad shoes, he had never seen such legs, and he stared fascinated at the way she kicked her feet up.

"With luck they'll manage to sell the estate this summer," she said, when she had smoothed her dress down again.

"What estate?" he said sharply, and instinctively pressed his bundle more tightly under his arm.

"The estate," she said.

"Aren't there many estates?" he said.

"No, I mean just this one estate—you know," she said. "Some people think that if it gets sold, things will start to improve."

"Are things going badly?" he asked. "What's going badly?"

"Do you see that rusty hulk out there at the anchorage? That's our trawler, *Númi*. Obviously, it was seized against the Regeneration Company's debts just about the time it was due to start fishing; so it won't be providing much food for the larder this year any more than previously. And the cutter *Júliana* was lost the year before last, as everyone knows. The Privy Councillor went to Denmark a long time ago, and the fish have all disappeared; no herring's been seen for as long as I can remember, and the Regeneration Company—that's just wind in Pétur Þríhross's guts, to say nothing worse in front of a total stranger. No, there's nothing here at all now, nothing, except for a bit of quarrying in the spring, and fewer get that than want it."

"Quarrying?" echoed the boy foolishly, not understanding a word of what the girl was saying.

"Yes, it's called government rock," said the girl. "It's been going on for three years now. It's the men who quarry rock for the government."

"What government is that?" asked the boy.

"Oh, it's just that damned pest of a government," said the girl. "It's that same old government it's always been, the government of the high-ups, the gentry, the ones in the south who own all the money. You can't be so ignorant that you haven't heard people talking about it. All I know is that the rock is called government rock, and it's down there on the foreshore just beside the anchorage, and my father's allowed to carry rock there to meet his account at the Regeneration Company for provisions. Some people say it's to be used for building some sort of harbor there eventually, but I suspect the ships that are to use it are in the same place as the new shoes I'm going to get for the Churchyard Ball this autumn, hahaha! It's more likely to turn out to be a cabbage patch, if you ask me. Can you dance?"

"No," he replied. "Unfortunately."

"You simply must learn to dance," she said. "There's really nothing in the whole world so much fun as dancing. Oh, there was such a lovely song I learned at the Churchyard Ball last year."

And she sang:

> " 'D'you think that Gróa's got some shoes,
> Got some shoes, got some shoes?
> Then I think she won't have much to lose
> When she starts to marry.
> Got some shoes, got some shoes,
> D'you think that Gróa's got some shoes?
> Then I think she won't have much to lose
> When she starts to tralalala.'

"Oh, here comes that damned parish officer!"—in a flash she was gone and had slammed the door, and the boy was left standing where he was in the roadway.

"Who are you, and what are you gaping at?" asked the parish officer.

He was a thickset, suspicious, waddling fellow with freckled hairy hands and an obstinate face, and not particularly civil in his manner of address, either. Ólafur Kárason told him his name. It turned out that the parish officer had not only heard about his supernatural cure, but had very decided views about his character. He said it was easy to guess how ill he must have been, if it needed no more than currents and vibrations from that young witch at Kambar to get him on his feet: "These are the sort of layabouts for whom honest men here in Sviðinsvík have to sweat blood, while you lot spend your youth in bed for fun and fill your bellies in far-off districts. No, it's certainly high time you had your share of quarry work, my lad!"

He waddled off at once towards the quarry with the boy, but the boy had difficulty in walking very fast because his legs were too long for him and, besides, his legs were unquestionably of uneven length and changed length at every step; he was therefore inclined to take too large a stride with the leg that was too long at any given moment, and had difficulty in walking straight, and sometimes he was almost in the ditch quite against his will and intention; in addition, he felt giddy in the head, rather like having the staggers.

"What's this, you young devil?" said the parish officer. "Are you drunk?"

"No," said the boy. "But my legs are too long."

"Rubbish!" said the parish officer.

Round them gathered untidy groups of children who had been playing in the ditch or on the barbed wire fences; they mobbed the boy because he was long and wearing a scarf, and they uttered all kinds of cries like animals sending distress signals.

The weather was beautiful, the sun shone from a clear sky, the sea a lovely blue, the fields revelling in contentment. More and more children arrived. Everything went black before the boy's eyes; he tripped over a stone and stumbled. The children let out a howl and showered abuse on him. Some of them played at barging into him to bring him down again. It is difficult to say how it would have ended if the children had not caught sight of an even more attractive entertainment. An old, half-blind woman came tottering round the corner of a house, feeling her way with a stick. When the children saw her they changed their tack and rushed at her, giving tongue as before: "Gudda bell, Gudda bell!" But some of them wandered over to two drunks who were standing in the road shaking hands endlessly, like a bridal couple, and heaped their jeers and abuse on them instead.

On the foreshore there were between twenty and thirty men carrying rocks; others were sitting astride large boulders and driving iron wedges into them. But above the shore the fragrant heather moors took over; farther off, a fertile green valley cut into the mountain range with its moors and grasslands. The rock-carrying went on in a gloomy, funereal silence that contrasted strangely with the cheerful melodious voices of the summer birds from the heaths and moorland; there was a sullen, cold heaviness in the faces of these rock-carriers, quite out of keeping with the effortless flight of the birds and that glad spring landscape, the warmth from that tranquil, blue dreaming sea, and the moss-grown ledges of the mountain. These men were obviously undergoing punishment for some terrible crime they had committed. Their unlovely, dirty faces seemed to reflect that condemnation which no acquittal can remove, no rehabilitation erase. Here surrender and despair had their ultimate abode, the individual at one with his own misfortune in a complete confession of his crime, in an acknowledgment of having no atonement except unconditional subservience to, and acceptance of, the disgrace of ruin, without hope of a single drop of mercy.

What had these poor wretches done wrong? What crimes had brought on the fearful punishment that was etched on these outcast images of misery, those sallow-gray, hopeless, wispy-haired faces, and on the contemptible rags which a cruel and omnipotent judiciary had obviously, as a mark of disgrace, hung upon these exhausted, stunted, starved, rock-carrying bodies?

Farther up the fjord, someone was riding up and down with two spirited horses, and the dust from their hooves hung like cloud banks over the dry bridle paths in the still weather.

"What's all that damned galloping over there?" said the parish officer.

"He's breaking in horses," said the men.

The parish officer took the parish pauper up to the path, where they waited awhile for the horseman. When he arrived, he all but rode them down. He was wearing a morning coat, a bowler hat, celluloid collar, pince-nez, and false teeth; his fiery young horses were dripping with sweat and blowing hard.

"What do you want, my lad?" asked the horseman.

"What do I want?" echoed the parish officer. "I want what I want."

The rider dismounted, all covered with dust and horsehair, patted his horses and talked to them caressingly, but showed no enthusiasm for hearing what the parish officer had to say.

"Take this man on at the rock-shifting for me," said the parish officer.

"Listen, my lad, what do you take me for?" asked the horseman. He had a very guttural voice.

"Oh, you should be grateful you're not called anything worse than your proper name, Pétur Þríhross!" said the parish officer.

"Shut up!" said the horseman, and tried to mount again and ride on his way; but the parish officer seized the reins of his horse right at the bit.

"Am I the parish officer in this village or not?" said the parish officer.

"Am I the manager of the Regeneration Company or not?" said the horseman.

"Whatever you are, it's as the agent of the parish council and the community, and this good-for-nothing here has been a particularly heavy burden on the taxpayers, and I direct the Regeneration Company to assist the parish under these circumstances."

"You can look after your damned parish paupers yourself, my lad; those who are in debt to the Regeneration Company will have preference in quarry-work for as long as I'm in charge," said the manager.

"What's the sense in giving well-to-do people these advantages and extra earnings, instead of trying to ease the burdens of the parish?"

"The Regeneration Company must have its due; otherwise it isn't a Regeneration Company at all," said the manager.

"The parish must have its due, too, otherwise it isn't a parish," said the parish officer.

"I'm busy breaking in horses," said the manager of the Regeneration Company, and did not want to listen to any more unnecessary talk. He made to mount again.

"Just one more word," said the parish officer. "I don't know whether you're aware of the fact that some people here on the estate are saying that it wouldn't be a bad idea if a few minor details in the management of the Regeneration Company were investigated a little more closely."

"And it won't be very long," replied the manager promptly, "before it's proved in court that you have misappropriated funds which have been squeezed out of the county for poor-law relief here in the parish, both by making out excessive bills for pauper funerals and by charging full clothing and footwear for bedridden lunatics, yes, and even coffee!"

"It's dangerous to blow with oatmeal in your mouth, Pétur," said the parish officer, and grinned. "Who was it who started life by selling the same horse to three different people? And if you think that the Regeneration Company is your private company, to which you can sell worthless merchandise and nonexistent goods and falsify all the accounts, and pocket the grant that the township gets from the state towards the building of a harbor, then it might well happen, my lad, that. . . ."

"No, my lad," the manager interrupted, and smiled. "If we're going to start discussing which of us is to be the first to have the honor of getting to know the locks in a certain public building, then one could introduce various matters which the parish paupers might enjoy hearing about!"

The parish officer shot a warning glance at the manager and gave him a furtive signal to stop.

"We can drop the subject if you like," said the manager, and smiled.

"I don't want any filthy language in front of youngsters," said the parish officer. He put his hand in his pocket, brought out a plug of tobacco, bit off a generous wad, and then offered the tobacco to the manager of the Regeneration Company.

"That's quite another matter!" said Pétur Þríhross, and put his hand into his breast pocket, brought out a flask of brennivín, took a pull, and then passed it to the parish officer with this mild reproof: "The trouble with you, I always think, old friend, is that you've never learned to think like an educated person."

The parish officer cheered up when he had had some brennivín, and he wiped his mouth with the back of his hairy hand.

"Well, Pétur," he said, "what are you paying me for my fish this autumn?"

"These are difficult times," said the manager, gutturally.

"Yes, you can say that again," said the parish officer.

"You'll get a fair price for it if you let me have it wet-salted," said the manager.

"No, thanks, my lad; that's where you're wrong. You'll never get it wet-salted," said the parish officer. "I've got plenty of layabouts and good-for-nothings to cure the fish this summer for their keep, people who would otherwise have to be supported by the parish."

"Do you think I, too, haven't got plenty of free labor to cure all the fish I care to buy?" asked the manager.

They went on haggling over their business transactions for a long time, while the boy stood there forgotten on the path without knowing what fate would be chosen for him; he was much too tall, and still felt uncomfortable when he had to stand upright for any length of time. Finally he resorted to lying down among the grassy hummocks while the others continued their bargaining. They were so engrossed that they did not notice for some time that he had lain down. The poet's mind immediately wandered off into space. At last they noticed that he had lain down.

"What the devil!" said the parish officer. "He's lying down! We can't have him lying down. Listen, Pétur, my dear old friend, do me a favor because I'm in difficulties, and give this wretch a job at the quarrying."

"It's quite a different matter, what I would do for you as a Christian and an Icelander, my lad," said the manager of the Regeneration Company. "Especially when it's the poor who are concerned."

The manager called out to the boy and said that Providence had looked mercifully upon him and was prepared, for special reasons, to allow him to shift a little government rock, even though he had no rightful claim to it. He told him to give his name to the foreman so that he could enter it in his book.

The township's leaders sat down, each on his hummock, and carried on discussing their business affairs after the boy had gone down to the foreshore. When everything was said and done it was apparently not a punishment and evil fate after all to have to carry rock to and fro along the shore in the fertile glory of spring: it was a blessing and a favor.

— 3 —

Although grace comes from above, that is not to say that everyone has the ability to accept it. The young poet, for instance, when it came to the bit, simply was not capable of carrying rocks. Providence may have the best intentions, no one would deny that, but it avails nothing if the person concerned is not worthy of it. The rock-bearers looked on and grinned wryly as he sagged at the knees; some of them laughed callously, perhaps it was the only amusement these men had had for a long time—hahaha, the man could not even carry rocks! However small the load that was placed on the barrow, however much he gritted his teeth in an effort of will, he just doubled up like a nail being driven into stone. They put him to loosening the rocks, but that was no better: his center of gravity moved into the upper part of his body and he fell forward onto his face.

"Have you got the staggers?" they said.

"Yes," he replied.

Here where every individual was judged by the load he could carry, Ólafur Kárason of Ljósavík could not carry anything; it took all his efforts to carry himself upright and, what was worse, he no longer knew what he himself was. His mind was dull-witted and vacant among all this abominable, accursed rock. The foreman came over and said, "You'd better go home."

"Home?" said Ólafur Kárason, in amazement.

"Yes," said the foreman. "Home."

It was time to eat. Women and children came and brought their menfolk boiled fish in jars and flasks of coffee in a sock. No one brought anything for Ólafur Kárason. He stood some distance away and watched the men sit down on the rocks and start eating.

"Aren't you eating anything?" they said.

"No," he replied.

"Why not?" they asked.

"Because I haven't got any food," he replied.

"What's that you've got in your kerchief?" they asked.

"It's my things," he said.

"What sort of things?" they asked.

"The things I own," he said. "Mainly books."

"Books!" they said. "What sort of books?"

"A few books of poetry," he said. "And *The Felsenburg Stories.*"

"Poetry books? And *The Felsenburg Stories?*" they said, and looked at one another in baffled astonishment.

One of them put an end to the matter by saying, "Stop asking the boy these silly questions. Can't you see he's a bit lacking? He's eccentric. Reimar fetched him from Fjörður on a stretcher for the parish council, and he was lodged with old Þuríður at Skálholt. We all ought to give him a share of our food."

So the eccentric was given food by more than twenty men, and drank coffee from twenty flasks. Apart from that the men paid no more attention to him than to a stray dog. But he felt uncomfortable in a crowd, and as soon as he had eaten his fill he shuffled unobtrusively away with his bundle, greatly relieved that he had stopped work. He stole away from the shore, and soon the men were out of sight. The two high-ups were no longer sitting on their grassy hummocks on the moor, but had gone. The village was a short distance away. Ólafur Kárason took to his heels and ran; all of a sudden his legs were of the right length, and he was quick to rise to his feet whenever he fell. He headed away from human habitation, over the hillocks of the moor, over the marshy bogs, over a hill and over a ridge below the mountain, and then he was out of sight. He came to a halt in a hollow and got his breath back. He felt himself freed of a great burden by getting out of sight of other people. The previous days and nights had been eventful, and he had lost himself. But now he was sure he would find himself again, like a dead man who finds himself, little by little, in the next world. In spite of everything, and although he was in reality a newborn babe in this new world, it was delightful to be born anew and to own a share of the sun like others instead of having to wait half the year perhaps for one little ray of sunshine.

He turned his face toward the sun like a lover, and there was really nothing now that separated them any more. Yes, he was undoubtedly a new being and no longer beholden to anyone; perhaps when all was said and done it was he who owned this world that others quarreled over and thought they owned. It was wonderful to be young and to let the sun shine upon one's face. He lifted his arms to heaven in rejoicing, as he had done when he was a child, exalted over the rest of mankind.

Yes, he was born anew, and stood up and started walking, and the ewes on the slopes looked at him with sympathetic eyes.

No, there is probably no way of making something cease to exist once it has come into existence. He was no longer afraid of the immortality of the soul, that doctrine which for a time had seemed to him the height of human cruelty. Today it was the many and varied abodes of the Creator which enchanted the mind. Over there was a little spring-water stream, as clear and pure as all streams; it had its source far up the valley and flowed by in quiet, almost pious, joy, a breath from perhaps an even higher sphere; its happiness was of the same kind as the poet's; the stream and the poet, they loved, and the sun shone upon them and death did not exist.

He walked on a long way beside the stream, far from all humanity. Finally the valley ended in a gorge with steep sides and a hollow under a shelf of cliffs; but at the head of the valley there was a turf-roofed sheep shed on a little, grassy hillock, and there the boy sat down at last, drunk with joy, among the dandelions and buttercups; there were also gentians, blue and white.

When he lay there among the flowers in that green lamb-field and looked up at the blue sky, while the brooks rippled by and the birds chirped at midday in tranquil contentment and the lambs dozed smiling beside their mothers in the noon quiet, and the mountains on the other side of the sparkling fjord merged into a mystical blue haze, he understood that Nature was all one loving Mother, and he himself and everything that lives were of the one spirit, and there was nothing ugly any more, nothing evil. He pulled out his poetry book and began to write about these exalted mystical perceptions, these lofty visions. He forgot the Edda and everything else he had learned from the time of the sloping ceiling and the bed in the corner, he forgot all his tendencies to adopt postures; the brook below the hillock gave him the note; it was not he himself who wrote, but essentially the impersonal joy of blueness and green:

> So bright the day,
> And glad the flowers whose thirst the dews allay!
> O life's green land!
> O green land of life, O Iceland's verdure mine!
> O let me love thee, and be mine.

> So sweet the day,
> And in the stream the little birds do play!
> O life's precious land!
> O precious land of life, O land of my brother,
> Of every little bird—O dream of our mother.

He went on composing poetry in this vein for most of the day, and reciting his poems to Nature and lying on his back on the grass and loving the sky. Late in the afternoon he drank some water from the brook. He was sure that the birds of the sky would bring him tidbits in their beaks whenever he got hungry. He was sure that just as Nature was the height of all grandeur and beauty, so was She also the height of all human love and magnanimity, not least when he had composed a eulogy in Her honor; no, he could not imagine that She would let a young and loving poet ever lack for anything hereafter.

And so the day passed in rejoicing over his regained contact with eternity and the inexpressible. The sun sank lower in the west, the shadows of the mountain lengthened; trustingly, his eyelids grew heavy in a healthy and natural way, until he woke up with a start, shivering with cold, and realized that he had slept. The night was certainly clear, but mist shrouded the landscape so that he could not even see the mountain, and his clothes were white with webs of dew. The purling of the brook was not as cheerful as it had been before he fell asleep; and no birds sang. He crawled into the sheep shed to the mushrooms, pulled out some hay from an old stack, lay down on it, and went to sleep.

When he awoke the birds had begun to chirp again, to be sure, but there was little enchantment about it now. There was a fine drizzle. His throat was a little sore, as if he were catching a cold. The glory of nature that had reigned in his soul before he fell asleep was over; he felt he had slept for ages and ages, and fingered his chin to see if he had not grown a long beard while he slept. One thing was certain—however determined he had previously been to take all his needs from divine Mother Nature, he was now equally eager to seek succor from men, even though no one was more aware than he how lacking these much-discussed beings were in both magnanimity and grandeur, to say nothing of beauty. He trudged back along the mountainside the way he had come, dull-witted and queer after a night's sleep in the darkness of old hay and mushrooms.

He racked his brains about where to go, where he should ask for help; but however much he thought about it, the only conclusion he came to was to give a wide berth to the household at Skálholt—Gísli the landowner, the naked heathen, the monster, and the happy old woman. "Anything, anything," he said, "except that!" But this conclusion was as impractical as it was negative; it was no solution.

His mind turned to the parish officer in the hope that even though the quarry work had failed, this great man would perhaps take pity on him and give him bread and coffee. But when he reached the village, it was empty and desolate. The life of the community had been wiped out. Even the children who had filled the village with their yelling had disappeared. Someone had passed through this place, either Doomsday itself or the Turks, and laid this famous estate waste instead of buying it and giving the people honey and new ships: not a wisp of smoke from a chimney, white webs of dew in the ruts of the road, the story ended. It was strange to wake up in an empty township, not knowing where one came from or where one was going—not even who one was. He sat down at the side of the road, helpless in an empty universe, with his hand under his chin and shivering inside, and he felt that God had deceived him. When he had sat for a while, he shuffled off again through that empty eternity. Thank heavens, one tern had been left behind, hovering over a nearby cabbage patch. Then he caught sight of a shapeless heap lying across the road not far away. He thought at first it was a sack, but when he came closer he saw it was a man. It was the man who had been left behind alone in the universe on the day after Judgment Day, at the end of the mystical Doomsday Turkish raid, the man who was overlooked on the road at Ragnarok,* the one who did not rise when the Last Trump sounded; he was lying there right across the roadway when God had finished judging the world, and he was dead, or at least sleeping. The poet bent down over him to see how dead he was. This was a small man with a moustache, and blood and dirt on his face. He lay directly across the muddy road, as if in a vain and forlorn hope that he would be run over by horses and carts, men and dogs. He had a tattered shoe on one foot, but only a ragged sock and much mud on the other. Ólafur Kárason decided to haul the corpse off the road and lay it out properly, and managed to drag it over to the verge between the road and the ditch. But when he had almost finished crossing the dead man's arms over his chest, the corpse sat up. It opened its dead, lusterless eyes, red-rimmed and bloodshot, and started to look around.

"Are you alive?" asked Ólafur Kárason of Ljósavík.

The corpse had difficulty in replying but fumbled inside its clothes for a flask and took out the cork and began to revive itself, and a powerful stink of medicine assailed the poet's nostrils. When the corpse had taken a gulp of the medicine, it began to revive; strange spasms convulsed its body here and there, particularly the face, limbs, and fingers, and at the same time the mouth and moustache began to writhe in various ways, and suddenly the man had jumped to his feet as if someone had touched a spring. He was a stocky fellow; his internal mechanism had been only temporarily out of order; but otherwise he was one of those who stayed on their feet for most of the time. He greeted the poet with a long, convulsive handshake, and blinked and grimaced, but no sound came for a long time. Ólafur Kárason watched carefully the way the man rose from the dead. Hosanna, this was undoubtedly one of the miracles; gradually the man began to utter sounds. He talked a strange language, mostly without syllables, though one could occasionally distinguish intelligible words like submerged skerries in this extraordinary surf of inarticulate angel-language, grimaces, blinks and finger-signs.

"What's your name?" asked the boy.

The man grimaced for a long time and mumbled something over and over again, but no matter how carefully the poet strained his ears, he could only make out one word in all the mumbling: "Jesus!"

"Where do you live?" asked the boy.

The man was so deeply moved by this that he was nearly beside himself, but no matter how he tried he could not manage any other answer than to gesticulate with his fingers and say, "Heave-up!"

The boy pondered for a long time over this incomprehensible reply, but finally gave up.

"No, I'm sorry; I don't understand you," he said, and shook his head sadly.

The stranger for his part was just as unhappy that their souls could not make contact; again and again it looked as if he were going to start crying. At last he grabbed the flask with its elixir of life and handed it despairingly to the boy, clutched his hand, and said, "My brother!"

But Ólafur Kárason did not want to taste the life-giving elixir on any account; he had never known such a vile stink in all his life. On the other hand, he allowed the stranger to express his respect and devotion in whatever way he liked—greeting him over and over again with protracted handshakes, pawing him with trembling hands, embracing him tearfully. They carried on like this for a long time. The poet thought with somewhat mixed feelings of his future here on earth with the One who was left behind when all other people had vanished. But then he suddenly saw smoke rising from a chimney, then from another and a third. His heart rejoiced at that; the village was not dead after all. It had only been asleep, now it was waking up: Jesus! My brother! Heave-up!

"I don't suppose you could please direct me to the parish officer's house?" said the boy.

The stranger led the poet to a garden gate and pointed to a home-field, cabbage patch, and a house, from which came a sound of hammering. Once again, to the stranger's chagrin, the poet declined to taste the elixir of life. If the stranger had had his way, he would have made the parting handshake last all day until nightfall. Finally the poet withdrew his hand from his trembling grip and gave him to understand that he could no longer tarry, that life called, that their ways had to part; it was a doleful moment. The stranger gave the poet a tearful parting embrace outside the parish officer's gate: Jesus! My brother! Heave-up!

— 4 —

When he had knocked for a long time a woman came to the door and asked what was the meaning of this damned racket? He bade her good-day, but she ignored that. Then he asked if it were possible to have a word with the parish officer.

"I've no idea," she replied. "It's nothing to do with me."

"Perhaps he isn't at home?" asked the boy.

"He's not tied to my apron strings," she said, and slammed the door shut in the boy's face.

The hammering was coming from a nearby outhouse; the boy went there and saw the parish officer at his carpentry, with sawdust in his eyebrows and wood shavings in his hair.

"What the devil do you want here?" asked the parish officer.

The poet always became tongue-tied when he was spoken to very harshly. He usually began to search his mind for a sufficiently mild and Christian reply, but sometimes had difficulty in finding it.

"What, can't you open your trap?" asked the parish officer.

"I had to sleep in the open last night," said the boy, in the hope of moving that cold heart to compassion for such misery. But the parish officer replied, "It'll do you good."

"I was thinking of asking you to give me some help," said the poet.

"Help! Yes, I'll certainly give you some help! Just do some work. Go and carry rocks. You're in good health. You're no concern of mine."

That was all the answer the poet got, and he had not the courage to prolong the conversation against such odds. But he remained standing in the doorway for a while after the parish officer had returned to his work. No, no coffee, no bread. This was the way the world's suppliants had stood since time immemorial. They stood there behind him, unseen and yet more real than anything visible, a thousand million wet, hungry men who had slept in the open, but unfortunately were neither half-witted, dying nor withered on one side of their bodies. He even felt a twinge of sympathy for all these men. Then he shuffled away.

The children were up and had started yelling in the ditches and on the fences. No, he had no fixed purpose any more. The household of Skálholt was the only place where he could conceivably find refuge— and yet he was not even in dire enough straits to qualify as one of the children of the happy old woman. Nevertheless, before he knew it, he was standing in the same place where he had stood the previous morning. And the girl in the cottage on the other side of the road was standing in the same place as on the previous morning, leaning against one of the doorposts with her toes braced against the other and gazing out onto the road. Her hair was dishevelled, and she had the bloom of youth in her cheeks, a high bosom and holes in her socks; it did not matter that she was wearing worn-out shoes, she was beautiful and rich in her doorway. He got palpitations and forgot his own misery, but she did not look at him today, she did not see him, just gazed far out, down the road.

"Good-morning," he said.

She did not reply, but went on gazing out, down the road; finally when he had repeated his greeting she looked at him askance, and rather suspiciously.

"It's raining a bit today," he said affably.

She made no reply.

"But even though it's not very much, one gets soaked through little by little nonetheless," he said, and coughed a little as if he were getting pneumonia.

Silence.

How he longed to thaw the icy armor of this young girl's soul and get a cup of hot coffee from her, but she no longer wanted to see him or hear him. She stood there frozen in her doorway at the height of spring, this newly blossomed flower.

Then he said as bitterly as he could, "It's awful to have nowhere to lay one's head."

She looked at him from far away and said, "To have what?"

"To have nowhere to stay," he said.

"Really," she said. "Is that so? Why?"

It was like a difficult long-distance telephone call from one end of the country to the other.

"Those who have nowhere to stay," he said, "have really lost their souls already."

"Ha!" she said. "Lost their souls! No, I've never heard anything like it in all my born days! Can't you stay with old Þuríður on the other side of the road at Skálholt there?"

"No, unfortunately I'm no longer confined to bed, not even withered on one side," he said with growing bitterness.

"It's awful the way you talk, man!" she said. "So it's true after all what they say about you?"

"What?"

"That you're eccentric."

"Who says that?"

"Everyone. And you look just like an eccentric, too. Why are you so tall?"

"It's because I have lain in bed for many years."

"And why is your hair so funny? And why are you wearing a shawl under your jacket? And why are your hands so long? You're obviously eccentric."

He did not have the courage to defend himself against these well-founded accusations, but stood where he was in the road, dull-witted and cold, with his books under his arm.

"Oh," she said, with a twinge of remorse at being so brutal to someone who was already down. "But in spite of everything I'll offer you some coffee if there is any; yes, and even if there isn't, hahaha."

"A thousand thanks," he said.

"I don't suppose you have any money for biscuits?" she said.

"No," he said. "I've never had a penny in my life."

"Never had a penny?" she said. "No, I don't believe you!"

"I swear it," he said. "I don't even know the difference between coins. I've only seen one coin. And that was a gold coin."

"A gold coin!" she said. "Are you crazy?"

"It's the land of coin that great poets and masters get from southern lands when they grow old," he said.

"You're obviously weird," she said.

It was a single-roomed cottage with a kitchen at the front and a living room at the back. She invited him to have a seat on a box beside the stove. The kettle was boiling, the warmth in the kitchen was very comfortable, especially after a night in the open, there were no worries in this house; peace and comfort for a lost heart.

"It's ridiculous, inviting guests like this," she said. "I've only got half a piece of chicory. But that doesn't matter, the chicory's good enough for us damned paupers, I suppose, hahaha; yes, and too good if we don't want it. But I can give you rye bread, and rye bread is rye bread. And there's even some poisonous margarine to spread on it, if you like."

"There are no words for such kindheartedness toward a stranger," he said. "And don't apologize; it's the kindness of heart that matters, not the coffee or the chicory."

Then he told her all his ordeals since they had last met: that he was not capable of carrying rocks, that he had slept in the open all night and had roused a corpse that morning, that the parish officer had turned him away empty-handed. On top of all that he was beginning to doubt whether God meant anything by testing those He loved.

She listened to him amazed at how blue and deep his eyes were and how clean his countenance; and that remarkable hair. She began to try to solve his problems and create a future for him, and said that he was more than welcome to have a bite of salted catfish with her whenever he had nothing to eat. He asked what her name was, and she was called Vegmey Hansdóttir, known as Meya of Brekka, and the cottage was called Fagrabrekka and the cow was called Skjalda, hahaha. He looked at her, spellbound, and asked, "Excuse me, but are you betrothed?"

"Why do you ask that?" she asked sharply, and looked down instinctively as if she thought something was showing on her.

"Because I can hardly believe that such a fine girl can be unbetrothed," he replied.

"No, I've never heard anything like it!" she said. "And you who can't even carry rocks!"

"I could perhaps compose a poem about you," he said.

She turned to him and looked at him in delight and amazement, clapped her hands and asked, "Are you a poet?"

"Yes," he said, serious and dignified.

"Well, then I'll have to run next door and ask the woman for a coffee bean and a biscuit if she has any," said the girl, and was gone.

He composed an excellent poem about her while she was fetching the coffee and biscuits, and when she came back he had finished the poem; it contained woman-kennings like "ocean's-current's-island" and "gold's-field." She had never in all her life heard such a good poem. She had a handful of coffee beans which she put into the mill and began to grind; a strong fragrance arose.

"Now at last I know what you ought to be," she said. "You ought to be a pastor."

He thought about this for a while, and then said, "I doubt if I am religious enough for that, or a good enough person. A miracle has happened to me, and yet in reality I feel as if nothing has happened. I don't even feel properly grateful. Sometimes I even doubt the victory of Goodness."

"Tcha, that doesn't matter," said the girl. "It makes no difference what pastors believe, and many people say they don't believe anything. The main thing is to become a fine gentleman and a great man, because that's what you ought to be and it's I who says so. And why the devil should they want to make a man with your hands and your eyes and your hair carry rocks? They ought to be ashamed of themselves! No, I'll tell you what you should do when you've finished your coffee. You should go straight to Pastor Brandur, he's very old now and he'll be dead soon, and tell him you want to study to be a pastor so that you can take over from him immediately after he dies."

That was how intimate an interest she took in his fortunes, and she was determined to bring him to maturity; he had never in his life got such good coffee as he got from her, and it never even occurred to her any more that he was an eccentric.

"Hurry up with the biscuit before these damned children come back," she said.

"A thousand thanks," he said.

"And now go to the pastor."

He was determined to do everything she said. He paused at the door after he had stood up and thanked her; he could not tear his eyes away from her. She came right up to him and looked into his eyes.

"Since you insist on knowing," she said, "I'm not engaged. But I was a little bit engaged to a man this winter; he wanted me very badly, I couldn't help it, but then he went away, and I said Thank God he went away, he can go to the devil, I only got engaged to him out of boredom, hahaha. And now I've told you more than I've told my father, and that's because you have such blue eyes and red hair; you ought to be ashamed of yourself."

She came right up to him and he felt her closeness for a moment as she opened the door for him and made him go, and he saw in her eyes that hot, wordless dreamland which is sometimes in a girl's eyes when she looks at a man, and then she closed the door behind him and he stood outside her door and looked at the cottage, entranced as if in a vision, and loved it. It had perhaps been one of life's loveliest mornings.

—— 5 ——

The whole village was up and about now. Life there had not declined since the last time after all; the children crowded round the unknown traveler, called him queer and worse, and made many remarks about his build and his clothing. They knew a host of bizarre terms of abuse and strange swearwords. The young men stood in groups against fences and walls with their hands in their pockets and told one another to go to hell, or jeered at the passers-by, or uttered awful howls and other peculiar cries.

"Do you walk in Christ, my good man?" asked the pastor, and dusted some fluff off his nose with his fingertips and snorted at the same time.

The boy was quick to recognize the note and replied without hesitation that with God's help he hoped that he walked in Christ, if that were the Will of the Holy Ghost.

"Huhu," said the pastor, and became cautious at once. "And who are your kinsfolk?"

Ólafur Kárason gave his father's name and his mother's, certainly, but hastened to add that he reckoned that God and good men were his kinsfolk first and foremost.

At this reply the pastor's face suddenly froze; he cleared his throat three times running, huhuhu: "And what brings you here, young man?"

The boy told the pastor his life story in the most theological language he could muster, and in an edifying parable style, and laid great stress on representing his years of lying ill in bed as irrefutable proof of God's glory: nothing in this world meant anything to him except the spirit. "The revelation of the deity has always been my comfort," he said, "and I am quite convinced that one's relationship with the Lord is all-important for people. That's why I have come to you to ask you for help," he added, using the informal "thee."

The pastor listened absentmindedly to the life story and dusted bits of fluff off, here and there, but when the life story was nearing its conclusion he stopped dusting himself and looked serious, even astonished. He pushed his spectacles higher up his nose and said, "One ought to get into the habit of using the formal 'you' towards one's superiors and using correct titles for the country's officials. I am Pastor Brandur Jónsson, pastor and rural dean of the deanery of Sviðinsvík, and I should be addressed by the formal 'you.'"

Until now the boy had been convinced that he had hit on the only note appropriate for God's servants, but he was now sorely disappointed; he blushed crimson and could not utter a word for shame.

"What was it you were talking about again, my friend?" asked the pastor.

"I have a strong leaning towards poetry," said the boy, trying to be straightforward.

"Tcha, for heaven's sake try to get that sort of idea out of your head, see," said the pastor, and went on dusting himself here and there. "Young men nowadays ought to set themselves the aim in life of not becoming a burden upon others. That's why they should also make demands upon themselves, above all, and never upon others. There is one man here in the village whom youngsters ought to look up to as an example, and that's old Jón the snuffmaker on the French site. Now there's a man who has shown how far one can get by industry, thrift and saving; and by never making any demands upon others."

"Unfortunately I have nothing to save except my own life," said the poet, and had now stopped talking theologically.

"Yes, but that's not the right way of looking at it, my friend," said the pastor. "Your own life, that's the one thing a man shouldn't try to save; old Jón the snuffmaker never spared himself. For thirty years he has sat in the same shed and chopped his snuff for God and man from six in the morning until eleven at night, and even though it's not considered an eminent task to chop snuff for people's noses, in his old age he has now become the richest man in the village. One should work while the day lasts, and set oneself the aim in one's youth of never going on the parish. Neither should one get into the habit of making excessive demands, least of all if one is someone else's servant. People never did that here in the old days, and that way everyone had something to live on for most of the year, and it hadn't become a habit to be on the parish all the year round and demand the impossible from both God and man."

"They tried me at the quarrying yesterday," said the boy. "But I'm afraid I didn't have the strength for it. I collapsed."

"One should get up again, my friend, when one collapses," said the pastor. "It is the duty of all Christian men to get up again. What do you think old Jón the snuffmaker had to endure in his young days? Jesus Christ collapsed seven times under the Cross."

"Yes, but he was the Son of God, after all," said the boy.

"Huhu, he was the Son of God, was he, and just what kind of talk is this, may I ask? Are you trying to be impertinent with me? Youngsters shouldn't get into the habit of answering back."

"I beg your pardon for being so stupid and uneducated," said the poet. "But don't you think that God would be willing to help me?"

"Help yourself, and then God will help you," said the pastor.

"I want so much to be a man of learning and a poet," sighed Ólafur Kárason.

"Tcha, where's the money?" asked the pastor.

"What money?" asked the poet.

"The money, you see," said the pastor, and brushed the dust from the sleeve of his frock coat. "Education is a question of money, my friend."

"I thought that true education expressed itself in doing something free of charge for those who yearn to see the light," said the boy.

"No, no, no," said the pastor. "I've never had anything free of charge. And old Jon the snuffmaker has never had anything free of charge. God punishes all those who try to get something free of charge. Even the Son of God got nothing free of charge, apart from a donkey which they borrowed without the owner's consent on the Saturday before Palm Sunday—and you know how that ended."

As a matter of fact Ólafur Kárason had already realized how pointless all this was. There was silence. Inwardly, the poet felt like someone being roasted. The pastor went on clearing his throat and brushing dust off himself.

"So you don't think, then, that God is willing to help me at all, Pastor Brandur?" said Ólafur Kárason.

"Oh, I don't rule it out altogether, my friend, once in a while, now that you have learned to address people properly," said the pastor. He stood up and pointed out of the window. "There's Hlaupa-Halla over there, who has had children by a number of men—go and help her weed the garden, and you'll get a dribble of something for it later in the day."

"A pipit in the pocket is said to bring wealth," mumbled Hlaupa-Halla without looking up from the weeding.

"Eh?" he said, perplexed by this observation.

It was still damp, a fine drizzle over homefields and gardens, and the poet grudged having to muddy his trousers, no matter how shabby they were, by kneeling in the wet soil; instead he bent down and carefully loosened a few shoots of chickweed and put them neatly to one side, taking care not to dirty his fingers.

"And when they pick the dog muck off the road," Hlaupa-Halla went on, "they say to themselves as they put it in their pockets, 'There's always a use for everything.' And yet even though they go on skimping and scraping all their lives, and even grudge the money for something to eat, they never become richer than petty fish-thieves, not to speak of wreck-looters."

"I'm sure you must be exaggerating a little, good woman," said the boy, straightening up because his back was already getting sore. "At least, I don't believe that any living person is so thrifty that he would pick dog muck off the road and put it in his pocket."

The woman stopped weeding and looked at the boy in amazement, and said, "Where on earth have you come from, you poor creature?"

She found him a sack so that he would not have to kneel on the soil, and taught him how to weed a vegetable bed. She was a little peevish with him because she did not know what sort of a creature this was, but he told her his life story, and gradually her heart was moved to compassion. "Poor wretch!" she said. "I think you'd have been better off if you had lain for another year under the sloping ceiling."

"I can only hope I'll get a roof over my head by and by," he said manfully. "And perhaps I'll get some clothes to cover my body eventually."

The woman made no reply, and in his mind he went on reveling in all the luxuries he hoped to have one day.

"It's also quite possible," he said aloud, "that somewhere there is some great man who wants to care for those in distress and help a friendless youngster to get on in the world."

"Yes, that's very possible," said the woman drily, and glanced at the boy not unsympathetically, without pausing in her weeding. "But," she added, "I've always heard that those who sleep with dogs wake up with fleas."

"I don't know what you mean," he said. "Who was talking about dogs? A great man, I said. Or have you perhaps never heard of great men like those you find in famous books?"

"No," she said.

"Really," he said. "That's odd."

This seemed to be one of those sad occasions in life when two people fail to understand one another.

"It's quite true, my lad," said the woman after a brief silence, "I've never done much reading in my time. But on the other hand I have had nine children in twelve parishes. Perhaps people have forgotten to write about it in books and famous stories, but if you haven't heard about it already I can tell you that my children were all thrown on the dung-heap as soon as they came into the world. I've never heard tell of the type of great men you're talking about; they might well be found in books, but they're not known in this part of the country. The only great men I've ever known all had one thing in common— they set more store by the jackals who showed them abject obedience than by these so-called friendless youngsters who want to get on in the world. And there were parish officers in my day, and even pastors, too—and I can scarcely believe they've all died out—who thought it a calamity that the Great Verdict had been abolished in Iceland."

"What Great Verdict?"

"Oh, there was never more than one kind of Great Verdict— drowning people in the river Öxará."*

"It's a great mercy it's been stopped," said the boy.

"Stopped?" said Hlaupa-Halla. "Only up to a point! What do the people matter in this country?"

"Whom is one to blame for being poor and homeless?" said the boy. "Isn't it God who governs the world?"

"Oh, I suppose it's easy enough to blame God for every misdeed and disgrace in the world," said Hlaupa-Halla. "But it certainly wasn't God who governed the world I lived in, while I lived."

"And yet I have heard a distinguished woman say that while the Privy Councillor was here, he provided for everyone," said the poet.

"Yes, but there was only one thing the Privy Councillor forgot," said Hlaupa-Halla. "He forgot to slaughter us before he went away. When his cow stopped giving milk, he drove her out into the snow instead of killing her, while he betook himself to the king in Denmark with his Privy Councillor's title and his million."

6

Like most people who actually live by a landlocked sound, bereft of hope of happiness, he had a particular aversion to any doctrines which left people without hope of happiness and told them that they lived by a landlocked sound. He did not have Hlaupa-Halla's obstinate, uncompromising, unbreakable temperament, which can endure lifelong despair without giving up.

It was now late, and the woman had gone. He stood in the road, alone under the care of Providence, soaked to the skin and already beginning to regret that he had not eaten more in the pastor's kitchen. And now he had reached the point where he no longer appreciated to the full the unbelievable miracle that had happened to him a few days previously, when he was elevated into that strange perpendicular condition which is man's answer to the law of gravity; instead he stared into the blue and asked the Creator of Miracles: If a person has been chopped into pieces and salted down in a barrel, is it a better deed to raise him from the dead or to let him remain in the brine?

Then Providence led him on his way, as it leads all people on their way. He began to wander round the estate in the night rain when everyone else had gone to bed. And it was not long before he was standing in the roadway between the two houses. He looked at them in turn, irresolute, his heart thumping almost in terror, and asked, "To be or not to be?"

For the third and last time he had to choose between those two houses. On the one side there awaited him a bed still unchanged from the dead patient who had last used it, where he would have lodgings in the shadow of death with Gísli the landowner and his companions until he himself was carried out feet first one morning. On the opposite side dwelt the beauty of the earth itself in all its rounded curves, in the image of a young woman, the hazard of life itself in one beguiling smile which promised you lifelong impassioned battle, probably lifelong unhappiness; but nevertheless, on that side of the roadway the concept of death had no place. And that is how it went; her young strong body, and the hot feminine look in her eyes that morning—the memory of these won, and he was suddenly determined to live. And he started hammering on the door.

When he had knocked for a long time, a man came to the window and asked angrily when these damned drunks were going to stop hammering on people's houses in the middle of the night. It was the girl's father.

"Is Vegmey at home?" asked the poet.

"Vegmey? At home? In the middle of the night? Where else would she be? Who are you? And what d'you want?"

He said he had been going to ask Vegmey if she would be kind enough to let him stay the night.

"You're as drunk as a pig," said the girl's father.

"No," said the poet. "But I've nowhere to stay."

"This isn't a guesthouse," said the man. "Go to hell!"

At that moment the girl herself came to the window with sleep in her eyes, to find out what was going on. And there was her eccentric back again, the one to whom she had given coffee and biscuits that morning!

"Well, is that you back again!" she said. "And soaked to the skin and covered with mud! Come into the kitchen at once, poor thing!"

The door was not locked, as is the custom among ordinary people because they have nothing worth stealing, or rather because everything has already been stolen from them; and he walked into the kitchen.

She came towards him, yawning; she had put on a ragged dress. "Poor boy," she said, "he hasn't got a home! Daddy, he hasn't got a home, hahaha, we'll have to let him stay the night."

"I've been hauling rocks all day and I'm not giving up my bed for anyone," replied her father.

"He can sleep on the kitchen floor," she said, but on closer inspection she saw that the visitor was too wet to lie on the floor, all the more because there was not much bedding available—he might catch pneumonia. She corrected herself and said, "I suppose I'll have to let you have my own bed."

She pushed him ahead of her into the living room, where the family was enjoying all the incomparable luxury of a clear conscience that characterizes sleep in these houses.

"There's my bed," she said. "Hurry up and get your clothes off and tuck yourself in well so that you don't catch cold."

Some people are rich, others are very poor; this was that true wealth which it is impossible to pluck from a girl at the wayside, even though unknown thieves had in other respects picked the house clean. He was allowed to wash, and bedded down in the warmth beside two warm children who lay at the foot, while Vegmey took a tattered bedspread and said Good-night and went into the kitchen and shut the door. He pulled the eiderdown up to his chin, and had never known a softer bed. There was a sound of breathing all around. The summer rain fell gently and sweetly on the roof; he soon got warm, all life's cares were wiped away—no one can be as happy as a homeless man. Hovering between waking and dreaming he worshiped this lovely girl who got out of her bed in the middle of the night to let one stay; what would it be, this world we live in, if there were no rich and lordly people like her?

He woke up in sunshine and there were fat bluebottles buzzing cheerfully against the window. The children had been got up quietly and sent out, and inside, in the kitchen, the young girl was singing a pleasant song and making a clatter with the kitchen utensils. He coughed a few times to show that he was awake, and she came to the doorway and bade him good-morning and laughed; she had even combed her ash-blonde hair, and the soft curls gleamed as she stood in the shaft of sunlight, her neck fair and strong. Her feet were bare in her shoes, her whole form was a revelation of that earthy line which is without doubt the most unfathomable vision of life, if not the measure of beauty itself; in a word, he had never known so rich a woman bid a poor man good-morning.

"Good-morning."

Today there was neither coffee nor chicory; the day's particular luck revealed itself in the fact that the household had come by some brown sugar, which she brought him along with some salted gill-lids and hot water.

"Eat as much as you can take of the brown sugar before the children come back," she said, and took a handful of sugar for herself.

Never had the young poet been brought such a lot of sugar, and so he chose this girl to be the queen of all the world's dainties; the sunbeams went on playing on her young hair, the buzzing of the flies at the window hummed like a voluptuous string, yes, the sun shone with true abundance into that house. He felt the house tremble with splendor and luxury. No wonder he forgot all other girls, all other loves at this moment; at her side he would walk fearlessly to the end of his days. She handed him his clothes all warm from the stove, and said she would go out while he was putting on his trousers. When he had put on his trousers she came in again because she said he was such a great poet that she wanted him to compose something about her every day, even if it were only just half a verse, hahaha, and they sat down together on the edge of the bed to talk, and the sun shone on them both as they sat there—and greater happiness it is impossible to imagine than two people and one sun.

Then she became serious and practical again and asked if he were going to carry on weeding for the pastor, and laid her elbow on his shoulder and looked thoughtfully into his radiant blue eyes.

"Unfortunately there is no more chickweed in the pastor's garden," he said.

"So what happens tonight?" she asked.

This was something he obviously could not solve, and he even felt it a little odd of her to be asking about it; this was a spring morning and the night was a long, long time away; the night did not exist, why should he have any worries yet about the night? He was seventeen years old and, what was more, a poet, who lives only one day at a time.

"Yes, but don't you think you have to live beyond this passing day, even though you're a poet?"

"I'll do whatever you tell me," he said.

"You must try Pétur Þríhross," she said.

"I daren't," he said. "People like him scare me. Besides, a distinguished woman I met yesterday told me that great men didn't exist in this part of the country."

"That's a lie," said the girl. "You'll see, if you speak badly enough of the parish officer in front of Pétur Þríhross, he'll do anything for you. They're both envious, you see, of what the other steals."

He turned this over in his mind for a while, but finally answered despairingly, "No, I don't think I can do it. I don't know how to speak badly of people. And that's because I think that wicked people don't really exist. If someone behaves badly, I always think to myself: this man hasn't heard the sonic revelation of the Almighty."

"The what?" said the girl.

"It doesn't matter," he said, "you don't need to understand it, because you are part of the sun."

"What a great poet you are!" said the girl. "You're such a great poet that you don't see human life, not even your own life. But you will live nonetheless, even though it's only me who says so!"

There was no point in trying to gainsay it; she had decided that he was to live, despite the fact that he was a great poet. Since he did not feel he could speak badly of the parish officer, she confided to him the only way that would work with Pétur Þríhross when all else failed, and that was to go and burst into tears and pretend to be dying. "That's what I do when his secretary has flatly refused us more credit and there's nothing to eat; then he can't stand any more and loads me with food from his own larder, because he's really a Christian at heart, the swine, and that's why he helps those who play up their misery enough and whine loud enough."

The boy was so impressed by the recklessness of her ideas and the ruthlessness of her methods that he impulsively leaned over against her bosom and laid his face against her neck to find refuge. "I know that I'm safe forever because I have you," he said.

"I've never seen a poet before," she said. "But I've always known they were like you."

"Now nothing can harm me any more," he said. "Never."

There was silence for a while, and then she whispered, "How nicely you breathe."

"What do you mean?" he said.

"Nothing," she said. "It's just so nice hearing you breathe."

There was another pause. She bent down over his face and gazed into his eyes for a long time before they kissed. Then they kissed. He had actually never kissed a girl properly before, and for a long time afterwards he thought about how soft it had been. Then he whispered, "Vegmey, do you think you would like to be my wife?"

At that she stood up and stretched her arms towards the ceiling and yawned and said, "Are you crazy, man? Do you think you can start proposing to me at once?"

He, too, stood up, but was very serious because this was the most solemn moment of his life.

"Forgive me, Vegmey," he said, "but I thought it right to mention it to you before I left."

"Go now," she said.

They went on kissing all the way to the door; and though she went on telling him to go, and pushing him ahead of her, it was not easy to tell which of the two found it harder to let go of the other.

— 7 —

Pétur Þríhross lived in a ribbed merchant's house with a high roof and low walls, a relic from the days of the Danish trading posts; the broad, dignified slope of the roof was broken only by an alien dormer window. The grass grew halfway up to the windows.

"Is it something important?" asked the maid at midday, when Ólafur Kárason had recovered sufficiently from the morning's adventure to think of asking for Pétur Pálsson, the manager.

"Yes," said the boy. Because he had been wandering round the village for hours on end in an ecstasy of love and was now hungry, and wanted the manager to help him at once.

After a moment the woman came back and said, "You can go in to the dining room and state your business briefly. He's having his lunch, actually."

She showed him through a kitchen which smelled of boiled meat, and left him at an open doorway through which he had a view of the manager and his family at their meal: red salt-meat, fat turnips, and thick soup, and a crowd of children and youngsters producing a cacophony of sound, and one lean woman who was silent, while Pétur himself sat at the head of the table in his morning coat and celluloid collar and surveyed the scene through magisterial eyeglasses.

"What d'you want?" shouted the manager when he saw the boy in the doorway; and at the sound of the harsh voice the visitor lost heart completely and truthfully no longer knew what he wanted and stood confused in the doorway. The young people at the table fell silent for a moment and waited for him to say something, but when nothing happened they broke into jeers and laughter that surged over the visitor like breakers.

"Be quiet for once, you idiots!" said the manager. "I can't hear what the man's saying."

"He's not saying anything," said the children. "He's weird and doesn't even know how to open his mouth."

At this taunt the poet plucked up courage, opened his mouth, and said, "I need work."

The manager had never seen this young man before, and what is more he did not even seem to recognize the language he spoke. "You need work?" he echoed in amazement, as if this were a quotation from some unfamiliar and alien language. "What d'you mean?"

"So—so that I can get something to eat and somewhere to sleep," said the boy.

"To eat? And to sleep?" the manager repeated in astonishment; he was so astonished that he stopped in the act of putting into his mouth the spoonful he had raised to his lips and looked helplessly at his children, who went on guffawing with laughter whether the visitor spoke or was silent. At last the manager looked enquiringly at his wife in the faint hope that she could offer some explanation for it: "To eat and to sleep? What's he getting at?"

"I don't know," said his wife.

"Who are you and where do you come from?" asked the manager.

The visitor said who he was, and the children roared with laughter at the incredibly funny idea that the man should have an actual name and come from an actual place. But the manager said, "That wasn't what I was really asking. What I meant was, who's playing you for a fool? Who's responsible for you?"

"I'm on the parish," said the boy.

"I might have known it was that damned parish officer!" said the manager. "Go back to him at once and tell him from me that he can go to the devil; and shut the door behind the man, Dísa dear, I don't want a draft in the house."

A clumsy, hoydenish girl of confirmation age, her face smothered in grease, stood up to close the door behind the boy as soon as he left; but the boy did not want to leave.

"The parish officer has thrown me out for good," said the boy.

"Huh, has the parish officer thrown you out? Yes, that's just like him! He's an idiot and a rat."

"He said I was to go and shift rocks," said the boy.

"Shift rocks is that what he said? So he said that, did he! To the best of my knowledge it's I who decides who shifts rocks in this village and who doesn't."

"Out you go!" said the hoyden, who was still waiting impatiently to close the door.

"What the hell are you doing, showing visitors the door, you brat?" said the manager. "Come in, my boy, since the parish officer has thrown you out, and tell me a little more about yourself."

The boy now stepped over the threshold and at once launched into his life story, but when he reached the point where he was sent to be fostered at Fótur-undir-Fótarfæti, the children made such a fearful racket that it made no difference even when their father ordered them to shut up.

"Pay no attention to these idiots shrieking and laughing," the manager shouted over the din. "It's a family custom here; these wretches have nothing better to do than to jeer at people and laugh at them, but luckily no one pays any attention to it. Carry on."

But the boy had lost the place in his life story and could not find it again; he saw nothing but a white fog and was drenched in sweat, and wrung his cap in agitation.

"Have you any aptitude for anything special?" asked the manager, when no more life story was forthcoming.

This question rescued the young poet; he was marvelously quick at recognizing sympathy in someone's attitude and taking advantage of it, and now he made haste to answer in the affirmative: he said he had a quite exceptional aptitude for everything intellectual.

"Eh?" said the manager. He stopped chewing and looked up mag-isterially, and the children broke into more jeering. "Woman, get these children out of here; I won't have these idiots in here when I'm talking to people."

Luckily the idiots had eaten their fill, but still they did not leave the scene without thumbing their noses at the visitor and jeering at him as they went past.

"What do you mean, you have an aptitude for intellectual things, my boy?" asked the manager when everything was quiet.

"Poetry and learning," said the boy.

At that the manager became a different person entirely and said, "Listen, sit down while I finish eating; we'll talk a little more together. You see, the thing about me is that if I hadn't become a manager I would have become a poet and a scientist. All my propen-sities lie in that direction. But such is the destiny of men, my boy; now I have to content myself with composing verses for the occasion now and again; that's to say I provide the material for them, because usually I get a woman I know to knock them into shape for me. Have you perhaps tried to write poetry yourself?"

"Yes," said Ólafur Kárason of Ljósavík. "I have composed eight hundred and sixty-five poems all told and have written them down in exercise books I got from my father. Over and above that I have composed many ditties and light verses I haven't kept."

"Listen, my boy," said the manager. "May I, as an older man, make one observation: you don't do any good by composing great masses of stuff; I never compose too much. One poem from time to time perhaps, for important occasions or sudden bereavements, that's quite enough in my opinion. But poems by the hundred with-out a reason—that usually ends in sourness and grumbling over some imagined sorrow, mainly because someone thinks he isn't living grandly enough. I never compose like that. I hope you're not one of those who compose like that. Poets ought to be wholesome: whole-some in joy and wholesome in sorrow. I acknowledge no poets except wholesome poets. I don't acknowledge these so-called modern realis-tic poets, like that damned fellow from Skjól,* who make a detour towards the dunghill solely because of their swinish natural desire to roll about in the muck. Poets should sing about 'the land where peace abides and equality resides.' D'you understand me?"

"Yes," said the poet, in the full realization that the most successful kind of intellectual talent was the one that could conjure into his mouth one bite of the manager's leftovers.

"Well, that's all right then," said the manager. "All young poets should get into the habit of writing poetry about what is beautiful and good. I'll let you hear my latest poem when I've finished eating. And as for learning and science, we here also have a great interest in that, because all that sort of thing helps to lift the common people to a higher level and accustom them to think about other things than mouths and bellies. That's why I've time and again thought of founding a small scientific research society here in the village, with my secretary, and the doctor, and the pastor, and perhaps the sheriff, even though he lives elsewhere. You see, I've been conducting some private experiments with a girl this winter, although to tell you the truth I haven't got irrefutable proofs yet; but it's getting better all the time. I'm hoping that she'll eventually let me make some sufficiently thorough experiments on her. I've taken a vow that I shall find the proper evidence through her or else die in the attempt. So you can see that we, too, are pretty intellectual here in Sviðinsvík, my boy."

"Yes," said the poet. "But I'm not quite eighteen years old, and therefore I'm not educated to understand everything you say."

"No, one can't expect that," said Pétur the manager, quite ready to forgive the boy's lack of education. "No one expects a parish pauper from the remote valleys to understand modern science in every detail. But I hope you understand one thing—if you've an interest in intellectual matters at all—and that is that the objective of all modern science has to be only one thing, and can never be anything else, namely the question of the afterlife. I don't acknowledge any other science or learning than that which makes the afterlife its aim and main object. Christian rationalism is my motto. I hope you understand that."

"Yes," said the boy.

"For what's the point of this life here on earth if there isn't another life hereafter?" asked the manager.

"That's true," said the boy. "If one is contented, one wants to live forever."

"And why aren't people contented? It's because they don't have the correct understanding of life; they lack Christian rationalism." With these words the manager wiped his mouth with his sleeve and the back of his hand, for he had eaten his fill, and rubbed a soup stain carefully into the lapel of his morning coat, then removed his upper dentures, sprinkled a layer of snuff on the plate, and put them back into his mouth.

"What is the correct understanding of life, my boy?" asked the manager.

That he did not know.

"Then I shall tell you," said the manager. "The correct understanding of life, let me tell you, is love despite everything. Love despite everything, that is the aim and object of life. Love, you see, is the only thing that pays in the long run, even though it might seem a dead loss in the short run. God is love. That's why I say that damned parish officer should be ashamed of himself. In fact I have always been what foreigners call a socialist. We human beings should strive to behave like the invisible beings in space. We should see light. That's what I call Christian rationalism."

The boy was sure the manager's voice almost broke at this solemn refrain of the miracles, and he had to remove his pince-nez to wipe the lenses. The boy, too, was rather moved, not least at hearing once again those winged words about the invisible beings in space, although he was on the other hand unable to fathom the mysterious connection between the manager and the great miracle girl of Kambar who had more or less raised him from the dead.

"I'm going to play a hymn for you," said the manager. He stood up and patted Ólafur Kárason on the cheek with the back of his hand, like a little child. "A hymn at midday, it makes one so wonderfully good; it casts rays over one's soul until well into the evening."

He sat down at the harmonium, adjusted his pince-nez, and

began to play the hymn "Praise the Lord, the King of Heaven" to his own singing. Ólafur Kárason was convinced that the manager was at heart the most affable of men even though he was a bit rough on the surface. As soon as you got to know him, you began to realize the sort of person he was; his singing was loud and powerful, the house quivered with the clamor of the harmonium; the visit had in fact turned into a church ceremony of the highest order. But however hard the boy tried to resist it, he could not take his eyes off the fat pieces of meat which had been left on the dish; that was how little of a poet he was, when all was said and done, so unspiritual that he was thinking about the irrelevancies of earthly life while Pétur Pálsson the manager was thinking about the cardinal point of existence—the afterlife.

Then the hymn was over and the manager got to his feet, his countenance transfigured, and patted the boy on the cheek again with the back of his hand.

"Would you like a pinch of snuff, my friend?" he said, and stuck the neck of his snuff mull into his nostrils one after the other, threw his head back, and inhaled hard.

"No, thanks," said the poet.

"Can I offer you a cigar?" said the manager; he took a cigar box from a shelf and lit one for himself.

"No thanks," said the poet.

"Well, that's all right, my boy," said the manager. "Tobacco's filthy stuff; people shouldn't use tobacco. That's why we refuse to handle any tobacco in the Regeneration Company. I never used tobacco either when I was just one of the common people. Now we'll go and visit Hólmfríður in her loft and see if she's finished my latest poem yet. I'm sure that rhymesters of your age would benefit from hearing a poem by an educated man with experience of life."

Then he bawled out, "Woman, where's my hat?"

"It's where you left it," his wife replied from the kitchen.

"It doesn't matter what you're asked, you never know anything!" said the manager.

Nevertheless he found his black bowler hat, and now they were ready to set off to visit Hólmfríður in her loft and hear the poem.

— 8 —

Pétur said they would have to look in at the doctor's on the way, and when he came out again one could make out the shape of a bottle in each pocket beneath his coattails.

"Now we're ready to meet the poetess," he said.

It was a long cow shed at the foot of the homefield right down by the sea. Half of the loft was used for human habitation, but the other half of the building from floor to rafters was a hay barn. Access was up some stairs with creaky steps. The door at the top of the stairs had been nailed together from odds and ends of wood; it closed of its own accord, worked by a weight on a string. The woman met them at the door and said that her husband was asleep.

"At the most productive time of the year?" said the manager.

"Is there anything more productive to do in Sviðinsvík than sleep?" said the woman.

She was a big, dark-haired woman with an intelligent, clear-eyed face, her voice oddly high-pitched and metallic, the more susceptible the tauter it was strung, and cracking at a certain pitch.

"I won't listen to any pessimism today, my dear Fríða," said the manager. "Today the weather is fine and we are all life's children. I've brought a young poet from the fjord valleys, a nice polite boy, as you can see. Would you let him hear my latest poem, if you've finished it?"

"I'm afraid I haven't had time to compose your new poem, the piebald cow didn't take with the bull this morning," said the woman with a tired, almost studied, lack of expression. In the lines around her mouth there lurked a kind of suffering the boy did not understand, something completely different from the common, coarse and stupid pain of poverty that is the easiest of all suffering and the least noteworthy; it was a delicate, rare and hard-earned suffering, a combination of hunger and sickness, and the boy felt he was kin to this woman despite the indifferent glance she gave him.

"Yes, you all pretend to be materialists," said the manager, "and behave as if the mating of livestock is more important than the soul.

But what a surprise they'll get when they die, poor things, as the poet says! How often have I told you that spiritual matters should come before livestock?"

This started a bit of a wrangle between them: Pétur the manager as the sensitive and emotional upholder of human feelings, the poetess snappish in her replies, brusque and dispassionate. The boy stood halfway up the stairs and listened as hard as he could. Then a torrent of curses and oaths was heard from inside the house; the woman's husband had woken up. He appeared in the doorway dishevelled, with feathers on his jersey, red-eyed and swollen, unshaven and toothless, jerking his shoulders and spitting. Ólafur Kárason stared in amazement at the man's wife, this woman with her fair skin and hawk-like eyes, her strong vigorous hair and her red young-looking lips.

"Have you brought a drink, Pétur?" asked the woman's husband, point-blank.

"I would expect to be invited in at least before I answer questions of conscience like that," said the manager.

"Come inside!" said the woman's husband.

They slammed the door on the poetess and the poet, and disappeared inside. The woman gave no reaction when the door was banged, but cleared her throat on a high, thin note, like the G string of a violin being plucked.

"They'll never quench their thirst," she said. "It's their life."

He did not know what to say.

"Are you in tow with him?" she asked, and took the boy into the kitchen.

"Oh, I don't know, really," he said, and added foolishly, "He played a hymn for me."

He could not stop looking at the woman: this wordless blend of inquisitive, ever-vigilant feminine perception and petrified indignation as if she were indifferent to everything and despite everything, indifferent in some indefinable, inverted way at once fanatical and impersonal, a hundred thousand million times indifferent, her introspective, precise replies as stilted as some kind of poetry—how was it that he felt he knew this soul? Before he was aware of it, he was saying, "I feel I've seen you before."

"Really?" she said. "It must have been in an earlier life. Where do you come from?"

He pondered her question in his mind for a moment, and then replied, "That's never occurred to me before. Where I come from, it was always said that another life came after this one. But now I see that it could just as well have come before this one."

"Do you believe everything you're told?" she said.

"I feel that what you say is true," he said. "I have known you in an earlier life."

"Aren't you hungry; don't you want to eat?" she asked.

"No," he said, and blushed because she was turning the conversation so abruptly to mundane and distasteful matters; and to tell the truth he was past hunger now.

"Didn't you get a hymn for your midday meal?" she asked.

At that he could not help laughing.

"I'll give you some fish now," she said, "and perhaps some bread."

"Well, perhaps just a very little, thanks," he said.

He thought she would just toss a cod-wing at him without ceremony, but she did not; instead she went to the rack and fetched a rose-patterned plate and a knife and fork and laid a place for him at the kitchen table, as if for an important visitor. He got into a festive mood, and went on studying her carefully while she was serving. Very soon the fish and bread had arrived.

She was a combination of two people, one half of each. Above the middle she was like a big, gangling adolescent, slender down to the waist, with that thin voice and that intelligent countenance; but below the waist she was gross, her legs (not forgetting her heavy, clumsy hips) were clearly those of quite another person; the upper part was like a sensitive flower which had been planted in a coarse vessel; he was convinced that if she were married to a bad man, her soul was not to blame for that. She paused in her work and threw him a glance, and he felt she had sensed what he was thinking, and he was ashamed right down to his toes, and silently prayed God to help him.

"Go on eating," she said. And when she saw how ashamed he was, she forgave him and said, "Let me hear some of your poetry."

He let her hear some of his poetry.

"Where did you learn all these kennings?" she asked.

"From an old poet," he said.

"Why do you write about love, at your age?" she said.

"It's probably because I've been in love," he said without looking up; then he added, as an excuse, and looked up, "But it didn't last very long."

"Love passes," she said, and it was the first time she smiled with her lips; but he felt that the look in her eyes hardened at the same time.

"It wasn't a very happy love, either," he said.

"A happy love is no love at all," she said.

"I would like to hear how you write about love," he said.

"I write about death," she said.

"Death? I don't understand how that comes into it."

"Oh, well," she said.

"Then you must be terribly unhappy—in your love," he said.

"My husband, he surpassed all others like an ash over thornbushes," she replied. "He had eyes that saw miles out to sea. When I saw him for the first time, I saw a hero. It is life that is disgraceful."

What was the woman getting at? Why this uncalled-for defense of her husband? Was she excusing herself?

"Unfortunately, he wasn't wicked enough for this criminal society," she added. "Unfortunately, he wasn't a criminal."

The boy forgot to eat and looked at the woman in surprise, but she did not even look up; she went on with her housework as if she had said something very ordinary.

"Take an oak tree and try to transplant it on to bare rock," she said.

He did not know what to say. "That's how I write about love," she said, and then said no more, and gave him his coffee and sugar in silence. Afterwards, when he had eaten his fill, he sat for a long time at the window and looked out over the bay, while she went about her work indoors and outside quietly and conscientiously, while the men in the next room sang "In Bethlehem a Child Is Born."

— 9 —

When the Bethlehem stage was over, "Oh, Thou Joy of the World" began. Finally came the Sprengisandur stage—"O'er the Icy, Sandy Wastes," with incredibly long pauses between the lines. That night there was a white mist over land and sea. Ólafur Kárason helped to fetch the Regeneration Company's cows and tether them, and stood in the barn and looked on while they were being milked. The poetess gave him milk to drink, warm from the cow, as much as he wanted and more. She had the task of separating the milk, churning the butter, preparing the whey, and making cheese for the manager, and the remainder of the milk she distributed at the barn door to the villagers who were on the books of the Regeneration Company. Towards midnight her evening work was done. Afterwards she sat in the kitchen and knitted very rapidly, but said nothing; the cat lay under the range and closed its eyes; the plates were rose-patterned, the curtains blue-checked; he sat at the kitchen window and looked out at the white mist, and the dew settled on the green grass in the summer dusk, and one could just glimpse the white sea like cream on the shingle a few yards away, and there was a shrieking of terns in the mist, and he felt that the night could continue like this forever. He tried time and again to start a conversation, but she would not talk; he wanted so much to hear one of her poems, but could not bring himself to say so.

Eventually no more singing was heard from the next room, just a vague mumbling now and again. The husband's name was called out a few times, but in vain. Pétur Pálsson came out of the living room, blue-black in the face and unsteady on his feet, minus his pince-nez and teeth, with tobacco stains at the corners of his mouth; he still had his celluloid collar on. He came over to the poetess, seized her hands and pressed them fervently, and spoke in a foreign language. When he had talked for a bit he tried to kiss her, but she wriggled out of his embrace.

"You'd be better to spare a thought for this young man you left hanging about here," said the woman.

"My name is Peder Pavelsen Three Horses," he replied. He talked twice as gutturally as usual, and his voice was very thick as well.

"What's happened to your eyeglasses, Pétur?" asked the woman.

"I'm no Icelander, s'help me," answered Peder Pavelsen Three Horses in Danish. "My grandmother's name was Madame Sophie Sørensen."

"And where's your hat and your false teeth?" asked the woman.

"Don't you bother about that," he said. "I'm going to sleep with you tonight."

She went in and fetched the manager's discarded emblems of dignity, wrapped the eyeglasses and false teeth in a newspaper and put them in his pocket, and placed the hat on his head.

"You are the greatest poetess in Iceland," said Peder Pavelsen, and began another handshake with the woman, and repeated in Danish, "I'm sleeping with you tonight."

"What for?" said the woman.

"I love you," said Peder Pavelsen.

"Is that so, poor fellow?" said the woman.

"I'm no Icelander, s'help me," said Peder Pavelsen in Danish.

"No, thank goodness," said the woman.

"That's the sort of thing you can say because you've got no soul," said Peder Pavelsen. "It's your fault that I'm no better than a corpse in this locality."

He sank down on a bench and wept.

"Don't cry, Pétur dear," said the poetess, and patted him consolingly on the shoulder when he had cried for a while.

"I'm not your Pétur dear," he said, sobbing. "You'll be the death of me. And take from me my afterlife."

The words were practically drowned in sobs, and the inflections of his verbs had gone adrift.

"If you do something for that homeless boy sitting there, you will attain eternal life, Pétur dear," she said.

At that the manager stopped crying, leapt to his feet, seized Ólafur Kárason's hand, squeezed it hard, and said in broken Icelandic, "You who are homeless, walk into my heart. If you are hungry, I shall give you a feast. If you have nowhere to live, I shall give you a palace. Love is the only thing that pays. My name is Three Horses."

He hugged the poet to his bosom and started crying again, overwhelmed by the thought of love in general and his own love in particular. Then he shook his fist angrily in the poetess's face and threatened in abusive and obscene language to drive her away and never let her compose his poems for him again, since she would not sleep with him. "We'll leave this jade to her own devices, my boy, she's never understood the Regeneration of the Nation anyway. But you understand me, and you follow me."

He lurched down the stairs, and the poet bade the woman goodnight and followed him. When they were outside, Three Horses grabbed his arm to steady himself. He discoursed at great length about Love and swayed and hiccuped and spat and wept, but talked for the most part in Danish, so that Ólafur Kárason unfortunately could not understand very much of it. It was past midnight, and the village was abed.

The shore road lay below a gravel-bank, but on the lower stretches between it and the beach were cobbled pitches for drying and stacking fish on both sides of the road, and at the far end of them there stood a large building right on the seashore, on its own, below the village proper. This building was grander than any man-made structure Ólafur Kárason had ever seen; nor had he ever dreamt any dream so far removed from reality that it had given him any suggestion that such a house could exist.

What especially attracted his attention at first were the three towers on the building, for he had never seen a tower before. There was a tower on each gable, shaped rather like a giant turnip and painted red, while the midtower was a four-sided pillar with concave walls and a very small roof. But on closer inspection the whole building was equally notable. The front faced out toward the waves of the sea, but right through the center of the building there was an open passage for the winds of the heavens. On the ground floor there was a large number of windows on the side facing the sea, and each window was designed to hold only one pane of glass, even though it was as large as the wall of an average living room. But unfortunately a pitiless war had raged there with such hatred and stone-throwing that all the panes were smashed or cracked or holed; yet there was still enough broken glass left at the front of the building to mirror the afterglow and give seafarers the idea that on this shore there were castles of gold. In the upper story the windows were elongated to a Gothic point, as in superior churches, and had many small panes, which had tempted the rampant armies all the more since they were higher up and made more demands on accuracy of fire and other advanced military arts, and indeed not a single pane was still intact. It was the same story with the cheerful little panes which had once adorned the midtower. But despite the shattered windows, the poet gazed in admiration at this mighty building, and before he knew it he had begun to count the windows in silent veneration.

"What's that in front of us?" asked the manager and pointed at the building with a lurch to one side.

"It's a house," said Ólafur Kárason.

"What house is it?" asked the manager.

This the young poet could not answer. He could not immediately find words for the strange feelings which gripped him as he faced the building. Even if he had said that this must be the biggest house in Iceland, that was really no reply at all; it was more likely that the house had been built by some higher being for some higher purpose that man's wisdom was incapable of figuring out, for example as a complement to the ocean, or as an assembly hall for the storms of heaven. And while he was racking his brains for a suitable answer to the manager's question, an old, mangy rat came crawling out through a crack in the wall, limped painfully over the paved yard, and disappeared among the stones on the beach.

Then the manager said, "That house was built by Tóti *smjör* (butter) from the banqueting halls he bought from the government the year after the king came. That house is built of four royal palaces from the government, and how much do you think it cost?"

The boy thought for a long time, because he did not know whether he ought to say a hundred, thousand or million; but then the manager asked if he were such an idiot that he could not estimate the cost of one house.

"A hundred thousand," the boy guessed.

"Idiot!" said the manager.

"A million," the boy guessed.

Peder Pavelsen had never known such an idiot in all his born days. Then the poet gave up guessing.

"No, my boy," said the manager, "when you do business with the government, you say, 'Not a brass farthing until I'm made a Privy Councillor.' And when you've become a Privy Councillor, you say to the government in Danish, 'I'm no Icelander, s'help me.'"

The manager bellowed with laughter at this witticism about Tóti *smjör* and the government, still swaying and lurching.

"But," he continued, "there was one thing that Tóti *smjör* never understood, even though he became a Privy Councillor and was therefore in a position to cheat the government. He never understood the present day. He was a rat. But it's me, Peder Pavelsen Three Horses, who understands the present day. Education, science, technology, organization, say I; but above all, spiritual maturity, love, light. D'you understand me? Everything for the people, say I. I'm what foreigners call a socialist. I'm in favor of Christian rationalism. D'you know what I'm going to do with this house that old Tóti *smjör* abandoned like a rat? I'm going to convert it into a fish meal factory and an observatory for the people, d'you understand me? And I'm going to convert it into a theater, shops, a net-making workshop and a church, because God is eternal, whatever that fellow from Skjól says. And I'm going to convert it into a bait shed, a restaurant, a hotel, a cold store, a scientific research society, a piggery, and a residence for myself, say I. It's me who's going to make this building a bastion of Icelandic culture for the people, a cultural center, if you can understand that. Do you want to be my poet?"

The manager tried to stand as upright as possible in front of the poet and glared at him with one eye at a time.

"If I can," said the poet.

"I like you," said the manager, and greeted the poet with one of those long handshakes reminiscent of a marriage ceremony. "You're a hell of a good fellow. You can undoubtedly make verses about the parish officer and others who want to get rid of me and think I'm some sort of small fry."

"If I had a roof over my head I would write large books," said Ólafur Kárason.

"A roof," said the manager. "It's a sin and a scandal that a major poet shouldn't have a roof. Major poets ought to have a roof. It is I, Peder Pavelsen Three Horses, who says so. Where would Fríða in the loft be if she hadn't been allowed to tend my cows and support the Regeneration movement? And where would her wretch and fool and idiot be, who planned to set up a shop here and compete with me? They wouldn't have a roof. They'd be rats. If you'll swear to be my poet, you shall have a roof."

"I don't know how to swear," said the poet.

"Well, in that case you can go to the devil," said Peder Pavelsen; he let go of the poet's hand and pushed him away.

The poet's upper lip began to tremble at once, and he said bitterly, "It's easy enough to push me away."

"Yes," said Peder Pavelsen. "You're a rat. Anyone who won't raise three fingers in the air for the Regeneration of the Nation is a rat."

At that the poet changed his mind and declared that he was ready to raise three fingers for the Regeneration of the Nation.

Then the manager loved the poet again, embraced him, and wept a little.

"Now we'll both raise three fingers and swear in the name of the Father, the Son and the Holy Ghost," he said.

They both raised three fingers and swore in the name of the Father, the Son and the Holy Ghost. The boy got palpitations, and silently implored God to forgive him if he were swearing a false oath. When they had finished swearing, Peder Pavelsen laughed one of those buoyant toothless laughs, and said, "The Regeneration of the Nation, that's me, you see, my boy."

Then he waved his arm in the direction of the palace and said, "There you are! There's your house."

"Eh?" said the poet, uncomprehending, his voice squeaky with horror in case he had sworn a false oath after all.

"The house is yours!" said the manager.

"Is it all mine?"

"That's up to you," said the manager. "You've sworn."

"Didn't you have other plans for the house?" asked the poet, his heart still thumping, in the hope of having the oath annulled in exchange for returning the house. "I thought you just said that you yourself were going to use the house for the people."

"Am I an Icelander?" asked Peder Pavelsen.

The boy could not give this question the answer it deserved; he was tongue-tied and could not put the oath out of his mind; he had sworn a false oath. Now it was his turn to feel giddy and to have to make a supreme effort to keep his balance.

"No, I'm no Icelander, s'help me," said Peder Pavelsen, and raised his black bowler hat to his poet and marched away with great dignity in an unsteady curve and disappeared round the corner.

The poet was left behind, standing on the pavement in front of his house. My God, he had sworn a false oath after all! He had developed a severe headache, perhaps his health was failing again. As far as he could see, the front door of his house had been nailed shut and barred. He looked for another door and found it, but that, too, was firmly closed. He stood perplexed and irresolute in front of his house in the night mist, and had sworn a false oath. A gray-striped feral cat came creeping through a cellar window and loped round the corner, but not without stopping for a moment to hiss in the poet's direction.

— 10 —

Next morning he told the woman that he had probably sworn a false oath, but did not dare to mention the fact that he had been given the biggest house in Iceland. The woman studied him for a long time with those deep, clear eyes whose depths he could not fathom, and then asked in surprise, "Are you such a child?" At that he thanked his lucky stars he had not mentioned the house; it was obvious that since it was childish to have scruples about perjury, then it was utter idiocy to accept the biggest house in Iceland. A long time later he asked her, out of the blue, just to find out where he stood, "What would you think of someone who became the owner of the biggest house in Iceland?"

"I wonder if you know old Gísli the landowner?" she said.

"Yes, but he's no landowner; he's mad and he's withered on one side as well."

"Yes," she replied, "he's mad and withered."

He was really relieved that she should have this opinion of landowners, and almost managed to put the problem of his property out of his mind for good.

"I own practically nothing," he said, and smiled with relief. "I was brought across the mountain on a stretcher like a corpse only the other day."

"Do have some coffee," she said. "And here's some bread and butter. Today I'll try to have some better clothes ready for you. When my husband gets up he'll take you with him to see to the lumpfish nets."

These were tranquil early-summer days, some time before the haymaking. The woman's husband was called Lýður. When he was sober he was usually silent and morose, because the universe, even though God had created it, could not bear comparison with the world which lives in a krónur's worth of methylated spirits, or a bottle of cough mixture from the doctor. Without drink he treated the boy like an impersonal phenomenon; the people you see with sober eyes had a tedious uniformity. But in the evening, when he had sold a few lumpfish, he went to the doctor's and bought some brennivín, and when he came back he was sufficiently revived to be no longer indifferent about anyone; in the spectrum of intoxication he saw Ólafur Kárason sitting in the kitchen eating lumpfish.

"What the devil's that red-haired lout doing here?" said the woman's husband.

"You keep quiet," said the woman in her cold, thin voice, unemotionally.

"Jade!" said the woman's husband.

"You go to bed," said the woman, and stared at her husband with that large, cold look from under her high, dark brows. And when he made as if to start arguing, she repeated calmly "Bed!"—and pointed to the bedroom door; and this big, strong man who could have pulverized her merely mumbled a few harmless curses to himself, and went to bed. That was how Ólafur Kárason got a job with the Regeneration Company.

Sometimes after a meal he was allowed to sit in the white-scrubbed kitchen and read her poetry books and other books, because she always had books in the same way that her husband always had drink. He came to know poets who were closer to the human heart than he had ever suspected was possible, and he forgot Sigurður Breidfjörð in that remarkably painless way we forget those we have loved most ardently. The poetess looked at his face and read there everything that was in the book, and the sun went on playing on his auburn hair. She did not say anything, and he did not say anything either. He was convinced that she could perceive whatever one was thinking, and so he tried to think only beautiful thoughts in her presence. When he looked up he smiled impulsively, but she did not smile back; instead she looked even deeper into his soul. She silently absorbed his enquiring smile without giving an answer to anything. Sometimes he made up his mind to ask her to let him hear some of her own poetry, but when he looked up, her soul was far away; and sometimes he felt, just like the manager, that she had no soul at all, only eyes.

He composed poetry wherever he was. His consciousness was all in verse, everything his eyes saw craved to be given syllabic shape; the poetry of existence affected him so profoundly that he walked around in a stupor and scarcely saw anything in his eagerness to put into poetic form the little he did see. The poetess gave him paper and exercise books, and then he would sit up late, sometimes all night, writing with all his might as if the end of the world could overwhelm them at any moment and everything depended on getting enough words down on paper before the sun, the moon and the stars were wiped out. He wrote down everything he saw and heard, and most of his thoughts, sometimes in verse, sometimes in prose. It could take him many hours to write in his diary a survey of one full day: everything was an experience, any noteworthy observation which some nameless person might make was a new vista, any insignificant piece of information was a new sunrise, any ordinary poem he read for the first time was the beginning of a new epoch like a flight around the globe; the world was multiform, magnificent and opulent, and he loved it. Fortune smiled on this young poet. He thought it unlikely that the guardian spirits which had opened new avenues for him this summer would begrudge helping him on his way in the winter—perhaps he would even earn some wages this summer and be able to go to the secondary school at Aðalfjörður whose existence he had only learned of recently. And his mother, who was now a person of standing in Aðalfjörður, even though she had once sent him away in a sack, weeping and helpless—she was bound to do something for him if she learned that he was on the way to becoming a major poet. He was more convinced than ever that all people were good, and he was not resentful towards anyone. All around him he heard wonderful harmonies. He saw light.

But—"Vegmey Hansdóttir, why don't you want to ask me in any more?"

No, she did not laugh as gaily and freely and entertainingly as she had laughed at first; instead she stood in the doorway and whistled, and shook her head in a blend of petulance and impatience, but it was the same melody.

"These damned pauper children. They're a terrible rabble. It's forbidden to rear them for slaughter and that's why no one can be bothered feeding them, least of all those who own the food and the money, and so these devils go round the village shrieking, swearing and telling lies about innocent people. But God knows I've just about had enough now, even if He doesn't exist."

"What a way to speak, girl!" said the poet. "What on earth has happened?"

"Imagine it, one's own brothers and sisters! They've been lying to the other children that I slept with you when you stayed the other night, and since then I haven't been able to show my face outside. These devils are all around me at once, yelling at me that I've been sleeping with an eccentric. And naturally the grown-ups do their bit as usual, as you can imagine. Everyone always believes everything nasty of everyone else, and especially if it's a lie."

"Yes, but when one has a clear conscience, it doesn't matter what people say," he said consolingly.

"D'you think it feels any better to be torn to pieces by cannibals even if one has a clear conscience?" she said. "And anyway, who says I've got a clear conscience?"

"How very angry you are!" he said.

"Yes, and no wonder!" she said, and laughed. And with that she was no longer angry.

"I thought we had become such good friends that it was only natural for you to ask me in, whatever anyone says."

"I'm such a fool," she said. "I've never known such a fool. I can't even be a friend. And I hate being a brother and sister." And she added in a nasal falsetto, half laughing and half whimpering, but still looking at him with those heavy, hot eyes of hers, "You should be ashamed of yourself for the other day!"

"Why?" he said.

"Tcha, you're a fool, too," she said, "you're just as much of a fool as I am. I've never known such a fool in all my born days."

"So you don't want to talk to me any more?" he asked.

"Am I not talking to you now?" she replied. "Are you deaf?"

"When can we see each one another?" he asked.

"Aren't you seeing me now?" she answered. "Are you blind?"

"I mean like the other day," he said.

"And how d'you think that would end? I've never known such a fool!" she said.

He stood on the roadway, obstinate and uncomfortable, and did not want to go away, but did not know what to say.

"I haven't time to talk to you any more just now," she said.

"You haven't talked to me at all," he said.

"You can write a poem about me," she said.

"I've done it," he said. "Would you like to hear it?"

"N–no," she said. "I don't want that."

"So that's the way you are?" he said.

"Don't be angry," she said, "you who are now in with Pétur Þríhross and soon to become one of the gentry. What am I? I'm nothing! Hahaha. Go away."

No, her laughter was not as clear and genuine as before, nor as wonderfully meaningless either; something had happened.

"May I never come again, then?" he said.

"You can walk along the road here tomorrow," she said.

"Thanks," he said.

Next day he walked by at the same time. She stood in the doorway and laughed a little. He wanted her to ask him in. She said, "No, I've never heard anything like it, to think that a girl would ask a man in!"

"You did the other day," he said.

"Ssssh," she said, and looked all around. "Don't talk so loud."

"I'll never ask you again," he said.

"You who live in the biggest house in Iceland, why don't you ask people in?" she asked.

"Any time," he said. "You're welcome whenever you like. But I'm afraid you'll have to crawl in through the cellar window, because the doors are nailed up."

"Are you daft, man?" she said. "You surely don't think I'm going to visit a man?"

"I can hardly call myself a man," he said, very unassumingly. "But still, I've got an old divan. And I can at least offer you a seat on it. But unfortunately there are no panes in the window; so if the weather's bad, the rain comes in."

"I hope you've got an eiderdown for yourself?" she said.

"Yes," he said. "I've got a big eiderdown for myself—and others."

"Really?" she said. "Where did you get an eiderdown?"

"Hólmfríður in the loft lent me it."

"Really?" she said. "That was lucky for you. She's a poetess like yourself, although no one's ever heard anything she's written, thank goodness."

"If you come to visit me tonight, you'll get a poem."

"No, I've never in all my born days heard such effrontery to imagine that a girl would go and visit a man! What sort of dreadful person do you really take me for? As far as I'm concerned you can just spread the rest of your eiderdown over Hólmfríður, who's a poetess like you! And now I haven't time for any more of this."

"May I walk by tomorrow, then?" he asked.

"D'you think I can forbid you to use the road?" she said.

"Then it's best we never see one another again," he said, theatrically sorrowful.

At that she laughed and said, "Yes, come again tomorrow."

And so it went on, day after day. This was not the first time that those who had at first smiled at him turned their backs on him and began to think of themselves instead of thinking of him. Sometimes it was as if you understood people's souls; a few days later, you understood nothing. One day you were kissed, and it meant everything; next day, you were not kissed.

——— II ———

He consoled himself by looking at his exercise books with the poems approaching the thousand total soon, and more. Perhaps the world would some day understand that the heart existed. Some day. Once upon a time there were two poets, the two greatest poets in Iceland; they were enemies because they served the Muse, each in his own way, but they both loved the Muse with all their hearts—yet perhaps they loved even more this nation which has the misfortune to foster poets. They both died young, penniless and forgotten, the one in Copenhagen and the other in Reykjavík; the grave of one is lost, and some say the other never had a grave. But their poems will warm every Icelandic heart for a thousand years. Who am I, Ólafur Kárason of Ljósavík, to expect greater happiness than they?

"Are you the one who lives in the palace?"

A man came walking towards him on the shore road late one evening. The stranger was shorter in build, but broader in the shoulders; his eyebrows grew in an unbroken line. He had light brown hair and a green glint in his eyes, and his face was drawn into a haughty pucker as if no one could tell him a thing any more. He had a deep voice, his neck was bare, and he wore tattered canvas shoes. Ólafur Kárason had not the faintest idea what the stranger had in mind, but he replied apologetically that he was allowed to stay in the building at night because he had nowhere to live.

"I know you," said the stranger. "You're the poet."

His hand was small and well shaped, the wrist thick, the middle of the hand beefy but the fingers slender and tapering like a woman's, with lone curved nails. But his handshake was firm and friendly.

"My name is Þórarinn Eyjólfsson," he said. "It's a name from antiquity, as you can probably hear, and that's why I call myself Örn Úlfar*; you're to call me that, too. The village calls me that fellow from Skjól."

He talked in an earnest, measured way, almost like a book, knitting his brows fiercely, screwing up his eyes and pulling down the corners of his mouth, and even when he was talking to someone and looking at the person he was talking to, his look seemed directed towards some undefined immensity. But in his face there was a strange beauty which made this haughty expression understandable and justified it. He spoke in a deep voice which had the ring of fine metal, and yet not without a mellow veneer.

"I was once a poet, too, like you," he went on in that proud voice of his. "Let us stroll along this shore road together. I feel we are going to become friends."

"Give me your hand again!" said the poet. "I've always longed so much to have a friend; I've never had a friend before. My name is Ólafur Kárason, and I call myself 'Ljósvíkingur' because when I was a small boy I often stood at a little bay called Ljósavík, and watched the birds."

"Ljósvíkingur," said Örn Úlfar, "I want to ask you one question. Why do you write poetry?"

This question took the poet so much by surprise that he forgot to keep putting one foot in front of the other. He stood stock-still.

"I l–love . . ." he said, but when he came to the object of the sentence he became tongue-tied—what was it really that he loved? He stood open-mouthed and waved his arms in the air like a man trying to catch a butterfly which has already flown by, and it was night and day at the same time, and a dead-calm, golden-clouded sea, and beyond the fjords the mountains were turning blue, one behind the other in an ever more unreal haze.

"You love," Örn Ulfar prompted. "What do you love?"

"I don't know," said the Ljósvíkingur, and set off again. "But probably it's beauty I love."

"What do you say about Sviðinsvík, in that case?"

The poet realized all too well how inadequate his answer to his friend's question had been, and went on gazing into that mesmerizing immensity of blue sky without being able to turn his mind from that unexpected question.

"The mountainscape here at Sviðinsvík is unique," he said at last.

"Do you know that these mountains you're looking at don't really exist at all?" said Örn Úlfar. "Or can't you see that they belong more to the sky than the earth? All this enchanting blueness which enthralls you is an illusion."

"What *does* exist, when it comes to that?" asked the Ljósvíkingur. "What isn't an illusion?"

"Human life," answered Örn Úlfar. "This life."

"It would be more natural if beauty and human life could be united and never more be parted," said the Ljósvíkingur.

"Beauty and human life are two lovers who are never allowed to meet," said Örn Úlfar. "Do you remember the poem 'About My Sister,' with these lines in it?

> *'She is glad in goodly weather*
> *Golden-bright her flowing hair.'"*

"Don't even mention it; that is sheer genius," said the Ljósvíkingur. "How on earth could he write so simply?"

"I didn't mean that," said Örn Úlfar.

"What then?"

"My sister," said Örn Úlfar; "she is dead."

At that the Ljósvíkingur did not know what to say; so they walked on in silence for a while. Then his friend went on:

"Yes. It's about three months now since she died. It was early in April. We're in the habit of saying here, 'Everything gets better in the spring when the sun begins to shine.' But she died. My last poems were three sonnets. She had golden-bright hair, just as in the poem, and blue eyes which believed and hoped and loved. That bright hair of hers—I thought perhaps we would be allowed to keep her with us because all the other brothers and sisters had died. But we weren't allowed to. I touched her cheek as she lay on the bier the morning she was buried. I also touched her hand. Death is one of the few things a man cannot believe, perhaps the only thing. I don't know whether you've ever touched a dead person. I don't know whether you know the sound of the first spadeful falling on the coffin lid. I don't care now. All I know is that I shall never write poetry again. I know that I, too, shall die of consumption one day. But that doesn't matter. I'm no longer afraid of anything. But nothing is beautiful anymore, either."

They walked together like that all night, and there was no night, just a slight unreality, a momentary trance, with mist here and there as if the landscape were about to dissolve, and then nothing dissolved and the mist had vanished again. There was a crimson glow on the highest mountain ridges, and shining birds swarming in their thousands over the flame-gilded, mirror-smooth sea. And they went on talking together. Ólafur Kárason had no conception of the passing of time; only that voice with its dark, silk-edged, golden tones reverberated through his consciousness. When a man has lost what he loves most, there is no need to write poetry; the timbre of a man's voice expresses all the poetry of life. How destitute the Ljósvíkingur felt at not having lost everything, or rather at never having had anything to lose!

"Since you have torn up all your poems, I'm convinced that my own poems have no validity," said the Ljósvíkingur. "I don't even know how to write a sonnet."

"We are two kinds of destiny," said Örn Úlfar. "I live in this curiously hollow sound of the first soil falling on the coffin lid. But you, poet, have been raised from the dead."

"When I have been in great distress," said the Ljósvíkingur, "I have always tried to concentrate on what is beautiful and good and to forget what is wicked."

"I acknowledge no beauty for as long as human life is one continuous crime," said Örn Úlfar. "If I did, I would regard myself as a degenerate coward."

"Are you accusing God, then?" asked the Ljósvíkingur.

"If you can convince me that it was God who never wanted daddy and mummy to be able to afford to buy milk for us when we were small; if it's God who prevented us from having enough food for months on end; if it's God who never wanted us to be able to buy firewood to warm our hovel in the winter frosts; if it's God who didn't want us to have clothes to cover our bodies; if it's God who never on any account wanted us children to be free of colds and tonsillitis, winter and summer—yes, then I accuse God. But to tell you the absolute truth, I simply don't believe you can convince me that it is God who governs this village."

"That's what Hlaupa-Halla says, too," said Ólafur Kárason of Ljósavík thoughtfully.

—— 12 ——

Örn Úlfar was, in the eyes of his softhearted friend, the rock against which the injustice of the world would be broken, a mighty, beautiful and awe-inspiring willpower. He did not have one view of life when the sun shone and another when the darkness fell; nothing could shake his convictions, his philosophy provided his feelings with a clear framework and was never their pendulum. Ólafur Kárason was like water which trickles through in various places but has no regular channel.

Admiration for this new friend, and the longing for his company, was a new state of mind, and with it came anxiety about disappointing his hopes, the gnawing certainty that he was not his equal in anything, and the fear of earning his contempt because of his worthlessness. If more than a day passed without their meeting, he gave up all hope, and thought, "He never wants to see me again." He set out in a kind of restlessness, but when he realized that he was on the way to see his friend, he turned back and walked in the opposite direction. When he stood at last in front of the tottering hovel at Skjól, he tried to persuade himself that it was by accident. He stopped at the gate, which scarcely reached up to his knees, and looked around in some embarrassment, like a stranger who has lost his way and finds himself at the wrong house.

"Wonderful weather," said the old fisherman. Because of poor health he was now incapable of doing quarry work, and was pottering about in his tiny cabbage patch.

Ólafur Kárason agreed, and could not take his eyes off him—he found it so odd that this should be his friend's father.

"Yes, such blessed fine weather in the skies," said the old man, still amazed at it all.

"Yes, it's strange," said the poet.

"One thought the night before last that it was clouding over and veering to landward, but it looks as if it will turn out fine after all."

"Yes, it's absolutely amazing," said Ólafur Kárason, and could not understand all this fine weather, either.

Örn Úlfar appeared in the doorway, barefoot in trousers and shirt, ran his fingers through his hair, drew down the corners of his mouth in a haughty horseshoe, knitted his brows and looked out to sea with the far-sighted eyes of a mariner; his face was an inscrutable contradiction to the surroundings. The words of the poetess came to the Ljósvíkingur's mind; face to face with his friend, he could not help asking himself whether it was only men like these who were doomed to become drunkards because they were not clever enough to become criminals, and because society was too abject to be able to create heroes.

His mother called out from somewhere inside, "Fie on you and put your shoes on, I say, and see that you keep your shirt buttoned up to the neck!"

He made no reply, but shrugged his shoulders, snorted, and pulled a face.

She came after him to the door: "I won't have you going out bare-foot and bare-necked, child! What d'you think people would say?"

He replied in his deep voice: "My feet are my own. And my neck, too."

The mother: "You know you've got a weak chest, child."

This child of beauty and renouncer of it—could anyone imagine a more alien guest in this tottering hovel, where the horrid hallmark of penury was branded on the living and the dead alike? No, he preferred to walk barefoot rather than to disgrace his feet with tattered shoes, and to go about bare-necked rather than cover his young chest with rags.

They sat together for hours on the sea crags at the foot of the mountain and looked back towards the village, and he told the Ljósvíkingur all about the conditions of the people who waited there to be bought and sold. It was well into the night before they realized it, but he went on talking. He went into great detail about everything; in the end it was as if his narrative became one with the expanse of the summer night itself, so broadly and quietly did he speak, and yet always in the background was the wild surf of midwinter. The destinies of nameless people, uneventful and monotonous, of people who were nothing, who did not even have a face in the world—suddenly they had begun to take shape, gradually they were beginning to rise up sonorously, beginning to matter, even to shout. There was no longer any escape, one had to listen, one had to answer, one even had to defend oneself; before one knew it, their pointless destinies had forced themselves into one's own blood.

A young woman came walking toward him on the road and peered at him, and the daylight gleamed in her white, crystalline eyes that seemed to reflect both red and green. Yes, she had recognized him all right. She halted on the road in front of him and smiled.

"Are you afraid?"

"No," he said. "Hallo."

"You were going to walk right past me."

"No," he said.

"Yes, you were," she said. "Fie on you!"

At that he said solemnly, "Þórunn, you are the last person I would pass by on the road. I owe you my life."

She looked at him with her ambiguous eyes, as she had done once before, first at his hair, then at his hands, then into his eyes, and finally away from him, sideways, in another direction, suddenly absentminded, and hummed a few bars from a new melody. But although she did not look directly at him he felt all too clearly that she had not let go of him, and his heart beat a little faster and he felt a little frightened, because the thought occurred to him that she might perhaps take his health away from him again.

"I've heard that you just say what anyone wants to hear," she said.

"You yourself know better than anyone what I have to thank you for, Þórunn," he said, but to be honest, he no longer understood the person (if he could call himself that) who had come to visit this strange semi-albino on a stretcher across the mountains to receive his life from her.

"Why do you look at me like that?" she asked. "You don't even shake hands with me. You're frightened."

Why did she keep on accusing him of being afraid? Did she have some evil intention? Surely she was not going to take his health away from him again? He gave her his hand.

"I simply don't know you any more," she said, and directed the cold light of her eyes on him, sideways. "How stupid it is to go to all that trouble for strangers! Even though you raise them from the dead, they've forgotten all about you in a week; they don't even recognize you in the road."

"You who get gold coins from all over the country for curing people!" he said.

"Shut up!" she said.

He shut up. Her new melody was much more restless than the old waltz, and not nearly so agreeable; he did not like to hear people singing while they were talking to you.

"Why don't you want to have a stroll with me," she said, "since I have given you your life?" And when they had moved off: "How very strange you are!"

He did not say anything.

"Why don't you say something?" she asked.

"You told me to shut up," he replied.

"I didn't mean it that way," she said.

"What am I to say?" he said.

"Anything at all," she said. "Say something to me because it's me. And because you're a poet. Say something so that I can find myself because you're a poet."

"What do you mean?" he said.

She hummed a snatch of her tune, absently. Then, out of the blue: "We've lost the farm. We couldn't pay. We were evicted yesterday."

"Why?"

"When you can't pay, you get evicted."

"Couldn't Friðrik help you?" he asked innocently.

She halted abruptly on the road, slapped him on the face, and said angrily, "Shut up, you should be ashamed of yourself!"

He put his hand to his cheek, even though it did not hurt very much, and said, "Why do you strike me?"

There was some blend of hatred and other suffering around her mouth, and he was afraid of it.

"Is that jibe to be the thanks I get for making him call you back to life when you were more dead than death itself?" she asked.

"Þórunn, I thank you with all my heart, all my soul, all . . ."

"Oh, shut your trap," she said.

They walked on for a while in silence, she did not even hum her tune. Suddenly she put her face on his arm and said with childlike sincerity, looking up at his face, almost pleadingly, "Ólafur, if you love truth at all, will you tell me the absolute truth about one thing?"

"What's that?" he asked.

"Do you really and truly believe that I cured you? Will you tell me the truth? Just one word, just this once. Then I'll never ask you again. Then you'll never have to tell the truth about anything again."

"What is truth?" he asked.

"Yes, I knew you'd be a damned Herod!" she said. "You're a damned Herod!"

"I came to you, a crossbearer on a stretcher and an outcast from humanity, and I went from you a conquerer of life," he said.

"I don't understand poetry," she said. "I'm asking for yes or no."

"Yes," he said.

"All right, then you can pay me ten krónur," she said.

At this unexpected suggestion he became acutely embarrassed and blushed to the roots of his hair. "To be absolutely honest, Þórunn, I've never had any money in my life. I've never earned ten krónur all my life. As you yourself know, I haven't been able to work at all for the last two years. But if I can get a job with the Regeneration Company this summer, then I can perhaps hope to have some money by the autumn."

"Work, work, work! It makes me sick listening to you," she said. "If you can't get hold of ten krónur at once, then I don't look upon you as a man."

"How am I to do that, Þórunn? Doesn't one perhaps always have to work first and get paid afterwards?"

"How incredibly stupid you are!" she said. "What d'you think you'll get out of working? D'you think I myself don't know what it is to work? It's ludicrous to work."

"But it's still the only way to earn money," he said.

"On the contrary," she said. "Working only teaches you to hate those who don't work, that's to say those who have the money. To work is to hate. To work is to be bored. To work is to have nothing to eat, it's to be unable to pay, it's to lose your farm, it's to be evicted. You are quite unbelievably stupid."

"Yes," he said, "it's true that I'm stupid. When I was little, I was always beaten with a birch for shirking. And if I said what I thought, my supper was taken from me and I was told I would go to hell. It may well be that I'm not independent enough to see the truth, much less to tell it if I happen to see it. One can't help the way one was brought up, Þórunn. You yourself know best what I was only a fortnight ago, when you called me back to life."

"Anyone who values his own life at all can always get hold of ten krónur, however useless he might be in other respects," she said. "I need ten krónur. From you."

"Þórunn," he said pleadingly. "What am I to do?"

"What if I strike you sick again unless you bring me ten krónur?" she asked.

At that he went weak at the knees and began to see a white fog before his eyes and broke into a sweat. This encounter was becoming an anguished dream, a nightmare. The time had to come when he would have to suffer his punishment for betraying God and Jesus, as he had suspected up on the mountain the moment he first heard about Þórunn and Friðrik. That time was now at hand. His life and his health were in the hands of irresponsible mystical powers; this Norn* could strike him down whenever she wished. . . .

"Well, if it isn't the spirit-girl with an earthly man on her arm, hahaha!"

He was startled out of his despair in front of Fagrabrekka, and there was Vegmey Hansdóttir standing in the doorway, jeering at them.

"What's the bitch of Fagrabrekka yelping about?" said the spirit-girl.

The girl in the doorway called out to a dozen children in the nearby ditches and fences and said, "D'you see the freak and the angel-girl, children?"

The children pursued them for a while with obscenities and abuse and dirt-throwing, and became twice as boisterous when the spirit-girl turned on them and gave them a taste of superior upbringing. But after a time the children could not be bothered chasing them any farther.

"Only ten krónur—from you; so that I can find myself. Even if it's only five krónur—for the truth."

"I wish I had a thousand krónur, Þórunn."

"Then I wouldn't want to talk to you," she said.

"I have an idea," he said, "and that is to go and see Pétur, the manager. . . ."

"I could get ten krónur from Pétur Þríhross myself," she said, "a hundred krónur, a thousand krónur. That's the one thing I don't want. Anything but that."

"I'll give you everything I have," he said.

"What have you got?"

"A few books," he said.

They were down on the shore road now, and when they reached the Privy Councillor's castle he asked her to wait while he went inside. He came out again with *The Felsenburg Stories*.

"This is my biggest book," he said, "and in many ways the most remarkable. It must be possible to sell it for five krónur or even ten."

They sat down on a boulder on the beach.

"This is just a tattered old book," she said. "Who d'you think would want to buy this old thing?"

"You've no idea of all the things that are contained in this book, Þórunn," he said.

"Are you fond of it?" she asked.

"This is a book of destiny; both the hopes and disappointments of life are bound up in this book," he said, and indeed he greatly regretted parting with the book, but would gladly sacrifice it for his health. "I wouldn't give this book to anyone but you."

"I wouldn't accept a tattered old thing like this from anyone," she said, and held it absentmindedly on her lap and began to hum her new tune again, which was not nearly so agreeable as the old tune. The fringes of the waves lapped at the boulder.

"You have reddish hair," she said in the middle of the tune and looked at him sideways, and her crystalline ambiguous look and her inscrutable smile shone on him as they had done that memorable night at Kambar. But it no longer enchanted him; on the contrary, the longer she looked at him the harder it was to bear it.

"Let me touch your hand," she said, and touched his long, slim hand, leaned forward over his hands and touched the palms and backs. "I've never seen a hand like that in my life. Do you remember the night at home at Kambar, when we sat in the homefield and you laid your head here?"—and she pointed to the place where he had laid his head.

He simply could not understand how it had ever occurred to him to lay his head there, and he looked away.

She said, "It isn't true what Reimar said about six men. I was once with a man a little bit, but I was just a child then. For a whole winter after that, I was determined to kill myself. But then I began to see into another world. Since then I have seen only into another world. As God is above us, you're quite safe in believing that I'm telling you the truth. Listen, is it true that there's something between you and that hussy at Fagrabrekka?"

"She's no hussy," he said evenly, but he went pale and something inside him began to quiver.

"So she's not a hussy? Well, if that's what you say, then it's quite obvious you're sleeping with her at night, like everyone says."

"No. It's not true."

"Then why was she jeering at me?"

"I don't know."

"Why don't you say something?" she said.

"What am I to say?"

"Oh, I don't know," she said, and tossed her head and made a grimace of impatience. "You're so damned boring, what the devil am I doing here with you?"

"We happened to meet on the road," he said.

"No," she said, "that's a lie, I was looking for you. You were the only person in the village I wanted to meet; it's because you have hair and eyes and hands that remind me of something, I haven't the faintest idea what. And because I woke you up from the dead. I hoped you would help me today, because if it doesn't happen today—listen, I want so much to ask you about one thing. Do you really think there is another world? Isn't it all just a lie? And do you think there is such a thing as truth, on the whole? Don't you think that spiritualism is just a lot of piffle? Don't you think you just pop off, just like any other damned carcass, which is all we really are, when you eventually expire?"

"I have often asked myself the same question," he said.

"Tcha, you just don't want to say it," she said. "You don't want to tell me. D'you know that last night I was offered a hundred krónur, a thousand krónur, a million? I was offered the chance of becoming a scientist and being famous all over the world."

"Really?" he said.

But when he was no more impressed than that, she became sad, buried her face in her hands and shook her head in despair. "You won't help me," she half-sobbed into her hands. "I'll die."

Then she took her hands away from her face and leaned over, staring at him.

"Your face!" she groaned helplessly, and was suddenly not a sorceress any more. "It's as if it were engraved inside me; I hate it. I don't care about anything now; d'you hear me? Anything!"

Then the look in his eyes turned as cold as ice; there was a hard grimace on her face, at once rude and malevolent; he had seldom seen anything so loathsome.

"And now you can go and be ill again!" she said, and hit him in the face with the book and then threw it into the sea as far as she could, and a few gulls dipped in their flight and thought it might be something for them.

She stood up and walked rapidly away toward the village.

—— **13** ——

That night he stood at the paneless window and looked at the drops dripping from the roof, because it had now started to rain; there was no wind, and the drops fell straight to the ground with a gentle sound that boded peace. He struck his chest with his fist, kneaded his abdomen and rapped his brow and temples with his knuckles to see if he could detect any signs of illness, but he did not even have a headache, let alone anything worse. He was dejected over having been unable to do anything for Þórunn of Kambar, apart from giving her that tattered old story book which he had not even bothered to read right through to the end; indeed the girl had not cared to own it and had thrown it at once to the illiterate gulls of the sea. On the other hand the boy was relieved that he was no longer beholden to this girl or to the mystical powers she controlled; and he was perhaps even happier because God, whom he still believed to be the most powerful of all the mystical forces, had not punished him for turning to secret mystical powers which were bound to be in more or less for-bidden competition with the One. Yet the strangest thing of all was that the stronger this young poet felt, the more often it occurred to him that perhaps, when all was said and done, he had some mystical power within himself, just as it says in the old Sagas about long-gone heroes, who had a remarkable mystical power within themselves which they called their might and main, and in which they believed, and their faith was justified no less than that of others, even though this power seemed to be of exclusively earthly origin.

But at the end of this day one memory remained in his conscious-ness like a wound. How could she have brought herself to call him a freak again, when he was walking innocently past her house with a girl from another world, yes, and what's more, after she had given him to understand that she had not meant anything by kissing him the other day? How could she bring herself to set all these awful chil-dren on a defenseless man, since she had not meant anything at all? Are human beings so inconsistent, not just in love and hatred (which is a different matter), but also when they do not care at all? Or do human beings, when it comes to that, not deserve to have people look up to them and expect great things of them and believe in them, the way dogs do? Luckily the gentle, peaceful rain of an early sum-mer night conquered the pain and conjured a dreamless sleep into the poet's breast instead of filling it with philosophical conclusions.

And he woke up from this deep sleep at the touch of someone's hand on his brow.

It could not have been long past midnight, because there was still no sign of that lightening which heralds the dawn, even in a clouded sky. It was just that time of a spring night when things are not real but unreal, the moment in which the consciousness has the greatest difficulty in believing and calls in question when day is begun. The girl from the doorway was sitting on the edge of his bed, and had put her hand on his brow. He opened his eyes and asked, "Am I awake, or am I dead?"

"Will you forgive me?" she asked, and stroked his hair, then took her hand away again.

She spoke softly, not loud and shrill, and she did not laugh at all.

She was flushed and breathless from running, her feet were wet from the sea, and there was sand in her footprints. She stared at him with large, wild eyes as if in anguish, and that cheerful, saucy expression was gone from her mouth.

"I couldn't sleep," she whispered.

He murmured her name, sat up, and put his arms round her, and when she felt him touch her she quickly moved right up against him.

"I wish I didn't exist," she whispered, and buried her face in his shoulder. "Didn't exist."

"What has happened?" he asked.

"Nothing," she said. "Nothing. Nothing. I couldn't sleep. Will you forgive me?"

"Will you kiss me?" he said.

When they had kissed for a while, she said, "You haven't got a crush on that spirit-girl, have you? Say no."

"No," he said.

"Well," she said, "that's all right then. A phony, pretentious angel-woman like her! When I get some flour I'll bake you a hundred thousand times better pancakes than at Kambar. But I haven't any boracic acid."

"It isn't very kind of you to speak so badly of the poor girl," said Ólafur Kárason. "If I hadn't been cured at her hands, I might never have got to know you."

"If she can cure one single person of so much as a cold, then I'll save the whole world from death and the devil!"

"It still wasn't very kind of you to jeer at us when we were walking innocently along the road, and to call me a freak. . . ."

"Will you forgive me, or do you hate me?" she asked.

"I love you," he said.

"What did she want with you?" asked the girl.

"It doesn't matter," he said. "She didn't want anything with me. Just to talk to me about something, be–because I stayed the night at Kambar the other day. Don't ask any more about it. Just kiss."

But the girl in the doorway did not want to kiss any more: "So you know how to lie after all? Who would have believed that of those blue eyes?" she said.

"No," he said, "I don't know how to lie. But I don't know what truth is, either. I always try to speak the way I think will cause least trouble to God and men."

"Oh, I know well enough what she wanted; there's only one thing she wants, that spirit-girl! I've known her to leave a Churchyard Ball here at Sviðinsvík with a man in a snowstorm and darkness at night."

"Leave?" he said. "I don't believe it."

"Of course she wanted to sleep with you!" she said.

"How can you think such a wicked thing of any girl?" he asked.

At that she nestled closer to him and said, "I really must be out of my mind. Oh, Jesus, I wish I didn't exist," and kissed him.

He loved her with all his heart, eternally, and was ready to sacrifice his life for her and walk through fire and sea, and nothing, nothing, would ever, ever separate them, but she had become anxious again, even frightened, and moved away from him with a start, opened her eyes wide and asked, panic-stricken, into the blue—"Is it wicked?"

"No," he said, without knowing what it was he was answering. "It is beautiful."

"Why do I exist?" she asked.

"To love," he said.

"Oh, Jesus!" she said.

"No," he said blasphemously. "Just you and I."

"Tell me I'm out of my mind," she said. "And I'll go."

"Love is always right," he said. "Everything you do is right."

"I wasn't even thinking about you. I had got the children to bed and wasn't thinking about you at all, and daddy had started snoring long ago, and I wasn't thinking about you at all; you didn't even cross my mind. I was in bed and had been lying in bed for a long time. And all of a sudden I was up. Had I then been thinking about you all the time?"

"You were thinking of making this haven of the winds the Palace of the Summerland," said the poet.

"I thought to myself that since the whole village says that he comes to me at night, then it's best that I go to him one night for a change! I opened the window above my bed and jumped out, so that daddy and the children wouldn't wake up when I went to the door. I ran straight down to the beach with a sack as if I were going to gather seaweed. Who was talking about wading through the sea? It was me who waded through the sea. I crawled round beneath the cliffs when the tide was coming in so that no one should see me, and waded through the water, can't you see that my feet are all wet, man? I really must be out of my mind, doing that on a bright spring night!"

"You came to bring me the greatest treasure in life and make me king over it," said the poet.

"No," she said. "I came to hear you breathe. Breathe for me."

"Oh, you who hasn't even wanted to laugh for me for days on end, and told me to go home instead," he whispered in her ear.

"You don't laugh when you've got a crush; if you laugh, then you don't have a crush," she said, and added hahaha from old habit, but it was not laughter.

"And today you jeered at me and set the children on me."

"Oh, you're such a great poet that you understand everything, and yet you haven't the faintest idea about anything. There's no one like you; I can't help the effect you have on me. I've never known anything so stupid, and I know perfectly well that I shouldn't and don't want to and won't. You're only seventeen and I'm eighteen, and where's the money to come from, and yet I love you so much that I hate you, yes, God help me. Love is such a wild beast, I'm not even myself; I waded up to the knees in seawater beneath the cliffs so that no one should see me. When you've got a crush you're like a criminal, God help me; I could kill someone and steal; that's how wicked I am—can't you feel I'm not wearing anything under my dress, man?"

The poetess gave him his morning coffee in silence and busied herself with her housework. He did not dare to look at her, but heard her clearing her throat in that high-pitched, silver-strung voice, it was as if she were far away. All the same he felt her nearness more than ever before. He had gained new perception from his experience of the night. The world was different from what it had been; he saw no man, no woman, in the same light as before. Suddenly he was beginning to think of how this woman would be, and was at once seized by a feeling of guilt. Her face, that indefinable blend of distance and nearness, yearning and denial, curiosity and indifference, that insolubly bewitching discord of to be or not to be—all at once he felt that no face had ever mattered so much to him, that this face really mattered more to him than his own face; and he had betrayed it; betrayed her; and he was convinced that she knew it, that she knew everything.

Yes, it was true; love was more precious than anything else. The supernatural was frankly ridiculous in comparison with the natural, in the same way in which miracles are contemptible in comparison with deeds. The living form of a young, loving woman—that is the key to beauty itself, the undertone of the world's poetry. And the sun shone on the face of this young man, and the clamor of the gulls was carried through the open window on the fresh sea breeze; but nevertheless in his consciousness there lingered a certain sense of loss, as if he had betrayed something that was more precious even than all this.

— 14 —

The trawler *Númi*, the property of the Regeneration Company of Sviðinsvík, had been allowed to lie rusting in peace in the anchorage, collecting rats and, some said, ghosts, because they thought they had seen a blue light flickering about on the ship on winter nights. During the years when she had been operating for the Regeneration Company's account on the best fishing grounds in the world, just offshore, she had only succeeded in amassing higher and higher debts at the bank, tens of thousands and hundreds of thousands in debts, sums which, together with the other debts of this powerful company, would have sufficed to make every single villager a count or a baron. On the other hand, it so happened that all the fish fled the sea as soon as the ship appeared on the scene. Two years ago, the board of the Regeneration Company had finally hit upon the brilliant idea of laying the ship up and letting her collect rats in the anchorage instead of debts at the bank. It was now the general hope that some good man or other would want to buy the estate from the Regeneration Company, just as it stood, debts and all; but buyers were not rushing to come forward. Finally the bank had made it clear that it had exhausted its Christian forbearance, which is such a hall-mark of these institutions, and was going to sequestrate the ship for unpaid debts and accumulated interest, and sell her off by auction in the near future.

Then one morning at the start of the haymaking season, when people happened to look out toward the anchorage as the fog was lifting (for there had been a very heavy fog), the people's trawler had disappeared completely. It was little wonder that everyone was a bit surprised—what had happened to the people's trawler? Had she been stolen? Or had the bank come for her? People went to see the man-ager and asked why their trawler had vanished, but the manager only replied, in Danish, that he was no Icelander, s'help him. But later that day word came that a rat-bitten life belt with the ship's name on it had been washed ashore farther down the fjord, and then it was thought unnecessary to make any further guesses about the ship's fate. Rats and rust had combined to gnaw through her, and she had sunk.

Strange as it may seem, the loss of the ship caused considerable emotion in the village; on the other hand it did not affect Ólafur Kárason at all, for he had no memories bound up with the ship, much less any hopes for the future. But he could not avoid hearing all sorts of things about the ship's disappearance, some whispered and some uttered openly. Only now did the people realize that they could probably have lived off this ship instead of carrying rocks for the government, year after year.

At least there had been some vague security in seeing the ship lying there, even though she was red with rust and manned only by rodents and revenants. While the ship had been afloat, it was as if the people nurtured in their hearts some obscurely reasoned hope that one day she would put out to sea with a brave crew from the village, determined to bring in a million-krónur catch from the inexhaustible stocks of the fishing grounds just outside, where other ships, some of them from distant parts of the country and others from foreign lands, harvested wealth and plenty before the very eyes of the local inhabitants. But now the ship had sunk. And when the ship had sunk, it was as if the village woke up halfway down a precipice.

The parish officer wanted to call a meeting of the board of the Regeneration Company at once and come to some decisions, but there were difficulties involved, because the directors were not available: the sheriff lived in another fjord, Pastor Brandur was making a visitation to the remoter parishes, the doctor had been mortal drunk every night for a week, and the manager, Pétur Pálsson, was no Icelander. No one on the board cared in the least, except the fifth member, the parish officer. And since it had proved impossible to arrange a board meeting immediately after the loss of the ship, he set off nonetheless to see the sheriff, leaving no one in doubt about the nature of his errand: he was going to demand a court of inquiry into the whole matter, and call for Pétur Pálsson to be sacked as manager and preferably arrested and taken south in fetters. No one doubted that he himself would be more than willing to undertake the management of the company, especially since the parish was now on the county.

Time passed. Finally word came that the sheriff certainly intended to come to Sviðinsvík at a suitable opportunity and hold a court of inquiry into the trawler case, but getting Pétur Pálsson sacked and taken south in fetters was reckoned to be much more difficult to arrange. Pétur had been appointed manager for five years and enjoyed the boundless confidence of the sheriff and the government, quite apart from the fact that he was the pastor's sole supporter in spiritual matters and by far the largest purchaser of brennivín from the doctor. In certain newspapers down south he was constantly represented as one of the most notable and capable socialists in the country. And although the village never tired of flaying him behind his back, he was nevertheless the only person the village turned to and trusted when the pinch came, not least the mothers and widows, because he was a man who could not bear to see misery and was always ready to do everything he could for other people.

What was the parish officer to do? This worthy boat-builder and crofter-fisherman, who was as honest as gold and did not know the meaning of fickleness, even though he was totally incapable of thinking and talking like an educated person, had now had enough of a good thing. When all else had failed, he hit upon the good idea of turning to the villagers, to the Regeneration Company's ordinary members, the small shareholders and those who had mortgaged their possessions to the company for provisions, and trying to get them together for a meeting. He enlisted the support of a few interested villagers, sent out notice of the meeting, and nailed an advertisement to the telegraph pole at the crossroads, in which he explained that since the majority of the board had other things to do, he himself, as the parish's representative to the Regeneration Company, was calling a public meeting of that company in the village hall tonight at eight o'clock, in order to combat criminal activity and autocratic conduct in the community and to pass a resolution to destroy the weeds and vipers that had been allowed to grow and flourish among the people here on the estate.

Fortunately, this tedious wrangle for the most part passed Ólafur Kárason by—this man who thought only about spiritual values and adored beauty and worshiped love as far as it was possible. And now a love affair had been added to all this, with the special experience it brings when it happens for the first time; his outlook, in a word, was lyrical. He got his friend, Örn Úlfar, to explain to him the mysteries of the sonnet one calm night when the sea was all gold and velvet, and now he felt that no other verse-form mattered.

But when his friend sided completely with the parish officer, that cold-hearted man who had no compassion for poor poets in delicate health who had to carry rocks, and suddenly started going from door to door to summon people to a meeting arranged by this unspiritual, obstinate man against Pétur Pálsson the manager, that friend of the spirit, Ólafur Kárason could not understand his friend any longer. "It's probably because he always sees his little sister on her bier and feels that she was murdered," the poet thought to himself, and was sorry for his friend and forgave him. "Perhaps I wouldn't write poetry either if I had brothers and sisters who had been murdered."

Haymaking: and over the village there lay this strong fragrance of new-mown hay that one only finds on the first days when the grass is put to the scythe. He was brimming with poetic sympathy for the young grass that was being mown by a scythe, and he himself was the mower—very stiffly at first, to be sure, but improving with every day. All experience is wonderful while it still retains the freshness of novelty and is material for a poem. It is poetic to mow hay—just a little, not for too long. When any experience has lost the novelty of freshness, the poet is no longer happy. It is intensely tedious to mow for a long time.

After a week he had begun to hope that the summer were over, so that he would not have to think about hay but could have the day to himself to compose sonnets. Sometimes inspiration seized him so powerfully in the meadow that he had to write the poem down on the handle of the scythe. Luckily the foreman was drunk and the pressure of work not so demanding. Often, early in the morning when the weather was fine and he had not yet become tired of mowing, he would recall his poems and be quite convinced that he was now a major poet even though he had not yet received any public recognition. He was determined to make his way to Aðalfjörður that autumn and have his collection of poems printed there, so that the public could enjoy the noble thoughts of a young man who had not only borne a heavy cross but had also been allowed to drink from the cup of joy. He was sure that as soon as he was recognized as a major poet his mother would ask his forgiveness for having sent him away in a sack in winter, and he decided to forgive her and stay with her if she so wished. Perhaps she would help him to go to secondary school, and he would not only be a major poet but a man of learning as well.

Recognition as a poet first came to him without warning one day, after great travail. That is how every poet's major victories come about. He was standing in the meadow one morning, little suspecting that fame was now on its way. It was the same day on which the parish officer had nailed his advertisement to the telegraph pole. One of the manager's children suddenly appeared in the mown field in front of the poet and handed him this note:

"Present yourself tonight as a living witness to contacts with the next world and compose a good poem about the necessity of science in human society, particularly spiritualism, and bring it to the Psychic Research Society of Sviðinsvík which intellectuals and educational pioneers are due to inaugurate tonight in my drawing room. You will be permitted to read your own poem aloud in your own name in the presence of myself, the sheriff, the rural dean, the doctor, etc. P.S. Bring your hymnbook with you."

Was it any wonder that this orphan poet was excited, this man who had until now been the outcast of humanity because of his loyalty to the intellect? That is how the wheel of fortune can turn. He, who in spring had been lying like mouldy meat-paste in a corner in a remote valley, was now, at harvest time, being summoned by the most important man of a great estate to help establish a society; yes, and what's more, a genuine and public scientific society of learned men and gentry to conduct psychic research, and there he was to be allowed to read a poem of his own in his own name. Often he had been on the point of giving up his chosen road. For two years he had lain helpless in bed after suffering the blows of beasts, men, and gods. But he had never given up. Now he was beginning to reap his reward; the time was at hand at last when, as he had always suspected, the spirit would be properly appreciated and would be victorious in men's lives. Everything, everything one had had to suffer in the battle for one's self, for the desire to exist, this one thing one possessed—everything, everything, everything was forgotten in the moment of victory, was forgotten and ceased to exist, like the baby's first tears, the mother's first anger, the first snowstorm. He laid his scythe aside and praised God.

The sheriff came over the mountain with seven horses and his clerk, because tomorrow there was to be a court of inquiry. He stayed with Pétur the manager as usual. Ólafur Kárason worked away furiously and composed a solemn congratulatory ode to Science and the

Soul on the occasion of their visit to the village, hoping that these two parties might find one another in Truth, without venturing to define their nature any more closely. An icy shiver of excitement went through him every time he remembered that the sheriff himself, the man who stood as far above parish officers as parish officers stood above parish paupers, was to listen to this poem, and in the evening he had no appetite, only nausea.

He had the poem in his pocket and was waiting the whole time for the poetess to ask to hear it, but she did not ask. On the other hand she offered to cut his hair so that he would appear before the gentry as an intellectual, and this he accepted. She lent him her husband's Sunday-best trousers and jersey, but there was no jacket to fit such a slender man.

"How lucky the manager is to have got himself a poet in my place," she said.

"Aren't you invited?" he said.

"I'm not spiritual," she said. "I'm grateful just so long as I'm allowed to stay in a barn loft."

Then he said, "I do so want to let you hear my poem."

"I don't want to hear it," she said. "Not before it's in ashes."

"I don't understand you now," he said.

"Poems are best when they're in ashes," she replied roundly. "When the lettering is faded and the book burnt, only then does the worth of the poem come to light."

"Still, I'm quite sure that I've seldom or never succeeded so well with a poem before," he said.

"If you succeed in writing it into the heart of the nation, then it's a good poem," she said. "There is no other yardstick."

She finished cutting his hair. She looked at him with her distant smile, and the evening sun shone through the window. He did not understand her and could not bring himself to say any more, because he felt that in conversation with her he became more stupid than in conversation with other people: those deep, sincere eyes that saw everything but said nothing. But the riddle remained: how was it that Pétur the manager was spiritual, while the poetess was not?

— 15 —

The gentry sat in plush armchairs in the manager's best room; the sheriff sat facing the door with his hands clasped and twiddling his thumbs, his paunch flowing over his thighs, his fat official's cheeks calling to mind that part of the body which is considered the least related to the face. The pastor incessantly brushed the dust off himself and snorted, his worsted suit threadbare from decades of brushing. The gaunt secretary, bespectacled, sat beside his master, Pétur the manager, swallowing saliva, the movement of his Adam's apple the only certain sign of life in him. The doctor sat hunched in a chair in front of his wife and stared out into the blue with the swimming eyes of a man who had long ago stopped knowing whether it was night or day. If a spoken word, or a passing face, provoked an association of ideas in his mind so that he felt a desire to express himself, his wife put her hand to his mouth at once and said "Uss!"; whereupon the doctor said "By God," and laughed in a mixture of bad temper and silliness and tried to bite her, but not hard.

On a row of broken-back seats, three-legged stools, and folding chairs that had been brought in for the occasion, sat three widows and four women who had recently lost their children, and who never moved a muscle, but sat staring straight ahead with an expression of petrified auguish as if their throats were about to be cut. One of them was the woman from Skjól.

The room had been arranged in such a way that those attending the meeting formed a circle. And in the middle of the circle, between the sheriff and the manager, there in a crimson dress and brand-new shoes as if she were going to a Churchyard Ball, with a string of pearls and a diamond ring, sat Þórunn of Kambar, the spirit-girl herself, ambiguous, semi-albino and crystalline, sniffing innocently. There was no seat there for the poet, Ólafur Kárason of Ljósavík, and nobody noticed his arrival except the manager's lean, taciturn wife, who said he could stand by the wall in the corner behind the door.

Since no others were expected, the manager began his speech.

When he had given the sheriff a particularly warm welcome to this inaugural meeting, which he said would mark a new epoch in the village, he turned at once to the kernel of the matter. He set forth once again the views which were no longer entirely unfamiliar to Ólafur Kárason, that nothing was nearly so important in this life as science, above all the science which was devoted to proving the existence of an afterlife. He said that the higher powers had become so tangible nowadays that even doctors and pastors no longer needed to feel offended, or feel put upon, even though the influence of intelligent agencies on human life was demonstrated beyond doubt. (The doctor, from out of his drunken stupor: "What are angels—birds or mammals? By God!")

"It gladdens me that our learned and distinguished doctor is no exception to this rule; he is both bird and mammal and angel in one and the same person, if I may put it that way. As for the pastor and Christianity, on the other hand, I would take the liberty of pointing out that we all know that the church has declined disastrously in Sviðinsvík and elsewhere over the past few years, to such an extent, even, that it has proved impossible to scrape up a congregation for services except twice or thrice a year at the most—for confirmation, Holy Communion, and Christmas Day; and sometimes it hasn't even proved possible to drive people into church at Christmas."

The manager said that the cause of this religious apathy was not that God had ceased to exist nor that we had an incompetent pastor. "No," said the manager, "God is eternal, and he certainly exists. And as for our pastor, I shall be the first and last to testify to the fact that it would be difficult to imagine a better comrade and guide in everything that concerns the prosperity of this village and its regeneration.

"On the other hand, the mood of the times is for science, not faith, and this is something no one can change, however good a pastor he may be, and indeed our own pastor has been the first to realize that the mood of the times demands proofs instead of sacraments, a tangible assurance of the soul's speedy and decisive victory immediately at death instead of vague promises of an uncertain resurrection on the Last Day. But it would only be half the pleasure to see the learned men of the county gathered here to establish a scientific research society, if behind the founding of this society there were not other pillars, I am tempted to say even stronger pillars, and by that I mean the nation itself, the people. By accepting our invitation to participate, the public has shown that it, too, is ready to honor the highest visions of science. It is with very special feelings, which I find it very difficult to describe, that I take the liberty of welcoming to this meeting the nation, the public, these poor and uneducated mothers and widows. Because for whom is science, the true science, the only essential science—spiritualism? It is for the poor, uneducated women of the people. It is chiefly for our wretched, blessed, poverty-stricken widows and mothers who have had to watch their loved ones depart to a better world in more or less harrowing ways. Because religious faith cannot show these destitute people that existence is by nature divine, then science must do so, and though we may have to do without some trivial things in this world, happiness awaits us in the Summerland to which our loved ones have gone before us. . . ."

"Give me another drink!" bawled the doctor, and bit his wife. "Give me some more of that damned poison!"

"Patience, my dear fellow," said Pétur Pálsson the manager. "And you, dear friends who are gathered here tonight—what was it I was going to say again? . . ."

"Mm—the English lord, English lord," whispered the secretary, after swallowing carefully.

"Yes," said the manager. "The English lord. It so happens that a famous English lord of noble rank, apart from the fact that he is a world-famous lawyer, professor and doctor, and really a most excellent man, hmmmm . . ." And the manager bent down to his secretary again and asked in a half-whisper, "What was his name again?"

"He's called Oliver Lodge," said the secretary. "Mm—Sir Oliver Lodge."*

"His name is Sir Ólafur Lodds," continued the manager, "and he has established with absolutely irrefutable evidence how earthly men can communicate, through mediums, with another world. This has revolutionized religious life in Great Britain and in America, and in a few years has transformed churches into purely scientific institutions. There are six hundred churches in England and I can't unfortunately remember how many in America which have changed into scientific institutions in this way in a very short time, to which millions of people flock every Sunday to receive proofs instead of sacraments. In the old days people fiddled with tables and glasses, but people stopped using inanimate objects long ago, and now one can get direct communication while the medium is in a trance and can speak to anyone one wants just like through a modern telephone exchange. There are even several instances from both England and America of the Creator of the world and the Savior being heard through a medium."

Finally the manager gave the village the glad news that it had now secured a medium with spiritual gifts of the highest order. "So now it will be within our power to seek information from a higher world whenever we are in difficulties, and receive comfort from our dear departed ones and from world-famous spirits in the Summerland when sorrows and cares afflict our homes.

"This girl, as some of you in the village probably know, has been in contact with supernatural powers and higher beings for some time, and many people in this part of the country have given evidence under oath that they were cured of various incurable illnesses through her mediation. But of all her cures, I reckon the most remarkable was that she as good as raised from the dead that young, promising, and poetical parish pauper standing over there in the corner behind the door, who has come here tonight at my request to present himself before this esteemed company and bear witness to the necessity for spiritualism, not only by his presence but also with a poem I have permitted him to write."

At this point the doctor began to retch, and the manager's wife slipped out to fetch a pail. The doctor's wife held her husband's forehead while he vomited, gave him water to drink when he had finished, made him comfortable in his chair, and spread a handkerchief over his face. There was a pause in the proceedings while the doctor was vomiting, and the promising young rhymester, parish pauper and miracle-ninny stood behind the door shaking with terror at having to make a public appearance at a scientific society. But then the sheriff stopped twiddling his thumbs for a moment and said that as things stood in this parish at present, esteemed members would doubtless have quite enough of seeing this parish pauper and knowing that he had been woken up from the dead at their expense, without having to start listening to him reciting poetry into the bargain, and anyway poetry had no place in a scientific research society; he permitted himself to hope that the experiments would start as soon as possible.

At that the manager said that the sheriff was quite right, they did not have time to listen to poetry tonight. "In a scientific society the only poetry that has any place is that which can produce proofs. British psychologists reckon that nothing is better suited to producing proofs than hymn-singing and the Lord's Prayer, and that's why I have asked everyone to bring their hymnbooks; but I hope most of you know a few bits of the Lord's Prayer already."

The manager now began to play the harmonium and asked the company to sing. Þórunn of Kambar had the lamp turned down. "Praise the Lord, the King of Heaven," all verses. The doctor was out for the count with the handkerchief over his face. Þórunn of Kambar settled herself comfortably in the armchair, took off her shoes, stretched her legs out on the floor and closed her eyes. By the time they reached the middle of the hymn her body began to twitch, she started gasping a little for breath, and a series of rattling noises and small cries came from her throat. When the last verse of the hymn was over she said thickly, "Put out the lamp, and turn your thoughts to the light."

The light was extinguished and they began to say the Lord's Prayer. "Again!" whispered the manager in near ecstasy, and the Lord's Prayer was recited over and over again. When the Lord's Prayer had been recited about twenty times, Pétur whispered, "Little Þórunn, Þórunn dear," but she didn't reply. "Are you awake, dear little Þórunn?" asked the manager, "or have you fallen into the trance?"

Silence.

"She has fallen into the trance," said Pétur. "Now we must sing and sing, and remember to call for light and strength from above the moment contact is made."

A few more hymns were sung, and the Lord's Prayer was recited a bit more. All of a sudden an unfamiliar man's voice, but not particularly deep, was heard through the prayer: "Good evening, hallo."

"God be with you," said Pétur Pálsson the manager.

"I am Friðrik the elf doctor in the next world," said the voice. "Some say I am one of the Hidden People, but that's due to a misunderstanding at the beginning. I am a spirit. I am the son of love and the friend of the light. Hallo and welcome my dear sheriff, and may the light be always with you. Welcome, welcome, Pétur Pálsson, my dear manager. The light is always trying to shine more and more upon you. And all hail and good wishes to you, dear Pastor Brandur Jónsson, minister and rural dean of the deanery of Sviðinsvík . . ."

Friðrik continued to address all those present in this way, in theological vocabulary and prodigiously Christian speech; but he got a little mixed up over the widows and mothers. Finally it was the poet's turn, and this was the only greeting which was not couched in flowery theological language: "It is you whom I greet with sorrow," said the elf doctor.

"Oh, why is that?" said the manager, who took it upon himself to reply on behalf of the poet.

"He is without gratitude in his heart," said Friðrik.

"It's strange to have no gratitude in his heart for being allowed to live," said the manager.

"I want him to speak for himself," said the elf doctor. "I don't want others to speak for him. Speak, Ólafur Kárason, say where you are."

"I'm here behind the door," said the poet in a small voice.

"We must have gratitude in our hearts," said the elf doctor. "And spiritual maturity. And lift our minds from base things, lift them to higher spheres, search for the right current. Not to think of ourselves but to raise ourselves to the light and love one another like invisible beings in space. If we do that we shall achieve gratitude in our hearts. And spiritual maturity. And shall get the right current like the invisible beings in space. That's why we ought to go to visit those who have contact with higher spheres, and show them gratitude. One mustn't talk much to the girl standing in a doorway, because she has a bad influence on spiritual maturity. She has a base current which ruins the right heart-current. She robs the wealth of the heart. She kills the light of the heart."

"What a hell of a lot the spirit's got to say to this boy," said the sheriff, rather displeased.

"Friðrik dear," said the manager, interrupting. "Can't you produce some proof for the authorities as quickly as possible, my dear friend?"

"There's a tall, dark-haired woman standing behind the sheriff," said Friðrik. "Now she's laying her hand on his shoulder and leaning down over him, I almost think she's going to kiss him. Does the sheriff recognize her at all?"

"She shouldn't be very tall if it's her," said the sheriff.

"Did I say tall? I thought I said small, at least I meant that she was small," said Friðrik. "That's to say, a little under average height."

"Can you give me proofs about yourself, my dear?" said the sheriff gently.

"Why did you have the sofa in the drawing-room moved over to the other wall, dear?" came a weak whisper.

At that the sheriff recognized at once that this must be his first wife, and started to explain why the sofa had been moved, and apologize for it. "But how are you feeling, anyway, dear?" he asked.

"Oh, I'm feeling so wonderfully well," said the sheriff's first wife.

"Can you let me touch you?" said the sheriff.

"No," said the sheriff's first wife. "I have long since lost my wretched, neurasthenic earthly body. And besides I haven't time, there are so many others here waiting to make contact tonight. But perhaps I'll be able to borrow a strong, good body somewhere, some time, and then I shall let you touch me as much as you like, but you mustn't tell Jóhanna your second wife about it, because then she'll send me a bad current. We must have spiritual maturity. Good-bye."

"Isn't that a wonderful proof?" said the manager.

"Yes," said the sheriff. "Particularly the bit about the sofa."

Soon came the husbands of the widows; they kissed them in the dark and tried to comfort them with assurances of how good a life they were leading in the Summerland. One had nothing to do but wander up and down through orchards and pick flowers and fruit the size of lumpfish, instead of carrying rocks on the beach at Sviðinsvík; and those who wanted to could build themselves palaces from different light rays when they had nothing better to do.

The women wept, each one harder than the next, and one of them in particular was inconsolable and kept on crying, "Grímur, Grímur, the cow died this winter, I wish I could come to you with the children, we don't have any potatoes left!" Another said, "You must remember our *Númi* here; it was on her that you broke your back just before you died. Now she's sunk. She sank last night."

The manager interrupted and called upon the women not to besmirch this sacred moment by harping on insignificant sorrows of the belly; truly no one needed to complain now about not living grandly enough, eternity itself was standing open before them. But when least expected, the widows' husbands disappeared and the weak crying of a child began, like an infant's crying, and Friðrik informed one of the mothers that her son was calling.

"My darling boy, my boy!" said the woman, and started crying herself.

"Mama, Mama," said the child.

"Oh my darling little boy, I've cried so much, but now I know you're alive."

"The grave and death don't exist, Mama," prattled the boy, and had suddenly got the voice of a two-year-old.

"How very small you've become again, my little darling, you were fifteen when I lost you," said the woman.

"A good boy becomes a little angel," said the voice.

"I wish you could come on my knee as you did when you were small," said the woman.

"Fly in the light; look after flowers," said the little angel.

"Yes, I might have known that you wouldn't want to come to me any more since you've become an angel and are looking after flowers," said the woman, a little disappointed. "How much I've wept, and weep still when I go to bed at night and start thinking that if only I could have got him that jersey he needed, he wouldn't have caught a chill at the quarry and got pleurisy."

"Tcha, tcha!" interrupted the manager, "don't start bringing that up again; he's forgotten all about that long ago. What do angels know about jerseys? Angels don't even know what jerseys are. It's you who are foolish and he who is happy, Katrín dear."

Then came the little girl, Örn Úlfar's sister, whom the couple from Skjól had lost early that spring.

"Oh, it's so good to be dead!" said the little girl.

"Yes, I've always known that it's better than being alive, Anna dear," said the woman. "And how are my two boys and your eldest sister? Are they pleased to be dead, too?"

"They're always playing at flying about on their wings."

"The darlings," said the woman. "God bless them. It's probably wicked of me, then, to be hoping and praying the whole time what I have been hoping and praying."

"What is that?" asked little Anna.

"It's perhaps not right of me to say it," said the mother. "But God knows what it is if he has heard me."

"I see God every day," said little Anna, inquisitive. "If you think He hasn't heard you I'll pass it on, so you can be sure that it reaches Him."

"I wanted to ask if my little Þórarinn, who is the only one I've got left, will also get consumption and be taken from me? But perhaps it's wicked to ask about that. And perhaps it's a sin to wish that I may keep him."

"God doesn't want any questions of that sort," said little Anna.

"Yes, I always thought so, too," said the mother, and wept into her apron with deep, pain-racked sobs. "But tell God that if he wants me to bear that burden, too, then I shall bear it like the rest."

"You must get more spiritual maturity, Mummy, and get into the habit of seeing the light," said little Anna. "Your mind is all on base things. To die, that's just fun and games for those who have spiritual maturity. It's like taking off your wet things."

"This is heavenly!" cried the manager. "More dead children! More dead children!"

More dead children came and had contact with their mothers, and this went on for a long time with tears and rejoicing in turn. At last the manager began to tire of listening to other people's proofs and getting none himself. He put a stop to these long-winded exchanges and called Friðrik by name and said, "Listen, why is it that no one wants to talk to me, my dear fellow? Tell them that we've had enough of minor proofs. Now it's Pétur Pálsson the manager who wants proofs, and nothing less than major proofs will do for him."

"There's an old woman standing beside the manager," said Friðrik the elf doctor. "She is beginning to lose her teeth."

"It can't be my mother," replied the manager, "because to my certain knowledge she hadn't lost a single tooth by the time she died, least of all her front teeth."

"Nevertheless, this woman is very keen to talk to you, Pétur, but she says she doesn't understand Icelandic," said Friðrik.

"Goo'morning," said the toothless woman, speaking Danish in a hard, broken, old-woman's voice.

"No, God be with you, it isn't old Madame Sophie Sørensen, my grandmother?" said Pétur Pálsson, and practically glowed in the darkness at this proof, and started at once to interrogate his grand-mother about her health.

"Yesyesyesyes," said the late Sophie Sørensen. "Goo'morning."

"Are you not extremely elevated now, grandmother dear?" the manager asked unctuously.

"I no Icelander," said the manager's grandmother.

"Have you no news to tell me, dearest grandmother?" he asked.

"S'help me, s'help me," said the grandmother in Danish.

"I see," said Pétur. "And what else can you tell me?"

"Goo'morning," said the grandmother.

The conversation continued like that for a long time with few variations, the manager went on asking for news from eternity with religious unctiousness and invocations to Jesus, and the late Sophie Sørensen went on replying Yes and Goo'morning and S'help me.

Finally the guide, Friðrik the elf doctor, became bored with this conversation and interrupted, saying, "Madame Sophie is gone, but another woman has arrived, much older, she's so old that she can't stand upright. She says she's your great-grandmother and comes from France, and that she understands nothing but French. Do you want to speak to her?"

"Tell her that I'm a bit weak in French, but that I pray Jesus to give her strength, on the other hand I can manage a little English," said the manager.

"Bisk-vee," said Pétur Þríhross's French great-grandmother.

"Yes," said Pétur Þríhross in English.

"Sakaria malistua," said the great-grandmother.

"Christ," said Pétur Þríhross in English.

"Bee-bee," said the French great-grandmother.

"This is absolutely extraordinary. May the good Jesus give her strength; she must have become a bird," said Pétur Þríhross. "And that reminds me of something, Friðrik. Some time ago, when I went in for shooting birds, I had a Spanish game dog whom I called Snotra, she was so intelligent that she understood human speech and could even read thoughts. I have never missed any living creature so much as I missed that one when she was killed. Now I want to ask you one thing, do the souls of dogs live on after death?"

He had hardly finished the sentence before a loud barking was heard from somewhere in the next world, and soon a friendly howling was heard in the room.

"Ah, are you there, poor beast," said the manager, with a catch in his voice. "Come here to my knee and lick my hand to prove that it's you."

"Bow-wow," said the dog.

"Ah, I've found you again," said the manager. "How are you, anyway, beastie?"

"She hasn't got so high yet that she can talk," said Friðrik the elf doctor. "But still, she has begun to see the light."

"Does she get enough to eat, poor creature, do you think?" asked the manager.

"Yes," said Friðrik the elf doctor. "In the afterlife, people never forget to feed the dog."

"Bow-wow," said the dog, and was gone.

"This is by far the most remarkable meeting I have ever attended," said the manager. "Now then, have we all had proofs now?"

"Mm—I don't need proofs," said the secretary. "I know. But there's still the doctor. And the pastor."

"To hell with the doctor," said Pétur. "Judging by his snores he's in the next world already and no mistake. But there's our blessed pastor. He certainly deserves to get strong proofs. Now then, my dear Pastor Brandur, isn't there anyone you particularly want to talk to on the other side, haven't you lost some loved one?"

"No," said Pastor Brandur, "I haven't lost any loved one. But I believe all the same. Proofs or not, you see, I believe according to the Word."

"Yes, you have lost a loved one," declared Friðrik the elf doctor, in flat contradiction of the pastor. "There is one loved one here on this side who wants to talk to you, but he is so peculiar in shape that I don't know to what I should liken him, he seems to me to be rather like a very large house in shape."

"He can't be wanting to meet me," said the pastor, and became evasive. "I haven't lost any loved ones, luckily."

Then there came a voice that sounded hollow, as if from inside an empty barrel: "Yes, you have certainly lost me, Pastor Brandur, no longer ago than last winter. Am I to believe that you have forgotten how much you missed me, you who took to your bed when you lost me?"

"This must be some sort of misunderstanding," said the pastor, "I never took to my bed. And if I did take to my bed, it must have been with a cold."

"Ah, do you no longer remember the little shed that stood at the south side of your house?" said the voice. "Don't you remember how I was torn away in that great storm in the middle of March, and my debris was blown all the way out to sea, and no one ever saw a splinter of me again?"

"Isn't this absolutely wonderful?" said the manager. "There one can see that inanimate objects, too, have a soul. Everything God creates has a soul."

"Pastor Brandur, I have become a palace in the next world, and rest on golden pillars," said the shed.

"This is contrary to God's Word," said the pastor, feverishly brushing the fluff off his nose in the darkness.

"May I make a short observation?" said the manager then, formally. "According to old theology and pure Lutheranism, only human beings have souls; that is not my view, to be sure, but it is the pastor's view as such, and therefore I take the liberty of proposing that he should get proof which is in accordance with his doctrine and can bring him joy and encouragement in his responsible task. Accordingly I want to raise a highly important point with you, Friðrik. As you must know full well from English and American spiritualist writings, it has frequently happened in Great Britain and America, when men of true doctrinal faith were present at a seance, that the Father of the spirits himself has looked upon them in his mercy and sent them a few words of encouragement directly through the medium. Do you think you can arrange it that He might look upon us in His mercy at this crucial moment of our lives?"

"It is undoubtedly extremely difficult," said Friðrik.

"Yes, but nothing is impossible for God," said the manager. "And think how often He has revealed Himself to people in various ways, both natural and supernatural."

"God is everywhere near," said Friðrik, "but those who live in darkness and have little spiritual maturity and lack the right current, they cannot hear him."

"Are we then so much worse than people in England and America?" asked the manager. "I have difficulty in believing that, at least as far as our Pastor Brandur is concerned."

"You could try singing 'Praise the Lord,' once," said Friðrik.

When "Praise the Lord" had been sung yet again there was a brief silence, and then a little whispering sound began to be heard, accompanied by strange rattling noises as in an old, asthmatic gentleman who had lost his voice. For a long time no words could be distinguished. "How should one live in order to achieve spiritual maturity?" whispered the manager, deeply moved.

"One should p–pay," said the voice, stammering and hesitating, from the great distance, and so low that it could scarcely be heard. "One should pay in money."

"Yes, isn't that what I've always said?" said the manager. "And what else?"

"One shouldn't interfere with girls who don't concern us," said the voice a little more firmly, "they can become pregnant and who is to look after the child?"

"Hmmm," said the manager. "Quite so."

"One shouldn't drink too much, either," said the voice.

"Quite so," said the manager, and was obviously a little disappointed. "That, too, is something I have always maintained. But can't we expect anything, even if it's only a couple of words, which could bring to the public joy and encouragement in the battle of life?"

At that the voice spoke plainly and directly, almost peremptorily: "The public is to have enough money and live a healthy life and get plenty to eat, meat six days a week and fish one day . . ."

"Huhuhu, that cannot be correctly reported," the rural dean was heard to mumble, "it cannot be the highest powers who say that the public is to eat meat every day, the public has to get into the habit of diligence, thrift, and saving in all things, and never to make demands upon others . . ."

But now God was annoyed that one miserable early wretch of a pastor should dare to interrupt Him with trite and captious wrangling, and He suddenly raised His voice and said angrily, "I won't hear any drivel about thrift. I have created enough for everyone; my world is full of the good things of life I created. Everyone can live well on my earth; all paupers could become wealthy if they had the sense to get rid of the thieves and plunderers and murderers . . ."

"Tcha, tcha, tcha," said the manager. "It can't be the Lord who has begun to talk like this; this is undoubtedly some stray spirit, probably from the underworld, who is trying to make a fool of us."

"Yes," said the pastor. "It is not the Father of the spirits who speaks like that. Let us say the Lord's Prayer a few times to drive this evil spirit away from us."

So a few Lord's Prayers were recited to purify the air, but it was easier said than done to get rid of the dreadful currents which had accompanied the evil spirit, and the medium was ill at ease for a long time. Eventually, however, Friðrik said that the right light was approaching; gradually the meeting managed to free itself from the influence of the Evil One and introduce an atmosphere of peace and love anew. Finally he announced that it was safe to bring the Lord's Prayers to an end—a blonde and blue-eyed woman had arrived from the fair country.

"Whom has she come to meet?" asked the manager.

"She is standing beside Ólafur Kárason," said Friðrik. "She loves him. She says that his blue, clear, kind eyes are her eyes. She asks whether he doesn't remember the sunny days when the two of them were alone in the fair country long, long, long before he was born?"

"Do you remember, my dear?" asked a tender and lyrical woman's voice from outer space, but not entirely free of affectation.

Ólafur Kárason was as unprepared for this sweet address as he was deeply moved by the secret, distant memory of the fair country, and for a moment he was quite incapable of finding a suitable answer.

"M–my mother isn't dead," he said at last. "She lives in Aðalfjörður."

"You must be mistaken, Friðrik," said the manager. "The description of this fair-haired woman fits perfectly my late mother, and the voice was quite clearly her voice." Then he called out, moved, "Mummy, mummy, come and kiss your darling little boy, who will never, never disobey you again."

But scarcely had the manager finished speaking before the medium suddenly started up from her trance and screamed, "Light the lamp quickly; I'm suffocating; where am I?"

The secretary lit the lamp at once.

Þórunn of Kambar stood in front of her chair, drenched in sweat and dishevelled, with distaste on her face as after a bad dream, and holding one of her shoes in her hand; the sheriff rested his paunch on his thighs and his cheeks on his shoulders and continued to twiddle his thumbs; the pastor took the opportunity, once the lamp had been lit, of brushing from his sleeve the fluff that had gathered there while the seance had been in progress; the doctor snored powerfully with his head on his wife's lap; but Pétur Pálsson the manager sat with his false teeth in one hand and his pince-nez in the other, ready to kiss his mother. The widows and mothers were moist-eyed.

Þórunn put a hand to her eyes as if the sudden brightness caused her sharp pain, and with the one hand shielding her eyes she turned first towards Pétur the manager and struck him a swinging blow on the face with her shoe, and said, "You beast!" Then she stormed across the room and struck Ólafur Kárason a similar blow and said, "You're even more of a beast!"

"Eh? Eh?" said the sheriff, and his thumbs suddenly stopped twiddling.

"They have bad currents," said Þórunn of Kambar. "They have currents that clash."

— **16** —

Sunday morning. Örn Úlfar knitted his brow and looked fiercely at the Ljósvíkingur.

"Hallo," said Ólafur Kárason.

He did not return the greeting. He stopped in the road in front of the poet and looked him up and down with hatred, contempt and disgust.

"Why are you looking at me like that?" asked the Ljósvíkingur.

"Unscrupulous dog!" said Örn Úlfar, and thrust out his chin. "You took part in mocking my mother!"

"Örn?" said the Ljósvíkingur.

"I could forgive you anything," he said. "You can join the criminals and liars any time you like. But this one thing, making fun of my old mother who has lost everything—that I can never forgive."

The poet's heart leapt into his mouth at this sudden and unexpected accusation, and he started to excuse himself at once: "God himself knows," he said, "that I have never knowingly made fun of any person, and never will. But if you mean the seance last night, I want to ask you one thing: Do you dare to assert that the soul doesn't exist? And do you dare to assert that God doesn't exist? I think that a man should investigate what he doesn't understand, I. . . ."

"I ought to give you a punch on the nose," said Örn Úlfar. "I'm ashamed of even knowing you."

"You are welcome to do that, Örn," said the Ljósvíkingur; he admired this friend of his so blindly that he could willingly suffer his anger after the blows he had had to take from the wicked. "But can I just ask you one thing before you strike me: Do you consider all those who believe in God and the soul, and the next world, to be criminals and liars?"

"The next world is cheap; it doesn't cost anything to dispense it with both hands. When they have sunk the people's ship in order to pay their debts with the insurance money, they give us a whole fleet in heaven."

"I don't care what you say about Pétur the manager," said the poet. "I don't believe he is a wicked person."

"What are you talking about?" said Örn.

"In fact I don't believe that any wicked people exist."

"What do you mean by wicked people?"

"I don't know," said the Ljósvíkingur. "Nothing, really."

"You are so stupid that it's practically impossible to talk to you," said his friend. "You suddenly come out with something you profess to advocate, but when you're asked about it, you've no idea what you mean or what you're talking about. You say that Pétur Þríhross isn't a wicked man; well and good, say I—but who's saying that he *is* a wicked man? Here in Sviðinsvík there are three kinds of wicked men: fish thieves, loud-mouthed drunks, and lechers who have children at the taxpayers' expense. None of them steals from the poor or lies to them. There is no more innocent phenomenon in our parish community than wicked people. If I accused Pétur Þríhross of being a wicked man, I'd be a fool. I accuse him of being a good man, a loving man, a noble-minded man, a spiritual pioneer, a friend of education, a champion of the faith and a benefactor of penniless poets."

"You are much more intelligent than I, Örn," said the poet. "That's obvious from the way you have never believed anything you have been told. I, on the other hand, have always believed everything I have been told. And when the world around me has been full of harshness and cruelty, I haven't had the courage to clench my teeth like you; instead I have instinctively withdrawn into myself and tried to live for beauty and the spirit."

Örn Úlfar made no reply, but laughed. It was not the kind of laughter that expressed joy, nor even mockery, nor pity, least of all kindness, just a primitive masculine antagonism to a helpless admission, to wretchedness. He was no longer angry. They walked along the road together. There was silence, and for a long time they listened to their footsteps on the road. Then Örn Úlfar began to talk: "You told me once about Hólsbúðar-Dísa, as we called her, Dísa from Skálholt, the crippled, naked wretch who crawled screeching from behind the partition on your first morning in the village. You thought she was going to attack you, and this picture haunted you, waking and sleeping, for a long time afterwards. You still haven't forgotten it. It's not so long since you told me that you found it quite incomprehensible that such creatures should exist. Yes, it is quite incomprehensible. I'm not going to try to explain it for you, but because you say you want to investigate whatever you don't understand, I shall tell you a story.

"When I was a small boy and sat here astride the fence with other boys in order to jeer at people walking along the road, because our life was nothing but one continuous shout of misery, Hólsbúðar-Dísa was a young girl with long, raven hair and these expressive dark eyes which concealed all the mystery of youth; she walked past wearing a shawl. We shouted at her the name of the man she loved, but she didn't look round, just held her head higher. Later, when her youth had been ruined and her life had been made an unbearable disgrace, I saw her being taken along this same road through the village, in fetters. It was on this very road we are walking on now. They had charged her with a crime and were getting ready to judge her, as they always do with the innocent when they have been struck down. They would gladly have given her jail for life, but when she went mad on their hands, they suddenly realized that they were poor and couldn't afford to send her to a mental hospital. The taxpayers couldn't afford the luxury of sending her to an asylum.

"Instead they farmed her out with the late Jón the murderer, because he was reckoned to have the strength of four men and therefore was the only man in the village they could trust to wrestle with her and beat her when she had her fits. He built a hutch round her in a corner of his bait shed, and there she languished on hard boards under a few tattered sacks for two years. When there was a thaw, the water dripped down on her; in frosty weather the walls of her hutch were covered with ice; her food was thrown to her through a hole. They have seldom been so lucky with their parish paupers here. You see, she could no more protest against anything that happened to her than a dumb animal. She just curled up like a snail under her rags, with her knees up to her chin, and she lay like that in cold and darkness for two years and was forgotten until old Jón the murderer died. When the bait shed was pulled down after his death, they hauled this hunched animal out of the hutch, and the people who saw her called upon the authorities to send her to a mental institution. But when the doctor and the parish council had examined her and ascertained that it would never be possible to straighten her again, they were so ashamed about her that they didn't dare to send her away from the village. They had such refined feelings that they couldn't bring themselves to let others see what the good men who ran a parish could do to a human being if they were only good enough, loving and noble-minded enough, pioneering enough in spiritual and educational matters, great enough champions of the faith and benefactors of penniless poets. So they were content with setting up a stall for her at the far end of the living room at Skálholt."

They walked for a long time after the story was finished, and still heard their own footsteps on the road; then Örn Úlfar turned off, with the Ljósvíkingur following. Örn Úlfar sat down on the grass and the Ljósvíkingur looked at him, in fear, then sat down on the grass as well. After a long pause he asked, "Why are you telling me this story?" And added, "I'm sure I shall never get over it."

"I hope you never will get over it," said Örn Úlfar. "But unfortunately you will get over it, and pretty quickly, too."

"When all's said and done, Hólsbúðar-Dísa is only one person in distress," said the Ljósvíkingur, "and luckily doesn't even know how much she is suffering."

"Hólsbúðar-Dísa is the village itself," said Örn Úlfar, without further explanation.

"I can't bear this," said the Ljósvíkingur and stood up and was going to run away. "I yearn for beauty, beauty, the spirit," he said and gazed almost in tears into the blue of the sky at the white clouds of midsummer which clustered into banks and then drifted apart again. But he did not turn away; he sat down again instead.

"I remember you once said that what you were most frightened of in Sviðinsvík were the children in the streets," said Örn. "So I can't expect you to enjoy listening to me. I am the children in the streets. I am the child who was brought up in the ditches and on the fences, the child who had everything stolen from him before he was born, the child who was yet another misfortune on top of all the other misfortunes of the family, one handful of dirt to add to the midden on which the cockerels stand and crow. But because of that, there's no need to talk to me as if no one has ever recognized the need for a more beautiful world except you. I know just as well as you what beauty is and even what the spirit is, even though you are the Ljósvíkingur himself and I am only called after the eagle and the wolf. Beauty—that is the earth; it is the grass on the earth. The spirit—that is the heaven with its light above us, the sky with these white summer clouds which cluster together in banks and then drift apart again. If there were any justice in the world I would have just one wish—to be allowed to lie on my back on the grass, in this heavenly light, and look at the clouds.

"But whoever thinks that beauty is something he can enjoy exclusively for himself just by abandoning other people and closing his eyes to the human life of which he is a part—he is not the friend of beauty. He ends up either as Pétur Þríhross's poet, or his secretary. He who doesn't fight every day of his life to the last breath against the representatives of evil, against the living images of evil who rule Sviðinsvík—he blasphemes by taking the word beauty into his mouth."

Two young poets sitting on the grass one midsummer day, talking about human life. Then there was a long silence. Örn Úlfar stared into the distance with that long-sighted look of his, the corners of his mouth pulled down, his face bearing an expression of unremitting suffering. The Ljósvíkingur sat straight-legged on the ground, feverishly tearing at the grass, clawing into the roots, down to the bare soil, dirtying his fingers. Then he suddenly stopped tearing at the grass, looked up, gazed at his friend with his sincere blue eyes, and said with expectant, childlike simplicity: "It needs an awful lot of courage to be a man. Örn, do you think I have the courage for it?"

"You can think about that in the autumn when I'm gone," said his friend.

— **17** —

One day Örn Úlfar was gone.

He went aboard a ship with a bag on his back, and traveled south in the hold. His mother said good-bye to him on the quayside with tears in her eyes, in the way in which all mothers have said good-bye to their sons who go away.

"Be sure to keep your scarf around your neck, child."

His father prophesied good weather.

But when the ship was out of the harbor, Ólafur Kárason noticed that the weather was raw with leaden clouds and a rough sea, no music in the air. Autumn; the golden plovers were gathered in flocks in the homefields. He stood alone on the quayside, watching with troubled eyes the ship receding in the distance; she was now far down the fjord. He felt he no longer knew what to do with himself now that his friend was gone. What was he to do? It was already starting

to rain; the first drops were being ripped from the heavy clouds as if
in anger. He walked home to his palace and crawled in through the
cellar window as usual. He hung a piece of sackcloth over the paneless window to keep out the rain. Seldom had he welcomed his
sweetheart with such heartfelt joy and gratitude as he did that night.

How remote youth's first sexual experience is from youth's first
love! It is as different as the dawn is from the day. Youth's dream is the
white glow of night on the mountain peaks when evening and morning, night and day, all become one without being anything. With
experience, the romances of the imagination no longer belong to the
world of poetry, fleshless and only half real. The meeting of two
lovers makes the whole kernel of poetry a reality which is sufficient to
itself; two lives have found one another, two bodies understand one
another, and it is everything in one—dream, expectation, joy, pleasure, satisfaction, remembrance and sorrow. This fulfillment of reality is so potent that it carries with it the danger that the divine and
eternal will never reveal themselves to the soul again.

The music of revelation, the soul's secret, sacred dream of the
Almighty's embrace—ah, what ridiculous vanity! He had suddenly
become a full-grown man, and it was her work. Her presence lived in
his body night and day, waking or sleeping. As the gentle swell stirs
on the beach on a clear-blue summer night, so he longed to rest
against her sun-white, loving breast, those rounded voluptuous
shapes which were the beginning and the end of all beauty, but at the
same time the very image of transience itself; nothing is more natural
than to die then and turn to dust. It was only a few hours since he
had been standing on the quayside with tears in his eyes watching the
ship sail away with his friend, but now he was suddenly glad that
Örn Úlfar was gone, so that there was no longer anyone to order him
to rise, to summon him to arms. Outside, it was raining.

"Oh, Jesus; no, there's no Jesus about it. We've got to start thinking of something," she said.

He woke up from a trance with a start, raised his head from that
precious pillow, and said, "Yes, there is perhaps nothing further
removed from reality than complete reality itself."

"Eh?" she said. "Reality? I don't know what you mean."

"Neither do I," he said.

"You're such a great poet," she said. "If only you knew how much I've dreamed of going with you to the Churchyard Ball!"

"Me, too," he said.

"I promised to teach you to dance," she said.

"We'll start tonight," he said. "I'll dance better than anyone else."

"It doesn't matter if you don't dance better than anyone else," she said. "And shall I tell you why? It's because no boy will have such deep blue eyes as my boy has, no one will have such golden hair and such small hands. And none, none of all the couples at the Churchyard Ball will be as happy as me and my boy."

She hummed once again the song she had sung on the first day they met.

"Some get shoes from Aðalfjörður," she said. "Some order them from the south. Some get them in any way they can."

"I've no doubt you'll get shoes," he said.

She was silent for a long time, and he could hear nothing but the autumn rain falling outside, steadily and unceasingly.

"No," she said at last. "I won't get any shoes."

"Why not?"

"And I won't be going to the Churchyard Ball this autumn."

"What's this now?"

"I'm pregnant," she said.

He raised himself on one elbow. He looked at her for a long time as she lay before him, young, white and loving, in the first darkness of the summer. He did not know whether to be happy or sad about the news, actually he just felt a little proud: I won't even be eighteen until September, he thought to himself, it isn't everyone who expects to be a father at that age. He leaned down over her and kissed her.

She said, "God in heaven, to think that I'm pregnant, that's how much of a fool I am, hahaha!"

"Now I'll publish my book of poems in Aðalfjörður this autumn and become a famous poet," he said. "And then you'll see whether you regret it!"

"I don't regret anything," she said. "But what are you going to say to the parish officer?"

"What's it got to do with the parish officer?"

"We're both on the parish. He'll kill us."

"Does he know about it?"

"Does he know about it? The whole village lies here outside the window every night counting the minutes I'm with you, as if they were the last drops of their lifeblood. Tonight Daddy threatened to tie me up."

"We'll get married," he said.

"Hahaha," she said.

"Don't you want to marry me, then, Meya dearest?"

"Yes," she said. "And then what?"

"Then no one can say anything."

"Are we going to live on anything?" she said.

"I can set myself up as a poet," he said. "Guðmundur Grímsson of Grunnavík is said to take two or even three krónur for an elegy."

She worked it out in her head for a while and then said, "So few people die, worse luck, that it's not possible to live off that. And in addition, the few who die can't afford to have elegies written for them. We couldn't afford an elegy for my mother. You're lucky if you get coffee at funerals nowadays."

They were no nearer to a solution.

"Perhaps I'll get some pay from Pétur Pálsson this autumn," said the poet.

"Yes, but don't you think you'll have to buy some clothes if you get any money, man?—which you obviously won't get, anyway, because Pétur Þríhross never pays anyone anything. Perhaps at best he might give someone two krónur out of charity. And the Regeneration Company has gone broke."

"What do you think we ought to do, then?" said the poet.

"That's for you to work out," she said. "You're the father."

His fingertips touched her body cautiously, inquiringly, reverently. "Is it really true?" he whispered. "How am I to be what you say?"

He looked at her for a long time on this late-summer night like a man watching a series of optical illusions and who cannot tear his eyes away from them, and his fingertips went on playing on her rounded form. Eventually his eyes filled with tears; he said, "I love you," and buried his face in her bosom. Thus the night went on passing.

At last she whispered, "Once I was frightened, and thought it was wicked. D'you remember how frightened I was? It was probably because I thought it wasn't true. Now I've lived it in my own life, and it's true after all."

"What is?" he said.

"Love," she said. "I feel now that we'll love one another for as long as we live."

"Yes," he whispered. "And never part again."

"Yes," she whispered. "And never part again."

A little later she was sitting on the edge of his bed and had put on her worn-out shoes.

"I must go now," she said.

"What are we going to do?" he said.

She sat with her elbows on her lap and her fingers between her teeth and gazed out into the night.

"Farther down the fjord here, if you walk for about an hour, there's a little cottage. It stands right down by the high-water mark, all on its own. And there's a tiny little homefield round it and a teeny-weeny little cabbage patch that needs weeding. There are flowers growing on the roof. And there's a landing place, and a boat on the beach, and a fishing line, and perhaps a bit of net. And there are flowers growing on the roof. Have you never walked past it?"

"Not yet," he said. "What else?"

"And the mountain, it stands above the little cottage, but not right on top of it; there's some level ground behind it which catches the snow avalanches, so there's no danger. And the front of the house is painted red and faces the sea, and there's white around the window, and the window needs a curtain; and there are flowers growing on the roof. And there's a little barn behind the cottage, and the cow grazes on the slope, and she has a little calf, and the cow's just called Skjalda, but the calf is called Ljómalind. And there are seven ewes with their lambs on the mountain."

"How simple life can be if it's lived right," said the poet. "I wonder who lives there?"

"And the little cottage at the landing place, everyone says it's so neat, and everyone admires how nice everything is around it. And the flowers grow on the roof . . ."

Suddenly she fell silent, and convulsive spasms seized her mouth, jaws, and neck. She bit the back of her hand for a moment, and then she lost all control of herself and burst into tears. She wept into her hands at first and shook her head and rocked backwards and forwards inconsolably; then she seized hold of his hands and covered them with her scalding kisses and tears.

He tried to whisper in her ear all the words of comfort he knew, but it made no difference; mere words were incapable of calming this surf, of restraining this elemental force. His hands were smarting under her tears. Finally he stared at her like a man standing by the sea on a stormy night watching a ship breaking up on the skerries only a few fathoms from land. Then she stopped weeping. She stood up and wiped away her tears with her arm and tore the sackcloth from the window. It was still raining. He felt he no longer knew her after the weeping, her face no longer had any definable features. She cleared her throat and sniffed.

"It's daytime," she said in a colorless, humdrum tone of voice. "I've got to go. Good-bye."

She did not give him her hand, but was gone. His hands were still hot and wet from her tears.

18

Two days passed, and he was always thinking about this one thing, but could hardly believe it—had she not just been joking, perhaps? But why, then, had she started to weep, this unsentimental girl? No one weeps for a joke, and tears are very close to the truth.

He still had not been able to decide whether he should be glad or sorry. His feelings kept changing. It was naturally in many ways delightful to beget a young and promising son, a true scion of his line, but it was easier said than done suddenly to have to start playing the paterfamilias in these difficult times, not to mention for a man who had been planning to go to the secondary school in Aðalfjörður that autumn and even publish a book of poems. When he began to think of all the things he had to do in the near future—publish a book of poetry, educate himself, have a son, buy sheep, get a loan for a fishing boat, set up as a farmer, and many other things—he was sometimes assailed by pessimism as he worked in the meadow, and wanted only to throw away his scythe and lie down for good. He felt overwhelmed by the responsibilities of life. But suddenly her brisk laughter sounded in his ears and he saw her before him, just like the first time, standing in her doorway and kicking her legs in the air one after the other. Then he suddenly became optimistic again and felt that the world was only half a calfskin and the future an unbroken, sunshiny road—"How can I possibly think of despairing when she is by my side? Didn't she have a solution for everything? Coffee, brown sugar, fish-gills—when didn't she have enough of everything?" There was no darkness so black that she did not see a glimmer; the last time she left, she had torn the sackcloth from the window and said, "Daytime." If she asked him for advice, it was just to test what he could do.

Probably she had already arranged to buy the cottage down by the sea without anyone knowing, yes, and the flowers on the roof, where they could live for the rest of their lives, just the two of them, in fact on the south side of the world and a little to one side of it, in shelter. In good weather he would row out into the fjord in the little boat and catch gleaming codlings for the pot. When the weather was bad he would sit in the living room and write famous books like Guðmundur Grímsson of Grunnavík and earn distinction in distant parts of the country; perhaps even in France; luckily the weather was often bad. The golden-haired toddler played in the living room at the poet's feet, but Ólafur Kárason of Ljósavík unfortunately could not help being a little shy about that. It was certainly manly to have the title of father, but he could not conceal from himself the fact that he was rather afraid of small children and felt that he himself was really the only small child in the world who mattered at all. On the other hand, he had no doubt that Meya would supply both the cow and the coffee.

Why had she then started crying?

All day, just like that. He was extremely restless and preoccupied, did not know where he was, did not hear what was said, saw nothing with his eyes in bright daylight.

Ever since she had come to him for the first time, they had never missed three nights in a row. Tonight he sat at the window and waited for her impatiently. He had seldom felt more clearly than now that she was his life's anchor, that without her he would go adrift and be shipwrecked in the next storm. Time passed, the late-summer night engulfed land and sea, but she did not arrive. First he was restless, then unhappy, finally apathetic; he leaned on the windowsill, buried his face on his elbow, and fell asleep. When he stirred again, sleep was stronger than unhappiness, and he threw himself down on the bed and slept on until his alarm clock rang in the morning. He gazed sadly out over the fjord, at the birds which had hovered over the smooth sea so many tranquil mornings after a happy night; all at once it was as if their wingbeats no longer concerned him. Why had she not come?

The following evening, when the day's meaningless toil was over, he was determined to go to her house. Her face in the doorway, the sound of her voice, just one word—he felt that his very life was at stake. In the gathering dusk of late summer a secret unrest was stirring in all young hearts. Boys and girls were meeting one another again by complete accident on the road, and talking for a long time together about absolutely nothing at all, with bursts of laughter and rocking and slapping of thighs, and had never in all their born days ever heard anything like it and were going to die of laughing. Three young girls came walking towards him in the late-summer dusk. He saw at once that the girl walking in the middle was his girl. The others fell silent when they approached, but she went on talking. The other two looked at him, but she did not see him. They stared at him with the brazen curiosity with which girls look at a boy who they know has been with one of their friends far into the night, perhaps until morning. They seemed not so much to be wanting to taste him as to devour him completely. To his own girl, however, he was as totally invisible as he was a feast for the eyes of her companions. At first he had intended to greet her and call her by name and ask her to listen to even half a word. But in the face of this pretense he was at a loss what to do; he did not know if behind it there lay some purpose he was meant to understand. But he did not understand. Only one thing was perfectly clear, however: she did not want him to pay any heed to her, in word or greeting.

At the last moment, just as she was passing by, she suddenly stopped talking. She turned her face towards him and flashed him a look, just for a fraction of a second. Then she had gone past with her friends, and was carrying on with her story. He was left standing in the road with her look burning in his heart.

At first it occurred to him that he had made a mistake, perhaps it had been some other girl after all. He had never seen those eyes before. In the past, her eyes had contained all the sunshine of the days. It was as if behind her there echoed the green and fragrant forest; the expanse which lay open before her happy eyes had no night. And now? The defiant pride of youth was broken, life's taut spring had slackened, the forest no longer echoed; and the expanse? One collided with things; and night had fallen. The eyes which looked at him tonight had been the eyes of a wounded animal. They were dominated by the dull and impersonal stupidity of pain; perhaps they do not even ask why, when their light is extinguished. His girl of the spring—that was how she walked past him in the autumn. Her companions looked back at him as he stood there in the road, but she did not look back.

It was Saturday night. He dreaded the thought of crawling into the darkness beside the rats and the feral cats. He wandered away and lay down somewhere on the moor. His sweetheart's glance occupied his soul like a terrible disaster. There was autumn in the ground. He waited until sleep had laid its gentle hand on the seething unrest of the autumn and given the village peace.

When he felt sure that she would be in bed at home, he set off again. He walked up to her window. There was a white cloth before the window, above her bed, so that he could not see inside. He looked all around carefully before he dared knock on the window. When he felt sure that there were no prying eyes in the vicinity, he rapped on the window with his knuckles, first once, and then, after a wait, once again. Then he waited for a long time, but there was no reply. Eventually he rapped for a third time, harder than before. There was no sign of life. Finally he was seized by such panic that he battered on the window as hard as he could with his fists, as if there were a fire, and the blows were accompanied by that bittersweet anguish which accompanies some dreams.

Suddenly the quarryman, her father, rudely awoken, was standing in the doorway, pouring abuse over the poet. Finally, when the poet managed to stammer out his errand, the father said he had no intention of being made a fool of by dogs in heat, and threatened to go in and fetch his gun if he did not clear off this minute. Unfortunately it never occurred to the poet to stand his ground and wait to see if the man would come out with a real gun. It was not until many years later that it occurred to him that the man perhaps had not owned a gun at all. He took to his heels.

He was standing by the sea, out of breath from running, and was turning over in his mind whether she had been asleep in her bed while he had been at the window. If she had been at home, would she have humiliated herself and him by letting him wake her old father with his knocking? Would she rather not have lifted the curtain in good time and given him a sign to go away? But if she was not in her bed, where then was she in the middle of the night? Was she perhaps sitting with her companions somewhere down by the sea; were they perhaps talking about life as the summer waned, like other poets? But it could also be someone else. Why not someone else, just like him? She was a passionate girl and, besides, Ólafur Kárason had not been the first.

"Farther down the fjord here, if you walk for about an hour, there's a little cottage. It stands right down by the high-water mark, all on its own. And there are flowers on the roof." Is true love, then, not indivisible? Is it possible to love two people as she had loved? Or is love perhaps not true, but first and foremost twofold or threefold?

Why should this little cottage not stand right down by the high-water mark? Why should she not have arranged to buy the cottage without anyone knowing? Why should she not slip over there at night to weed the garden even though summer was almost over, or to put up curtains at the little window that faced the sea?

He wandered off, not up the fjord, but out by the sea, as she had said. The sky was cloudy, but it was not raining, and there was mist on the mountaintops, the murmur of the sea like the tranquil pulse of a supernaturally huge beast in its sleep, a swarm of terns on a sand-spit. There were bridle paths along the fjord, with the mountain on one side; sometimes the path had to climb a low mound, sometimes as it hugged the mountain it veered round a cliff. Sometimes at the water's edge it had to round another cliff and was lost in the sands; he walked over the smoothed beach and the wet seaweed clung to his legs, and then he caught sight again of the path running up off the beach between rocks. He saw two cottages, but both of them stood right up by the mountain and he did not recognize them from the description; no, they were not her cottage. Her cottage stood down by the high-water mark, and there was a little landing place. He went on like this for a long, long time, long after it had begun to grow light. He saw many small landing places and bays, and he looked around carefully into every cranny, but there was no cottage. Then it was morning over the land with the sound of the sea heavier now, with a chilly breeze from the ocean, a cold, ponderous gull. He had been walking all night.

What if she were determined to forsake him? If she never wanted to see him again? Did not know him any longer? If he were to spend the rest of his life without her, alone?

It was she who had really given him life in the spring. She was the healing spirit who had nurtured him and revived him at her breast when he had no way out—the loving spirit that gives living creatures not only health and fertility but also hope and faith, and lifts our faces towards beauty itself at the same time as it clears the blindness from our eyes—she was not only his physical health, but also his spiritual life. Without her, no life.

It was a gray and dreary late-summer morning. He lay exhausted on the withered grass, and the swell washed over the stones in complete indifference, as if it were saying over and over again: It doesn't concern me at all; it doesn't concern me at all. Was this perhaps life, then?—to have loved one summer in youth and not to have been aware of it until it was over, some sea-wet footprints on the floor and sand in the prints, the fragrance of a woman, soft loving lips in the dusk of a summer night, sea birds; and then nothing more; gone.

> *You kissed my hand one twilit night*
> *While autumn rains battered the ground,*
> *Remorseless, deadening as a blight—*
> *In autumn tears our love was drowned.*
>
> *Your passion was a storm-tossed sea,*
> *Fierce as the ocean's raging tide*
> *That crushes cliffs to sand and scree—*
> *Till "Is it wrong?" you asked, and cried.*
>
> *With morning came the daily round*
> *Of pointless toil and dreary strife;*
> *You left my bed without a sound*
> *To start again your mundane life.*
>
> *Yet you know well that he whose love was real*
> *Was cut to the quick, and will not quickly heal.*

He was not sure himself how he got home. But it was the soul's good midwife, the Muse of poetry, who raised him to his feet and supported him and protected him. He woke up late in the day. It was Sunday. He was told that Vegmey Hansdóttir had been married at the pastor's that day. Her husband was a fisherman-farmer from another village; that was their boat disappearing down the coast, under full sail.

— 19 —

Most of the board were agreed that there was now nothing else to do but to declare the Regeneration Company bankrupt and hand over its property to the bank to meet the claims for repayments and interest. By this decision, the Regeneration Company of Sviðinsvík was in effect wound up and turned into a Psychic Research Society.

A few wonderful late-summer weeks went by, with good drying weather for the hay, but unfortunately people did not know what they were drying; people brought in the hay, but did not know what they were bringing in. People had long ago mortgaged their homefield and the cow to the Regeneration Company, and now the Regeneration Company had become the property of the bank, along with the cow and the homefield. No one knew what the bank would do with the cow; as far as people knew, the bank was not a person and therefore not endowed with common sense. It was just as likely that it would slaughter the cow for the winter and sell the hay. What were people to think? Pétur Pálsson, the manager, was away traveling all over the place, on spiritualist expeditions and horse trading; the foreman went on drinking and did not care if the employees did not start work before midday; the whole estate hovered in limbo; only the hay showed any thrift and initiative, and dried of its own accord in the fine weather for the bank.

Some people were wishing and hoping that this much-discussed estate would be sold by auction before they were all dead. But then the same question was bound to arise that no one had been able to answer for years on end: who would buy it? Lopsided, ramshackle, rotting hovels on a gravel-bank and a slope, a palace for the winds of heaven, a fleet of ships at the bottom of the sea, millions owed to the bank, six hundred people and scarcely any potatoes—it was certainly no easy matter to find a good man who would care to buy such a useless place. From now on, every day was shorter than the last; soon it would be winter with snow hanging from the eaves, and what were they to use for firewood, not to mention footwear?

And then, all of a sudden, Pétur Pálsson the manager was seen

strolling to and fro about the estate with a stranger: mysterious per-
ambulations, frequent halts, speculations, much pointing with walking sticks, rocking and swaying from side to side. It was little wonder
that hope now stirred again in some hearts. This was a distinguished
gentleman wearing boots and a new coat and a broadbrimmed hat of
a style unknown in Sviðinsvík; he did not have a dent in the crown
like other people, but let the crown keep its full shape. The hope was
that this man would now decide to buy the estate.

No, the manager had certainly not brought any small fry this
time. This was nothing less than one of the big boys. This was Júel J.
Júel, the son of the well-known Júel Júel: Grímur Loðinkinni*
(Hairy-Cheek) Ltd.—two fishing stations up north and five trawlers.
All the Grímur Loðinkinni trawlers had one virtue over the late
lamented *Númi*—they could all catch fish. It was little wonder that
the bank had greater confidence in Grímur Loðinkinni than in the
people of Sviðinsvík whom that dreadful creature, the rat, had shipwrecked. Pétur Pálsson himself made it known that Júel J. Júel had
half a mind to establish a station here at Sviðinsvík, but what kind of
station no one seemed to be quite sure; some thought a whaling station, others said a herring station, and others a radio station. But
everyone was agreed that any kind of station could save the estate.

As can be imagined, these base considerations had little effect on
Ólafur Kárason of Ljósavík. He had more serious things to think
about, having newly suffered a tremendous love sorrow. Few things
are so enriching for the imagination, or altogether so maturing for
the spiritual life as a whole, as suffering a love sorrow, especially for
the first time.

So it was not because the grief-stricken poet was concerned about
the present and future state of the village that destiny so arranged
things that he should get to know the station owner himself, but for
other reasons. He was summoned one day to act as groom for Pétur
the manager and the distinguished visitor, who were going to ride
over the mountain to pay a visit to the sheriff. The poet was provided
with a pair of the manager's cast-off riding boots and a tattered jacket
of unknown origin to make him fit company for the gentry.

He was to look after the six riding horses which had been thought necessary for the journey, and to hold the stirrup when the gentry mounted. Júel J. Júel had his big hat on, and was in all other respects dressed with such distinction that Ólafur Kárason forgot his cares in amazement at this novel sight—that clothing should exist which did not seem primarily designed to show contempt for the human body, but the contrary. When he looked at this man, he felt in his heart like a wretched and clumsy farm implement beside some rare work of art, a chased and engraved ornament. He had not realized until now that there could be such a difference between two people on this earth. The station owner looked around with magnificent disdain, and smacked the house with his whip as he turned the corner. He lit a cigarette with a grimace of distaste on his handsome, polished face, pulled gloves over his manicured hands and stared at the same time with unqualified disdain and heartfelt boredom at Pétur Þríhross as he walked splay-footed and bent-kneed out of his house, wearing his morning coat, celluloid collar, pince-nez and bowler hat, with a half-chewed cigar between his gutta-percha dentures.

The journey began with Ólafur Kárason having to hold one of the manager's fiery horses while Júel J. Júel mounted. But no sooner was the station owner in the saddle than he swung his whip with all his might at the horse's groin, and the fiery beast was seized with panic, knocked Ólafur Kárason down as it reared, and disappeared in a flash up the road, right through the village, out onto the moor, over fences, bogs and earth slips, until it pulled up, trembling with terror, against another fence and looked round wild-eyed, whinnying. Júel J. Júel, on the other hand, had been left behind in the bog, and had lost his hat. He did not stand up when Pétur Pálsson came up to him, but pretended to be dead.

"A fall means fortune on the way," said Pétur Pálsson, consolingly, and hauled the station owner out of the bog and laid him on a hummock and began to clean him up.

"Leave me alone, you damned fool!" said the station owner, when the manager began to scrape the mud off him with his pocketknife. "I've got a concussion."

"You went off a little too fast," said Pétur Pálsson.

"No, it was you who was trying to kill me with that damned hack," said the station owner.

"He's a very fine horse, my dear chap; he just doesn't take to the whip too kindly," said Pétur Pálsson.

"What the hell's the use of having a horse if you can't whip him?" said the station owner, and rose angrily to his feet. "I demand that you shoot the damned beast at once."

"My dear friend and brother, no bad language," said Pétur Pálsson. "We must remember to set off more slowly next time."

"I'm not moving another step," said the station owner. "I've got a concussion."

"If a man's got concussion, there's nothing better than cognac," said the manager.

"It's my cognac," said the station owner. "You don't have to advise me to drink my own cognac. I decide what I do with my cognac."

But Pétur Pálsson had no intention of losing his temper; he handled everything with great adroitness and psychological understanding, fetched the station owner's hat from the bog, and began to examine it.

"This is a hell of a fine hat," said Pétur Pálsson.

Júel J. Júel pulled out his handkerchief and dried his face sullenly.

"What did you pay for this hat?" asked Pétur Pálsson, and went on examining this treasure from every angle.

"Bring me the cognac," said Júel J. Júel.

The manager opened a bag, brought out a bottle of cognac, and gave it to the station owner without a word, then continued his examination of the hat. The owner rummaged in his pocket for a corkscrew.

"Where can one get hats like this?" asked Pétur Pálsson, who had now turned out the sweatband to see how the lining was fastened inside it. "I simply must get myself a hat like this," he said.

By the time the owner of the cognac had put the neck of the bottle to his mouth and was beginning to drink from it, Pétur Pálsson had become so enamored of the hat that he whipped off his own bowler in order to try on the station owner's hat. But when the latter saw this he stopped drinking, tore his hat out of Pétur's hands, and put it on.

"Let's go!" he said.

He caught sight of Ólafur Kárason the poet at a distance, and asked why that good-for-nothing was standing there gaping, and shook his whip at him: "What are you gaping at? Be off with you at once and get the horses, or you'll know all about it!"

The station owner was given another horse and they set off. He said he still had a concussion and refused to go at more than walking pace, and took care not to dangle his legs nor touch the pony's groin, but sat hunched with the cigarette smoldering away in the corner of his mouth, with his hands in his pockets, and let the reins lie loose on the pony's mane.

Pétur Pálsson suggested that they should dismount again soon and have a drop from the bottle. When they had ridden a few hundred yards, they halted again in a hollow not far above the village, where the road began to zigzag up into the pass. Júel J. Júel lay down flat on the ground with his hat over his face and began to utter all kinds of expressions of ill-temper and boredom. Pétur Pálsson did not spare the cognac meanwhile. Then Júel J. Júel half sat up and drank. When he had had a pull, and grumbled a little more, and had another pull, he said, "No, let's be friends again, my dear Pétur," and offered Pétur Pálsson his hand. Pétur Pálsson was seldom slow to accept a proffered hand when there was alcohol nearby, and indeed the handshake was long and firm and not unlike a betrothal ceremony. Then they drank again. Then Júel said, "Listen, Pétur, why didn't you bring the damned girl along, too?"

"We are married men, my dear Júel," said the manager piously, taking out his upper dentures, spraying snuff over them and thrusting them back into his mouth again. The station owner watched these proceedings with murder in his eyes, despite their newly pledged friendship and the handshakes.

"Eat shit!" he said.

"No bad language, dear friend," said Pétur Pálsson the manager.

"I don't call it much of an excursion when there are no women," said the station owner. "I want that girl, do you hear me?"

"It's not quite so easy to have her," said the manager. "She's not cheap, old friend."

"Yes, perhaps with someone like you who hangs around her all day long and frightens her," said the station owner.

"I know her from a spiritual standpoint," said the manager. "I have been making scientific experiments with her for more than a year, first in private and now, recently, in public."

"I would have had her a long time ago," said the station owner, "if you hadn't been nosing around in the corridor until all hours. What the devil were you nosing around in the corridor for?"

"Please don't talk like that, my friend, we're not only married men, but what's more important, we are educated men," said the manager.

"I'm turning back," said Júel J. Júel.

"No, don't do that, my dear Júel; I'm sure you wouldn't treat the poor sheriff like that," said the manager.

"To hell with the sheriff," said the station owner.

"The roast's waiting on the other side of the mountain," said the manager.

"I want the girl," said the station owner.

"The sheriff has a young wife," said the manager.

The station owner wavered at that, and he said after a little thought, "Let's be friends, my dear Pétur. You're not so stupid as some people think. But that I should drink from the same bottle as you—never!"

They brought out another bottle and shook hands again for a long time and gazed into one another's eyes like lovers, and the station owner said, "Grímur Loðinkinni never fails its friends."

Eventually the manager leaned over to his friend and asked confidentially, "Has she told you how much she wants for it?"

"I don't care a damn," the other replied. "Money doesn't matter if you need a woman—just don't go wandering about in the corridor until all hours; it frightens her."

"Are you prepared to pay her price?"

"Such as what?"

"Her price is a trip to England."

"Yes, you've made her take leave of her senses. What the devil does she want to go to England for?"

"She wants to be world-famous. And I can well believe that she might become just that."

"You must be out of your mind," said Júel J. Júel.

"She has the most remarkable talents," said the manager.

"It would be unthinkable in any civilized country to pay her more than five krónur," said the station owner, and suddenly caught sight of the poet Ólafur Kárason of Ljósavík.

"What's that boy doing hanging around here, may I ask?"

"He's a versifier and a harmless wretch I've taken under my wing," said the manager. "Pay no attention to him."

"He's eavesdropping," said the station owner. "If he doesn't hop it to the horses at once, he's going to catch it." And he grabbed the whip, so that the poet jumped to his feet in alarm and hurried over to the horses.

It was noticeable that the more often the gentry halted for refreshments and shook hands and became better friends, the more of an irritant Ólafur Kárason became in the station owner's eyes. About the time they had got as far up the pass as they were far down the second bottle of cognac, the station owner announced that he could not bear to have that jackass near him, least of all sober, and that they would have to pour some cognac down his throat.

"He doesn't understand that sort of thing," said Pétur Pálsson. "He's in bad health, poor creature. He has enough difficulty keeping the horses together even when he's sober."

"It's none of your business what I do with my cognac."

"It's not that I grudge the cognac," said Pétur Pálsson. "But as everyone who knows me knows perfectly well, I have always believed in teetotalism for others, particularly for youngsters."

"Yes, you've always been a damned socialist all your days," said Júel J. Júel. "Grímur Loðinkinni Ltd. won't have anything to do with fellows of that sort. Fetch me the boy at once; that cognac is going into him."

"No, thank you," said Ólafur Kárason from a distance. "There's really no need."

"Leave the poor wretch alone, my dear Júel," said Pétur Pálsson the manager.

"The cognac's mine and I decide what I do with my own cognac. If I say he must down my cognac, then my cognac he must down," said the station owner.

"Run and fetch the horses, friend," said Pétur Pálsson.

"Stand still," said Júel J. Júel.

Everything began to go black before Ólafur Kárason's eyes. Nothing had such a paralyzing effect on this poet as when the authorities of the nation went to the trouble of fighting over his soul. But Providence so willed it that Pétur Pálsson should stand up and stagger in pursuit of the owner of the cognac and grab him by the arm. They scuffled a little over the poet's soul, and the station owner said that Grímur Loðinkinni Ltd. would not have anything to do with notorious damned socialists, while the poet took the chance to make his escape and went to fetch the horses.

With every halt for refreshment, it became more and more difficult to get the gentry back into their saddles, particularly the station owner, for he was lanky and swayed inordinately, and the horses were nervous. Ólafur Kárason was full of foreboding about the rest of the journey; it was already late in the day, and they still had not reached the highest point of the pass where the mountain path proper began.

It was one of those quiet late-summer days, with white sunshine and no birdsong, like a young girl who has become old. He tried to forget his companions and life as a whole, and to listen to the late-summer stillness that seemed to have no limits. Nature herself hesitated, at once amazed and questioning, in memory of the sounds that had died away.

Up in the pass there was a cairn where for the past two hundred years had rested two luckless people who had been executed there in their time. The fanatical and intolerant mood of the age, which could neither understand nor forgive, had grudged them the pleasure and satisfaction of being allowed to lie in consecrated ground. These two long-dead corpses, which had to face the afterlife so high above sea level, had during their lifetime borne the name Sigurður Natan and Móeiður, but a prejudiced and coarse populace had distorted these names and called them Satan and Mósa. This was the cairn of Satan and Mósa.

Their story, briefly, was this: At Kirkjuból, to the west of the heath, there lived fully two hundred years ago a couple named Jón and Móeiður. Jón was a prosperous farmer, but was thought to be less doughty in more manly exploits. His wife Móeiður was said to be a very energetic and hard-bitten woman. Their marriage was thought to be a somewhat precarious one. It is said that one autumn, the farmer hired a young and able fellow called Sigurður Natan or Natansson, who hailed from the south. Sigurður Natan, according to those who knew, was a very artistic fellow, an excellent carpenter, a good singer and versifier. But it was rumored that he was not quite such a faithful servant, and he was thought somewhat fickle in his love affairs. To cut a long story short, early that winter the housewife and the farmhand fell in love so desperately that neither felt able to live without the other. They agreed to get rid of Jón the farmer, seize his money, and then go abroad where they could enjoy their love in peace. They both attacked Jón one night when he was asleep in bed; the wife undertook to hold him down while the farmhand struck. This done they emptied his money chest, and to hide the evidence of their handiwork they thought it best to set fire to the house and burn it down. All the buildings burnt to ashes during the night with every-thing they contained, both the living and the dead, including five servants, four cows, three children, two old women and a dog, in addition to the farmer. Satan and Mósa were convicted at the Þingskálar Assembly next spring and executed up in the pass on Midsummer Day and buried under a cairn. They were both said to have walked a great deal after death, and for more than two hundred years they had been considered the worst ghosts in the district.*

"Poor blessed creatures," said Pétur Pálsson thickly. He sat down beside the cairn overcome with grief, took off his pince-nez, and wept.

"Eat shit!" said the station owner.

"The love was nothing, my friend, compared with burning down the house," said Pétur Pálsson, and shook his head in despair as if all were lost. "My dearest Júel, it's so dreadful to burn down a house."

"What the devil does it matter! What was the house worth?" said the station owner.

"Oh, it was a lot of money, Júel, and no insurance in those days," said the manager.

"Haven't I told you over and over again that money is worthless if you need a woman?" said the station owner. "Either you're going where you're going, or you're not going where you're not going; a hundred thousand million, what do I care?"

"Yes, but the people, dear friend: four cows, three children, two old women, and a dog, what d'you say about that?" said the manager.

"You should deny facts if they're inconvenient," said the station owner.

"People are still people," said the manager thickly, and he went on shaking his head over all this loss of life.

"People!" said the station owner. "What do I care? Grímur Loðinkinni Ltd. doesn't stand for any nonsense."

"My dear, beloved Júel, my dear friend and loving brother, who's going to help me and us and this damned estate that neither God nor man wants to own! Forgive me for just this once if I, as an older man and an intellectual and president of the Psychic Research Society, ask you as a five-trawler man and two stations up north: If money's worthless, and people are worthless, and everything's worthless, and nothing's worth anything, what then is worth something?"

"Fish," mumbled the station owner and closed his eyes and let his head fall forward, with a newly opened bottle of cognac between his legs. "Fish. Fish."

"Fish?" echoed the manager, weeping. "Fish—and nothing else?"

"Nothing else? Yes, of course," said the station owner and looked up with a sudden hiccup. "Roe and liver are also worth a lot. Fish offal and whale oil are worth a lot. Even muck is worth a lot. It's only people who are worthless. And money if you need a woman. Grímur Loðinkinni won't have any damned socialism."

As he threw out these winged words he caught sight of Ólafur Kárason who had forgotten the danger again and was sitting a few yards away. The station owner's instinctive wrath at the poet flared up anew. He jumped to his feet, this time without any warning, threw himself on the poet, and sat down on him astride his chest with one hand at the neck of his jersey and the bottle of cognac in the other. It was useless now for Pétur Pálsson to beg for mercy for the poet, not even when he let it be understood that this was his own poet whom he had been feeding all summer; the station owner refused absolutely to have any people in full possession of their senses near him: "Poets should be given enough drink to make them mad," he said, and tried to hold Ólafur Kárason's head in such a way as to force the neck of the bottle into his mouth. "And if they don't want to drink, then they can starve; they will be trampled underfoot into the mud."

But at the moment when the poet felt he was going to be robbed of his last scrap of human dignity because it was not possible to rob him of anything else, at the moment when he was going to be deprived of the most fundamental human right of self-determination, at the moment when he actually felt the gentleman's boots on his face, he suddenly felt that it did not matter. He thought of his poems: when everything was said and done, he owned a fortune that the station owner's hands could never touch. He thought of the thousands of poets whom the station owners of the world had trampled into the dirt with their boots before him. Time passes, and grass grows on the graves. But long after the station owners have sunk into the dark night of oblivion, shrouded in the contempt of the centuries, the songs of the poets will still sound on the lips of living and loving people.

Pétur Pálsson had at first watched the proceedings idly, but at this point he put on his pince-nez and stood up.

"Your name is Júel Júel Júel, my lad, and that is a fine name," said Pétur Pálsson, and grabbed the station owner's shoulder. "But I'm no

Icelander, s'help me, if you want to know. My grandmother was called Madame Sophie Sørensen."

"It'll be a long time before Grímur Loðinkinni Ltd. helps such rats as you, who sink ships, embezzle funds, falsify books, and burn down houses," said the station owner when the manager had dragged him off the poet. They scuffled for a short time in earnest on the grass beside the cairn. But just when the manager seemed to be getting the better of the station owner, the latter spewed a jet of vomit straight up into the manager's face. At this unexpected attack the manager retired, removed his teeth and his pince-nez and put both in his pocket while he wiped his face with his sleeve. The station owner went on spewing. After a moment he fell asleep in his vomit. Pétur Pálsson also lay down beside the cairn and went to sleep. Ólafur Kárason sat some distance away and kept an eye on the horses, but occasionally he watched how these pillars of society went about going to sleep.

And the day turned to evening.

—— **20** ——

On the following evening, after an eventful journey, he was sitting in the poetess's low-ceilinged loft at the open window, while the swell broke on the gravel beach with a slow, regular murmur and the sea gleamed in the moonlight. He had finished eating and telling the story of the journey, and the woman had cleared the table and washed up the dishes. That white-scrubbed kitchen with its open window had both a kind of universal dignity and an impersonal warmth, which made you happy in the midst of the adversities and sorrows of life. The friendly rose-patterned plates in the rack, the ladle on the wall, the blue-checked curtains, the woman's knitting on the windowsill, the warmth from the cooking stove, the cat, the aroma of coffee, the moonlight, the sea—it was perhaps not many krónurs' worth if you tried to sell it, but all the same it was the world at its fairest and best.

Then there came a commotion on the stairs, a violent blow on the outer door, a knocking on the kitchen door. But it was not the woman's husband after all; it was the manager's hoydenish daughter. She said she had a letter for Ólafur Kárason from Júel J. Júel, and then was gone.

The woman came over to him at the window while he was tearing open the letter. He took out of the envelope a piece of paper decorated with pictures; he turned it over and studied it from all sides in the moonlight, but did not know what it was.

"It's a fifty-krónur note," said the poetess.

He was absolutely flabbergasted. It was the first in his life he had ever come into any money. It took him a long time to realize what blessings a gift like this could bring. Finally he clutched the poetess's arm and said, "Now I can buy myself some clothes! And probably boots! And perhaps I can get to Aðalfjörður to have my poems published and to visit my mother."

She did not say anything. Eventually, after a long silence, she cleared her throat in a high-pitched note.

"Don't you think it's a lovely present, perhaps?" he said.

"No," she said bluntly. "I think it's better when the mighty abuse the lowly free of charge—and indeed that's undoubtedly their dearest wish."

He was speechless; to be honest, he did not understand what she was getting at. She went over to the side of the kitchen that was in deepest shadow, and vanished.

"It's a poor overlord who hasn't the guts to kick a pauper in the teeth without opening his purse afterwards," she said. "There's no creature on earth so despicable and loathsome as a rich man with a conscience."

Her thin, silver-clear voice cracked and became a whisper.

"Hólmfríður," he whispered, alarmed. "Where are you? Come here. Sit beside me."

She crossed the room twice before she sat down. Then she sat down on the little bench beside him. She turned her back to him and looked out at the sea.

"Hólmfríður," he said again; but she did not answer, just sighed and picked up her knitting.

"I'll throw this money out of the window if you like," he said.

There was a long silence. She knitted very rapidly. At last she said in her clear, silvered voice, having regained her composure: "I can't give you anything in return."

He replied after a long silence: "Yes."

There was another long silence.

"What?" she whispered out into the moonlight, almost inaudibly.

"You know what it is," he said.

Silence.

"No," she said.

Silence.

"Yes," he said.

The conversation went on like that for a long time, with meaningless monosyllables, long silences and the breathing murmur of the waves breaking their green-white fringes on the gleaming pebbles of the beach.

"Hólmfríður, you who see everything," he said, "you know what's wrong with me."

"How should I know?" she said. "No one knows what goes on in someone else's heart."

"You surely know that I've suffered a terrible sorrow."

"Sorrow?" she said. "No, I don't know that. What sort of sorrow?"

"A love sorrow," he said.

He had suddenly begun to think to himself that a little sorrow was actually worthwhile if one could afterwards enjoy consolation from such a woman. But then she said bluntly, as if nothing were amiss, "Love sorrows don't exist."

He was a little disappointed that she should reply like that; she used a special tone of voice; it was very difficult to get close to her.

"You can call it what you like, Hólmfríður, because you're so intelligent and much more of a poet than I am, what's more," he said. "But for the past few weeks I have felt as if life's days were getting shorter and shorter, darker and darker, and that soon everything would become one unending night."

"Soon everything will become one unending night," her weak, silvered voice echoed in the moonlight, but the woman went on knitting.

He continued to listen after the words had died away; finally he shivered and moved closer to her, involuntarily, put his hand on her shoulder and said, very seriously, "No, Hólmfríður, you mustn't say that."

"They were your own words," she said.

"Yes, but you mustn't repeat them," he said. "If you want to save my life . . ."

"Child," she said, when he fell silent. "How strange you are! You're so equivocal that one never knows whether you're being serious or joking. And yet so simple that one feels sorry for you."

"I am that which craves consolation," he said.

"But who is to console me?" she said.

This question took him aback, and he felt ashamed and blushed to the roots of his hair. He had always seen himself as the only person in the world who was in distress; it had never occurred to him that she, too, was in need of consolation, this reserved, clear-sighted woman, this weak voice.

"I've wanted so much to read you my poems all summer," he said. "And yet I've wanted something even more, and never more so than tonight—to hear your poems."

"I have burnt them," she said.

Autumn sounds from the sea. The moon was only a short distance away, it was on this side of the mountain, it was almost over the middle of the fjord and yet really even closer, it hung right over the gleaming stony beach, scarcely more than an arm's length from the window. As a child one would have stretched out a hand and caught hold of it; its beam on the fjord was a path one could walk—because if something is beautiful enough, one believes in it. This simple scene was for a long time the only sequel to their conversation. Finally he laid his face against her neck and whispered, "Will you let me kiss you?"

"No," she replied bluntly, without taking offense.

"Why not?" he said.

"I could be your mother."

"Then be my mother," he said.

"Promise me one thing, little Óli—don't be a womanizer when you grow up. We others cannot imagine anything more disgusting than that," she said.

"Just one kiss," he implored. "Then I know I'll see life in a new light. Then all the sorrows of life will be wiped away. Then I shall have a seed which will live in my heart until next spring."

"We mustn't play with fire," she said.

"Just this once," he begged. "And then never again."

"For that very reason—no," she said.

They heard the stair creaking, and the outer door was torn open.

"Quick, get up, he's coming!" whispered the poet in confusion.

But she did not move, did not even look up, just went on knitting. Then the woman's husband was standing in the doorway. Even though he was drunk he saw them at once, silhouetted against the window; he looked at them for a moment, growling to himself. Then he began to pour abuse on his wife. She carried on knitting for a long time without moving, but eventually she gave a start as if she had been stabbed: he had said "whore." But she did not ask for mercy; she merely said in her coldest and most silvery voice, "You'd better go to bed."

"If that boy ever comes into my sight again, I'll murder him," said the woman's husband.

At this, Ólafur Kárason became not a little uneasy. Of all dreadful things, nothing is more dreadful than murder. On the other hand, the woman seemed to think differently. It was not until the man had repeated that one word that she made any move. But then an amazing thing happened, the like of which Ólafur Kárason had never seen. This youthful-looking woman with that girlish bosom, that slight voice and the impassive, preoccupied thoughtfulness in her large dark eyes—she stuck the needles into the ball of wool, went over to her husband, and gave him a box on the ear. And for whatever reason, this gigantic, formidable man, who looked as if he could have crushed her with one hand, stopped swearing, wiped his face with his hand as if it had been splashed, and then gaped speechlessly at his wife.

"There," she said, as if she had been chastising a child. "Do as I say and go to bed at once." She turned to Ólafur Kárason and said, "It's getting late. You'll come over for morning coffee at your usual time."

Then the couple were alone in their home, and Ólafur Kárason was standing outside.

He was far from contented. The road to his bed had become the Way of the Cross for him each day. With the onset of autumn he was the only person in that empty building which had previously been part of the warm winds of summer. Each time he approached the building he felt it was teeming with evil forebodings all around; it was as if it were besieged by evil thoughts. And he discovered that the whole building was tenanted by dreadful wild animals. As soon as night fell, the rats began to scratch and scrape, squeak and squawk behind the walls, or even to fight and scream; sometimes they fell several feet behind the wainscoting, and he could count up to five before their bodies came down somewhere with a thud. Even if he got out of bed and hammered on the walls, it had little more effect than waking a snoring man—after a few moments the fun would begin again. But the yowling of the feral cats in the cellars was perhaps even more horrible than the rats themselves. Around midnight (not to mention when there was moonlight like tonight) it was as if evil spirits took possession of these man-shy, broad-jawed creatures which otherwise lay in hiding all day; their discordant howls, either in frightful solo or shrill chorus, gave the night the character of hell itself and everlasting torment, and robbed this sensitive poet of both sleep and peace of mind so that he could hardly bear it.

He tried to kill time as much as he could, stopping at every other step and looking at the moonlight on the sea. And then, as so often before, the good spirits of the world smiled upon this young poet with the uncertain future: he found Eilífðar-Daði in the dirt. This Jesus-brother and drinker of cough mixture was lying, as was his custom, directly across the road, with one cheek in the soft mud, asleep.

The poet recognized him at once and tried to rouse him. He had met him once before, in the spring, before the summer began; he had then thought him the only person left in the whole world. Now he met him again in the autumn, and it was wonderful to meet him again when the summer was over, because even if he perhaps was not the only person in the world, as the poet had once thought, he was at least a person in the world. Jesus! My brother! Heave-up!

His name was Daði Jónsson, and he was called Eilífðar-Daði (Eternity-Dave) because people were convinced that he had achieved eternal bliss already in this world; some called him Eilífðar-Dauði (Eternity-Death). He was said to be a good seaman, he was even much in demand as a fisherman, and he never missed a fishing season. At the end of the season he would come home to his sister, the mother of a family in Sviðinsvík, and hand over most of his pay to her if there were any; but the rest he would deposit with the doctor for cough mixture, and usually he managed to achieve bliss in the course of the first day. Cough mixtures—they were his family, his million, his hotel. He left his sister's house and slept on the road, always directly across it; but the chariots of the Lord would on no account run over this strange consumer. It was difficult to avoid being fond of such a man, who loved the whole world without doing any harm to anyone except himself. Few people could boast a more courteous and humble soul, even among those who were reckoned to be in their full senses. On dry land, Eilífðar-Daði Jónsson never said anything but those three familiar phrases: Jesus! My brother! Heave-up!

He took a sip from the flask of cough mixture when he woke up, and his face was convulsed by the most incredible grimaces. He said "My brother!" and greeted the poet tearfully and with long handshakes and embraces. Ólafur Kárason considered himself a good and loving person to have found an individual who was even less able to shift for himself than a poet, and he was determined to take him to his palace and invite him to be a fellow lodger and soul mate because it was now autumn, and because he was alone in the darkness, surrounded by wild animals and evil foreboding; and there was no longer any consolation.

___ 21 ___

Momentous tidings at Sviðinsvík: Satan and Mósa had materialized at a seance of the Psychic Research Society, and now wanted to be disinterred. They lamented their sad fate and said that the angry thoughts and harsh judgments meted out to them on earth deprived them of peace of soul and prevented them from attaining the joys of heaven. They took the liberty of reminding the Psychic Research Society of the words "Judge not, that ye be not yourselves judged." It was not much fun being called a ghost for more than two hundred years, and each time a calf fell into a pool or a cow went dry or the roof fell in on people, it was always that damned ghost. On the other hand it was quite true that one had had very little spiritual maturity during one's time on earth, and looked for the right current but did not find it. One longed to see the light but there was no light, one loved carnally instead of loving like invisible beings in space; but life was not all fun and games, far from it. Times were difficult, God was not always near, one was forced to commit adultery, one was forced to murder people, one was forced to steal money, one was forced to burn down houses; yes, unfortunately, five servants, four cows, three children, two old women, and a dog, in addition to the farmer himself. But might one ask: would these people not have died anyway? None gets a seal for a stay of death, as our dear Hallgrímur Pétursson put it. Let him among you who is without sin cast the first stone. Who among you has achieved perfect spiritual maturity, found the right current, seen the light, loved like invisible beings in space? Vengeance is mine, saith the Lord. We humans must practice forgiveness, most particularly towards the dead. Let our riches be in reaching heaven, says the poet. If you who now live on earth want to promote spiritual maturity and ensure your contact with the right current, you should open up the cairn which an unfeeling age heaped over us up in the mountains, and transfer us to consecrated ground, said Satan and Mósa.

To begin with, the manager was not disposed to pay any attention to such talk. At first sight there were many more urgent tasks to be done on the estate than disinterring this excellent couple, but after repeated appeals from Satan and Mósa at seance after seance, the upshot was that he no longer felt able to turn a deaf ear to their pleas, and raised the subject with the pastor and the secretary. Now, church life had been rather apathetic in the past few years; it was practically impossible to drag a single old woman into God's house any more, except for funerals, which were unfortunately much too infrequent to keep the people spiritually awake. So the pastor seized upon this rare ecclesiastical opportunity with relief, and said he was prepared to take upon himself the burdensome duties associated with the disinterment and transport of bones, along with the appropriate divine service, including an address to the congregation, memorial sermon, funeral oration, prayers, etc. He brushed the dust from his sleeve and blew on it at the same time.

"The main point in this business," said the pastor, "seems to me to be who will undertake to pay the funeral expenses? And where are we going to get a coffin for the bones?"

"Don't worry about that, old boy," said the manager. "The one who always pays for everything in Sviðinsvík will pay. The main point in this business, from my point of view, is that God should forgive us as we forgive our debtors."

So it was decided by both the spiritual and temporal authorities that both God and men should forgive Satan and Mósa in accordance with the Lord's Prayer; it was proclaimed that it was not in the power of humans to judge those who lived in the vale of sorrow.

One day late in September Pétur Pálsson the manager set off on an expedition up the mountain with three laborers from the estate. They took with them pickaxes, spades, crowbars, and brennivín. There are no reports of their journey except that they were away all that day. That evening they did not return from the mountain. People waited up for them far into the night, and some people began to get certain ideas. Some voiced the opinion that the ghosts' theological drivel about forgiveness at the Psychic Research Society had been nothing but lies and deceit—all that the couple had wanted was to lure people up to their cairn and murder them.

But those who were up early next morning had the consolation of seeing Pétur Pálsson come riding down off the mountain, admittedly somewhat the worse for wear, extremely muddied, without his hat, his teeth and his pince-nez, but undeniably in a comparatively unmurdered condition. And though he had lost his outer emblems of dignity and was so worn-out that he could scarcely sit on his horse, his journey had not been in vain. Across the pommel of his saddle he was carrying the bones of Satan and Mósa in a bag. Although his outer dignity had gone, his sight, hearing, sense of smell, taste and feeling all gone, the body's sense of balance disturbed, the laws of gravity in disorder, and heaven and earth threatening to disintegrate, there was nothing which could make the manager part with this ultimate treasure of the soul, this symbol of forgiveness and current, spiritual maturity and light. The last seen of him that morning was when he clambered off his horse at his door, crawled to his bedroom with the bag and locked himself in with a key. He was not seen for the rest of the day. That evening the coastal steamer called at the harbor on her way to the capital, and then the manager was observed to embark, accompanied by the pastor and the secretary, who bade him an affectionate farewell and wished him a good and successful journey.

As for the gravediggers, they came straggling back to habitation one by one as the day wore on, two of them on the other side of the mountain, the other on this side, and had lost their horses. They were in poor shape; they had spent the night in the open in slush and autumn darkness, crazed with drink and very ill; but they had little to report about the opening of the cairn, whether it took a long time or not, except that one of them had a very vague recollection of having caught sight of a horse's tooth. On the other hand, the pastor gave notice on the church door and the telegraph pole, by agreement with those properly concerned, and by leave of the bishop, that next Sunday, from this parish church, the funeral would take place of the luckless bones of the late Sigurður Natansson and the late Móeiður, which had in accordance with their own wishes been disinterred and brought to Sviðinsvík.

—— 22 ——

But while all this was going on, there was one person who was walking about the estate with fifty krónur in his pocket and did not care at all—the poet Ólafur Kárason. When it came to the bit, he had not thrown this large sum of money out of the window after all. Certainly he knew in his heart that there was something odd about slaving away all summer without anyone mentioning payment, and then getting a vast sum of money as a reward for maltreatment, but all the same he was determined to get himself a pair of boots. If footwear were available in accordance with justice, then who would be wearing shoes?

The secretary was leaning against the writing desk behind the counter, poring conscientiously over a large, closely written ledger filled with the gravity of the world. The shop occupied a small room at one end of the Privy Councillor's palace, with entry through an uninviting door. There was no sign, either on the door or the window, to indicate that activity of any kind went on there; indeed it was late in the summer before Ólafur Kárason discovered this modest commercial enterprise in his own palace. He had never set foot across its threshold before now.

"Good-day," he said.

Most of the shelves were empty, but the stocks that were visible to the eye were limited to crumpled strips of moldy shoe leather, a few packets of five-inch nails on a shelf, a few cups and saucers with incredibly colorful raised roses on them, gray-white gossamer-thin corpse stockings that could also be used by women, all bundled together in a heap on the counter, and three extremely broad-brimmed straw Mexican hats. Judging by the smell, most of the trade seemed to consist of petroleum and creosote.

After a long pause the secretary looked up from his serious reading, swallowed so that his Adam's apple took a steep dive; he pushed his rusty spectacles higher up his nose, looked at the poet for a long time and finally said, "Mm—good-day."

"Do you have any boots here?" asked the poet.

"Mm—not that I know of," said the secretary.

"I would very much like to buy a pair of boots," said the poet, and smiled apologetically.

"Mmya, just so," said the secretary. "That is undeniably a rather peculiar desire. Or at least, as far as I can see, you are wearing shoes on your feet. Mm—on the other hand we have here some quite good pieces of leather for those who have no shoes."

"Aren't there any clothes for sale in the shop here, then?" said the poet.

"Clothes?" asked the secretary. "Might I ask what you mean, young man?"

"Clothes to wear," said the poet.

"Clothes to wear?" echoed the secretary. "Not that I know of."

"I don't suppose one could buy a scarf?" asked the poet.

"A scarf," said the secretary. "I don't know what that is; I've never owned a scarf. Mm—on the other hand we have some light-colored women's stockings here as you can see. Mm—and there should be some shoelaces somewhere, if they haven't rotted, so we'll say no more about that. But anyway I have a little business with you on behalf of the manager, so it's just as well I saw you."

The business was that since other poets were not back yet from their summer jobs or the herring, apart from those who had fallen prey to hysterical whims and eccentricities, the committee of the Psychic Research Society had agreed to get Ólafur Kárason to compose a hymn on the occasion of the funeral next Sunday. If the hymn turned out well, the secretary himself was to write it out on duplicating paper and make several copies of it and have it distributed, so that the congregation could sing it at the church service.

"I wrote a poem once this summer, but when the time came no one wanted to hear it," said the poet.

"It was the sheriff who decided that," said the secretary, "and it didn't really matter, because that was an unimportant occasion compared to the ceremony which is to take place next Sunday. The whole nation will be watching what happens here in Sviðinsvík on Sunday.

And it's also extremely likely that various foreign countries will be taking notice of it, too, at any rate, Great Britain."

"Really," said the poet, without enthusiasm.

"Mm—you say 'Really,' young man?" said the secretary. "That is undeniably a rather peculiar reply. Might I ask what you mean by that word?"

"I mean that I'm such an insignificant poet that it isn't worthwhile getting me to compose a poem," said Ólafur Kárason modestly.

The secretary gave the poet a stern and searching look and finally said, "I no longer understand young people nowadays. It's as if nothing serious or important makes any impression on young people any longer. The modern craze seems to be to squander money needlessly if possible. But luckily it isn't possible. Even you, young man, who are said to have a poetic bent, yes and some say you even possess a modicum of intelligence, you just say 'Really' when you're invited to take part in a ceremony which is destined to revolutionize the religious, scientific and moral life of the nation."

"I have so little education," said the poet.

"It doesn't need any education to understand the glad message of forgiveness, young man," said the secretary. "Judge not, that ye be not yourselves judged—these words weren't spoken to the educated, but to the human heart. Nor does it need any education to understand the science of the afterlife; all that is needed for that is a human soul."

And before this young poet realized what he was saying, in his ignorance and lack of conviction, he had blurted out the words which were at once the most utterly forbidden and the most unforgivable of all words which the human tongue could utter in Sviðinsvík; he said, "If I am to tell you the honest truth, I have grave doubts about whether I have a soul."

The Adam's apple of the man behind the counter seemed about to plunge below his diaphragm, and the spectacles also came right down to the tip of his nose. First he looked at Ólafur Kárason absolutely rigidly, then he turned aside abruptly as if he were going away, then he opened his mouth and screwed up his eyes as if the stars were hurtling down from the firmament, finally he coughed weakly into his hand. He looked like a frightened puffin which was trying to do everything at once to save its life—swim, fly and dive. Eventually he assumed a cold official expression and asked in an impersonal voice, "Might I ask, isn't Pétur Pálsson the manager your benefactor?"

"Yes," said the poet.

"Is he perhaps familiar with the mm—independent and undeniably rather peculiar views you have acquired for yourself on important matters here this summer?"

"I don't know," said the poet.

"You presumably don't feel you owe any debt of gratitude to the manager?" said the secretary.

"Yes," said the poet. "And indeed I'm quite prepared to compose in his honor as fine a poem as I am capable of, any time at all, for instance for his birthday, or at Christmas. But to compose a eulogy in honor of ghosts like Satan and Mósa—I'm not enough of a poet for that."

"Mmmmm—you need say no more," said the secretary. "This is the second time today I have received the same answer; on the first occasion it also came from a person not far removed from the generous hand of Pétur Pálsson. One begins to understand who have been conspiring together all summer at his expense. This isn't the first time that Pétur Pálsson has nurtured snakes at his breast. But fortunately there's no need to explain to him in what direction materialism is bound to lead the individual."

An unhappy tobacco addict came into the shop and begged, almost in tears, for a little tobacco to soothe his soul. But the secretary had no knowledge of any poison being available there, although there were some cigarette papers left over from the Privy Councillor's time, somewhere up in the loft, but he was afraid the damp had got at them. The poet used the opportunity to sneak away.

In this shop there was really nothing for sale except the soul and what pertained to it—forgiveness, the afterlife, and so on. The poet stood on the shingle with a warm fifty-krónur note in his hand and a troubled conscience as if after a murder. He knew in his heart that something had just happened which would bring in its train an irrevocable judgment on his future. He had not been content with saying that terrible word "really," but had also cast doubts on the soul and had called the two saints "ghosts."

Gradually, Ólafur Kárason began to understand that it was more difficult to be a poet in the world we inhabit than many people think. One can see things this way, one cannot see things that way; speak this way, not speak that way, entirely according to who gives one food to eat. How did Jónas Hallgrímsson* and Sigurður Breiðfjörð manage to be poets in such a world? What did they say if they were asked to write a eulogy to a ghost? Poets should drink to make them mad, the station owner had said, and had sat down astride the poet's chest with a bottle in his hand; but they should not get anything to eat. What was the position in regard to Jónas Hallgrímsson and Sigurður Breiðfjörð? Did they get enough to eat? Or did they get too much to drink?

The anger of Pétur Pálsson the manager and of other good men menaced him; remorse for these ill-advised, light-hearted words to the secretary assailed him. Perhaps, despite everything, he ought to try to cobble something together about the late Sigurður Natan and the late Móeiður, in order to buy himself peace. In Rome one must do as the Romans do. He sat down on the beach and tried to think about this subject for a poem. But no matter how hard he tried, he simply could not derive any inspiration from this dreary couple. They remained the two most insufferable ghosts he could imagine. Could he then not forgive Satan and Mósa like the manager, like the pastor, and the secretary, like all good men—probably the sheriff, too—since they had been dead for two hundred years and there was no way of punishing them more than had been done already? Why was it that he could not be good, could not love them and understand them and forgive them and take them to his bosom, these two unhappy departed souls? Why was it that he felt sick?

— 23 —

A pitch-dark autumn night, without a moon.

He had been allowed to sit in the kitchen and read a book by the woman's lamp; her husband sat at home with the newspapers, without a drink; nothing was said. Then the evening was over. Ólafur Kárason got to his feet and said Good-night. But no sooner was he outside the door than someone came up to him from the shelter of the house, seized his arm in a fierce grip, and uttered his name in a breathless whisper: an agitated woman; he thought he could sense her heartbeat in the darkness, unnaturally fast, her manner unbalanced and ethereal.

"I have so much to say to you," she said. "I thought perhaps I wouldn't find you."

"What do you want with me so late?" he said.

"Why have you stopped believing in me?" she asked, without any preamble.

"Was that all?" he said.

"That all? Really? Was it so trifling, then, to lead you out into a homefield, fully recovered, this spring? Have you forgotten the night we sat among the sheep and understood one another utterly, even though we had never met before?"

"No, Þórunn," he said. "I've told you already that I shall never forget it."

"Shall I tell you, Ólafur—it was the only time I've felt deep down, deep inside myself that Jesus Christ was right. Believe. Believe. Believe. Tell me now, do you think it's all a lie?"

"I have difficulty in thinking as quickly as you, Þórunn," he said. "You think too quickly. I don't understand how you think."

"D'you know that I'm going to England?" she said.

"Really," he said, and bit his tongue a little afterwards.

"I've never known anyone to become so corrupted in one summer!" she said. "You don't believe anything any more."

Silence.

"It's quite possible that my psychic phenomena aren't all genuine, Ólafur, but what am I to do when there are spirits with horns and cloven feet all around me?"

Silence.

"Why don't you say something? Am I such a wicked person, then? What a damned fool you are! I can tell you that I have every right to talk to you, because I'm many thousand times older than you are. I could almost be your mother."

Silence.

"I know perfectly well what you're thinking even though you don't know anything about what I'm thinking. But tell me something. How is one to have any respect for a world where nothing else matters except who can lie the most plausibly and steal the most?"

Silence.

"You don't believe me, but can I ask you something else? Do you perhaps think that Júel J. Júel owns all the fifty-krónur and hundred-krónur notes he carries around in his pockets? No, he has stolen them all. I don't care what you say. I'm not yielding to anyone. I'm going to England. Am I a pig?"

"Þórunn," he said at last. "You've been drinking."

"Yes," she said, "I've been drinking water. Mad people drink water. Wicked people drink water. Pigs drink water, worse luck."

"I desire nothing so much as to understand you, Þórunn," he said. "I know that there is something very great in you, and I can well believe that you are destined to become world-famous. But the more famous you become, the harder I find it to understand you."

"It's said that people will always hate those who save their lives, and I know perfectly well that you hate me, whatever you say. And yet, yet, I'm standing here in the roadway tonight to save your life for all eternity, all eternity . . ."

"Þórunn, I wish I knew what to say to make you stop talking the way you talk. In the first place, I don't hate any living person; in the second place, I don't know what hate is; and in the third place . . ."

"Yes, and in the third place you've always got something to say for yourself when you want to," she said. "But if you care for me at all, why wouldn't you compose a poem? Why did you answer the secretary with mockery?"

"Mockery?" he said. "I may well have answered stupidly. Can I help it if I have no education? But to call it mockery to say that one doesn't know what the soul is—that's being more touchy than I can understand."

"D'you think I don't know that the two of you are conspiring to work against us and humiliate me, that cow queen and you? You pretend you don't have souls. You talk about 'ghosts.' But have a care, say I. I utter this curse and lay this spell, that one fine day you shall have souls. And that day you will both come crawling on all fours like ghosts to Þórunn of Kambar!"

To be sure, he had stopped being afraid of her curses and spells, but nonetheless he felt uncomfortable in her presence and valued neutrality and peace more highly than ever before.

"Let's meet again tomorrow in broad daylight, Þórunn," he said. "People talk more reasonably in the daytime than at night."

"No," she said. "Truth belongs to the night. The day is nothing but excuses. I won't be wicked any longer. I'll be good. Let's be friends. It doesn't matter if you don't want to write a poem about a ghost, ghost, ghost. It doesn't matter if we rot like the damned corpses we are when we die, die, die. Come on, let's run away, away, away."

She seized his arm and ran off as if she were fleeing. Her frenzied restlessness infected him and he, too, took to his heels; they ran through the pitch-darkness along the wet road, up to their ankles in mud, splashing through puddles, heading up the fjord, away from the village. Then she suddenly stopped.

"What are we running away from?" he said.

"I'm frightened," she said, panting, and came right up to him and put her arm round him and breathed all over his face.

"There's nothing to be afraid of," he said bravely.

"Yes," she said. "Everything one does is a sin. Can't you see anything?"

"No," he said.

"Let's go on," she said.

They went on.

"Everything one says is a lie," she said.

Silence.

"Everything one wants is evil."

"I would give so much to be able to understand you," he said.

"All your life is a crime and a disgrace, crime and disgrace, if you can't steal money," she said. "A lot of money."

"My life?"

"Everything you say is a lie while you're not stealing money. Money is truth. Everything you do is evil if you haven't stolen money. Money is beauty. You are a wicked man if you don't steal money. Money is love. How I loathe this damned penniless dog's life that makes a person less valuable than fish offal and whale oil! Can't you see anything?"

He thought then that he saw a sudden quick glow over the Privy Councillor's palace, as if someone were walking outside it with a lantern.

"Come on," she said.

"Where to?" he said.

"I'm going to show you something down by the shore here," she said. "Something that concerns only you."

"It's past midnight," he said. "Shouldn't we rather say Good-night and go to bed, in the hope that we shall understand one another better tomorrow morning?"

"No," she said. "Don't leave me, I'm alone. The manager's old woman has forbidden the children to talk to me, and would undoubtedly kill me if she knew how to kill anyone. My mother, who's an invalid, has been farmed out with some wretches away out on Outer Ness, and Daddy, who's old and infirm, wandered from place to place all summer looking for work and found nothing anywhere. Yesterday he wrote to me and asked me to recommend him to the high-ups at Sviðinsvík for quarry work. You remember my sisters, how close the three of us were; we were inseparable. They're now wandering about somewhere in the south, one of them with a two-year-old child. And my friend Friðrik, who made my days at Kambar a festival and a romance, he's now in a higher sphere and doesn't come to me any longer. And you, you whom I raised from the dead, you won't even talk to me, and you say that no one has a soul."

"If it's any comfort to you, Þórunn dear, I shall walk with you all night," he said, and tears came to his eyes, for he now saw that this was not as complicated as he had thought; she was just a lonely girl, penniless and in distress.

"Are you feeling sorry for me?" she asked then.

"No," he replied, afraid of having offended her again. "But when I was small, I heard a strange music behind the universe. Whoever has heard that music never forgets it again, but understands everything in the light of that music."

"I know that you're not like anyone else," she said. "Thank you for being willing to walk with me. We've now nearly arrived at where we were going."

"Where were we going?" he asked.

"To the house on the shore," she said.

"What house is that?"

"The house on the shore," she said, as if thinking of something else.

He didn't know of any house that far up the fjord and went on asking what she meant, but she was preoccupied and did not reply for a long time. Finally she put her arm around his shoulders and leaned against him and whispered into his face: "You know, of course, the blue palace that the heaven has held in its embrace all summer?"

At first he had no idea what she was talking about, but when she began to describe this building in more detail, he half felt he recognized the description and that he had seen this house before, but whether it was in a book or in a picture or in a dream he could not be sure. One thing was certain—a secret shiver of pleasure went through him when he heard her talking about this house; the girl's voice had suddenly changed register, and she was now talking in a quiet, deep, warm tone with a suppressed excitement, as when someone is starting a long story.

"There is a lantern on the balustrade, so that you can see your way up the steps," she said. "Then you walk up the steps. You come to a huge oak door such as you find in foreign story books. And when you press a button on the doorpost, the double doors open wide without your seeing anybody, and you step across the threshold. You come into a large and silent antechamber where only one light is burning. Then you go on through the next door, and then suddenly you're standing in a vast hall. It is hung all around with red velvet, but here and there you can see carved dragons' heads protruding between the drapes. And your footsteps drown in the softness of the carpet. And there is a scent of flowers you don't recognize, as in a dream. And you see a long decked table, the whole length of the hall, laden with choice food and wines. You can hear the heavy, autumnal roar of the sea, and you can feel a cool draft from outside through the open balcony doors, and see how the wax has formed into icicles on the candles beneath the charred wicks because the draft makes the flames flutter. You look down at your feet and see that the floor is covered with heavy, dark-red roses. And you stop in the middle of the floor and look around you in awe and whisper, 'There has been a great feast here.'

"And the old, silver-haired woman dressed in black who looks after the house curtsies to you, without a flicker of expression, and whispers back, 'Yes. There has been a great feast here.'

"And you hear her whispered words echoing from wall to wall throughout the house; it's as if the roar of the breakers carries it in off the sea, as if the draft breathes it through the open doors: 'There has been a great feast here.'"

And now the poet suddenly recognized the house. He stopped in the roadway and said, "It is the Palace of the Summerland!"

But at that very moment it was as if a flash of lightning flared behind them, with a sudden glow over the whole sky. They both looked round. The big building of the Regeneration Company, the Privy Councillor's palace, was ablaze. In a very few minutes the whole building was on fire from end to end. The flames were shooting furiously from every window, the air around was filled with glowing embers. They watched in horror for a moment, and then Ólafur Kárason of Ljósavík remembered his poems, and in the same instant he was running away from the girl towards the blazing house.

— 24 —

"Why wasn't I allowed to burn with my poems?"

He came to his senses again with this question on his lips. There were some men standing round him, pouring seawater over him. The building was still burning. They had caught hold of him as he was rushing into the flames and had dragged him unconscious out of the smoke with his clothes smoldering. They thought at first that he had suffocated, but the freezing seawater brought him round.

"Is the boy mad?" they asked. "I wouldn't be surprised if he had set fire to the building himself."

He was shaking violently in their hands after the drenching, and they did not know what to do with him. Finally they let him go, with the warning that they would not rescue him again if he tried to run into the flames a second time.

Everyone who could move had run to the scene, men and women, children and decrepit old people, many of them still in their night-clothes, some with buckets, others with jugs, one woman with a tiny mug. All of them were greatly excited and ran to and fro in disorder, many of them shouting meaninglessly or giving one another orders that were not obeyed, some of them quarreling about how the fire-fighting should be organized.

Eventually the poetess came out of the crowd and took Ólafur Kárason by the arm, and said, "What's this I hear, boy! Come home at once!"

"My poems are burnt!" he said.

"You're shivering," she said. "Here, take my arm."

"Don't you understand that I've lost my poems?" he asked.

"You're all wet," she said. "And probably burnt as well. What were you doing in the fire? Come on."

"No," he said. "Leave me alone. I've no poems left. I haven't got anything left. My whole life is burnt. Why wasn't I allowed to burn with my own life?"

"Stop this nonsense," she said. "Come on."

She led him away, and he reeled dully beside her.

"A poet's like a cat," she said. "He has many lives. What does it matter if one of them is gone with the wind? You're eighteen years old."

"My poems," he said, "they were all my lives. In times of adversity I fled to them; if someone tried to harm me I consoled myself with them. And now they are burnt."

"Didn't I tell you once, this summer, that poems were best in ashes? I burnt all my own poems myself," said the woman.

There were burn marks on his clothes, and a spark had singed his skin and it was sore and she put ointment on it. She told him to take off his clothes and throw them into the firewood box, and gave him a blanket to wrap around himself. Then she gave him hot coffee.

"Örn Úlfar also burnt all his poems," he said. "Am I then that much less of a poet than all the others?"

"Don't worry," she said. "You are reborn. You're in swaddling clothes."

"It's no use trying to humor me; I cannot smile," he said.

"I didn't expect you to have learnt to smile yet," she said. "When one is born, one only knows how to cry. It's only very gradually that one learns to smile."

He looked in amazement at his naked feet sticking out from the blanket, and let himself be convinced by her, and felt he was a child who was discovering his toes for the first time.

"You're my child tonight," she said, unemotionally. "But since I didn't have you by my husband, I don't properly know what I'm to do with you."

"Put me out to die of exposure," he said dramatically. "I won't return to haunt you."

From the passage one could get to the hay barn through a trap-door under the rafters; she placed a ladder against the opening, removed the hatch, and crawled onto the hay, and told him to follow her. It was pitch-black. She removed the damp top layer of hay and made a bed for him, and told him to lie down there with the blanket around him.

"Tomorrow I'll have some clothes ready for you," she said. "Try to sleep now."

"Don't go," he said.

"Yes," she said.

"Talk to me a little. I've got no one now except you."

"What nonsense," she said, but nevertheless she sat down beside him in the hay so that he could feel her presence. "Tonight you own a fortune that is the first and last wealth possessed by everyone on earth, all their wealth put together, their only true wealth."

"I don't understand you," he said.

"You have your naked life," she said, and he thought she came even closer to him so that he felt the warmth from her loins, and yet her voice, that characteristic sound of a muted G string, seemed to come from far, far away.

But when she started talking about his wealth, whether she did it to console him or to mock him, or both—for where is the dividing line to be drawn?—he suddenly remembered another man of wealth, and he gave a start in the darkness and clutched her arm in horror.

"Dear God in heaven, Eilífðar-Daði Jónsson has probably been burnt with the house!" he said.

"Old Eilífðar-Dauði?" she said. "Well, perhaps he's been burnt, the poor old fellow."

In the darkness, the poet saw the contorted, helpless face of the person who for the past few nights had told him so much about how difficult it was to be a man here on the estate: "Even though he could only say these three or four words, I felt I understood him better than most others," said the poet. "He was my friend, yes, probably the only one."

At this declaration, which came quite unbidden to the poet's lips as if born of a sudden inner illumination, he was so moved that the tears streamed from his eyes. He buried his face in the poetess's lap and wept with grief.

It lasted a long time. She laid her hand on his head and stroked his hair and wet cheeks and let him cry himself out. Then he had finished weeping. When he had finished weeping, she raised his head from her lap and said, "Now I don't need to be with you any longer. Your new life has begun to burgeon at once. Tonight when I am gone you will compose an immortal poem about your only friend, who was burnt to death."

She made ready to stand up.

"Don't go," he said.

"Good-night," she whispered, and stroked his hair once, very quickly, as she stood up.

"I implore you to stay," he said, and caught hold of her leg and tried to stop her leaving.

But the poetess whispered Good-night again, and slipped out of his grasp.

— 25 —

> On the road our life goes with the light,
> Empires and great lands go speeding past;
> Summer has bidden you good-night,
> And all your sunshine days are gone at last.
>
> The palace that brought you luck and health,
> Music and scent of roses late at night,
> Tapestries and carpets of unimagin'd wealth—
> It died in autumn's ghastly bonfire bright.
>
> You flotsam of the shore, forgotten freight,
> Oh, happy Jesus-lover, drunk in bed;
> Heave-up, my brother, my cough-mixture mate—
> Our palace is burnt down, and you are dead.
>
> Tomorrow, oh, and ash, alackaday,
> And ha and tcha and pooh and tut and see,
> And wheest and amen, ho and hey,
> And rags and toil and pain, and oh, dear me.

—— **26** ——

And now Pétur Pálsson the manager stepped ashore with his pince-nez, teeth and a hat. Until now, he had always worn a black bowler hat, but now he was wearing a grey felt hat which resembled Júel J. Júel's hat, except that the station owner's hat had been an extremely unusual hat whereas Pétur Pálsson's hat was an extremely ordinary one. Júel J. Júel's hat was broad-brimmed, but Pétur Pálsson's hat was narrow-brimmed; Júel J. Júel's hat had a narrow band, but Pétur Pálsson's hat had a broad band. Júel J. Júel's hat had a low crown, but Pétur Pálsson's hat had a high crown. And so on. So why was it that people should think that these hats were identical? Was it because Pétur Pálsson had no dent in the crown of his hat, but let it stand straight up, like Júel J. Júel's? Or was it because people had heard over the wires the previous day that Pétur Pálsson had bought the Sviðinsvík estate from the bank, and assumed that Júel J. Júel had helped him to do it?

But of all the gratifying and notable things that Pétur Pálsson brought home with him on this occasion, the most gratifying and most notable was the coffin. Such a coffin had never been seen in Sviðinsvík within living memory; yet it would be a shame to say that the people of Sviðinsvík were especially unaccustomed to burying folk. Here in the village, when one's nearest and dearest were being buried, the most important consideration had always been to ensure that the bottom did not fall out of the coffin at a critical moment and, secondly, that it should at least be as pitch-black on the outside as the life which its occupant had just departed, the darkness which had engulfed him, and the grief his death was supposed to cause. But now Pétur Pálsson the manager stepped ashore on this memorable autumn morning with a lovely, white infant's coffin in his luggage, as if the child he loved most dearly had passed away into eternal light. This beautiful coffin was made from special wood, its boards carpentered together with matchless skill and precision. Under the coffin were some peculiar runners or feet which made it higher and more stately than was customary in this part of the country.

The lid alone was a superb work of art. Near the head end there was a cross emblazoned in gold, and below it two sorrowing golden hands which took their last farewell and forgave everything. The lid was screwed down with many gilded angel-heads with wings in place of ears. This was not only the most beautiful coffin that people had ever seen, but also without any doubt the most magnificent piece of furniture to come to the estate since the days of the Privy Councillor, and it was downright tragic to have to watch such a work of art disappear into the black soil.

As can be imagined, it was no small ordeal for the manager to come home to his newly acquired estate in its present condition. It was no more than three days since he had increased the insurance on the estate's major building by a hundred thousand krónur, with a view to converting the building into a cultural center for the people. But when he got home, the prospective cultural center was nothing but an insignificant heap of ashes. He stopped at the scene of the blaze with his hand under his chin, his elbow on his knee, and one foot up on a rock, and remained in that posture for a long time, deep in thought, and let the pastor and the secretary watch him.

In the midst of all this desolation and ruin there was one thing that the elements in all their fury had not managed to destroy. That was the estate's huge safe. Inside the palace it had been a sort of kingdom within a kingdom, made of fireproof steel; now it towered over the ruins, alone and invincible. This enormously strong and mighty safe stood on specially cemented foundations which were sunk deep in the ground. No force known to man could shake this edifice. In this repository had been stored all the Regeneration Company's books and accounts, documents and papers. But unfortunately someone had forgotten to close the safe the last time it had been opened—perhaps the lock had been out of order. The flames had made a clean sweep of its contents, every single scrap of paper, so that not a fragment was left unburnt that could give any idea of the financial affairs of the late Regeneration Company.

As soon as Pétur Pálsson came to after his profound reflections beside the ruins, it was time to start thinking about the funeral.

It was the first time for many years that it had proved possible to bring people to church in any numbers here in Sviðinsvík; actually no one had had any inclination for such luxuries since the great years of the Privy Councillor, when people went to church on the more important festivals in order to have a look at the Family. Now it was forgiveness and the nearness of the next world which drew people to the sacred place. Until now, God had been righteous, and the next world a kind of child's toy, to soothe people who had had the misfortune of being robbed of their own world while they were still alive. The value of Pétur Pálsson the redeemer lay in the fact that he had compelled God to forgive us our debts and established the next world as a sort of station here on the estate.

These people who were for sale—they stood there in their dilapidated churchyard one sun-white autumn day, about the time when the hoar-frost was drying on the withered grass. The menfolk roamed restlessly around in circles between the lych-gate and the church door, and had no tobacco. Half-dead women stood in embarrassed groups around neglected graves and wiped away yet another tear. Boys and girls looked around inquisitively, but did not quite dare to look one another in the face in the churchyard. The summer was past; there had been no work, at most perhaps one might have managed to scrape together enough hay for the bank's cow which had now become Pétur Pálsson's cow. A few had been allowed to cut peat on the moor and carry it home on their backs, but otherwise there was not much fuel, nor very much to cook for that matter. And soon it would be winter with snow hanging from the eaves and the incessant crying of sick children in the house; the days were becoming shorter and shorter. Was it any wonder that these people longed for some glimmer of light in their dungeon? With terror-stricken eyes, like helpless little children who have been thrashed, like dull-witted vagabonds who have been chased by dogs, like half-lost foreigners who have wrecked their ship on a sandy desert, these helpless people roamed around their churchyard one autumn Sunday in the hope of hearing even one word that would carry them forward through the darkness of the coming winter, the snowstorms and prolonged bad weather, over the living death that was their life. These were murdered people.

Six veteran quarrymen walked bareheaded under the coffin, bent-shouldered and dejected, as if in the knowledge that the world's crimes had been laid upon their shoulders, every single one, and they had to atone for them all. Behind the coffin walked the pastor in his cassock, with his family; next came Pétur Pálsson the manager and his wife, then Þórunn of Kambar with a red ribbon round her hair, peering about in bewilderment in the white sunshine and soon to set off for England; then the secretary and his wife and children, the doctor's wife with her adolescent daughters, and then various members of the public who had attended the service at the manager's house; many of them had come from distant parishes to be edified by this momentous religious ceremony.

The men laid the coffin down on the grass while someone went to look for the key of the church. The pastor and the manager stopped beside the head of the coffin with solemn, pious faces; the last remnants of human characteristics had been brushed off them so thoroughly that there was not even a speck of dust left on the pastor's nose.

Then a woman detached herself from the cortege, walked over to the coffin, stopped at the foot facing the two holy gentlemen and cleared her throat slightly to call attention to herself. It was Hlaupa-Halla. The pastor opened one eye and looked at her, but the manager let nothing disturb him at his devotions.

"Excuse me, may I ask a question?" said the woman meekly. "I don't suppose I might be allowed to see what's in the coffin?"

"There's nothing in the coffin that concerns you, Halla dear," said the pastor.

"I know that well," said the woman. "My children were never buried in a coffin like that. When the life had been crushed out of them they were put into a tarred wooden box; yes, and what's more, it often cost quarrels and rows to get even that. But it's easy to see from this coffin that it wasn't squeezed out of the parish."

Until that moment, Pétur Pálsson the manager had been completely lost to the world; he held his new hat in front of his paunch with bowed head and moved his thick lips in prayer now and again. But now he suddenly stopped praying, looked up, and said, "We don't have to account to you for this coffin, my good woman; there are other and higher powers to whom we have to account for our deeds."

"Let's not pay any more heed to things that don't concern us, Halla dear," said the pastor.

"I thought perhaps it wasn't asking too much to let the public see what the public is having to bury," said the woman politely.

"Luckily, your disposition is not entirely unknown to us, Halla dear," said the pastor. "It has, you see, always left something to be desired."

"Really," said the woman. "Since you know my disposition so well, Pastor Brandur, then there's probably not much point in my trying to hide what I think. But I thought there was no need to dig up from the ground many centuries-old riffraff, incendiaries, murderers and thieves to say prayers over; I thought we had enough of them above the ground."

With these words she stormed away, while the holy gentlemen were left standing there with red faces.

Then the coffin was carried into the church.

— **27** —

"My dearest beloved, whom I nevertheless scarcely dare to address as I do because you stand as high above me in faith in God's mercy and redemption as the sun stands above the earth.

"When I heard this summer that you had had to endure martyrdom for my sake, and evil people had driven you away on a stretcher over mountains and deserts because your light had shone upon me, then I said: God be merciful to me, a sinner, and give me health to lay down my life for Hallgrímur Pétursson reincarnated.

"I haven't seen your letter nor heard the hymn you composed in my honor, because both were torn up, but since the mighty heavenly

Father hears even the prayers of this sinner, Jarþrúður Jónsdóttir, how much the more must he keep the Ljósvíkingur's own poetry in his all-knowing heart!

"All summer I have been looking for someone I could trust to write to you, because although I can read, particularly religious matter, I am very bad at writing because I was brought up beneath the feet of men and dogs that I would rather choose death than the humiliation of letting a great poet see anything so terrible, and now I have at last got to know a young pastor's wife whom I dare trust with a secret.

"I have always been looking for someone to love, like everyone else, but it's now ten years since I began to turn to Jesus and pray to him to forgive my sins, for seldom has any person sinned as I have done, and that's because I lay beneath the feet of men and dogs, as I said earlier, and couldn't provide for myself because of ill health. I have never managed to rise above just earning my keep. I had often heard you spoken of as an example to all those in distress, and I had always wanted so much to see you and hear something from your own lips, but when I saw you for the first time on our wedding day this spring, I understood then what it was to have found what one no longer dared to look for. The moment you spoke your first words to me I felt I was your mother. Jesus Christ, oh, you who laid down your life for me, give me strength to lay down my life for him! Help me to come to him and I shall never, never forsake him again.

"Since you love me, I don't care in the least how small our hovel is. I can do a great deal of work. I am accustomed both to baiting hooks and mending nets and everything else to do with fish; yes, and I've even been out fishing, what's more. I can also do everything connected with sheep and cattle and even horses. I can do all manner of washing, and I also know all about working wool, even spinning yarn, for that matter, although unfortunately I have seldom had the opportunity to do it. I can also do all the jobs involved in haymaking, and have spent many a summer at the scythe. I have also had to work at land reclamation, both cutting turf, digging trenches and carrying stones for drainage. All these tasks I have carried out under constant threat of terrible bouts of illness and with a heavy burden of sin in my heart, but from now on I shall do everything that's required with a glad smile so that you can compose immortal hymns about God's mercy and the redemption of our Lord and Savior Jesus Christ. I have now given in my notice here at Gil, so you can expect me at the end of the harvest season; I am going to try to come to you over the mountains directly, before the weather gets worse."

A turbulent sea, yellow moors, rain showers billowing over the withered grass, pastures bitten down to the roots, not a single flower, two ravens. He roamed about in the rain, and the letter burned in his hand like a punishment. The brook from springtime now poured past, muddy from the autumn rains, and the little lamb field from springtime was cropped close by cattle; no hay had been cut for the stack, but someone had torn off the roof of the shed and taken away the timbers, and only the roofless walls remained standing. He tried to find shelter there from the stormy squalls of autumn.

Once upon a time there was a destitute poet in a corner and although he was not considered to be a human being, he was sometimes asked to compose a poem when much was at stake, for instance if someone wanted to conquer an impregnable heart. He himself was not allowed to come near the festivities he had instigated with his poems; someone delivered his poem to his beloved and conquered her heart with it completely and utterly; but when the invitations went out for the wedding no one remembered this living corpse in the corner under the sloping ceiling. And when other people's wedding celebrations were at their height, another soul had appeared through the hatch at last, someone as unhappy as he himself, and they had found one another. "Poor blessed birds"—and she had sat down on the edge of his bed. A few days later he rose from the dead, a new man to a new life. A straw is of great value in sea peril, but of little value on dry land—and she was such a straw. Yes, it was impossible to deny that he had composed a hymn in her honor; he had written her a letter of proposal; yes, he had even married her, what's more, in a supernatural way, and for that matter she referred to her wedding day as if it were an accepted fact. But nonetheless he had forgotten her as swiftly as he had married her. Is it then perhaps the intention that one should love all the women one marries? No, thank you, he thought. All summer he had not even remembered she existed. One sees a particular woman in a particular place at a particular time. One loves her above all because of the place and the time, because a woman in the first instance is a place and a time. It is like a surf that rages over the beach one day and even blots out the stars in the vault of heaven. Next day it is calm. The waves throw themselves ashore with less and less force, at longer and longer intervals, until finally the sea is stilled and the stars mirror themselves again in the flat calm.

This summer which was now passing—never had anyone lived such a summer! Nature had given him the happiness of a blossom. She gave him love and a palace, and put precious poetry into his mouth; it was all one long, unbroken romance. And now everything was lost, his poems, his love and his palace, withered, burnt; forlorn and helpless, he faced the desolation of winter.

If the poetess had been willing to kiss me that night, she would have saved me, he thought. She would have left in my heart a seed that would have survived the winter, and this seed would have sprouted in a new spring and become the loveliest flower on earth.

But she had not been willing to kiss him. Her eyes were the same unresolved riddle in the darkness of autumn as in the day-bright nights of spring. But even though she had no soul, like the mermaid about which Jónas Hallgrímsson wrote somewhere, he still felt that she alone could protect him from the autumn sweetheart who was coming to him over the mountains with the stormy weather.

___ 28 ___

He had had his morning coffee in the loft early that morning and everything had been as usual—the woman at her morning tasks, the husband still in bed. When he came back at dusk, hungry and wet from having roamed around in the open all day, the loft was empty of people, all the couple's household belongings gone. He looked round the kitchen that had been the living room of the home, and although the furnishings had never been extensive and certainly never luxurious, suddenly it was as if a whole fortune had been removed. No plates in the rack, the kettle gone from the stove, the ladle vanished from the wall, the woman's knitting gone, likewise the cat, the friendly blue-checked curtains removed from the window. The little bench at the window was gone, too, where the poet had sat for his meals, where he had also been allowed to sit on Sundays, and the sun had shone in and white gulls had hovered over the blue fjord. He had also sat there in late summer when the nights had become longer and the moon had lent its reflection to the sea. The atmosphere of tranquil security and culture which creates a home and is above all worldly wealth had reigned there in that room that morning. When he came there tonight it was like any old closet in the loft of an outhouse. Yet the stove was still warm. It was like the corpse of a dead room.

Ólafur Kárason was told that at noon that day the new owner of the Sviðinsvík estate, Pétur Pálsson the manager, had summoned the couple into his presence and dismissed them. The former owner who had employed them was bankrupt and sequestered, and his documents burnt. The new owner could not allow himself the luxury of having unreliable drunkards in his service in these difficult times, much less a poetess who not only refused to support the cultural efforts of the place but was also suspected of corrupting young men and even conspiring against her employer and benefactor. The couple had collected their things in haste and put out to sea in a small boat in bad weather, with one companion.

Everything comes and goes in succession, there is no point in praying for anything, nor in begging to be saved from anything; that was how the summer passed away with everything it had given to the poet Ólafur Kárason of Ljósavík. In the end there was nothing left; perhaps they had even been caught by a squall and their boat had capsized. He was left standing alone on the beach; and it was autumn.

That night he crawled into the barn and bedded down in the warm hay as on previous nights. His clothes gradually dried on him while he was thinking about the impasse his life had reached. When he eventually fell asleep he dreamed that he found himself in dire straits on a precipice. He hauled himself along narrow ledges in a vain search for a path, the cliff beetled out above him, the abyss yawned below. Again and again he woke up gasping for breath and felt he was falling. Once he thought it was day and crawled out to look at the sky, but it was pitch-dark and still raining. His disquiet and anxiety had increased rather than diminished with sleep. He wandered off to try to calm himself down, but there was no one about. It rained and rained, and he sought shelter beside a wall.

At last it began to lighten. Other people got up, each in their own homes, and started to drink their hot coffee-water or milk-blend, or perhaps eat bread, and some, even, to have biscuits. Now when he no longer had any hope of coffee, it dawned upon him who it was who had kept him alive that summer. In fact he had never thought about the woman in the loft from this point of view before; in his eyes she had above all been the poetess, and he had never dared to associate her with the more primitive needs of human life. Now he realized that it was precisely these primitive needs of his that she had looked after at the same time as she was refusing to attend to his higher desires; yes, she had even burnt her poems rather than let him hear them.

She had seen to his needs in such a natural and simple way that he had not noticed it. She gave him an eiderdown and bed sheets and a pillow and a blanket. Then she gave him an alarm clock so that he would not oversleep. She had given him a change of clothing, inner and outer, socks, shoes, a cap, even a handkerchief. His dirty clothes had vanished without his noticing and come back clean. If there was a hole in his socks, it had been darned before he knew it; if there was a hole in his shoes, it was patched; if his hair got too long, she cut it for him. At her table he ate better than he had ever known before, milk, whey, cream, cheese, butter, sugar, fresh fish, potatoes, flatbread, meat, sugared pancakes on Sundays, sometimes doughnuts. Yes, she had even given him paper and writing utensils with which to compose his immortal poems for the fire, and to write his life story. It was she who had held a summer-long banquet for him in her taciturn, tranquil way. She inhabits a higher sphere, he had thought; but the reason why she was raised above the humdrum plane was simply that she did not shrink from any humdrum work but had it all under control without difficulty—a poet who dwelt in the high halls of beauty at the same time as her hand was automatically writing down the stupid, monotonous letters in the alphabet of human speech.

At breakfast, when he had not tasted food for twenty-four hours, he plucked up courage and went to see Pétur Pálsson the manager. There was a new doorkeeper now and it was no longer as easy to reach the manager as it had sometimes been before—but then the estate no longer owned him any more, he owned the estate. The woman who came to the door seemed to have spent all her life as a doorkeeper for Privy Councillors. She told the visitor to wait until the manager was ready to receive him; then closed the door in his face. He tried to press himself as hard as possible against the outer door to take advantage of the shelter of the eaves. There was a smell of coffee from inside the house. His fingers were numb with cold. Finally he plucked up courage and knocked again. The same woman came to the door and looked at him as if she had never seen him before.

"Could I perhaps have a word with Pétur?" asked the poet.

"If it's the manager you're referring to, I don't know whether he's ready to receive visitors," she said, as if the manager were some kind of duchess.

Eventually the poet was allowed in to see the manager as he sat in his private office poring over large documents and muttering figures in an undertone, with his new hat on his head, sucking a cigar with a lordly expression of hauteur which seemed to have been borrowed from the south because it did not really belong on his own face. The poet felt he did not know this man; he was almost becoming afraid of this new manager in advance. Finally, though, he had the nerve to clear his throat, take off his wet cap, brush his hair from his forehead, and say, "Good-day."

The manager went on for a long time mumbling tens and hundreds of thousands and writing these figures down on various sheets of paper with an authoritative and responsible expression and groaning. The poet counted up to two hundred. Eventually the manager laid down his pen and said sharply, "Good-day."

"Good-day," said the poet again.

"Yes, have I not just said Good-day, man?" asked the manager. "As far as I'm aware I've already said Good-day. Where are you from? And what d'you want?

"D–don't you recognize me?" said the poet. "My name is Ólafur Kárason. I've been with you this summer."

"Ólafur what?" asked the manager. "With me? What's all this drivel; no one's been with me this summer. Tell me what you want quickly; I haven't any time."

"Have you then forgotten that you're my benefactor?" said the poet.

The benefactor sucked at his half-chewed cigar and let out a cloud of smoke.

"I was going to ask you if it was possible for you to do something for me this autumn, as you did in spring," said the poet.

The manager replied, "I have always been prepared to sacrifice everything for a good cause. But those who have no soul, I reckon it's best to bury at once. That's always been my opinion, my lad."

He stuck the half-cigar into his mouth and pulled again with all his might so that the smoke lay like a fogbank round his head.

"I composed a long poem this summer, but no one wanted to hear it, so I thought perhaps the same thing would happen this autumn," said the poet, who realized at once which way the wind was blowing.

It then transpired that the manager recognized the boy perfectly well. He said that all excuses were unnecessary—"I know exactly what words you used in front of my right-hand man about this matter. Those who work against the cause of the estate have to support themselves. I'm no idiot, if you must know."

Until now, Pétur had been speaking in a rather impersonal managerial style, but now he abandoned this boring tone, banged the table, and went on: "D'you think I don't know that you and that p–person I've been keeping off the parish for two years have been conspiring to make me look ridiculous here on my own estate and to mock my most sacred ideals, and using the opportunity while other poets who are a thousand times better poets are not yet back from working at the hay harvest or the herring, like for instance Reimar Vagnsson, and refusing to compose an ode in honor of those whom God has forgiven, and calling them ghosts and saying to my right-hand man that the soul doesn't exist? You must think I'm just one of these damned small fry! But you'll find out that those who won't use their poetic talents for the spiritual rebirth of the nation, and who betray me at a sacred hour—they'll learn what it's all about. I hold you on a par with that wh–whore and her drunkard who didn't even have the energy to spread dung on the homefields, to say nothing of making people work. It was reckoned an achievement this summer if you were seen straggling into the meadow before midday, while he himself was lying in bed with a hangover. No, from now on there won't be any kid-glove treatment on my estate, if you must know, my lad. And incidentally, since you've got the effrontery to show your face in front of me, let me ask you one thing—who set fire to the house?"

The poet felt giddy and replied in falsetto, "I don't understand it; it's quite incomprehensible. I was out for a walk along the seashore with Þórunn of Kambar . . ."

"I'm not concerned about any Þórunn of Kambar, and anyway that girl's left this estate and is going abroad. I ask, what do you know about it, as the only person who went near the building that night?"

"I didn't go near the building that night."

"That's a lie!"

"I swear it. I sat all evening in the loft with Hólmfríður, and was reading a book."

"Yes, d'you think I don't know that you've corrupted one another with lies, slanders, insinuations, and gossip about me, that wh–wh . . ."

Then the poet interrupted with a sob in his throat and tears in his eyes: "That's not true, Pétur; I've never known a more honest person in word or deed than Hólmfríður in the loft."

Pétur Pálsson removed the cigar from his mouth, absolutely flabbergasted, and sat open-mouthed for a moment. "It isn't true?" he asked in amazement. Then he went on with growing force: "So what I say isn't true? Here? In my own house? Then what is true, may I ask? No, if a fellow like you is going to tell me what's true and what isn't true at home, here in my own private house, then the time has undoubtedly come for the sheriff to have a word with you in court, and with a vengeance, so that no one is left in any doubt where materialism leads the individual. You can stop thinking, you so-called intelligentsia who are nevertheless the most useless riffraff of all the riffraff, that I'm such small fry and such an idiot that you can tell me this is true or that isn't true at your pleasure. It's I, and not you, who owns this estate, and it's I, and not you, who decides what's true and what isn't true here on this estate; and those who don't want to sacrifice anything for me and my own cause on my own estate, they'll sooner or later get to hear the voice of the law, and with a vengeance. Who knows but that the law will look with different eyes on my cause than you so-called intelligentsia, my lad."

"I see," whispered the poet, and leaned back exhausted against the wall like a man about to be shot. "So perhaps I set fire to the house, too."

"I won't express any opinion about that; it's the law that determines that," said the manager and was not angry any longer, because he saw that the poet was on the point of collapse. "Here's two krónur, and out you go."

He took the poet by the arm, opened the door, and steered him out through the doorway.

— **29** —

So he had set fire to a house, too, then.

The autumn rain was of the kind he had once written about in a poem: "In autumn tears our love was drowned." He felt that the end must be approaching.

In his mind's eye he was already standing before the judge, his hands and feet manacled, with an indelible crime on his conscience, because crimes are only the misdeeds which others believe you have committed; he was the enemy of his benefactors, an arsonist and a thief, and probably a murderer. As the day passed, the more it rained and the more hunger assailed him, the more of a criminal he felt himself to be; his difficulties seemed insoluble. To be sure, he was walking around with fifty-two krónur in his pocket and was probably the wealthiest man in the village in ready cash, apart from the mysterious Jón the snuffmaker, the pastor's example, and could have bought himself porridge and probably fish, too, for cash in any house he chose, if such a thought had occurred to him. Instead he wandered around the wet streets of the village or the yellow moors round about or explored the beach, and drank the rain as it fell.

Yes, the end was approaching inexorably. But it was not until nightfall that evening that he finally made up his mind. He walked to the doctor's house and knocked on the door. He was shown into a long passage and told to wait. There were doors on both sides. He waited for a while and wrung his cap out on the floor. Eventually the doctor's wife appeared and asked him what he wanted.

He said, "I'd like to have a word with the doctor."

"The doctor's busy," said the woman.

Then she caught sight of the water on the floor and asked, "What's that puddle on the floor? Are you ill?"

"Yes," he said.

"How disgusting, that's what I say!" said the woman, and looked at the puddle on the floor with horror.

"It's from my cap," said the poet.

"I hope there's nothing seriously wrong with you?" said the woman.

"Yes," said the poet. "I'm extremely ill."

"Oh, you can hardly be so ill that I can't deal with it," said the woman. "Tummy ache or a cold?"

"No," said the poet.

"Headache, toothache?" asked the woman.

"No," said the poet. "Insomnia."

"Oh, just insomnia," said the woman. "I don't call that an illness. What do you want me to do about it?"

"I want to buy a sleeping draught," said the poet.

"How much money have you got?" said the woman.

"Fifty krónur," said the poet.

"A sleeping draught for fifty krónur?" said the woman. "Do you think I'm crazy? Or is this meant to be some sort of a joke?"

"Two krónur," said the poet.

"Two krónur," she repeated. "There's something very odd about you; I wouldn't be surprised if you didn't have any money at all."

At that the poet brought out both the two-krónur piece and the wet fifty-krónur note from his pocket and showed them to the woman.

"Where did you get that fifty-krónur note?" asked the woman.

"I got it from a man," said the poet.

Then the woman told him to go into the waiting room, while she herself disappeared into the pharmacy to look for medicine for insomnia. She came back after a moment and handed him a pint bottle of medicine; it cost only two krónur. She told him to take one spoonful before going to bed—"but anyway it's quite unnecessary to suffer from insomnia," she said. "Insomnia comes to people having no aim in life and therefore not enough to think about; I never suffer from insomnia." The poet thanked her, stuck the bottle in his trousers and said Good-bye.

But as he was walking down the passage on his way out he thought he saw one of the doors being stealthily opened, and as far as he could make out there was someone spying through the chink. He paid no attention but went straight on toward the exit. But as he walked past this open door it was suddenly thrown ajar, a hand stretched out through the gap, took the poet's arm in a firm grip and pulled him in over the threshold.

He found himself in a room with bookshelves on the walls, a writing desk, deep armchairs, a cupboard in one corner, and in the other a medical instrument cabinet and a rifle, all shrouded in cigar smoke. In front of him stood the doctor himself; he was laughing. Then he peered out carefully through the chink again and put his finger to his lips to indicate that the poet was to keep quiet. When the doctor had made sure that there was no particular danger lurking outside, he closed the door again and whispered to the poet in explanation, drawing one eyelid down in a wink: "I thought they were perhaps in the passage, the two old ones with the twisted horns."

He turned the key in the lock and put it in his pocket, then walked over to the poet and greeted him with strange talk and a handshake that seemed never-ending. In his expression and behavior there was some blend of strange glee and anxious unease, even fear, which so affected the poet that he felt anything but safe.

When the doctor had talked very rapidly and in the oddest manner about all kinds of things, without Ólafur Kárason managing to make head nor tail of anything, he pushed the patient down into an armchair under the window, put before him a tumbler full of brennivín and told him to drink, while he himself went over to the cupboard and drank, turning his back on the poet as he did so. After that he started another handshake with his visitor and went on talking. He said that he was well aware that Ólafur Kárason was a poet, and what is more a major poet, that is to say a man who imagined he had caught the end of the lightning. "But by God," he added, "it doesn't alter the fact that you're a fool. Everyone who thinks he's a major poet is off his head. I've been thinking of getting hold of you all summer and having an evening with you to let you hear a novel I've written. Drink up, I say. Shall I show you my gun? All major poets have guns. Arms and the book, that's always been my motto. Both Pushkin and Lord Byron died with a gun in one hand and a novel in the other. Drink up."

The doctor opened his drawers to look for his novel and rummaged about for a little, until he drew out a bunch of papers covered with sprawling handwriting so large-lettered that on some pages there was no room for more than four or five lines. Then he took the gun out of the corner, checked to see that it was loaded, let the poet look down the barrel for a moment, and then sat down facing him with the gun in one hand and his novel in the other, and started to read. The poet was extremely frightened, not least because the gun was pointing menacingly in his direction.

It was a grim description of a storm at sea. A ship which had lost its sails and rigging was being tossed from one huge wave to another, waiting for the one that would finish it off completely. Finally came the long-awaited wave which sank the ship, and the poet was beginning to hope that the story was over, but far from it; now there began a series of long natural history descriptions of various whale species, walruses, sharks, monster halibut species and other deep-sea fish, but particularly those of the leviathan family that have a long tusk, a horn, or other form of snout. The relationship of these creatures to one another or to the fate of the ship or to other phenomena was not made clear from the content, and Ólafur Kárason listened to this obscure composition, ill with hunger and sweating with fright, with the barrel of the gun looking at him. It was hopeless to think of going out, because the door was locked and the key in the doctor's pocket, but when he shot a glance at the window to one side of him he noticed that one of the lower panes was fastened with two hooks, so that a daring man in peril of his life could open the window and squeeze through.

"As I say," said the doctor, "the ship is sunk and the whales are ruling the sea. What do we do next?"

"I don't know," said the poet.

"Think about it," said the doctor. "If you're a major poet you're bound to know what to do next. What would you do?"

"I simply haven't any idea," said the poet.

"My God, no one can be a major poet if he doesn't know what to do when one gets stuck," said the doctor. "I'll give you three minutes. I'll put the gun here."

He took out his watch, got to his feet, set the gun like a doll in the chair facing the poet, went over to the cupboard, mixed himself a drink, looked at it against the light, and turned his back while he drank it.

The sweat continued to run down the poet's brow. He racked his brains about whether it would be any solution to the problem to let another ship sail the same course and reach land, or whether the readers would accept it if one of these wide-mouthed whales of the sea swallowed the ship's crew at the last moment and spewed them all out on land somewhere, unharmed, after three days. But neither this solution nor any others seemed satisfactory, as the story now stood. Finally, the poet clasped his hands in despair and stared straight ahead with infinite stupidity and saw no way out of this terrible novel but to let the doctor murder him. The three minutes passed.

"Well then?" said the doctor with an ambiguous grin. "The time limit I gave you is up. What do you do?"

"I don't know," said the poet.

"Drink up, by God," said the doctor.

"Thanks," said the poet, and raised the glass to his lips.

"Your glass is still full," said the doctor. "Perhaps you'd rather have cognac?"

"No, no, no," said the poet, with a start. "I'd much prefer bren-nivín."

"Well, then, by God, get some brennivín down."

"Thanks."

"What d'you do next?"

"I—I'm such a small and unimportant poet . . ."

"You're a fool and a good-for-nothing," said the doctor.

"Yes," said the poet.

"At first sight," said the doctor, "it seems that there's nothing that can be done, the way things stand. As you can see, everything's sunk and gone to hell ten times over. But then I do what is actually the most remarkable thing in all this, although it's so simple that any child could have said it once it was told. I save the cook."

"Really," said the poet.

"Really?" repeated the doctor. "Are you saying Really? What d'you mean? What a damned fool you are, boy. It can cost you dear to say Really, let me warn you. Drink up, or I'll tie you up and pour it down you throat."

"Thanks," said the poet. "I've had enough to drink now. I'm afraid I must be getting on my way. I'm in a bit of a hurry, actually."

"No hurry," said the doctor. "I've got a lot of things to talk to you about still. I've got a lot of other things to show you. To tell you the truth, I always want to talk to rational beings every now and again. It's no life to have to listen to the creaking of one's own coffin all the time."

"It's terrible," said the poet, and a shudder went through him.

These reflections made the doctor distinctly uneasy; he put his ear to the door for a moment, then tiptoed over to the poet, leaned over him and whispered, "Listen, friend, I don't suppose you noticed anything strange around the house when you came here?"

The poet said No to that.

"No goats or anything like that?" asked the doctor.

"No, I didn't notice any goats," replied the poet.

"And no animals with horns at all?"

"Horns?" asked the poet.

"Yes, I mean—you didn't see two old rams with twisted horns on the doorstep outside?"

"No," replied the poet.

"Oh, well, that's all right then, lad," said the doctor more calmly, and patted the poet on the cheek. "And drink up now."

He raised the glass to the poet's lips and poured the brennivín into the poet's nostrils and down the neck of his jersey. Then he started rummaging through his desk again and finally brought out some more papers, this time drawings.

"These are copies of drawings I have sent to the university for further examination," said the doctor.

The poet no longer dared say that terrible word Really, for fear of offending the doctor, and said instead, "Is that so?"

"I'm going to point out once and for all that I don't believe in psychic phenomena, whatever Pétur Þríhross says," said the doctor. "As a doctor, a scientist, and a realist I'm not at liberty to hold with any nonsense. In my eyes, all phenomena are scientific phenomena. I was brought up with a scalpel in my hand, and therefore I demand investigation. It's perhaps a harsh doctrine, but by God I say precisely what I mean. I have no more respect for a ghost than a man, whatever Pétur Þríhross says. And even less do I want to hear about any damned spirits. Investigation, investigation, investigation, science, science, science, d'you hear me? Drink up, or else I'll knock you out."

The doctor had another drink in front of the cupboard, turning his back on his visitor while he did so, then came back and went on talking.

"One night early in spring I was sitting in my surgery doing a urine analysis—that was the start of it. This was just like any other ordinary, routine urine analysis, the sort of analysis one does a hundred thousand times a year or more, by God, without anything to write home about. But what happened? When I began peering through the instrument, suddenly I began to see strange pictures the like of which I had never seen before, pictures which I can safely assert neither I nor any other doctor has ever seen before under similar circumstances.

"These pictures had not only form and perspective, they also had continuity; they had some sort of time-space characteristics in full accordance with Einstein's theory, but were in other respects, if I am to liken them to anything, most like a remarkable film, except that in it occurred things which no filmmaker could reproduce. For instance I saw a huge river, both broad and fast-flowing, rather like the Mississippi River; it rushed between wooded banks, as you can see on drawing number one. Suddenly I saw a gigantic beast swimming, with enormous horns such as I've never in all my born days seen on any other living animal; they towered to the heavens like fearful, awful pillars, I have them here in a separate drawing, number four. But no sooner had the creature climbed onto the bank and started to shake itself than there was moonlight and hard-frozen snow, and then I suddenly saw a flock of satyrs riding through the forest on unicorns, and in the van rode a woman with twisted horns, God help me, on a green horse, I swear it. Here you can see drawings of this cavalcade in detail, and here you can see a picture of the queen herself; her horns were grooved in exactly the same way as a ram's, and yet that's a female horn, I swear it. But what scientific significance these grooves on the horns have in themselves I'm afraid I cannot determine here. I lack all the proper equipment; the university will have to decide on that. The only thing I can assert for the university is this: I have looked at them with my own eyes through scientific instruments; I, a man with my scientific education, I, a man who flatly refuses to acknowledge anything supernatural and could never dream of believing in an afterlife—I don't care if Pétur Þríhross has bought the whole estate himself and can therefore report me to the authorities. They can chop me up into squares if they like; neither heaven nor earth will ever get me to acknowledge the existence of so much as a paltry angel, let alone anything else. But I know you won't let it go any further, friend, because then Pétur Þríhross would go absolutely mad, even though the estate is his only on paper, and obviously the man's right in one respect—that here on the estate it's absolutely essential that people believe in ghosts, because what the hell else are they to believe in? The afterlife is a matter of national importance which has significance first and foremost for this life, and that's why I think, as a member of the nation, that a single Psychic Research Society can't unfortunately give people this life, to be sure, but someone has to give the people an afterlife instead of potatoes, shoes and peat, since the church is dead and gone to hell. You can quote me on that to anyone you like, even if Pétur Þríhross had paid for the estate on the nail, by God, I swear it, say I. Drink up."

"Thanks," said the poet.

He spread his drawings over the table and chairs, walked to the cupboard again, turned his back on the poet, and drank. "Now I'm afraid I must be going," said the poet, and stood up.

"What nonsense," said the doctor. "You're not in any hurry. It's not so often you're my guest. We'll have a game of cards. Knock some of that back and we'll have a hand of piquet."

"I really must go," said the poet.

"It's out of the question until the glass is empty," said the doctor, and pushed him down into the armchair again. "You're my guest. We haven't really started to talk yet. When you've finished that glass, then we can first start talking together."

"I—I'm afraid I don't know how to drink brennivín," said the poet.

"Then you'll just have to learn," said the doctor.

"I—I'm afraid of alcohol," said the poet.

"Then you can't be a poet," said the doctor. "Nor a man, either. And least of all an Icelander. Brennivín is the beginning of all life."

He stood up with the glass in one hand, and put his other arm round the poet's neck, thrust his finger in between the poet's teeth and tried to pour it down his throat. But the moment the brennivín met the poet's lips he jumped, like a virgin being touched for the first time, and hit the glass with his shoulder so that the doctor dropped it; it fell to the floor and broke. The doctor looked at it for a moment with frozen drunken eyes but said not a word, without a flicker on his face; he went over to the cabinet with measured calm and firmness as if he were going to perform a major operation, took out another glass, filled it, and placed it in front of the patient. All this took time because the doctor did nothing in a hurry, but on the other hand the patient got the opportunity of unobtrusively unfastening the window. When the doctor had put the fresh glass of brennivín in front of him, he examined the gun again with the greatest care. Then he began to shift the chairs out of the way, doing everything with the careful precision of an operating theatre. Finally he took up position against the wall on the other side of the room, raised the gun with one hand, and pointed at the brennivín with the other.

"Drink up!" he commanded.

But then something very extraordinary happened in this poet's life. He jumped to his feet without warning, threw open the window without thinking, and saved his life. He was over the windowsill and out into the darkness before the doctor had time to bring his rifle up to his shoulder and take aim. The shot which blazed through the open window a moment later missed its mark.

— 30 —

What was the mystical power which saved this destitute poet from sudden death in the doctor's room? He got to his feet out of the mud below the window and ran as hard as he could from the volley of shots. At the fence of the homefield he paused and looked back. The doctor had stopped shooting and had closed the window. The poet reckoned he was out of danger, and crept between the wires and went on his way.

He knocked on the kitchen door of the post office and said, "Can one send a letter, please?"

"Yes," said the postmistress. "If one has an envelope. And if one has money for a stamp."

It so happened that he had fifty krónur in ready cash, but neither an envelope nor change for a stamp.

"Oh, I don't think it will do you any good to write letters," said the postmistress. "People do insist on doing it. But I've noticed over and over again that it's pointless to write letters."

"Actually, I wasn't really going to write a letter," he said.

"Well, isn't everything all right, then?" said the woman.

"No," he said. "Unfortunately I have to send a little something to someone."

"Can't you deliver it to her in person?" said the woman.

"No," he said. "I'm going away tonight. And she's not arriving until tomorrow."

The upshot was that the postmistress gave him an envelope and promised to deliver the letter free of charge if she came across the addressee in the village. He put the fifty-krónur note in the envelope, stuck the flap down, and wrote on the outside: "The Girl Jarþrúður Jónsdóttir from Gil, expected at Sviðinsvík within a few days, sender Ólafur Kárason, urgent."

The woman put the letter on a shelf, and he bade her Good-night.

"So you're not going to the Churchyard Ball tonight like the rest of the youngsters?" asked the postmistress kindly; she would probably have given him coffee if he had shown any inclination to hang around. But he was in a hurry; he did not reply, and was gone. There was no doubt about it, he was eccentric all right. Perhaps he had not even heard the Churchyard Ball mentioned. Jarþrúður Jónsdóttir— how had this parish pauper come by so much money to send to a woman? Was it true then that he had set fire to the building and robbed the safe? At all events, there had certainly been a fugitive look in his eyes. And he was on the run. And said he was going away.

Early that morning he had chosen for himself a little bay between the cliffs down by the sea, where the sand was smooth. When he had come this way that day the tide had been out. It was bound to be low tide now; after an hour or so it would be coming in. His idea was to drink the sleeping draught, then lie down on the sand, fall into a deep sleep, and let the tide come in over him; and this wretched mortal life would be ended.

The autumn darkness was like tar, heavy rain, the sound of the sea. He sat down on the wet sand. His consciousness was in darkness; he was in that state of mind when every word of comfort is like a mutilated corpse washed ashore; no memory was beautiful any more, but sore and bleeding, every recollection like being clawed to the quick. From out of the deadly darkness of the future there gleamed not even a single feeble star. At such a moment you do not draw up a balance sheet of your past life, as on a peaceful deathbed: what was good, what was evil, what was beautiful and what ugly. At such a moment you have only one enemy, and you know nothing else. That enemy is your own life. He put the bottle to his lips and drank.

Originally he had intended to drink it all down in one go, in order to fall asleep both quickly and soundly, but he had not allowed for how vile the medicine would taste. He had to force it down with pauses between each gulp; he felt sick so that he almost vomited, again and again, and broke out in a cold sweat. Finally he had to stop drinking, even though he was scarcely halfway down the bottle. I hope it works all the same, he thought, remembering that the doctor's wife had even suggested that one spoonful would do. Then he lay down on the sand, with his cap under his cheek.

Strangers have the idea that a Churchyard Ball is a dance that is held in a churchyard among the graves, but that is not so. The Churchyard Ball is a dance that the pastor holds in the village hall every autumn, in aid of the churchyard. But not everyone went to the Churchyard Ball this autumn who had looked forward to it in spring.

When everything was said and done, youth is beautiful nonetheless. You realize it by the light of an oil lamp and the sound of a harmonica one autumn evening; life is wonderful, beyond all words. Young hearts, two pairs of enchanted eyes which discover one another during the dance, two inexperienced lovers who meet for the first time—is that not marvelous? Is anything more marvelous than that? But unfortunately we all have too little money. If it is God's will that we should have money, then someone has stolen our money.

And while the youngsters danced away, the poet lay on the beach and waited for death. He had not expected that it would take so long. It is both more difficult and more complicated to die than people think. Even though the soul craves for nothing but extinction and oblivion forever, the body is a conservative master which will not give up until the very end. He had expected to fall asleep from the drug in two or three minutes, but now he grew terribly cold without becoming drowsy, and it was unfortunately the sharp cold of life, not the dulling cold of death. Seldom has any person been so wide awake as the poet Ólafur Kárason after this medicine.

For a long time he tried to lie motionless on the wet sand, but when the side on which he was lying got pins and needles from numbness, he turned over. Time passed. Death would not come. Eventually, however, he thought he heard a sound of singing above the sound of the sea, and his heart rejoiced in his breast, for he had never lost the idea from his childhood learning and the *Book of Sermons* at Fótur-undir-Fótarfæti that when one died one was welcomed to heaven with singing. But when he started to listen more carefully, he realized that the singing was not in heaven but here on earth. It was the Churchyard Ball. Unfortunately the singing of this world refused to leave his ears, even though he tried filling them with sand; again and again he sensed the notes from an old, familiar dance tune mingled with the sounds of the autumn night—

> *D'you think that Gróa's got some shoes,*
> *Got some shoes, got some shoes?*
> *Then I think she won't have much to lose*
> *When she starts to marry.*

In the midst of this earthly singing he was suddenly seized by a dreadful suspicion. Surely the sleeping draught had not been adulterated? In panic he grabbed the bottle with his frozen fingers, put it to his mouth, and drank that fearful poison to the dregs. Then he lay down to sleep again. But he was so convulsed by shivering spasms after the drink that it was practically impossible for him to lie still on the sand; his body demanded movement despite everything, life. Again and again he was on the point of jumping to his feet and beating his arms to get warm. And when this struggle was at its height, a wave suddenly washed over him, submerged him and lifted him up and dragged him out with it, all at once, but only to leave him lying there on the beach facing the opposite way as it fell back. The next moment Ólafur Kárason was on his feet. He ran as hard as he could farther up the beach to escape the next wave. Soon he was so far up on land that he was in no further danger from the sea. It is as it says in an old proverb—no one is drowned whom the scaffold awaits. This was the second time in one evening that the body had taken over and saved him from the dark decisions of the soul.

Drenched with salt and fresh water, with a sleeping draught in his nerves and sea in his nostrils, frozen hands thrust deep into soaking pockets, he shambled up to the road in the autumn darkness. Perhaps he was dead and was walking again, a ghost. He bumped right into a man who was also doddering around in the darkness. They practically fell over one another; but they did not fall, just came to a halt. Ólafur Kárason's teeth chattered, but he could not utter a word. The stranger also made several attempts to say something, each more despairing than the last. One could hear the creaking of his jaws, face and throat, but unfortunately without any results. Finally, as a last resort, he started to embrace Ólafur Kárason in the darkness; he laid his wrinkled cheek against the poet's soaking bosom and said, "My brother!" And Ólafur Kárason did not heed the reek of cough mixture from the man, but was seized with joy and gratitude at having found again this extraordinary mirror of the soul, and embraced him in turn.

"Heave-up!" said Eilífðar-Daði.

He had been ill in bed at his sister's for a few days, but last night he had got to his feet to fetch some cough mixture, and was now back in his proper element again. He was on the way to the Churchyard Ball, like other good men, and took the poet by the arm. Perhaps they were both dead.

"And to think that I composed an elegy for you!" said the poet.

Eilífðar-Daði stopped on the road to give the poet a special embrace for such generosity. How many people have to be content with dying nowadays without getting an elegy! Then they turned into the path to the village hall. Two men. And yet in reality the same man. The soul. A refreshing aroma of coffee from the Churchyard Ball met them. Eilífðar-Daði showed the poet the contents of his purse, he had both one-króna pieces and two-krónur pieces. They stood for a long time in the light from the window and listened enraptured to the singing and the sound of the dancing, before they ventured any farther.

> *D'you think that Gróa's got some shoes,*
> *Got some shoes, got some shoes?*
> *Then I think she won't have much to lose*
> *When she starts to tralalala,*
> *Got some shoes, got some shoes,*
> *Tralala ralala ralalala.*

Not everyone went to the Churchyard Ball this autumn who had looked forward to it in spring.

After all, it was Ólafur Kárason of Ljósavík who went to the Churchyard Ball, not in the way it had been decided that summer, certainly, but in a new life, after the Palace of the Summerland had burnt down.

BOOK THREE

THE HOUSE
OF THE POET

I

High up the hillside, where you look out over the roofs of the houses, there crouched a wooden shack with a slanting roof and a porch, one room with a stove, and a little closet; and at the window early in spring a pale man sat lulling his sick child in his arms—the poet Ólafur Kárason of Ljósavík. Whoever has a sick child has a house. This house was called The Heights. There was sunshine on the sea, the lagoons dead calm. That morning when the poet's intended had woken up, she had praised her God as usual and hurried down to the fish yards to earn some money. The poet gazed out over the roofs of the village, over the blue fjord, out towards the mystical haze of the mountains on the other side, and dandled his child. Anything was better than working for money. He bent down over the little girl and kissed her brow, and she smiled at him.

"My little darling," he said, and now for the first time he felt fond of little Margrét; or at least he thought he felt fond of her. While she was healthy and merry he did not care—healthy, merry children do not worry anyone. Leave them be; we have obligations only to those who suffer, we love only those who are in distress. Although he had never even noticed before if she fondled his cheek, he now felt there was nothing he would not take upon himself for her sake. "My little darling," he said, and hugged the sick child to his breast. "When the weather gets warmer and little Maggie's strong enough to walk beside her daddy, then Daddy and little Maggie will go down to the beach to look for shells."

"A-a," said the girl, weakly.

"Broad cockleshells, narrow mussels, fine pink scallops," said the poet. "Perhaps even sea snails."

"And a bow-wow," said the child.

"Yes, and then we'll meet a bow-wow," said the poet.

"And a miaow," said the child.

"Yes," said the poet. "And then a pussy will come along and say miaow."

Then he saw a man coming up the hillside with his hands behind his back, tall and lean and a little self-important, and not the type of man to go visiting on a spring morning without a purpose; there was frustration in his eyes. The poet went to the door to welcome the visitor.

"Faroese-Jens! Hallo and welcome," he said. "It certainly isn't every day that skippers venture so high above sea level. I hope you're not bringing the Devil with you up the hill?"

The visitor offered the poet a plug of tobacco in greeting, and took a chew himself.

"I walked up the hill here mainly to work off my bad temper," he said, without any unnecessary banter.

"I'm afraid Jarþrúður, my intended, isn't at home, so I can't offer you any coffee," said the poet. "On the other hand I can lend you a spittoon so that you can spit out your own tobacco while you're here."

"Oh, there's no need at all," said the visitor vaguely, but came in nevertheless.

"Well," he said when he had listened absentmindedly to the poet's inanities for a while. "It now looks as if it's been decided to take away the people's livelihood for good and all."

"Oh, really?" said the poet. "And none too soon either."

"I'm not joking," said the man. "Do you see these?" And he pointed at three trawlers which were fishing at the mouth of the fjord. "They never move out of the seaweed; they scrape the bottom as if they were scouring a pot. You should be grateful you don't have them coming into your cabbage patch. Two men had their nets destroyed this morning and have lost everything."

"Where are the fishery patrol boats?" asked the poet.

"They're down south, of course, ferrying the gentry as usual," said the skipper.

The poet did not quite know what to say; unfortunately he could not get very excited about it. "Yes, that's how it goes," he said.

"It's really no life at all any more," said Jens the Faroese. "And one can't even call it an honest war either, dammit. I go out with a dinghy and a bit of net, you go out with a trawler and a trawl. Is that an honest war? If two parties fight, and one of the parties is an unarmed dumb infant and the other is a fully armed berserk biting on the edge of his shield, is that war? No, it's murder."

"Oh, I wouldn't say that, perhaps," said the poet cautiously. "But it's certainly stealing, at least."

"And now the fish merchants have conspired to lower the price of fish, and Pétur Þríhross flatly refuses to buy a single fin over and above what he needs for his own curing station, to give himself a monopoly over what little employment there is on the estate—and over who gets work. And now he has announced an all-round wage reduction in the government quarry."

"Has anyone tried to complain to the authorities?" asked the poet.

"Are you off your head, man? You surely don't believe in the authorities!" said the visitor.

The poet was stuck. Visitor and host sat for a while in silence. What on earth could have driven this severe, pessimistic skipper to visit a poet? Finally the visitor broke the silence and said, "And yet these are just trifles."

Was the visitor not unnaturally pale? Was there not a white gleam in his eye? Surely he had not turned to Jesus? The poet began to feel a little uneasy; he could feel his heart beginning to beat faster. Granted that powerful thieves were scooping up the catches that could save the lives of the poor and the humble; granted that they were scouring the bottom of the fjord and ruining the bits of nets and lines which these little folk had acquired through unbelievable sacrifices; granted that the fishery patrol boats were being used for pleasure trips for the gentry while all this was going on; allow that the people were to be robbed not only at sea but on land as well, by means of all the price cuts and reductions and frauds which can be used against the poor, and that the authorities themselves no longer deserved our full confidence—but if all these were just trifles, dear God, what more was there to come?

But Jens the Faroese was unwilling to elaborate, and turned the conversation to unimportant matters. The poet did not know what to think. Finally Jens the Faroese said, "Hjörtur of Veghús—there's a great man for you."

"Oh, yes, he's always fiddling around with something, that fellow," said the poet.

"Yes, you're a poet and therefore you don't look at what's happening on earth," said the skipper. "The rest of us, on the other hand, look at what's happening on earth. And for my own part, I regard Hjörtur of Veghús as a real man."

"Oh, I wouldn't say that, perhaps," said the poet. "But at least he has introduced hens to the place."

"There are many people here who make fun of hens," said Jens the Faroese. "But what birds are more useful than hens, may I ask? None that I know of."

"That's quite true," said the poet. "Hens are very remarkable creatures even though they can't fly."

"But apart from that, Hjörtur hasn't stopped at hens. Didn't he bring a cow as well? Hasn't he shown and proved that little folk can own a cow even after their souls have been mortgaged and their fjord cleaned out? I call that a downright stroke of genius. Previously people had to be at least Privy Councillors and Þríhross's before they could even think of having a cow. Now everybody's talking about cows."

"Moo-moo," said the little girl, weakly.

"Yes," said the poet. "Moo-moo; perhaps Mummy will be bringing some milk from a moo-moo."

"And in addition, Hjörtur of Veghús has raised some sheep. In his hands, every beast seems to have two heads. Who ever thought of keeping sheep here on the estate before him? And have you heard what he's thinking of doing now? He's going to re-seed the Privy Councillor's old fish yards where the terns have been nesting for the last few years."

On reflection, the poet felt that his visitor's enthusiasm for Hjörtur of Veghús was not entirely misplaced. This man who had come to the estate by chance a few years back, empty-handed after losing everything he owned in another village, and had managed to squeeze a patch of gravel slope out of the manager—he signified in his own way the strange ups and downs in the history of mankind: the Creator's inventiveness knows no limits. In the beginning God created the world, then came the Privy Councillor, and then the Regeneration Company, then the Psychic Research Society, and finally the terns took over the fish yards and foreign poachers occupied the fjord. But in spite of that, the history of mankind was not finished; a new man came, a new woman, new children; and poultry came. But the new man did not stop at hens; he could make grass grow on the land. This was the greatest and most astonishing miracle that had ever happened at Sviðinsvík-undir-Óþveginsenni.

Out of the blue, the skipper now told the poet that Hjörtur of Veghús had been twice married. His first wife had died many years ago; he had had a daughter by her, who had been brought up by her mother's people in the south. But her foster parents were now dead, and she had come to stay with her father a few days ago. She was twenty-three years old, and her name was Jórunn.

"Is that so?" asked the poet.

There was a reverberating silence, as when one raps a pitcher while holding it by one lug. Finally, however, the poet said, "And is she a promising girl?"

"Promising?" echoed the skipper. "I don't know about that. But I've just been telling you that even though everything has been stolen from everyone here on the estate, these are just trifles. I'll say no more. Here are five krónur in cash. And I would like you to compose a poem to this girl for me."

Ever since the poet Reimar had had to leave on account of an ill-chosen epitaph he had penned for twelve Sviðinsvík voters who had been drowned on trawlers down south, the poet Ólafur Kárason had been to all intents and purposes the only focus and switchboard for the emotions here on this estate. He composed love poems and letters of proposal on behalf of enamored suitors, and poems of requital and letters of acceptance in reply from lucky maidens. A love poem or a rhymed letter of proposal cost from a króna and a half to two krónur, often with a small percentage if the suit succeeded. A letter of proposal or an ordinary love letter—"Honored Miss, my most cordial greetings. It is not unlikely that you will be surprised to receive a letter of this kind from me. But I have resolved to write this to you and to none other. I love you in spirit, I adore you"—high-flown piffle of this kind, on the other hand, cost only half a króna. He also composed for people congratulatory poems, birthday poems, marriage poems and epitaphs; but he refused to compose lampoons, even if he were offered ten krónur, and he always took care in his poetry not to criticize those who owned the estate, or other property; that was the mistake the poet Reimar had made in his epitaph for the twelve voters and, indeed, Pétur Pálsson the manager had declared that this Reimar was a pornographer who defiled the hearts of the young. Reimar had been dismissed and evicted with all his brood in the middle of winter from the shack in which he had lived.

"Yes, it's just like you to loiter at home like a mare over a dead foal and scrawl godless rubbish on a piece of paper instead of trying to give a little help to the parish which has supported you all winter," said Jarþrúður Jónsdóttir, his intended, when she came home after a day's work at the fish yard.

"Someone has to stay with the sick child," said the poet.

"That's something new, if you're now wanting to stay with the sick child, when hitherto you've scarcely wanted to know the child existed! It couldn't be that this sudden concern for the child arises from the fact that you were offered work at Pétur Pálsson's today?"

"Didn't I stay up every night with little Kári last year before he died?" asked the poet.

She was preparing to cook some porridge, but the cooking stove would not kindle. Whenever she had difficulty in lighting the fire she always talked to the poet in the second or third person plural or the third person singular neuter—you, they, it.

"Though I live to be a hundred I shall never understand people who can look at other people without it ever occurring to them to want to become something. Nowadays when everyone's copying Hjörtur of Veghús with his beasts, there isn't even any attempt to acquire some hens, not to mention anything more ambitious."

"I don't really feel that hens are birds at all," said the poet.

"Yes, that's just like you!" said the poet's intended. "To the best of my knowledge you never believed in the victory of Goodness, neither in small things nor great."

"Jarþrúður," he said. "I feel that birds ought to fly in the air. I repeat that I can scarcely call any creatures birds if they cannot fly in the air. Do you remember, Jarþrúður, when we first met, there were birds flying past the window at Fótur-undír-Fótarfæti? They were free birds. They were birds that could fly in the air."

"In the eyes of those who love God, hens are the most beautiful birds on earth," said the poet's intended. "When I first saw you, I was stupid and ignorant and thought you were Hallgrímur Pétursson reincarnated. But when all's said and done, you think you're cleverer than both the Heavenly Father and the Savior put together, and you look for excuses to sit idly at home on your bed when you're offered work, and I'm not even allowed to call a hen a bird."

"Little Maggie and I are going to go down to the beach to look for shells when we're better, and perhaps even sea snails," said the poet. "Then we'll meet a bow-wow and a miaow-miaow. Jarþrúður dear, in the five years we've lived together I've always wanted so much to have a dog and a cat . . ."

"Yes," his intended interrupted, "it's not enough to be on the parish yourself, you have to have a dog and a cat on the parish as well! Wouldn't it be more to the point to have a few sheep, and try to provide one's own meat?"

"Excuse me, Jarþrúður dear, I hadn't finished what I was saying—you can see I'm sure little Maggie would enjoy having a dog and a cat, and I myself think a house isn't complete without a dog and a cat; a dog and a cat are part of man himself, you see. But if I'm to tell you my honest opinion of sheep, then I don't think it's nice to have sheep except at the very most one or two sheep for one's own enjoyment inside and around the house. And I think one ought to allow them to die a natural death when they're old. I think it's a sin to raise animals around one in order to kill them; it's like making friends with people in order to make it easier to murder them. But when you say that I look for excuses to sit idly at home on my bed, I would permit myself to point out to you that I have earned five krónur today in cash by composing a poem for somebody. And when everything's said and done, I doubt whether many poets have produced more than I have in such a short lifetime. I'm only twenty-three years old, and yet my poems now top the thousand mark and a bit more if I count everything I've composed for others. In addition, there's my novel, *The Outer Isles Settlement,* which I wrote in my twentieth year. Further, there's the *Register of Poets* in this county for the past hundred and fifty years, with the fullest biographies possible, which is a work of nearly eight hundred pages; and at present I'm in the middle of the *Stories of Strange Men.*"

At this the poet's intended, Jarþrúður Jónsdóttir, buried her face in her sooty hands, near to tears: "That's not much consolation to me, who has been allotted nothing but sin and remorse and the righteous anger of God while others have been pretending to write famous works! You still refuse to make an honest woman of me; instead you leave me to burn in this terrible sin, and the child's obviously caught the same disease as the boy had, what's more, and nothing but damp seaweed to put under the pot. How can any person who nevertheless believed in God fall into such terrible sin? What was I being punished for, dear Jesus, to have got to know such an awful person, yes, and even think he could be Hallgrímur Pétursson!"

When the little girl saw that her mother was starting to cry, she started to cry, too.

If it ever happened that the poet felt a little obstinate and complacent, perhaps even touched with a certain arrogance at being a poet, such feelings vanished the moment his intended started to cry—not to mention if the little girl started crying as well. It was hard to say which was strongest in the poet's soul—the desire to please or the fear of hurting. When happiness came to this poet in his solitary moments, he was free and did not have a house. When he saw before him their tear-stained faces, he suddenly had a house. To be alone, that is to be a poet. To be involved in the unhappiness of others, that is to have a house. He took the little girl in his arms and repeated foolishly that now we shall be going down to the sea to collect shells, mussels, cockles, scallops, even sea snails. And then a bow-wow will come along and then a miaow-miaow. Dearest little darling. He put his arm around his intended's shoulders and said, "Jarþrúður dear, remember that Hallgrímur Pétursson had leprosy. And his wife was a Mohammedan. Aren't we perhaps happier than they?"

And thus the poet went on consoling them in turn, until they stopped crying.

"And you're going to make an honest woman of me, then?" she asked, and looked at him imploringly, and the tears still shone in her dark eyes. "And we'll put an end to this living in sin?"

That night he sat at the window very late and imagined to himself that he was alone. He was composing in his mind, revising lines over and over again without being satisfied. Eventually he lit a small lamp and wrote down a few verses. Underneath he scribbled the words, "Love poem for Jens the Faroese, paid." Then he put out the lamp again, and sat at the window for a long time and looked at the mountains on the other side of the fjord outlined against the sky of the spring night.

> Here where our late Privy Councillor
> Once dried his fish on pegs,
> Now grow only weeds and wild madder,
> And the tern now lays her eggs.
>
> Helpless in his homeland
> The sturdy patriot grieves,

Since all that he owns and works for
Is secretly paid to thieves.

While some people worked for the catches
And others stole their part,
A third one came sweet from the southlands
And stole away my heart.

Oh, where is the champion to strengthen
These wretched people's hand,
Who are fighting a desperate battle
Against this robber band?

It was here that the late Privy Councillor
Once tried to shape our part.
Oh, where is the champion to strengthen
My trembling little heart?

—— **2** ——

Hauling fish from the sea—what endless toil. One could almost say what an eternal problem.

Every conceivable effort had been made by the men of Sviðinsvík to lure these strange, tapering creatures from the depths of the ocean, and yet these people were still as far from a satisfactory solution to the problem as ever before. The Privy Councillor had had fishing smacks, cutters and finally trawlers, but just when the fish were well on the way to dragging a million krónur of his fortune into the deeps, not counting the human lives they had managed to lure down into those cold, wet places, the man had come to his senses and fled to Denmark to a warm, dry place. Since then the men of Sviðinsvík had made many desperate efforts to trick the fish, but they had all ended in the same way—the fish had tricked them. Nor had the fish been content with dragging men down into the deeps; all these adventurous attempts by the latter to catch the former had been the direct cause of loading one and all with such a crushing burden of debt to the bank that there was no hope of rising above it in this life, and very little in the next, unless people were made to repay it with the soul's eternal sojourn in a very hot place. Everyone ought to remember vividly how the trawler *Númi* had sunk from rust, rats and revenants here in the anchorage a few years ago, with the result that the high-ups of the estate had seen no alternative but to establish an afterlife here on dry land in order to answer the demands of the shipwrecked about footwear, potatoes and peat. When the men of Sviðinsvík then elected Júel J. Júel to Parliament the following year, it was because both Pétur Pálsson the manager and the station owner himself had convinced the people that they would never have another opportunity of catching fish unless they voted for money. Not everyone gave his vote to money, of course, nothing like it, but enough did, all the same.

Twenty picked voters were rewarded by being invited south to the fishing the winter after Júel became Sviðinsvík's representative. A new Golden Age was in prospect. Unfortunately, twelve of these voters were left behind in the watery ballot box of the sea, and played no further part in elections at Sviðinsvík. When it came to the bit, Júel's ships turned out to be no better able to grapple with the fish of the deeps than the little Sviðinsvík dinghies, perhaps even worse; the fish went on having the better of it and catching men.

At this time Ólafur Kárason was living in extreme poverty and enjoying little fame as a poet, since Pétur Pálsson the manager had suspected him for a long time of being against the Soul, which was just about the only asset which the people of Sviðinsvík could call their own at the time after the demise of the Regeneration Company. On the other hand, Pétur Pálsson the manager had appointed the poet Reimar as the folk poet of the estate that year, and had declared that this gentleman supported the Soul in his poetry. For this reason he had obtained for the poet an official post carrying the mails. But one day Jarþrúður Jónsdóttir went in tears to see Pétur Pálsson and begged him to take pity on her fiancé. The manager explained to the

fiancée that this wretch of a versifier had not been very loyal to his
interests and had instead supported those who worked against the
Soul, but he said that there would soon be a turning of the tide here
on the estate, and therefore it was not entirely out of the question
that he might give this poetaster and wretch another opportunity of
becoming a major poet and a somebody. He then explained that he
had decided to hold a big religious ceremony here at his own expense,
in memory of the twelve people of Sviðinsvík who had been lost on
trawlers in the south, and to mark the occasion he had decided to
commission a personal elegy for each of the drowned trawlermen, as
well as one short but heartrending epitaph for all of them together.

Finally the manager asked the fiancée which of the two tasks she
would choose for her intended if the opportunity arose—the twelve
elegies or the one epitaph. The fiancée reckoned that twelve poems
were bound to make at least twelve krónur, but one poem only one
króna, and was quick to choose the twelve elegies. Thereupon the
poet Ólafur Kárason set to work and toiled like a slave to compose
twelve elegies. He tackled the task extremely conscientiously, inter-
viewing the survivors' mothers, wives and sisters to establish what
good and fine things one could truthfully say about each of these
men, and then tried to introduce a special individual expression of
sorrow into every poem, as well as trying to squeeze out all the spiritual inspiration he had at his command. The result was that these
poems were considered some of the finest elegies that had ever been
composed in Sviðinsvík.

Reimar the folk poet had been away on a journey when the elegies
were being allocated. When he returned he was told the news that
Ólafur Kárason had now composed twelve elegies for the manager,
and that only the one collective epitaph remained for him to write.
The poet Reimar did not think much of these tidings, but composed
the epitaph in a trice and delivered it to the manager, with the message that he would not be requiring any payment. But the outcome
of it all was that Ólafur Kárason's twelve elaborate elegies were forgotten even though they were brimming with artistry and inspiration, and each one was enhanced by a particularly personalized

mourning; rather, they never went into circulation. No one recited them for real consolation in sorrow even though Pétur Pálsson had valued each one of them at two krónur. But the one free-of-charge epitaph by the poet Reimar spread through the whole county like wildfire and was sung in season and out by old and young alike until it ended up as a cradlesong. This is how the epitaph went:

> *There once were twelve good fellows,*
> *And each one had the vote,*
> *And off they went a-fishing*
> *In the leakiest tub afloat.*
> *And none of them returned,*
> *And every widow weeps,*
> *The fish pulled all the fishers*
> *Into the watery deeps.*

After this, Pétur Pálsson the manager announced that the poet Reimar was a poetaster with a filthy tongue and an even filthier mind who poisoned the thoughts of the young and besmirched the Icelandic language as well as Sviðinsvík's reputation. He said that as a democrat, a Christian and a socialist he could not countenance this kind of libel being composed about the common people when they drowned; and the folk poet was promptly dismissed from his job of carrying the mails. Soon afterwards he was also evicted from his house, so that he was left destitute with all his brood in the middle of winter. On the other hand, Pétur Pálsson now let it be known that Ólafur Kárason had a real talent for rhyming and would probably become a major poet in time, and gave him a shack which he told him to move farther up the hillside so that he could keep himself to himself, and then chose for the poet's house that lofty name of The Heights.

But while the struggle between men and fish had brought no more positive results than a change of poets on the estate, people from far-off countries continued to have their own opinions about the Sviðinsvík fishing grounds and to stand by them. They reckoned that these fishing grounds were neither more nor less than the finest in the whole world, without exception. Could that be right? One thing was certain—the foreign fishing vessels frequented these fishing grounds incessantly, and there scooped up catches worth one million after another while the fish continued to drag the men of Sviðinsvík down to the bottom of the sea or, what was worse, into that morass of debt which had no known bottom. And while the trawlers which were associated with Sviðinsvík's trusted Member of Parliament were either sunk or sold, or mortgaged against debts of millions at the state bank, the day never passed without a foreign fishing boat sailing away from the fishing grounds of these destitute people, laden to the gunwales with wealth for the benefit of foreign millionaires.

There is no denying that at this time some grumbling was heard in Sviðinsvík, because people thought that the station owner, Júel, perhaps did not own as much money as they had thought when they elected him. Rumor also reached Sviðinsvík that Grímur Loðinkinni Ltd. would soon perhaps be declared bankrupt. It was at this time that Pétur Pálsson the manager first put forward his idea that it was essential for the people of Sviðinsvík to build a new church to commemorate the fact that Guðmundur *goðl* (the Good)* had broken his leg there in a storm at sea some seven hundred years ago; he also said it was imperative for them to get an airplane, or at least to secure the use of an airplane, and talked about floating a company for this purpose. But a few people who were getting tired of Pétur Pálsson's ideas now took the bit between their teeth and went all the way south to have a word with Júel himself. They told him frankly that they would not elect him to Parliament again if he did not have enough money. Júel at once pulled out his checkbook and asked, How much? They said they wanted to catch fish. That was the first of the drafts endorsed by Júel for a number of people in Sviðinsvík to enable them to indulge in the luxury of losing money on fishing enterprises. People were satisfied with their representative again for another year. But no sooner had Júel paid up their drafts than they started to become restless again. On top of everything else it transpired that the two trawlers which Grímur Loðinkinni still managed to keep afloat had more than once, according to what people asserted, joined company with the foreign poachers fishing within the Sviðinsvík territorial waters.

That is how the estate's fishing problems stood one April morning soon after the Faroese's love poem had been composed, when the poet Ólafur Kárason wandered down to the fish yards at the manager's invitation and his intended's promptings to take part in the day's work. His way led past the parish officer's house. There were four men standing at the gate talking to the parish officer in the morning quiet, and the poet raised his cap and said Good-morning. But as he walked past them he suddenly felt they were looking at him in a peculiar way, so that he became a little afraid of them and began to wonder what he might have done wrong now.

When he had gone a stone's throw past them, one of them called out to him and said they wanted to talk to him. He turned and walked back to them, raised his cap again, and said Good-morning. He thought they looked a little odd. The parish officer stood there, bowed and dejected, with sawdust in his eyebrows and chewing a chip of wood, his face and hands smeared with pitch. Two of them were boat-owners, two were quarrymen.

One of the quarrymen said, "You're getting work at the fish. I don't get any work at the fish."

"Really?" said the poet.

The other quarryman: "What does Pétur Þríhross mean by letting you work at the fish?"

"I don't know," said the poet.

"I do," said one of the boat-owners. "Pétur Þríhross doesn't keep poets in food unless he needs to bribe them—either to speak or to be silent."

Then the parish officer said, "There must be some reason why you get work at the fish yards for full pay while men with large families to provide for have nothing, and a pay cut in prospect for those who work for the government."

"Pétur Pálsson the manager has always been good to me," said the poet.

"Yes, it's obvious enough he's got you in his pocket," said one.

"Tell me, Ólafur," said the parish officer, "why did you make the parish pay your food bill at midwinter when you're so well in with Pétur Þríhross? Why didn't you make Þríhross supply you from the shop without my intervention?"

The poet: "I had already got so much on credit from him before Christmas, he thought it was reasonable for the parish to pay the midwinter bill since I couldn't meet it myself. And this spring he allowed me more credit once again without the intervention of the parish. And after that my intended, Jarþrúður, began to get work from him on odd days, splitting fish and suchlike. I hope to be able to pay off all my debts some time, both to the parish and to him."

"So you don't consider yourself under an obligation to him?" said one.

The poet said, "I don't consider myself under an obligation to anyone, except perhaps to my little house, if you can call it a house."

"What do you say to looking in at Guðmundur's here tonight?" said one.

"It's an unexpected honor," said the poet, "especially if it's the parish officer himself who is giving the invitation."

The parish officer said nothing.

"He's good at writing," said one of the quarryman.

"Oh, I don't suppose there will be all that much writing to do," said one of the boat-owners.

"Poets get a lot of good ideas," said the other quarryman.

"Yes, but can they use their fists?" asked the other boat-owner.

"I hope there isn't going to be any fighting?" said the poet.

"No," said the parish officer. "But you're not being invited to a party, either, if that's what you think. And there's no need to say that anyone's spoken to you."

"I don't understand," said the poet.

"You're to keep quiet," said the man.

"I'm going to be late for work," said the poet.

"After eight o'clock tonight," they said.

He raised his cap and went.

At the fish yards there was a girl whom the poet did not know. She wore her head scarf differently from other girls, she wore it farther forward, and yet one could not help noticing her eyes—some eyes interest you even before you can describe them, or were they just unusually wide open? She was strongly built, solid but not stout, but otherwise dressed in the usual way for fish work, so that the clothing gave only a hint of the figure underneath. He did not look at her, really, and would not have admitted to anyone having seen her. He was thinking about something else: he was deep in thought about the conversation at the parish officer's gate that morning; but even so he could not help wondering why she pulled her head scarf farther forward than the other girls. It struck him as a protest—but a protest against what? Was this perhaps a nun? Or had she been beguiled, but only once, and was now determined never to let such a thing happen again?

But he was really thinking about something else, and it did not occur to him to ask who she was. He avoided talking to anyone for fear of becoming embroiled in other people's affairs any more than he already was; perhaps his gullibility had got him into trouble already. As the day wore on he became more and more worried— what on earth had he pledged himself to keep silent about? Had he perhaps allowed himself to be snared, had he already been trapped into keeping his word about something, or tricked into supporting something or opposing something, and thereby losing his freedom, his independence and peace of mind? Perhaps he was already a member of a conspiracy or a criminal band, perhaps at war with Júel J. Júel; perhaps he had already become an opponent of the government?

With an old woman he carried fish on a barrow until early evening, but his mind was yearning for unrelated values. He wished that the evening were over with its cares, and everyone asleep except him. Then suddenly the foreman had turned on him and was asking what he thought people were being paid wages for here? It was very far from Ólafur Kárason's mind to shirk his work, and if he refrained from overloading the barrow it was the kind of accident caused by his subconscious regard for fish. "I'm afraid I didn't notice that there was too little on the barrow," he said politely. The foreman called the

poet a lazy layabout and a moron and ordered him to turn back and
add at least half as much again to the barrow. The poet turned back
at once, with the old woman muttering behind him. Somewhere a
burst of laughter was heard. But when he had put the barrow down
again to add to the load, full of shame at this humiliation, the girl he
did not know was standing in front of him. Her eyes beneath her
wide, thick eyebrows were large and piercing, hooded by strong lids
and long lashes. She looked at him.

True repentance is the feeling of shame at having been punished.
He felt much worse about being sent back with the barrow than
about having cheated over loading it. Committing a crime is nothing
compared to being caught at it, and to let oneself be turned back
before the eyes of an unknown girl was a greater disgrace than perse-
vering in obduracy without accepting correction: anything is better
than a woman's scorn. The worth of any deed depends on how it is
assessed by the onlookers. To load too little onto a barrow is good if
one gets away with it, bad if the foreman sees it, a calamity if the
bystanders laugh; because once you have made yourself ridiculous
you go on being ridiculous whatever you do, perhaps for the rest of
your life. But your deed only becomes an eternal humiliation when
you meet ridicule in the eyes you have maybe dreamt about without
knowing it, or even compassion for your uselessness, perhaps contempt. Thank goodness, that was not the case now. In that unknown
girl's look there was challenge and encouragement. And she said to
him these words:

"Do you let yourself be turned back?"

That was all she said.

— 3 —

Work on the one side, the home on the other—they were two walls
in the one prison. Every time he was allowed to go out, and not on
some routine errand connected with his livelihood or his home, it
was as if he were being given the world for a little while. However

small a digression it was from his everyday routine, the Voice began to echo at once. It was the same Voice as of old. The difference was that when he was a child he thought he knew what it was, and that he understood it, and he gave it a name; but the older and wiser he became, the more difficult he found it to say what it was, or to understand it, except that he felt it called him away from other people and the responsibilities of life to the place where it alone reigned. He no longer knew its name now—far from it; just that its music sounded ever sweeter in his ears as time went by, so much so that he sometimes felt that the day might come when he would abandon everything to listen to it alone. Ah, sweet Voice, he said, and filled his lungs with the cool evening breeze of the north, but he did not dare open his arms to it for fear that people might think he was mad.

In the parish officer's room there was a crowd of men and a few women. There was a lot of talking going on; everyone was so engrossed that no one noticed when the poet joined them. People were all talking without any attempt at order, sometimes many at a time and all eager to have their say, but for some reason or other it was not made to look like a formal meeting. Some were agitated and angry, others despondent and grim; only a few seemed to be enjoying themselves. The poet had difficulty in making out the subject under discussion at first, and although he asked two people on either side of him what it was all about, he got no reply. After he had listened for a while, he came to the conclusion that the debate concerned Pétur Þríhross's family, but especially his grandmother. It was little wonder that the poet began to prick up his ears.

There were not many who could have boasted before now of knowing much about Pétur Pálsson's ancestry—even genealogists reckoned that some of the most important branches of his family tree were uncertain. The only thing the public knew for sure about his family was that his grandmother, Madame Sophie Sørensen, had occasionally made herself heard at seances during the time when the Psychic Research Society of Sviðinsvík was flourishing. About the lady's nationality there seemed to be some ambiguity. When Pétur

Pálsson was drunk he asserted that she was Danish and that he was therefore no Icelander; but at the Psychic Research Society, learned people had thought that the old lady's speech had inclined more toward some unidentified language such as Faroese or Norwegian, and on the only occasion on which Madame Sophie's mother, the manager's great-grandmother, had appeared at the Psychic Research Society, there had been various indications that the ancestry was French. The poet Ólafur Kárason had been present when the ladies had made themselves heard from the next world; it therefore came as a considerable surprise to him suddenly to hear Madame Sophie Sørensen now being talked about as if she were still alive, and so for a long time he could not believe his own ears. He got the impression that the woman was not nearly as deceased as she had pretended to be at the Psychic Research Society, but was somehow present in this part of the country, even here in the village, although she unfortunately did not seem to enjoy the best of health. He realized, certainly that there was no little secrecy about the elderly lady's health, and indeed about her whole existence; but often when the postmaster became extremely drunk he would allow some of his closest cronies to see copies of the telegrams concerning Madame Sophie Sørensen's health that Pétur Pálsson was now sending to his relatives in the south, sometimes daily, sometimes at intervals of only a few hours.

When the postmaster was questioned more closely about these telegrams he did not reply directly, but let it be understood that he knew more about the affairs of the Þríhross kin than was good for anyone outside the family circle to know. In this way he had for years had knowledge of the grandmother's health from one day to the next, and knew every detail of her multifarious setbacks and recoveries. People believed that a not unusual day in Madame Sophie Sørensen's life went like this: at dawn she woke up with an epileptic fit, by midmorning she had dyspnea, at noon she had a slight stroke, by midafternoon she had broken both thighs, but by evening she had gone out for a stroll to Aðalfjörður and sent her greetings to her friends and acquaintances. . . .

"What's all this damned nonsense!" said one man. "As if any person in their right mind would set off for a stroll just before nightfall over mountains and deserts to Aðalfjörður and with both thighs broken at that!"

The man who had got the story from a friend of the postmaster's replied by asserting that there could be no mistake about it, for on the very next day a telegram had come for Pétur Pálsson from relatives in Aðalfjörður to the effect that grandmother had arrived there last night and was feeling well, but that she could easily take a turn for the worse in the morning. No sooner had Pétur Þríhross received this telegram than he had wired to relatives in the south: "Grandmother in good health in Aðalfjörður, could perhaps get a touch of appendicitis tomorrow."

One person laughed louder than anyone else over Madame Sophie Sørensen's health. He laughed in ascending cascades, and in between he looked around with tears in his eyes, ready to laugh more; he made no other contribution to the discussion. This was Hjörtur of Veghús.

Beside him sat a fair-haired girl in a blue dress, with a large face and a complexion that had a suggestion of coarseness, slightly oblong dimples, and brilliant eyes under those strong, thick eyebrows. Her expression bore witness to a passionate temperament; her silence was full of vehemence, almost articulate. It was the unknown girl who had spoken to Ólafur Kárason at the fish yards. Across from her, three seats away, sat Jens the Faroese, gazing at her in wonder as if he scarcely believed that such a girl could be true. Then Ólafur Kárason realized that this must be the girl to whom he had composed the love poem, the Jórunn Hjartardóttir of Veghús who was a greater thief than all the foreign and inland trawlers put together. She had powerful shoulders and a sturdy bosom, curved breasts that sat high.

"Had I known she looked like that, I would have written a very different poem," thought the poet.

Someone said it would surely be easy to get the postmaster drunk enough to pump him of everything he knew. But that was no longer possible. Someone else explained that Pétur Pálsson the manager had recently signed the pledge with the postmaster.

"What, has Pétur Þríhross taken the pledge now?" asked one man, thunderstruck, as if a comet had been sighted and the Last Day were at hand.

"Yes, and even given up tobacco and coffee," said someone else.

"Good God!" said many of them. "Has he gone completely mad?"

"He says it's to keep the aura pure."

"Aura? What the devil's that?"

"It's a halo, like the one round the baby Jesus and the Virgin Mary; it vanishes if you take snuff."

"Poor fellow," said one man. "I know for a fact that since he gave up tobacco he goes around with a quid under his tongue and secretly swallows the juice."

Then someone else said, "You'll all have heard, of course, about this new stuff he's got; it's called vitamins and it's meant to be better than anything else that's ever been known before, including snuff, chewing tobacco, women and brennivín."

Hjörtur of Veghús laughed so much you could see right down his throat, but his daughter frowned and clucked her tongue with displeasure. Someone had heard that this vitamins business was a new way of fooling the people.

"No, it's not entirely a hoax," said one, "because otherwise he wouldn't be eating the stuff himself all day. He's even got hold of some litmus ribbon from Germany which he has to moisten in a particular way which I would describe more fully if there weren't any ladies present; if the moisture produces the right color in the ribbon, the body and the soul have had their fill of vitamins and have regained complete health."

Now everyone who could laugh began laughing, but Hjörtur of Veghús sat with tears in his eyes and his mouth open and could not laugh any more, while his daughter snorted and bridled.

The parish officer now began to speak and said he had not intended people to come here to amuse themselves; he said that on the whole he himself did not feel like laughing, and indeed it was not right under any circumstances to be facetious in these very grave times for the whole nation. He said he had been building boats for people here so that they could make a living, not to have their living stolen from them. He said that if people had well-founded suspicions that a conspiracy was at work here with the object of helping poachers to evade the fishery patrol boats and starve out the nation, then he would do his best to bring the sheriff into the matter, but he said he did not care in the slightest how Pétur Þríhross passed his water.

"Hear, hear!" people said, and became serious again.

One other matter was no less urgent than the violation of the fishing limits, and Pétur Pálsson was involved in that as in everything else. As everyone knew, the manager was the government's agent as regards the estate, and the estate's agent as regards the government. He had never been so firmly in the saddle as since Júel J. Júel had become his Member of Parliament and stood in his stirrups down south. Among other things he had a completely free hand with all government enterprises here on the estate. At long last they were about to start building a breakwater, and for that, cement and iron had to be bought with the government grant; that would lead to reduced employment; it would lead to a reduction in wages. The parish officer said that this was tantamount to forbidding people to reduce their debts to the parish, apart from the fact that it could be the beginning of total destitution in the village.

One after another, people vied with one another to repeat the main points of the case: the outlook was terrible; not a fish out of the sea, the foreigners were catching not only the Sviðinsvík people's fish but also their fishing gear; the nation was in danger; but what was all that compared to the fact that Pétur Þríhross was now going to squander this destitute parish's government grant on luxury wares and extravagances like cement and iron! And anyway, what was the point of starting to build a breakwater—what ships were going to sail into that harbor? The few tubs that existed would be better in the fire than on the sea. One man asserted that this harbor which had given people the opportunity of shifting rock for a decade would never come to anything; the site the government engineer had chosen for it was on dry land except at high tide; there was every likelihood that the harbor would be more suitable for growing potatoes than for docking ships. Hjörtur of Veghús had started laughing again.

The poet listened to the meeting in a trance, thankful that it was not turning out to be a plot against the government or something even worse, and was happy to be away from his home for a while. He envied Hjörtur of Veghús for being able to succeed on his own at anything he chose to do while at the same time finding all problems laughable. In the sensitive eyes of his new-found daughter, the father's unquenchable vitality expressed itself in a fanatical expectation of great but undefined things.

Everyone felt that something had to be done, and several proposals were put forward: to send a telegram to the government, to write to Júel, to talk to Pétur Þríhross. But all these had been tried umpteen times on similar occasions, without any visible results. Finally, some of the men had got the idea that the best solution would be to form a union; they had heard reports of successful unions in various other places. Others opposed the forming of a union, and cited the societies which had previously been established here on the estate, such as the late Regeneration Company which had brought everything to ruin, and the Psychic Research Society which followed in its wake and was to give people an afterlife here on the estate but had only achieved one thing before it passed away— the resurrection of two murderers. Someone asked, "How can we here in Sviðinsvík form a union against the government, the manager and foreign countries all at once?" Another maintained that unions and associations would be no earthly use until there was a radical change in the attitudes of each individual. The parish officer was in favor, up to a point, of the idea of forming a union to back their demands, but he said there was one drawback to laborers' unions which called for the utmost care: he foresaw the danger that such unions might use their strength against society as a whole, which was surely in dire enough straits already.

"What damned society?" shouted Jens the Faroese.

"The thieves' society!" said one cynical man by way of explanation.

The parish officer said there were examples in other places of unions being formed against society in general.

Someone said the time had come to overthrow the dogs who were always stealing from people. "What does Ólafur Kárason of Ljósavík say? He's a poet."

"Yes, that's right—Ólafur Kárason!" clamored the meeting, and people were now ready to listen to inspiration.

Ólafur Kárason said nothing, but got slight palpitations when he heard his name mentioned. He felt all eyes upon him. He was being challenged to contribute to the discussion. The daughter of Hjörtur of Veghús gazed at him with the expectation that commands something to come from somewhere and get something done.

"What am I to say?" said Ólafur Kárason.

"You're a poet, man, stand up and make a speech!" they said.

He stood up, accustomed to doing as he was told, looked around in confusion for a while, felt giddy, ran his hand down his forehead and over his eyes and down over his face as if he were bothered by cobwebs, and heaved a deep sigh.

"How can I say anything, a man who is outside everything?"

But the meeting would not let him sit down again without speaking, now that he was on his feet: "You're not above accepting support from our parish in order to live; so why should you be above sharing our interests?"

Then the poet began, little by little, to speak.

"I find it so difficult to speak," he said. "Quite apart from the fact that I think that all of us who live on this estate are blind. If I'm to say anything, I think that this estate is ruled by an almost omnipotent enemy who ceaselessly demands our lives, but yet I feel we never see the battlefield we stand on nor the actual enemy who rules over us, and that is because we are blind. Sometimes I feel as if the enemy himself is part of our own soul. Perhaps there is no enemy other than our own blindness. Perhaps we would be free of our own accord if our blindness left us. I don't know. What do you think?"

"Go on, carry on speaking," they said. "Try to offer some conclusion, man."

Then the poet said, "I find it difficult to speak. I said just now that I was blind. I said we were all blind. But I'm more than blind, and have an even harder furrow to plough than those who have lost their fishing gear and are in danger of having their wages reduced in the quarry or of losing their jobs altogether. I am a poet. I am the man who could never carry rocks, let alone have a share in a boat—that was what I meant when I said I was outside everything. I'm the village good-for-nothing whom everyone jeers at because I stay up at night and write books about men who were just as useless as I am myself. But for that very reason there is no thief so powerful that he can steal anything from me. Some say I'm allowed to work at the fish yards because I'm in tow with Pétur Pálsson the manager, but that's not true; I have never done anything for the manager except to compose twelve elegies for him, which is the least one can do for anyone. But even though both king and bishop allowed me and no one else to work in their fish yards, and promised to pay me in gold and diamonds, I'd never dream of touching a single fin, except only because fish are the same color as the sunshine, and because the smell of fish matches the breeze off the sea."

The meeting had already begun to interrupt him occasionally, but the poet Ólafur Kárason had now started and did not want to stop.

"Yes," he said, "I can hear what you say. I have never thought of anything except being a poet and a scholar, and so I don't care what others call me—fool, good-for-nothing, layabout, every bad name imaginable. But whatever I'm called, it doesn't alter the fact that whoever is a poet and a scholar loves the world more than all others do, even though he has never owned a share in a boat, yes, and not even managed to be classed as a quarryman. The fact is that it is much more difficult to be a poet and write poetry about the world than it is to be a man and live out in the world. You hump rocks for next to no pay and have lost your livelihood to thieves, but the poet is the emotion of the world, and it is in the poet that all men suffer. 'From the hoof of this damned world, O Lord, remove the small nails,' says the old hymn. The poet is the quick in this hoof, and there is no stroke of luck, neither higher wages nor better catches, which can cure the poet of suffering—nothing but a better world. On the day the world becomes good, the poet will cease to suffer, and not before; but at the same time he will also cease to be a poet."

He fell silent, looked around, and realized that the cobweb was gone from his face. And what he saw before him was wide, blue eyes, hot with the expectation of great, great things. Was it they which had called forth all this eloquence? He was not finished even yet.

"To be a poet is to be a visitor on a distant shore until one dies. In the land where I belong, but which I shall never reach, individuals have no cares, and that is because industry runs by itself without anyone trying to steal from others. My land is a land of plenty; it is the world that Nature has given to mankind, where society is not a thieves' society, where the children aren't sickly but healthy and contented, and young men and women can fulfill their aspirations because it is natural to do so. In my world it is possible to fulfill all aspirations, and therefore all aspirations are in themselves good, quite unlike here, where people's aspirations are called wicked because it isn't possible to fulfill them. In my land one can be content with looking at the clouds being mirrored in the sea, or lying on the grass listening to the brook purling through the dell. And when the great storms rage, people stoke their home fires generously, happy to own a sturdy house. And we hear a Voice which doesn't express any pain, and makes no demands, but which never sounds sweeter than when the poet is silenced at last; and in my land, all men can hear it. But here on this shore . . ."

The men were getting restless and were searching their pockets for tobacco; it caused them almost physical pain to hear someone baring his soul like this. But Jórunn, the daughter of Hjörtur of Veghús, stood up in a trance, walked over to him, gave him her long, strong hand and said:

"It is the Dream of Happiness."

The girl's father bellowed with laughter.

Everyone had started mewing at one another again. The poet felt that no one had understood him except this girl, who had certainly been the cause of his speech, and yet he doubted whether she had understood him correctly; her unexpected handshake burned in the palm of his hand. Her hand was larger than his and undoubtedly stronger. But what worried him most was to have aroused Faroese-

Jens's jealousy, because suddenly the lovelorn skipper got to his feet
and declared that everything Ólafur Kárason had said was useless
poetic nonsense; he said he bought that sort of stuff when he had
need of it and paid what he thought it was worth; he said he had not
come here to listen to drivel but to make plans to put an end to injustice and tyranny, and to overthrow the thieves' society. People urged
him to carry on. "There's nothing for it but to combine," he said.
"Form a union, get a reliable leader, start fighting!" At that the poet
became uneasy. Soon afterwards he left.

The moment he was out in the open he realized that the air in the
house had been stuffy. It was an unspectacular April evening of no
particular beauty, lovely only because it contained a promise of
spring, in the way that a young girl has no need to be pretty. He
thought to himself that since he had been allowed out that evening
without too much trouble, he would take the opportunity of going
for a walk along the seashore. How the dickens had he strayed into a
meeting full of people discussing Pétur Þríhross's grandmother, and
poured his heart out there? Obviously, all that talk about the millen-
nium must have struck the people there as mockery, or at best as
lunacy. He bit his tongue, but it was done now. In the evening stillness down by the sea, when he began to think about it honestly, he
realized that he would never have spoken like that if the girl had not
been there with those eyes. People had laid their problems before
him and he had responded to their trust by romanticizing about a
dreamland for a girl. What distressed him was that he felt he had
stolen the girl from Jens the Faroese; he had sold the skipper an ordinary key to her heart, but he himself had opened it with a golden key
so that she walked over to him in public and gave him her hand and
spoke to him. The truth was that he had needed to reinstate himself
in this girl's eyes for having been turned back with the fish barrow
that day. But had he the right any longer to keep the five krónur he
had accepted from the skipper?

— **4** —

When he had walked far along the seashore and had turned back and was going past Veghús on his way home, he met the girl. She was coming from the meeting. He pretended not to recognize her in the twilight, raised his cap, and asked who it was, and she came over to him and gave him her strong hand once again.

"It's me," she said. "Jórunn."

She stood very close to him, and he felt that this was a powerful girl who could probably carry him on her back.

"Please forgive me for shaking hands with you in front of everybody like that," she said. "But my feelings sometimes run away with me, that's my problem."

"There's nothing to forgive," he said. "You must forgive me, because I think I didn't myself understand what I was saying."

"It doesn't matter," she said. "I understood you. Other people understand one better than one does oneself. And poets think one's thoughts better than one does oneself. I have written a novel, three hundred and fifty quarto pages—it's called *The Dream of Happiness*— and that's why I understood you. Even though I'm sensitive I do everything I can to understand others. So please forgive me for interfering at the fish yards today."

"Ah yes," he said, "I let myself be turned back. Perhaps that wasn't right. But I reckon one has to do something for those who get pleasure out of turning people back."

She gazed into the twilight thoughtfully for a moment, pondering this reply, and finally said: "How very mature you are! I'm not as mature as that. And yet I felt, when you were speaking tonight, that you were speaking from my own heart, at least in the way I used to think when I was small. In my novel there are a young man and a young girl who change a whole parish into a Dream of Happiness, just as in your speech."

"I, too, have written a novel, called *The Outer Isles Settlement*, which is about two young men, friends, the one poor and the other rich; they couldn't endure the world being so full of injustice and so empty of understanding for the individual, and so they went off in search of an uninhabited island out in the ocean, and found one, and settled there."

"Were they alone?" asked the girl.

"Yes, more or less, at first. But there was another island close by, where an excellent couple lived with their two grown-up daughters. This couple also had settled in the Outer Isles in order to create a beautiful life in solitude. The young men now married the daughters, and at the end of the story the Outer Isles had become a perfect paradise on earth."

"Just like my settlement, except that mine was larger," said the girl. "I thought I would never meet anyone who thought the way I used to think when I was small. It's strange to hear one's fairest dreams from others. And moreover, you used the very words I have always wanted to say but never found. Do you mind if we take a short walk along the road?"

He turned with her.

"There's one thing I've always taken very much to heart," she said. "You see, I can't write poetry. I've so often wanted to write a poem. But however hard I try, I can't get the words to alliterate or rhyme, can't find the right words either. What should one do to find the right words? For example, I've been trying to write a poem to a man now for the last few days; I know that the right word is there, somewhere, but no matter what I do I can't get hold of it."

"Isn't that because you lack the right feelings?" asked the poet. "If you have the right feelings, the right word comes."

"I've always had the right feelings," replied the girl, almost resentfully, and the poet was afraid he had offended her.

"Do you love him?" asked the poet.

"Why do you ask so directly?" she said.

"If you love him, I shall write a poem to him for you; it costs one and a half krónur at the very most."

"Do you believe in love?" she asked.

"What a question!" he said.

"Why are you being evasive?" she asked.

"It's you who asks too directly," he replied.

"He is ready to do battle with anyone at all," she said.

"Yes, he's undoubtedly a man after your own heart. I am quite sure you love him."

"He has sent me a poem which could well have been written by himself," she said.

"Indeed," said the poet.

"He has a boat, and a house he shares with his mother, and money in the bank, no doubt. And has been sailing on foreign ships. And it doesn't matter if he's a little older than me. I never look at very young men. Do you ever look at very young girls?"

"How old are you?" he asked.

"Twenty-three," she replied. "But when I wrote *The Dream of Happiness* I was only seventeen. For the last five years of my foster mother's life, I had so much to do that I didn't have time to write novels; I was keeping house for her."

"House!" said the poet. "Yes, I understand that."

They were at the gate of Veghús.

"You have turned me back," he said.

"Thank you for seeing me home," she said.

"Now I've let myself be turned back twice in the one day," he said.

"'One has to do something for those who get pleasure out of turning people back,'" she said.

"Never forget your Dream of Happiness."

"I'll never forget the pleasure it gave me to hear you speak. I shall go on thinking about it until I fall asleep."

"Well, good-bye, and good-night."

But when he had gone a few paces he stopped and called out, "Are we going to think about the poem at all?"

"Oh, I'd nearly forgotten all about it," she said from her doorway. "Yes, let's think about it."

"How would you like it?" he asked.

"Any way you like," she answered.

"Do you want it to be long?" he said.

"As long as you think suitable," she said.

"Some people want to get as much as they can for their money," he said.

"Let's say three verses; it could be five, but on no account more than seven. But anyway, do it your own way."

"True love needs few words," he said.

"Who knows but that my love is so true that even poets cannot find the right words for it?"

"Then you wouldn't have asked me to write a poem," he said.

"You're making fun of me now," she said, and opened the door and went inside. He stood on the roadway outside the house without having understood her completely. It was difficult to write a love poem to Faroese-Jens, the way things were now.

—— 5 ——

There was a light on in The Heights. It occurred to him that one of his intended's cronies was with her, telling her that a young girl had shaken the poet by the hand in public. What could he say to excuse himself, not to mention if word had already reached her that he had been seen taking a walk with her in the dark? News traveled like lightning on this estate. But when it came to the bit, this was no gossip-monger. It was none other than Pétur Pálsson the manager himself who was sitting at the foot of the baby's cot with his pince-nez on his nose and a gold chain across his paunch.

"Can you imagine it; this blessed man has come here to bring us a whole tin of life-giving vitamins for the child," said his intended. "May my dear Jesus in Heaven reward these wonderful people now and always."

"There's no need to mention these trifles, my good woman," said Pétur Pálsson the manager. "Are we not all true Icelanders?"

"Yes, I hope God grants we shall always remain true Icelanders for all eternity," said the intended.

But the poet opened his eyes wide at this far-fetched prayer. "I don't suppose one has the choice of being anything but an Icelander for the time being anyway," he said, not without a hint of impatience at Pétur Pálsson's unexplained presence.

"That's what I like to hear from a poet's lips," said the manager. "I can see now that you're a freeborn Icelander and not a pornographer."

"I'm so terribly sorry not to be able to offer our blessed manager some coffee," said the intended.

"Down with all poison!" said Pétur Pálsson the manager with a gesture of renunciation and disgust. "We Icelanders are descended from Nordic vikings who drank raw cod-liver oil to quench their thirst, yes, and didn't mind the sediment, either. I know of old shark fishermen who were shipwrecked on the outskerries in winter and drank hot seal's blood instead of brennivín. And these weren't any Irish slaves, my lad, they were freeborn Icelanders from Iceland, who would never have dreamed of forming a Bletherers and Murderers Union against industry. Instead, they kept their aura pure."

"Yes," said the intended. "They were wonderful people, bless them!"

"I'm afraid I don't know what an aura is," said the poet. "And that's because of my lack of books."

"A poet, and he doesn't know what an aura is!" said the manager in amazement. "Well, you don't know much, I must say, my lad. My right-hand man and I, on the other hand, we know what an aura is, we've got a first-class book from England. One can tell from the aura whether people are true Icelanders or not; those who won't make any effort for industry in these difficult times aren't true Icelanders. Listen, you're a poet; we need to compose a little something together. You see I've been thinking of writing a play; drop in and see me tomorrow or the next day and we'll have a chat over a bottle of cod-liver oil. I hope you don't use tobacco?"

"No," said the poet. "I'm afraid not. And I'm probably missing a lot because of that."

"No, no, no—no immoral views, my lad," said the manager, holding his hand up to stop the poet. "The difference between a tobacco-less aura and a tobacco aura is like the difference between raw flatbread and a burnt pancake. That's why we shouldn't use tobacco. We ought to have ideals instead of tobacco. We ought to be patriots instead of tobacco men. But at the same time we have a responsibility to do something for culture here in Sviðinsvík. We lack high culture. We lack avant-garde culture. Listen, what do you say to having a cultural beacon erected here, to burn night and day in memory of Þórður of Hattardalur* or one of those sages of old?"

"Eh, who?" said the poet.

"Well, it could just as easily be someone else; we can always discuss that later. The main thing is to think up something to draw people's attention away from the bletherings of the unpatriotic so that they don't bring industry to ruin. Incidentally, how did that meeting go tonight? Was a union formed?"

"I don't really know," said the poet. "I heard someone or other mention a laborers' union, but I left the meeting early and went for a walk along the seashore."

"A laborers' union!" said Pétur Pálsson the manager. "They must think I'm some sort of small fry! They must think they can intimidate me by creeping together into a lousy union which is basically an idlers and riffraff union. But they'll soon see what's what. Let me just tell you that if they form a laborers' union, then I'll form a craftsmen's union, and if they form a craftsmen's union then I'll form a champions' union. And if they think they can form a materialists' union against me, I'll just show them: I shall unleash such spiritual forces here in Sviðinsvík that they'll have no need to call the doctor. We true Icelanders of Sviðinsvík must start fighting for a fine church. I've had someone in mind for that for a long time, old Jón the snuff-maker on the French site there, who really should have been dead ages ago and will be popping off soon with any luck, because he'll undoubtedly be worth fifty thousand krónur when he dies, apart from what's in the church fund already. In addition, we need to buy an airplane here in Sviðinsvík to elevate the people, or at least secure the use of an airplane. Here are two krónur for the child, Jara dear. But to digress for a moment, my lad, who d'you think is the leading idiot in all this? Hardly that rat of a parish officer? A man who was out having a look at the weather told me that that new wench from

Veghús, who has had work in my own fish yards, was hanging around there. May I ask, do you think that Faroese-Jens, who's an idiot and a rat, has had a letter from that damned fellow from Skjól, the one who lets his parents die off here like a couple of curs?"

"Örn Úlfar has been in a TB sanatorium," said Ólafur Kárason.

"Yes, one should spit on them. These idlers and wretches who can't be bothered working for themselves or for others, they all crawl off to a sanatorium. There they're fed like lords and barons and have Marconi earphones on their heads at the country's expense. But I'll show him, that Irish slave, that anti-patriot whose parents I kept off the parish for ten years, if he's sending letters here against me, yes, and even trying to worm his way into my own family, he'd better watch out, and those who are his friends had better watch out, too. I shall crush them, I shall grind them, I shall have their guts out, they'll see! What we need here is a fine church with pillars and painted windows which reflect the history of this county back to the time of Guðmundur *góði* at least, who was caught in a storm at sea here and broke his leg. That's what Sviðinsvík lacks. But as poets and idealists we also need to look ahead. A church alone isn't sufficient, we must also have aviation."

"As you know, I have always liked to call myself an idealist," said the poet. "Nothing is so essential as elevating the people. But don't you think it would be better to keep these two things separate, the church on its own and the airplane on its own?"

"What's the difference between Christianity and aviation?" asked Pétur Pálsson the manager.

The poet could not answer that.

"You see, my lad?" said the manager. "You can't tell me any difference between Christianity and aviation! Some say Christianity but not aviation, others say aviation but not Christianity. I say not just Christianity AND aviation; I don't even hesitate to say Christianity IS aviation, and aviation IS Christianity. Listen, if you want some vitamins free of charge for yourself, just come to the shop and talk to my right-hand man. I can even get you some litmus ribbon from Germany to piss on."

"Many thanks," said the poet, and his intended prayed once more that Jesus would give the manager strength. "But as an uneducated poet of the people, I would very much like to ask you one thing, Pétur. What are we to do with an airplane here in Sviðinsvík?"

"What are we to do with an airplane?" said the manager, scandalized. "Are you quite right in the head, my lad? Can't you understand what we're to do with an airplane? We are obviously to fly in the air, man! An airplane, that's modern times."

"I thought that modern times first and foremost meant having food and clothing," said the poet.

The manager was flabbergasted. He opened his mouth, speechless, as if Ólafur Kárason had suddenly started quoting proverbs in Chinese, and in his amazement over the sound of this remote language, a dark muddy stream came welling out of one corner of the manager's mouth and trickled in a curve down his chin.

"Say no more, my lad," said the manager at last when he had recovered, and sucked the trickle back up into his mouth again. "It's quite obvious where you've been this evening. There's no concealing the spirit of the Russians. Their souls are frozen. But let me just tell you that poets who become Irish slaves had better watch out. There are no guarantors for poets, my lad. The poet's house can be blown down. It can burn down. If you think that modern times means having food and clothing, you're very wrong. Modern times means service; it means having a fatherland to starve for and to drown for if industry requires it. Modern times means being ready to give one's last drop of blood for the nation's history and future hopes. Modern times means not being a Russian. Modern times means not being an unpatriotic Irish slave. Remember what happened to Sigurður Breiðfjörð! Remember what happened to Jónas Hallgrímsson, my lad!"

"These are big names to be mentioned in such a little house," said the poet. "I am ashamed. If they deserved to die of penury and hunger, hounded and mocked, then what am I worth?"

"All right, my lad; if you stop talking thoughtless drivel, you'll come to no harm," said the manager. "Because if we really examine what you were saying, who is there in Sviðinsvík who doesn't have food and clothing? To the best of my knowledge I provide everyone with food and clothing. I'm a democrat. I've always been a good socialist. I'm in favor of all the latest scientific discoveries. I've just bought vitamins for the village for more than a thousand krónur. Let other estate owners beat that. What industry demands is labor conscription, not paid labor where people get into the habit of unpatriotic blethering and would kill us, the freeborn, if they could, just like Irish slaves, and sell Icelanders into the hands of Danes and Russians. Listen, what do you say to having the cultural beacon up on top of Óþveginsenni in memory of the settler Úlfur *óbveginn* (the Unwashed)?"

"It mustn't be allowed to confuse ships and make them sail onto the rocks on shore," said the poet.

"You're not so stupid, my lad," said the manager. "You're quite smart. We'll have the cultural beacon of Sviðinsvík beside the church so that ships aren't endangered. We must do everything for our dear seamen. The main thing is to have ideals, as well as a blazing, seething faith in life, man. 'On wings would I float,' my lad. The morality of modern times demands not only a healthy life but also a holy life, as in days of old: spiritual maturity, light. One must keep the aura pure, as Skarpheðinn Njálsson* said to me at a seance in the south the other day. So that damned girl from Veghús was also hanging around there this evening? That's news, I must say. She has undoubtedly got syphilis. She had better watch out. Keep away from her, my lad."

"My God, dear Jesus!" said the intended. "What people are these you're hobnobbing with, Ólafur?"

"Er," said the poet, and blushed to the ears.

"I think I have the right to know what people you meet," said his intended. "You're the father of my child, after all."

"Oh, let's not go into that now," said the manager, "it would be too long a story; it's difficult to be unfaithful in the right way. What I wanted to ask you now, my lad, was whether you didn't need new clothes? And underwear? Have a word with my right-hand man tomorrow. And tell me now, briefly: what was the main subject of discussion at the meeting while you were there?"

Despite his lofty ideals, the manager had a remarkable ability to come down to earth occasionally, not unlike a seabird which in a twinkling swoops down from the sky and dives for a sprat.

"Oh, it wasn't anything important," said the poet. "They were arguing about the usual thing that mustn't be mentioned but which everyone's talking about: people keeping body and soul together on margarine and chicory, houses falling to bits, scarcely a whole pane of glass in the windows, last winter no one but the gentry could afford a piece of coal. They were talking about how much the powers which rule Sviðinsvík must hate the people. And they were being amazed at how incredibly resilient a creature a man has to be not to be completely exterminated in this struggle . . ."

"Unpatriotic creatures are too resilient; they should all be thrown off the end of the pier," interrupted the manager. "And what else?"

"They were also talking about how strange it was that the people of Sviðinsvík couldn't catch the fish in the way the foreigners do. They were wondering why it was that the Sviðinsvík ships should either be lost on account of rats, rust and revenants here in the anchorage, or their crews dragged down into the deeps by the fish, while foreign millionaire enterprises go on robbing the people of their plenty before their very eyes."

"It's quite clear that these men are under orders from the Russians," said the manager, who had got to his feet, rather swollen in the face. "In other words, there is a party in the making here which obviously intends to fight against the nation. I am in no doubt at all that propaganda is reaching this place in letters from a man who doesn't even belong to this parish according to the new residence qualification laws and has therefore no right to meddle with whether I hang my people or cut their throats here on my own estate. But he'd better watch out. Did I give the child the two krónur; did I give the child its two krónur, say I!"

"Yes, and there's no one but Jesus who can reward that," said the intended.

"Listen, my good woman, it occurs to me that you might need a new hymnbook," said Pétur Pálsson the manager, and put his hand in his coat pocket and took out a new hymnbook with gilt edgings and gave it to her.

The tears were not slow in coming to the intended's eyes.

"It's a pity we don't have a harmonium here," said the manager. "How appropriate it would now be to say good-bye by singing one hymn together."

The intended gazed at her new treasure with tears in her eyes and could not utter a word, but flung herself like a grateful child into the manager's arms and kissed him.

"We shall sing 'Praise the Lord, the King of Heaven,' " said the manager. "No other hymn lifts the mind so quickly and completely to the heights."

Pétur Pálsson took the book, looked for the hymn and found it, and at once his face had taken on a strange pious expression.

"I am afraid the child might wake up," said the poet, "she's so ill, poor thing, and those moments she manages to rest are precious."

"Whoever awakes to a hymn awakes in heaven," said Pétur Pálsson, and started hunting for the note. Then he thrust his thumbs in his waistcoat pockets, took up position in the middle of the floor with his legs astride and his Júel-hat down over his eyes, distended his paunch, and sang so that he swelled up and went blue in the face. His voice was very powerful. The intended tried to pipe up as well. It was a church ceremony of the highest order. But as Ólafur Kárason had foreseen, the child woke up and started to cry, and he had to take her in his arms and rock her to soothe her terror. At last the hymn was over. The manager took off his pince-nez so that the tears could course more freely.

"How good and true one hymn can make you!" he said. "I always feel that the day is lost in which I don't sing a little hymn."

He embraced the poet's intended and kissed her with all his might as he said Good-night.

"I think I gave the child her two krónur," he said. "The poor thing's not very well; it comes from eating sweets. Children should live a wholesome and natural life and go about with a mussel in one corner of their mouths and a shrimp in the other instead of sweets; that's what French children do. But I hope the poor thing will soon get better. Vitamins are the life-giving substances of modern times. But on the other hand if she dies, then never mind that, because death is just a vanity and a delusion; we all become reincarnated, and children who die with their auras in order are dealt a better hand next time."

"Yes, what a dear, wonderful man!" said the intended when Pétur Pálsson had gone. "I never thought it would be my lot to talk to a great man and a noble man as a friend. And to think that he was penniless to start with and on the parish! Yes, it's certain-sure that those who never lose their faith in the victory of Goodness will be exalted by Jesus in this life and the next."

"I can hear from the way you speak, Jarþrúður dear, that you are a true Icelander," said the poet.

"I know that well," said his intended. "And it's just like you to take sides with loose-living harlots and scoundrels against your benefactor. Give me the child at once; it's my child."

But the poet did not give his intended the child; he laid the little girl carefully into bed and tucked her in. She had almost recovered from her fright. She had fair curls. Her face was too hot, her eyes were half-closed, her breathing too rapid; he bent over her and looked at her, and felt that here was his house.

"Is someone not coming to bed?" asked his intended after a while, and was under the covers already.

"Yes," he murmured absently, and went on gazing at the child without moving. His intended had started muttering her evening prayers. Soon she had settled down to sleep, but she had not stopped muttering. He stayed where he was, sitting beside the child's bed. His intended fell asleep. Now night had come, and he was free. He tiptoed over the floor and brought out his writing desk, sat down with it on his knees by the head of the child's bed, took out his manuscripts, and began to write.

— 6 —

Jóhann *beri* (the Naked) was a fugitive for twenty years from his mistress. The story began when he was a married man with a farm in the north. Then came the mistress; at the mistress's arrival, the wife left home. But after a short while Jóhann *beri* began to hate his mistress and tried to resurrect a corpse to set upon her, but conjured up his mother by mistake. His mother flew at him and wrestled with him in the churchyard for most of the night until she overpowered him. She laid a curse on her son, that he would be a fugitive wandering all over the country for twenty years, pursued by the creatures of darkness; they would tear every piece of clothing off him so that he would never have a stitch to cover his body. Of all his journeyings about the country, the most memorable was when he crossed the hinterland in the middle of winter, and was eighteen days in the uninhabited waste-lands. He could not bear to listen to God's Word being read. He had a little knapsack with him, containing a pair of socks, a pair of tattered shoes and the *Passion Psalms*. Jóhann *beri* was a taciturn man.

The poet's Strange Men were in general all distinguished in that they had no possessions other than the clouds in the sky or, at best, the sun. But it was noticeable that the author never referred to anyone in his stories, no matter how wretched they might be, without proper respect. Just as he never referred to Jarþrúður Jónsdóttir in everyday life without adding "my intended," he always took great care to give everyone he wrote about a proper title, and in some cases two titles: "rhymester and horseman," "poetess and seamstress," "singer and housemaid." Simple titles for men were: "book lover, diarist, widower, coffee-seller"; simple titles for women: "housewife, house-help, house-keeper"; a man who owned only one goat would be titled "goat-owner." Jóhann's title was *Hinn Beri*, written with initial capitals, like His Majesty.

The poet's courtesy drew no distinction between people by position, occupation, appearance or character—or had irony become second nature early in childhood to this orphan, who had been brought up at the feet of powerful sheep-farmers and boat-owners? He was never biased against anyone in his stories, he never passed moral judgments on a deed or its doer, any more than when Snorri Sturluson* recounts the exploits of kings or gods. This man who himself could do no harm to any living creature—in his stories there

never appeared any hint of indignation over so-called misdeeds; he
told about them simply because he thought them worth telling. Nor
did he ever use exaggerated terms about so-called good deeds or edifying attitudes, and nowhere in his writings was there any enthusiasm for conventional morality or any propaganda for accepted
orthodox behavior—the classic ideals of the common man. The person who wrote the books was quite different from the meek adherent
to conventional orthodox behavior who went around every day eager
to please everyone he met.

Of all his destitute people, Ólafur Kárason was fondest of Jóhann
beri. His story would soon be a whole book, and this book would
surpass the *Stories of Strange Men* in that here the author had entirely
parted company from the scholar who uses natural uncut stones as
toys, and identified himself completely with his hero's fate, lived it
and experienced it as his own struggle with the Creator, as a poet
does. That was why he would stay up many a night over one sentence
which he would then cross out at dawn and go to bed cold, tired and
disappointed like a man who had lost his all and would never see a
happy day again.

A few days went by. He put off going to see Pétur Pálsson to write
a play with him over a bottle of cod-liver oil. He passed the time
indoors at The Heights as much as possible, and let his intended go
down to the fish yards. He got the impression that party strife was at
hand, and did not want to know about it. If there were thieves and
robbers everywhere lying in ambush for the poor, he did not think it
worthwhile to form a union to put a stop to their highly enjoyable
activities, because it might simply provoke them to steal the last drop
of blood from people as well. Just let them think up new ways of
stealing by ever more cunning methods, and new laws to protect
themselves against those they had fleeced. Everything, everything
was better than having anything to do with them; the thought of
being called upon to exterminate them was just as intolerable as having to take their side. The individual's finest fortune in Iceland is the
clouds which cluster together in banks and then drift apart again.

He spent a whole day trying to compose a love poem to Faroese-

Jens, but no inspiration came, probably because he did not know how deeply the girl loved the man. Perhaps he had not been shrewd enough to interpret her replies concerning this question. He labored and labored, but to no avail. Time and again he started up from his doggerel like a man overtaken by fog on a mountain path, and asked in despair—"Does she love Faroese-Jens, or does she only want to toy with him?"

"Daddy," said his little daughter.

She just wanted to know if she was so wealthy as to have a daddy still. "My little darling," he said. There was a red-checked cover on her eiderdown. The head of the bed had been raised so that she would not have to look at the ceiling all the time but could look out into the world as well, and she gazed with half-closed eyes at this little world which was in reality such a large world, and clutched in her hand a bird carved from a haddock bone, the symbol of human life; but she had not the strength to play with this symbol. But when her father had stood at the foot of her bed for a while and looked at her, a tiny gleam of a smile kindled in her face, like an enchanting message from a higher world, and yet just an earthly smile—that is how happiness reveals itself in the midst of suffering. In her smile there lay a suggestion of delightful teasing, with a dimple in one cheek; formerly, when she had been well and had smiled at him with all the magic that the face of childhood can contain, he had often said to her, "The boys had better watch out when she grows up!" And in her face he had seen a whole woman's life with exciting romances and endless escapades. Gradually the smile died out and the poet was overwhelmed by grief. That was how simply the sorrow and happiness of life met in the house. This little house, which could scarcely be called a house at all, became both wider and higher until it was as large as the whole world.

But when a few days had passed and Jórunn still had not come to fetch the poem, he began to fear that he had worked in vain. He was thinking of taking it to her, and yet not—that could lead to a misunderstanding. Instead he put the paper in his pocket and sometimes went out in the evening in the hope that he might meet her on the road. But he did not meet her. He felt a little annoyed with her for having asked him to compose a poem and then not coming for it. She should surely have realized that this was his occupation; this was his money. He was often restless, particularly late in the evening, and sneaked out of the house time and again, and walked rapidly along the seashore looking all around like a criminal; but he did not meet her.

"Well!" said his intended breathlessly one evening when she came home from work. "From tomorrow, everyone is forbidden to work here on this estate unless they join the Idlers and Riffraff Union."

"Is that so?" said the poet. "I'm sure that no one would join a union with such an ugly name for the fun of it."

"But I say for my own part," said his intended, "that I shall never betray my homeland and become an Irish slave."

"I don't know what you're talking about," said the poet.

"I do," she said. "Those who live outside human life can afford to talk. But I've been told that if I arrive for work at the fish yards tomorrow, I shall be beaten up."

"Well, well," said the poet. "No one would surely want to start beating you up, Jarþrúður dear; there must be some misunderstanding."

But his intended stormed on and talked about industry, true Icelanders and the victory of Goodness, all of which was to be pulled down now. She said that now they would see what stuff the poet was made of, and challenged him to fight for his benefactor Pétur Pálsson tomorrow, and not to allow unpatriotic men to trample underfoot everything good and noble they had ever been taught.

"In my world there is peace," said the poet, and had only one wish—to be able to sneak out. Then one of the women from the fish yards called, and the poet had a chance to disappear while they talked; he flew away as if his shoes had wings, reached the road in a twinkling, and walked for a long time along the shore. The weather was calm and the evening had brought fog; a fine drizzle was falling which settled like hoarfrost on the hairs of the back of his hand.

On his way back he thought he saw a giantess coming toward him, but despite the fog the evening was not so dark that he did not recognize her when she came closer. He raised his cap. She shook him by the hand, and once again he felt that warm, strong grip going right through him, instantly filling him with pleasure.

"Where have you been?" she asked.

"Where have *you* been?" he said.

"You're walking like someone a little drunk," she said.

"That's because when I rose from my childhood sickbed," he said, "I thought my legs weren't the same length."

"Walk a little with me," she said. "Don't let's stand here. I need to talk to you."

They set off, and she touched him.

"I need to talk to *you*," he said. "I've got something for you. Why haven't you called for it?"

"What is it?" she asked.

"A poem," he said.

"Ach, I'd forgotten all about it," she said, and took the poem and folded it carelessly and put it in her coat pocket but forgot to say thank you, let alone bring out her purse.

"Will you sign a vote of censure on Júel with us?" she asked.

"What for?" he said.

"It's been proved that his rusty tub of a trawler has been here inside the fishing limits."

"Those people who have trusted Júel J. Júel deserve neither better nor worse," said the poet.

She asked, "Are you a villain, then?"

"Quite possibly," he said. "But I've never been a Júelist."

"Are the wretched people to be punished for whom they elect?" asked the girl. "They thought the damned scoundrel had money and would give them plenty of alms, and then he goes bankrupt. It's said that the last rusty tub will be taken from him this summer."

"Well, that will be one fewer inside the fishing limits," said the poet. "And one ship's crew fewer to feed to the sharks."

"The postmaster has been summoned south," she said.

"Really?" said the poet, who had no interest in the postmaster's movements. "You're a strange girl . . ."

"Why?" she asked.

"To be talking about such matters," he replied.

"What do you think is worth talking about?" she said.

"I can't answer that when I'm asked so brusquely," he said.

"You probably don't think it worth talking about the fact that Júel Júel is known to be spying on the movements of the fishery patrol boats on behalf of foreign trawler-owners, and has operatives near all our best fishing grounds. Pétur Þríhross is an agent for these foreigners here on this estate and is in contact by coded telegrams with other spy stations in the vicinity night and day."

"I was seventeen years old when I first made the acquaintance of Madame Sophie Sørensen," said the poet. "That same summer I earned some money for the first time, with Júel J. Júel. Nothing can surprise me now. But we who meet so seldom ought to be able to think of more pleasant things to talk about."

"It's you who are strange," she said. "Talking to you is like talking to someone who has no shadow."

"I know what you're getting at," he said. "You mean a ghost."

"Can you clench your fist?" she said.

"Not very much," he said. "Just a very little. Practically not at all."

"Clench it as hard as you can," she said, and stopped.

She had a very broad bosom; there was a cleft between her high, curved breasts. Her face was as strong as the bows of a ship—the forehead high and arched, the mouth broad with a full lower lip, the eyes bright and wide under the thick brows. He clenched his fist.

"Hit me!" she said.

"You're a woman," he said.

"Hit me wherever you like. I dare you to!"

"Jórunn," he said, and put his hand on her shoulder and touched her bare neck. "Are we friends or enemies?"

She said nothing, but set off walking in silence.

When they had gone another few steps, she said, "What's the point of the Dream of Happiness if one can look on calmly while evil people cheat innocent people?"

When he had pondered this for a long time he asked, "What do you want me to do?"

She replied, "We have formed a Laborers Union and are demanding the right to negotiate about working conditions, and for members to have preference when jobs are available. We have stipulated our own rates of pay. Why don't you join this union? Why don't you make those in your care join it?"

"At night I stay up and write books," he said. "Other work means nothing to me. I am a poet."

"Ólafur Kárason," she said. "Will you tell me just one thing. Are you for us or against us?"

"I don't want to harm anyone," he said.

"Ólafur, say Yes or No."

"Yes or No, I am here only as a visitor . . ."

"Oh, shut up!" she said. "The fish yards have become a battlefield. The battle will be fought tomorrow and you will have to side with one or the other. Either you fight for the Laborers Union or you fight for Pétur Þríhross. There is no third choice."

"I shall be at home," he said. "I have a sick child."

"In other words, you're going to send poor Jarþrúður into the battle, while you yourself stay at home."

"You must be off your head," he said. And when they had walked a little farther in silence: "Am I to be torn apart once again?"

"It's your move," she said. "It's your choice."

"Let me say Good-bye to you here," he said. "I'm a little pressed for time."

She gave him her strong hand.

"Are we friends or enemies?" she said.

He left the road and jumped over the ditch. "I have something to do up the hill."

"Are you angry?" she asked.

"I'm undoubtedly a fool," he replied, and climbed over the barbed-wire fence at the roadside. "And probably also what you said earlier—a villain."

"Why are you so angry?" she called out to him from the road.

He walked away quickly across the moor, toward the mountain, without replying.

— 7 —

Five years ago, when she had come over the mountains with the autumn storms at her heels and sought him out and found him, a failed suicide, it had been her mission to nurse pastor Hallgrímur Pétursson reincarnated and support him. She was not in such straits that it was enough for her to live for herself alone, and therefore she was determined to live for him. She said she had never forgotten his eyes; she was sure the world misunderstood them, she thought he stood above all other men, and said it was of vital importance for him to have a mother.

He said, "I once had a mother. She sent me away in a sack one winter's day. I cried so hard in the storm that I haven't recovered yet, and never will recover."

"I shall never forsake you," she said.

He looked at her. Youth had faded from her cheeks, and her brownish eyes had the moist sheen of seaweed and reminded him of the sea one cannot drown in.

"What I long for most of all, since I couldn't drown, is to be allowed to hear the music of revelation anew," he said.

"I shall ask Jesus to whisper in your ear night and day," she said.

"Oh, where I was brought up, there was never really any Christmas," he said, downcast. "My friend was Sigurður Breiðfjörð."

It was as if the sun had clouded over a little. Perhaps this was the first time she had suspected that he did not stand above all other men, perhaps she had not understood him completely; it was her first disappointment over Hallgrímur Pétursson reincarated.

She had a cousin in the parish at the head of the fjord, where there was a vacancy for a very low-paid teacher to instruct children in reading, writing and Christian faith. Jarþrúður Jónsdóttir had come to fetch the poet and move him to this place.

He had not succeeded in catching pneumonia, certainly, but he had often shuddered at the thought of the murder that had failed, and he had some difficulty in getting used to the idea of being alive.

He dreaded to think that a frustrated death should be followed by a frustrated life. The children in the parish looked at him with fear. He said he was in pain and asked if he could go to bed early; Jarþrúður had already taken over the duties of the barn.

He was shown to a bed in a semi-outhouse near the front door of the farm. Round about lay farm implements, packsaddles and seed potatoes. There was a strong smell of fulmar from the eiderdown, to be sure, but it was warm, and there was a lamp hanging from a post. When he had got under the covers he realized that one's circumstances are never as bad as one imagines beforehand; he brought out his notebooks and pencils and began to write down what can happen to one individual. Within a short time the chill had gone out of him and poetic inspiration had taken its place; perhaps it was not impossible that he might yet hear the right music once again.

It was late in the evening and the farm had been quiet for a long time when he heard someone fumbling with the door handle. From old habit he hastily hid what he had been writing under the bedclothes. Jarþrúður Jónsdóttir pushed the door open, but only just enough to be able to squeeze herself through. He looked at her in alarm, but she said she just wanted to see to his clothes. Her colorless hair was braided into two plaits. She was pious and burdened with sins, but despite that she had hair, eyes and teeth which suggested an animal. There were holes in his socks and in his shoes, and she sat down on the edge of the bed and began to mend them. Nothing was said for a little while. Then she said, "You don't say anything."

"What am I to say?" he asked.

"Last spring you said so many things. I've thought of it all summer. Talk to me about the Voices of the Light. Talk about Jesus in human life."

But he was no longer in the mood to talk about these things. He who had got to know Meya of Fagurbrekka since last spring, that earthly, natural girl who left sea-wet footprints on the floor and sand in the prints—how could he ever set his mind on Jesus in human life again?

There was silence for a while and he studied her pale cheek. Her neck and chin began to tremble, and then the tears came. Then he suddenly felt he was being cruel, because he had actually once written a hymn to this girl and proposed to her, even though the letter had gone astray. Was it not just as disgraceful to deceive a girl even though she was getting on in years? Or did the poet no longer appreciate this woman for having traveled all the way from another county to make a man of him again after things had gone so badly for him that he could not even have an accident any more—could not even catch pneumonia no matter how long he went around in wet clothes, nor die of starvation when he got nothing to eat, nor fall on the battlefield when he was shot at. Why, even the sea refused to accept him for drowning. Finally he made this confession, in utter despair about his own character:

"Unfortunately, I'm afraid I'm not Pastor Hallgrímur Pétursson reincarnated, Jarþrúður dear."

She started to cry aloud at that, and asked Jesus if He were determined to deprive a sinful woman of her last hope. Ólafur Kárason was more and more moved. Finally he asked if she could not possibly imagine having someone other than Pastor Hallgrímur Pétursson for a son, and at that she looked up with a new gleam of hope in her moist, seaweed eyes and whispered, "Yes." And since that was the case, he brought out his poetry book from under the eiderdown and said she was more than welcome to hear the poems. She recovered completely at that and stopped crying. But while she listened to his poetry, he was sure she saw something quite different in him from the person he was; perhaps he also saw something quite different in her from the person she was. But when she had listened with staring eyes for a while, she suddenly fell to her knees beside his bed, put her hands on his naked body and said, "Shouldn't we pray?" This was in the middle of a poem, and he winced a little at the touch of her cold hands, and put down the poetry book in amazement.

"Eh?" he said.

"Pray," she said.

"You pray, I'll listen," he said.

So she prayed.

He was now called Ólafur Kárason the schoolteacher, and had attained thereby a certain standing. He was not expected to share the work in the house, and so he often had time on hand to pursue his own studies. Every second day he went to the next farm to give religious instruction, and there was a young girl there who sometimes looked at him. He talked to her for the first time by the farm brook one day at dusk when she was rinsing out some clothes. Later he met her in the doorway of the farm; then he met her in the kitchen where he was getting coffee. She talked easily. The weather was often wet at midwinter and two young, scintillating eyes were just as good as the sun. When he got back home the memory of those eyes inspired him to write a poem about freedom and the blue expanse of spring which beckons us with infinite promise; such eyes were enough to abolish the thought that spring was just a folktale and a pleasant fantasy about a Golden Age which in reality had never existed in Iceland. Then someone called to him as he sat working at his poems and he was told to come quickly: Jarþrúður had had a fit. She was lying in the mud between the barn and the farmhouse, this always fastidious woman who could not bear to see dirt anywhere, and her cousin, the housewife, was standing over her and had thrust a nail between her teeth. The poet got muddied from carrying her into the farmhouse. When he had laid her down, he looked in amazement at how the holy sickness that had struck her down had given her another soul, another body and another face, the face of ecstasy; he would not have recognized the woman had it not been for the claw-like hands which had seized the chance of touching his naked body in the middle of the prayer and laid claim to dominion over a poet. That night he lay awake with the seed potatoes and saw mysterious islands beyond the mouth of the fjord, far out to sea, toward which two young men made their way as the sun ascended the heavens, in order to find freedom; and found nobler people than are to be found in the Sviðinsvík district; and more beauty. Complete happiness reigned there. It was the beginning of the novel *The Outer Isles Settlement*.

It was no use denying it, the answers he got from the girl on the next farm had the hot rush of the blood in them. One says Hallo shyly and gets a smile in return, one feels one's way with an observation about the weather and gets a snatch of verse or a proverb in return, or even a paradox; and the game is on. But did she not forget one again the moment one disappeared round the corner of the house?

On a moonlit night one evening when he was on his way home he met her behind the farmhouse; she was carrying the usual cinders out, and had spread her sacking apron over the ash trough so as not to get ash in her eyes.

He said, "You are too lovely to be carrying ashes."

"I'm nothing more than dust and ashes," she said, and laughed.

"What do you think of the evening?" he said.

"It's like porcelain," she said, for the moon was glittering on the frozen snow.

"Then it's the first time that dust and ashes have turned to porcelain," he said.

"Tomorrow the porcelain will be broken," she said.

"You're so intelligent I think you ought to come for a walk with a poet, beyond the homefield," he said.

She undid her sacking apron and forgot about the ash trough, and made a slide over a frozen puddle with a poet, and laughed. When they were beyond the homefield she said, "Well, now I'm going back before the blessed housewife starts getting any ideas."

"Walk over to the boundary brook," he said. "When I meet someone high-spirited I am reborn."

"Why should one worry?" asked the girl. "The world surely isn't as serious as some people think."

"But if it had nevertheless been created in all seriousness in the beginning?" replied the poet.

"I don't care," she said. "Nothing will make me hobnob with any but the cheerful ones."

"Even though you're dust and ashes?" he asked.

"Precisely because of that," she answered.

When one hears pretty girls talking, one cannot help thinking that even their most light-hearted replies contain some deep, deep meaning: yes, even some hidden wisdom, and perhaps they do; perhaps it is only beauty that contains the highest wisdom—that remains to be proved. He felt she was uttering a special wisdom which she was playing against his own wisdom, in the same way, moreover, that she was playing her own life against his life, with a definite purpose.

"Be careful what you say," he said. "Who knows, I might also own an island out in the ocean where happiness reigns entire and intact. Perhaps I'll write to you one day from a famous island."

"The woman will be starting to get ideas now if I don't turn back," she said.

She was eighteen years old.

A little farther on there was a small lake covered with mirror-smooth ice. They could not resist running over to it and having a slide, because they were the same age. They crossed it twice one way and twice the other, and she held on to his arm, but there was nothing in her grip that suggested wantonness, nor wanting to lean up against him and dally. She was just companionable and straightforward, totally free of that duplicity and dishonesty on which love is built. So they had yet another slide, and five, and ten, and her face was flushed in the moonlight.

They noticed nothing until someone was standing at the side of the lake and calling angrily to Ólafur Kárason. Jarþrúður Jónsdóttir said that a person in delicate health should be at home in bed rather than indulging in this tomfoolery in the middle of the night with folk he knew nothing about.

"Folk?" said the girl from the next farm, and laughed. "Am I folk?"

"What do you want with this boy?" asked Jarþrúður Jónsdóttir. "Have you any right to him?"

"Have I any right to him?" said the girl. "I thought people had a right to themselves."

"Oh, so you're one of those!" said Jarþrúður Jónsdóttir. "Ólafur, as your mother and sister, I order you to come away from this person."

"Mother and sister!" repeated the girl from the next farm, and burst out laughing, but it was not a laugh of derision; it was a laugh of sheer amusement as when one laughs at a joke. And it was precisely this—that she should find it funny—that hurt Ólafur more than malice and derision would have done. He felt he was ridiculous in the eyes of the girl from the next farm suddenly to have such a mother and sister, and he walked away alone without saying Goodbye. Jarþrúður stayed on for a while and heaped abuse on the girl. When she had satisfied herself, she came running after him.

"So you had to make me suffer this, too, Ólafur," she said when she caught up on him.

He did not reply.

"Aren't you ashamed of letting me find you in the clutches of that wanton creature?" she asked.

"I'm not in anyone's clutches," he said. "And she's not a wanton creature."

"Yes, go on, take her side against me!" said Jarþrúður, and started crying in the frost. "D'you think I need to do more than look into her eyes to see what she is? The time will come someday when you will reap such punishment from God that you will realize properly what you have done."

He had certainly realized for a long time that she and God were allies, but though he was sorely tried he could never bring himself to utter a wounding word to a grief-stricken human being and her God. And moreover it could well be right, however hard it might be to understand, that it was advisable for a poet not to go sliding on the ice with a carefree young girl.

She often stayed up late at night, knitting for him, or sewing new clothes for him out of old garments she got hold of, and there was never a crease or a speck to be seen on his clothing, let alone a hole; she never tired of washing, she enveloped him in an atmosphere of soft soap. And many was the tidbit she came by for him both late and early. But it was not long before he discovered that she was keeping a constant watch on him. During the daytime when he was teaching he would suddenly see a glimpse of her at the living room door; when he was at the next farm giving religious instruction it happened more and more frequently that she would be waiting for him at the homefield fence of the next farm or behind the farmhouse, and then she would lend him her protection on the way home. But when the days began to lengthen and the realm of the sun expanded, he was often overwhelmed by a throttling melancholy, like a prisoner. The mountains called him and said it was better for a poet to die of exposure in their embrace than to live as a slave on a farm. The summer sky used every opportunity of whispering to him like a dangerous lover who is trying to entice a young girl all day. Even the late-winter snowstorms were just the lover's disguises and strategems. The poet Grettir Ásmundarson* lived in the wildlands and died on an uninhabited island, but earned himself immortality thereby in the hearts of the nation.

One day when he was on his way back home he overtook one of the girls from his confirmation class. She was carrying a sack on her back. He thought she was too slender to carry the sack, but did not know whether it was morally right for him to take any notice of it. Until now they had had no other communication than matters concerning Abraham, Isaac and Jacob. There was a storm blowing up.

"What's in the sack?" he said.

"Mussels," she said, panic-stricken, because her religious faith depended upon this man.

"I'll carry the sack for you; the wind could blow you over," he said.

"No, thanks," said the girl.

"You're much too slender to carry such a heavy sack in bad weather," he said.

She was called Stína. Her farm lay halfway between the sea and the mountain. Her clothes were much too thin, and her stockings were hanging down her thin legs. The wind was straight in her face; she seemed to get thinner and thinner the harder it blew. He took the sack from her and took her arm.

That was all.

"What people are you walking arm-in-arm with beyond the homefield in the middle of the day?" asked Jarþrúður.

"People?" he said. "It wasn't any people. It was just one of the girls from my confirmation class. Her name is Stína."

"That's all I needed, to have to watch you behaving in such an unchristian way with one of your confirmation girls before the very altar!"

"How can you possibly speak the way you speak," he asked, "about an innocent little girl?"

"Oh, they're certainly not so innocent as they pretend," she said. "They're all dirty sluts descended from dirty whores, and they don't know the meaning of shame. They'll accommodate strangers on the highway long before they reach puberty, and both Jesus and God know that if I meet that nasty little worm I'll give her ears such a warning that she'll remember to leave people alone next time."

In her eyes, only Ólafur Kárason existed, and the rest of the world was an unending collection of whores; life was a battle in which she fought single-handed against this unappetizing army of enemies; day in, day out, all the womenfolk of the world, both young and old, besieged this frustrated Hallgrímur Pétursson, her poet, in a ceaseless effort to seduce him. He turned away from this woman, his mouth dry and his throat twitching, and walked over to his outhouse and began to put his books into a sack along with a few clothes. When he was almost ready to leave, she came in and asked him what he was doing.

"I'm going," he said.

"Where to?" she said.

"Away," he said.

"Away from me?" she asked.

"Yes," he replied.

First of all her face emptied, then it was shaken by spasms, and finally it disintegrated in weeping.

"I who was ready to die for you," she said.

"There's no need," he said. "I'm going to die for myself."

"What am I to die for, then?" she said.

He said, "For your God."

Her strength gave out then. She sank to her knees in front of him as if before an idol, clasped his knees, buried her face against him and whined: "Even though I'm nothing but a worm beneath your heel, I am nevertheless carrying your child."

The cold cruelty of the freedom-fighter had seized him suddenly like a flash of madness, like poetic inspiration that turns all obstacles into trifles, all fetters to dust; he had seen the mountains, the resort of the fugitive, rearing up in all their glory, and was ready to trample one worm underfoot. But at her words he saw light. To trample one worm underfoot was to trample all worms underfoot. And he saw once again where he stood. He felt as if he changed suddenly from one substance into another. The fear of hurting was once again dominant in his being—the desire to please. He looked back as he softened, and saw himself splitting in two: the freedom-fighter, the madman, the villain and the poet were left behind in the distance, and forward stepped the socially conscious, Christian, boring and unpoetical man, the warrior who could not toss children on his spear point, the meek adherent of conventional orthodox behavior. He took his things out of the sack again, the books and the clothes, and put them back in their place; besides, it was getting late, and there was a din of worsening weather from the mountains.

— **8** —

This notice was pinned to the telegraph pole:

Icelanders! You are the descendants of Nordic vikings! Down with Irish slaves!

Long live the commonwealth of Iceland even though civil order needs to reduce wages! Be freeborn!

All those who own a cabbage patch or a boat—defend your nationality! We demand war against the Danes and Russians!

Support the True Icelanders in their crusade for aviation in Sviðinsvík! Down with the unpatriotic!

We want to build a great church in Sviðinsvík and erect a cultural beacon! Down with the pornographers!

Remember to keep the aura pure!

The Committee.

NB. Cod-liver oil for children is on sale at give-away prices at My Shop. Also vitamin pills. Vitamins are the life-giving substances of modern times. P. P.

Early in the morning, when the poet's intended, Jarþrúður Jóns-dóttir, was about to hurry off to her work at the fish yards as a true and freeborn Icelander, the poet Ólafur Kárason was standing in the doorway.

"I want to ask you to stay at home, today, Jarþrúður dear," he said quietly.

She looked at him speechlessly for a moment, and then she said, "Am I to believe, Ólafur Kárason, that you are siding with those who would rather obey men than God?"

"It could well be, Jarþrúður dear, that God wants people to work for the old wages and is against people working for the new wages. But I'm sure that if God and men quarrel, then happy the one who stands aside from that quarrel."

The power that caused this neutral poet to bar his intended's way when she was trying to become a True Icelander was stronger than his deep-rooted desire to please and his fear of hurting. Without any conscious logic, as if by some secret instinct and yet with the irrefutable certainty of revelation, it had come to him that it was wrong to go to work at Pétur Pálsson's fish yards today, and right to stay at home.

"Stand aside from that door, or else I'll call down God's anger on this house," said the intended.

"Well, then," he said, "let your God do to this house what my God has always tried to abstain from."

It is more than likely that fisticuffs would have broken out elsewhere that morning if a remarkable thing had not happened to divert the attention of the village from its disputes. The Danish warship *Valur* had pulled off the unbelievable exploit that very night of catching a foreign poacher within territorial waters. It was a British trawler. Just as matters were coming to a climax on land, the Danish fishery patrol boat steamed into the anchorage at Sviðinsvík with the culprit in custody. Pétur Pálsson the manager had already killed the fatted calf and put on his best morning coat by the time the Danish ship had cast anchor, but the notice had disappeared entirely from the telegraph pole. And within a short time the sheriff had arrived and the court was convened. That night, when the poacher had been sentenced to a fine of ten thousand gold krónur and its fishing gear had been brought ashore and Pétur Pálsson the manager had bought the catch, he gave a party at his home for the Danish officers of the fishery patrol boat and the sheriff.

The manager had now bought enough fish to save all the people of Sviðinsvík for the time being, and he offered a lump sum for the whole job: unloading, gutting, splitting and salting. With that, the dispute over wage rates was over for the time being; the fish yards did not become a battlefield and people refrained from coming to blows. The Danish party went on all night while the unloading was going on—and it was not only cod-liver oil that went down their gullets!— and in the morning before the sheriff went to bed the fishing gear of the British trawler was put up for auction in the presence of the pastor, the secretary, and a few drunks and children, not forgetting the manager himself, who stood on the quayside with his legs a little apart, somewhat dark around the mouth and puffy in the face. And although he perhaps was not thinking absolutely straight, he was not so far off course as to bid any more for the gear than was absolutely necessary, a few hundred krónur for many thousand krónur's worth, and got it all knocked down to him. The business was over in two minutes, and the manager took the sheriff's arm and led him away. The Danish warship had put to sea and the notice had reappeared on the telegraph pole; but some joker had scrawled this observation underneath: "Grandmother is well again."

The following evening the manager manned a motorboat with a lighter in tow to return the fishing gear to the trawler which was waiting off the mouth of the fjord.

But during the night of the party, while the populace had been toiling to unload the trawler and work on the catch, there were two other freeborn Icelanders who had not been idle either—the pastor and the secretary.

It is significant to note that there are always worthy individuals to be found who are ready to save the community even though they themselves are not invited to the celebrations. While Pétur Pálsson was feting the Danes with the fatted calf and wine, sparkling, sweet and heady, until no one could tell the difference between Danes and True Icelanders any more, these two Icelandic sobersides went round all the houses with a document in which people were required to make and sign a solemn declaration that they preferred continuous work this summer to high rates of pay this spring. Most of them made haste to sign. After all, man is not a butterfly which lives for one day to spread its beautiful wings to the sun, nor a tiger beetle which is content to fly for one month at midsummer and then be more or less dead for the rest of the year; no, unfortunately, man has to live all the year round.

A few days later, the Society of True Icelanders was founded in Sviðinsvík with general participation. A lot of people preferred to be True Icelanders rather than Laborers, apart from the fact that human beings are, generally speaking, unselfish creatures, always ready to support ideals (particularly if these ideals are sufficiently unlikely to improve their own lot) and to fight tooth and nail against enemies if they are sufficiently insignificant, unbelievable and incomprehensible, not to mention if they are simply bogeys. It was agreed to fly in the air, build a great church and have a cultural beacon, and war was declared on Irish slaves and anti-patriots. Further, it was agreed to celebrate Midsummer Day in honor of St. John the Baptist with a poem by Ólafur Kárason and a lecture about the aura, followed by communal cod-liver oil drinking. The inaugural meeting was held in the primary school, and on the blackboard was chalked in large letters: "Keep the aura pure. Skarpheðinn Njálsson. Vitamins are the lifesavers of modern times. Pétur Pálsson, manager."

Thereafter there was peace on the estate, and the spring sun reigned alone in the sky. The clouds clustered together in banks and drifted apart again, all in a much simpler way than one had suspected. The poet avoided going out-of-doors for fear of meeting people. As a rule he sat with his little daughter and looked at the sky and the earth through the window. But with the coming of summer the poet's daughter revived; she wanted to make her fish-bone bird start flying like other birds. Other little girls from the village came up to show her their toys, and one day she was out of bed and playing with them on the floor in the sunbeam. Another day she sat with them beside the road and played with the flowers. The poet stood on the threshold of his empty house and looked out through the doorway, out into the universe. And then it was as if his house slid away into the distance from under his feet, and he was left standing alone in the middle of infinity watching his house moving off, sailing farther and farther away into the distance, concerning him less and less, until it had vanished; and he did not have a house any more.

Was he not sorrowful, then, at the disappearance of his house? Did he not find everything desolate around him? Did he not feel that God had forsaken him? Far from it. He felt he was left standing in an orchard of fruit trees and roses. He composed this:

> *Dear earth, you turn your once discordant ear*
> *To the wilderness in which the heart once slept;*
> *And every single creature now can hear*
> *That luminous word in which God's smile was kept.*
>
> *This lowliest soul, oh, Lord of all the skies,*
> *This wordless poet, this most worthless worm,*
> *Is once again a child who snugly lies*
> *Warmed by Your smile, Your light, Your loving word.*
>
> *How eagerly I gaze upon Your glorious face*
> *You showed me dimly when I was a boy.*
> *My happiness o'erflows: oh, endless grace,*
> *Oh, ecstasy of life, oh, infinite sea of joy!*

—— 9 ——

Then it was autumn again, and the raven sharpened his beak on the eaves of the houses.

"Why have you been avoiding me all summer?" asked Jórunn one wet September day. It was at the corner by the shop, he had not had time to escape, they bumped into one another. "Am I so frightening?"

She looked him straight in the face, without blinking, even though the rain was beating on her face.

"Good-day," he said, and raised his cap.

"I asked you why you always avoid me if you see me coming in the distance."

He replied, "I never try to avoid anyone except myself."

"I have time and again wanted to speak to you this summer, but you always run away. Why are you running away?" she repeated.

"Where is Faroese-Jens?" he asked.

"Faroese-Jens!" she said. "So that's it—Faroese-Jens! Are you perhaps still angry since that time in the spring?"

"I wouldn't say that," he said, when he saw he could not get away from her. "But I've been living in great luxury this summer, and sometimes I've been afraid that someone might come and disturb me. I have been afraid that someone might come and involve me in a fight."

"Fighting's as it should be," she said. "What's the meaning of life if one has no enemies? What's the meaning of life if one doesn't fight? What's the meaning if one doesn't win—or if one gets defeated, what's the meaning if one isn't human?"

"It may well be that fighting is normal," he said, "like having something to eat. Peace, on the other hand, is a luxury. The only thing I yearn for is to live in luxury."

"What have you been doing then?" she said.

"I have been looking at the sky," he said.

"You don't need to talk in riddles," she said. "I know perfectly well you're a great poet."

"I'm not much of a poet," he said, "worse luck. On the other hand, I'm an extremely wealthy man. I own the sky. I have invested all my capital in the sun. I'm not bad-tempered, as you seem to imagine, nor do I bear grudges. But like all wealthy men, I'm a little frightened of losing my fortune."

She half turned away and became thoughtful; it became her well to let the rain fall on her sunburnt face, healthy and strong, and one could see her thoughts marching across her face like clouds, almost like regiments of troops.

"Why do you despise humanity?" she then said through the rain.

"Incidentally," he said, "what became of the battle that Faroese-Jens was wanting to wage?"

"You're such a great poet that I'm glad I have burnt my *Dream of Happiness,*" she said. "And yet I'm disappointed in you, Ólafur Kárason."

"Yes, I know you think I'm a villain," he said. "And you're quite right; he who examines the heavenly light is a villain. The earth is and will always be an accident in his eyes. To examine the heavenly light is to harden the heart utterly. Such a man, if you can call him a man, is beyond saving. That's why I ask you to leave me in peace. In peace."

The expression round his mouth tightened with emotion as he repeated these words, and she watched him and his emotion pitilessly.

"You are two-faced," she said.

"Really," he said.

He was going to raise his cap to her and go.

"Stop that silly cap-raising," she said. "Tell me instead why you dislike me so much."

"I've already told you what I most yearn for," he said.

Afterwards he walked for a long time, restless in the rain. The autumn birds held their coal-black assemblies on the moors with strange antics beyond human comprehension, and a few dogs who were worn-out by chasing them lay not far away with their heads on their paws, ears cocked and tongues hanging out, keeping a close watch on the tantalizing movements of these haughty creatures while they gathered their strength for a fresh chase.

It is good to have a house if one is wet enough. The intended was cooking; there was steam and the smell of fish boiling. She fussed around as usual because he was wet, she did not understand folk who got themselves wet unnecessarily, some people made no attempt to protect their clothes even though they had nothing to change into, and so on; he usually did not reply, because her talk was seldom of the kind that required an answer. But while he was taking off his wet things he looked at her obliquely as she stood in the corner behind her barricade, the stove, pale and thin and with that strong, impersonal hair which seemed to live a life of its own like the hair that grows on a corpse, and he asked himself: If I cast her out, who is then to thrust a nail between her teeth so that she doesn't bite her tongue off when she has her fits? Why should I make her suffer because she no longer has young warm hands, a high bosom, a strong fair neck, lips that melt under your kisses? Why make her suffer because her voice no longer has a young, sensuous excitement, because her speech doesn't have an attractive, cultured choice of words? Was it her fault? Had he, who had chosen her for his lot, the right to punish her—for shortcomings she couldn't help? When he had been seeing an attractive young woman, he felt pity for this one more keenly than ever before, and the pity fettered him more than any love could. She was a representative of that humanity with which he himself was inextricably bound up, burdened with emotions, sensitive and sorrowful in its quest for a way out of the darkness and the severity of its origins. Was one to despise and betray this humanity, one's own humanity, because its instinctive quest for something finer and more beautiful hadn't succeeded? To abandon her and run after another was to abandon one's own life for a will-o'-the-wisp. Once upon a time this one, too, had been young and glamorous like all other girls. And all other girls would one day no longer be young and glamorous, any more than she was today. He was as determined as ever to avoid all meetings which might contain the risk that he would betray her—and his peace. His compassion was so strong that no asceticism was too severe, no dungeon too dark or deep or fetid, as long as that companion was satisfied.

On a pale, quiet autumn day without ravens, a young man and a girl came walking up the hill, with that slightly uncertain gait which bears witness to the fact that the betrothal is not of very long standing. It was Jórunn of Veghús and Jens the Faroese. Yes, times had changed since Faroese-Jens brought the Devil with him up the hill! And now, although the gait had this suggestion of waywardness and uncertain equilibrium, the poet was much too experienced in such matters here on the estate to think of interpreting such a walk in any other way than one—a formal engagement. By walking up the poet's hillside, they were giving the poet special intimation of this event. Although the poet had affected ignorance the other day, he knew perfectly well that Faroese-Jens had been away on another fjord all summer; he must have only just come back, perhaps yesterday. That they should be together already like this suggested it was serious. He had probably earned quite good money. He was big and strong and discontented and militant, and wanted to overthrow society and manage to make money at the same time—in short, he was the right man for her. It was to be hoped that the poem the poet had written to him on her behalf, and which was still unpaid, had played its part in making this match—at least, the poet found some comfort in thinking so. He started to tidy the room, because he thought they were perhaps going to call on him. But when they came near The Heights the girl pointed in a different direction and they turned off the path. Then the girl gave her companion a sign that they should sit down, and they sat down on the scree a stone's throw from the shack. They sat for a good while and talked, in full view of the poet's window. Neither of them looked in his direction, as if he did not exist. After a while the girl stood up, then the young man stood up; she started walking and he, too, started walking. Then they were gone. When they were gone, the poet heaved a sigh as if a danger had passed. He had violent palpitations.

What had he been afraid of? Had he feared that they would visit him in the shack to show him that tedious, innocent, nauseating faith in life which is the substance of every new betrothal and which irritates all those who want to be left in peace with their lot? Or was he secretly afraid of the opposite—that his wealth, his peace of mind, would grow still more, and grow too much, now that the girl was finally disposed of?

All summer he had lived in the delightful danger that she might deprive him of his peace, and had run for cover if he saw her in the distance. When all was said and done, a lack of peace is a prerequisite for desiring peace. He was so ambivalent still that when the couple had disappeared from sight among the houses down below, he was seized with regret at having lost that secret hope of unrest which made peace so desirable. Her image, that strong long hand that could enclose the poet's small hand, that bold, demanding life, belonged to someone else. In a sad vision in the fading light of an autumn day he saw how the hours could come and go without excitement, as they did long ago, with only a heavy swell of boredom like crossing a desert. In that instant he felt the cold breath of the many winter mornings ahead, with rime on the window, when he would wake up only to find his life flowing quickly past without joy and beauty, without any satisfaction for these secret yearnings of the soul, in the full knowledge that his loyal moral life, which was founded on pity for those who were closest to him, was in the first and last instance completely false.

—— 10 ——

The child was still ill; the poet's house which during the spring had sailed away into the universe had returned long ago. And when the little girl leaned back against her pillow, pale and silent in the morning instead of throwing herself laughing into the day's embrace, he suddenly remembered that he had not kept the promise he had made last winter to take her down to the beach and look for shells. In remorse over this omission he determined to be kinder to her than ever. He got three kinds of medicine from the doctor's wife, in addition to the vitamin pills he had already got from Pétur Pálsson, and when it was obvious that the child only accepted these remedies with disgust and nausea he simply went to the shop and bought her sweets for twenty-five *aurar*. He sat with her for hours on end and played with her toys for her or told her stories. Sometimes the child was racked by suffering, and then it was he who nursed her in his arms and crooned foolish words of comfort to her and snatches of verses.

The rainstorms of autumn were at their worst, with incessant downpours and the heavy growling of the sea between the squalls of wind. On many a stormy night the poet and his intended did not go to bed, so as to be ready for anything. One tempestuous evening when the shack was creaking under the lash of the wind and the child continued to whimper with half-closed eyes, the outer door was suddenly thrown open and a visitor appeared on the porch. It was at the time of day when sober people were no longer out and about, and the poet began to fear that in addition to the bad weather he would now have to spend the night in that hell he associated with drunks. But the visitor who greeted them in the shrill whining of the wind through the open door was not a drunk after all but a traveler from afar, weather-beaten from walking in the storm, wearing strong boots and a coat and carrying a knapsack. But it was no meek visitor who thrust his head through the doorway and surveyed the room with leonine eyes.

"Örn Úlfar!" said the poet, and jumped to his feet. "Where have you come from; what brings you here?"

His ship had not been scheduled to call at Sviðinsvík; so he had walked from the next fjord, across the mountain.

"You are welcome to stay the night here, even though there isn't much to offer," said the poet.

"Who is this man?" asked the intended, and fled behind the cooking stove. "How are we to put up a fine gentleman like this? This wretched hovel could be blown down over this sick child at any moment. Wouldn't he be better to look for shelter with Pétur Pálsson the manager?"

"Örn," said the poet, "I ask you to look upon this little house and everything in it as your own. Jarþrúður, he is tired after his journey and hungry; what can he have to eat?"

"I was half expecting that someone might have been asking for me here tonight," said Örn Úlfar. "Has anyone called?"

"Who would that have been?"

"Oh, just someone. A colleague. He has a rather large-boned face and a dark curly beard, and he chews tobacco."

No, no one like that had been in. Ólafur took his friend's coat and invited him to sit on the bed and made him as comfortable as possible. "Jarþrúður, isn't there a pinch of flour so that we can bake pancakes?" And he broke with long habit by stoking the fire himself, fidgety with eagerness, his eyes aflame.

"What a carry-on!" said the intended.

"He is my friend and my guest," said the poet. "The house is his."

"There's no flour," said the intended. "But there are some potatoes. And there's some salted skate soaking in the tub."

The visitor did not say Thank you in spite of the fact that he was being given the house many times over, and behaved as if he did not hear the exchanges between host and hostess; he leaned across to the poet's writing desk which was lying at the foot of the bed, and began to leaf through the manuscripts, the corners of his mouth pulled down and his brow furrowed. Instead of giving a more detailed account of his own travels he asked bluntly, "Do you still write for the same reasons as before?"

"I've forgotten the reasons why I wrote before," said the poet when the fire was going. "I am writing some stories about Strange Men."

"What are strange men?" said Örn Úlfar.

"Jóhann *beri* was a fugitive from his mistress for twenty years, wearing rags like a beggar. Thereafter, I'll be writing the story of Jón *almáttugi* (the Almighty)."

"Why do you write about these wretches?"

"Probably because I'm sorry for them," replied the poet.

"Why are you sorry for them?"

"I don't know. Perhaps because I see all humanity in them."

"Will you make any sacrifices because of this pity?" asked Örn Úlfar.

"I don't care if I have nothing to eat," replied the poet. "I don't care if my house is blown down in the next squall."

Then his intended, Jarþrúður Jónsdóttir, said: "I don't call it being like pastor Hallgrímur Pétursson to care nothing about shame or honor and never to write anything one can recite to redeem one's soul. But to sit up in bed at nights like a ghost with his knees up and to disarrange the bedclothes like a dog chewing a piece of fish skin instead of lying still; and then to get his head down in the morning and sleep all day; and to look on in cold blood while his own children waste away—that's his way of life. Needless to say, those who try to keep this place going never get any thanks for their trouble except silence."

The visitor looked at the intended impassively and coldly for a moment, like a man who hears a sudden creak in a piece of furniture from which sound was unexpected. But the poet said, "A well-formed sentence and a true rhyme in a poem are generous reward for a day's hunger and a sleepless night. In the future when I have long been dead and gone, it won't be asked what the poet had for his meals or whether he slept well at nights, but—was his style Icelandic? Was his poetry pure?"

"And the spirit?" asked Örn Úlfar.

"I used to stand outside human life, particularly my own life. But now—human life has come closer to me than before, particularly my own life."

"Don't you mean that your death has crept closer?" asked the visitor.

"I was trying to answer you about the spirit," said the poet. "What I was thinking of was that the world has certainly become more materialistic than it was when we last talked together and, it's quite true, more transient. But nonetheless I still hear the good Voice; and however poor my life may appear from the outside, that makes it rich."

"Yes, you believe in Ýmir," said the visitor, and smiled at his friend after all these years.* The poet looked admiringly at his neck-linen, at how neat it was even after crossing the mountain in rain and darkness. His complexion had recovered from the storm, his features were at once refined and strong like his whole physique; perhaps this man was unnaturally healthy rather than ill, and Ólafur Kárason counted himself lucky to have such a man as his friend—and his judge.

"Well," he said at last, "now I've told you everything about myself. Now you must tell me something about yourself."

"What do you want to know?"

"You must have some reason for being in these parts," said the poet.

"I'm going to become a Member of Parliament," said the visitor.

"A Member of Parliament!" said the intended. "And crossing the mountain on foot!"

"Örn Úlfar, M.P.—yes, I like that very much," said the poet.

"Then don't let me down," said the visitor. "There's to be an election in the spring."

The poet then realized that his friend was perhaps in earnest after all, and he asked, "What does Pétur Pálsson the manager say to that?"

"We'll thrash the living daylights out of that bloodsucker," said the visitor.

"Oh, I wouldn't say that, perhaps," said the poet, and glanced rather anxiously in the direction of his intended.

"You must write," said the visitor, "a challenge to the people of Sviðinsvík to defeat Júel and throw out his agent, Pétur Þríhross, so that your children and all the others you are sorry for here on this estate can get a chance to live."

The intended from the other side of the cooking stove: "I'm leaving this house! People can cook their own skate!"

"We must be careful what we say," whispered the poet to his visitor, and out loud he begged his intended not to be offended by an innocent joke.

"I can't bear jokes about what I hold sacred," said the intended. "And least of all do I want to have to listen to filthy talk about my benefactor."

"If he has given you vitamin tablets, my good woman," said the visitor, "then I can tell you that you have to take thirty pints of water with every tablet if it is to have the same effect as one crowberry."

"Dear God and Jesus, to have to endure this kind of thing from strangers, yes, and under His very own roof!" said the intended, and the tears had begun to flow. She found a dark shawl and put it on and sniffed and sobbed. The poet had got to his feet to soothe her. Was she out of her mind to think of going out in this weather in the middle of the night, and how could she ever let herself get so furious over the harmless pleasantries of two old friends who had not seen one another for God knows how long?

"Since he now owns this house and everything in it jointly with you, as you said before, I'm obviously not wanted here," said the intended.

"I'll go," said the visitor, and stood up.

But now Ólafur Kárason was beside himself and said, "If you go, Örn, I'm going too."

In other words it looked as if the poet's house would be left standing empty; everyone was prepared to leave it for good and abandon a dangerously ill child to her fate, along with the salted skate in the pot.

But in the middle of these midnight emotions the porch door opened again, and the wind came raging into the house once more. A tall girl with a red silk scarf tied round her black curly hair, wearing an expensive coat and carrying a basket on her arm, said Good-evening.

"God help me, Védís Pétursdóttir; what are you doing here in this terrible house? And in the middle of the night at that!"

The manager's daughter who had roamed around the estate here in bygone days, hoydenish and disagreeable, had long since become the best match in the Sviðinsvík district, quick and clever, educated in the south, with boyish movements in her long body, and shrewd eyes which never gave anything away, her coloring dazzlingly healthy.

"Someone said your little girl was very ill," said the hoyden. "All at once I felt so sorry for you in the storm; I suddenly wanted to do something for you; what can I do?" And then she was suddenly taken aback at seeing the poet's unexpected visitor: "Örn Úlfar, is that you, or am I seeing things?"

"No formalities, Dísa," said Örn Úlfar. "Anyway, you're a godsend; the whole household was disintegrating because I said thirty pints of water were needed with your father's vitamin pills. I rely on you now to unite this household again."

"Ach, you're always the same villain about the old man, poor Pétur Þríhross, but let me just tell you that his real vitamin is me, and no one needs to take thirty pints of water with me, my lad!—and with that let me give you my hand and bid you welcome."

"Thanks, Dísa," said the visitor. "Let me have a look at you. Have you changed?" And he added by way of explanation to the others: "Dísa and I have met in the south."

"Védís, an educated girl!" said the intended, dumfounded. "Am I to believe my ears that you not only use a nickname for your father but mimic him as well? And in the presence of—these people?"

The child whom the manager's daughter had come to visit had been almost forgotten, and the poet showed her where she lay but said they had better not waken her; it was best for the sick to sleep. The girl bent over the child and murmured a few affectionate words, but perhaps without that quiet inner tenderness which characterizes true love. Everyone had given up the idea of abandoning the house. The intended had also forgiven the girl for talking disrespectfully of her father, and had begun to extol the high-mindedness of these wonderful people whom God wakes up in the middle of the night to comfort the poor.

"I can tell from the smell that you're boiling fish, Jarþrúður dear," said the hoyden. "Take it off the stove for this once. It occurred to me it was perhaps a long time since your little girl had tasted meat. I'm just ashamed of myself for not having thought of it before."

She opened her basket and brought out a fine, brown, roasted leg of lamb for the child, golden sugar-fried potatoes and peas, a splendid pudding, exotic fruits, and a bottle of wine. The poet and his intended stood there speechless while the princess laid a cloth on the rickety table, put out plates and cutlery, brought out all the delicacies and began to serve them. Örn Úlfar frowned and was silent while the banquet was being prepared, and then said, "Have you taken leave of your senses, girl?"

"Dinner is served," said the hoyden.

"This is an affront to the house," said Örn Úlfar. "I'm not touching this food. Give me the skate."

The girl stopped serving and looked at him. Disappointment made her face suddenly childish: a little girl who had been hurt, almost brought to tears, in the middle of her unclouded happiness.

"Örn," she said. "When you come at long, long last, and everyone, everyone's been waiting for you, and then . . ."

Then she pulled herself together, bit her lip a little, and said, "It doesn't really matter. If you don't take any of it, there will be all the more for us, and besides it wasn't meant for you but for the little sick girl. Jarþrúður dear, you just give him some rotten fish and preferably some cod-liver oil dregs for coffee."

In the end they all took their share of the roast except the one for whom the roast was intended, the little girl; she was allowed to sleep on. The daughter of the estate lavished all her care on the traveler instead, anticipating his every wish, never tiring of making him comfortable: "You know how ill he's been," she said by way of explanation. And the host and hostess gradually overcame their shyness and let themselves be entertained in their own house instead of abandoning it, and that leaky house with its mysteriously incompatible party guests ate and drank and was merry.

Örn Úlfar suggested that they might hear the *Stories of Strange Men* by Ólafur Kárason of Ljósavik; the table was cleared, and the poet brought out his books and begged his guests to make themselves as comfortable as possible on the bed, while he seated himself on a stool at their feet and began to read. Jarþrúður the intended barricaded herself behind the cooking stove. The wind had suddenly dropped and the sea had died. The insecurities of heaven and earth were forgotten. The saga of Jóhann *beri* reigned in the house. One poet, and two royal listeners in the high seat, and this little house was a royal house. The girl leaned back against the visitor's breast and laid her curly head under his cheek.

It was late at night and the poet had come to a stop. Then the intended said, "It doesn't look as if he's going to come, the man with the beard the visitor was expecting here tonight."

"Yes, you're right," said Örn Úlfar. "But it doesn't matter. Maybe I'll meet him all the same."

"My dear fellow, don't worry about that," said the Ljósvíkingur. "You're sleeping in this bed tonight. We can lie down anywhere ourselves."

Then Dísa got to her feet and said, "No, you can't sleep here, Örn."

"Oh, really?" said Örn. "You're not thinking of making me sleep with Pétur Þríhross?"

"Not directly," she said.

"But indirectly?" he asked.

"Leave that to me," she said. "I know of a place where you can sleep. The one you waited for will not let you down."

Soon afterwards they bade Good-night and were gone.

—— **II** ——

Örn Úlfar had undoubtedly looked deep enough into his old friend's mind that first evening to realize that he was not the man to lead the attack in a battle, and that it would be advisable to try somewhere else first if there were to be a call to arms; in any event he never called on the poet for support in the party strife which now began on the estate, this time under his own leadership. But because he himself did not feel a scrap of admiration for conventional orthodox behavior, he knew better than anyone else how to talk to a poet, and so there was no more welcome visitor at The Heights, and the hours flew by when the two of them wandered together in Poetry's meadow, that meadow where human destiny is given meaning.

And the winter passed. The Laborers Union had been reconstituted long ago with Faroese-Jens as president, but with a more distinguished name; it was now called the Sviðinsvík Trades Union. To be sure it proved to be difficult to find anything for this union to do as things now stood, because there was less work available than ever and therefore there was no opportunity to fight over wages being too low. The difficulty was that the land part of the harbor was now completed, but the government had reserved the right to decide whether deeper water would affect the possibility of growing potatoes in that part of the harbor which was likely to be under water at high tide and while this decision was held up, no money was available for quarry work on the estate. The union could only insist that there was little prosperity in the village, and therefore it sent one resolution after another to the government, to Júel J. Júel and to Pétur Pálsson the manager, demanding money, ships, stations, fields, poultry, a just society. But the shop became emptier and emptier, and after New Year there was, apart from chicory and margarine, not much left on the shelves except hardtack biscuits in barrels and vitamins in packets, and people were allowed to have these remnants on credit as long as they lasted, against drafts drawn on the parish funds in the hope of a grant from the treasury.

On the other hand, all those who owned a sack of saltfish and a barrel of potatoes wanted to be freeborn Icelanders and to do everything they could to protect their nationality against the unpatriotic. The shares in Irish slaves, Danes, and Russians were not very high at that time. The Society of True Icelanders in Sviðinsvík now began to collect funds for a new Icelandic church with pillars and painted windows in memory of Guðmundur *góði* here on the estate and, as it turned out, donations started pouring in from all quarters, some in kind, some in promises of work or in ready cash, because there has never been such lack of prosperity in Iceland that it has not been possible to raise unlimited money for building churches. People who would rather have been flayed alive than spend a halfpenny on themselves laid five krónur in pure silver on the table; yes, and two men from the Outer Nesses even brought a shiny rix-dollar.* If old Jón the snuffmaker on the French site would now contribute ten thousand krónur or so, it was practically certain that the church could be built that summer, and not just the church, but beside it also the cultural beacon in memory of Þórður of Hattardalur and Úlfur *ópveginn*, which had for a time been the fondest dream of Pétur Pálsson the manager. Likewise, the True Icelanders of Sviðinsvík had managed to secure the use of an airplane. The chairman assured the society that as early as next summer the members of the society would be given the opportunity of floating on the gentle breezes of heaven above this troublesome estate of Sviðinsvík-undir-Ópveginsenni.

But none of these enterprises affected the poet's world. What caused him more concern was the fact that it was now becoming impossible to get the child to take Pétur Pálsson's vitamin pills or his cod-liver oil, and when they eventually began to try giving her warm fresh milk from the manager's own barn, it was too late; the child continued to waste away. It was a wonder that she managed to draw breath at all.

With every day that passed, the problem of what the child's parents themselves were to have for their next meal became more and more difficult for a beginner and amateur to solve. It required neither more nor less than a scientific solution; it required the wisdom of the world. Money did not grow at this time of year, any more than green grass. If it so happened that someone was forced to commission an elegy in these difficult times, the poet was lucky to be paid with a sack of peats, or even a load of sheep droppings. But if there had been good fishing weather and people had caught anything, the Ljósvíkingur was sometimes to be seen wandering along the shore, and then people would perhaps throw him some fish with some such remark as: "We must give the poor fellow some fish heads for the pot; he's a useless wretch and a poet; he'll bring blessings or famine upon us with his poetry according to the way we treat him." But unfortunately these occasional acts of charity made no provision for the future.

More and more frequently he would return home empty-handed even though his intended had driven him out into the frost with the threat that she would not open the door to him until he came back with sugar, rye meal and groats. Her prayers to God, which she shouted on her knees, loudly, as if she were on a bad telephone line, together with incessant hymn-singing, required eardrums of leather. He himself could starve with equanimity, and had he been a free agent he would have gone to bed, pulled the covers over his head and waited fearlessly for the start of a new order in human affairs. But now the usual outcome was that the intended herself set out to see Pétur Pálsson the manager, and got him to give her some food from his own larder for the only currency with which the poor can trade with the rich when all else fails—a beggar's tears.

One day when there was one half-dried fish tail hanging outside the porch, the sum total of the house's wealth, the poet found himself on the road in an icy snowstorm, having been forbidden to come home empty-handed. He pulled his old peaked cap down over his ears and wrapped his scarf twice round his neck. His nankeen jacket had long ago ceased to keep the wind out, and he felt the icy blast blowing through his bones like a whistle.

It then occurred to him—it was something he had really never completely forgotten—that the girl from Veghús had omitted to pay him her debt from last spring. To go dunning a girl of her kind for such a trifling sum was certainly no pleasure outing, and something very different from what he had imagined at the time when his speech and her novel of *The Dream of Happiness* had found one another. Luckily he himself had fled up the mountain in time, but his poetry had, as so often before, been able to bring two hearts together in one truth. But in view of her love and happiness, how could she justify withholding from a poet the reward due to him for having given her a little key to the heart of so excellent a man as Faroese-Jens? She was bound to see for herself that it is not possible to bring two people together in love so artistically for nothing.

His arguments for the justice of this claim became weightier and weightier the longer the icy wind played through his bones. No, it could not in any way be called degrading himself. It would be an untimely act of gallantry to give the poem away for nothing. What does this girl matter to me? Whether her eyes are hot or cold does not concern me at all. The main thing is that I sat up for a whole day and a whole night to execute an order for her; work is work, business is business. People must not imagine that poets are above ordinary human necessities.

And so on, over and over again.

The farmhouse of Veghús looked just as the poet had always imagined a house should look. It was in such a house that he had dreamed in his childhood that his mother lived, with the front door on the side that faced the road and friendly windows on each side of the door, a roof, a chimney. He trudged up the path to the house with the icy wind in his face and met the farmer in the yard, jovial, ruddy-faced and smiling, with a sou'wester on and bits of moss on his jersey. The farmer laughed in the driving snow and asked what brought the poet there.

"Oh, I'm just having a stroll to pass the time," said the poet.

Then the farmer laughed even more; he had thought that poets had better ways of passing the time than that.

"What do you think of the weather; what's it going to do next?" asked the poet.

"Oh, it's just the sort of winter weather you'd expect, eh?" answered the farmer. "And what's news with you?"

"Nothing I can think of," said the poet.

"Everyone hale and hearty in the village?"

"As far as I know," said the poet.

"And how far are you going on your stroll?"

"Oh, this is probably far enough for today," said the poet. "I just came up to the house because I saw you in the yard. You mustn't think I had anything in mind. I just find it so remarkable that here, where there was only a gravel slope and a stretch of moor a few years ago, there should now be a farmhouse and a homefield; and people and sheep; yes, and the terns' old fish yards down by the shore soon to be a meadow."

"Perhaps you might like to have a look at my hens, eh?" said the farmer.

"Many thanks. A lot of people make fun of these birds because they can't fly, but can other birds lay more eggs?" asked the poet, who had suddenly started to side with these birds.

"Those who make most fun of these chickens wouldn't say No to their eggs," said the farmer.

The animal sheds were behind the farmhouse, all under one roof including the hay barn; everything was as clean as if it were Christmas Eve—all the paving swept, the stalls and flooring brushed, not a speck of dung on the legs or tails of the two cows, any more than on the farmer's conscience. At the other end of the barn were twenty plump hens in a wooden cage, cackling unemotionally in their hen language in the midday quiet, apart from the cockerel which bridled and crowed reprovingly at this intrusion and shook his comb and wattles. Ólafur Kárason thought the birds really were remarkable, particularly the cockerel, and looked at them for a long time. At the other end of the building twenty sheep were chewing the cud, in blissful peace like saints, innocent and lovely.

"Feel one of them and tell me what you think," said the farmer.

But the poet excused himself and said he did not know how to feel a sheep. To tell the truth he was a little afraid of sheep. Then the farmer took hold of one of the ewes and showed the poet how to feel a sheep: the brisket and back to see how meaty it was, the belly to see if it were eating well, the udder to see if it were filling with milk. "I shall take the liberty of saying that if these ewes were a little farther down the Fjörður, they would all be True Icelanders and would form a society and erect a cultural beacon," said the farmer, and laughed gustily, and everything pointed to the fact that the man and his livestock were one. Their well-being was one of the characteristics of his soul.

"My heartfelt thanks for letting me see these delightful creatures," said the poet. "I'm always becoming more and more convinced that animals are much more perfect creatures than human beings, and probably human beings will never get as far as they have. Everything that concerns animals is beautiful. And now I'd better be heading for home. Good-bye."

The farmer, for his part, was grateful that the visitor should have liked the animals and appreciated them properly, and he now asked if the poet would not step inside to have a look at the womenfolk as well. "Perhaps a poet knows how to fondle them a bit better, eh?"

"There's no need at all, thank you," said the poet.

"They often have coffee," said the farmer.

"Indeed," said the poet. "Well, perhaps, thank you."

She was radiantly pure like a plant in blossom time, newly sprung, full of invisible rich coloring that appealed to hidden senses, and she pushed back a lock of hair behind her ear when she saw it was a man.

"It's out of the question to invite poets into the kitchen," she said, and led him into the living room with her strong hand. She apologized for her appearance; she was wearing a big loose-knit jersey and a coarse woolly skirt which concealed her figure. She ordered a lanky youth to fetch coal and kindling, lit the fire in a twinkling, and told the poet to make himself comfortable. What could she offer him?

She was no less energetic at home than outside, brought up in a large family, accustomed to running a household and receiving visitors; she shooed out the children, her brothers and sisters, who came to look at the man, and the stepmother withdrew; the farmer had gone to see to his tasks; in a short time there was an aroma of pancakes in the house. The fire crackled and the room became warm, and the window started to steam up.

Alone, the poet looked around the room, enchanted. There was a picture of a waterfall in a ravine, and another of the Great Geysir erupting; casual cushions on a corner bench nailed to the walls, with a table in front but no chair, woven rugs and braided mats of different patterns on the floor, embroidered hangings on the walls, a broad divan with a multicolored, woven covering and several embroidered cushions, a washstand with a bowl, toilet water, soap, powder box and a jar of cream which all gave the room a fragrance; there was also a *Book of Dreams* and an inkstand. On the wall above the washstand were pinned three postcards of male film stars, all looking rather sugary, and only one female film star beside them on a fourth postcard, slightly indecent and not very good-looking. Against the middle of the wall facing the window stood a loom with a half-finished blanket on it. The poet sat marveling on the divan among these magnificently patterned, embroidered cushions and had never imagined that such a room could exist. To the fragrance from the washstand was added the aroma from the kitchen next door. He could hear the batter being ladled onto the pan with a delectable seething noise which was associated with all of life's greatest festivities, and on top of that came the smell of coffee. At last the girl came in, a little flushed after the baking, having changed out of her jersey into a close-fitting dress which showed her full, mature figure to best advantage; she laid a cloth on the table and brought in strong coffee with cream so thick you could hardly pour it, and pancakes baked over a fire so hot that the edges were crisp, smothered in butter and sugar.

"I think I must be dead and in heaven," said the visitor when he had put sugar in his coffee.

"A poet was the last thing I expected," said the girl.

"I never thought that such a room existed," he said.

"When I arrived last year, this was the drawing room, but I threw out all the rubbish and put in my loom here instead. I made that corner bench myself; then I painted it and made these casual cushions for it. Don't you think it looks nice?"

"Don't ask me," he said. "Everything I see here is way above me. I have nothing to compare with it. I own nothing."

"Who then owns the poem you wrote last spring?" she said.

"You," he said.

"No," she said. "Don't try to flatter me. But Pétur Þríhross wouldn't own it either even if you had recited it at his party. It is and will always be your own poem. And yet I would rather stand barefoot in the frost in a storm like today's than not know it by heart."

He stopped eating and drinking and looked at her for a moment as she stood there in the middle of the room, and his eyes moistened a little with tears. Even if he had said something beautiful, how worthless it was in comparison with what she said merely by existing. Her figure was of a quality that left nothing more to be said, neither in a poem nor a story nor a picture nor in divine revelation.

"Jórunn," he said, and gazed into her eyes imploringly with those deep, sincere, serious eyes of his. "Have mercy on me."

"Have something to eat with the coffee," she said, and smiled.

"These pancakes," he said, and had recovered himself. "It's like eating auras."

"Hardly of saints, though," said the girl.

"No, thank goodness," he said. "Listen, who's that woman on the wall over there?"

"It's me," she said.

"I cannot believe," he said, "that you've ever lifted your dress so high in other people's presence."

"Higher—before a poet," she said. "Before a poet, one is always naked."

"And those three men beside her?"

"Do you think they're genuine?" she asked.

"Their hair is at least well cut and groomed," he said.

"May I cut your hair?" she said.

He thought for a little while and then said, "I don't dare to."

"Do have some more coffee," she said, and laughed at him. "What are you afraid of?"

"I could catch a chill if I lost my mane," he said. "Why is there no picture of Faroese-Jens?"

"You and your Faroese-Jens!" she said and laughed a little, and there was a glint of recklessness in her eyes as she laughed, experienced rather than light-hearted, and the poet felt he understood better than before the picture of the girl on the wall.

"Yet you walked together up the hillside last autumn," he said.

"What hillside?" she said.

"The hillside," he said.

"I met him outside a house," she said.

"Outside a house? What house?" asked the poet.

"A house," she said.

She breathed on the frosted window pane for a while, as if she were thinking, and then she said out of the blue, "How is it that you who write poetry for Pétur Þríhross aren't rich and happy?"

"Luckily I am poor," he said. "The one thing for which I thank God is for having given me nothing except myself. While I have nothing, I am free to look upon myself as a human being."

"That's odd," she said.

"It's quite true," he said. "A person first begins to exist when everything has been taken from him. And besides, I don't write poetry at all for Pétur Pálsson the manager. I write poetry for those who will be born after I am dead. My life is an accident. But the nation which has the spirit of poetry is eternal."

Her eyes warmed at seeing him a little vehement.

"I always think there are birds perching on your hands when you speak," she said. "You ought to live in a high tower on a wooded heath and sit there by the window and look out over the whole world and live for all eternity and let the birds fly."

"Birds? Fly? Where to?" he said.

"To me."

"What would Faroese-Jens say?"

"You speak that man's name in derision," she said. "You have no right to do that even though you're intelligent. But since you have mentioned him again and want to hear about him, then let me tell you that though you're a great poet and have birds on your hands, he has certain things over and above you that are decisive. He hates injustice and is ready to do battle for justice."

She was suddenly red in the face, and her eyes were flashing.

"What do you mean when you say that this is decisive?" he said.

She looked down and bit her lip a little. She was an impetuous girl. Her whole life was lived in hot waves and she had no control over it herself; before she knew it, she had given away too much.

"I mean—I mean that one day you might discover that Örn Úlfar is a better friend of Faroese-Jens's than of yours."

"That could well be," said the poet. "And yet I know of someone who is a better friend of Örn Úlfar's than both Faroese-Jens and me put together."

"Dísa Pétursdóttir is an intelligent girl," said Jórunn. "And she's an educated girl. She understands that justice is worth more than house, home and family, as it says in the catechism. She is ready to do battle against injustice even though it's her own father. So is Faroese-Jens. He has a house and he has a boat and he has money in the bank, but he is still ready to do battle against injustice. And Örn Úlfar himself, who is so intelligent that he could have become anything he wanted—he has never seen anything except the one thing, one star, one star that shines, and that is justice. But he has therefore never known where his next meal was coming from, except when he was in the sanatorium, and I am convinced we shall one day see him die for the cause of the poor. I love Dísa Pétursdóttir for loving him."

"I understand you much too well," said the poet, and had stopped eating. "Whiplashes cannot be misunderstood. You draw pictures of great men in order to let them reflect a picture of a little man and, what's worse, a picture of a coward, a picture of a man who lacks the courage to live life—in a word, a picture of me. My heartfelt thanks for all your kindness, Jórunn dear. I've never had such wonderful pancakes since the time, many years ago, when I was raised from the dead. Now I'm going to leave this lovely warm room, this prosperity where nothing is lacking, not even the proper love of justice, and go home."

Then she saw that she had hurt him, and came right over to him and said his name without raising her eyes and said, "Why am I worse to you than to other people? Can you tell me that?"

"Good-bye," he said.

"No, don't go," she said. "I know quite well that it needs courage to live your life; yes, even inconceivable courage at that. Forgive me for being so unreasonable, and don't go yet."

"I have work to do, and should have been gone a long time ago," he said. "It was only by chance I came at all, anyway."

"Thank you for coming," she said. "But all the same you have misunderstood me a little—yes, and perhaps quite a lot, Ólafur, do you realize that? I know I can't express myself, but I beg you not to hold that against me. I couldn't bear it if we didn't part friends on this one occasion you found your way here by chance. Ólafur, often when I recite your poems to myself, I want so much to do something for you in return. What can we here do for you; isn't there some little thing you need . . .?"

"No, thanks, I have enough of everything, enough of everything," he interrupted, withdrew his hand from hers and made for the door. "My little sick child at home cries for her daddy if he's away any length of time."

Then he was standing outside in the driving snow again, and he pulled his old cap down over his ears.

— 12 —

And now Pétur Pálsson the manager took the bit between his teeth and set off for the south. At first no one thought this particularly remarkable; the manager had a lot of traveling to do. But this time it was not long before the rumor spread that the manager's journey was not just a matter of routine. Soon everyone was saying that he had been summoned south by the authorities to appear in court. A special investigating judge had been appointed to inquire into the widespread stories of espionage which various highly placed personages in the land had been involved in recently, with a view to helping foreign poachers to plunder and rape the people's livelihood; and arising from this, a close investigation into the health of Madame Sophie Sørensen, Pétur Pálsson's grandmother, had been set on foot. At these court hearings it was disclosed, and of course publicized in the newspapers of the capital, that the headquarters of this espionage system on behalf of foreigners had been run by Júel J. Júel, M.P., in the south, but his agents had been operating near all the country's best fishing grounds. It was proved that Pétur Pálsson had been an agent for the foreigners at Sviðinsvík. The spies were all given fines, the leader being fined the heaviest, of course, but Pétur Pálsson was also given a very tolerable fine, which under the circumstances could be considered rather to have enhanced his credit than weakened it—it was in any event a respectable five-figure sum.

In Sviðinsvík, on the other hand, certain powers left no stone unturned to undermine the general confidence which is bound to be felt in someone who is given a heavy fine. These people maintained that Júel J. Júel was on the verge of bankruptcy, and that his last rusty tub and killer-boat was sure to be sequestered in part payment of the fine. The Trades Union passed a vote of censure on both the manager and the Member of Parliament, and spread the word that they were both broke and in no way to be trusted. For a time it seemed that even a number of freeborn Icelanders were in two minds. To be sure, the Society of the True Icelanders carried a resolution to the effect that the disgraceful attacks on the manager and the Member of Parliament were just one more aspect of the persecution campaign which the anti-patriots were running against the nation, the unpatriotic against the homeland, but nevertheless every day more and more freeborn people were beginning to doubt whether Júel and the manager had very much money. Naturally, all freeborn men were sorry for Pétur Pálsson for having run foul of more or less unpatriotic agencies, such as, for instance, modern justice, but they secretly asked themselves whether one could be sure that men who had been engaged to carry out risky duties for others would be able to afford to pay their own fines? Can we rely on getting money from someone who lets himself be used in risky work for others instead of doing it on his own behalf? In other words, it could no longer be concealed that confidence in the pillars of society and the providence of the estate was beginning to waver where it had least right to—let alone if it was correct that Júel's last rusty tub was soon to be sold by order of the court. Where then was the independence of the nation? If Júel did not succeed in proving that he had enough money, he could well be in danger of losing the Parliamentary elections in the spring. Really, these were difficult times for the nation. A few of the freeborn now secretly left the Society of True Icelanders to join the Laborers Union.

People asked themselves expectantly: "How will our dear pillar of society and benefactor look when he comes ashore again here after his journey to distant parts?" People no doubt pictured this to themselves in different ways, each according to his own conscience, because people are apt to give others their own image; and yet probably no one suspected that his arrival would turn out the way it actually did. No one could possibly attribute such fortitude to anyone else in this part of the world. It was now seen how much Pétur Pálsson the manager surpassed other men.

One day a Norwegian freighter came sailing up the fjord and headed for Sviðinsvík; she did not ask for a pilot—she knew the course exactly. A short distance away from the village, down the fjord a little, the Norwegian cast anchor. Here was Pétur Pálsson the manager, wearing a hat both broader in the brim and higher in the crown than ever before; it appeared to be one of Júel's own hats. The manager was surrounded by a handsome retinue of learned gentleman with hats, walking sticks and spectacles, like himself. They walked in procession onto the estate.

What the devil was brewing now? It was briefly this: Júel Júel had plenty of money. Grímur Loðinkinni Ltd., which had gone bankrupt last June and owed the state bank millions, had now obtained a new loan running into millions from the same bank to build the long-awaited station at Sviðinsvík, and here was Pétur Pálsson with a ship laden with materials for the station, as well as engineers and foremen; an immediate start was to be made on constructing quays and building factories. On the very same day a meeting of the Society of True Icelanders of Sviðinsvík was called, and this society was fortified by the glad news about the station in the same way as the palsied man who rose to his feet, took up his bedding and walked. People declared themselves ready to work on the station for low wages. Iceland's Cause was held in high honor in Sviðinsvík.

But Ólafur Kárason of Ljósavík sat by his child's sickbed and the news of these outside events reached his ears like a rumbling in the distance. What concerned him was her suffering, which had grown worse in the last few days; it overwhelmed that little body in waves, with brief respites, and he sat up beside her, pale and sleepless, awaiting each new wave with a heartfelt prayer to the Creator of suffering that this surf might break over him instead of the child. Everything humanly possible had been tried, even to the extent of fetching the doctor.

The child had had a terribly difficult night before Pétur Pálsson's return to the village, and both her parents had stayed up all night without going to bed. On the following afternoon she fell into a coma; her breathing, which had been much too rapid, was now only just discernible, and every now and again weak spasms went though her body. The poet's intended fell into a deep sleep early that evening, but Ólafur Kárason stayed up beside the bed with his head drooping, overcome by that exhaustion which lies in the body like a bittersweet toxic pain and carries the mind and senses away into the drunken world of symbols and dreams.

Suddenly he started up, thinking he had seen a lion thrusting its head round the door and gazing around with that resolute look which, allied to its lack of pity and sensitivity, has made it the mighty king of the beasts—that face which knows it is superior to everyone else and is therefore the most perfect face on earth and the face most remote from humanity.

The poet stretched and tried to tear his eyes open to see if this unreal world would change its appearance, so that another picture might replace this one by way of explanation. The lion's head in the shadow of the doorway gradually changed into another face, not much more comprehensible than the other, certainly; it was the perfect face of his friend peering around carefully, like an animal on the lookout, before he came into the open.

"Are you the only one awake?"

"Yes," whispered the poet. "I'm the only one awake."

"Can I sleep here on the floor tonight?" whispered Örn Úlfar.

"You don't need to ask for anything in this house," said the poet. "This is your house."

"I had a room with the True Icelanders," said the other, "and that was paid in full. But tonight I was thrown out on the ground that the Home Rulers had won. How are things with you?"

"It's touch and go," said the poet.

"Have you tried calling the doctor?"

"Yes, he came here this morning."

"And obviously didn't do anything."

"Yes, he drank all the medicine his wife had prescribed for the child for the last few weeks, the dregs of three bottles. He also ate up all the cream he had got to rub on her where she felt pain."

Örn Úlfar walked quietly over to the child's cot and looked at her for a moment; one could read nothing in his expression.

"She no longer knows her mother and me," said Ólafur Kárason. "For the last three days she hasn't been able to smile at me."

"Are you going to stay up?"

"Yes, I'm going to stay up; I slept a little today. But Jarþrúður, my intended, didn't sleep at all last night, and didn't sleep at all today, either; so the bed is occupied, unfortunately. But I can lend you a blanket to wrap around yourself."

"If you're staying up, I'll stay up too," said Örn Úlfar. "It's no worse for me than for you. I can sit on that box there on the other side of the girl's bed and lean against the wall, and we can perhaps talk together."

"How very glad I am that you should have found your way here," said the poet. "I've been sitting here for a long time and seeing hallu-cinations. Now I'll warm some coffee for us. And you can tell me all the news."

First there came some smoke from the oil stove, then the whistling of water on the boil, finally the aroma of coffee. The two friends sat one on each side of the child's bed and sipped coffee at long intervals, and the visitor recounted everything happening on the estate. He told all about Pétur Pálsson's travels and the court case he had been involved in, about the bankruptcy and wealth of Júel J. Júel, about money in Iceland and for whom it is minted, and about the penniless populace, those toiling or unemployed but at the same time good-hearted margarine- and chicory-eaters who above all must not be called Icelanders in their own land, but were either called antipatriots or were named after races they had never heard mentioned, from Celts to Slavs, to justify the economic war being waged against them. Then the visitor told how the first thing Pétur Pálsson had done when he stepped ashore that day was to summon a meeting of the society of those in his pay and to promise them work at a wage rate he himself would determine, in a phony enterprise into which a hun-dred thousand krónur or so would be poured before the elections. The Sviðinsvík Trades Union had also held a meeting that evening and had agreed not to budge from the wage rates it had demanded last spring nor the claim for the right to negotiate about working conditions here on the estate—failing which, it would declare a strike. This decision had been communicated to Pétur Pálsson that same evening, whose first reaction had been to reply that whoever lis-tened to Örn Úlfar's was not only an enemy of the soul but also an enemy of Iceland and would be treated accordingly; and in the sec-ond place, the hoyden now being placed under house arrest in her room at home, with her door locked on the outside and a guard at her window.

The poet listened not entirely absentmindedly to this story, which in Örn Úlfar's mouth was long, colorful and dramatic, told with much embroidery and innumerable digressions—definitions, deduc-tions and conclusions—which were totally alien to the poet's empirical and objective way of thinking. The visitor's impassioned story, told in a temperate, almost whispering, voice across the poet's dying child, gave a human content to the chilly solo of the cold night and sustained the poet through that jungle of waking nightmares which otherwise this lonely night would have brought while the sweetest light of his life was being extinguished. What his friend actually said did not matter all that much—the poet was deeply grateful that his voice should be there under his roof on this particular night. When the visitor had been talking far into the night, with the poet gazing into the blue and listening, the poet said: "I am so grateful to the Almighty for letting me hear a noble-minded person talking, tonight of all nights, and letting me forget that man is a creature of dust."

Örn Úlfar looked sharply at his friend with renewed attention and replied in a different register: "A normal person is noble-minded, but I am not. And man isn't a creature of dust."

"You always belittle yourself, Úlfar—that's a characteristic of good people. They feel they never do anything for anyone. Love for others is as much a part of their natural life processes as eating and drinking."

Örn Úlfar sat thinking for a long time without acknowledging the handsome compliment he had been paid by his friend. And when he eventually replied, it was quite out of keeping with the dispassionate, hesitant stillness of the night: "I don't believe in love," he said. "I don't even know what love is."

"Love?" said the poet, a little unsure of himself at having to define such a commonplace thing without warning, and repeated the word in embarrassment: "Love, that's feeling for others—as I feel for my child when the waves of suffering break over her."

"Man has only one characteristic that equals the most commendable qualities of animals, one mark of nobility above the gods; he chooses justice," said Örn Úlfar. "He who doesn't choose justice isn't human. I have little fondness for that pity which the coward calls love, Ljósvíkingur. What is love? If a loving person sees someone's eye being gouged out, he howls as if his own eye were being gouged out. On the other hand he isn't moved at all if he sees powerful liars utterly rob a whole people of their sight and thereby their good sense as well. If a loving man sees a dog's tail being trodden on, he suffers as if he himself had a tail; on the other hand, it doesn't touch any string in his heart if he looks upon demented criminals trampling half of mankind into the dirt."

"But because of this pity for mankind, God sent his only begotten Son to suffer on the Cross—don't you then see anything magnificent in that ancient story, Örn?"

"Yes," said Örn Úlfar, "that pity for mankind should have caused the death of the god."

"Don't you think it right, then, that I should feel pity for this little child who lies here at death's door between us?" asked the poet.

"It is justice, not love, that will one day give life to the children of the future," said Örn Úlfar. "The battle for justice is the one thing which gives human life rational meaning."

"Örn," said the poet, "hasn't it occurred to you that it's possible to fight for justice until there's no one left alive on earth? 'Though the world should fall, justice shall conquer,' says an old proverb. I can't imagine any proverb more suitable as a motto for lunatics. If the battle for justice calls forth Armageddon, Örn—what then?"

"You're quite right; the battle for justice *will* call forth Armageddon," said the visitor.

"Justice is a cold virtue," said the poet, "and if that alone is victorious, there will be little left to live for in the world. Man lives first and foremost by his own imperfection and for it."

"Man lives by his own perfection and for it," said Örn Úlfar.

"You cannot deny, Örn, that man is by nature indigent," said the poet.

"Man is by nature rich," said the visitor.

"Look at that little child lying there between us . . ."

Örn Úlfar did not look at the child, but replied at once: "There is nothing so inevitable and natural as dying. Death should be as welcome to man as everything else that comes at the right time. A normal person isn't afraid of death, either. Christian cynics who maintain that man is sinful have used death to frighten him with Hell; that is the propaganda of misanthropy. You said just now that man was a creature of dust, but that, too, is a Christian vulgarity, a Christian superstition, a depraved, perverted attitude. Man is first and foremost the being that has raised himself above the dust. Burying people in the earth isn't hallowed by someone believing that man is related to earth, but because those who bury people despise man and equate him with the basest thing they know. Physically, man is mainly water; although twenty per cent of him is a compound of other earthly substances, he is in a certain sense a water-being; but his vitality depends primarily on air. But in the first and last instance, man is a fire-being. He is the being which stole fire from the gods, and whatever he is, he is because of fire."

Outside the night wind whispered at the eaves and doorways, the intended's light snoring was a voice from another sphere, the child slumbered on in her deep coma and the poet bent over her bed, his thick red-gold hair flowing over his brow and cheeks. And when he looked with tired eyes at his friend sitting on the other side of the sickbed, he felt as if Örn were talking to him from an infinite distance, the gap between them mystical and unbelievable, beyond measurement, unrelated to exterior proportions, and yet the two of them were an indispensable condition for one another, two poles. The poet said: "Tonight when I listen to our voices in this strange calm which is touched with the presence of death, even though the breeze is rustling so innocently at the door and the roof, I feel as if we were two gods on the clouds of heaven, with mankind dying between us."

Then the poet suddenly noticed that the little girl had opened her eyes and was looking at him. She was awake. There was life and health in her face again, her lips moved, he felt she was going to say something to him. He bent down over her and kissed her once again on the brow.

"Daddy," she suddenly said aloud in a clear voice which went through the house like a ray of sunshine and summoned everything to life and lit up the shadows of night after the long whispered conversation of the two friends, the toneless susurration of the wind. "Daddy and little Maggie will go down to the beach . . ."

"Soon the spring sun will be shining through the window, my darling," said her father. "And then we'll get up early one morning and go down to the beach to look for shells: broad cockleshells, and narrow mussels, and fine pink scallops, perhaps even sea snails."

Then she smiled at her father in deep joy and said nothing more, because now everything was complete and perfect. How rich she was, how profoundly happy to have him still and to know he was beside her, loving and wonderful, to feel his soft, kind hand on her brow and his dear eyes shining upon her; and to have this wonderful journey to look forward to with him one sun-bright morning. Her eyes grew heavy again, certainly, but the smile never left her lips any more. Then there was silence for a long time. Örn Úlfar sat motionless on the other side of the bed and gazed into the distance without expression as if none of this concerned him at all; or as if it concerned him too much for him to want to see it. A little later a few spasms went through the child's body once again; and then nothing more. The poet took his hand from her brow. Her eyes were only half-closed, and the smile was still on her lips. The poet looked at her and her smile for a while and whispered to himself over and over again, nodding his head a little as if in agreement: "I bid him welcome, I have always known he is a good friend."

Then he closed her eyes with his slender poet's fingers.

— **13** —

When the poet Ólafur Kárason begat a child, the first thing he did was to go out and borrow a spring-balance to weigh it. When he lost a child, he went out to borrow a few krónur so that he could buy a small coffin. The two friends parted at the door next morning; the one went off to inspire the poor to do battle for justice so that the children of the future might live, the other set off in search of kind hearts so that he could bury children. But the kind heart that was willing to bury his daughter was hard to find. Several people gave him hot chicory-water and one or two gave him hardtack biscuits, but no one wanted to support the poet's mission with a cash contribution. On the other hand they offered him the consolation that a new Golden Age was at hand; the station was coming. What did it matter if people had to work for fifty *aurar* an hour if people could protect their nationality? Others were pessimistic and said that Pétur Pálsson's aura was not worth fifty *aurar*. Both sides had this in common, that they wanted to form powerful coalitions; both sides strove to win the poet over, and forgot that he had to bury a child. When the poet had listened to their overtures for a while he said that if he were given one wish, he would want to be a spirit in the mountains—and made his farewells.

The pastor saw many obstacles to burying a child for the poet under these circumstances; it was out of the question to lend him money for a coffin—it required more than a little impertinence to ask such a thing of a poor servant of the Lord on top of everything else. These were difficult times; there was civil war in the air; and the dust gathered by the pound on the pastor's nose, as well as all the fluff on his sleeve. He had suffered a great sorrow, in that a large plaid blanket he had placed at the bottom of his silage-pit last autumn, to save pressing and perhaps even cutting off the nap, was found missing that winter when all the hay in the pit had been used up.

"The people no longer walk in Christ," said the pastor.

When the poet pressed him further, the pastor said bluntly that his conscience as a pastor would no longer allow him to carry out his clerical duties unless he had some guarantee that he would be paid; pastors had to live no less than poets and he was not obliged to bury anyone unless the funeral fee was paid in advance—let alone provide the coffin. The poet looked at the pastor with deep, serious eyes, and asked: "What would Christ have done in your shoes, Pastor Brandur?"

The pastor blew a pound of fluff off his arm and said sharply, "I won't have that sort of talk in my house! How dare you prattle about God here, my man? I have good reason to believe that you have no faith in God. Those who talk like you have no faith in God."

But the poet had not the courage to quarrel with the rural dean about God: "I'm afraid I don't know who has more faith in the other,

I in God or God in me," he said. "But one thing is certain—relations between Him and me have never been other than good. But as regards my worldly difficulties, I feel I have to turn to men rather than to Him."

"Yes," said the pastor, "I hear the tone, and I recognize it. It's the tone of the Russians, that awful, terrible tone. Have no faith in God but demand everything from men; that's their watchword. Respect for the purses of those who do something for industry simply doesn't exist. But to compose chronicles about sheep stealers and men who maltreated their wives and were louse-ridden into the bargain, and all sorts of riffraff who never existed here on this estate—that kind of thing calls itself modern literature and expects to be admired! Anything goes if it serves to disgrace the village as much as possible and demean its reputation elsewhere!"

"Really," said the poet. "Well, I think I'd better be pressing on. My heartfelt thanks and apologies."

When the pastor saw that the poet was truly humble he softened a little and said, as he saw him to the door: "The only thing that occurs to me, since everything else has failed, is old Jón the snuffmaker on the French site. He's a splendid and honorable man; the one man, apart from our manager, who has shown how far one can get in life if one makes a practice of never making demands on others. For nearly forty years he has chopped snuff for God and man from six o'clock in the morning until eleven o'clock at night. His reward was that when the Frenchmen left the estate they gave him that large site farther out, along the bay, for having looked after their equipment while they were stationed here. And two years later he sold the land to the Privy Councillor for a fortune. Such men are a model for other people and uphold the good name of the village, and these are the kind of people one should write books and compose poetry about, not dishonest scum and naked vagabonds. It's about men like our old Jón that the Lord has said, 'Thou hast been faithful over a few things, I will make thee ruler over many things.'"

The plutocrat allowed himself only one luxury, and that was pitch. He tarred his shack every year while other houses were allowed to become discolored from weathering. Inside there was a stink of lamp smoke and oil, sour snuff and ammonia. The snuffmaker was sitting on his bed under the small window; he was a grimy, gray-bearded man with incipient cataracts in his eyes, dressed in rags, and he was shredding a coil of tobacco with blue, bony hands knotted with veins. At the head of the bed there was a blue coffee pot on an oil stove, and in front of him a four-legged tobacco-cutting table. The plutocrat spat on the floor. Then he reached up to a shelf above him where the tobacco-jar stood, and asked:

"D'you want twenty-five *aurar* or fifty *aurar* worth?"

"I'm afraid I don't take snuff," said the poet.

"Eh?" said the plutocrat.

The poet repeated his apology.

"Who are you?" asked the plutocrat in surprise.

The poet said who he was.

"No one gets anything for nothing here," said the tobacco king.

"I'm just paying you a call because the pastor has spoken to me so often about you."

"The pastor?" said old Jón the snuffmaker, and began to be wary. "Tell him that the church will come when I'm dead, and not before. I want to be left in peace while I'm alive. I don't want any fuss. It's becoming impossible to stay here for all the whining and pestering. I've never had anything for nothing."

"Oh, I had no intention of pestering you for anything," said the poet, "but it occurred to me that you would have many stories to tell, like so many elderly men, and I would very much enjoy hearing a part of your life story some time. Perhaps I could even write something down for you, if you thought it worth preserving for posterity."

"No," said the old man, "I don't want to have anything written up. Everything that needs to be written up has been written already, and that was done by the late Snorri Sturluson. I have my genealogical tree and that's enough for me. I am a direct descendant from the late King Haraldur *hilditönn* (War-tooth).* These modern people in this country nowadays, they're nothing but dishonest rogues and idlers. In my heyday I dealt with Frenchmen. Tell the pastor they won't get a church from me until I'm dead."

"But you must have some pleasures in life, like other people?" said the poet.

"No one is happy before his dying day," said the old man.

"I lost my child last night," said the poet.

"Yes, that may well be so. I've never had any children," said the old man. "I've never tied myself to anyone's apron strings."

"I didn't mean to have children either," said the poet. "I've always felt I was a child myself, and still do. And yet before one knows it, one has started to live life nonetheless."

"I've heard you're a wretch," said Jón the snuffmaker.

"Yes," said the poet. "That's quite true. I'm a wretch. But who isn't a wretch, come to that. Man is a wretch."

"Oh, the men of old weren't wretches. Göngu-Hrólfur (Walker-Hrólfur)* conquered Normandy, I was told that by the Frenchmen. And old Órvar-Oddur (Arrow-Oddur) was eighteen feet tall, and lived for three hundred years.* And I'm kept busy chopping snuff from morning to night despite all the damned whining about starvation in the community, yes, and often have to get up in the middle of the night, what's more, to get out the snuff-bag. But a church they won't get before I'm dead."

"It's obviously hopeless to suggest that you might give a little help to someone in difficulties," said the poet. "Perhaps I could pay you back later, if only by composing a poem about you?"

"I never help those who are in difficulties," said Jón the snuffmaker. "Wretches have never made good, and never manage to make good even if they're given some help. If I give help to anyone, I give help to people of substance. Then one knows what becomes of the money. Wretches—that's like throwing money into the sea."

"But when we stand outside in the winter cold, bent double, and even the earth is locked against our dead children, let alone heaven?"

"I don't feel sorry for anyone," said Jón the snuffmaker. "They can die for all I care. It's only right that those who can't stay alive should die. I'll die like a shot the moment I can no longer stay alive. And no one will help me, neither on earth nor in heaven."

"Then why was Jesus Christ born if we are not to help one another in distress?" said the poet.

"Jesus Christ can help his own wretches himself," said Jón the snuffmaker. "And He won't get the church before I'm dead."

"But what do you say, Jón, to letting Jesus Christ build his own churches when you're dead, and you use your money while you're alive to help your fellowmen when they're in difficulties?"

"I've never had any fellowmen and don't want any; you won't catch me out that way," said the old man. "They're all the same damned rabble; the one's as bad as the other. I don't care a damn what happens to them."

"Who knows but that I'm a man of substance when everything's said and done, Jón?" said the poet. "Who knows but that I could pay interest if you lent me, say, ten krónur?"

"Oh, no," said the old man, "you're not the man for me. My man has always been my ancestor, the late Sigurður Fáfnisbani (Fáfnir's-Slayer).* He was really rolling in it, that fellow! On the other hand I reckon that Grettir Ásmundarson was just another damned wretch, and Gunnar of Hlíðarendi* was never anything but a layabout and a good-for-nothing. But if there's anyone worth calling a man here in Sviðinsvík, it would be poor little Pétur Pálsson, I suppose. I was a shipmate of his father, old Palli, for many years a long time ago. He was both a thief and a liar, and was said to have killed a man, so the family wasn't particularly distinguished. But it's better to be a scion of an undistinguished family than a page-boy in a great one, and if I were to give help to anyone in this place, I might possibly help poor little Pétur. You can have one pinch of snuff free of charge, but that's all you're getting. And you can tell that fool of a pastor they're not getting any church before I'm dead!"

It was now late in the evening, and the poet had drunk enormous quantities of chicory-water, but his child was just as far from getting into the ground as in the morning. On his way home that night he thought back over the events of the day. He knew quite well that he had now looked for help in every place except where he was certain of getting it. But he did not trust himself to produce that salty nectar which nourished Pétur Pálsson's heart, and yet there was one other place where he felt still less able to divest himself of the rich man's dignity and sybarite's cloak—Jórunn's house. The man without a coffin went home. He had no illusions about the reception he would get when he arrived, but he was so dulled after a day-long humiliation on top of his sleepless vigils that he dreaded nothing any more. He saw clearly the same solution for this problem as for many others: tomorrow his intended would go to Pétur Pálsson and cry for a while—and a coffin would come as a matter of course.

In a shed beside the road, at the foot of the hillside, there were often clothes hanging out to dry, which fluttered in the night breeze and made the people of The Heights even more afraid of the dark. The poet walked past unsteadily, defeated, without looking around. Then suddenly a creature loomed up before him from the direction of the shed, well wrapped up and with a shawl round her head, and confronted him.

"I need to talk to you," she said.

"What do you want with me?" he said.

"Why do you go to everyone except us?" she said. "Are we so much worse than everybody else?"

"I had no business at your house," he said.

"Don't be so silly," she said. "I know perfectly well you need money. That sort of thing gets around. People are glad to see others in need of help—like themselves."

"We mustn't be seen here," he said. "Come into the shadow."

"I have nothing to hide," she said. "Here's some money; I'm sorry it's so little. And promise me never to go from door to door again if you need something. I can't bear it."

"I can go cap in hand to everyone in the world except you, Jórunn," he said. "Everyone, everyone can despise me except you. Only in your eyes do I want to appear rich. Why wouldn't you let me live on in the delusion that you thought me rich? By handing me these alms you take from me the last thing I had left. You help to bury my little girl, of course, but into that same grave disappears my last vestige of manly pride . . ."

"You have fettered youself of your own free will, man—break the fetters!"

With this harsh order she broke through his despair, and he felt her strong hands on his thin arms, and her impassioned breathing on his face.

"Pity is man's nobility," he said. "Suppose I wanted to cast her out, this woman to whom I am betrothed—call her what you will—do you really think it would make me free? No, I would never see a happy day again. If she were young and beautiful and rich, if she had family and friends and the capacity to get a lover, the capacity to make others feel fond of her, in a word, if she were endowed with all the world's graces, that would be another matter, because everything is safe that God protects. But she has nothing—nothing. She is the human being in all its nakedness: ill, defenseless, without a friend, without anyone to feel fond of her or give her a helping hand and thrust a nail between her teeth when she has a fit. God and men and Nature have taken everything from her . . ."

"You don't believe in life!" said the girl. "You think that the Creator cannot keep the world going without your idiotic pity! You—you who are a poet, come down off this disgusting cross!"

At the same moment he felt her lips on his mouth, hot in the frost, almost fierce; only for an instant, and then she was gone.

—— 14 ——

The Laborers' dealings with Pétur Pálsson the manager had no results. He flatly refused to acknowledge their union as having a right to negotiate and said he would provide work at the wage rates of True Icelanders and not of anti-patriots. The struggle went on all day, and the Norwegian freighter was not unloaded. On the next day, when the True Icelanders tried to go to work and launch the lighters to unload the ship, the anti-patriots barred their way and prevented them from doing any work. These were mostly young men, right down to confirmation age, but there were some middle-aged men there, too, who still had not succeeded in understanding the Soul—including the parish officer, who had always had the parish purse as his God, and believed that it would be better off if people could push their wages up. Here, too, the skipper, Faroese-Jens, was going berserk, but he was first and foremost a Faroese. On the other hand the young men could see their fathers and kinsmen facing them among the True Icelanders, old quarry laborers who had been part of the place for decades on end, owned variously by the Privy Councillor, the Regeneration Company, the Psychic Research Society, and now finally by the station owner who was revealed in the person of Pétur Pálsson the manager. The fellow from Skjól was here, there, and everywhere, issuing instructions and setting father against son. The manager was also out with his stick, morning coat and high-crowned hat. He said he was not really surprised that people with Irish slave-blood in their veins who had let their parents die like dogs were now rebelling against the nation; he could also understand Faroese-Jens, who was a Faroese and therefore wanted to bring Icelanders under Danish rule anew after a four-hundred-year struggle for independence; but he thought it was going a bit far when the parish officer, Guðmundur—who like all other honorable embezzlers and forgers had made out bills for footwear and coffee for bedridden lunatics and had charged twice for the same coffin for skinny old parish paupers—should now find himself in company so far beneath his dignity.

But one thing was obvious: Pétur did not think it advisable to encourage the True Icelanders to attack, and when people had been standing for a few hours on the beach, on the pierhead and on the quay, looking at one another and exchanging sardonic comments, the manager summoned his men to a meeting for a renewed bout of national awakening and hymn-singing in the primary school. A little later it was reported that he did not have enough confidence in the fighting qualities of the True Icelanders, because he mounted the pastor and the secretary on his best horses and sent them up the valley to enlist reinforcements. Peasants who wanted to earn themselves some fame were urged to come to Sviðinsvík and there support the nation's cause against foreign political extremism. Iceland's independence was in danger; Russians, Danes and Irish slaves were rampant on the

estate and tyrannized all those who wanted to protect their nationality for fifty *aurar* an hour. The older and more sober-minded farmers
snorted into their beards and said they had never heard that Egill
Skalla-Grímsson* or Gunnar of Hlíðarendi, who had no need to
apologize for their nationality to Pétur Þríhross and this Júel Júels-
son, had ever allowed anyone to ask them to fight for fifty *aurar* an
hour, and they refused to take part in a battle where such meager
booty was offered. But there were a few younger farm workers, of a
different temper from their elders and less familiar with the Icelandic
Sagas, who thought it more honorable to follow the standard in
Sviðinsvík than to bother with the back-ends of cows in the remote
valleys.

So it was no easy matter to get the child of a neutral poet into the
earth as things stood. When Ólafur Kárason went to see the pastor
again, this time with the funeral fee in his pocket, this chaplain of
God had gone on a military mission up country; and when the poet
tried to ask the parish officer to make a coffin for him for hard cash,
he had become a military commander down on the beach. Everyone
was intent on shooting people, yes, just shoot them, shoot them, but
no one seemed to have any interest in getting into the ground a child
who had already been shot.

He walked back home again in the late afternoon after his fruitless
efforts in all directions, but, despite everything, feeling grateful and
glad that he had a dead child and private sorrows, and with that a
deeper understanding of human fickleness, when other people were
so committed to the economics of this wretched life that they were
hell-bent on shooting. He was disturbed in these reflections by an
unexpected sight; around his shack there was a crowd of men with
cudgels in their hands, while others were in the doorway, and inside
it. At first he was extremely frightened. Since he belonged to neither
of the warring parties, and despite the fact that he knew most of
these men to speak to, it was impossible to say which were friends
and which were enemies of poets in uncertain times like these; perhaps they were lying in ambush for him in his own house, ready to
murder him simply because he loved peace—that sort of thing had

happened before. But there was no mistaking one thing—the war had occupied his house first, the friend of peace. He stopped and looked irresolutely towards his house in the dusk of early spring.

Then the men shouted: "Come here, poet! There's no need to be afraid. We're fighting for you. We're fighting for all the poetry of the world put together."

The poet was grateful for this handsome invitation and stepped closer. At that moment his friend Örn Úlfar came to the door and repeated the invitation, saying hospitably that the poet was welcome in this house. The men were sitting wherever they could, and had turned upside down everything with a bottom to use as seats; a few were sitting on the floor. The poet first looked to see that everything was in order in the closet behind, and so it was: the little corpse lay there under its shroud on its humble bier. But when the intended, who was standing tear-stained behind the cooking stove, saw Ólafur arriving, she drew herself up and screamed: "They are disturbing the peace of the living and the dead, they are desecrating my house, they are dishonoring my corpse—heavenly Jesus, let fire and devils rain upon them, they are criminals!"

A few of the men grinned, but most of them paid no attention to her.

The poet was told what was going on. Örn Úlfar was to be arrested and taken to Aðalfjörður for breaking the laws—of TB prevention. He had left the sanatorium without permission. Telegrams from the health authorities confirmed that he was still an infectious case; the district doctor at Sviðinsvík had reported him to the sheriff and asked to have him removed so that he would not infect other people on this healthy estate. The anti-patriots had immediately mounted a guard to protect Örn Úlfar. Could they stay there that night?

"The house is yours, Örn," said the poet.

At these words the intended let out a wail and started to pray aloud in even more specific language than before. Some of the men looked in rather foolish amazement at this Jesus-crying creature, but many of them turned away because it offended their sense of decency. Those who had tobacco in one form or another brought it

out and treated themselves and others to it, then cards were produced, and the friendly cursing and swearing of the visitors took over
from the housewife's prayers. Someone fetched oil, another fetched
water, a third coffee, and sugar appeared from somewhere. The poet
helped to serve. In the end the intended stopped praying and sat
exhausted behind the cooking stove with her knitting.

Late in the evening, when several of the defenders had given up
hope of any action and had gone home, they got warning of the
manager's troops: "You in The Heights—be prepared!" Soon afterwards a crowd of men moved up the hillside with lanterns and cudgels. Both doors in the poet's house had been barred as carefully as
possible, the light was put out, and inside the men took up defensive
positions at doors and windows. Soon there came a knock at the
door, and when the visitors thought there was not a quick enough
response, they started hammering on the walls. The poet went to the
window, opened the upper pane, and asked who was there.

"Nationalists!" came the reply. "Icelanders!"

"Indeed," said the poet, for he had not the nerve to utter that
wicked word "really."

Then some stranger declared that he was here by the sheriff's
authority to fetch a tuberculosis patient. "Will you hand him over?"

"My child died of tuberculosis yesterday," said the poet. "Perhaps
you good people will help me to bury her?"

"Open the door and hand the man over," said the emissary of the
authorities.

"I'm afraid I've gone to bed," said the poet.

Now Pétur Pálsson came waddling up; he had fallen behind coming up the hillside, because he was too short of breath for climbing.

"There's no need to ask anyone to open the door, I own this
house," he said. "It is I who says when and how this door is opened.
But first I'm going to say a few words to Ólafur Kárason. Ólafur
Kárason, you who call yourself a poet, I've come here to tell you that
you are no longer a poet at all. You're a pornographer, a blasphemer
and a foul-mouth who poisons the minds of the young. For too long
have I tolerated an idiot and a rat like you. I have forgiven you even

though you besmirched the name of Sviðinsvík by writing about people who have never been known on this estate, thieves, drunkards, naked vagabonds, and louse-ridden men who maltreated their wives. And though you have turned against God and the Soul both in word and in deed, I have forgiven you and never tired of giving you a chance of becoming a good poet. But all my efforts to make you a good poet have been in vain. And now my patience is exhausted, my lad. We knew one another to speak to before, right enough, but when you become an official emissary for the anti-patriots against the Home Rule movement, against the nation's independence, against me, we no longer know one another. I'll just show you all, I shall crush you, I shall grind you, I shall have your guts out! Don't think for a moment you can hold someone in defiance of my wishes. Boys, if the door isn't opened, make the ropes fast and pull the house off its foundations."

Nest morning the poet's house lay on its side.

During the night the True Icelanders had fastened ropes to the shack and overturned it to have easier access to the nest. But this act of war had not succeeded in its object. The anti-patriots had managed to extinguish the True Icelanders' lanterns, they had scuffled in the darkness for a while, and in the tumult Örn Ülfar had escaped. The result was that the poet was left without a roof with the corpse of his child in his arms and a Jesus-wailing intended who nevertheless had not been enough of a True Icelander for her fiancé's poetry to escape the severest criticism. They were allowed to take shelter with the corpse and the poetry in the nearest house. But at dawn the anti-patriots returned and put the poet's house back on its foundations.

— 15 —

The day after the failure to arrest Örn Ülfar the state of war at Syiðinsvík-undir-Óþveginsenni reached a higher pitch than ever before in the history of the estate. These were difficult times for the leader of the Home Rule movement, Pétur Pálsson the manager.

Throughout the night people had been searching up hill and down dale for the Irish slave, and the guard on the hoyden had been doubled. Early in the morning, after a sleepless night, the manager drew up the troops which had been pressed into service the previous evening and issued them strong cudgels; one or two of the men from up country had brought breech-loaders with them. All teaching came to a stop in the village; the primary school was turned into the Icelanders' headquarters, the church was converted into a medical center and stocked with first-aid equipment, and the secretary was sent up into the steeple with orders to ring the bells as soon as Pétur Pálsson gave the signal to attack, for this was a holy war. The True Icelanders' plan was to drive the Laborers off the quay into the sea, and the attack was to be launched from three sides. But now it transpired that the Laborers had not left it to the True Icelanders alone to call out troops; they, too, had been out in all directions raising an army and had not only found good support in the nearby valleys but had also (which was more important) attracted reinforcements from other fjords, and it was quite clear when the armies appeared on the field of conflict that morning that the Home Rule movement would have their hands full in a battle. Indeed, Pétur Pálsson the manager ordered his men not to attack for the time being.

It was a mild spring day with a calm sea. Various guesses were now made about what the manager's tactics would be next. He was known to be utterly unyielding, and if he failed to come up with a stratagem today, even though he was up against overwhelming odds, it would be for the first time. He was seen to summon two stalwart seamen. Then he had a motorboat launched, and headed down the Fjörður with all the speed the engine could produce.

A few people shouted that the manager had fled the field.

The explanation for this move spread from the True Icelanders' camp. It so happened that the Danish warship which had been entertained at Pétur Pálsson's party the previous year had been patrolling the nearby coast for the last few days and was still visible off the mouth of the fjord. This was the ship with which Pétur Pálsson suddenly had such urgent business. It was never possible to establish irrefutably by sworn evidence just what this business was, to be sure, but all the same the purpose of his sortie was on everyone's lips that day and later; and though it was often denied, sometimes not without a touch of nervousness, there was no one who ever thought this story more incredible than anything else that could happen at Sviðinsvík. When it became clear that the anti-patriots were a match for Pétur Pálsson the Homelander and could easily seize control of the estate and thereby acquire a homeland for themselves, he thought it best to seek assistance from the warship and to impress upon the Danish commander the necessity of bombarding the village with his guns, or at least of lending the True Icelanders a cannon.

As things stood, it was little wonder that people did not worry very much over one poet who wandered from house to house with his corpse, his writing desk and his intended; no, the times were too serious for that. The most remarkable thing that happened that day, however, was that Ólafur Kárason of Ljósavík himself forgot that he had to bury a child. Of course, no one would suggest that much would be lost if the Danish warship were persuaded to reduce to ruins this little fjord village which unfortunately could not boast too many True and Freeborn Icelanders. "Worse things have happened," would have been its epitaph. On the other hand it could not honestly be denied that Icelanders, whether true or untrue, had been under the Danish yoke for the last four or five centuries, a flogged, robbed and cheated people; and it was now only a few years since these true and untrue people had succeeded in throwing off this foreign yoke once and for all. But though the hearts which beat in a little village under high mountains could only in a limited sense call themselves truly Icelandic and freeborn, and were only run-of-the-mill Icelanders, if that, there was no heart so indifferent that it had not been uplifted when the Danish yoke was thrown off. And therefore things had come to such a pass today that even the poet Ólafur Kárason, who had only a run-of-the-mill Icelandic child on the bier, had had enough when True Icelanders tried to persuade Danes to fire cannons at this dead child.

He had left his corpse and his intended behind, and before he knew it he was standing as a recruit in the ranks of the anti-patriots on the quayside by the fish houses. The prospective M.P. for Sviðinsvík, Örn Úlfar, was making a speech, and the people were packed all round him. It was clear from people's expressions that they believed what he was saying; many of them nodded at one another, others could not tear their eyes from his lips. It gave them great confidence and pleasure to have him among them, so unlike them and yet flesh of their flesh. They all felt themselves grow greater by having him for a friend, and when he was present they felt they had the measure of their enemy, and when he spoke they felt that now for the first time they understood their own thoughts, now at last they saw who they were and where they stood. Ólafur Kárason, too, was in a state of exaltation. There was a throbbing in his temples and a lump in his throat, and although this condition made it difficult for him to understand the spoken word and appreciate rational arguments as they were delivered, a certain faculty of mind asserted itself which absorbed the mood of this meeting and had a deep-rooted understanding of its soul.

Örn Úflar said that our banner symbolized the lifeblood of all mankind. He said we were the representatives of all men on earth who yearned for liberty and fought for liberty. The others, he said, the others think that your cause would be lost if I were removed from here by force. What shortsightedness! No, it is not my image, nor the image of any single individual, which will decide the outcome of this struggle. My image will soon be obliterated; it was only an illusion. But, he went on, even though I may fall, even though my image may be obliterated, there is one thing that will never fall and can never be obliterated, and that is the yearning of those in chains for liberty. It could well be that the ideal of liberty is not a particularly remarkable ideal, but it is the noblest ideal of the fettered, and as long as there is a single slave left in the world it remains valid in the same way in which the ideal of repletion remains valid as long as there is a single hungry person left in the world. He said that the history of mankind was the history of the struggle for liberty, and in that struggle nothing could be lost because mankind was by nature triumphant. He said that mankind was standing on a firmer footing than ever before.

The law of life was on our side. He said that the enemies of the people could never bring any charges against us which were not first and foremost ridiculous; and even though these enemies of mankind fired cannons at us, he said that did not matter. He also said it made no difference how many individuals among us were killed on the field of battle or how often we had to retreat; our defeat could never be anything but an illusion, because we had nothing to lose and everything to gain, and our victory is an inevitable law of life, whatever the others do, and on the basis of this law the whole world rests.

The poet no longer recognized his friend as the man he had known. That somber, taciturn expression had disappeared like a discarded mask. The look in his eyes and his features had been freed and exalted to a quality which did not concern this man alone but was stronger than any one man, the quality of human harmony—impersonal, unfettered and prophetic, exalted beyond place and time. He was the hidden, undeclared thought of them all, spoken out loud, both those who happened to be there as well as those who were dead and those still unborn. Such was his secret; he awakened this murdered people from death.

Under the red banner that symbolized the lifeblood of mankind stood a young girl, fair and enraptured, with a high strong bosom and the light breeze of spring ruffling her hair; and the poet said to himself, "She is the Living Image of Liberty," and suddenly he understood her image to the full. On his lips still burned the hot kiss she had given him in the frost, as the sun kisses the earth in spring, and he felt he might blossom forth at any moment.

But suddenly in the middle of his speech Örn Úlfar fell silent. He gasped as if he were suffocating, then bent forward and clutched at his chest with one hand and his face with the other, and sank to the ground. Something had happened to him. People crowded round him in agitation. In a fever of haste Ólafur Kárason pushed his way through the crowd, slipped through like an eel until he reached the center of the ring where Örn Úlfar was being supported by Faroese-Jens and someone else, pale as death, eyes closed, with blood at the corner of his mouth.

"Ólafur, take the banner," said the girl, while she herself started

policing the crowd, calming people down, keeping them away, sending for a blanket; and the patient was carried away by four comrades.
Ólafur Kárason was left standing by the banner.

A moment later the girl came back and said, "It's not too serious.
But Faroese-Jens is nevertheless going to start up the engine of his
boat and take him to hospital in Aðalfjörður. Now I'll take the banner again."

"May I carry it a little for you?" said the poet.

"No," she said. "Not for me, but for those who will overcome
their enemies because the law of life is on their side."

Örn Úlfar was carried to Faroese-Jens's boat and made comfortable in the cabin. A few stalwarts had been called in, and not a
moment was wasted. But as they were about to cast off, a girl came
running down to the quay. She was bareheaded and her dark-brown
curls were unkempt; she had just thrown a coat over her shoulders
and pulled on a pair of rubber boots over her pale silk stockings.

"I'm coming, too!" she shouted breathlessly, and waved to the
men. "Don't leave without me!"

The men paused for a moment and looked suspiciously at the
manager's daughter, and pretended not to understand what business
she could have in their boat.

"Someone has to look after him," she said.

"You least of all," said Faroese-Jens.

She did not wait for his permission but jumped on board and disappeared down into the cabin in a flash.

"The damned girl's mad," said one of the deckhands.

Faroese-Jens peeped into the cabin and saw her sitting on the edge
of the bunk, leaning over the patient.

"Is she out of her mind?" said the deckhand, ready to chase her
out of the cabin.

"We'll cast off," said Faroese-Jens, and bit off a chew of tobacco
and grinned as he went to the engine room. "The goddess of love has
made her a hostage."

A few quick puffs from the engine, and the boat was under way.

At the same moment, Pétur Pálsson's motorboat ran onto the

beach in front of his house. People now assumed that the secretary would shortly be given a signal to ring the bells; but things turned out differently.

The manager asked where Faroese-Jens was off to.

"He's gone off with Örn Úlfar and your daughter," someone said.

"Where to?" said Pétur Pálsson the manager.

"I don't know," said the man. "Some say they're going to get married."

At first the manager looked blankly at the other for a while and said "Eh?" But he was not angry; he was speechless. He walked out to the end of the little pier in front of his house and waved his hat idiotically at Faroese-Jens's boat, and called out three times "Dísa!" loudly at first and then in a whisper. But no one paid any attention. Faroese-Jens's boat receded rapidly into the distance. The manager stayed there at the end of the pier for a while, his legs apart, bowlegged, looking anything but a military commander, with his Júel-hat in one hand and his pince-nez in the other, and went on gazing after the boat, and the wind ruffled his thin, graying hair and flapped his coattails.

If he had gone out to the Danish warship like a lion, he stepped ashore like a lamb. It was obvious that the Danes neither wanted to shoot at Sviðinsvík nor lend the True Icelanders any cannons. Instead of climbing the church steeple and making the shivering secretary announce that the sword of the Prophet had been drawn from its scabbard, Pétur Pálsson went into his home and made a telephone call to the capital.

"Well, my dearest Júel, Grandmother's in a bad way now."

The station owner in the south: "Shut up!"

Pétur Pálsson the manager, in Sviðinsvík: "She's a corpse. She's dead and gone."

The station owner: "Oh, go to Hell!"

Pétur Pálsson the manager: "Icelandic nationality is up against it in Sviðinsvík."

The station owner: "Yes, you've always been a damned blithering idiot."

Pétur Pálsson the manager: "They would rather shed their blood

than work for the True Icelanders' wage rates. Can you send reinforcements from the south?"

The station owner: "I'll send men straight from here to give you
such a thrashing there won't be a bone left unbroken in your carcass."

Pétur Pálsson: "Are we then to surrender Icelandic nationality
unconditionally to the lash of the anti-patriots?"

The station owner: "If you cost me the constituency, I'll murder
you myself with my own hands."

Pétur: "All right then, good-bye my dearest Júlíus, and may God
always be with you."

The station owner hung up without replying.

And with that the great war over wages in Sviðinsvík was over, and
the secretary, stiff with cold, was recalled from the steeple. Next day,
preliminary work on the station was started at the Trades Union
rates.

That evening the poet found himself alone in his resurrected
house, a new man, and thought back over the events of the day while
his intended slept. In two days' time his daughter was to be buried;
and as soon as the first earth had been sprinkled on the coffin, what
would there be left to tie him any longer to this wretched house
which had been pulled down the night before? There were hail showers blowing straight at the window; there were cracks in the panes
and the hailstones were trying to get in; in between squalls the wind
dropped and the clouds parted and there was clear, green sky; and he
saw one star shining. He closed his eyes, but without wanting to
sleep, and felt this star stepping down to him from heaven, and
between sleeping and waking he heard its dancing footsteps outside,
blended with the memory of the historic tumult of the day that had
passed; and to a music that streamed forth in sad delight he heard
deep in his breast a song being sung about the girl he called the
Image of Liberty:

> *Oh, how light are your footsteps,*
> *And how long I awaited thee;*
> *There is hail at the window*

And a cold wind that whines.
But I know of a bright star,
Of a bright star that shines,
And at last you have come here,
You have come here to me.

These are difficult times, dear,
There is squabbling and strife;
I have nothing to offer,
Not a thing I can give,
Except my hopes and my life, dear,
Every moment I live:
This one thing you gave me,
That's my all, dear—my life.

But tonight the winter is over
For every toiling hand,
And the sun will shine tomorrow—
It is their summer sun.
It is our summer sunshine,
It is our life begun;
And for you I shall bear the banner
Of this our future land.

___ 16 ___

Jón *almáttugi* (the Almighty) came from the south originally, and was said to be of good stock, but born out of wedlock. He quickly became highly accomplished in mind and body and could turn his hand to most things, but he was unsettled and thriftless. He was at home in every part of the country, and everywhere he went he did skilled work which few were capable of doing, both out-of-doors and in. He was a smith in wood and iron, he had an intimate understanding of all machinery, he was a fish-breeder, a weaver, a fox-hunter, a midwife, an accordion-player, a vaccinator, a singer, an animal-gelder, a fine skier, and a swimmer; he could reckon the calendar on his fingers, he knew Danish and orthography, and could improvise verses. Needless to say, Jón *almáttugi* was enormously popular with the ladies. The years went by, and Jón *almáttugi* went on having the whole of Iceland as his home, and was a welcome visitor all over the country. He would stay for a week in the east and the next week he would be in the west; it was here, there and everywhere as far as he was concerned. In many places Jón *almáttugi* was awaited with long-ing, and sometimes was seen off with regret.

But one day, when Jón *almáttugi* was well into his thirties, misfor-tune overtook him in the guise of good fortune. A young and hand-some daughter of a pastor in the north brought about Jón *almáttugi*'s downfall. They got married and settled on one of her father's farms, and rebuilt the farmhouse in their very first year, because the wife had ample means. The farm yielded produce from both land and sea. But it quickly became apparent that the woman loved her husband to excess, and accordingly disliked most people who came near him, but in particular hated all other women. She could not bear to let him out of her sight for even an hour. Jón *almáttugi* was as capable a fisherman as he was at everything else, but the woman became so afraid for her husband that she had hysterics on the beach each morning she thought the weather not good enough for going fishing.

In some seasons his boat caught only half as much fish as others did; indeed, there was many a day of reasonably good weather when she would cosset her healthy husband in bed with egg punch, hot pancakes and pickled lamb's flank. Often she sat numb-fingered with him as he baited fishing lines on autumn evenings, and in spring when he was out herding his sheep she followed him up to the moors and chased every ewe with him. In summer she forbade all other women to rake behind his scythe. If he had business elsewhere she would accompany him or would soon be on his heels. Should he need visit the outside privy in the middle of the night she would get out of bed with him and stand scantily dressed outside the privy door, even in a storm.

That was how matters now stood for this man who once had

owned the whole country and belonged to it. Pale and withdrawn, dull-eyed, not daring to look anyone in the face, Jón *almáttugi* wandered round his house and yard a shadow of his former self, weighed down by the burden of the great and true love this young and wealthy woman bestowed on him.

It is said that one night, as usual, the housewife brought her husband the finest steaks and other delicacies with loving tenderness, and took infinite care as always to serve him to perfection. Jón *almáttugi* ate his meal quietly and without saying much. But when he had finished all the delicacies he took out his razor-sharp clasp knife and cut off his genitals, then handed them on a plate to his wife before staggering off to bed, castrated.

While Ólafur Kárason the poet was preparing to write down the story of this Strange Man, his thoughts kept dwelling on his own problems. The young girl who had handed him the banner of mankind, this strong, noble, burgeoning life which was ready to embrace him with all her richness, occupied his mind throughout these long days as well as the short nights which would soon be ending.

In a poem he had composed subconsciously one night he had said that his life was hers every moment he lived, but as usual what he said as a poet was far removed from his life as a man. The poet's visions were subject to no fetters; but outwardly the man continued to be a prisoner of the life he had once chosen for himself and called his destiny, continued to sacrifice his life to his loyalty to the partner to whom he had once pledged himself, despite the fact that he had long been a different person to the one who had made the pledge, and she a different woman, the world a different world. This fidelity to those who depend on you, this contradiction of Love's instability, duplicity, unsociability and dishonesty—perhaps there would be no human society without it.

But sometimes the poet roused himself from his thoughts and asked himself: "Isn't this fidelity contrary to manliness if one lives for it at the expense of love? Isn't fidelity first and foremost the characteristic of a dog? Can it be reconciled with the land of the future? This fidelity—isn't it, along with the pity from which it springs, the very opposite of virtue, a lack of courage to be a real man? But when is a man real, then? To lack courage—isn't that precisely the same as being a real man? Does one belong to oneself, or does one belong to others? To what extent was Jón *almáttugi* within his rights when he resorted to that despairing operation to spite his wife? Or is the only solution to the problem to drown oneself, as was for a long time the only way out for men who were too much loved by their wives, in accordance with the old fundamental principle that it was best that a man and his manhood went together?"

Out of an innate sense of caution, Ólafur Kárason had tried to keep one loophole open: he had always shrunk from actually marrying her. It was as if he had an obscure hope of being able to escape by flight for as long as he could avoid the public seal of society on his cohabitation with her; but when it came to the point of decision in his mind about flight, he always realized only too well that outward ties were chaff and vanities—the real knot was the one he had tied within himself. To break the outward forms was easy, yes, just child's play; to disengage himself from the fundamental substance of his life was certainly possible in moments of inspiration but, when the intoxication had worn off, the poet discovered that the reality that mattered was not outside himself. It lay within his own conscience, independent of all outward forms, and nowhere but there.

When he awoke in the morning after troublesome dreams, he looked around in anguish and did not recognize his own senses. He felt they were as utterly alien to him as a hideous world of sorcery, and sometimes he felt that no princess could ever release him from this spell, not even the princess of the future land herself, the girl with the banner, the Living Image of Liberty.

Where, oh, where was that free, mad and villainous poet he had taken leave of on the roadway once, long, long ago?

— **17** —

Luckily there are not many who are surprised at being human when they wake up in the morning. Most people simply go about it as if nothing could be more natural, even happily, particularly in times like these when there was plenty of work to be had: the prospect of building a pier, a cod-liver oil refinery, a fish-meal plant—in short, a station costing a hundred thousand, a station costing a million, high wages and an abundance of goods in the shop. And only now, when there was work for all and welcome, and no one had to worry about where the next meal was coming from, and there was plenty of money, the poet realized what sort of place Sviðinsvík-undir-Óþveginsenni had been in the years gone by, when there was nothing to do and no one had anything and every meal was a blessing of fortune, and those who wanted to could stay at home and compose poetry and write stories about Strange Men. The poet felt that every hour he was away from his writing desk was wasted; but now, after his children were dead, he had no excuse any more for staying at home all the long spring day. But Júel J. Júel seemed to have plenty of money, worse luck, and there was no hope that this tiresome wrangling over work would end in the foreseeable future and poets could turn their minds anew to things that mattered.

One day when the spring was at its brightest, battle was joined once again in Sviðinsvík, this time the election campaign. Two candidates for this distinguished office popped up in the village, and people were rounded up for meetings. Júel brought his motorcar with him, a most magnificent vehicle with a chauffeur, to drive children and old people to and fro about the district as far as the roads permitted. It was also reported on good authority that the airplane that had been promised last year would be coming this summer, if people voted the right way, and the low standard of living of people on this estate would be raised to a higher level at the station owner's expense. He also donated a thousand krónur to the new church which was to be built here. And now there began in Sviðinsvík a round of parties with cognac, pony excursions and skull-fractures.

But Júel J. Júel's opponent was also a character, even though he was a more modest one. He was not the man, of course, whom the common people had seen and loved in Örn Úlfar and had been ready to follow to the ends of the earth. Nevertheless, the opponent was said to be the spokesman of the workingman and, furthermore, something which most people found harder to understand, the government candidate. The opponent unfortunately did not have a car, let alone being in a position to make promises about an airplane the way things were in these difficult times; on the other hand he had brought a walking stick. And while Júel made his chauffeur drive children and imbeciles to and fro about the estate, night and day, with frantic hooting and grinding of gears, the opponent, the government and people's candidate, went from house to house with his walking stick. It was obvious from his demeanor that this walking stick was not just his badge of honor and scepter but also his wealth, and indeed he looked after his stick as if it were the apple of his eye. He carried it carefully in front of himself, and a little to the side, almost upright, and stepped cautiously along as if he were bearing a lighted candle in a slight draft or rather as if he were delivering a magnificent bouquet on some very solemn occasion; in other respects he walked like a man who had lost his toes. The opponent's solemn, solo progress was bound to earn him respect and confidence. But now it was no wonder that people asked: was the opponent's walking stick such a treasure that it merited such care, such devoted self-control, such pious and steadfast reverence? There was no easy answer. Perhaps this walking stick was something exceptional in the eyes of God and even in the eyes of the government. But in the eyes of men, this was just an ordinary one-and-a-half-króna stick with a curved handle, and had originally perhaps been painted yellow or even red, maybe with a little tin ferrule at the bottom. But if so, all such superfluous fripperies had rubbed off long ago; the stick had long lost its color, it was worn at the bottom and the handle had become almost straightened by constant use.

Jarþrúður went at once to see the station owner, was given a ride in the car, and used the opportunity to cry a little and say that her house had become a little lopsided during the last storm and could be demolished altogether in the next one. But the station owner had no time to listen to any blethering; he gave her fifty krónur at once and told her to be off. Then she went to the stick-bearer, wept the same tears and repeated the story of the rickety house. The opponent invited her to have a seat and was ready to discuss the matter thoroughly. He said he would think the matter over. He said he would make a mental note of her request. He said he would do everything he could possibly do and everything that could be done as things were in these difficult times. But he said he would need to consult some other more highly placed officials before any final decision could be given. He said he could give an assurance that the government had every intention, if the elections turned out as expected, of increasing the grants to Sviðinsvík for quarry work, so that a new breakwater could be built that would reach even farther out to sea than the existing breakwater. He said that the main thing for the people of Sviðinsvík was to be patient and to work for their objects gradually: in a word, he was determined to take a mental note of it all. And now Good-bye.

The intended could not find enough words of derision for the opponent, for his mental note-taking, for his walking stick and government rock, and prayed to God that the one who suffered defeat in the elections would be him. But Júel Júel, she said—what a glorious and darling man! To think that people existed on earth who carried fifty-krónur notes in thick bundles like Bibles in their pockets, and built churches for a thousand and stations for a million—that was something no one would ever have believed where she had learned her catechism! She looked upon the station owner as yet another proof of the glory of God.

"Jarþrúður dear," said the poet, very seriously, "I want to warn you that if you vote for Júel in this election, you are voting against me."

"I know," said the intended. "It's just like you to say that one should obey that Skjól fellow who tried to incite the accursed mob to plunder and murder, rather than to obey those in whom God is pleased."

"Poets and mobs are always friends," said Ólafur Kárason. "And it's an old story that when there's trouble, they are one."

On a Sunday in June, polling day, the poet was standing with a group of laborers outside the primary school, watching people coming to vote. The clear solstice sky arched over the village by the mirror-smooth sea, and once again there reigned in Nature that mood of delight and tranquility which makes sorrows and cares so improbable in Iceland.

Júel J. Júel's shining luxury car drove up to the door of the polling station with yet another load of True Icelanders who were to be allowed to rule the country for a while. The car doors opened, the chauffeur called on some of the others to help him unload the car, and some True Icelanders were hauled out from the luxurious comfort of the seats. It was old Þuríður of Skálholt with her people. Gísli the landowner was the first to be pulled out. Although this landowner had now been bedridden for many years, he still had enough life left in him to open one eye and wave one fist angrily in the air and shout defiantly: "It's I who owns the estate!"

Behind the landowner, Jón Einarsson the heathen was carried into the building, slobbering with delight over the sunshine, the car ride, the elections and Christian people in general. "Vavva-vavva," said the heathen, and laughed. "Vavva-vavva."

Finally the Creature was hauled out of the station owner's luxury car, Hólsbúðar-Dísa, who had for long been kept in Jón the Murderer's bait shed but who had of late been hidden behind a partition in the living room at Skálholt. It was this creature whom Örn Úlfar once, long ago, had regarded as the image of the estate. She, too, had now come here to support the cause of the True Icelanders. She was carried in a sack from the station owner's luxury car to the polling booth. From out of the sack there peered a demented face without human features, no longer emaciated but shapelessly swollen from dropsy, framed by black hair which once had been wispy but now was matted. The mad, long-frozen eyes stared blankly at the clear sky.

And when these three True Icelanders had been pulled out, who should bring up the rear, dressed to the nines in her Sunday skirt, and a new cardigan under a fichu, combed and washed, with a tassel-cap, ready to take her place in the ranks of the True Icelanders against the unpatriotic? None other than Jarþrúður Jónsdóttir, the poet's intended. She walked with firm, solemn, determined steps into the polling station, looking neither to left nor to right. A few unpatriotic youngsters greeted the True Icelanders with jeers.

Other spectators joined the crowd from all directions when word went round that the inmates of Skálholt were out for a drive; people crowded round the door of the polling station and waited impatiently to see them emerge again after doing their civic duty. After a moment a commotion was heard from within the building. Suddenly the Creature appeared in the doorway on all fours; in the polling booth she had escaped from the sack and slipped out of people's grasp. She had eaten both the voting paper and the pencil and was uttering dreadful cries. It took a little time to catch her and cram her back into the sack.

A little later the intended from The Heights came out of the polling booth again, her eyes aglow with that inner peace, that embrace of mercy which characterizes a communicant who has been granted communion on the Day of Resurrection itself. In this state of bliss she went back into the car without seeing anyone. And the honest voters were escorted back home from this luxury car ride which was to last them until the next elections.

When the spectacle was over and the shining vehicle had driven away, Ólafur Kárason came to his senses again. He shook off this appalling sight and was about to take to his heels—he did not know where to, just away, as far, far away as possible. But then a hand was laid on his shoulder, and the young girl was standing by his side again; he met her smile and those warm, bold eyes under the solstice sky.

"Ljósvíkingur," she said. "Which way are you going?"

And at the same moment he had changed his mind about running away.

"With you," he replied, and gazed entranced at how well the solstice sky became her.

Then they linked arms and walked away together.

—— **18** ——

No one had much doubt who would win the seat in this election; but even so, interested voters stayed up through the night while the counting of votes continued, waiting for the result. Some people had been lucky enough to get hold of brennivín, and there was cursing and swearing, shrieks, vomiting, fighting, broken bones and other amusements. Many were lying helpless in the ditches by the road. Júel and Pétur Pálsson walked up and down in a zigzag along the main road with the stick-bearer between them, all drinking from the same bottle, while a few sober anti-patriots watched the Fatherland owners for a while, one lesson the wiser—or the unwiser. They all knew now that it had just been a joke when the station had opposed the stick-bearer and the stick-bearer opposed the station—because where did Júel get his money from? From the stick-bearer, of course. The stick-bearer was both the government candidate and the spokesman of the common people, and the money came from the common people and was put into the state bank for Júel to build stations, erect churches and buy constituencies. The necessary arrangements had already been made to unite the Laborers' Union and the Society of True Icelanders under the leadership of the parish officer. There was really nothing left but to let the station go bust, and everything would be perfect. The opponent went on carrying his stick as if it were a cross between a candle and a bouquet, and Júel J. Júel and Pétur Pálsson the manager bent over him in turn as they led him along, and kissed him behind the ear where the mental notes of Jarþrúður 's request were kept.

"They thought I was an Icelander!" said Pétur Pálsson the manager, and roared with laughter. "But I'm no Icelander, s'help me! My name is Peder Pavelsen Three Horses. And my grandmother was Madame Sophie Sørensen."

And the village went on celebrating.

The sun was high in the sky and the shadows were beginning to shorten when the poet got home to his shack. He made as little noise as possible in the hope that he would not wake his intended. But it was to no avail; she heard him come in—perhaps she had been lying awake for him. He went straight to his writing desk and took out his writing materials in the rays of the morning sun. She half sat up in bed and started abusing him at once; there was a dangerous glint in her eyes.

She said she had taken him under her wing wet from the seashore, defiled by whoredom; she had nursed him, given him life, rehabilitated him, made a man of him again when it was obvious that neither God nor man thought him worth helping. For all that, she said, she was ready to endure whiplashes. She said she had also borne him two children and aborted a third; she had sacrificed her virtue and honor to him in sin and shame and thereby put the salvation of her soul in eternal jeopardy; she had endured without complaint all his evasions to avoid making an honest woman of her and calling in the pastor. And on top of all that she was ready to endure as many whiplashes as need be. Whiplashes, whiplashes, she repeated greedily over and over again, as if such a treat were some sort of blessing. Hunger and cold she was also ready to endure. With gladness of heart, she said, she had watched her children give up the ghost after protracted tuberculosis; she had stood calmly over their clay as she commended their souls and hers to the Savior's almighty mercy and grace. Even her own death she was ready to endure at the hands of this dreadful man, Ólafur Kárason. She was even ready to forgive him when he stole a glance at women here in the village, as long as they were respectable. But though she could endure from him whiplashes, hunger, cold, sin, death and respectable women, there was one thing she could not endure, and that was that he should lie with whores all through a bright spring night and come home in the morning with syphilis.

The poet looked up from his writing while she ranted on, but did not straighten up and made no attempt to interrupt. His expression betrayed nothing beyond a hint of amazement at this extraordinary eloquence, and curiosity about what would come next or how long she could keep it up. Like a man who knew he was innocent, nothing was farther from his mind than trying to excuse himself. Perhaps his silence hurt her more than words; she raged more and more furiously; finally her speech was nothing but incoherent curses, dire prophecies and oaths, and ended in a loud storm of weeping. He was not moved. She writhed about on the bed for a while, howling, then the paroxysm left her and at last she lay face down, exhausted, racked by sobs, with the corner of the pillow crammed into her mouth. A long time afterwards, when her sobbing had begun to subside, he laid his pen aside and calmly put his manuscripts tidily away in his writing desk; and a voice which he himself really did not recognize, even though it came from his own larynx, said these words: "Jarþrúður dear, we won't be staying together any longer now. Tell me where you want to go, and I shall take you there."

For a long time after these words had been spoken she went on lying as before, face down, motionless except for the sobs, with the pillow in her mouth. But when she did not reply and he had begun to doubt whether she had heard what he had said, he asked: "When do you want to leave?"

At last she raised her head warily and peered at him with the eyes of a cornered prey that knows the wild beast is standing over it, ready to tear it to pieces. But when she saw how calm he was, how far removed from letting emotion affect his decision, she slid very gradually under the eiderdown and pulled it over her head without answering him. He waited for a long time yet, but she did not stir, and when he had completely given up hope of a reply he wrapped the blanket around himself and lay down on the floor to sleep without taking off his clothes.

He awoke at nine o'clock in the morning to the smell of pancakes.

Now, it so happened that hot pancakes were the greatest delicacy which this poet knew, the pinnacle of epicurism, and he sat up amazed in this aroma, and in his half-awake, half-asleep state he did not know where he was.

She was standing behind the cooking stove, baking, looking at him tenderly as if nothing had happened, searching for a conciliatory gleam in his eyes. Then she made the coffee and brought it to him with hot pancakes. But sleep had not melted him; his resolution was not to be shaken. He drank the coffee without a word, but did not touch the pancakes. It was as if he had changed completely; he was suddenly a totally different person from the Ólafur Kárason of Ljósavík whom Jarþrúður Jónsdóttir had known before.

"I shall help you pack your things, Jarþrúður," he said. "Where do you want to go?"

She let herself sink down on a chair and started to cry into her blue, gnarled hands which for all these years had laid claim to dominion over a poet, had worked for him, touched his nakedness, nursed his children in happiness and sorrow and closed their eyes for the last time. But this time she wept without violence, a quiet weeping, just with deep, wordless grief.

— **19** —

A few days later, Ólafur Kárason removed his former intended, Jarþrúður Jónsdóttir, from his house. It had been decided that she should go back over the moor to the farm at Gil where she had been staying before she came to live with the poet. They crossed the fjord on the ferry, and on the other side there was a horse waiting for her which had been sent across the moor. The poet had decided to escort his former intended to the county boundary, and be back home in Sviðinsvík himself by nightfall. The route was the same as when he had been taken on a stretcher by the poet Reimar long ago.

The journey was rather a silent one. He walked ahead, threading the winding bridle paths up the mountain, sweating, bent, with his hair in his eyes. He was in no state to look back and see how the vista widened behind him the higher up they went, nor to breathe in the fragrance from the green dells of the mountain; he plodded onwards like a soulless old jade and never lifted his eyes from the path. She sat astride her belongings, wrapped in black shawls and wide skirts in the June sunshine, and the tears fell in brief showers with clear periods in between, and dried of their own accord before the next shower. Finally they reached the brow of the mountain and were met by the fresh, cool breeze off the highlands.

Halfway across the moor, at the boundary line—a little brook reddened by bog ore—the poet stopped and said: "This is where I turn back, Jarþrúður. I want to be home by tonight."

"Home?" she repeated tonelessly, and could no longer weep; defeat was frozen into her face.

"I've no doubt you can find your way from here," he said. "You traveled this route by yourself when you came."

No reply.

"I'm sorry I'm not in a position to give you a present now that we're saying good-bye. But so as not to part from you like a dog, I want you to accept my watch."

He had got this old timepiece in payment for a poem the previous year, and although he had never discovered how to make it work for any length of time, and seldom accurately, it was still the only thing this poet possessed which could be valued in money.

"Keep your watch yourself, Ólafur," she whispered.

"No," he said. "I want you to have it."

He thrust the watch into her skirt pocket, whether she liked it or not.

Then she said: "Ólafur, aren't you even going to pray to Jesus for me?"

"I know there's no need," he said. "Your invisible friend will be with you whatever he's called, perhaps Jesus, perhaps Hallgrímur Pétursson. Whoever you believe in will be with you. And now I ask you to take this parting sensibly. Remember that all people have to part sometime, however much they have loved one another, yes, however much they still love one another. It's better to part before anything happens which could leave a stain on one or both of them. It is beautiful to have been together, Jarþrúður, but it is also beautiful to part. It is right to have been together, but it is also right to part. And now, good-bye, Jarþrúður. And thank you for everything."

He gave her his hand and made haste to take it back again. He was even so hard-hearted as to give her horse a little smack as she started crossing the brook. Then she was over the brook and in another county.

He hurried away in the opposite direction. His steps were as light as a criminal's leaving the scene of the crime, or a man walking over burning coals; and yet he avoided running, so as not to hurt her if she happened to look back, but he quickened his stride as the distance between them grew, feeling anything but secure while she was still within hailing distance. At last when there was a hillock between them he took to his heels. He was ready to run to the ends of the earth. He ran as hard as he could, he ran with seven-league strides, he vaulted over everything that stood in his way, he flew. He had never run like that before, nor had anyone else. Yet there was no effort to this running, quite the contrary; it was supernatural running, it was redemption, it was freedom itself. The land beneath his feet was small and distant as in a bird's-eye view. He sang, he yelled, he shouted the names of trolls, gods and elves he had never believed in before; in a dell he started to turn somersaults and walk on his hands or else lift them to heaven thanking the Almighty with tears—"God, God, God."

Finally he lay flat among the grass willow and dwarf azaleas of the highlands, a free man under the blue sky, and listened to the beating of his heart. There is nothing so glorious on earth as to have been in a dungeon and to be freed. This was the most wonderful moment he had ever experienced, or anyone had ever experienced. He felt as if his childhood would now return to him anew with all its mystical music.

— 20 —

On a bright night he stepped ashore at Sviðinsvík a free man. After six years in a dungeon he saw this village in the light of a new promise. He was not quite twenty-five years old.

The village was asleep; there was a soft night-murmuring of birds gliding softly over the creamy-calm sea. It had been arranged between them that the girl would be waiting for him when he returned from this journey. His expectation, the knowledge that he would be meeting her as a free man and staying with her without interference from God or man made him feel dizzy, made his blood seethe with joy, brought a hot flush to his cheeks, animated his body with a feverish lightness as if he had taken a drink.

When he walked up to her house he saw a glimpse of her behind the curtains of her room. He closed the garden gate as quietly as he could. As he walked up the steps the door opened as if of its own accord. She was standing inside; she gave him her hand and pulled him quickly across the passage and into her room, and locked the door carefully behind them. Then she came to him. Nothing was said, they embraced one another blindly, drowned their shyness in each other's kisses.

And the night went on passing. All life's threads were entwined into one cord, all its laws reduced to their fundamentals, love reigned alone. The first rays of the morning sun found a man and woman, naked, smiling mankind's eternal smile at one another, and the murmur of the birds had grown louder and the sea was ruffled by the morning breeze, and they had started whispering to one another and telling one another the story of their love.

"What on earth kept you her prisoner for all these years?" asked the girl.

"I wasn't her prisoner," he replied. "I was the prisoner of those in distress. But when you looked at me at the fish yards one day and said 'Do you let yourself be turned back?' I felt then that something had happened in my life, which would never let me be the same person again."

"Here," she said. "Here in this room is your home—if you like. Nothing shall happen to you ever again which isn't worthy of a poet. You shall never go without again. We here in Veghús have green fingers—everything we touch comes to life."

In the glow of dawn he looked around this room which surpassed all other human abodes, profoundly moved, grateful and speechless like a sinner who awakes in paradise after death. Was it true that in this lovely house he was yet to compose the immortal poems of his adult years and write thick books about mighty heroes, who were not perhaps entirely real but were at least more real than living people, and who made the world new or at least made beauty more alluring than ever before? Was it true that he was yet to stand pensively at this curtained window on many a tranquil summer's day and look at the sky mirrored in the deep? Was it true that on countless winter nights when the roar of the sea and the storm could be heard outside, he was yet to sit here safely by the fireside and lamp, wrapped in her love that was the symbol of all that was noblest in earthly life? Was it true?

"I'm going off now to burn my shack with all the loathsome lumber it contains," he said.

"What will the owner of the estate say to that?" she asked.

"No one can say anything if a man burns his own house when he's tired of it," he said. "Don't you think it's a wonderful feeling to see the past ascending to heaven in flames and to rise from the ashes oneself, a new man?"

She asked him to leave before her stepmother came downstairs; it would take time to prepare her for the news of this betrothal, but she was nevertheless going to tell her about it at once, that very day. She embraced him again and again and said, "Kiss me, Ljósvíkingur, hold me tight, let me feel you, no one has ever loved so passionately as this."

The parting kiss at the door was never going to end, and it was touch and go that everything would not start up all over again.

He roamed for a long time alone, out in the cool of the morning while the sun rose higher and higher; he was tired from lack of sleep and lethargic after a night of burning love, and longed to slip into a deep slumber.

He stopped on the hillside at The Heights and contemplated his shack, which was still a little lopsided after the war damage of the spring, and looked forward to setting fire to it. No one had ever hated any house so much as the poet had hated this house. No one could ever have suffered more in any house, and yet escaped with his life. In this house he had never passed a happy hour. In this house he had never been himself, never spoken a true word, always kept silence about his real inner self like a crime. Every single time he had stepped across this threshold in all these years it had meant a victory over himself, a victory which often demanded all his strength. This house was not only the one place where every life-process had been an agony for him, but also the only place where he had been as wicked as deep down in his consciousness as everyday conduct reached, deeply and inevitably wicked. He had wasted the six best years of his life in Hell—and it was this house. What a joy to be able at last to see this Hell going up in flames!

He opened the door, and the smell of the house assailed him after being away for twenty-four hours—putrid fish, rancid old puffin feathers, the ever-present stench of smoke, mildew. But as he stood in the doorway, wrinkling his nose at this familiar stink, he caught sight of a heap on the floor, wrapped in black clothes covered with mud and dust and horsehair. It was a human being.

At first he had some difficulty in believing his own eyes—had he gone mad? He went inside with hesitating steps in the hope this vision would dissolve before he made himself ridiculous by trying to touch it with his hands. But the vision did not dissolve. And he touched the heap on the floor. He took it in his arms and raised it to its feet. And it turned out to be alive.

She opened her terrified, tearful, beseeching eyes.

"Jarþrúður!" he said. "I don't understand. Why have you come back?"

She sank down at his feet, embraced his knees, and begged: "In God's name, kill me!"

"Stop it," he said, and pulled her up again. "Tell me what you want."

She fell against his shoulder, weeping, with her arms round his neck.

"Dearest Ólafur, dearest darling Ólafur, my own one, if you will let me die here with you, I shall belong to you in death just as I have borne your children and buried them. But if you let me live, I shall endure any suffering you want to cause me. If you think me wicked you can beat me, if you think me ugly you can go with other women, anything, anything except casting me from your sight into the outermost darkness!"

At that he stroked her awkwardly on the cheek, his eyes a little troubled, and said: "Poor little Jarþrúður, how could I ever imagine that I, the poet, could forsake those in distress? Stop crying, my dear, and I shall try to be good to you."

He felt her lips burning on his skin, and her salt tears, and into her weeping there came an exalted, convulsive jubilation as if she were about to fall down again.

"Are you then going to go by the will of merciful God, Ólafur?" she asked through her tears.

"God and his mercy have nothing to do with me," replied Ólafur Kárason. "On the other hand, I'm going to go by the will of man. Soon we shall publish the banns. But at this moment I only ask you to come away from here with me."

"Yes, I shall come," she said humbly. "Where are we going?"

"Away," he said. "Away—to the west, over the mountains, to far-off places, perhaps up into the remote valleys, perhaps to another corner of the country, just so long as we come away at once, before the sun is high."

"And leave everything behind?" she said.

"Leave everything behind!" he said. Everything. All his dreams. All his poetry. All his hopes. All his life. Everything.

He sat down at the table by the window and looked out dully over the roofs of the village. She wanted to make coffee before they left. She lit the stove and it smoked; she opened the cupboard and out gushed a smell of stale bread. He leaned forward on his elbows, put his palms against his temples, and went on staring out of the window. Like a man in a stupor he perceived without seeing or hearing, he knew without reasoning or thinking; cowardice or compassion, whatever it was called—he did not go back on his pledges to life at the hour of decision; or rather—he *did* go back on them. He was a real man. With his hair over his forehead he continued to stare at the first light of day for a while with the glazed eyes of a condemned man. Gradually his eyelids grew heavy. He sank down onto the table, stretched out his arms, buried his face and slept.

BOOK FOUR

THE BEAUTY
OF THE HEAVENS

—— I ——

Where the glacier meets the sky, the land ceases to be earthly, and the earth becomes one with the heavens; no sorrows live there any more, and therefore joy is not necessary; beauty alone reigns there, beyond all demands.

While people in the remote bay were toiling to lay in their winter supplies, and the wife, Jarþrúður Jónsdóttir, was working at the haymaking for the bailiff in Greater Bervík, the husband was lying on the grassy slope in front of Little Bervík, a landless, deserted hut, contemplating this remarkable meeting of land and sky where heaven and earth at last understood one another to the full.

"It's fine weather today," said the wife when the sun shone from a clear sky at breakfast time. "You should go and rake hay with the Bervík folk to make yourself useful."

"Please leave me alone," he said imploringly.

He drank the milk she had brought him the night before and gave her back the empty bottle, went out into the aroma of summer, and lay down on the grass. A bluebottle was already up and buzzing at the wall of the house, there was still an echo of nesting time in the chirping of the birds, the dandelion was not yet in bloom.

It was best to forget one's own world, both the world one had to endure and the world one longed for, the world one had lost and the world one might perhaps achieve, forget one's own life in the face of the beauty where mortality ends and eternity takes over: perfection, beauty as the supreme arbiter. No day which gave a clear view of the glacier could ever become commonplace; as long as the paths of heaven were open, each day was a festival, peaceful and yet without any connection with death, beyond poetry and painting. Other people's animals came and grazed on the slope around the poet.

Some other day he got to his feet and wandered off like a sleep-walker. The river was called Berá, or Bergá; it was clear spring water with no trace of clay although its source was at the roots of the glacier. In the upper reaches it ran through ravines, but lower down it flowed over sandbanks. The poet walked upstream toward the mountain, the valley narrowed, the ravines deepened, the current grew stronger, a waterfall. He sat down on the brink of the ravine and listened to the purl of the water in the narrows blended with the shrill, echoing cries of a pair of merlins which flew in circles over the ravine, where they had their nest. There were copses in the hollows, small bushes growing on the ledges in the ravine, rosewort and ferns in the cracks. From here one could see out over Bervík parish, this small, remote community with its infertile lowlands, its sandy harborless bay sheltered on two sides by almost-barren mountains; their nearest trading post lay in another district, on the other side of a mountain pass.

The poet made his way farther up alongside the gorge, towards the glacier. And suddenly there was a little valley with yellow-green mossy bogs along the banks of the river and small, marshy patches below wooded hillsides, and here at the foot of the forest slope he suddenly came upon a tiny farm in a homefield facing the sun. There was an age-old man scything the homefield and a girl, with a head-scarf pulled down to her nose, was raking behind him. On the mown grass lay the pet lamb and the farm dog. When the poet approached, the dog began to bark, but the lamb stood up and stretched itself and tossed its head and wagged its tail. On the doorstep sat a little boy, who started to cry and called out to his mother.

"Who is the man?" asked the farmer, and began to whet his scythe.

"My name is Ólafur Kárason of Ljósavík."

"And where would he be going?" said the old man.

"I don't know," said the poet. "I didn't know there was a farm here."

"Oh, it's a farm only in name," said the old man. "You might be a stranger in these parts?"

"I'm the funny man who got married the other day and moved into the house at Little Bervík," said the poet. "Most people think I'm crazy. There's been some talk of letting me give the children religious instruction this winter. You must have heard of me."

"Nothing but good," said the farmer. "Helga dear, show the man inside and ask mother to make some coffee."

The daughter was somewhat taciturn, with a rather simple expression and eyes like a scared animal; it was hard to guess which of them was the more hostile to the visitor—the girl or her son on the doorstep.

"The summer mornings are nowhere as bright or long as in this nook of the glacier," replied the old woman, when the poet asked politely about their health. "We can feel the fragrance of the forest in our sleep."

The couple's other daughter was paralyzed. She lay bedridden under the window, silent, and was called the Invalid, and had a little mirror which was hanging from a nail on the bedpost.

"Our daughter lost the use of her limbs when she was fifteen years old," said the old woman. "But God has given her patience, and patience is stronger than might. The mirror is hung in such a way that she can see the glacier in it. She sometimes watches the glacier all day in the mirror. The glacier is her life."

"Forgive me, old woman, if I make an observation. Isn't it the beauty of the skies that is her life?" said Ólafur Kárason.

"I'm told you are a poet," said the old woman. "How lovely it is to be a poet."

"Tell the little boy that he has no need to be afraid, my dear," said the poet. "I am a child myself, even more of a child than he is. I am still in swaddling clothes."

"Little one," said the old woman, "we only need to look into the man's eyes to see that he is a child like us."

After the coffee he asked the old woman for permission to lie outside on the garden wall and look up at the sky.

The glacier was no more than a few feet above the top of the wooded slope; its presence was the image of pure divinity, lovely but merciless. The poet felt that those who lived in the presence of such a magic whiteness must be preternatural; this was the realm of mythology.

The old man mowed his field until evening. He neither swung the scythe nor disturbed the grass, but did everything smoothly and effortlessly, with barely perceptible movements. He let the sharp edge of the scythe do all the work; he cut the grass at the roots without felling it; his working methods were those of Nature herself. The old woman came out with her rake; the little boy fell asleep on the mown grass beside the dog and the lamb. The late-afternoon work went on under the still glacier. Then the day was over. At suppertime the poet still lay on the garden wall. They said it would not be much but invited him to have supper with them.

The daughter had gone to bring home the cows, the old woman put on the porridge, the farmer seated himself on his bed, took out his clasp knife, and began to whittle some brazilwood for rake teeth, taking care not to let the shavings spill from his palm to the floor. They did not say much unless spoken to, but dealt with all questions most conscientiously and always spoke as one. When the farmer was asked how long he had been farming there, he looked at his wife and said, "Mother, how many years has it been?"

"We've been crofting here for fully forty years, Father," said the woman.

Then the farmer answered the visitor and said, "Oh, forty years we've been scratching a living here."

The visitor asked if they had had many children, and the farmer looked at his wife as if he expected her to answer the question direct.

"It was sixteen children we had, Father," said the woman.

"Yes, sixteen were the children we had," said the farmer.

The children had all scattered to the four winds long ago, of course, apart from these two girls, the one paralyzed physically, the other morally. Half of them had died in childhood; some of the sons had been lost at sea; some had settled down as farmers in far-off places. The most the old couple had managed was two cows and twenty sheep.

"Have you always loved one another?" asked the poet.

The farmer stopped whittling for a moment and looked at his wife in some embarrassment.

"We have always loved God," said the woman.

It was as if the poet awoke from a dream; he looked up in astonishment and asked, "God? What god?"

"We have always believed in the one true God," said the woman.

"Yes, the one God we have believed in," said the farmer.

They looked upon their lives as a living example of how God loves people and is good to them. The poet said Thank you and prepared to take his leave.

"Patient girl," he said, "if your mirror should ever break, will you allow me to give you a new one?"

"Poor dear man," said the old couple, and the little boy was no longer frightened but brought his toys—sheep's leg-bones and shells—and laid them at the visitor's feet in farewell. In the faces of these people was the image of the long, bright summer mornings with the fragrance of the woods through their sleep. Not only did they have souls, but so did the things around them. Although everything was on its last legs—the little cottage, the farm implements, the household utensils—every object was in its place, everything clean and polished. It was not thanks to the cohesion of the material that the articles here did not fall apart. What would happen to this wooden bucket if they stopped milking into it morning and night? It would fall apart. The cottage would cave in the day they stopped walking in and out, turning the door handle gently, and with careful, kindly steps on the floorboards. It was unknown here to treat things as if they did not matter. Even the ladle in the pot was an important, independent individual with duties and rights; nothing seemed ever to have been done here haphazardly or casually. Every humblest task was carried out with a rare respect for Creation as a whole, with

affection, as if each task had never been done before and would never
be done again.

He threaded his way down the sheep paths alongside the ravine; in
some places they were extraordinarily close to the edge. The fragrance
of the grass and the heather blended amiably with the smell of the
path. He met the farmer's cows, grunting with repletion, their udders
bulging, curiosity shining from their eyes, ears and noses, but not
unmixed with the disdain of the sated. He stepped politely off the path
so that they would not have to inconvenience themselves for him.

The girl was sitting on a jutting rock, staring down into the ravine.
She had taken off her head scarf, the curls of her auburn hair were
bleached by the sun, she had red cheeks and a not-very-intelligent
face, and had lost her happiness all summer. She pretended not to see
the man approaching. The lamb lay innocently at her side with its
head held high, chewing the cud with rapid jaws, while at the other
side lay fidelity itself, the old farm dog, and it could not be bothered
barking at the same man twice in one day. The merlin in the ravine
was still flying round in circles, calling, and its cries went on echoing
from the cliffs.

He raised his cap and said Good-evening, but she scarcely
acknowledged his greeting.

"Don't look down into the ravine for too long, little girl," said the
poet. "There's a bird of ill omen in that ravine. But in the glacier
there lives a divine nature; you should look at the glacier instead."

She made a reply, but glanced for a moment at the glacier to see
whether the man was speaking the truth. Then she looked down into
the ravine again. It could not have been because of wantonness that
such a girl had had a baby; on the contrary, it must have been from
an excess of modesty.

"Perhaps you don't dare to talk to me because you think I'm
crazy?" he asked.

She looked at him, and an attempt to answer flickered in her eyes;
then she shook her head and gave up trying to say it.

"I'm one of these madmen who do no one any harm," he said.
"I'm in search of peace. That's all."

This time there came a suggestion of warmth into her eyes, like a warning of tears to come. But she did not know how to weep, either. She looked down into the ravine.

"The day comes when one forgets those one has loved," he said. "On that day one can die in peace. The deepest wounds heal so that you'd hardly notice."

Then the girl said, "It's no use talking poetically to me; I don't understand what you say. And there's nothing wrong with me."

"There's no point in being so formal with me," he said. "I'm neither a major poet nor a national poet, not even a district poet, and I've never had anything published. If I'm a poet, I'm my own private poet. Apart from that, I'm just a person near a glacier, like you."

"I don't understand you," said the girl. "Don't talk to me."

"But what if I have business with you?" he said.

"Business? With me? That's impossible."

"A message."

"A message? For me? From whom?"

"From a man," he said. "A man you knew not so long ago."

"Leave me alone; you're crazy," she said.

"He asked me to remind you that whenever people's lives appear to be harmony itself—perfect love, an ideal family, comfortable circumstances—life isn't real, either, and certainly only half a life. A whole heart—half a life. He asked me to tell you that life is governed by opposites and is always in conflict with itself, and that's why it is life. To have lost what one loved most is perhaps the only real life. At least, anyone who doesn't understand that, doesn't know what it is to live; doesn't know how to live and, what's worse, doesn't know how to die. That's what your friend asked me to pass on to you."

"As if he'd talk nonsense like that!" said the girl. "He never talks nonsense."

"Yes," said the poet. "A lot of people think he's become a bit funny of late. But I think, on the other hand, that he's become more experienced and mature than he was."

The girl forgot her shyness for a moment and now looked him full in the face; the lamb and the dog had also raised their heads sternly and were looking in the same direction as she. He felt as if he were standing before three judges.

"Are you lying to me? Yes, you're lying to me," said the girl.

"No," he said, looking as sincere as he could. "I call all good spirits to witness that I'm telling the truth."

"Then didn't he give you any other message for me?" she asked wide-eyed, from the depths of her heart.

"Yes," said the poet. "He asked me to deliver this poem."

> *If my poor heart is all that is most fickle,*
> *That's how I'm made,*
> *And I must be as destiny has shaped me,*
> *As fate ordained.*
> *Yet never since the gods of old, my darling,*
> *First came down here,*
> *Has any girl so sweet as you, my darling,*
> *Been loved so dear.*
>
> *But understand my fickle heart, my darling—*
> *How hard it is*
> *To love, and hope, and trust, and wish, my darling—*
> *And then know this:*
> *That my half-heart, inconstancy's true symbol,*
> *And my whole life,*
> *Will never disappoint, nor harm, nor hurt you,*
> *Nor cause you strife.*

— 2 —

But when the summer had passed and autumn weather was raging, and the grassy slope with its expanse of sky was no longer a sanctuary for other people's animals or for anyone who longed to live in luxury, the householder at Little Bervík realized that he had forgotten to lay in supplies for the winter. As a children's teacher, the poet was to get free kerosine from the parish, but the rumor got around at once that he was using a light in the evenings after bedtime, and the bailiff called on him officially and solemnly announced that the parish council would not be responsible for paying out money for such extravagance in these critical times for the nation. In the first snow-storms the snow came in through the eaves, in rainy weather the roof leaked, and on top of that there was no fuel. One evening during a snowstorm, the poet and his wife were intensely cold. At his wife's request, the poet then went to see the bailiff in Greater Bervík and said they needed fuel and matches, and asked for the loan of a few peats.

The parish office replied promptly, "You'll get damn all peat from me! Those who can't make provision for themselves in the autumn can stew in their own juice."

But after some moralizing, he said that the poet could go out to the moor and take twenty-five peats from a stack he owned there—against payment. Thereupon the poet asked the parish officer if he would be so good as to sell him a box of matches for cash.

"No," said the bailiff. "If one knows one has fuel, there's no need to light a fire."

That evening the poet and his wife had to burn the mattress from their bed to cook their porridge, since it was impossible to fetch the peat from the bailiff's stack because of the weather.

Some time later the education committee called on the children's teacher to discuss the start of a school term. There were three of them: the bailiff, Pastor Janus, and Þórður of Horn—old Bervíkings every one, coarse-tongued and practically fossilized. The pastor was a totally godless man, living entirely in ancient learning, with only a limited interest in modern times and none at all in everyday life. Þórður of Horn sat rocking to and fro, his mind full of disasters and other catastrophes which he wanted to have taken down in writing, including the life of his mother-in-law. The bailiff was endowed with official dignity and social conscience. When these three men were all together, it was as if three deaf men had met; they did not appear to see one another, either. In the same room, they talked as if they were in different corners of the country and had never met, and would never meet, had never heard one another, and not even heard of one another; and yet they all gave the impression of being the same person. Ólafur Kárason was the fourth deaf man in this gathering, the fourth sightless man, the fourth corner of the country.

"My men tell me that not just twenty-five peats are missing from the moor, but a whole stack," said the bailiff. "What have you to say to that, Ólafur?"

"I wouldn't like to swear to it that the occasional lumps of peat weren't frozen together; it was freezing hard and I couldn't always break them apart."

"If one wants to steal, dear boy," said the pastor, "then for God's sake one should never steal from the rich. A rich man has a hundred peats, and then suddenly he has only ninety-nine left: one of them has been stolen. He won't forget that even on his deathbed. A poor man has only one peat and is just as poor if it's stolen; and by the next day he has forgotten all about it. The wealthy man will inevitably get you into trouble if you steal from him; the poor man doesn't even bother to mention it. That's why all genuine thieves have the good sense to steal from the poor. The only really dangerous thing to do in Iceland is to steal from the rich, and the only really profitable thing to do in Iceland is to steal from the poor, dear boy."

"I shall pay in full for every single peat," said the poet.

Þórður of Horn: "My wife and I have wanted so much to meet someone who could compose a nice elegy for my late mother-in-law who perished in the great snow avalanche at Eyrarfjörður a few years ago, and preferably someone who could write up her whole life story. I'm a bit short of fuel myself, of course, but one can always spare a load of sheep-droppings if there's a chance of a good poem, lads."

"What we need in this district above all isn't poetry," said the bailiff. "We need honest people, not intellectual people and not educated people either, but truly Christian and industrious people; people who are content with little. We need people who don't indulge in amusements in these critical times; people who don't go to the moor and burn other people's peats. That's what has to be impressed on our children. We want a serious society. We don't want to have the sort of society they have at Kaldsvík over on the other side of the mountain: at the last Faroese Ball there, two men had their noses bitten off, a third had his ear torn off, and women were lifted up by the legs in the middle of the dance floor and various other offenses."

"Hlaupa-Halla had nine children in twelve parishes over more than thirty years, and was forgiven everything until she became a sheep-stealer, dear boy, but then she was sent to prison," said the pastor. "No crime has ever been recognized in Iceland except sheep-stealing."

"I really think there's an urgent need to write a poem about the snow avalanche in Eyrarfjörður while there are still people alive who remember it," said Þórður of Horn.

"The most important thing in life is not to be a burden upon others," said the bailiff. "Not to be dependent upon anyone, never to need to ask anyone for anything—that's as good as being given every human virtue as a christening gift."

"If one wants to become somebody," said the pastor, "it's a good idea to start early collecting useless bits of string, rotten sticks, rusty nails, old whetstones, dried dog muck, and so on. But some people have grown rich from killing the survivors of shipwrecks. Many people favor witchcraft in order to acquire wealth. For instance, the late Finnbogi Bæringsson always went about with a pocket in his shirt where he kept a few krónur that had been stolen from a poor widow, as well as a heron's claw, a mermaid's purse, a wishing-stone, an orchis and an abracadabra. Others reckon that using a wren is an infallible way of becoming well-off: you have to catch it alive, then it's split in two, dear boy, and the one half is placed in the chest where you keep your money, while the other half is buried in the ground according to certain prescribed procedures. Actually, the person who catches the bird catches ill luck, too, but there's a way round that. You only have to get someone poor to do it for you, dear boy."

"Four farms were destroyed in that avalanche," said Þórður of Horn. "In Syðrivík one eighty-five-year-old man suddenly woke up with snow in his mouth—he was the only one on the farm to survive. At Steinar only a cat survived. At Hólm a woman in confinement christened her newborn baby in the darkness under the avalanche, and named it after her husband and son, both of whom perished. I don't know what's worth writing about if it isn't that sort of thing, lads."

"And the use of kerosine beyond reasonable needs I have always criticized, and reserve to myself the right to criticize in the future and take such steps as may be necessary," said the bailiff. "I am not aware that it is written anywhere that the Icelandic nation should provide lighting and heating for people who, under the pretext of making poetry, think they're too good to make provision for themselves in the autumn. To the best of my knowledge, the Icelandic nation has never asked for poetry from anyone."

"You can take everything from me," said the poet, "except the freedom to look up at the sky occasionally."

The pastor, who until now had been rattling on about various ways of acquiring money, abruptly dropped the subject for the time being and fixed his peering eyes on the poet, not unlike an actor who suddenly forgets his part because of an accident in the auditorium; and into his eyes there came an expression of that rare presence of human characteristics which perhaps belongs nowhere so indubitably and eternally as in the eyes of an old boar squinting momentarily up from its swill.

"By the way, dear boy, who are your people?" asked the pastor.

Ólafur Kárason named his parents and grandparents, which was all he knew. But he had no need to go any further back, the pastor had the rest of the family tree at his fingertips. He started droning on again in the same style as before, with the expression of someone reading aloud from a boring book, with occasional grunts and groans in between. "It's positively a lineage of the highest distinction on both sides, further back, dear boy," said the pastor, "alternating sheriffs, pastors, and factors of royal estates. You are, like me, descended from Bishop Jón Arason, and at least two other bishops of Hólar. Your poetic gifts you've probably inherited from Björn, the son of a bishop, who was the best versifier of his time at Hólar, and sailed to France to study and was drowned at sea. But I haven't yet mentioned the most important part: your ancestor is the same man as the ancestor of Queen Victoria of England and that family—Auðunn *skökull* (Shaft), who lived at Auðunarstaðir in Víðidalur, the father of Þóra *mosháls* (Moss-Neck)—and the line of descent from her has been worked out in the newspapers and published in England, although little has been heard from the English on all this."

"Sometimes when we meet privately I'll tell you my late mother-in-law's life story," said Þórður of Horn. "At present I'll content myself with telling you about my father's death, in case you would like to compose an elegy for him. Fatal accidents have for long been the favorite subjects of poets. It so happened that he was fowling for fulmar down a cliff and slipped on the rock face just above the farm. He could be heard screaming for twenty-four hours, and people could see where he lay on a ledge. But there was no way of reaching him. The birds could be seen tearing the body to pieces. Next spring, fowlers came from Latrar and collected the bones."

With that, the education committee went home.

A few days later the schooling began. The courthouse stood in the bailiff's yard, the meeting place of all the tempests of heaven. Twelve children made their way here, blue in the face and a trifle louse-ridden, with colds that went round the group in waves and never quite disappeared. The bailiff had contracted on behalf of the parish to supply the school with peat and droppings, but winter came early and the icy winds blew from all directions right through their meeting hall. The bailiff thought the fuel was disappearing rather quickly and blamed the teacher's extravagance; teaching soon became a secondary issue in the battle over peat and droppings. And when the school's weekly ration was exhausted by midweek and the children had aching fingernails, chilblains, pains and temperatures, the poet saw no alternative but to close the school. The bailiff called officially to say that he would not only report the teacher to the education committee and have him dismissed, and to the parish council and have him deported to his home parish, but also to the authorities and have him punished if he did not open the school at once. The poet took this very much to heart, even though he found it difficult to imagine any punishment more severe than having to teach ill, numbed, and therefore dull-witted children in a building where all the tempests of the far north held their assembly. He did not know to whom he should turn for help in this crisis. Finally it occurred to him that perhaps Pastor Janus would give him the benefit of his kinship with Þórður *mosháls* and the British Royal Family, and decided to go to see him.

"What am I to do, pastor Janus? It's as if the snowstorms blow from all four directions on the courthouse, and the bailiff refuses to supply any more peat this week, so that I can't be sure of keeping the children alive. On the other hand, the bailiff threatens to dismiss me if I close the school, and even take me to court."

The pastor replied: "I'm not surprised at anything the bailiff says or does, dear boy, I know his lineage too well for that. You see, he's descended from the so-called Sperðling family, which wasn't in fact any family at all, although it can perhaps with some dexterity be traced back to Þorgils (Knoll-Muck), who was of Danish origin according to some. There's never been any talent or distinction in that lot, but plenty of villains and riffraff, dear boy, like for instance Þorgarður *drangur* (Ghost) and a fellow called Tumi who stole the candlesticks from Sómastaðir Church and sold them to the Dutch for a keg of brennivín, with his six-year-old daughter thrown in as well; the son of Þorgarðyr, the son of Smyrill *tvítóla* (the Hermaphrodite), who flogged at Kollabaíðir Sands; his daughter was Hunda-Karítas, whom everyone knows about, reference the *Lives of the Sheriffs*. She was convicted of fornication and executed by drowning at the Althing, and her son was Jón *sperðlingur* (Sheep-Guts) who killed a man at the Eysteinseyrarleitur (Eysteinseyrar Sheep-Drive) and was a notorious sheep-stealer and scoundrel to boot, dear boy, and besides his parents were cousins on both sides and he himself was said to be a changeling."

"It may be a consolation to some poor people to know that men of power can be descended from base families," said the poet. "Unfor-

tunately it needs more than that to bolster up my courage. Though it
was sometimes difficult to be a poet and a somebody at Sviðinsvík,
where I was a poet for five years although I never succeeded in
becoming a somebody, it seems to me twice as difficult to be a poet
and a somebody in Bervík."

"As you so rightly say, it's two different things to be a poet and a
somebody, and for that reason I shall take the liberty of giving you
my answer in two parts, dear boy," said the pastor. "*Primo,* no one
denies that it's difficult to be a somebody in Bervík, nor indeed has it
ever been tried to the best of my knowledge since the country was
first inhabited. In the year 1705 the parish pastor of Bervík wrote to
the authorities about his parishioners, to the effect that they were the
very lowest of the low, both in intelligence and conduct. We can
expect to find emerging in Bervík, sooner than anywhere else, that
animal species which will inhabit the world when men and monkeys
have died out as a result of their own actions. It has never suited the
Bervíkings to have a school. For more than a thousand years their
luxuries have been lice and colds while other nations had plenty of
tobacco and brennivín. For that reason you mustn't be surprised if
they keep the school short of peat and threaten to deport the teacher
to his home parish. But *secundo,* dear boy, as for the other point, I
disagree with you entirely that here in Bervík it isn't possible to be a
scholar and a poet. I have written thirty books since I was ordained
to Bervík forty years ago. One writes books for oneself because one is
among people who cannot be classed as human beings. If you feel
you lack the courage to write books in Bervík, it would be salutary
for you to remember that precisely here, on this harborless coast, was
written and preserved for centuries one of the greatest books ever
written in the North, namely *Korpinskinna,* which Árni Magnússon
himself called the most important manuscript ever to come into his
hands.* He wrote a letter in his own hand to this country, offering
not only his own wealth but also the wealth of the Danish crown,
without restriction or limit, if it were possible to get hold of the
eighteen sheets which were missing from the back of the manuscript
when it was found. In this book, which was found in a poor man's

kitchen in Bervík in 1680, are collected some of the most notable Sagas in the world. It is now kept in a strong underground vault in Copenhagen, and considered so valuable that no greater loss could befall Denmark than to lose this book."

The poet found this remarkable indeed. He had heard of *Korpinskinna,* of course, as one of the greatest books in Nordic literature, but he had never realized that it had originated here. The pastor brought out his own works, genealogies, historical writings, and philological treaties, to prove that one could still write books on this harborless coast, and soon the poet had forgotten all his difficulties over the school, confronted by these closely written volumes. They talked until the night was almost over about those matters which have always been close to the hearts of scholars and poets in Iceland. In the small hours, the poet walked home in the moonlight and hard-frozen snow; it was as bright as day. From the brow of the glacier there shone the kind of light one can only read about in more advanced doctrines. The poet now felt that it did not really matter at all if the bailiff at Bervík was too mean to supply the school with peat and droppings. He saw this place in the light of *Korpinskinna,* suffused with incomparable beauty, a literature which would live for as long as the world existed. However wretched human life could be in its retrogression towards monkeys and other creatures, he thought it did not matter so long as poets existed: human life was a minor detail, practically nothing. Beauty was the only thing which mattered, and in reality a poet had no responsibilities to anything except that. He suddenly felt that his finest poems were still to be written.

— 3 —

There had never been any talent or distinction in that lot, the pastor had said of the bailiff's lineage.

On this harborless coast the dignity of human life was an improper concept, no less than the heavenly light; stupidity, servitude and penury were the true virtues of his serious society, its divine

Trinity. This dark dictatorship gave each child an impenetrable breastplate to shield it from all danger of talent or distinction, but especially from the influence of beauty.

It was no wonder that the poet was delighted to see among his group of children a face that was in complete contrast to soot, fulmars, saltfish, cold germs and lice, encouragingly fresh, endowed with the faculty of being exalted to understanding and enlightenment. It was like finding a colorful, tender flower on the moor among the rushes and sedges. Those clear but rather cold eyes constantly sought a purpose in everything they saw, that bright but rather weak face listened by some inner command for every sound that betrayed opposition to the divine Trinity of the place.

This thirteen-year-old boy came of by no means distinguished parentage, nor had he been reared among wealthy people where more polite manners are found. He was an illegitimate child in the care of his mother who had come to the bailiff's as a maid; the boy's father had been residing in the south for a long time now, and had no contact with the mother or her son. Whatever the boy's origins, there was no concealing the fact that little Sveinn of Bervík was of a different mold than was customary here. Perhaps the reason was that he had a rather special mother who had taught him to wash and wash again, over and over again, and always. One thing was certain, it was as if no dirt could stick to him; he even had clean nails. His hair was combed and, though his clothes were poor, his mother had cut them carefully, and there was never a stain or a wrinkle to be seen on them, and therefore he always seemed to be in his Sunday-best. Cold germs and lice seemed to have a dislike for this boy and gave him a very wide berth.

Sveinn of Bervík learned naturally without difficulty or effort. But though he surpassed all the others in understanding, there was in his conduct a certain reserve which forbade him to push himself to the front or take the lead. It was his nature to observe unobtrusively, to be a pure voice in the midst of coarse clamor, to have ready the obvious, simple answer, without any conceit, when the others had given up.

One day Ólafur Kárason asked the boy if he would mind coming with him part of the way home that day after school; he said he had been wanting to ask him something privately for the last few days.

"No," said the boy, and blushed.

But when they were alone in the dusk the poet was tongue-tied. They walked silently side by side for a while. At last the poet plucked up courage.

"Since I first noticed you, I have wanted to ask you one question," he said. "I hope you won't feel offended if you think it rather an odd question. Do you ever hear a strange music when you're alone?"

The boy looked up at his teacher, amazed at such a mysterious question, very serious, a little embarrassed and perhaps not entirely unafraid.

"Music?" he said. "What sort of music? Like, for instance, birdsong?"

"Like birdsong," said the poet, and was now in difficulties himself, "and yet not like birdsong. No, actually, not like birdsong at all. Perhaps not even music, but rather a light, an inner light, a joyous light, an omnipotent light, that Light, that Music which no word had been created to describe."

"Really," said the boy.

The poet was disappointed; he felt he had made a fool of himself by saying so much in one breath. The boy's reply made him suddenly sad. They walked on in silence for a while. Then the boy said, "Will you teach me to hear this music? And see this light?"

"That's something that cannot be taught, my dear," said the poet. "All the world's wealth, all the earth's luxuries are only a poor imitation of it and recompense for it. But sometimes when I look at your face in class, I feel as if you were born to hear it and see it."

"I'm so sorry I haven't heard it and seen it," said the boy, and felt utterly shattered.

"My friend," said the poet, and decided to try once again. "If you stand by the sea on a calm summer day and look at the clouds mirrored in the deep, or lie in a green dell at midsummer, with a brook purling by, or if you walk on the withered grass on the banks of a stream on the last day of winter and hear the first barnacle goose honking—don't you feel anything special then?"

Then the boy said, "Always when I see or hear something beautiful I forgive everyone everything; I want then to be a great man so that I can do something good for everyone."

Then the poet seized his friend's hand and said gratefully, "Thank heaven you have understood me after all."

But the boy was not quite clear what he had understood, and wanted to clarify it, and added, "I want so much to be a scholar and a poet."

At that the poet fell silent again. In reality, this was not what he had been asking about. But though he had suffered another disappointment, it would be wrong to show it; as a matter of fact he had expected something from the boy which a poet has no right to demand from anyone else.

"You must come home with me and have some coffee," said the poet, to change the subject.

"I have to feed the horses," said the boy. "If I shirk, I get into trouble."

"I understand," said the poet. "I, too, was beaten by gods, men and horses. But you have a mother and perhaps even a father. Perhaps you will one day become a scholar and a poet."

But though Ólafur Kárason had been a little disappointed in his pupil, particularly over the Music, he could not avoid being interested in this young man. Their friendship grew and throve for a while like a seed which has found a handful of soil in a desert. The poet had never before been aware of being at the giving end of a friendship, and the knowledge of this gave him confidence in himself at a difficult time. How would this winter ever have passed without Sveinn of Bervík? He forgot all his other pupils and saw only him and talked only to him. He put those tedious Jewish chronicles on a shelf along with the rest of the Bervík bailiff's favorite subjects, and brought out the *Núma Ballads* and the *Poems of Jónas Hallgrímsson*, and turned the talk to the sanctity of poetry and the omnipotence of beauty; nor did he forget the majesty of transience.

One day the teacher noticed that the boy did not want to stay behind at the end of the class, but hurried away without saying Good-bye. When he kept this up, the poet waylaid him one day and asked him why. The boy would not talk. But when he was pressed, he admitted that he had been thrashed.

"What for?"

"For talking about poetry," said the boy.

"I, too, was beaten at your age," said the poet. "It was gods, men and horses. But poetry is the Redeemer of the soul, and it never occurred to me to break faith with it."

The boy wanted to run away despite all persuasions.

"Don't run away," said the poet. "My wife will give us coffee. And we'll read a love song by Sigurður Breiðfjörð.

"There is no beating that can affect a poet," said Ólafur Kárason. "Poets are stronger than gods, men, and horses."

"I can't stand being beaten," said the boy.

Then one Sunday morning the bailiff appeared in the yard at Little Bervík. He asked the poet to come outside.

"You are corrupting the children," said the bailiff. "You've filled the head of the most promising boy with such nonsense that he's started to make strange remarks; and even started to mess about with pen and ink. But I'm not having any ink-work in my home. I'm not having any weird speculations in my home."

"Is that so?" said the poet.

"If you carry on like this you'll turn the boy into a useless wretch like yourself and the same sort of criminal as Sigurður Breiðfjörð, who sold his wife for a dog and was sentenced to twenty-seven strokes of the lash."

"Oh, I wouldn't say that," said the poet.

"I've come here to tell you that if you go on leading the children astray with worthless speculations instead of teaching them honest conduct, then you'll be in for it. We here in Bervík believe in Christ. We have agreed to build a twenty-thousand-krónur church and we stipulate that others should believe in Christ. We oppose tooth and nail those who want to turn the young from work and honesty and to indolence and crime under the pretext of poetry."

"Really," said the poet.

"You say 'Really,' you damned fool?" said the bailiff. "Maybe you'll live to pay for that word in full before we are finished."

This conversation had its consequences for Sveinn of Bervík. The first thing Ólafur Kárason did when he went inside again was to melt his ink; then he sat down and wrote a letter to the south for the first time in his life.

The boy's parents had not been on speaking terms since his birth; the mother had raised the boy on her own. Ólafur wrote to the boy's father, not just without the mother's knowledge, but even despite her opposition. He wrote it on his own responsibility; he told his own life story and asked a complete stranger to save his own life—from being reincarnated at a new Fótur-undir-Fótarfæti. Never had this poet pleaded a case with such passion. And an astonishing thing happened, for this turned out to be one of the few occasions in life when a letter brought some results.

More than a month later, Ólafur Kárason was in a position to take Sveinn of Bervík aside and say to him these words: "In your life will be fulfilled what I was born to yearn for."

Then he explained to him that the boy's father had written to him and said he was willing to pay for the boy to be educated according to the boy's own wishes.

"How can I thank you for bringing this about?" asked the boy, when he had wiped the tears from his eyes.

"My reward is to know that you will be living the reality which was my dream," said the poet. "You'll go to school now and become a scholar and a poet."

"Even if I go to every school in the country, I shall never have been in more than one school—your school," said Sveinn of Bervík.

They felt as if the moment of parting had arrived, and looked at one another from a fateful distance.

"If a destitute folk poet from an unknown harborless coast should knock at your door, do you think you would recognize him again, Sveinn?"

"When you come to visit me, Ólafur, I shall have a room of my own, and a lot of books," said Sveinn of Bervík. "That room is your room, and all the books are your books. Everything of mine is yours. At night I shall have a bed made up for you on the divan."

"No, thank you!" said Ólafur Kárason with his polite smile. "I won't want to go to sleep. We'll stay awake all night. We'll sit up and talk. We'll talk about what has been the Icelanders' illumination in the long evenings from earliest times. You will be a scholar and a poet, I'll be the visitor who comes to learn from you. Will you promise me not to go to sleep, but to stay up with me and talk to me?"

"Yes," replied Sveinn of Bervík.

"Will you promise me something else?" said Ólafur Kárason of Ljósavík.

"Yes," said Sveinn of Bervík.

"Will you promise not to look at me with contempt even though I am ignorant and hapless, and perhaps shabbily dressed in comparison with those you'll be in the habit of associating with—and not to feel sorry for me, either?"

"I will never see in you anything but the best man I have ever known," said Sveinn of Bervík.

"And then there's only one thing left that I want to ask you," said Ólafur Kárason. "May I tell you what it is?"

"Yes," said Sveinn of Bervík. "What is it?"

"When we have stayed up all night, talking, and the first rays of the morning sun are on your walls, will you go with me to the churchyard and show me one grave?"

"What grave is that?" said Sveinn of Bervík.

"It's the grave of Sigurður Breiðfjörð," said Ólafur Kárason.

"Everything I can do, I am ready to do for you," said Sveinn of Bervík.

"I have heard that on his tombstone there is a stone harp with five strings," said the poet.

— **4** —

And so five years passed in that stealthy way in which time steals away from the heart, not only among the fleshpots and bright lights but also in a harborless bay behind the mountains, until one wakes up, questioning, from a long sleep in a dark night.

He woke up in the depths of the night, stranger in his own life, a penitent for the sins he had not committed, his good deeds long since drowned in pity; he woke up far away from himself, lost in the wilderness of humanity and the way back too long for one mortal life. No one gave him an opportunity to smile any more, and he had not known a happy moment since he lay under the sloping ceiling at Fótur-undir-Fótarfæti, sick and sore, waiting for the sunbeam. If he got up and lit the lamp and looked at himself in the mirror, he would be afraid of this beggar who lodged here with a woman fifteen years older, and a three-month-old son.

"Who am I?" he asked. "And where?"

And got the answer: "Your wait is nearly at an end; the life that was intended for you—lost."

He realized how indifferent he was to life on the morning on which Jón Ólafsson was born. The cottage was full of that silly but good-natured midwives' humor which characterizes the atmosphere in a house where a woman has been delivered of a child. No, he said, I'm afraid I have no desire to know how heavy the baby is. And when other people had fetched a spring-balance and the baby was being weighed on it, he asked to be excused from having to read the weight. A newborn child was not a novelty any more. He had experienced to the full a child's whole life from its birth to its death, the first crying, the first smile, the first time it said Mama, its first faltering steps, the sickness, the suffering, the wasting away, the last breath—always the same story. And he knew that on the day when he would be told to go out to borrow a little coffin for little Jón Ólafsson, he would cold-bloodedly reply with that adage from the Jewish chronicle: Let the dead bury their dead.

But it so happened on the morning after Ólafur Kárason of Ljósavík woke up in the wilderness, that a stranger came into his life; an unimportant occurrence, of course, nothing at all in the normal sense, but nonetheless the beginning of unforeseen events as is usually the case with the most fortuitous occurrences. Later, he often asked himself what hidden connection there might have been between the night's fear and this visit which in itself was of no importance. Would I have paid any heed to this unexpected call to life, he asked himself, if the voice of the void had not reached my heart a few hours earlier? Does life call your name out loud before the anguish of death comes upon you?

In itself, it was really one of the thousands of events which happen unnoticed in one's life in the quiet flow of the years: A man from the Outer Nesses, Jason the lighthouse keeper from Taungar, arrived with a child for the school, and came to see the teacher to ask him to keep an eye on the child. The poor thing had never been away from home and had never been to school before, but was to be confirmed in the spring.

A large, beefy girl gave the teacher a brawny, calloused hand molded by milking and rowing, and he saw in front of him coarse dark hair in thick braids, growing low down on her forehead; a large plump face with massive jaws and straight teeth, thick and shapeless lips, oily skin, and the eyes of a well-fed beast; but physically she was more full-grown than half-grown. She brought with her an atmosphere of horse-flesh, fulmar and fish roes as she stood there in the poet's living room with her coarse stockings round her ankles, and sniffing.

"Jasína Gottfreðlína has had a little instruction in reading and writing, but has had little opportunity of practicing it," said her father, a big, thickset, coarse-tongued man. "And I've told her a little about the Sagas, so that at least she knows something about the Ramstad people in Norway and the most important of the ancient kings of Scandinavia." But now the poor thing had to be confirmed in the spring, he went on, and therefore it was very important for her to learn this so-called Christian faith this winter so that she would not need to feel ashamed about it in front of others.

The girl's father had put her up at his sister's, a widow living in one of the Eyrar cottages on the other side of the river down by the estuary, and he asked the teacher to give the poor thing shelter if the river was ever impassable during a thaw. He offered extra payment if he would give her special tuition in the Christian faith early that winter, in the hope that she could catch up with her contemporaries in this subject and keep pace with them by the spring.

Ólafur Kárason looked in amazement at this untamed daughter of the Outer Nesses, this overgrown, pagan child, and brushed his hair back from his forehead in perplexity. To tell the truth, he could see no point whatsoever in trying to cram Jewish adages and fables about Jesus into such a hump; Christianity was the last thing one would think of teaching Jasía Gottfreðlína.

When she took her seat in class among the other children, she stood out because of her strength and physical maturity. She seemed to have her origins in chemistry, charged with an impersonal power from the earth and the sea that was completely unrelated to any concept of the soul. She overwhelmed the school, so that the other children vanished in her shadow, gray and skinny, or dissolved into patches of mist.

This pupil knew how to handle every living creature that moved on Iceland's coasts or in its seas, whether it had cold blood or hot, and knew its nature alive or dead; but unfortunately she could not answer the simplest question about natural history. On scores of mountains and moors there was no fog so thick that she would ever lose her way when herding sheep. She knew every landmark by name, not only on her father's land but much farther afield as well, both wastelands and mountain pastures: names of hills, hollows, brooks, bogs, marshes, moors, earthbanks, sheep sheds, ruins, cliffs, boulders, mountain peaks. In the same way, she also knew the fishing grounds, but to try to din into her head the most simple elements of geography—that was out of the question.

Perhaps she was at no higher or lower a stage of maturity in relation to the supernatural, not to mention the fundamentals of morality, than the nation has ever reached since this country was first inhabited, but her reluctance first came to a head when the subject of Christianity was raised, because she thought that Christ had been some sort of ancestor of the Danish merchant Kristinsen at Kaldsvík. She had never even heard of God, did not know that he existed, and did not believe it, either, even when she was told. But she did not know how to feel ashamed of her ignorance, and when everyone was laughing all around her it did not occur to her that she could be the cause of it. Often, Ólafur Kárason felt that actually he was the fool, to carry on pestering and questioning someone over and over again about vain trifles—a person whose only fault it was to be more original, more genuine, than other people.

During the breaks, the poet stood at the window and looked at the children playing tag. Jasína Gottfreðlína was always "it." No amount of agility could match her purposeful, impetuous energy; and after the game she would stand in the yard, glowing with health, with a horse-like gleam in her eyes, hot, her braids undone, her stockings down. And though the children jeered at her she paid no attention; she tidied herself where she stood, pulled her skirt up over that coarse knee, and adjusted her garters quite openly.

The teacher took her to his house that evening to explain the Creation of the world to her, the Fall and the unusual downpour that this Fall caused in Armenia in Noah's time, together with the other main points of this subject in which she knew less than other women.

The pupil stared into the blue.

"Do you understand what I'm saying?" he asked.

"I don't know," she said. "I'm not thinking about it."

He became a little uneasy at this and said, "What do you think your father will say if you don't think about the things you have to learn? Who went into the Ark?"

But she had forgotten by then what the man was called, it was such an unusual name—"Ach, that fellow you were talking about," she said.

"And why did Noah go into the Ark?" asked the poet.

"The rain came," she said.

"Rain?" said the poet.

"Yes, but not as much as you said, I'm quite sure," she said.

"Why did the rain come?" he said.

"I've no idea," she said. "I don't suppose it could have stayed dry much longer."

"What do you think your father will say if he hears the way you answer?" said the teacher.

"I've heard my daddy say that everything in the Bible is just a pack of lies," she said. "I don't believe any stories except the Sagas. I don't want to go to school. I want to go home."

Into her face there came an expression of boredom and despair, and he was both sorry for her and angry with her for being such a simpleton. And at that moment his little son Jón woke up crying.

Jasína Gottfreðlína stood up with a start, went over to the baby's cot as if she were suddenly at home here, picked him up in her arms and began to dandle him. In a twinkling, Ólafur Kárason saw God and Noah vanish completely from the girl's face, together with the unusual downpour associated with these two preposterous characters. The reluctance was gone; the obstinacy was suddenly replaced by its opposite. She knew how to hold a child to her breast in the classic and immortal fashion beyond Christianity, beyond education and civilization, to bend down over it, to stand rocking on her feet while she lulled it, to croon a nursery rhyme which contained more of the magic of the race in its cadences than any poetry. Soon the child was asleep. But she could not bring herself to put it down again, and went on dandling it and rocking back and forth on her feet and crooning the same rhyme, the same cadence, without melody or meaning, over and over again for a while, as if she had rocked herself into a trance. The poet put the Bible stories under his pillow and went out.

Some time afterwards there came a thaw after a snowstorm, and the river was in spate. It was for this kind of disastrous weather that it had been arranged that the pupil would spend the night in the teacher's cottage and at the same time have the benefit of special tuition from him. On such a day she sat behind after school in the living room at Little Bervík, and had to answer questions about God's Ten Commandments.

"Thou shalt have none other gods but Me," said Ólafur Kárason. "What's that?"

"I've no idea," said the pupil.

"The God of the Jews was an absolute God, who believed in other gods himself, to be sure, but forbade me to obey them, contrary to our own beliefs in the North. We have many gods and obey them all, and they us, the god of the sea and the god of the land, the god of thunder and the god of poetry . . ."

She stared dully into the blue, but when he had been harping on about the Commandments for a while she lost patience and said: "Can I go over to Greater Bervík and stay up with a cow tonight? The bailiff's Skjalda is about to calve."

He heaved a sigh, rose to his feet, and was about to say something serious, but changed his mind and gave the girl a light blow with the catechism. "Oh, off you go, for heaven's sake," he said.

Smacking her was like tapping a rock-cliff. She did not understand humor, but put on an injured expression, as if her dignity had been offended. Then she was gone, and he was left standing there with the catechism, not knowing what on earth to do. Since she did not understand even the Old Testament, which after all speaks to the lower senses, it was not very likely that he would succeed in explaining the New Testament to her, which after all speaks to the soul. Luck seemed to have turned against the poet, by sending him such a pupil; indeed, this was the first time in his life that he had ever wanted to strike a living creature.

But next day the river was still in spate, and before he knew it he was listening to his own voice once again trying to explain the fundamental principles of the faith. He talked rapidly and without pause, to conceal from her his own lack of interest; he told her the most fantastic stories about the deity in hope of arousing wonder in her, of how the Lord was His own Father and Son at once, as well as being born of an immaculate virgin, and of how the Holy Ghost was elected to the Trinity by a majority of one vote after fierce argument at a famous Synod. But not even divine tokens and miracles were potent enough to move this strange pupil.

"Are you paying any attention to what I'm saying?" he asked at last.

"Oh, I suppose I hear you all right," she said.

"You seem to be so absentminded, somehow," he said. "Perhaps I'm not explaining it properly?"

"Why are people always talking to one about these gods?" she asked.

"You're probably too old to start on Christianity," he replied. "One probably has to learn Christianity in infancy."

"Do you think I can't tell from your face that you're making it all up?" she said.

He fell silent. Perhaps the explanation of her slowness lay in the fact that the doctrine he was teaching was not true. This simple, natural girl sensed intuitively his duplicity; she listened out of politeness for as long as she could endure it, like someone sitting through a tedious sermon or an unsuccessful play, but saw through his words to what he was really thinking. He had an urge to laugh, which he had the greatest difficulty in keeping down; he rose to his feet, closed the catechism, and gave the girl another cuff to signify that he gave up.

But now she had had enough. She came of an Outer Nesses aristocracy that knew neither oppression nor inferiority, well-practiced in wrestling not only with her younger brothers and sisters but also with her father, brought up in the spirit of the kings and heroes of old. She sprang at the teacher and started wrestling with him.

This was something that Ólafur Kárason was not prepared for. In actual fact, he had never been in a fight. Physical exertion was not at all to his liking and he was in the habit of avoiding it, but suddenly his dignity was in jeopardy against this young giantess who preferred strength to intellect, and understood only physical things. As a man, he had no right to let himself be worsted in this exchange, either as an adult against a child or as a teacher against a pupil, least of all as a man against a woman. One thing was certain; she was in deadly earnest. He had no alternative, under the circumstances, than to meet the challenge. So they fought.

A fight was the only way of reaching a satisfactory conclusion; to win a fight was to have been proved right. She was determined to get him down and annihilate all his Christianity; she gritted her teeth and grimaced. Her father had not taught her any other wrestling holds than a trial of strength by bear hug; if all else failed, it came quite naturally to her to use her teeth, and she bit. But when he tripped her she lost her balance, fell backwards, and pulled him down with her to the floor.

Later, he often thought about whether this fall had not been the beginning of the misfortune: could he not have prevented it; did he have to let her pull him down with her? He could argue about it with himself for a long time, but perhaps it was a minor detail. The main point was that all of a sudden he felt her young, brawny body pressed hard against him, her life against his life; and astonishingly enough, at this point she no longer put up any resistance. On the contrary, her body yielded to his body as naturally as she had earlier taken his child and comforted it. Just as it had been her spontaneous reaction to defend herself when he had cuffed her, it seemed just as natural for her, now that she was down, to abandon her defenses and expect him to take advantage of the fall. One moment—and then the door in the passage was opened. He leapt hurriedly to his feet, picked up the catechism from the floor, and sat down.

The schoolgirl Jasína Gottfreðlína stood in the middle of the floor, scarlet in the face, out of breath, her eyes hot, and had just smoothed her skirt down when the housewife, Jarþrúður Jónsdóttir, came in. There was dust from the floor on her back; but she did not say anything and was not ashamed of anything.

Next day the ice on the river was bearing.

— 5 —

By tradition, Ólafur Kárason got three days' leave from the school to enable him to do some Christmas shopping at the trading station like all other good men. The route lay across the valley, over the river, up the mountain, through the Kaldsheiði Pass, and through another parish to Kaldsvík-undir-Kaldur, which was a big place. He was leading a packhorse. When he had a full load he set off homewards. It was two days before Christmas. A storm was blowing up and rapidly getting worse, torrential rain and gale-force winds and dreadful conditions underfoot. He had the wind against him. Darkness caught him on the mountain. But when he got down off the mountain at last that evening he shrank from tackling the Berá. He knew how much it rose in that kind of weather, and since he was not much of a traveler himself, he decided to seek shelter for the night on this side of the river. He made for the place where he thought he was most likely to be given refuge, and that was with the widow at Syðrivík, the aunt of his pupil Jasína Gottfreðlína.

The teacher was received with open arms in this little cottage and was treated with all hospitality. The cottage was only a shack, with two wooden walls and two of turf, standing on a grassy bank down by the sea, with seaweed spread on the homefield. The widow lived there with her half-grown son and a fifteen-year-old daughter and two younger children. They had some sheep and a cow, but the greatest luxury of the place was the surf with its eternal cadences of coming in and flowing out.

The poet was drenched to the skin, because he did not have much in the way of protective clothing; there was not a dry stitch on his body. The woman's children stabled the pony and brought the baggage in to the porch, while she made the poet go to bed at once and waited on him herself, spread his clothes to dry on the cooking stove, and gave him strong coffee laced with brennivín. Gradually the chill went out of the poet's body. Before long she brought him meat and soup, fresh milk and scones. She was a talkative woman, and she chatted to him from behind the stove and thanked him for her daughter Dóra, who had attended his school and learned some fine poems. She said that fine poems were the best capital any youngster could be given before starting out in life, rich and poor alike.

"Yes," said Ólafur Kárason. "Poetry is the Redeemer of the soul."

"So long as God gives the Icelandic nation poets, we shall never have cause to despair," said the woman.

Even though the house was small, the conversation contained the murmur of the farthest ocean.

The schoolgirl, Jasína Gottfreðlína, and her cousin Dóra sat side by side with their soup bowls in their laps, Dóra rather anemic and flaccid, talking in undertones and leaning against her friend and giggling, whereas the pupil did not know how to speak in undertones, and when she laughed it was open laughter, physical and straightforward, with moist gleaming teeth as if one were looking into the maw of a cub. The widow's young son came of the same giant line, insensitive to anything around him; he sat near the door, sunk in a heavy stupor over his soup and meat. The younger children had been put to bed. There was a fire in the stove, and the living room was warm. The widow recited some beautiful poems she said she always recited when things were difficult—shortage of food, illness, family bereavement—and when life smiled on her she also recited fine poems.

"Yes," she said. "It's absolutely true; poetry is the Redeemer of mankind."

As time passed, the poet became slower and slower to respond. It was so wonderful to be staying the night in a warm, dry place after the storm on Kaldsheiði, and to hear poetry appreciated properly, with everyone eating soup and meat, and the din of distant oceans reigning in the house. The present and the everyday, the remote and the eternal, merged into one in an almost supernaturally blissful way; and then he was asleep.

It was the sleep of a tired man, peaceful and deep and long. When he opened his eyes, there was a dim light burning in the living room. There was no fire in the stove and the room was rather cold, the storm had died down, no wind on the roof, and quiet apart from the desolate sound of the surf. He took his watch out from under the pillow and saw that the time was a few minutes past six. The two youngest children were fast asleep in a bed farther along the wall, but on the other side of the room the schoolgirl, Jasína Gottfreðlína, was half sitting up in bed and spelling her way through the *Children's Christian Primer* by the feeble light of the little lamp. There was no one else in the living room. He looked around carefully and was debating with himself whether to reveal that he was awake or pull the eiderdown over his head and go back to sleep. For a while he did not draw attention to himself and listened to the girl muttering; her method of reading was to say the words half-aloud to herself. He felt he would not be able to go back to sleep.

"Good-morning," he said.

But Jasína Gottfreðlína did not know how to bid someone Good-morning.

And then a strange thing happened; for when Ólafur Kárason had been lying there quietly for a while, he began to have a strange feeling in his nerves—later, he compared it to hanging by a thread—he was gripped by a strange trembling that started in his groin and then spread right through his whole body and became a steady shivering, and he could hardly breathe. He half sat up in bed in the hope of being able to shake it off, gasped for breath, and asked: "Where's the woman?"

"She's in the barn," replied the girl.

"And the older children?"

"They've gone to see to the sheep."

There was a short silence, and Ólafur Kárason went on shivering and the girl went on learning Christianity. Then he asked: "Are the people coming back soon?"

"No," she replied. "Not for ages yet."

"What about the little ones?" he said.

"The kids?" said the girl. "Can't you see they're asleep?"

"Do you think they're fast asleep?" he whispered.

"They sleep like hogs," said the girl. "They're always allowed to sleep until breakfast. I'm always woken up very early to do my lessons while the children are sleeping and the people are out."

"Yes, you're a good girl," he said.

"No, I'm not a good girl at all," she said.

"Soon you'll understand everything in the catechism," he said.

"I'm a simpleton and don't understand anything," she said. "Least of all the catechism. No matter how I go about it, I can never apply my mind to it. I'll undoubtedly never get confirmed."

"Yes, Jasína dear," he said. "You will be confirmed. When have I ever said that you're a simpleton? I say you're a good girl. If there's anything in the catechism you don't understand, I'll try to explain it to you."

"Just now?" she said.

"If you like," he said.

"I don't know how to ask," she said.

"I'll show you," he said.

He got out of bed, turned down the lamp so that the room was almost in darkness, and got into bed and under the covers beside her, took the *Children's Christian Primer* from her, and kissed her. At first she did not know what this was; then she opened her mouth. She was wearing tattered knitted drawers and she let him tear them off as if nothing were more natural. On the whole she made no attempt to prevent anything, she received him without any resistance, she just winced for a moment and bit her lip as if at a sudden and relatively harmless attack of gripe which was over before there had been time to cry out. She laid her young, strong arms round the poet's shoulders. A few minutes later he got out of her bed again and turned up the lamp. He said nothing, but the girl said, "What did you do with my catechism?"

He picked up the catechism off the floor and handed it to her, and she started spelling her way through it again in the same way as before, saying the words out loud as she read them. He went back to his own bed and waited for the woman to come back and give him his clothes which had been drying. He was no longer shivering, and felt very well. The children slept as before. The drowsy sound of the surf went on being the voice of the place. Then the widow came back, said Good-morning, asked how the visitor had slept, and began to light the fire.

Outside the weather was calm and it was freezing again; the river was bearing, the thaw had been too brief to affect the ice. The woman gave the visitor his clothes, dry and warm, and brought him steaming coffee to his bed. He wanted to leave at once when he was dressed, but she would not hear of letting him go before he had had breakfast. It was not so often they welcomed good visitors. The younger children got dressed, and the schoolgirl, Jasína Gottfreðlína, was also up. The two girls helped each other make the beds and clean the house. The woman went on talking, but Ólafur Kárason was now somewhat restless and quite a different person from the night before. He noticed that over Jasína's bed the girls began whispering as if they had found something unexpected, and next moment they had both vanished from the living room. When they came back, Ólafur had the impression that the widow's daughter was in a state of excitement and looked at him strangely, but Jasína Gottfreðlína was her usual self. The poet did not have much appetite. He managed to get hold of Jasína alone in the doorway when he was leaving, and was quick to whisper to her these words: "You must keep quiet about what happened; it can be a matter of life and death for us both. Remember that nothing happened."

She looked at him in amazement, slow on the uptake, almost nonplussed, but he had no opportunity to say more to her. The woman and the children came out into the yard and helped to put the packsaddle on the horse, bring out the baggage and load it up. Then they said Good-bye to the poet and bade him farewell, grateful to God for such a visitor.

6

Early on the morning of Christmas Eve a man passed the homefield at Little Bervík leading some packhorses, heading towards Greater Bervík. The poet was standing in front of the house; it was his custom when he saw travelers in the vicinity of the cottage to go to meet them and offer them coffee.

"Good-day!" he shouted.

It was Jason the lighthouse keeper at Taungar. He did not return the poet's greeting. Ólafur Kárason said Good-day again. At that the traveler halted and shouted back: "I'm not in the habit of greeting criminals! You have grossly harmed my daughter! This insult shall be avenged!"

"I don't understand what you're talking about," said Ólafur Kárason.

"I'm talking about the disgrace you have done me and my family. My family and I, we are of royal lineage; my genealogy goes back to Sigurður Fáfnisbani (Fáfnir's-Slayer). When Icelanders were worthy of the name, it was considered an accepted duty to avenge with a sword the sort of crime you have committed against my family. It's a bitter thing to be living at a time when one may not challenge to single combat the man who has disgraced one's family, and carve a blood-eagle on his back!"

"Your way of talking condemns itself, sir," said Ólafur Kárason. "I shall make no reply."

"If there is a trace of justice left in this land, your deeds will bring you to the gallows!"

"No fear of that, sir," said the poet. "We'll all end up where we belong in good time. That's why there's no hurry. So let's talk about this calmly and fraternally, like men."

"I would be ashamed to be descended from the men of old if I talked fraternally to a scoundrel," said the man, and went on his way.

Ólafur Kárason remained standing on the doorstep for a long time after the visitor was out of earshot. Then he went inside.

His wife pulled her long, pendulous breast out of her cardigan and started feeding the child. The poet paced about the room for a long time. Finally he brushed his hair from his sweating brow and addressed her.

"Jarþrúður, I have something to tell you that weighs heavily upon me," he said.

"It must be quite something if you're taking the trouble of telling me about it!" said his wife.

"I must ask you to try to wear a human expression on your face, Jarþrúður," he said.

"Dear Jesus in Heaven!" she said. "Are you going to frighten me?'"

"If you put on that kind of expression, as if you're on intimate terms with the deity, I cannot talk to you, Jarþrúður," he said.

"I've always had the feeling you would one day bring down some terrible calamity upon me!" she said.

"Very well," he said. "In that case I'd better not tell you anything, and let you hear it from others instead."

"In the name of the Father, the Son and the Holy Ghost!" she said.

"Yes, of all the imperfect things that man has created, the gods are the most imperfect," he said impatiently.

Then the woman removed her breast from the infant's mouth and asked simply, "What has happened?"

As soon as she stopped invoking the Holy Trinity, they calmed down, and he began to talk. He told her about his difficult journey over the moor the day before yesterday in the teeth of the wind and the rain, and how it was dark by the time he came down off the mountain, with the river unsafe, so that he sought shelter for the night at Syðrivík. He was exhausted and in a bad state, and the widow made him go to bed at once. To get the chill out of him she gave him some brennivín in his coffee. But when he woke up in the morning he was feeling very odd, he did not really know what it was, there was such a feeling of strangeness about everything, a feeling of desolation, he felt as if he were hanging by a thread, and the pounding of the surf was the heartbeat of this place. He felt as if the ocean were reigning in this house, and he had no control of himself any more and began to shiver. He had not the slightest idea what it was that was affecting his actions, but one thing was certain. He got out of bed and into another bed, and in it there lay a young girl who was learning her catechism, and he turned down the lamp and took her catechism from her.

"And then what?" asked the wife.

"She was practically naked," he said, unnaturally calm.

"And then?" asked the wife.

"It's really extraordinarily simple to be human," he said. "I've never understood how it's possible to think of guilt and sin and such-like in connection with human life; and yet I think it's even more ridiculous to imagine the god being angry in connection with it."

"What did you do?" asked the wife.

"Do?" he repeated. "What does anyone do? One lives. That's all. Is there anything more natural? Is there anything more simple? On the other hand, it certainly wasn't very prudent of me to go to the girl. The Conscience of the Nation passed by just now and wanted to carve a blood-eagle on my back."

"Who was the girl?" asked the wife.

"One of my pupils," he said. "Jasína Gottfreðlína."

"I knew it!" said the wife. "Do you think I hadn't noticed those mare's eyes of hers? Creatures like that should be flogged beforehand."

"There's no point in speaking ill of this young girl," he said. "And there's no question of flogging anyone, before or after. To do something is just as right as not to do something; to be is just as right as not to be. Let's not concern ourselves with the fact that the gods that man has created are stupid and imperfect, and their laws likewise. The problem is to know how to behave prudently in conformity with human society; and that's something I have never known how to do in anything. This ignorance has often cost me dear, but seldom have things looked as black as they do now. A dark shadow may fall over this little cottage of ours, Jarþrúður."

What surprised the poet most was that when he had confessed to his wife she did not rage or storm or invoke the gods, but received this information with the same kind of stoical calm as the natural death of a child. After some thought she asked if he suspected that something would be done in the matter.

He told her that the lighthouse keeper must have spent the night at his sister's, on his way home from the trading station; and he had just passed by on his way to the bailiff's.

The wife was silent for a while, and then asked, "How's the river today?"

He said the ice was bearing.

"Then we'll walk over to Syðrivík," she said. "We'll take the little baby with us. It could be that even if they don't want to have mercy on us, they'll have mercy on the child."

Hope springs eternal in the human breast. All of a sudden, God's Word had been stanched in her, she even stopped abusing Jasína Gottfreðlína; he listened in amazement to her saying "we" and "our" about his case. Perhaps today for the first time he was really seeing the person who had been his companion for ten years.

After that the couple gave themselves and Jón Ólafsson a thorough wash, put on their Sunday-best clothes, and dressed Jón Ólafsson in his best frock. It was a calm day with a slight frost, frozen snow, solid ice on the river. They walked down to the river without a word, Sunday-suited and grave, the husband carrying his son wrapped in a blanket.

The Syðrivík widow greeted the couple from little Bervík reasonably well, but her cheerful cordiality of the previous morning had cooled somewhat; there was another atmosphere about the house, the sea was dead. The widow told them not to stand outside in the cold with the child, and invited them inside.

"Thank you, there's really no need," said the poet's wife. "We only wanted to have a word with little Jasína Gottfreðlína, your niece, who is staying with you."

They went inside. The two girls were finishing their Christmas cleaning, there was only a small corner of the living room left to scrub. The schoolgirl, Jasína Gottfreðlína, did not take off her sacking apron when she was summoned to meet the poet's wife. She had just finished drinking some coffee, and she wiped her mouth on both forearms, one after the other. The housewife ordered the younger children outside, and called her daughter over to the other end of the living room.

"Little Jasína," said the poet's wife, and lifted the baby to her breast and hugged it as if to protect it. "We want to ask you something which is perhaps unimportant, but which could affect all of us, not just this innocent little baby and Ólafur, but also you and me. Do you think, if you had to swear to it before God on the Day of Judgment, that Ólafur has done you any harm that you have to make a complaint about?"

The girl answered at once, in a loud voice, "Make a complaint? Me? I haven't made any complaints. I just told what happened. And it wasn't anything."

"All right, Jasína dear," said the wife. "Since it wasn't anything, as I'm sure it wasn't, then it doesn't matter either if you tell me exactly what did happen."

"You should ask him," said the schoolgirl, and pointed to Ólafur. "I can't be bothered going over something again and again that wasn't anything. It wasn't really anything much, and it's all the same to me if it's all the same to you, and I'm not angry at all if you're not angry."

"Are you then ready, Jasína dear, to declare anywhere and in front of anyone at all, both God and the authorities, that it wasn't anything?"

"I'm never going to mention it again, least of all before God and the authorities," said the schoolgirl. "And I would never have mentioned it to anyone if it had been something. I only mentioned it in fun because it wasn't anything."

Then Ólafur Kárason said, "To whom did you mention it?"

The schoolgirl: "I only mentioned it to my cousin, Dóra."

The poet: "Why?"

"Just for a laugh," said the girl. "Dóra and I are always thinking up things to laugh at. How on earth was I to know that Dóra was going to start blabbing about it? The first thing I knew this morning was that Daddy, who stayed the night here, said I deserved to be flogged in public. And so I naturally told him just to try to flog me if he dared."

Then the widow came forward and spoke: "I know that you're not such a simpleton, Ólafur Kárason, as to imagine that individuals can settle this sort of thing according to their own wish and by agreement; you must realize that it's the law that settles this sort of case. But it wasn't because I wanted to get anyone into trouble that I told my brother about this, but because I think it's a hazard to have someone so misguided in charge of the instruction of the young."

The poet asked if it had been decided to report him to the authorities and have him arrested.

"I'm not reporting you to any authorities," said the woman. "But God knows that I would rather have lost one of my own children than to have this happen under my own roof. I asked myself, What is the point of fine poems if poets are wicked people? And not least was I distressed when I thought of your Jarþrúður; and your child. But I would have considered myself an accessory to this . . . misfortune that has happened under my roof if I hadn't told the girl's father the truth about what took place."

Then Jarþrúður said, "It doesn't matter at all about me, a wretch in body and soul, as everyone knows, and corrupted by sin from childhood; but if they're going to make Ólafur Kárason out to be a criminal and wreck his home and cast an indelible shadow over his little child, then there is no justice on earth any more, and not in Heaven either, may God forgive me. Because if ever an innocent and pure-hearted person has been born on this earth, a person who couldn't hurt any living creature and has never thought ill of any living person, but has tried to embrace everyone with affection and gentleness, it is he."

For the second time that day, Ólafur Kárason looked as in a dream at this unknown woman who shielded his child in her arms as if to protect it against axe-blows and spear-thrusts. In her moist seaweed eyes there was a new radiance; her defense was governed by an unshakable natural certainty and instinctive reaction, utterly free from any weeping or whining; this was completely new to her husband. The schoolgirl Jasína had until now been standing facing her rival with her head held high, her legs apart and her stomach forward, with obstinacy in her eyes and electricity in her hair, not fully understanding the deeper significance of this encounter. But now, when she realized that she had a share in wrecking her teacher's home and casting an indelible shadow over the little child, her bearing suddenly sagged, and she bent her head, lifted her sacking apron to her eyes, and burst into tears.

"If I had known that Ólafur Kárason would be made to suffer for it, I would never have told anyone about it," she said through her tears. "Ólafur Kárason can always, always do to me everything, everything he wants to, and it will never, never have been anything!"

Further discussion was unnecessary for the time being; the solution of the affair was in the hands of the fates, or rather of those powers which see to it that everything comes to an end in one way or another. The teacher and his wife waited while the widow made coffee, and Jón Ólafsson was given a stick of brown candy to play with. The schoolgirl Jasína and her cousin Dóra made haste to scrub the last corner of the living room, because it was almost the holy hour of Christmas Eve. They did not say anything, did not even look at one another, but sniffed in turn. Nothing much was said after this; everyone was deeply troubled about the future despite the approaching Christmas festival of the Savior. When the visitors had drunk the coffee and eaten their bread in silence, they stood up and took their leave, and people wished each other a merry Christmas and a good and happy New Year.

— 7 —

Between Christmas and New Year, Ólafur Kárason was summoned
to Kaldsvík to appear in court. He set off early in the morning with a
scarf round his neck and a few slices of bread in his pocket. His wife
wanted to accompany him with Jón Ólafsson, because she had the
peculiar belief that the court would be moved at seeing a baby; but
the poet flatly refused to accept this escort. He reached the trading
station shortly after noon, and went to the courthouse where he was
to present himself; it was just like any other courthouse—rusting
corrugated iron, creaking walls, broken steps, faulty door-handles
and sagging hinges. Inside, a small group of people sat waiting on
benches made of unplaned wooden boards; their breaths made a
freezing mist in the air; the windowpanes were thick with hoarfrost.
Ólafur Kárason raised his cap and said Good-day, and got only a
reluctant response. He could just make out the bailiff's face through
the mist, as well as the schoolgirl Jasína Gottfreðlína, the lighthouse
keeper, and the mother and daughter from Syðrivík. Everyone was
freezing.

"Is the sheriff not here yet?" said Ólafur Kárason when he had
been sitting for a while and was getting cold.

The bailiff explained that the sheriff had come specially for this
court-sitting from Aðalfjörður that morning—"And when have
scoundrels and suspicious characters refrained from inconveniencing
the authorities and other honest men in the middle of winter in a
hard frost, yes, and even in the middle of the Christmas festival?" The
widow from Syðrivík said that at the moment the sheriff was at
table in the home of Kristinsen the merchant. The lighthouse keeper
said he did not understand how the people who lived in Iceland at
present could be descended from the men of old. Ólafur Kárason
said nothing. People went on waiting and freezing, and the young
girls blew into their hands. Eventually the bailiff started pacing the
floor and cursing, and said that the sheriff had been eating for three
hours. The lighthouse keeper said that the Danes had corrupted the

Icelandic nation; he said that Danish merchants had always cowed the common people and led the officials astray. The widow from Syðrivík tried to smooth things over, and said that the merchant Kristinsen was only Danish by descent, and only on one side at that.

"Then why don't we get roast meat?" asked her brother, the lighthouse keeper, angrily.

"Did we come here to eat roast meat, then?" replied the woman.

"I don't care what you say," said the lighthouse keeper. "In my eyes, all merchants are Danish."

Finally the bailiff said that as bailiff he could not justify keeping the witnesses waiting any longer in this damned cold; he appointed the lighthouse keeper to deputize for him, and set off in search of the sheriff. And they went on waiting.

At last, heavy footsteps and loud voices were heard in the vestibule, and the door was thrown open. The sheriff appeared in the doorway—a mountainous man with the outsize face of a red sea perch, wearing several overcoats, a fur hat, and high boots. In his wake came a number of lesser officials, including the sheriff's clerk with the court record books under his arm, and the county doctor. The sheriff sat down at a table, took off his fur hat and clapped a little skullcap over his bald pate, ordered the record books to be opened, and gave instructions for the witnesses to be kept in the vestibule and brought before him one at a time.

First he made the widow from Syðrivík give evidence of identification of the schoolgirl, Jasína Gottfreðlína Jasonardóttir, and then about the arrival of the primary schoolteacher, Ólafur Kárason, at Syðrivík two nights before Christmas. What was the visitor's condition that evening, what were the circumstances in the house next morning, what had the girl said about what happened while the others were out? About the latter, the widow testified that her daughter Dóra had taken her aside when Ólafur Kárason had gone, and said, "'Mummy, Jasína says the teacher got into bed with her this morning.' 'Into bed with her, what nonsense is this?' I said. Then my daughter said, 'There's blood in the bed.' 'What nonsense you talk,' I said. But when I took a look for myself, it was true. And when I asked the girl herself, she said that all of a sudden he had got into bed with her and taken her catechism away and put out the light. 'Did you let him harm you?' I asked, and she replied, 'I hardly felt a thing, and he was away in no time.'"

The cousin, Dóra, was called next, and was asked how the school-girl Jasína had described what had taken place between her and the teacher that morning. The girl was more dead than alive from cold and anguish, and her teeth chattered in her mouth. The sheriff's questions soon became too coarse for this sensitive body, and when she did nothing but tremble in front of the sheriff, delicate and ane-mic, there was nothing for it but to remove her and put her into someone else's hands.

The schoolgirl, Jasína Gottfreðlína Jasonardóttir, only just four-teen years old, said she had been reading the *Children's Christian Primer* that morning after the housewife and the older children had gone out to see to the sheep and the cows. When she had been read-ing for a while, the visitor, her schoolteacher, woke up and said Good-morning. She said she had not made any reply. He had spoken a few more words to her, she could not remember what about, except that he had offered to explain the catechism to her. Then what? Then nothing. Did he not get into bed with her? Not really to speak of, he was feeling a little cold, he had scarcely touched her, then he went back to his own bed at once and she went on reading her catechism. What had she told Dóra? A lot of nonsense! They were always mak-ing up things to laugh at. Then the sheriff became very friendly and asked how Jasína Gottfreðlína liked Ólafur Kárason as a teacher and a person. Jasína Gottfreðlína said that Ólafur Kárason was a very nice person. The Sheriff asked with an oily fish-smile if she did not think Ólafur Kárason handsome.

She replied, "I'm not telling anyone that."

At that the smile vanished abruptly from the sheriff's face, along with all the more agreeable characteristics of the sea perch, and in its place came the expression of a sea scorpion. He glared at her with cold, empty, slimy eyes and started asking her the sort of questions that at their mildest were at least on a par with ordinary rape, while some of them would undoubtedly have made even the most hard-

ened prostitute blanch. At first the young girl did not know what he
was driving at, and was tongue-tied; but when she began to feel out-
raged, she replied bluntly, "I'd never even dream of answering such
drivel!"

At that the sheriff asserted himself more forcefully and asked if the
witness were aware that she was standing before the authorities?

The schoolgirl replied, "There are no authorities over me."

The schoolteacher, Ólafur Kárason, described how he had come
to Syðrivík, cold and exhausted in darkness and foul weather, and
asked for shelter for the night. The widow made him go to bed at
once and gave him some brennivín. He said he was quite unaccustomed to brennivín and the effect had been that first he had fallen
fast asleep in the middle of a conversation with the widow, and later
had woken up extremely early with a strange feeling in his nerves as if
he were hanging by a thread, and cold shivers. He said he was anxious to avoid saying anything which might be construed as ingratitude for the hospitality he had received, but undeniably the eiderdown
had been on the short side and the bed cold. He also explained that
there had been a strange soughing sound of surf in the house. To get
rid of the cold shivers, he said he had crept into bed beside his pupil
but had gone away again quickly when it occurred to him that this
move might be misinterpreted. He firmly denied that he had done
the girl any harm. The sheriff now started questioning him insis-
tently, but Ólafur Kárason was a past master at evading awkward
questions; finally, however, he said that he did not dare to deny on
oath that he had had an ejaculation in the warmth under the schoolgirl's eiderdown, but on the other hand he steadfastly denied that he
had had criminal intercourse with her. Then the sheriff instructed
the clerk to read out the certificate that the doctor had signed after
examining the schoolgirl the day before; this examination had revealed
injuries for which there was no natural explanation for a girl of her
age. The torn pieces of a pair of drawers, and bedclothes with blood-
stains on them, were produced as evidence against the teacher.

Then the witnesses were brought in again and again and interro-
gated until weakness had overcome them and every trace of modesty
had been expunged from them as thoroughly as from the authorities

themselves. The girl had started to give answers to various questions about her earlier relations with the teacher which did not concern this case at all: she told the story of his light cuffs and their scuffle one evening, of how she had flown at him in a temper as she often did with her father, and how he had tripped her and thrown her to the floor. The sheriff asked if he had not lifted her skirt, but at that she hastily said No; the sheriff asked if he had not unfastened any of her buttons, but she said that was a lie. But when this point had been reached, her evasions were nearing their end. When her modesty had been sufficiently dulled, and cold and hunger had allied themselves with the sheriff against her strength, she suddenly blurted it all out before she knew what she was doing: yes, he had done this on the morning before Christmas Eve; and he had also done the other; yes, first this, then the other. And then she came to her senses again and realized she had said too much, and hastened to add that she had not really felt a thing, it did not matter at all, it was not really anything, it was not even worth mentioning.

On the other hand, Ólafur Kárason stuck firmly to his earlier testimony despite hunger, cold, and weariness; no, he had not done this and he had not done the other either. The girl must be imagining things. The sheriff was sustained by the merchant's roast beef and was livelier than ever, and the questions went on raining down. It was late in the evening. Finally Ólafur Kárason stopped answering, let his head droop down on to his chest, and closed his eyes. At that the sheriff ordered him to be arrested, and adjourned the court.

8

The sheriff decided to ride home to Aðalfjörður through Gamlafellsdalur that evening, and asked for men and horses to transport the prisoner, whom he was going to take with him. As soon as the hearing was over, he himself went to the merchant's for supper with his retinue. He deputized Jason, farmer and lighthouse keeper, to guard the prisoner while he was having his meal.

The mountain from which the village took its name was called

Kaldur. It was freezing hard, and the snow was drifting a little; a half-moon glistened on the sea and on the rime-covered cliffs where the surf growled menacingly in the night breeze.

The prisoner and his guard stood in the open yard in front of the merchant's house down by the sea, with orders not to move from there before the sheriff was finished. The news of who was in the yard soon spread, and a few young girls went out of their way to have a look at the criminal. It was difficult to say offhand which of them was the criminal, but the majority of the girls inclined to the view that Jason the lighthouse keeper would be the one. A few young men from the village also arrived. One of them thought he knew who they were, and said that Jason the lighthouse keeper was not the criminal; it was the lanky one. At that the boys and girls raised their voices and jeered at the poet with tolerably witty jibes, from ordinary obscenities to the foulest language imaginable. But when it came to the bit, Jason the lighthouse keeper could not avoid feeling that he was, despite everything, related to this poet now, and realized that blood was thicker than water; besides which, the crown authorities had placed this man in his custody; so he thought he was within his rights to speak to this mob as roughly as he pleased, and told them all to go to Hell.

Gradually the young foulmouths dispersed, but in their place came two drunks who asked why these damned peasants were hanging around here. No doubt they were waiting to waylay the merchant to trick some work out of him which belonged by rights to honest folk and good Kaldsvíkings; they said they would live and die for Kaldsvík, and invited the strangers to the sort of trial of strength in which one or other, but not both, would live to tell the tale. Jason the lighthouse keeper fought them both and put them both down and sent them home and told them to go to bed, while the prisoner stood in the lee of the wall of the house and blew into his hands and stamped his feet to pass the time.

"Well, then," said the lighthouse keeper when he had put the Kaldsvíkings to flight, "it was a stroke of luck to get these damned ruffians to warm oneself on. By the way, aren't you getting hungry, lad?"

"Oh, just a little, perhaps," said the poet.

"Have you brought anything with you?"

"I've got some slices of bread in my pocket, certainly," said the poet. "But I thought it perhaps wasn't appropriate to start eating, the way things are with me at present; at least, not without permission."

"Of course you must eat, whatever the circumstances!" said the guard. "Nothing ever made Halldór Snorrason* lose his appetite. None can act on an empty stomach. As your guard I give you full permission to eat."

It was a matter of honor for Jason the lighthouse keeper to carry out his custodial duties most conscientiously, but not without tempering justice with mercy.

The poet took the bread out of his pocket without stopping shuffling and stamping his feet; his hands were so numbed that he had to hold the bread between his clenched fists when he bit into it. He became a little warmer when he started chewing. A few gulls came gliding in from the sea over the yard, and the poet broke off some pieces of his bread and threw them to the birds. The guard had some food in a kerchief, better and more of it than Ólafur Kárason had, and he gave the prisoner a slice of smoked lamb. They sat down on the steps of the merchant's house and ate in the frost, and there was a ring around the moon. There were lights in all the windows of the house and sounds of great revelry from within, loud arguments, funny anecdotes, nose-blowings by the bailiff, singing, the clatter of cutlery, the clink of glasses. Now and again they caught the fragrance of roast, coffee and tobacco smoke.

When the prisoner and his guard had fed for a while, the latter broke the silence anew.

"Well then, lad," he said. "You're a poet, and that's why I want to know what you think about Gunnar of Hlíðarendi. Don't you think that Gunnar of Hlíðarendi is the greatest man who ever lived in Iceland?"

"Oh, I wouldn't say that," said the poet. "But he was undoubtedly one of the great men in many respects."

"Oh, he was a great man in every respect, man," said Jason the lighthouse keeper. "And, he was the only man in the Sagas of whom it was said, clearly and explicitly, that he jumped his own height forwards and backwards wearing full armor. It even gives the place and the time: if I remember rightly it was out east in Estonia, in the battle with the brothers Hallgrímur and Kolskeggur on the occasion when Gunnar won the halberd. He leapt backwards over a boom on the ship to avoid a lethal spear-thrust, and saved his life thereby."

"Yes," said the poet. "And here we sit outside other people's doors."

"Eh?" said the guard. "Who was saying anything about that?"

"No one," said the poet. "But all sorts of things can come to mind."

"Gunnar of Hlíðarendi comes to my mind on many occasions," said the guard. "In moonlight like this, it comes to mind that he was one of the few Icelanders who have composed just as good poetry after death as when they were alive. It was on a night like this that he turned in his cairn, looked at the moon, and said:

> "'Hogni's generous father,
> Rich in daring exploits,
> Who lavishly gave battle
> Distributing wounds gladly,
> Claims that in his helmet,
> Towering like an oak tree
> In the forest of the battle,
> He would rather die than yield,
> Much rather die than yield.'

"I regard that as the best verse that exists in the Icelandic language even though it was composed by a dead man. And it's a great spiritual inspiration for someone from the Outer Nesses to think back to the time when the nation really could be called a nation and lived in the land. There's no fighting in Iceland any more, except when infamous poltroons and wretches molest innocent folk in a drunken frenzy."

Then Ólafur Kárason said, "And here we sit on someone's threshold shivering in the night, you a hero and I a poet: two beggars."

"What? Are you out of your mind?" said the guard. "When was I ever a beggar? If you're cold, here's some twelve-year-old shark-meat—or rather, thirteen-year-old."

"Many thanks," said the poet. "I've no doubt that shark-meat is wholesome food, but unfortunately I cannot stand either the smell or the taste of it."

At that the lighthouse keeper became impassioned, and said that this was these damned modern times all over: to prefer to die rather than smell. "It's a scandal and a disgrace to call such people Icelanders who are ashamed of smelling of shark-meat!"

"I hope you won't be angry with me, my dear Jason, if I put one question to you," said the poet. "I must emphasize that you don't need to answer it if you don't want to. Do you think that Kjartan Ólafsson ate twelve-year-old shark-meat on the day he proposed to Guðrún Ósvífrsdóttir?"*

"I can't be sure about that," said the lighthouse keeper. "But I do know that the men of old had nothing at all in common with the present band of leaders who despise the common people. And Guðrún Ósvífrsdóttir wasn't ashamed of doing her washing in a stream even though she was a great woman: and she spun twelve ells of yarn on the morning Kjartan was slain."

When they had finished eating they sat on the steps for a little while longer, but the festivities inside the house showed no signs of ending. The guard was beginning to grow uneasy.

"For my own part it's obviously immaterial to me what becomes of me, the way things have turned out," said the poet. "But I wouldn't be surprised if I had developed pneumonia by tomorrow."

"No man could stay in Jómsborg* who lost heart or showed fear in the face of danger," said Jason the lighthouse keeper. "Take a turn along the shore to get some warmth into your body."

The poet Ólafur Kárason now started to flail his arms and jump about in the yard with bizarre gestures; the guard paced to and fro under the merchant's windows, glowering, but after the twelve-year-old shark-meat he was impervious to cold. Finally the prisoner grew tired of jumping about and came back into the lee of the house.

"Did that warm you up?" said the guard.

"I'm afraid not," said the poet. "I've got a stitch in the chest."

Jason now found himself in a dilemma. As a veteran public servant in the Taungar lighthouse, he was aware of the importance of carrying out faithfully the duties entrusted to him by the authorities; and according to the letter of the law it was his task to guard this prisoner whatever happened, irrespective of whether the man got pneumonia or died of exposure out here in the yard. But nonetheless, compassion continued to sway in the guard's breast; the duty of one human being to another is above the law and above public office, irrespective of what is entrusted to us by the authorities, irrespective of whether it concerns a criminal who has disgraced our family, or a good friend and son-in-law.

"Perhaps the sheriff has changed his mind about taking you to Aðalfjörður tonight," said the guard.

"Perhaps he's forgotten all about us," said Ólafur Kárason.

"If you like, I could knock at the door and ask on your behalf, as the party directly concerned, what the sheriff intends to do," said the guard.

It was a long time before anyone came to the door. After protracted knocking, a woman opened the door and asked what was going on, was everything in heaven and earth going mad, or what? The guard explained in his best official voice that two men were waiting here outside, a prisoner and his guard, and the former wished to know whether the sheriff was still determined to ride through Gamlafellsdalur that night.

The woman promised to make enquiries, disappeared into the house again, and shut the door behind her. After a while, someone came to the door once more. The sheriff's clerk lurched into the doorway, very drunk, and asked, not without arrogance although his speech was thick, who was presuming to disturb the state's officials at this time of night?

"The prisoner asked me to ask the sheriff . . ." began Jason the lighthouse keeper, but the clerk interrupted at once and said, "The sheriff says the prisoner can go to Hell!"

With that the clerk slammed the door in the guard's face.

After this brief and pithy message from the banquet, the two cold men of the night went on sitting side by side on the doorstep for a long time without exchanging a word. The surf creamed itself on the glistening rocks and threw its spray against the silk-smooth seaweed in the moonlight, and the drifting snow swept across the ice-covered yard in eddies as in a dance where the dancer whirls round and vanishes in a swirl of snow-white veils. Finally the guard broke the silence anew.

"You who are a poet," he said, "and therefore see matters more clearly and profoundly than other people, will you answer me one question? Aren't you sometimes, when you're alone, appalled at the oppression which we Icelanders have had to suffer from the Danes down the centuries?"

"If I'm allowed to see a little corner of the sky," said the poet, "then I'm prepared to forgive everyone."

"My grandmother told me that in her great-grandmother's day there came an ordinance from the king that all the copper in Iceland was to be taken abroad. They went into every church in the province and made a clean sweep of them all. Candlesticks and chandeliers, all of them choice treasures, were torn away and carried off to ships. But the worst of all was when they took down the church bells in Bervík church, which were famous throughout the land for the beauty of their chimes. They had been there since before the Reformation. These lovely-sounding bells the Danes broke into small pieces so that they were easier to carry in packsaddles and transported them down to the shore. Then the copper was melted down and used for palace roofs in Copenhagen."

"I've never had a grandmother, a great-grandmother, nor a great-great-grandmother," said the poet. "I never even had a mother. I have certainly missed a great deal of love thereby, but fortune has compensated me by not giving me the capacity to hate anyone, neither nations nor individuals. If candlesticks and church bells have been plundered from my ancestors, then I'm only grateful that I'm so ignorant about genealogy."

"In my family there was a man who farmed a tenant's cottage near

Bervík, who inherited the last six sheets that were found of *Korpin-skinna*, whose every sheet was assessed at a hundred hundreds in land values; and if these sheets could have been kept in the family I would now be the wealthiest man in Iceland and could order the government about. But the king got the pastor at Bervík to wheedle those sheets from my ancestor in exchange for some stockfish, and they were sent to Denmark, where the main part of the codex had already been taken. And now it's called the greatest book ever written in the North and the finest treasure in the whole Danish empire, and it's kept in a special palace in Copenhagen; but the Icelanders never got anything in exchange from the Danes, except hunger."

By the time the lighthouse keeper had recalled a few more instances of Danish oppression, and the humiliations the Icelanders had had to suffer at the hands of that race, he was in a towering rage. The party inside the merchant's house was at its height: singing, laughter, and other sounds of revelry came pouring out in waves into the night into the still assembly of stars where these two eternal Icelanders sat, the poet and the hero. At last the guard stopped talking and was gazing up at the window with a not-very-amiable expression on his face. It was already long past midnight. Finally he made his decision, went up to the front door for the second time, and started knocking. No one showed any sign of coming to the door. He knocked with increasing force. Eventually the door was cautiously opened, and the same woman as before peered out and asked what on earth was going on in the middle of the night.

"I'm the one who is knocking at the door," said the man. "My name is Jason Gottfreðsson, farmer and lighthouse keeper from Taungar, and tonight I was deputized by the sheriff to guard a prisoner while he was having his meal. It's now almost morning and the sheriff has been eating all night, and I refuse to hang around here any longer and I demand to know what is to be done with the man."

"The sheriff certainly won't want to attend to any official business now," said the woman. "He's a private citizen tonight."

"I insist on talking to the sheriff, or else I shall renounce all responsibility for the prisoner," said Jason the lighthouse keeper.

The woman went back into the house and shut the door, but after a short while someone came to the door again. This time it was the groom; he was extremely drunk.

"I demand to speak to the sheriff!" said Jason.

"You've got a nerve, being cheeky to the authorities!" said the groom.

"As the guard of this prisoner, I demand to speak to the sheriff!" repeated Jason.

"The sheriff says the guard can go to Hell!" said the groom, made a grab at the door-handle as he staggered, and slammed the door as he reeled backwards.

The man on the outside shook his fist at the windows with appropriate curses, and said that without any doubt those who were quickest to condemn others deserved the gallows most of all; he said he spat on all justice in Iceland, and stamped off in a rage. Such was his abrupt parting with his prisoner. Ólafur Kárason gazed after his guard for a while, but soon lost sight of him in the darkness and drifting snow. But when he showed no sign of returning, the prisoner became uneasy and set off into the village to look for him. "Jason!" he called out. "Jason Gottfreðsson, where are you?" But it was all to no avail. Perhaps the man was already on his way home? What was Ólafur Kárason to do? There were no lights in any windows, and he had no friends here he could expect to give him shelter for the night—least of all the way things were with him now. He was left standing there alone in the depths of the night, a prisoner without a guard, and the drifting snow swirled around him mournfully in the blue moonlight.

— 9 —

When the sheriff woke up next morning, he was somewhat bad-tempered and not feeling too well in the head. He drank a few raw eggs and turned his face to the wall again; but then the clerk arrived, who was feeling even more fragile, and said that the prisoner had escaped during the night and had probably killed his guard and hidden the body.

"Hidden the body?" said the sheriff, and sat up again.

One thing was certain; neither hide nor hair of the two men was to be found. No one had seen them since late the previous evening when a few girls had taken a stroll down to the yard to have a look at the criminal. The sheriff now forced himself to crawl out of bed and ordered a posse to be raised in the village to hunt for the prisoner. People were sent out to the surrounding districts, and a search was also made along the shore for the guard's body.

But luckily it quickly came to light that all this alarm was just a mild attack of delirium tremens in the sheriff's immediate entourage. At breakfast time the prisoner was found sleeping in a little cottage half an hour's walk from Kaldsvík. He had woken up the people there in the early hours of the morning, more dead than alive from cold, and begged for help. When the authorities' searchers arrived, he was sound asleep and dreaming dreams. But it was not long before he was disturbed from this congenial occupation, dragged out of bed, and handed over to the sheriff again. The sheriff and his clerk, as well as the groom, were still in a state of feeling afraid of their own criminals, and were therefore convinced that a man like Ólafur Kárason would stop at nothing. The sheriff ordered the prisoner to be tied to the tail of a horse to ensure that he did not run away, and since most of those involved turned out to be unfamiliar with this technique, he supervised the work himself and gave instructions as to how it was to be done. First the man's hands were tied behind his back, then a rope was passed under his armpits and round his chest and shoulders, and then securely fastened to a horse's tail.

At a certain point a man ceases to care, and in its place there comes another capacity which is at once a more effective weapon and a stronger shield: the capacity to endure. The fish wriggles on the hook, it is said that the sheep is begging for mercy if it bleats in the slaughterhouse, the cat shows its claws in the snare and spits in its murderer's face; but no one can deny a man his last shred of dignity and personal liberty with impunity. There comes a point when no act of violence can hurt a vanquished poet's pride any more. Ólafur Kárason of Ljósavík had an invisible friend whom no one had ever succeeded in naming. Not only did he dull the feelings the more, the sharper the weapons that were used, but he also laid life's healing balm on every wound. He lent the face of the humiliated a majesty which was beyond life's fortitude, so that even the most powerful enemy appeared trivial.

Ólafur Kárason of Ljósavík was not angry with anyone. Nothing was personal any more. He no longer saw individuals, but only the whole world; even less did he impute evil motives to anyone for any single action. He was face to face with justice, not people, least of all individuals. And this was the first time in his life since he was kicked on the head by a horse that he was not afraid of anything any more, perhaps the first time in his life he had felt well, the first time he had felt like a truly happy man, a man whom no misfortune could befall any more.

When the expedition had set off at last and the village spectators had had their fill of entertainment for the time being and had gone home, and the sheriff had whipped up his horse and ridden on ahead with his clerk and groom, Ólafur Kárason's physical senses began to come to life again; he began to distinguish individual features in his surroundings, to see people, horses, earth, even clouds.

"Well, well, my lad, I knew we were bound to have another journey together sometime!" said his escort cheerfully.

"Why, hallo, if it isn't Reimar the poet!" said Ólafur Kárason. "How very nice to see you again! Where have you been all this time?"

Reimar Vagnsson, major poet, had been living in a number of different fjords, because a man, and particularly a poet, is not a plant but a creature of mobility; he was traveling a lot, often as a postman, always ready to cross a mountain or two if the government had need of a reliable man.

"I'm ashamed of myself for not recognizing you at once," said Ólafur Kárason. "Yet I have every reason for remembering our first journey, and the joy that reigned in the world then."

"Yes, there were no cares in the world then, my lad," said Reimar the poet.

"Yes, it was fine weather then, all right," said Ólafur Kárason. "Why won't the Lord create the same day more than once, one day of happiness like that one, and then repeat it forever from then onwards? Do you remember how I was raised from the dead?"

"Oh, our Reimar can never go past Kambar now without shedding a tear," said Reimar the poet. "Those girls there really knew how to give contact! They gave contact on both a natural and a supernatural plane; contact with heaven and earth; in a word—contact; what a current, what trembling, my God! Yes, they were glorious creatures!"

"To me they gave contact on a supernatural plane," said Ólafur Kárason. "But I was never quite clear what they gave you. But don't think for a moment that I'm going to start asking you about matters of conscience after ten years, my dear friend."

"Look," said Reimar the poet, and grew serious as people inevitably do when they start talking about their own subject. "The Kambar girls were obviously no exception to other women in that they needed time and opportunity. Women aren't machines that can be set in motion by pressing a button; women are first and foremost human beings. I had had my eye on Þórunn, because she was the most peculiar of them, and it has always been my fate to fancy peculiar girls more than pretty girls. But I'll confess to you now, because ten years have passed, that despite honest efforts all night long, both with her and with the middle sister, I had to make do with the fallen one in the morning when the sun was high in the sky. So it was little wonder that I was sleepy and bad-tempered next day, for which I ask your pardon, my lad, however belatedly; but this was in the days when one still thought oneself cheated with a fallen woman—as if they wouldn't all fall some day! And besides, they've all fallen a long time ago now."

And thus they trudged out of the village: Ólafur Kárason the poet tied to the tail of a black jade, with Reimar in front leading the horse, walking practically backwards all the time in order to carry on this fascinating conversation about their overnight stay at Kambar; the sheriff went farther and farther ahead. When they had more or less exhausted the subject of the former glory of the Kambar girls, and there was a pause in the conversation, Ólafur Kárason said: "Well, since we've started reminiscing about the old days, Reimar, it's little wonder that I call to mind Sviðinsvík-undir-Óþveginsenni where we were both poets together once. You who travel widely and hear many things: what news can you tell me of Sviðinsvík-undir-Óþvegin-senni?"

"Oh, it's the same old story of unrest at Sviðinsvík-undir-Óþve-ginsenni," said Reimar the poet. "Things aren't any better for our friend Pétur Þríhross."

"No, he never had a very easy time, poor chap," said Ólafur Kára-son. "If I remember rightly, the Danes and the Russians were his ene-mies, quite apart from poets. Yes, that was quite a struggle."

"Yes, it's terrible the emotional upsets he used to suffer in those days, our friend Pétur Þríhross," said Reimar the poet. "Örn Úlfar has now vanished with the hoyden to some distant land whose name I can hardly remember. And the war with the poets is over, with the result that the poor old fellow is writing plays himself for the Society of True Icelanders."

"Yes, poor chap, he always had such a strong desire to be an intel-lectual," said Ólafur Kárason. "And seldom has anyone been more opposed to materialism than he. He never thought poets were intel-lectual enough; they were never sufficiently indifferent to what was happening on earth. The last winter I was in Sviðinsvík he had become so tired of me that he even had our shack pulled down around our ears."

"Yes, he has certainly provided plenty for his epitaph," said Reimar the poet. "By the way, you've no doubt heard that old Jón the snuff-maker on the French site is dead? Yes, at long last he went to the devil. And naturally he left all his money to Pétur Þríhross except for the miserable two thousand krónur he bequeathed to the pastor for the new church. Now, I don't know if you remember a celebrated spot up in the pass behind Óþveginsenni where criminals used to be executed in the olden days? Pétur Þríhross once had a revelation that he was to dig up some murderers who had been buried there in olden times, and transfer them to consecrated ground in Sviðinsvík. When old Jón the snuffmaker died, Pétur Þríhross had another divine reve-lation, this time suggesting that this old place of execution for criminals should be declared a sacred precinct, and that the great men of Sviðinsvík were to be buried there. He had Jón the snuffmaker's corpse transported up to the mountain and had God's Word bellowed over it for three days on end. Then he got the pastor an author's grant from the state to write up Jón the snuffmaker's life story in two volumes. And now he himself has started to have an elaborate sepulcher built for himself on the site where he once dug up the bones of Satan and Mósa."

"Yes, he was always full of ideas," said Ólafur Kárason. "And perhaps a greater poet than both of us put together, even though he never understood the secret of poetic form."

"You've no doubt heard of the National and Cultural Drawers Society?" said Reimar the poet.

No, unfortunately, that was something Ólafur Kárason had not heard about.

"It so happened that the year before last, a society was formed in Sviðinsvík with the object of providing destitute children in the village with footwear; it was Faroese-Jens and his wife, Jórunn of Veghús, who organized it. Through this organization they managed to provide poor children and youngsters with socks and shoes at very reasonable prices. Pétur Þríhross, of course, realized at once that a society of this kind must have been inspired by Danes, Russians and poets, and hastened to seek a grant from Júel Júel to start a society to provide Sviðinsvík kings with free drawers. 'If the Danes, Russians, and Poets start a Socks Society, then I'm starting a Drawers Society,' said Pétur Þríhross. 'I insist that everyone, both old and young, men and women, go around in free drawers from me. And my society won't be any treasonable Socks Society but a True-Icelandic, High-Cultural and National Drawers Society. And my Drawers Society will crush all socks and shoes in Sviðinsvík; it will grind all socks and shoes; it will have the guts out of all socks and shoes!' "

"The name of Pétur Þríhross will live for so long as Iceland is inhabited," said Ólafur Kárason.

"And yet he will have to share his fame with Jón the snuffmaker for a long time," said Reimar the poet. "Or did you never hear of the ballot that was held in the Society of True Icelanders in Sviðinsvík last fall?"

Far too many things had passed Ólafur Kárason by in that remote corner of the world, Bervík, including this particular ballot.

"Good heavens, yes!" said Reimar the poet. "They held a ballot in the Society about who was the most exemplary man who had ever been born. Now, I know you'll think it was Pétur Þríhross who got the most votes, but you're wrong there, my lad. Out of almost two hundred votes, Jón the snuffmaker got sixty-one, and Pétur Þríhross only sixty. Napoleon the Great got seventeen, Júel Júel Júel fifteen, and the secretary five. Jesus Christ got only one."

But by now Ólafur Kárason was growing tired of hearing about Sviðinsvík and regretted that he had ever started talking about this place which he had at one time done his best to forget.

"Well, Reimar," he said, "changing the subject for a moment, you haven't told me anything about yourself. What's the news of you and yours, and above all, what poetry have you been composing? This would be just the time to hear a good ballad."

"Then I'll have to untie you from the mare's tail," said Reimar the poet. "I'm not reciting poetry to a bound man. Free men, free poetry! We'll let the damned sheriff get out of sight."

They lingered for a while until the sheriff and his companions disappeared round the shoulder of a hill. Then his escort freed Ólafur Kárason from the horse's tail and unfastened the rope around his wrists.

When Ólafur Kárason was free, Reimar the poet said, "I've made it a habit never to criticize someone in fetters, but now that you're free I can't contain myself any longer. What a damned silly ass you are, man!"

"Oh?" said Ólafur Kárason, not quite sure what he had done wrong this time.

"You had an affair with a gabber," said Reimar the poet.

Olaf Kárason was greatly disappointed in his friend at this, and said sadly, "You, too, Reimar!"

"Yes, and I'm not taking it back; the Lord forgives people everything except their own stupidity," said Reimar.

"May I remind you, Reimar, that it's only a few years since a pregnant girl was confirmed in Grenivík Church. And what's more, it's an old saying in this country that the children of children are fortune's favorites."

"That's not what I'm talking about," said Reimar the poet. "No one feels sorry for gabbers as such. Gabbers are no good, as it says in the Sagas. But if one wants to commit a crime, one should do it in accordance with the law, because all major crimes are done in accordance with the law. A man of your age should know that law and justice apply only to idiots. A man of experience always plays it safe, my lad. And to the best of my knowledge, no one has ever got it signed and sealed that a gabber would keep her mouth shut over trivialities."

"Everything that God protects is spared," said Ólafur Kárason. "I have never been spared. But it doesn't matter so much for myself; it only really matters when one's own transgressions hurt those who are dependent upon one."

Then Reimar the poet said, "Please don't think I'm being an old pastor's wife. The sin is not in being unfaithful, far from it. Those who aren't unfaithful are usually villains and scoundrels towards others, especially towards their wives. The sin lies in being unfaithful in such a way that before you know it, you find yourself tied to a horse's tail."

"How very different we are as poets, Reimar Vagnsson!" said Ólafur Kárason. "I have always had one ideal as far as love is concerned: one woman. I only love one woman, and could never love anyone but her. All other women are a crime or a misfortune in my life."

"Who is she?" asked Reimar the poet.

"I don't know," said Ólafur Kárason. "Fortune hasn't allowed me to find her yet."

"You'll never find her," said Reimar the poet. "No one ever finds her. Monogamy is a mixture of monasticism and self-deception."

"Every man is his own world," said Ólafur Kárason. "My world is my law, your world is yours. I love one girl and haven't found her, but am tied to my wife through compassion, which is perhaps stronger than love. My whole life is like the mind of a man who has lost his way on a fogbound mountain."

Then Reimar the poet said, "I'm now as old as my beard suggests, my lad, and I haven't yet strayed from the right road in life—never composed a verse with half-rhymes or failed to find a word to rhyme with another. And if I've sometimes been a bit malicious in my versifying, it's not because I've ever felt any malice towards anyone, but because they were an easy target. I've been married to my old woman for nearly thirty years, and we've had seven strong and happy children whom we have given a good start in life, and I'd like to see the father who has been better to his children and his old woman than Reimar the poet. For instance, I'm going to use this journey to get hold of some stockfish at Aðalfjörður, and a man on the Kaldsvík coast has half promised me a side of beef."

"This is another point where we are miles apart," said Ólafur Kárason. "I have never provided for the home. To bring up fat, contented children is an ambition I have never understood. On the other hand, I don't think it's my nature to retreat from the belief that true love between a man and a woman is indivisible. That's how I regard my responsibilities—and mourn my shortcomings."

"You could well be a tolerable hymn-writer and satirist some day, my dear Ólafur Kárason of Ljósavík," said Reimar the poet. "But someone who has no notion of a man's duty towards a woman can never be a great poet. The moment a woman is in flower, she wants children and yet more children, that's what a woman wants. A man's love doesn't give a woman her fulfillment; it's first and foremost children: five children, ten children, fifteen children to bear in her womb and bring forth in pain and bring up in riot and disorder, children to wake over at night, to spank and caress in turn, children who either scatter all over the country and settle in far-off places or die of all sorts of ailments, children to bury in the ground and sing hymns over. A married man has only one duty towards his wife in order to make her happy, and that is to ensure that she is constantly pregnant, and with a child in her arms."

"What a very happily married man you have been, Reimar!" said Ólafur Kárason.

"My old woman's a good old woman who has always looked upon

me as a great poet and a great traveler and has always been ready to take my side," said Reimar the poet. "She has always looked askance at the women who turned up their noses at me; she thought it showed bad taste and was therefore an affront to herself."

They had the wind behind them, these two old acquaintances, fellow poets and traveling companions, who were no doubt just as far apart today as when they had traveled together for the first time. Yet this was the second time that Reimar the poet had had a hand in freeing Ólafur Kárason from his bonds: the latter had changed places with the black mare, despite the wishes of the authorities.

"Two people can never understand one another's lives," said Ólafur Kárason. "But poetry is the Redeemer of us all."

And then the ballads began.

—— **10** ——

When Ólafur Kárason the poet had been kept in the cold and dark so-called prison at Kaldsvík for three days, and faced two more court hearings, he began to weaken. The sheriff's frowns and whisky bass got the upper hand. Finally he was ready to confess. He made his confession with the preamble that he had not held out from fear of punishment—that was neither here nor there. He had been thinking of his wife and son; he said he had shrunk from causing them humiliation and sorrow. Whatever a crime might be in reality, and human behavior generally, crimes had to be proved and admitted in order to be called by that name. On the other hand it is a minor issue whether a person knows that be has committed it or whether a person actually has committed it, or whether other people know that one has committed it, or whether crimes actually do exist: with the proof and the confession, the crime becomes a fact. And Jarþrúður Jónsdóttir and Jón Ólafsson were sacrificed.

He said it was quite true that on the morning before Christmas Eve he had woken up when the widow at Syðrivík had gone out to tend the livestock with her older children. Jasína Gottfreðlína, whom

he regarded as a grown-up girl however little she might know about
the Christian faith, was lying in the next bed; he had gone into her
bed, turned down the lamp, lain down beside her, and slept with her.
And she had received him willingly for the simple reason that a
grown-up girl in love with a man thinks that nothing is more natural
or inevitable. And that was all.

He found himself standing that evening in the county town, in
the dim light of the scattered streetlamps.

It was here, to this place, that he had dreamed of coming in the
old days; it was here that he had intended to go to school and
become a man of learning and a famous poet; and last but not least,
it was here that he had hopes of a mother who lived in a real house
with a window on each side of the door. It was to her, over countless
mountains, that he had wanted to flee when he was in distress in
alien places.

He wandered about for a long time in this big place, no longer a
weeping child, unfortunately, but an unshaven, hungry law-breaker
with a cold, who had forfeited his right to a mother. The days were
gone forever when he had been so happy that he believed that the
height of unhappiness was to carry heavy buckets from an icy spring.

But even though his situation was now such that he no longer had
any claim to a mother in a real house, nevertheless an old defiance
against this more or less imaginary woman arose in him, anger over
her treatment of the little boy who was put in a sack and taken away
in a snowstorm, a lack of any desire to whitewash her even though
she was a great and noble woman while he was a convicted criminal.
If he knocked at her door and she resented meeting a forgotten past
in the person of a son awaiting sentence, he was going to say: If such
things had happened to him in the snowstorm of life, who was it
then who had sent him out into that snowstorm, crying in a sack,
when all he had wanted was to have a mother and to rest against her
bosom? That's how he was going to justify himself in relation to this
woman.

Of course the house where she lived was not anything like the real
house of his hopeful dreams; on the doorstep he felt he had lost his

way and that his dream-mother was not only better but also truer than reality. The shadow of the house convinced him that the woman he had dreamed about did not exist. But he had already knocked on the door, and all forebodings were too late.

He was shown up long, narrow stairs where the permanent smell of boiled fish from years gone by assaulted him. In an untidy attic under a sloping ceiling he was directed to the apartment of the woman he had asked for.

She was short and bloated, her face with its plump, shiny cheeks reminded one of enameled clay; her eyes were like fractures in old iron. Never had Ólafur Kárason suspected that he had a fat mother. He asked if he had the name right and she said Yes, and then he offered his hand and said Hullo, and she replied curtly and asked who this person might be.

"My name is Ólafur Kárason," he said.

"Ólafur Ká . . . ?" she said, wide-eyed with surprise.

"Yes," he said. "I am your son."

"Well, I never!" said the woman, and there was no doubt that she almost fainted at the visitor's unexpected news; but she recovered quickly and gave him her hand. "Do come in," she said.

"Many thanks," he said.

She shut the door and looked at him.

"Well, I'm absolutely flabbergasted!" she said. "Do have a seat."

"Thank you," he said and sat down, and brushed the hair from his forehead.

"I would never have thought you looked like that," said the woman. "How old are you?"

"I'm thirty-one," he said.

"My God, was I only seventeen when I had you!" she said, and the words seemed to him to be a blend of self-reproach and excuse. "Am I seeing right? Are you red-haired?"

She came right over to him and ran her fingers through his hair and had a good look to see if he was red-haired all the way down to roots. "Yes, you really are red-haired! My God, no one in my family has ever been red-haired! I'm simply speechless!"

"How is your health?" he asked.

"Health?" she said. "Don't even mention it. I haven't any health at all."

"Haven't you been to see a doctor?" he asked.

"Yes," she said. "I've been to every doctor I can get hold of. Whenever I hear of a new doctor somewhere I either write to him or go there myself. They'll soon have tried on me every mixture there is, but nothing helps. I've often thought of having an operation. It's no life at all."

She had a bed, a sofa, a chest of drawers, and a broken-down sewing machine. There was no sign of any work in hand; but there was a picture on the wall of a noble lady in a broad-brimmed hat meeting a huntsman at a gate in the road, and there were some other foreign pictures in color, but no family portraits. On a corner-shelf there stood an oil stove and some tin jars and ladles.

She did not ask him any personal questions, which he interpreted as meaning that she knew his circumstances and did not want to know any more. The silence was fraught with embarrassment on both sides.

"You're a seamstress, I'm told," said Ólafur Kárason.

"That's all over," she said. "Some are in fashion, I've never been in fashion. I've always been misunderstood all my life. Nobody has ever been so misunderstood as I've been. Actually, I've never been anybody at all."

"Yes, you're not the only one," said Ólafur Kárason.

"Your father was the one who misunderstood me first. My God, how that man misunderstood me! And everyone else. Yet he misunderstood himself most of all."

"I've no way of judging that," said Ólafur Kárason. "I have never seen him. What news can you give me of him, by the way?"

"News? Of him? Me? No, I can't give you any news of him, for the simple reason that there has never been any news of him; and never will be. He really wasn't a person at all. I never knew what he was. I think he wasn't anything."

"Oh, I wouldn't say that, perhaps," said the poet.

"It's at least twenty years since I heard his name mentioned," said the woman. "He must surely be dead long ago; or else gone to the north."

"He sometimes sent me writing materials when I was small," said Ólafur Kárason.

"Yes, of course, that's right," she said. "You're said to be a poet. Won't you have some coffee?"

"Thank you," he said. "There's really no need."

"You've never sent me a poem," she said when she had put the kettle on. "I really would have loved to get a poem!"

She had false teeth, like a woman of importance, and that helped to widen the gulf between them.

"I often thought of sending you a poem," he said. "I was even thinking of coming myself. I was often in distress."

"You should use the opportunity to write a poem about me while you're in town. How long are you thinking of staying?"

"I'm going home tomorrow," he said. "If I only knew where to stay the night."

It was noticeable that she did not need to ask where he had been staying the last few nights. In his shoes, she said, she would stay at the Salvation Army; she had heard that a bed cost twenty-five *aurar*.

"I have a poetry book," she said. "You ought to compose something for it while I'm making the coffee; a lot of poets have written something in it."

He said it took him a long time to compose poetry, and that he had to be in a very special mood for it.

"I know lots of poets who can make poetry wherever they are," she said.

"Just so," he said.

"I'm so terribly fond of poetry," she said. "I'm sure you've inherited your gifts from me and my family. You should go and see the editor of *The Alfirðing* at once tomorrow, he's got a black beard, and get him to publish a book of your poems so that you'll be famous. He has a big printing plant."

The visitor made no reply to this suggestion but stared vacantly into the blue, and she looked at him sideways, half furtively; how pale he was and haggard, and though his eyes were almost unnaturally bright, there lurked in them such grief that it was difficult to imagine that this man had ever known a moment's happiness all his life.

"It isn't really enough just to be a poet, I suppose, far from it," she said at last. "Why have you never thought of being something?"

"I don't know," he said.

"You should have become something," she said.

He was very hungry because he had had nothing to eat except coffee and hardtack biscuits in the prison that morning before the court hearing. "Mummy, give me a piece of bread" was really the only thing he wanted to say, but between him and this woman were thirty years with thirty winters of snowstorms and innumerable mountains. The kettle was coming to the boil, and she had started to crumble the chicory into the coffeepot.

They heard noises on the stair and in the attic, coming closer and closer; then the door was thrown open and an unsightly drunk appeared in the doorway. He growled a little at the visitor at first, then lurched across the room, cursing, turned to Ólafur Kárason, grabbed him by the lapels and started to shake him.

"Who the devil are you, eh? What the devil d'you want, eh?"

"My name is Ólafur Kárason," said the poet.

The newcomer lost control of himself so completely now that he might have been called a comparatively peaceable and courteous man hitherto. He started to heap on the poet the worst abuse and the most obscene insults imaginable, and ended by saying that a man who had brought upon his mother's name such everlasting disgrace should get out of her sight at once. He did not stop at mere words, but hauled Ólafur Kárason out of his seat and across the floor, and threw him out of the room; then he threw him down the stairs as well.

And the Ljósvíkingur's old dream of having a mother came to an end.

II

Next morning he went to see the editor, a short man with a generous paunch, an underhung jaw, a black goatee beard and foxy eyes behind pince-nez. He greeted the editor and said that his name was Ólafur Kárason, but the editor was in some doubt about the attitude he should adopt toward this voter and went on writing for a while behind the shelter of his pince-nez. When it suited him, he laid his pen aside, having decided to be amiable to Ólafur Kárason, said that he knew him by repute, said that he was a poet himself and had had books published. He said he had heard some of Ólafur Kárason's poetry and rather liked it, but that it would do him no harm to spread his wings a little more vigorously and also, perhaps, apply himself a little more to Egill Skalla-Grímsson's discipline of form.

"A f–friend of mine suggested to me yesterday that I should call on you and ask how much you think it would cost to publish what I have written," said Ólafur Kárason.

The editor asked the poet to give him some idea of his works, and Ólafur started to enumerate them: novels, collected poems, biographies, stories of strange men, registers of poets—scores of written volumes, thousands of pages. Finally the editor assumed an extremely mathematical mien and started calculating; the calculations were accompanied by deep sighs and groans and a grave air of quite exceptional responsibility, but eventually he laid aside his pencil, leaned back in his chair, and asked: "Can you put two hundred and fifty thousand krónur on the table?"

"Oh, I wouldn't find much difficulty in raising that," said the poet.

"If you really are going around with masses of money in your pocket," said the other, "then I, as an older and more experienced man, would point out to you that this cash could be used in a much more rational way than for having books published. For two hundred and fifty thousand krónur one could at the very least secure oneself six medium-sized constituencies, build both churches and fish stations, apart from all personal guarantees of loans, and still have money left over. And even if you had brought your gold here in casks to ask me what to do with it, I would advise you to get a boat and row your casks far out to sea and sink them there, rather than to have books printed. To have books printed is to throw money in the fire and lose everything except your shirt. I once had to print two books, a book of poems and a collection of short stories, because I had been given an author's grant by the state, but if I hadn't had so-called ownership of a printing plant, I still wouldn't be free of debts because of these books, even though I am well known not just here in this part of the country but down south too. No, my friend, to have a book published is the last thing you want to do with your money. Would you like a cigar?"

"Thank you," said the poet, "but I'm afraid I don't know how to smoke cigars. But there's something else I'd like to say to you if you'll allow me to sit with you for a moment. I have come to you in all sincerity, and therefore I beg you not to scoff at me; and I shall not try to hide anything from you. The fact is that a grievous calamity has befallen me; I have been accused of a crime. To be sure, I denied it for a long time, for fear of bringing disgrace and unhappiness upon my wife and children, and upon my mother, apart from the fact that I myself take the view that what I did wasn't really any more of a crime than anything else I have done in my life. But last night I lay awake and was thinking that if I am found guilty and thereby branded for all time in the eyes of the nation, like Sigurður Breiðfjörð who was sentenced to twenty-seven lashes, it would perhaps help somewhat to rehabilitate me a little in the eyes of posterity if I had a book published just about now, however small."

At this confidence, the editor's mathematical mien vanished entirely, and over his face there spread the fat smile of the politician: "Since we're both poets and therefore brothers," he said, "I can tell you that in my opinion it's only natural that men should grow tired of their old women when they reach a certain age and start fancying young girls; but on the other hand I think it was quite unnecessary of you to bother the sheriff for nearly a week with these damned trivialities. Because it isn't crimes or breaches of the law that cause people's downfall nowadays, as you know; people fall by being on the wrong side in their views and turning against the National Movement. By the way, Ólafur, how are the prospects for Our Movement up in Bervík?"

"I can't speak for others," said the voter, without quite knowing what this was leading up to, and beginning instinctively to feel his way, "but for my own part I can assert that I have always had a very strong desire to be on the right side in my views and support the National Movement to the best of my ability, and to the best of my conscience."

"As you know," said the editor confidentially, and leaned forward into the shaft of sunlight with butter in his smile, while the raven-black beard, the underhung jaw, and the pince-nez all glistened—"as you know, we editors and party leaders can whitewash anyone at all if he has the right perception of the right powers."

"The right perception of the right powers," said Ólafur Kárason. "That has always been my deepest longing."

Not only butter but honey as well dripped from the editor's smile; he patted his visitor on the shoulder, almost kissed him, and said, "Sometime soon you must send me a poem—about the right subject. It doesn't need to be long—three verses would do—but if I like it, I'll have it printed in a good position in the paper. And we'll both be doing ourselves a favor."

"I have," said Ólafur Kárason solemnly, "been thinking for a long time of writing an ode to the sun."

To love the sun, and to praise it above all other things—Ólafur Kárason thought that no one, neither man nor poet, could get much further in having the right views about the right powers here on earth. "But unfortunately," he added, "I can't say whether I can get everything I would like to say about this subject into three verses."

What the poet found most surprising was that the editor seemed suddenly to lose all desire to kiss him; the butter and the honey vanished from his smile as if they were no longer friends. He leaned back in his chair and put on a serious expression.

"If I might give you some good advice," he said rather distantly, "then I think it would be better for you not to compose a poem about the sun."

The poet looked at the editor, perplexed. It was obvious he had failed to feel his way towards the glimmer of light in that dark forest which can separate two people.

"You mean . . ." he tried to say, "that–that–that the s–sun is perhaps rather far away?"

"Yes, I suppose it is," said the editor, and started looking out the window.

"But I still think," said the poet ingratiatingly, "that despite all the coldness that sometimes seems to reign in the world of men, the sun is nearer to us than everything else, all the same."

It was now the editor's turn to be perplexed by the conversation, and Ólafur Kárason saw himself suddenly become a strange animal in the editor's eyes, some kind of odd species of fish, or even a two-headed calf.

"Are you an idiot, or do you think I'm an idiot?" the editor asked at last.

"God help me!" said Ólafur Kárason.

"Shall we agree to talk like people in their right minds?" said the editor. "Or shall we bring this conversation to a close?"

Ólafur Kárason looked at him in alarm for a little while and could not utter a word; he got the impression that further attempts would be fruitless and said, as he got to his feet, "I–I'll go now."

But then the editor was undecided about this confused voter and did not want to let him go. "By the way," he began, in the tone of voice of a teacher who is making one more attempt to explain to a slow-witted child the mysteries of the multiplication table, "aren't you acquainted with Pétur Pálsson the manager at Sviðinsvík?"

Ólafur Kárason did not deny this, but said it was now five years since they had had anything to do with one another.

"How did you and Pétur get on while you were living on his estate?"

"I always had a tremendous liking for him," said the poet. "He's a very fine person. If any misunderstandings ever arose between us, it was always my fault. He was both an idealist and a national hero at once, while I was never anything more than an insignificant poet."

"I don't know if you're aware of the fact that we're thinking of making Pétur Pálsson the Member of Parliament for that constituency in place of Júel Júel, who has resigned his seat and is now in charge of the National Bank."

"I am truly delighted to hear this news," said Ólafur Kárason. "Pétur Pálsson the manager richly deserves to be made a Member of Parliament. Few men have had so many and varied interests as he. If people were measured by the number and diversity of their interests, I think Pétur Pálsson the manager deserves the highest honor that Iceland can bestow."

"You have presumably heard that Pétur Pálsson has now decided to clothe all the people of Sviðinsvík, from the ankles to the midriff, free of charge?" said the editor.

"Yes, it's absolutely astonishing what that man can achieve," said Ólafur Kárason, and tried to see into the editor's soul, behind the spectacles and the foxy eyes, in the hope of finding some landmark in this desert.

"He's decided to bury all great men in the pass behind Óþvegin-senni, and is now erecting an imposing sepulcher there," said the editor.

"I think that no grave is too fine for really great men," said Ólafur Kárason.

"Many good men have had the idea that he ought to become the president of the republic," said the editor, and there was butter in his smile again.

"That seems to me only right and proper," said Ólafur Kárason; but even if his life had depended on it, he could not have said how sincere was this solemn talk about Pétur Pálsson the manager.

Finally the editor said, "Have you considered whether it wouldn't be advisable for you to compose a few verses about the old fellow sometime?"

The poet realized with a shock that he had fallen into a trap.

"Is there any hurry for it?" he asked.

"Oh, no, not really, at least not as far as Pétur's concerned," said the editor. "But for various other reasons it might perhaps be advisable if you did it fairly soon, before sentence is pronounced. I hope now you realize that I'm doing you a good turn?"

"Yes," said the poet, with emotion in his voice. "I feel that I've found a good friend."

"It also occurs to me that it wouldn't do any harm either if you were to write a nice article in *The Alfirðing* about the nation's most distinguished man and Iceland's greatest leader of the modern era."

"Yes, excuse me, who would that be, again?" asked Ólafur Kárason, scratching himself behind the ear.

"Who would that be?" asked the editor in amazement. "Who do you think it is? Our new National Bank manager, of course!"

"Of course, how silly of me!" said the poet. "It's quite true, too. Of course I ought to write something about Júel Júel. It's a disgrace that I've never written anything about him."

"And it wouldn't do any harm," said the editor, "if you gave the Russians and the Danes a little dig in the ribs, and also those poets who in fact don't belong in Iceland but in other countries. All voices that aim at strengthening the Security of the Nation in these critical times are gratefully accepted."

"I'll do what I can," said the poet.

"When you bring the poem we can have another word about the most practical way to work for Our Movement in your part of the world," said the editor.

"And we'll just forget that thing about the sun?" asked the poet as he took his leave.

"Anyone who has the nerve to write about the sun in these critical times for the nation is against Pétur Þríhross," replied the editor. "He is against the Bank; he is against the National Movement; he is in danger of being judged."

12

One day in midsummer when the heat-haze made even what was near look distant, so that the stones at the roadside had also become blue (that was the extent to which distance and unreality were mingled in everything), three people were on a journey, a man, a woman, and a child, leading a horse along the route over Kaldsheiði. They took turns at riding with the child.

There was a heavy fragrance of ling and brushwood and precious mountain plants. The chirping of the birds was quiet and soothing in the summer stillness; all Nature lay in an uninterrupted trance of bliss.

Sometimes it is as if man is the poorest of all the things in Nature; but today all cares were dulled; today their journey lay not through human life but through a dreamland. And this blue, shimmering dream, this almost airborne blissfulness where the next bend in the road held all the enchantment of a distant mirage, gave no sustenance to grief.

And the poet was wearing a new suit. His wife, Jarþrúður Jónsdóttir, had said that no one from this part of the country had ever been known to go south without a Sunday-best suit; she had suddenly become very proud on behalf of this part of the country, and she said that that rabble in the south, the same slaves who in their time had almost tormented the life out of our late blessed Hallgrímur Pétursson, would have to find something other to laugh at than a man from Bervík without his Sunday-best. She had got hold of a jacket off an old man who had died in the district last year; it had been his Sunday-best jacket for more than forty years and he had never worn it. True, the jacket was both too short and too wide for a tall, thin man like Ólafur Kárason, but who could say what the fashion might be down south? One thing was certain—well-fitting jackets are never in fashion with the well-dressed, they are always too long or too short. The origin of the trousers, on the other hand, was shrouded in some mystery, but even so the poet had a suspicion that they had come from afar. They were gray in color, of a material which was not above criticism, certainly, wide where they should have been narrow and narrow where they should have been wide. When one put them on, some of the most important seams burst, and when they were buttoned up for the first time, the buttons fell off. By accident, shortly after the trousers arrived, the poet happened to meet a traveler from Sviðinsvík who was wearing trousers of the same make, and then it dawned on him that these would be National and Cultural Drawers from Pétur Pálsson the manager, sepulcher-owner and prospective president of the republic. But wherever these trousers might have come from, the poet was grateful for the advantage of having a prudent and resourceful wife in these critical times for the nation.

And when they reached the trading station she did not stop at jacket and trousers, but went into a shop and bought him a pair of boots; and that was not all: when he had put on the boots she also bought a stiff collar, a dummy shirt-front, and a tie, which she got the shopkeeper to fasten round her husband's neck. Never in all his life had Ólafur Kárason been so well dressed.

A boat had arrived to take the passengers on board the steamer. Down on the quay a few souls had gathered, all wearing their Sunday-best suits, stiff collars and sheepskin shoes, people of the same type as Ólafur Kárason the poet and his wife, people setting off on a journey.

Jarþrúður Jónsdóttir told her husband to give her the boy, and he was really rather relieved to get the child off his arm; but as he handed him over he noticed how unhappy and forlorn he looked, his face almost that of an old man. And when it occurred to him that these little blue eyes would perhaps live a long time without seeing mankind becoming free he grew sad, and all of a sudden he began to feel fond of this boy at the moment of parting and to wish that Jón Ólafsson, too, might have a share of the sun. He kissed the boy in order to ease his conscience, and had forgotten him the same moment. And just when he had kissed the child and forgotten all about him, something unheard of in this household occurred: this poet's penniless wife brought some money out of her skirt pocket and gave it to him, real bank notes with the king's portrait on them, no less than twenty-five krónur in ready cash. "Use this to enjoy yourself with," she said.

He stared in amazement at this huge sum of money and held it tightly between his fingers so that it would not blow away. In the poet's house, money had never been an everyday sight; for years on end the gleaming metal had been kneaded in places unknown to him; he hardly knew one coin from another. His knowledge of economics consisted of ensuring that what he bought on credit from the merchant did not exceed the pay he could expect as a primary schoolteacher during the winter and for casual labor with the Bervík bailiff in summer. He went on seeing his wife Jarþrúður Jónsdóttir in a new and ever newer light right up to the last moment; on top of everything else she had been hoarding money. He felt that neither he nor anyone else could ever have a more understanding wife or one better qualified to take charge of a difficult marriage in critical times. Men with good-looking wives never had a happy moment, never had a moment's peace; Jarþrúður Jónsdóttir's epileptic fits, on the other hand, became milder and less frequent with age; besides which she had undoubtedly been good-looking once, like other women.

"There, put the money in your pocket quickly so that no one sees it, or else it will be stolen," said his wife. "They're beginning to call the passengers down on the quay. Ask God to redeem our souls and forgive me, and may Almighty Jesus go with you, and now Good-bye."

People sail out into the world in different circumstances, but it is always a pleasure, not least the first time, however late one starts; the unknown is itself a promise. The strips of grassland on the mountainsides between the gullies and the gorges reached right up to the sun-gilded cliff-belts; between the mountains lay grassy valleys with lazy rivers, enchanted valleys from the world of myth or fairy tale; the mountain trails entranced the seafarer's eye. The poet felt completely free now as he stood there on the deck in his collar and boots, sailing past new and ever newer districts; even if he did not own this land's resources, he owned its beauty. In the distance towered the glacier, his greatest wealth, his thousand, his million. The beauty of things is greater than the things themselves, and more precious; most things are of little or no value in comparison with their beauty, above all the beauty of the glacier. The poet was the wealthiest man in Iceland because he owned the sight of this beauty, and therefore he had no apprehension about the world. He felt he was not afraid of anything. Some people own a lot of money and large estates, but no beauty. He owned the beauty of all Iceland and all human life. He felt kindly towards everyone; he was reconciled with everyone. The music that sustained his soul was the music, along with the nightingale's, that will triumph when the world destroys itself. Here sailed a wealthy poet. Happy and victorious is the nation which has wealthy poets! He could not understand why the Creator of the world had given him so much. "God, God, God," he said, and gazed towards the land, and the tears streamed down his cheeks without anyone seeing them. "Thank you for having given me so much!"

Then the storm clouds began to gather and a cold breeze blew up, the ship was out past the headland, out in the open sea; there was even a suggestion of slight rolling. At first the poet found the swell comfortable, but soon he began to feel cold as he stood there at the rail, then he began to feel strange in the head, then he began to feel sick and broke into a cold sweat; finally he leaned out over the rail and vomited. Afterwards he dragged himself, sick and exhausted, down into the hold where he had his bedding, and made his bed with difficulty among other souls in a similar condition, and lay down. Life's joy had vanished.

— 13 —

By the end of the journey the traveler's collar was much the worse for wear. The starch had gone out of it long ago; it was no longer a stiff collar. The tie had fallen off during the seasickness and had been trampled underfoot in the dirt on the floor of the hold. The dummy shirt-front turned out to be cardboard, and it sagged into his trousers when the buttonhole got torn; the poet had thrown it away long ago. He threw away the collar also. But the suit was fine, except that the forty-year-old jacket gathered a lot of fluff, and the National and Cultural trousers from Pétur Pálsson the manager were all too prone to wrinkle. Word came that the ship was entering harbor. It was early in the morning. The steerage passengers got themselves on deck, some of them rather fragile from seasickness or hangovers, others, including Ólafur Kárason of Ljósavík, looking solemn and full of expectation for the unknown whose doors were being opened. A little later he stepped ashore.

This was the capital of the country. At long last this poet had left the valleys and outer nesses of the farthest coasts and had been lucky enough to see the place which contained the grave of Sigurður Breiðfjörð.

"Country bumpkin, country bumpkin!" shouted a few children, and pointed at him as he stood there at a street corner with his sack.

But hardly had he realized that he was this country bumpkin before the children had disappeared. Here there was no time to think about the same thing for long. He remained at the street corner for a long time, deep in thought. Then two gentlemen came walking across the street in a slow slalom, stopped at the corner beside the poet, greeted him effusively, and called him their friend. They were a little puffy in the face and red-eyed, and had not shaved for the last few days or had their shoes polished. The First Gentleman squinted with one eye at a time at the people in the street and asked in amazement: "Young man, can you tell me why these people don't go to bed?"

"I'm afraid I can't say with any certainty," said the poet. "On the other hand, I presume that they've just got up."

"Yes, what terrible morals we have in this town nowadays," said the First Gentleman. "This rabble sleeps all day and then goes whoring all night, even five-year-old children. Listen, friend, what's the sun doing over Mosfell District at this time of day?"

"It's shining," said the poet.

"It can't be a real sun," said the First Gentleman. "It's an artificial sun. I want these children sent home to bed. Will you be honest with

me and tell me the plain, unvarnished truth: Are there any morals
here in this town? Can the birds be right at this time of day? And
what sort of a sun is that? Is it I who have lost my bearings or you,
who comes from the country?"

"It is I who have come from the country," said the poet.

"Friend," said the Second Gentleman, and embraced the poet.
"The Bank's been closed. The English have closed the Bank."

"Just so," said the poet.

"And why have the English closed the Bank?" asked the Second
Gentleman. "It's because there's no money left in the Bank any more.
Júel has cleaned out the Bank. Júel has squandered all the money the
English lent this ill-starred nation out of the goodness of their hearts.
Júel has sunk all the English money in the depths of the ocean. That's
why the Bank's been closed."

"Really?" said the poet.

"D'you say 'Really'?" said the Gentleman. "How dare you say
'Really' here in the south?"

"He needs to go to bed; he's sleepy," said the First Gentleman.

"He'd better be careful about saying Really," said the Second Gentleman. "D'you know who I am? I'm a political editor. I'm a leader. I
can prove that you're a traitor to your country and an anti-patriot. I
have the proofs to hand. Whoever says Really is against our kinsmen,
the Finns, I can prove that. Listen, have you got a króna?"

The poet found a króna piece in his pocket and gave it to the men.
Then they asked if he had two krónur. He dug into his pocket and
found two krónur and handed them over, and thus bravely bore the
banner of the lending activities which the English had stopped by
closing the Bank.

"Now we'll take him out on the tiles," said the Second Gentleman.

But the poet thought that The Tiles was the name of some very
high mountain, and said that unfortunately he did not have time to
climb The Tiles.

"What d'you drink, then?" asked the Second Gentleman.

"Milk," said the poet.

"Milk!" repeated the Second Gentleman. "God help me, I blush for shame! So you drink milk? In other words, there's no limit to how far people will go in shamelessness nowadays. May I ask: Are you making fun of people here? Or have you really got V.D.?"

Then the First Gentleman said: "You, as a political editor and town councillor, don't understand countrymen, whereas I, as a lawyer and a sheriff and spiritual aristocrat, understand countrymen—let me speak. Friend! Milk isn't just the most boorish and unpoetical drink ever known, but also the most vulgar drink which has ever been invented on earth. No one with an uncorrupted aesthetic sense can announce that he drinks milk, at least not in public and without prior notice. Milk is taboo, my dear friend; milk is an obscenity; d'you understand me? On the other hand it's a matter for negotiation, and I'm quite prepared to consider the matter at a suitable opportunity, how one should classify cattle. As a spiritual aristocrat I incline in the main to the doctrine that cattle are cattle, as far as that goes. And I willingly admit that when I see a cow chewing the cud, I wouldn't dream of denying that in these disgusting creatures there may reside a certain philosophical, I'm tempted to say metaphysical, power which . . ."

"That's a repulsive point of view," said the Second Gentleman. And mercifully for the poet's purse they forgot all about him and staggered away, bickering.

He shouldered his sack and set off into the town. There was some sand blowing about, as on Sprengisandur, and everyone was thinking about himself. He was still feeling a little peculiar after the voyage, and knew of no way of finding something to eat in a capital city. He went up to various people and asked where the sheriff was, but people only asked in return if he were an idiot. Finally he met a policeman, which was lucky for him; for this gigantic, uniformed man neither made fun of him nor took money off him nor was suspicious of him on sight, but went out of his way like the good Samaritan to help a stranger, in the spirit of the Gospels.

A midsummer stillness reigned in the police station; no one was in any hurry to take the trouble of coming to the counter to ask this lanky countryman what he wanted. The visitor was allowed to kick his heels for a long time by the door. But when there was no longer any hope that he would go away without bothering people, an elderly gentleman got up from his chair in this mighty sheriff-house, walked with measured stride to the counter, stopped there, and tapped the lid of his snuffbox.

"Good-day," said Ólafur Kárason.

"Good-day," said the man.

Ólafur Kárason offered him his hand. "Are you the sheriff?" he asked.

"There's no sheriff here," said the gentleman, taking the visitor's hand rather reluctantly. "This is the police. What do you want?"

"I'm the man from Bervík," said Ólafur Kárason.

"Bervík," said the gentleman. "So there's a Bervík, is there?"

"Haven't you heard of me?" said Ólafur Kárason. "I'm the one who committed the crime."

"Really?" said the man, a little absentmindedly. "You committed a crime, did you? What crime was that?"

Ólafur Kárason took from his wallet a copy of the judgment and a document from the sheriff to prove his story, and gave them to the officer.

The man spelled his way through the document and called some of his colleagues over, and they all spelled their way through the document; some of them were wearing ordinary gentlemen's clothes, others had gilt buttons. They nodded amiably towards Ólafur Kárason when they saw what was up; some of them asked the news from his district about the weather conditions, the grass-growth, and the fishing. The poet said that the grass-growth was well above average in Bervík, and the hay crop was doing well so far this summer; on the other hand there was not much fishing at our place. One man offered him some snuff. These were splendid people. They asked if he could not come back tomorrow.

Ólafur Kárason was disappointed and replied, "I'm a stranger here in the capital, and don't know any people here apart from the one house I'm to go to, and I haven't got much money. I'd prefer to be allowed to start serving my sentence as soon as possible."

They said there were several difficulties about admitting him immediately to this highly desirable residence which they managed; of that house it could truly be said that many were called but few were chosen, all the documents had to be in perfect order. Did he not have any friends in town?

Ólafur Kárason blushed. One man in this capital city, certainly, was his friend from the old days, but he did not even know himself any more, let alone old friends. He wanted to delay meeting this man until he had served his sentence and was a free man again. But all things considered, there seemed to be nowhere else to turn for the time being, and a policeman was sent with the poet to look for his old acquaintance.

They walked for a long time until they came to the house where the poet's friend lived; the policeman went to the back door and said Good-day, and a middle-aged woman came to the door, a little scared because she thought someone was going to be arrested, but it turned out to be only a stranger asking for Sveinn of Bervík. She said that her stepson was out at work and would not be back until six o'clock. The woman asked who the visitor was, but when she learned that it was the children's schoolteacher from Bervík her face filled with sheer anguish. The policeman said that the man was a stranger in town, and asked the woman to afford him shelter until his friend came home. With that the policeman disappeared, and the woman stood in the doorway and looked in dread at this terrible man, Ólafur Kárason. She called out to three adolescent girls and told them to leave the house at once. Then she took Ólafur Kárason through the kitchen into the living room. He asked if she could please sell him some food. She said this was not an eating house, but perhaps she could give him some food. He was grateful for being allowed to sit in her living room for the day, because as a stranger, an idiot and a criminal he did not have the courage to wander about in this town, even though it contained the grave of Sigurður Breiðfjörð.

That day while he was waiting for his friend was extraordinarily long. The woman brought him food with fear in her eyes, and if he tried to start a conversation with her, she became even more scared.

Everything he said seemed to have the same effect on her as delirious ravings; there was no doubt that in her eyes he was not merely a hardened criminal but a lunatic to boot. He looked out the window at lightly clad children playing in the street, and in his thoughts he had already become a prisoner, an outcast of mankind, and despised by society. Again and again he was on the point of sneaking away before his friend returned.

Around six o'clock he heard a young man's cheery greetings outside; it was the boy coming home from his work with no thought of anything untoward. But his voice was quickly hushed and whispering began, and after that it was whisperings and suppressed emotions that reigned in this house. Blushes of shame came and went in the poet's cheeks.

After a long time his friend Sveinn of Bervík came into the room. He was a tall, fine-looking young man in a blue suit and brightly colored shirt, extremely well-washed, smelling of hair-oil, with his hair carefully brushed, his hands scrubbed to remove all traces of the day's work as thoroughly as possible, his shoes polished. He offered his hand to the visitor with grave courtesy, and when the visitor had examined him more closely, he was grateful that he had not tried to pretend a friendly smile. In a flash the visitor saw that all his secret plans to try to make his life comprehensible to this young favorite of fortune were ridiculous. To try to excuse himself to this young man was merely to accuse himself. He understood now as never before that a man must conquer or fail in his own eyes alone.

"Sveinn, I–I know no one; you don't need to know me if you don't want to," he stammered, and felt, as he always did in the hour of trial, that he was a foster child at Fótur-undir-Fótarfæti and was in the wrong, alone against the world. Once upon a time these two men had been in the same situation; now the difference between them was like the difference between a wish and its fulfillment. The one was what the other had dreamed of, and therefore they did not know one another any more. He who has wishes, yearns for a friend; but when the wishes have been fulfilled, the friends are the first thing we forget.

"You are a man of learning now," said Ólafur Kárason, and could not hide the admiration in his eyes as he contemplated this young, handsome, intelligent and well-dressed man whom he in his insignificance had discovered in the darkest cranny of the country and had helped to push towards maturity.

"I'm an undergraduate," said Sveinn of Bervík, with a slightly self-satisfied expression round his mouth.

"And you're no doubt a great poet now," said Ólafur Kárason of Ljósavík.

Perhaps the unreserved devotion in the visitor's eyes struck this young man as being merely dog-like, because a shadow of distaste passed over his face at these words, and he looked at Ólafur Kárason's Sunday-best suit not without disgust.

"I've decided to become a theologian," said the undergraduate.

"A theologian!" repeated Ólafur Kárason. "That's wonderful! Oh, how that pleases me. I always knew you would become something; something special; something out of the ordinary."

He smiled his gentle, fervent smile at his friend, but to no avail.

"Did you have a good trip?" asked the undergraduate.

"Yes, thank you," said Ólafur Kárason. "But I was a little seasick the first night. And my neckwear was ruined, unfortunately, so now I haven't got any neckwear."

"What do you think of our capital?" asked the undergraduate.

"Thank you, I like it," replied the poet. "I haven't actually had a chance of looking around very much, but that doesn't matter. But there's one thing I would like to see here in the capital, and that is Sigurður Breiðfjörð's grave. Would you like to show me where it is?"

"I know where the cemetery is, of course," said the undergraduate. "But I've never looked for any particular grave there. I wouldn't be any quicker at finding this tombstone than you yourself. If you want to find the cemetery, you walk west, then turn south. By the way, where are you staying the night?"

"I'm ashamed to say I really haven't thought so far ahead yet," said the poet. "I—I know no one . . ."

No one knows another man more than once, any more than a

woman. The friend you took leave of yesterday is a different man today, you do not know him any more, the world changes overnight, not even loyalty can conquer time. Whatever a man possesses, he possesses only for a fleeting moment—a friend, a sweetheart, his own life—just for a moment, the moment that is passing; the next moment it does not exist any more. And Ólafur Kárason's Sunday-best clothes were ridiculous rags in comparison with this man's everyday clothes.

"Is there any news from Bervík?" asked the undergraduate.

"Not that I remember."

"Reasonable weather?"

To think that he should know how to ask such ordinary questions, the poet thought to himself, and reported to the best of his ability that the grass-growth had been well above average and the hay crop was doing reasonably well so far this summer. "But there isn't much fishing with us, of course; it's the old story, as you know. On the other hand, there have been good catches at Kaldsvík."

Then there was silence. The undergraduate was becoming rather impatient; he drummed his fingertips on the table or put his finger into his mouth and bit at a nail or suddenly noticed a speck of dust on his shoes that had to be brushed away. Of course he had never intended to listen to the poet's report about the weather conditions in Bervík. Between these two men lay a gulf that could not be bridged. Neither of them knew what to say. Ólafur Kárason looked at his friend with pleading eyes and the sweat streamed from his forehead; it was like a dream about a ledge on a precipice, about drifting helplessly in a boat without oars.

Finally the undergraduate said, "I'm afraid I've got a rather special engagement tonight. I didn't know you were coming, you see . . ."

"Yes, I'll go now," said the poet, and stood up and wiped the sweat from his forehead with the sleeve of his jacket. "But I couldn't help it," he added, "I wanted so much to see you." And he smiled once more at his friend that gentle, remote smile, and his throat was dry.

— **14** —

At their parting, his friend gave him the address of a hotel which bore the proud name of "The Mountain Queen," and said that some woman from Sviðinsvík was running it. Ólafur Kárason wandered around the town that evening and asked his way to the hotel. Well-dressed young gentlemen stood at the street corners in groups and criticized the passers-by. When Ólafur Kárason came along in his forty-year-old jacket and National and Cultural Drawers from Pétur Pálsson the manager, this attire aroused only scant admiration and earned all the more severe criticism. The poet felt as if he were coming to Sviðinsvík for the first time and did not know how to put one foot in front of the other.

Over the door of the hotel there was a large signboard with a painting of Mount Hekla on it, and on top of the volcano there sat a beautiful woman in national costume looking out over the whole world. Underneath was printed "Mountain Queen Café." The poet drew from this the conclusion that the mountain queen was called Safé, which must be a modern version of the name Sophia. He felt so much respect for this house that he scarcely dared enter it. From the elegant vestibule, however, he eventually edged his way into an elegant lobby where he met an elegant girl. He took off his cap and said Good-day. The girl looked at his forty-year-old jacket and cultural drawers and did not return the greeting, but softened when she looked into his eyes; so he plucked up courage to ask if it would be possible to talk to the woman.

"What woman?" said the girl.

"I–Isn't there a woman from Sviðinsvík here?" he asked.

"I don't know what woman you're talking about," said the girl. "I don't suppose you're talking about Madame Félgor?"

Gradually the visitor and the inmate succeeded in understanding one another, and the girl set off to look for the woman.

While he waited, the poet had a chance of getting to know the atmosphere that reigned in this house.

In the dining room sat some extremely noisy men of foreign and native extraction, busily courting some almost unnaturally beautiful women with lavishly curled hair and crimsoned cheeks that put all shame to shame; and from another room came a clamor of unidentifiable musical instruments not unlike a rattle, a banger, and three tin buckets rolling down a staircase. Happy couples danced past the doorway.

Then a door in the lobby suddenly opened and a woman came walking towards Ólafur Kárason, and face to face with this sight the poet suddenly knew where he was. He perceived the house in its natural setting; this house was just a continuation of a fairy tale from the past. Once upon a time there was a man, or rather, once upon a time there was not a man but a living corpse who came riding across the moors on a stretcher; and there were fairy maidens; and he was woken up from the dead.

Þórunn of Kambar came sweeping toward him, an energetic woman with black wavy hair, darkened eyebrows, rouged cheeks, and false teeth, and thick spectacles to shield these mysterious, semi-albino eyes which no colorist has ever managed to capture, wearing a rustling silk dress, rather plump with two or three bracelets and several rings set with precious stones, a half-smoked cigarette between nicotine-stained fingers. But it soon became obvious that the hostess's ornaments were not just vanity—they were the outward symbols of her inner virtues, for she was the only person in this capital city who did not seem ashamed of greeting a humble guest who had neither hit upon the right fashion in jacket and trousers nor acquired the art of mixing with distinguished people.

"Ólafur Kárason of Ljósavík, you are welcome here!"

She still spoke in that well-remembered ambiguous voice which fitted both night and day, but the twilight best of all.

"I don't suppose you'd be so kind as to let me stay the night here?" said Ólafur Kárason.

"Of course!" she said. "How delighted I am to see you! You're almost exactly the same as you were. Let's get out of this din at once and go to my own room."

She still had not lost her tendency to lay hands on people; she laid her hands on Ólafur Kárason instinctively as she made him sit down beside her on a dark-red plush sofa. She wanted him to smoke a cigarette and drink a glass of wine, but he said he was too old now to learn that sort of thing. In her room everything was of plush and more plush, cushion upon cushion, tablecloth upon tablecloth, picture upon picture, mirrors mirroring themselves in one another.

"Do you remember when I raised you from the dead?" she asked.

"Yes," he replied, "and I thank you for it with all my heart. Unfortunately I was never in a position to repay you. But when I look around me in your house, I can see that it's been proved once again that God pays for the poor. I myself haven't acquired much more than I had when I came to you dead that time, and learned very little more than I knew."

"On the other hand you haven't lost anything since then," she said. "You have the same eyes, and the golden sheen in your hair and these long, delicate hands."

She took his hands in hers, as she had done so long ago, and studied them. Then she said, "There's a barber in the house on the other side of the street; go and have a shave and a haircut, and when you come back I'll give you a new suit I've been keeping since the spring. I took it in lieu of rent from a very nice man. Dinner will be served soon."

A little later be was shaved, trimmed, and bathed and wearing new clothes from top to toe. She herself tied his tie under his shirt collar. She looked at him and started humming a tune which was coming from the room below, and he stared at himself in the mirror.

"There," she said at last. "Stop looking at yourself in the mirror. Come and talk to me. Tell me why you could never fall in love with me."

"What a thing to say, Þórunn! I was always so terribly attracted to you," he said. "On the other hand I didn't always understand you. You knew more worlds than I did. You even made me a little afraid of you sometimes. But you always had a very overpowering personality. I was only seventeen."

"And it was another girl who came to you through a window. All you wanted to give me was some damned old book."

"What was I to do?" he said.

"If you had fallen in love with me, nothing would ever have happened to me," she said. "Nor to you, either."

"You have everything at your feet, Þórunn," he said. "Even this world is your world, too."

"If you mean that I'm wicked enough even for this world, too, it isn't true," she said. "One can never be wicked enough for this world. No one is wicked enough for this world."

Then the look in her eyes was drowned in the refraction of the glasses, and she started to hum to herself, absentmindedly, and the smoke from her cigarette curled upwards.

This girl had at one time gone to England to become world-famous for spiritualism, but her inexperience of miracles was too great for them to be able to use her. Pétur Þríhross and Júel, whom she called unprintable names, forgot to send her any money, a stray Icelandic country girl alone in a world city. "You said just now that I was intelligent enough to live in this world, yet I wasn't even intelligent enough to be a successful woman of the streets in a large city, and that sort of failure is the crowning misfortune that can befall a woman."

She had started singing again. No one knew what she was looking at. The poet paced the floor deep in thought: "You have always been a little cynical in the way you talk, both about yourself and the world," he said. "Will you promise not to be offended if I ask you in all sincerity: did Friðrik never exist?"

She often did not hear what was said to her, and she went on singing; the cast of her features had been of a particular kind originally, and could only accommodate a particular kind of experience, but now the experience had long ago settled in these features and marked them in harmony with their nature and origin. But while he was still puzzling over her, she had long since made up her mind about him.

"When the devil has taken care of old Félgor, I'm going to marry a man with your face," she said, "your brow, your golden hair, your eyes, your hands."

"Thank you," he said. "But who was the other man you mentioned?"

"It's my husband, whom I had just finished undressing and laying to rest when you arrived. He died at seven o'clock tonight. He's lying there in the next room."

"Good God!" said Ólafur Kárason. "Is your husband dead?"

"Yes, he died today," said Madame Félgor. "But don't grieve over it. He also died yesterday. And he died the day before yesterday. He dies every day. Shall I show you?"

She led the poet against his will into the next room; he did not dare do other than tiptoe out of respect for this great and constantly repeated death. In the marital bed there lay an obese corpse, bald, blue in the face, with its mouth open and its teeth on the bedside table; the flabby shoulders protruded from under the bedclothes, and one arm hung limply over the edge of the bed; it was absolutely true, this man was dead to an unnatural degree, and yet there was in him some ghost which made a curious whistling noise in his nostrils.

"Look at him!" said Þórunn of Kambar. "I'll even show you all of him." She pulled the covers off him as if she were displaying a newborn child, and the poor fellow lay there completely naked and completely dead and snorting quietly; very short, with two breasts and straggling wisps of black hair between them, a potbelly like a round of tallow, thighs like a woman's. Ólafur Kárason was filled with revulsion.

"Is it the cognac?" he whispered, for he had the strange idea that this liquid was the most dangerous poison known to mankind.

But she did not reply to questions about minor details; she covered her husband again, without a word, and the show was over.

"He was a chief steward on a Danish liner on the Icelandic run," she said when they were sitting down again. "The poor wretch saved my life. I was standing weeping on the quayside in Copenhagen, and couldn't get home."

"Weeping? You?" he said.

"Yes," she said. "They were real tears, as any analysis would have proved. What else do you think it was?"

There was roast meat on the table and silver cutlery and porcelain dishes, and for the first time a banquet was being given for this poet.

"I feel I don't know how to eat," he said.

"Let me pour you some red wine," she said.

"Don't you think our souls might suffer?" he asked.

"I know exactly where I stand," she replied, and her bracelets jangled on her bright wrist as she lifted the bottle and poured the wine into the glass, and it poured in a jerky rhythm that reminded one of a heartbeat.

"If I didn't know that the gold you wear is a symbol of human virtues, I would be frightened," he said.

"There's supposed to be good body in this wine," she said, and raised her glass and drank to him.

But when he had gone to bed that night she came into his room and sat down in the armchair, as inscrutable as ever, and went on smoking and humming; the look in her eyes through the spectacles confused him because of its mixture of red and green on top of the wine he had drunk.

"I don't suppose I could ask you to take off your glasses?" he said.

"No," she said. "Once I asked you to tell me what truth was, and you wouldn't tell me."

"You yourself said that money was truth," he said. "If I had had a hundred krónur I would have given them to you."

"You asked me earlier," she said, "whether Friðrik the elf doctor ever existed. The gods that we ourselves create exist, and no others."

"I know," he said. "And yet . . ."

"And yet what?"

"There exists one Music," he said, "one Voice."

"Why did you say a hundred krónur? I only asked you for five, at the most ten. But you gave me a useless old book. And it was another girl who came in through your window."

"Haven't you then forgiven me yet, Þórunn, you who have had all your soul's wishes fulfilled? Excuse me, of whom is that picture hanging on the wall over there?"

"Oh, it's that devil, Napoleon the Great," she said. "He goes with all second-rate hotel bedrooms."

She took off her glasses.

The dusk never grew any darker; this was the owl's light. Outside the open window it had started to rain, and the soft and gentle rain of midsummer blended with the sound of footsteps in the street and the noise of carriages hurrying past in blissful, unrelated distance. Þórunn of Kambar's eyes were green.

"Listen, Ólafur," she said. "What did you think about me when they had sent me abroad?"

"I thought: she has cured the sick and raised the dead, she will one day become famous throughout the world."

"You're lying," she said. "What you thought was this: she is mad and has hallucinations; she's a criminal and has let herself be used to set fire to a house; she's a whore, she . . . she . . . she . . . that's what you thought."

She stubbed out the cigarette in the ashtray, and the lines around her mouth twitched in a way he could not interpret, everything between hatred and grief, callousness and tenderness and yet none of these things. Then she began to take off her ornaments slowly, one by one, and throw them on the floor. This was the one true Þórunn of Kambar, of whom one never knew from which world she was being controlled; one never knew either when she was being genuine, and when artificial, nor where in her the dividing line between fiction and reality lay.

"If you didn't know before what to think of me, you know it now," she said, and kicked the last bracelet so that it rolled under the chair. He was as far as ever from knowing what to think of her. What will she look like when she starts gathering up her jewelry tomorrow morning when I'm gone, he thought, as she fell to her knees beside his bed, without any finery, and leaned against his breast, babbling deliriously.

— **15** —

In a village in Rumania there lives a man whose profession is swallowing knives, forks and other tableware. In Australia recently a calf was born with eight legs, six of them below, and two growing out his back. Rama the Fifth, king of Siam, had three thousand wives and three hundred and seventy children—a hundred and thirty-four sons and two hundred and thirty-six daughters. In England a dog has been taught to speak; in Germany a horse has learned to write. In one African state, betrothed girls are kept for three years in pitch-black cellars and forbidden to utter a word.

Ólafur Kárason had never suspected that such momentous events could be happening in the world as those one could read about in the family weekly *Heimilið*, which was an exceptionally popular publication in the prison. For the first few days, the poet never tired of pondering over the wonders and miracles that this periodical preached with a view to enlivening family life in the land. Just as the annalists of old used to record comets, he jotted down some of the more remarkable events printed in that family journal, with his own questions in brackets for closer attention at a more suitable opportunity.

In the family weekly *Heimilið* there were recorded also lengthy descriptions of bank robberies, burglaries, poisonings, and double murders, all of which seemed to be an indispensable condition for a happy family life. For the first few days the poet was far from being unconcerned about who had murdered whom. He read about these great tidings with genuine interest and sometimes sat up all night by the light of his little lamp in the hope that the right murderer and the real thief would be found, and suddenly the dawn would be breaking over a sleepless and exhausted man, almost with blood on his hands. But the more volumes of *Heimilið* he read, the less he was affected by the kind of news with which an ordinary family concerns itself. Soon it no longer upset him to hear about a murder; eventually a multiple murder evoked only a sleepy yawn in this poet's face; finally he had reached the point where he was merely slightly irritated if someone mentioned murder, and instinctively sided with the murderer against the victim. This made him afraid that he was becoming a wicked man, and he decided to stop reading this family literature completely. The summer passed. He began to think about the flowers of late summer, and how blissful it would be now to be able to smell the fragrance of meadowsweet, to put a forget-me-not in one's buttonhole, and to taste a mountain dandelion.

"Today there is peace and quiet and blessed calm in all God's creation." The voice was deep and warm, but rather brittle and extremely old. "But there is even more peace and quiet and blessed calm in the soul of a Christian person who acknowledges his Savior at a time of trial."

Then the door opened. And after this preamble an elderly gentleman appeared, wearing a black overcoat in the sunshine and high galoshes in the dry weather, with a snowy-white, high, wing collar round his shriveled neck and a few pamphlets in his hand.

"My brother," he said, and gave Ólafur Kárason his blue, silky-smooth old man's hand and looked at him with mild, impersonal affection. The light in those old eyes was of the kind which knew no shadow. He had a large and manly beaked nose and thick, dark eyebrows, a skin like old parchment, and snow-white hair. Ólafur Kárason thought him a handsome man. He shook the visitor's hand and said instinctively, "I can see that you are a friend of the heavens."

"That's far too high praise, my brother," said the old man. "I'm only a poor cathedral pastor. But it's certainly true, heaven is beautiful. And the Lord has bestowed his grace upon mankind."

He asked the prisoner where he came from and who his parish pastor was, and asked Ólafur Kárason to give him his greetings when he returned home. He said he could not stay long this time, but to make up for the shortness of the visit he was going to leave a little booklet by a famous man in Norway: when the soul is sorely tried, it is often good to have beside one a little book about something beautiful. The poet thanked him.

"God sometimes leads a man along mysterious paths to meet his Redeemer," said the cathedral pastor. "Nature in her midsummer finery is full of warmth and gentleness and blessed peace, and yet the grace of God can work the greatest wonders within cold walls. It is glorious, my brother."

"It's certainly very strange, at least," said Ólafur Kárason. "Indeed, I've often thought how much God and Nature can be at variance with one another."

"If Nature listens to God's voice, heaven is our wealth, my brother," said the cathedral pastor with his kindly, remote smile, a mild wayfarer who despite his many responsibilities in the town was never in too much of a hurry to say a kind word to his brother in passing. He promised to come again soon in order that they could talk more about God's grace.

Ólafur Kárason was left with the cathedral pastor's booklet, *Komið á fund Jesú*, and he opened it in two or three places before he put it on the shelf beside the New Testament. It was one of those Christian books in which everything was attributed to Matt, Luke, Cor, and Rev, and behind these names stood strange numbers with commas in between, like some kind of decimal fractions, and with brackets round them, as in algebra. He was far from feeling any ill will towards writings of this kind, but ever since he had grown up under the dominion of the *Book of Sermons* at Fótur-undir-Fótarfæti it had become second nature to him to pay no regard to any books in which God and Jesus were mentioned.

The family that lived in this establishment was perhaps a little unhappy because they were far from meadowsweet and mountain dandelions, but they were not any unhappier than the rest of mankind, far from it, and as people they were undoubtedly no worse than the average run of people who are outside prison—with the exception of drunks. The drunks were a special category. No one had less business in this peaceful, civilized house than these lunatics who were thrown in here at night, fighting and cursing, and set the whole place by the ears. When they sobered up, they thought they were a cut above everyone else and behaved as if they had landed in here solely through the injustice of the authorities and the malevolence of the police. These monsters, who could not even be counted as people, let alone animals, dared to presume that this house was beneath their dignity, and that they as nonresidents were in some way better than other folk. The drunks were the criminals whom the others all agreed ought to be shot out of hand, without warning.

"Oh, I wouldn't say that, perhaps," said the newcomer.

It was the first day.

They were standing outside in the yard on a bright summer's day, chatting together after their meal before going back to their cells.

The drunks had kept them awake all night, and they were all rather bad-tempered, except Ólafur Kárason, who wanted to turn the conversation to other matters. There were tufts of grass growing beside the prison wall, and there the poet caught the eye of a little dandelion. He took the nearest man by the arm and pointed to the dandelion.

"Look at that little dandelion," said the poet. "It's the first hawkweed I've seen this summer. It's strange that this type of dandelion is never seen until well into the summer—I wonder if it's because it grows so late? Or could it be because the other flowers are so beautiful that one doesn't notice it until they are gone?"

But the man he turned to happened to be the murderer, the pride of the house; he was a man of under thirty, auburn-haired, pale and handsome, wearing a leather apron because he was the prison cobbler. The murderer made no reply.

"I don't think he appreciates flowers," said the household's moonshiner. "What's the point of talking about poetic matters to men like that, who can't even see the sun shining from a clear sky?"

There was a short silence. Then Ólafur Kárason happened to look at the prison wall in front of him and said, "That's a very high and well-built wall!"

"Hell's bells, yes, eh!" said a conceited sneak thief; it was the only thing he knew.

Then the murderer said drily, "Only a useless wretch couldn't get over the wall if he wanted to. That wall's nothing."

"He has no respect for anything," the moonshiner said to Ólafur Kárason. "It doesn't matter what you talk about. If it's flowers, he doesn't answer; walls, that's nothing. He's so proud of having done away with some useless creature that nothing impresses him."

The murderer paid no attention and made no reply, but Ólafur Kárason was upset that people should always be throwing the murder in his teeth for no reason, and was at once ready to take his side.

"It's an expensive luxury that a man pays for with twenty long years," he said. "In my opinion he has every right to be proud."

"That's absolutely true," said a forger. "It takes a lot of courage to get married, but even more to kill someone. The moonshiner needn't talk. He stinks. He distilled his stuff behind his cows' backsides, then buried the brew in a dunghill so that the authorities wouldn't find it, and sold it out of the muck to his customers."

"Hell's bells, yes, eh!" said the sneak thief, and wriggled with pleasure.

"Aw, shut up," said the forger. "Being an idiot is a poor reason for sitting in prison."

"He's only a youngster," said Ólafur Kárason, and took the sneak thief under his wing. "Don't be unkind to him."

"Yes, I don't know what youth's coming to nowadays," said the forger. "I spit on this small fry who breaks into shops to pinch biscuits, malt extract and shoelaces; or goes into workships at night and sneaks out with one file and a few three-inch nails; or runs off with a louse-ridden overcoat from someone's vestibule. But it's the last straw when this damned trash call themselves criminals. Sneak thieves should be put into homes for mental defectives."

The moonshiner was a broad-minded man with a fondness for poetry, as is usual with people of his calling, and he asked Ólafur Kárason if it were true that he was a poet.

"Oh, nothing to speak of," said Ólafur Kárason.

"What would it cost to make a poem about us?" asked the sneak thief.

"For friends and brothers, I do it for nothing," said the poet.

"Make a poem about me," said the sneak thief.

"My dear friend, I'm afraid I'm no good at composing poems about men," said the poet. "But if you needed to write one to a beautiful girl who was your . . ."

"Hell's bells, yes, eh! There was a new one scrubbing the corridor this morning," said the sneak thief.

"It's a crying scandal that decent men have to live with people of this kind!" said the forger. "People like that should be locked up in a box with the drunks."

Soon the poet had become the main attraction of this bright company in the yard within the wall; they all came to him except the murderer, who stood aloof, and the sneak thief took hold of his sleeve and tried to pull him over.

"He can make poems," said the sneak thief.

"Really," said the murderer.

Ólafur Kárason was shy, and tried to get away. Several of them offered to recite poems they themselves had composed if Ólafur Kárason would recite one of his. The murderer made to go away.

"Don't go," they said to the murderer. "Stay and listen; there's some poetry coming."

"Poetry bores me," said the murderer, and headed inside to his work.

"Why?" they shouted.

"It's meaningless," said the murderer, and vanished into the house.

Not flowers, not walls, not even poetry. Was all human endeavor then, even the beautiful of the world, of so little consequence compared with murder? Were the flowers themselves so contemptible in comparison with this potent and mystical experience? He was at once the prison's justification and its *raison d'être*, its man of distinction, its bishop, its millionaire, and its internal authority; his fate was a silent secret that made other men small.

It is strange how similar the inmates of a prison are to those outside; by the time the bell rang they were all falling over themselves to recite their own poems and had forgotten that they had been going to listen to the poet Ólafur Kárason's poetry. In actual fact, each and every one of them liked his own poetry best and did not care a damn about the poet's poetry. The murderer was the exception; he had said he did not want to listen to Ólafur Kárason's poetry, but neither had he himself composed anything which he forced down other people's throats at the first opportunity.

A little later the cathedral pastor came back. He was still wearing his heavy, black overcoat, galoshes and wing collar, and teetered along the corridor with short, old man's strides, and his knees sagged with age at every step.

"How warm and bright the days are getting!" the cathedral pastor mumbled affectionately as the warder opened the door. He smiled with his good eyes and bad teeth, a man who in the endless chores of the day thought it his prime duty, and a necessity that overrode all other necessities, to stop in his brother's house to say a kind word. It was not just the smile; his whole demeanor, together with that affectionate, habitual talk which did not seem to be directed at any particular person, had the same effect as a hearth in a cold house when a fragrant log fire suddenly starts burning in it; and the poet welcomed him.

"How warm and bright the days are getting, full of blessed peace, when one knows that God's grace is truly their source," said the cathedral pastor. "May I sit down on the corner of your little bench here, even though I haven't really time to stay? But when one is old, my brother, one's legs become as unmanageable as a little child's."

"When I am old, I would like to have a face like yours," said Ólafur Kárason, and gazed at the cathedral pastor, fascinated.

"If I have a face that rejoices in God's grace, my brother, it is because I have learned more from those who have lived within these walls than from those who live outside them," said the cathedral pastor. "I have learned more from those who have fallen down than those who have remained upright. That's why I am always so happy in this house. God bless this house."

"What do you think of the murderer?" asked Ólafur Kárason.

"Uhu," said the cathedral pastor. "Christ doesn't judge men by what they have done, my brother, but according to whether they feel the true meaning of the hours and days deep in their souls. I am an old man now. When age begins to tell on a tired man, he doesn't talk about sin any more, my brother. The joy at having found God's grace, that is the Joy. Those who understand that trial and grace are two sisters—their house is a large house; it is a beautiful house; and it stands high upon a rock."

He brought a small booklet out of his pocket and gave it to the poet. "May I leave with you a small pamphlet by a famous man in Denmark?" he said. "It is called *Come to Jesus*."

"Thank you very much," said the poet. "This is the same book you lent me the other day."

"Well, well, my brother, I'm so glad," said the cathedral pastor. "I am quite sure you have felt the blessed warmth that radiates from this little book."

At this, the poet had to admit that he unfortunately had not read the book yet.

"Perhaps my brother doesn't care for books much?" said the cathedral pastor.

"I was brought up on such a tedious *Book of Sermons* that I doubt if I'll ever recover from it," said the poet.

"Dear me, how unfortunate," said the cathedral pastor in the same tone of voice, but ready to vindicate everyone. "It must have been Árni's *Sermons*. He was sometimes a little long-winded, bless him. Some people are long-winded about Jesus; some are brief. But it doesn't really matter, and you mustn't despair simply because some people are long-winded about Jesus. The main thing is to speak about Jesus neither briefly nor at length, but to yearn for Him in silence; to have a place for Him in one's house; and to be glad."

Ólafur Kárason was silent for a long time, fascinated by this talk, and went on contemplating this old, peaty-brown, parchment face under the silvery hair, where every passion had long ago been transformed into gratitude; was anything on earth more blissfully happy? In the presence of this man there was shelter against all weathers.

"I hope nonetheless," said the cathedral pastor finally, and stood up, "that I may leave this little book with you before I go. It's by a famous man in Sweden and it's called *Come to Jesus*. Just as bad books are bad if they are bad, so good books are good if they are good, my brother."

"Thank you very much," said the poet; he accepted the book, and laid it beside the other copy on the top of the New Testament on the shelf.

"Now, it's possible that we won't see one another for a while," said the cathedral pastor. "I have a daughter in Copenhagen. She and her husband have built themselves a house there and invited me to Copenhagen to see their new house."

"I'm sure that nothing but good can happen to you, but let me wish you a good journey nonetheless," said the poet and clasped the cathedral pastor's hand, and his eyes moistened a little because he was so happy for the old man to have a daughter in Copenhagen and to be going to see the house.

"I've really got two long journeys ahead of me now," said the cathedral pastor; he was trembling a little with age, and there was a glint of humor in his smile, as if he were going to say something daring. "I have ahead of me a journey to Heaven. And I also have ahead of me a journey to Copenhagen. To tell you the truth, I am looking forward even more to going to Copenhagen. Have you any friend in Copenhagen to whom I can give your greetings, my brother?"

"If you should ever on your long journeys come across a despised poet and poor man like me, then he is my friend, and I ask you to give him my greetings," said Ólafur Kárason of Ljósavik.

"Thank you, I shall remember that," said the cathedral pastor, perhaps a little absentmindedly. "And now good-bye; with all my heart I wish you all the best in body and soul, now and always; and a happy Christmas. May the grace of Our Lord Jesus Christ be with you all."

This was in the middle of August.

Ólafur Kárason was sorry that the cathedral pastor was going abroad, and at once began to look forward to his return.

—— 16 ——

And it was not long, unfortunately, before the prison ceased to be an enjoyable novelty for the poet; its attraction was exhausted, even the murderer was no longer an interesting or desirable companion. In place of the cathedral pastor there came occasionally a tall and tedious curate, and they all felt he came there only from a sense of Christian duty and not because he loved his brothers in a simple and natural way, let alone because he thought he learned more from the inmates of a prison than from those outside it or felt happier in this house than in other houses, like the cathedral pastor. Sometimes there came also a skinny missionary who understood God but not people, and knew all the less about people the more he knew about God.

One night the poet woke up with internal pains. He was convinced that he was about to die. Suddenly he remembered that he was not a free man. He sat up in bed and felt for the pains in his innards in a panic; yes, one was sure to die of such pains. What frightened him most was that the hope of being allowed to live before one died had vanished. Perhaps he now for the very first time appreciated liberty to the full. The irresponsible life of the prison, carefree, at the expense of others like the life of the rich—what was that compared with being a despised poet and a poor man on the outside? Without liberty there was no life. To live in penury as a parish pauper, beggar, versifier and figure of contempt, his honor blemished, and even in poor health—nothing mattered if you were free. Liberty was the crown of life and the most precious of all precious things—the freedom to lie in a green dell beside a brook, the freedom to look at the sky, the freedom to see a girl in the distance, the freedom to sing, the freedom to beg. And now suddenly he was about to die. He got out of bed and touched the cold windowpane with his fingertips and gazed for a long time at the stars shining in the sky, like a penniless child standing outside a shop window full of expensive toys.

From that night on he was tormented by the fear of the emptiness around him: of being alone, of knowing no one in the world; of loving no one, of knowing himself to be loved by no one; but above all else by the fear that true love did not exist but was only a jug of water in the heat of the sun. His days passed in a foreboding of death. He tried to drown his anguish by wrestling with poetry and prose, but the visions of the land rising obliquely against reality would not reveal themselves to him; and the winged word associations had taken flight.

When he finally got a letter from his wife, Jarþrúður Jónsdóttir, his eyes filled with tears, not because she wrote so movingly, because she did not write her letters herself, and not because she was so noble at keeping faith with a husband of his sort, but because money is reality, and out of the letter rolled two silver krónur. This woman who could not forget how the southerners had treated Pastor Hallgrímur Pétursson understood the necessity of not running short of pocket money in the south. But how the poorest woman in the poorest district in the country could conjure minted silver from her sleeve—

that was a miracle that made even the forger himself an ignoramus and a sneak thief.

This wife, who thought that she herself had committed sins the size of elephants, said not a word about his own transgression. On the other hand she mentioned that Helga, the daughter of the ravine farmer at Berá, had gone out to collect firewood that autumn and never returned. People thought she had been pregnant, but it was not known that she had been associating with a man. True, a boy had been staying at the cottage since spring, but he was so recently confirmed that no one could believe that he could have had any ideas about women. But if it had been so, the girl's disappearance had only been a proof that over us human beings there hangs an awful sword of justice. Finally the wife said that if the bailiff flatly refused to reinstate Ólafur Kárason at the school when he came back, she would try to arrange with the pastor that he would get some kind of official post in the future, at least as Bervík's dog-doctor.

Towards Christmas, when the darkest shadows lay over the world, he thought he might find relief in starting on the long-desired poem about the sun, despite all the advice of the sages in Aðalfjörður. But the weeks went by without producing a single couplet which he thought worthy of the subject. The anguish of the heart was still stronger than his belief in the sun, and the poet went on lying awake at night, sweating, with palpitations and bouts of shivering. Often he was convinced that he would die before he managed to compose his poem about the sun; seldom has a distant heavenly body made life so difficult for a poet. His mind wandered off along ever more dangerous paths. Finally he had begun to wonder if the fiery furnace of this orb was not just an accidental blaze caused by an explosion or some other disturbance in matter, or simply some breakdown in space, this soulless space, this eternal void, which actually seemed to be the only rational and justifiable condition possible. He asked if the solar system had not come into existence through some mysterious accident, if the life that sparked from this ill-starred energy was anything but a corruption of matter, and if it would not be extinguished after a calculable, yes almost foreseeable, number of years, and with it the buttercup in the homefield and the fine poems of the poets. In a word, his thoughts led him to the point where one ceases to understand the sun. Christmas passed this wretched poet by; in a fog he saw old, sin-laden women from the missionary society spying at the door or bleating hymns around a Christmas candle, and also the lanky, boring curate, but there was no Music and no Light; and on Christmas Day the poet got up and said to the warder in a strange voice:

"Soon I shall be dead."

At this, the warder became a little alarmed.

"Isn't the cathedral pastor coming soon?" asked the poet.

"He'll be away for a year. He's in Copenhagen with his daughter."

"Thank goodness," said the poet, and cheered up a little at knowing this delightful man to be in the one place that was better than being with God.

But one morning not long afterwards, the poet could not get up, but lay still. He said he had unbearable pains all over, and claimed that old ailments that had afflicted him in his youth had flared up again. He did not eat anything, he did not talk to anyone, he turned his face to the wall. A doctor came and listened to his chest and took his temperature. He was asked if he had any friend in town, but he said he had no friend. The doctor said it would be best to take him to the hospital. He was carried out on a stretcher to an ambulance, but unfortunately he was in no state to enjoy life to any extent while he was being driven from the prison to the hospital. He was examined for a few days with magic methods, hundred-thousand krónur apparatuses and frightful medicines, and X-rayed body and soul; but science found no ailment to speak of in him apart from this ailment of matter, these accidents in the ether, this misunderstanding in space, which is called life. He asked politely if science thought he was lying in bed for fun?

"Well, what's wrong with you, then?" asked science.

"I can no longer understand the sun," said the poet.

At that, science gave him a mass of mixtures and tablets and sent him back to the prison.

And the long, dark winter went on passing.

The inmates of the house were very worried about their poet; they all wanted to cheer him up or do something for him. The thief brought a pack of cards and wanted him to play Snap for money with him and another thief; the moonshiner brought a brew from a midden which someone outside the prison, a colleague of his, had managed to smuggle to him in a flask; even the murderer came to share silence with him and look at him from his unapproachable distance from which all things seemed to be nothing but trivialities, except for one exception. But it was all to no avail.

The poet was certainly neither ill-natured nor morose, just taciturn and exhausted like a consumptive. With a gentle but strange smile he declined the invitation to play Snap with his young protégé, the thief, and to drink dunghill-brew with his poetic friend, the moonshiner. Even the pride of the prison and the company's internal ballast, the murderer, was not able to elevate the ailing soul of his brother, the poet, to a higher level.

And then one day it so happened, if one could talk of days any more in the life of this poet, that he dreamed a dream. He had dreamed many dreams, certainly, when he dozed, but they were difficult dreams, for there was no waking thought so pygmy that it did not take on a giant's shadow in sleep; but this was an exceptional dream, perhaps not just a dream but a portent and a revelation, a higher perception, a reality, and yet only four words, or rather, one name.

He did not know what time it was nor what day it was, for he had long since stopped asking about the succession of the hours or the names of the days. A bound man, his heart frozen, in the midst of that endless death which brooded over the world's most insignificant life—and then suddenly he was seized by the presentiment that Sigurður Breiðfjörð had now driven down from the skies after all this time. Divested of the cloak of visibility, the poet had now returned, perhaps inhabiting higher spheres than before, where neither color nor form reigned any more. Whatever heaven he inhabited, his golden chariot was here. And he spoke four words. He spoke one mysterious name. This name echoed through that myth-like dream, and in a flash it was woven with letters of fire across the soul's heaven: "Her name is Bera."

And then the dream was finished. He sat up wide awake and looked around. The first sunbeam of the year was on the prison wall above his bed.

"Is her name Bera?" he asked.

He got up on his knees on the bed, put both palms against the wall and touched the sunbeam. He rose to his feet and let the sunbeam fall on his face.

"I would never have thought that her name was Bera," he said.

He forgot the shadow of death; his mind went on dwelling unbidden on these saving words, on that name, that key to the future, this unknown happiness, this life. When it was dark, his mind dwelt on the message from the poet's golden chariot; and when there was a knock at the door, he expected to see a woman with a white headdress and a golden diadem on her brow. But it was only the warder with his supper.

"Has anyone been asking for me today?" asked the poet.

"No," said the warder, relieved that the prisoner should be speaking to him at last after a month's silence. "Are you expecting someone?"

"Yes," said the poet. "If a woman by the name of Bera asks for me, tell her that I'm waiting."

— **17** —

It was midsummer again. Ólafur Kárason of Ljósavik stood in his new suit, the gift of Þórunn of Kambar, outside the gate of the prison, a free man. He was very pale, his eyes as clear and blue as ever, the sheen of his hair just as golden, his gait as unsteady as it had been when he came to the village of Sviðinsvík for the first time, out of accord with the solid ground he was treading; this man could start floating without warning.

He took care not to venture far from the side of the houses, probably for fear of being surrounded. At the shipping office he was told that the coastal steamer was sailing the next day, but would be traveling the wrong way round and would take at least ten days to carry the poet home. If he wanted a more convenient passage he would have to wait for a fortnight; but it hurts the purse to be a free outsider in the capital, and Þórunn of Kambar had gone for a holiday to the country with her husband, so that no one knew the poet at "The Mountain Queen Sophia." He decided to take advantage of the sailing tomorrow.

His route zigzagged from the prison to the churchyard. The man who had been his first friend and who had visited him in a golden chariot when everyone else had forgotten him—that was the man he was going to meet.

Nothing the poet had seen in the capital could equal this churchyard. How remarkable it was that such a park should flourish around dead bones! One could hardly believe that the flowers were real, so lovely were they. And it was difficult to imagine that anywhere on earth there could be a greater assemblage of celebrities than could be read here in golden letters on artistically carved tombstones. There was not a single resident of this place who during his lifetime did not appear to have carried the crushing burden of conventional, orthodox behavior with ease and complete mastery. It was amazing. And more people than anyone could have suspected had borne the mark of true greatness, held high office, received titles and honors, performed outstanding taks for the good of the fatherland. The women had not only been beautiful but also virtuous. Ashamed of the smallness of his own reputation, this useless poet greeted the righteous folk who dwelt in this park.

But no matter how he searched, he could not find the grave of his friend Sigurður Breiðfjörð. He wandered around the cemetery for most of the day and stopped at every tombstone. Finally he had given up all hope of finding him, and now felt that his journey was only half complete if he had to turn back home without finding what he sought. The sun was already low in the west. Then he met a poor woman who was sitting beside an unpretentious grave and talking to it, and he imagined that this must be a widow who had lost her son and now had no one left in the world any more. He took a króna piece out of his pocket and gave it to her and told her to buy herself some coffee. She thanked him and said, "Do you belong to the churchyard here?"

"No," he said. "I don't belong here, in a manner of speaking."

Then he asked her if she could show him the grave of the poet Sigurður Breiðfjörð.

The woman: "Does he lie under a stone, or does he not lie under a stone?"

Ólafur Kárason of Ljósavík: "I've heard that he lies under a stone."

"Then he's one of those I talked to last year," said the woman. "I won't be talking to him this year."

"Just so," said the poet. "May I ask why you won't be talking to him this year?"

The woman: "Last year I talked to all those who lie under a stone. This year I talk to those who don't lie under a stone."

Then the poet said, "I hope it's not too impertinent to ask out of curiosity what you talk to them about?"

"I am trying to prove to them that death doesn't exist," said the woman.

"You may well be right, my dear," said the poet. "I only know one person here, and he isn't dead, at least not in the usual way."

"None of them is dead," said the woman. "Didn't their mothers perhaps love them? When you look into the eyes of those you love, you understand that death doesn't exist."

"How can that be?" said the poet. "One day every eye is extinguished."

"Beauty itself lives in the eyes you love," said the woman. "And beauty cannot be extinguished."

"Beauty?" said the poet in surprise. "What beauty?"

"The beauty of the heavens," said the woman.

He raised his cap to the sibyl and hurried away, taking care to avoid listening to any more, but letting these words echo in his mind in the certainty that more would not be said however much was added; and he wandered around this park for a long time. But when he was on his way out, through a little gate in the wall, despairing of finding the grave of his friend the poet, he happened to look to his left, and there was the grave. It was really too insignificant for anyone to notice it except by accident, a gable-shaped dolerite slab reaching just above a man's knee. All the other monuments in the churchyard

were of costlier and more enduring stone. This stone was weather-
worn and covered with a yellow-green crust, for only Nature tended
this grave; the grass grew up to it unchecked. On the front of the
stone were carved these words in deep, antique Roman lettering,
which grew shallower the more the stone wore away: *Sigurður Breiðfjörð
1799–1846*. And above the name a harp had been carved on the stone,
and it had five strings.

He was the greatest of all the penniless folk poets in Iceland.
While others went to the university in Copenhagen to study profound sciences and fine arts, he was sent to Greenland to cooper barrels. While the smart set performed heroics of conventional orthodox
behavior—set up house, made a delightful home with a beautiful
wife and well-behaved children—he sold his wife for a dog. While
others rose to the heights of fame and gained high office, titles and
honors, he was sentenced to twenty-seven lashes. The leaders of the
nation, the major poets and intellectual pioneers, proved by their
learning and eloquence that he was a doggerel rhymester and a fool.
While worthy men died in style in the bosom of their family, and
loving hands laid them to rest, he died of starvation in a cold outhouse and the parish council had the corpse carted away. But the
spirit of this penniless folk poet, whom the learned dismissed and the
major poets despised, has lived with the Icelandic nation for a thousand years, in the smoky farm cottage, in the destitute fisherman's
hut under the glacier, in the shark-catcher off the north coast when
all fishing grounds are lost in the black midwinter night of the Arctic
Sea, in the tatters of the vagabond who beds down beside a hill
sheep in the willow scrub of the moors, in the fetters of the chain
gang convicts on Bremerholm: This spirit was the quick in the life of
the nation throughout its history, and it was he who made this
poverty-stricken island in the western ocean into a great nation and a
world power and the unconquerable flank of the world. The five
strings of the poet's harp were the strings of joy, sorrow, love, hero-
ism and death. Ólafur Kárason of Ljósavík first stroked the cold
stone carefully with his hands, then let his fingertips touch the five
strings of the stone harp in the name of all the penniless folk poets

who have ever lived in Iceland, and he thanked the poet for having come down to him in a golden chariot from the heaven where he had his dwelling.

—— **18** ——

When Ólafur Kárason went to the ship with his luggage the next morning, the sun was dissolving the white mists of the night. The land which emerged, green and blue, from this magic shroud was the kind of land which had nothing to do with functional things but was first and foremost ornamental. The bustle of the quayside and the clatter of the ship's winch had no part in this world. The breasts of the hovering gulls gleamed like silver over the mirror-white smoothness of the sea. The gods create the world every day, to be sure, but never had they created a morning like this one. This was the one true morning. The poet stood apart from the crowd and gazed entranced at the green mirage of haze where this immortal morning-land was being born.

And as he stood there under the spell of the morning, looking around in the midst of the bustle of humanity but apart from it, a being suddenly appeared at his side, young and fair, and stared in silence into the blue as he did. And as soon as he looked at her for the first time he realized that she and the morning were one, that she was the morning itself clad in human form.

The young girl had halted at a distance from the crowd and remained standing there as if she were waiting. She was wearing a light coat, bareheaded, with quite a large suitcase by her side. What attracted his attention before anything else was the youthful freshness of her skin, the unbelievable wholesomeness of her coloring; yet she was closer to being pale than ruddy. Although something in the skin was related to the creaminess of summer growth, she was nonetheless closer to the plants, especially those which bear so tender a flower that the lightest touch leaves a mark. To protect her, Nature had covered her with a sort of magic helmet of invisibility: this was not the conventional beauty which was obvious to everyone immediately, which conquered its surroundings while it was there and demanded to be loved, admired and worshiped at once, quickly, and by everyone, as if it might be in danger of withering by sunset. Instead of the gleaming golden sheen which arouses immediate delight, there was an ash-gray color in this hair; the locks fell without coquetry in long, simple curves about her neck and cheeks, unevenly bleached by the sun, the fairest on the outside. There are eyes that rouse a man's admiration in a trice, wild with joy like conquering legions; but what characterized the eyes of this girl was a calm, clear depth, mingled with a hint of innate sorrow.

When he had looked at her for a while he addressed her and asked, "Are you sailing with this ship?"

She noticed him now for the first time and looked at him in surprise, a little offended by being suddenly accosted by a stranger; but she did not know how to deliver a snub. She just gave his question a silent assent and looked as far away from him as she could.

"May I carry your suitcase for you?" he said.

"No, thanks, I can manage it myself," she said.

She was not entirely at ease; the time of the ship's departure was approaching and whoever she was waiting for had not come. She pushed a lock of hair behind her ear and the expression on the young face grew more and more downcast. At last the ship hooted for the third time. She gave a start, grabbed her suitcase, and was going to carry it on board in a hurry, and then this stranger was still standing there ready to help her.

In the general confusion when the ship gave the signal for departure, she forgot to object to his willingness to help, and he seized her suitcase and they went on board. There was a mass of people saying Good-bye. She went over to the rail, still hoping to see someone on the quay, and he still stood there at a distance and studied her ethereal profile, the soft slender neck, and the curve of the bosom, which was really more imagined than real. And yet she was not a child, though the line of the leg was so finely drawn, from above and down, that it made the normal almost vulgar. It was precisely the line from hip to ankle which removed her young figure from the world of childhood's sexless mystery and made her a part of our world where all ideas about beauty are heresy except against the background of ugliness, and all beauty is the more enchanting the more its precincts approach the superior power of its opposite. Then he could no longer restrain himself, but addressed her again and said, "Is your name Bera?"

She realized to her annoyance that this tiresome man still had not gone from her side; but she did not know how to be nasty, and only replied with a quick, colorless No, shook her head at him a little, and went on staring ashore over the rail, full of anxiety and apprehension.

The ship lingered for a few more minutes after the final blast had been blown. But at the moment the moorings were being cast off, the young girl breathed more easily, stretched out over the rail and started to call out.

"Daddy, Daddy!" she cried. "I've been waiting for you for such a long time. Why are you so late? Now I can't say Good-bye to you!"

Her father was a tall, slim man, middle-aged and graying at the temples. And even though he was unshaven and swollen in the face and not a little drunk, with a battered old hat which had obviously been taken by mistake from someone of lower status, he bore clear signs of having known better times. His clothing, his features and his bearing all retained remnants of education and distinction which no ravages can erase completely. He came right to the edge of the quay, took off his hat and crumpled it before his breast, wrung it in his hands with all his strength in feverish desperation, and the tears streamed down his cheeks.

"My darling child!" he shouted, weeping. "My only dearest darling, I beg you in the name of Almighty God, don't go away from me; don't leave me!" He went on wringing his hat, his hands raised in supplication toward the ship, and the bystanders grabbed hold of him and pulled him back lest he fell into the sea.

"What can I do?" he cried to those who had saved him from falling into the sea. "Her mother is dead and she's the only thing I've got, and now I'm losing her!"

"Daddy!" cried the girl with greater vehemence than one suspected her capable of. "Can't I tell Uncle that you're coming north in the autumn?"

But either he did not hear what she was asking or did not care to reply; instead he shouted after the ship, weeping, "She is my treasure, my jewel, the light of my life. In the name of God's holy Son be good to her, spare her, give her life. Jesus Christ shield the only thing I possess; protect my innocent darling who is the most precious thing that has ever, ever been created in the world!"

Soon the ship had turned from the quay, and the father was lost to sight among the crowd on the pier. On the other hand the stranger who had carried her case was still by her side, and when she was out of hailing-distance from her father he said, "Bera, will you let me help you as he would have done?"

For the first time she looked at him properly to size him up, but without any inclination to become acquainted, only in silent inquiry. Finally, however, she said, "Why do you call me Bera?"

"Someone told me," he said.

"It must be some other girl," she said.

"No," he said. "It's you."

"Who says so?" she said.

"It's a remarkable voice," he said.

"Voice?" she said.

"That voice never tells an untruth," he said.

"You must be hearing things," she said.

"That would be something new, then," he replied.

"Where do you come from?" she said.

"From Bervík."

She did not recognize his place of origin and did not want to know any more; she leaned forward over the rail without paying any more attention to him and became distant.

"You don't ask me my name?" he said.

"Why should I ask you that?" she said.

"There's no need to be formal with me," he said. "I don't understand it when people are formal with me."

She did not say anything, and had no idea how to get rid of him.

"I'm called the Ljósvíkingur," he said.

"Really," she said.

But when she had gazed pensively for a while at the shimmer on the surface of the water, she remembered her suitcase. It was still standing where the poet had left it in the crush when people were crowding on board.

"You're no doubt traveling First Class," he said, and was still beside her and had his hand on her suitcase.

"No," she said.

"May I carry your suitcase below for you?" he said.

There was much hustle and confusion. Finally she managed to find out where her cabin was. He struggled with the suitcase. Soon afterwards she was gone, her door closed. She had forgotten to thank him for his help. She did not have breakfast and he walked past her door again and again, but it remained closed. That young, tender heart—how tired she must have been, he thought to himself, and wished her pleasant dreams.

— **19** —

It became known early in the day that among the passengers there was a heartthrob from the east coast, and the women naturally wanted him to start telling ghost stories at once. The heartthrob, however, would not hear of it while the sun was still up. But as the afternoon passed, the news spread round the ship that the heartthrob would be telling stories that evening. Dusk was awaited impatiently.

When she came out on deck again in the rays of the evening sun, her skin was more radiant than ever before; there was hidden gold in her cheeks and hair. The poet suddenly noticed that she was standing some way off, in a crowd of other girls. The morning's sadness had gone from her expression, and the smile that had replaced it was youth itself, impersonal and unshadowed. He thought her figure looked fuller and softer after the rest.

"What a long sleep you've had!" he said when the group of girls had dispersed and she was left standing there alone. "And what pleasant dreams you had!"

"How do you know that I slept and whether I dreamed?" she said.

"Forgive me for always talking to you," he said. "But it's because I feel that I understand you."

"Understand me?" she said, surprised. "That's impossible. Besides, I haven't said anything."

Then he said, "If you look at my face and study it closely, don't you feel that I'm the person who understands you—even though you don't say anything?"

She looked at him with her mouth closed, searchingly; in her face there was once again trouble and sadness, questioning and anxiety, as there had been this morning when she was waiting for her father. But when she had looked into his eyes for a while the smile shone through again, and everything was fine, the sun appeared.

"What did I dream, then?" she asked at last.

"That would be too long a story," he said. "The whole of Nature was involved in that dream, the sky, too."

"You see, I didn't dream anything at all," she said, and laughed. "I never dream anything."

"You don't understand yourself who you are," he said. "You are the dream of some other being. It is I who understand you."

"No," she said, a little vehemently. "You don't know who I am at all. Why are you trying to frighten me?"

He touched her arm with his fingertips to soothe her, and said in a trance, "Bera, nothing bad must ever happen to you, d'you hear, nothing but good, ever."

That fine-drawn face with its thick, ash-blonde eyebrows over those bright blue eyes, and the light upper lip which often half-disclosed the white, chisel-shaped teeth in an unintentional smile—the longer he looked at this face, the more enraptured he became by this voluptuous, hypersensitive dream of Nature itself, the more convinced that only a poet could understand this vision to the full, this amber radiance amid the gleam of metal, this fifth between trumpet and bass.

In the gloaming of the summer evening the passengers seated themselves in the saloon and waited for the storyteller—mostly women and their admirers. The lights were put out and the curtains drawn, because the night could not be trusted.

"The ghost stories are about to begin," said the poet. "Don't you want to hear them?"

"No," she said. "I'd rather go to bed and read a good book."

"It's a heartthrob who's telling them," he said.

"Ugh!" she said.

"And yet ghosts undoubtedly exist," he said. "At least in the soul."

"No," she said.

Then they went in to hear the ghost stories. She sat down on a corner-bench with some girls, and he had the sense to creep in without attracting much attention and without annoying people too much, and before she knew it he was sitting by her side.

The heartthrob was an awkward-looking countryman who studied folklore to get into print and become known among learned men in the south. He held the view that anyone who did not believe in Þorgeir's ghostly bull was off his head; otherwise he seemed to belong in some ordinary political meeting. He told ghost stories in the traditional way, with appropriate genealogies, topographical descriptions, details of employment, economics and meteorology, with imitations of people and animals, as well as endless references to worthy men and virtuous women. He overcame the listeners' skepticism with descriptions of moors and valleys that could not be faulted; he gave the lineage of everyone concerned in the story, so that people were convinced that this was not just a question of truthful and honest folk but also even of real folk, who might well be related to the listeners themselves. He described meticulously the weather conditions and farming methods in the districts where the hauntings took place, not forgetting the Anno Domini, the month, the day and the time when some worthy man or virtuous woman was ridden by a ghost. And when this mind-numbing textbook information with its stupefying weight of fact was over, people were at last in the mood to believe as the crown of all reality that headless women and trunkless men had rubbed their cold, bleeding necks in the faces of living people.

The poet was too agitated to attend closely to protracted literary realism and storytelling of this kind. The nearness of beauty made him forgetful of more realistic matters, not excepting ghosts. He heard snatches of the life story of a man who was drowned in a river one autumn on the way to see his sweetheart and now walked again, along with his horse and its harness—in particular a loudly jangling bridle. Thereafter he always rode into the yard of his sweetheart's farm late at night when autumn came, and went to her room; the horse whinnied, there was the sound of hooves in the lanes, the bridle and bit jangled. The heartthrob had achieved perfection in the art of making the ghostly bridle jangle and the ghostly horse whinny wildly, the storm come sweeping into the house when the door was thrown open. The women screamed. The girl beside the poet gave a little start and moved farther along the bench, closer to her neighbor.

Time passed, and the poet had no idea of what was happening. It needed nothing less than a child murder to make him come to himself again. All the genealogical, topographical, economic and meteorological preliminaries to this terrible crime had passed him by; the first thing he knew was that the mother had murdered the child and placed the body in a chest of drawers. But since this poet had become more or less inured to murders and other grim deeds from Christian family journals, his attention wandered again before long. He did not notice whether the mother was murdered, too, or whether she did herself in. One thing was certain: At night she used to come in through the closed door, go over to the chest of drawers, kneel down by it, and start tending the corpse in the drawer. Worthy men and virtuous women alike had watched this unusual spectacle between mother and child every night for more than a hundred years. The poet yawned slightly. Whenever a light was put on, the woman dissolved. The young girl shuddered, and she moved a little closer to the poet.

A certain farmer was traveling through a strange district one autumn—a long genealogy, descriptions of the whole county with a catalogue of place names along little-used tracks, industries, economic conditions, year, month, weather. Evening came, and darkness fell.

He found a small farm down by the sea, climbed onto the roof, and shouted down the smoke-hole "God be here!"

After a long pause there came a reply from within:

"There is no God here."

"Of course God's here!" said the man crossly, and made his way into the deserted house. He settled down on the floor and fell asleep. But when he had been sleeping for a while he suddenly woke up with something being thrown at his chest. He fumbled all around and found that it was the head of a cat; but he was not going to let that affect him, and threw it back at once in the direction from which it had come, then lay down and went to sleep again. When he had slept for a while, he woke up again with something being thrown at his chest, much heavier this time than the time before. He fumbled for the object and realized that it was a seal's head, and now he was getting angry; he took the head in both hands and hurled it furiously in the direction from which it had come, then lay down again and went to sleep. For the third time something was once more thrown at his chest, and this time much the largest object. The farmer woke up gasping, fumbled for it, and found that a woman's head had been thrown at him, with long, flowing hair he could wind round his hand. And at that the farmer said these words: "Is the devil in earnest, then?"

He got up, took the woman's head and threw it back with all his strength in the direction from which it had come, then lay down again; but the story did not relate whether the farmer got much sleep for the rest of the night.

A soft and unsteady hand, cold and clammy, had sought refuge in the poet's palm like a sparrow from a bird of prey; the girl was sitting pressed close against him; he could sense the fragrance of her hair. But at that moment the steward opened the door and said it was midnight; the saloon had to be closed. Several people got up at once, relieved as birds at the coming of dawn, without waiting for the end of the story—or had that been the end of it? Bera had gone. Was it just the poet's imagination that she had sat there and put her hand in his?

—— **20** ——

Next morning she looked at him with her deep blue eyes, that neutral spring sky which betokened endless promises without ever
vouchsafing anything that could be put into words. It was as if she
had not seen him before. The ship was moored at the quayside of a
little trading station under the mountains. He started to converse
with her.

She had had two parents but no brothers or sisters, born in the capital but brought up in a distant county since she was three years old by
her aunt and her husband, whom she called Uncle; he was a pastor.
That spring she had been allowed to go south to visit her mother and
stay with her for a while. Then she said no more, but the poet knew
the rest: she had sat by her mother's deathbed to the very end.

"Your late mother will undoubtedly have been in poor health?" he
said.

"My father drinks," she said.

She spoke curtly and dispassionately, without any desire to reveal
her feelings, and stared out over the unfamiliar fjord. Behind her
father's farewell twenty-four hours ago, Ólafur Kárason sensed a long
story: an intelligent and educated man starts drinking heavily and
drags a young wife down with him into misery and degradation. The
little girl is saved from the morass when she is three years old and
brought up in a respectable pastor's home far away. But why had her
mother not divorced the father when things went wrong, in order to
look after the child and safeguard her own health? Perhaps she had
loved him so much that she had forgotten her child and taken to
drink with him. Thank goodness the child had been saved from this
sad home and spared many a tragic sight. The poet went on regard-
ing her cheek as she leaned out over the rail and gazed across an
unknown sea toward unknown mountains. Had her mother looked
like that once, perhaps? Can the world really corrupt anything that is
beautiful by nature? Or are these sensitive people, whom the gods
particularly love and have chosen to endow with beauty, in greater

danger than others of being trodden into the mire, just because beauty is closer to ugliness than anything else? Would it also be this little girl's fate to love a wicked man one day?

"Shall we go ashore?" he said.

"I'm waiting for a couple of girls," she said.

"Where are you going?" he asked.

"I don't know," she said. "Where are you going?"

She had stopped using the formal "you," but apart from that there was no hint of familiarity. He did not know where he was going, he was an inexperienced traveler, all places were unknown to him. Now the girls arrived. He did not ask to be allowed to accompany them, because he thought she might feel he was chasing her. But when she was on the quay she looked round for a moment, and he was still standing on the deck following her with his eyes. Then he went ashore alone. Soon afterwards he found her outside a shop.

"Are you alone?" he asked.

"They went into the shop," she said.

"Why didn't you go, too?" he asked.

"Because," she said.

"Were you going anywhere particular?" he said.

"Yes," she replied.

"Really," he said. "Oh, well, good-bye then." And he raised his cap.

Then she said, "I don't mind if I walk with you."

Long afterwards he sometimes wondered if the girls had really gone into the shop, or if it was she who had given them the slip and stopped outside that window to wait for him.

In this place there were no lowlands.

"Shall we go up the mountain?" he said.

"Not too far," she said.

"We'll see if we can't find some flowers we know," he said.

His strides were too long; she had to walk rapidly to keep up with him; she was almost tripping; perhaps her heels were too high. He could not stop looking at her as she walked by his side on the road, so slender and serious but bright and new, with that precious air of sunshine and spring about her hair, her lips and her cheek.

"Don't you think it funny that we should be alone here in a strange place?" he asked.

"No," she replied. "What about you?"

"In reality we have never existed until this moment," he said.

"I don't understand you," she said.

"You and I were somewhere else before, certainly; but not We," he said. "Nor the place, either. Today the world was born."

"Now you're trying to frighten me again," she said, but looked at him and smiled a little, so that he would not think she was angry.

The Creator had given her that addition to conventional art which is sometimes associated with the unattainable, the mysterious pencil-stroke that everyone is aware of but no one can say exactly where it is drawn in the picture, that note which is impossible to interpret because it lies between all explanations and makes nonsense of every definition, and yet is both One and All. She herself had no inkling of this wonder and did nothing to exploit it; there was not a trace of coquetry in her behavior, no suggestion of wantonness. He was afraid that the man who first paid her compliments would break this enchantment with one blow.

The dew was still on the lady's-mantle. They sat down, each on his own stone, and looked out over the roofs of this unknown place at its calm fjord, the blue-green mountains, and the clear, unknown sky.

"It's so pleasant to see the world for the first time on a morning like this," he said.

"Really," she said.

"Bera," he said. "Will you teach me to talk to you?"

"No," she said.

He stood there defenseless before her perfect eyes, which made poetic talk sound silly.

"Sometimes I feel as if your world is above human feelings," he said.

At that she shielded her eyes from him, pursed her lips, and closed her mouth and once again had that anxious, forsaken face which could just as well have been the beginning of an ill-starred, sorely tried woman whom everyone had deceived and whose every hope had turned into a will-o'-the-wisp. For a moment she seemed on the brink of saying something, but she could not find the right words; she stood up and walked away by herself.

"Have I said something wrong now?" he said. "What am I to do?"

"I'm going aboard," she said. "My heels are too high for this terrible path."

He was distressed over his clumsiness and went on apologizing. Then she found a few flowers which she picked and showed him, and said, "Crowfoot, speedwell, meadow violet."

"Where did you learn these strange names?" he said.

"From my uncle."

"How lucky you are," he said, "to have an educated uncle. I was brought up at Fótur-undir-Fótarfæti. There were two brothers there; they fought over who was to be my master. Sometimes the blows landed on me. Once I was ill in bed for four years. When I was a youngster I was the unhappiest person in all Iceland."

But when she looked into his eyes he felt it had been worthwhile to have endured it all and then be allowed to meet these eyes when it was over. He was surprised to find that youth had such gentleness and calm. When she had gazed into his soul she touched his arm and said, "Let's walk where it's smooth. Let's not walk where the ground is rough."

"Forgive me for stopping talking about the flowers and starting to talk about myself," he said.

"Talk about yourself," she said.

"No," he said. "No more. It's not pleasant."

"Not pleasant?" she said. "Why?"

"Because in your presence, my whole life should be burned to ashes and blown away, vanish," he said.

At that she put her palm against his chest as if to push him away from her, and said, "No, you're making me frightened."

When they had walked in silence for a while, she asked out of the blue, "Why are you so strange?"

He replied, "This winter, when gods and men had taken everything from me, not just the sun but my liberty, too, I thought for a time that I hadn't a single friend any more. But just as I was dying I was suddenly given one sunbeam. It was thrown on a wall for me from heaven, and I heard a voice that spoke about you."

"Me?" she said. "That's impossible. Why do you talk such nonsense?"

"Bera, even if I've talked nonsense all my life, I'm not talking nonsense now," he said.

"My name isn't what you think at all," she said.

"What are names?" he said. "The Revelation of the Deity, Sigurður Breiðfjörð, Ýmir, the Invisible Friend, Bera—it makes no difference to me. I don't ask about names."

"I don't know what you're talking about," she said. "I don't know who you are, either."

"I'm a poet," he said.

"That's what I thought," she said, and it was as if she were rather relieved to hear it.

"Why did you think so?"

"I felt it in your hands," she said, but without looking at his hands.

"Bera," he said, "may I compose beautiful poems about you?"

"Yes," she said simply, as if it were a very small favor to ask, so small that one could grant it however preoccupied one might be, and without looking at the supplicant. He wanted very much to find out if she really was without any feelings at all. When they had been walking for a while he asked, "Did you cry very much, Bera, when your mother died?"

"No," she said.

"Bera," he said. "You are undoubtedly rather unfeeling."

"Really," she said.

After a while she asked, "What makes you think I cried?"

He said, "If I had lost my mother at your age I would have cried, even though she sent me away in a sack in winter. But when I discovered that I had never had a mother, I was too old to be able to cry."

After some thought the girl said, "I would perhaps have cried if I had been away; and if I hadn't heard from her; if I had known that no one was with her. But I went south to be with her. And I talked to her before she died. And I was with her."

At these simple words he understood the whole story: a forsaken and despised mother in the city, a daughter who in the middle of the joy of spring travels from a secure home far away to tend her on her deathbed, to shrive her, to take leave of her in the last lightening before death, to sit by her bed while she drew her last breath, to lay out her body, to follow her to the grave.

"I'm sorry," he said at last. "I forgot for a moment that it takes a greater poet to conceal feelings than to reveal them."

She smiled at him as when the whole spectrum suddenly appears in a crystal, unreservedly, and he was once again seized with the grief that beauty always aroused in his breast.

"Those were true words your father called out to you when we were sailing away," he said, and was going to repeat them, but she put her hand over his mouth.

"Don't," she said. "It's not right of you to repeat them. My mother is lucky to be dead. It's my father who is suffering."

They were on a stony path and he took her arm and guided her. They sat down on a grassy bank above the path, where all the world could see them. They saw all the world, the mountains, the sea, the sky. He sat at her feet and looked at her ankles, but she gazed silently towards the unknown paths.

"Why are you called Ljósvíkingur?" she asked at last.

"When I was a small boy I sometimes stood down by the sea in fine weather and looked at the birds. There was a little bay there, it was called Ljósavík."

"I thought you had a little house, and that it stood beside a little bay, and the bay was called Ljósavík, and that was why you were called Ljósvíkingur," she said.

"No," he said. "It's the glacier that faces my door. And the god dwells in the glacier."

She did not ask who the god was, but which glacier it was, and when he told her its name she smiled again and said, "Then it's our glacier."

It turned out that they lived on either side of the glacier. But when she said "our glacier," what did she mean by it? Did she mean her glacier—her uncle's and her aunt's glacier? Or had she made him, the poet, joint owner with her? Did she perhaps mean their glacier—Bera and the Ljósvíkingur?

"Yes," he said. "It is our glacier."

"You're lucky to live near it," she said. "Between me and it is a two-day journey through uninhabited desert; from where I live, it's like a distant cloud."

"One day I'll come to you over the glacier, nonetheless," he said.

"No, we'll meet up there," she said, and smiled.

___ **21** ___

The more passengers who disembarked from the ship at each port of call, the easier it became to distinguish one person from another. People formed into groups. At first it was the great men of the heart-throb's class who had been to the fore, now it was leaders of lesser caliber who took the stage. On deck, between Bera and another girl, strolled a plump and jovial student from First Class. He was talking. The Ljósvíkingur kept watch on them from a distance, how she squandered her smiles and glances on this little man as if she had at last found the one she understood. This came as a shock to the poet, but it was no use denying it: in the company of this man she was in her element—neither suspicion nor reticence, doubt nor fear, just unreserved approval. Seldom had Ólafur Kárason understood so plainly where he stood. A poet and man of learning, what was the point of that? It was the fat conversationalists who conquered in the world, this world with its glorious women; it was their world, the self-satisfaction in their gait made one sick, but what did that matter? God liked them, that was why He created so many of them; He never sent any of their sort to Hell. The poet went below and sat with his head in his hands for a long time. Much later, when he walked past the door of her cabin, he heard cheery voices and laughter from inside, boys, girls, and brennivín, and if he was not mistaken it was

Bera herself who was laughing the most wildly. Everything went black before his eyes. So that was how the dream of winter was to be fulfilled: the wanton and thoughtless laughter of one girl—that and no more was what a poet's life was worth.

That evening the ship was again in harbor. It was raining. The poet stood on deck and looked at the rain coming down. There was a streetlamp; it glinted on the fish offal on the quay in the summer twilight. Cheerful passengers in raincoats were waiting for the ship to tie up; they were going ashore.

"We're going to a café," said Bera. "Are you coming, too?" She put her hand on the poet's arm momentarily.

"No thanks," he said. "I don't know how to go to cafés. I'm going to stay here and look at the rain."

"He's a poet," said the student. "Some call him Ljósvíkingur, others call him Bervíkingur. Poet, which are you?"

"Do come," she said.

"Where have you been all day?" asked Bera's girl friend.

"With myself," he said.

"He's been with himself!" said the student. "He's a poet. Heeheehee!"

One girl came over and said, "Isn't it fun being a poet?"

Another said, "Will you write a poem about me?"

"Come on," said Bera. "We're going to a café."

"The ragamuffin gave a hop," said the student. "Humpty-dumpty saw him bop. Can you finish that one?"

A chorus of laughter; and the whole crowd went ashore. He stood at the rail and looked at the lights in the village. It went on raining into the mud. She was in a new, off-white raincoat, with a black pillbox hat on her head; how slender she was; and she tripped slightly as she walked. In the light of the streetlamp at the top of the pier she looked back; the light gleamed on the rain behind her as if she were standing in the middle of a harp with silver strings—what was she looking for? For a moment he thought she might call out, but she did not. Could it be that she had been looking back for him? No, it could not be. She went on with the crowd.

But when she had gone ashore, he was seized with impatience and he wandered off the ship by himself. He walked first up the main street, and then along smaller streets. If he saw a nice house, well-lit, he thought it was the café, for he associated such establishments with bright lights and luxury. He peered through windows, tiptoed up doorsteps, listened but could not hear her voice anywhere; he became more and more agitated, he started running, landed in puddles, muddied himself; it rained and rained. A man came out of a garden and stepped into his path and said harshly, "What's all this?"

The poet came to a dead stop in the street, as if he had been shot, and stood in front of the man, panting and guilty-looking like a criminal with blood on his hands.

"Why are you running like that, boy?" said the man.

"I'm searching," said the poet.

"For what?" said the man.

"For someone," said the poet.

"For whom?" said the man.

"I don't suppose you've seen a crowd of people going into a café, a young, fat man and a fair-haired girl with a pillbox hat on her head?"

"Pillbox hat?" said the man. "No. And the café went bust a long time ago. It doesn't pay to have a café. These are critical times for the nation. On the other hand I can sell you some excellent dried halibut, as white as a newly fallen angel, twice as cheap as in the south. It's a giveaway bargain, man. And if you want some coffee, I'll wake up my old woman free of charge. And I can also show you the most delectable spring haddock, man, red through and through like an untouched maiden, the best fish God ever created."

The poet needed all his diplomacy to escape without any stockfish from this simile-rich man. When he at last got away, he decided to walk very slowly so as not to frighten himself or others. A river flowed through the village. The crowd was standing on the bridge, talking loudly above the babbling of the water.

"Ljósvíkingur!" said Bera, and took his arm while her girlfriend took the other. "Why didn't you come with us?"

"The ragamuffin gave a hop, Humpty-dumpty saw him bop," said the student. "How does it finish, poet?"

The crowd moved on, except for the two girls and the poet; they hung back and were left behind on the bridge; he never knew who decided that, but there they stood, leaning over the railing, with him between the two of them, and looked at the river flowing in the midnight dusk and the rain falling. He wished that this moment would never end. An unknown bird flew past them. Did she lean up against him? If she did, then nothing seemed more natural nor more straightforward. He was the proudest poet in the world.

A moment later they heard a shout, the crowd was waiting for them, did they want to be left behind, the ship would be leaving soon.

"Excuse me, but how old are you girls?" asked the student. "Have you forgotten what I told you? Little girls should beware of Bervík poets."

Ólafur Kárason gave a start as if he felt a knife against his bare skin: what had this man told them? Now for the first time he realized that obviously all his fellow passengers must know what had happened to him. It was a small nation; everyone knew everything about everyone else, he alone had forgotten that. He let go the arms of both girls.

"You go on ahead," he said. "I'm staying here."

"You'll miss the ship," said Bera.

"It doesn't matter," he said.

She took his arm and said, "Come on."

Then he whispered, "Bera, let me talk to you privately afterwards."

There was no opportunity to exchange any more words. No sooner had the crowd gone aboard than she disappeared below decks; and soon the ship had put to sea.

He was uneasy in his mind. It was long past midnight, the passengers had all turned in, he went on pacing the deck in the nightgloaming, the rain had stopped, a single star peeped out.

He had really no right to think that he was expecting anyone, he had not arranged any meeting, he did not even know if she had heard what he was asking of her, or had paid any attention to it. But he was too agitated to go below and rest. He tried to calm his mind with this one star that shone on the wake of the ship; but not even a star could bring him peace.

Was she asleep?

If the student had told her, what was she thinking now? Why had she allowed a criminal to squeeze her arm on the bridge; why had she even leaned up against him? If she was sleeping, what had she been thinking about when she had fallen asleep? Why had the god laid this upon him on top of all else, to show him this image precisely now, in this trough of life?

There was a whiff of the new morning in the chilly breeze; he was cold. But just as he was about to go below, he suddenly became aware of her standing beside him. She had thrown her raincoat over her shoulders, the breeze ruffled her long locks, her face was paler than usual, from her eyes there shone a strange mystery in the gloaming just before dawn, a night-woman, and behind her the land of sleeplessness. Perhaps she had been standing there for a long time and staring out over the sea before he had noticed her.

She did not look at him until he had whispered her name a second time.

"Is it you?" he said. "Or am I seeing things?"

"I couldn't sleep," she said slowly.

"How can you stand beside me, Bera, after what you've heard?"

"What have I heard?" she said.

"Don't you despise me?" he asked.

"What kind of a person do you think I am?" she replied.

"What did the student say about me?" he asked.

"I didn't listen," she said.

She looked at him with her deep, steady eyes for a long time. If he had previously thought it essential to explain his position to her, he now felt, at this look, how trivial all accusations and excuses were. With one glance the eyes of beauty, wiser than all books, could wipe away all the anxiety, guilt and remorse of a whole lifetime. She had come to see him in the secrecy of this night to rehabilitate him, to give him the right to live a new life where beauty would reign alone. He put his arm around her slender waist and kissed her warm lips in the cool night breeze. Afterwards he looked around in alarm; she was not alarmed and did not look around. But in the same instant she had gone.

Only the solitary star was left behind, pale in the light of the early morning—and the memory of the time he had found her, three mornings ago, radiant in the glow of a new light.

> *We met like passing ships upon the ocean,*
> *While meadows basked in autumn's russet gladness.*
> *Our destinies were strung 'tween time and motion*
> *Like all who meet in joy and part in sadness.*
>
> *We stand in silence, you and I. The trailing*
> *Mists of morning melt from heaven's spaces*
> *And clear the path for the one who home is sailing,*
> *And for the one who sails to unknown places.*
>
> *Oh, wonder of mine eyes, I welcome thee!*
> *Or is this greeting only the good-bye*
> *Of one condemned to separate from thee?*
>
> *Am I the one who goes—or do I stay?*
> *I only know your beauty now will guide me*
> *In every step along life's endless way.*

—— **22** ——

The loveliest flower lives in hiding; very few people ever manage to see it, many overlook it, some do not understand its value, while those who discover it will never see another flower again. All day one thinks about it. When one sleeps, one dreams of it. One dies with its name on one's lips.

The jovial student had found her, and never left her side all day. He was endowed with all the accomplishments the Ljósvíkingur lacked. His cheerfulness seemed as if it could be measured only in horsepower, his energy bordered on frenzy, he was always ready with a quip, he could talk to many people at once, his speech was sleek and polished by nature, with no inner effort, whereas a poet has to buy his simplest expressions with protracted suffering and his poems, even the bad ones, with almost unbearable sorrow, with unquenchable grief. In the presence of this man the poet suffered physical torments, like a child visiting a sawmill for the first time. He fled if they approached; but he could not stop watching them.

Who could understand the heart? Last night she had deliberately lingered on the bridge when the student's crowd had moved on—yet this morning she was bestowing on him her guileless glances, each of them a treasure in itself. She smiled at him with all the candor of daytime, she flaunted the golden-smooth color of her cheek and the ethereal wave of her hair before his lovelorn eyes; only the discretion of daylight seemed to prevent her from offering him her lips. Does infidelity no less than cruelty have to be the inseparable companion of beauty, then? Is fidelity just the excuse of the ugly? Or was it just the poet's imagination that she had come up on deck to see him in the secrecy of the night?

That evening the ship sailed up a long fjord and tied up at a quay in a large town; a crowd of people disembarked here, and the last of Ólafur Kárason's cabin companions got ready to leave. It turned out that here, in these green and red houses with their beautiful gardens, was where the student charmer lived. Ólafur Kárason heard him inviting the girls to a party at his home. His mother, a formidable woman, had come on board to meet her son; these were distinguished people. In his mind's eye, the poet saw Bera being received like a queen with unrestrained delight by wealthy people in a great mansion; in his imagination he confused the student's invitation with the caliph's feasts in the *Thousand and One Nights*—and he himself was one of the beggars outside. The evening sun turned the windows of the town to gleaming bronze, and the lavish embellishment of the sunset played its part in justifying the poet's ideas about the oriental splendor of the town; there was also a new moon. But at the head of the fjord there was a wide valley with broad, green grasslands, and the river flowed silver-clear through the valley into the evening sun, the green of the slopes and the yellow, newly mown meadows turned red in the euphoria of the evening.

"I'll come for you all at ten o'clock," said the student charmer, and raised his hat and bowed, and Bera took leave of him with her calm smile in which every thought of deceit seemed an impossibility, and every promise a certainty.

Like a light eiderdown the dusk of this mild summer night settled on the warm mountains and the still sea; the moon and the stars took charge of heaven and earth. He was wondering whether to stroll ashore by himself and have a look at the town, but to tell the truth he was not in the mood for anything; seldom had his own wretchedness been weighed down by such a vast burden of other people's happiness. And then he saw the girl standing not far off, bareheaded, in her light coat. At first there was nothing to suggest that she had noticed him. She leaned against the rail and looked ashore; it was nearly ten o'clock. The student charmer was bound to be coming soon to fetch his guests to the party. Ólafur Kárason had not the courage to let on that he had seen her, let alone speak to her. But then it was she who did not think it beneath her to notice him. And since he did not come to her, she came to him.

"Ljósvíkingur," she said, and her smile and her voice, that ethereal hair and the pallor of her cheek along with the dusk of the midsummer night and the young half-light of the new moon—everything was one.

He did not say anything.

"Why haven't you spoken a word to me all day?" she said.

She had her own melody, a rather eager tone of voice in keeping with her tripping, slightly stubborn gait, but simple and free of affectation; her pronunciation revealed a certain aristocracy of the common people, with a strong flavor of the country in it.

"You have found someone better than me," he said heavily.

"Ach, why are you being like this?" she asked reproachfully, but without any resentment.

"He is intelligent, well educated, congenial, well dressed, and undoubtedly rich," replied the poet.

"Whom are you talking about?" she said.

"The student," said the poet.

"Yes," she said. "He's all right, I suppose."

"And he's giving a party for you," he said.

"What's the time?" she asked.

The poet: "He's bound to be here any minute."

"I don't want to go," she said. "And anyway, the party isn't specially for me."

"You accepted with thanks," he said.

"I didn't promise anything," she said. "It was the other girls who promised to go."

Then he asked eagerly, "Are you not going to his party, then?"

She looked the poet in the face with her deep, deeply perfect eyes and said, "No." Just that one word.

"Aren't you going ashore, then?" he said.

"I don't know," she said. "Are you?"

"Will you come ashore with me?" he asked.

"Yes," she said.

But after they had gone ashore he was tongue-tied. He was too agitated, and besides, he did not know her language; she did not even seem to listen when he talked, although she was talkative and quick to laugh when she was with others; it was as if her reactions ceased in his presence. When they had walked in silence for a while he started again: "I thought you found this student attractive?"

She, curt and toneless: "Why did you think that?"

"You've been talking to him all day."

"He wouldn't leave me alone."

"What effect does he have on you, then?"

"Oh, none at all, really."

"Then at least he doesn't have a bad effect on you?"

"Oh, no, not particularly."

"Well then, since he doesn't make a bad impression on you, you could just as well fall in love with him."

"Why are you behaving like this?" she said.

"I'm sorry."

"If you insist on knowing," she said, "he bores me stiff. He behaves as if he owns me, and that I cannot stand. And now let's not talk about it any more. Say something nice."

She had never said so many words to him at once, and he was astonished to hear her say all this.

"Bera," he said, "when I walk beside you, and particularly when I look at you, I feel that everything I'm going to say is going to be banal and empty. And yet I now understand for the first time why we have a sun."

"Why do we have a sun?" she asked.

"For your sake," he said.

She did not answer for a long time, but her portrait said more than speech; her changes of expression were more eloquent than words. Once again there came over her this anxious questioning, this other face, this foreboding of lasting sorrow. And she said, finally, "That's not the way to talk to any human being."

"I ask your forgiveness once again," he said. "Perhaps it is I who am not a human being."

"Yes," she said, "it's you who are different from everyone else. And I, on the other hand, am just an ordinary girl, except that I'm nowhere near being pretty—can't you see how ugly I am when I close my mouth? Everyone says that I'm too flat, and I'm too long in the waist, with thick legs and not at all nice hands."

"Really?" he said. "Perhaps you're one-eyed, with a wart on your nose and hag's claws? Then it's just my bad eyesight which has endowed you with beauty; my ignorance which says that the sun was created for beauty's sake; my madness which says that beauty belongs to that sphere where the concept of death is incomprehensible. But if that is so, let me never be cured."

"Don't say madness," she said. "It's wicked."

"It is my love that cannot acquiesce in believing in anything less than immortality," he said.

"Don't speak," she said, and laid her hand in his for a moment. "Some people think it's necessary to talk, but it isn't necessary to talk."

Broad, flat meadows with the fragrance of mown grass from the haycocks, the evening star and the sickle moon reflected in the sedge pools and rush-grown ponds, or glittered in the placid flow of the river; and this simple splendor of the skies reigned over the land. But

from the lakes a white, thin vapor rose in the dusk of the summer
night and spread slowly over the damp meadows. In light such as this
was the Soul born.

They stopped on the grassy bank of the river and saw a few harle-
quin ducks swimming in the moonlight; from the distance came the
call of the old-squaw duck in the meadow ponds: a-aa-a, over and
over again, with a long *a*.

"That's a strange bird," said the girl. "What do you think it's
saying?"

"He's saying, 'We a–are to,'" said the poet.

"No," said the girl. "How can you think the bird says such nonsense?"

"Birds are strange," he said.

"Yes, but they're not as strange as you say they are."

When they sat down under a haycock on the riverbank, with the
summer fragrance of the earth in their nostrils, he wanted to kiss her,
but she would not let him.

"We a–are to," he said.

"No," said the girl. "We a–aren't to."

Then they kissed.

The evening went on passing.

"You don't say anything to me," she said after a long while. "Why
don't you say anything?"

"You have forbidden me to talk," he said.

"I would much rather you said something I could understand
than that you kissed me so much," she said. "I don't know how to
kiss very much. Dear God, if my uncle knew of this!"

"Would you understand if I said that I love you . . ."

"Will you please leave me alone?"

We a–are to, we a–a–are to, said the bird, with a longer and longer *a*.

"No," said the girl, "we a–aren't to."

Considering what a natural and obvious thing love is, Nature is
still remarkably conservative over the first lover. Perhaps a woman
only loves her first man. At least she loves her first man despite her
suffering; it is the pointer towards motherhood; she loves him

despite herself—that is sacrifice. The one who comes afterwards receives her pleasure, certainly, but not her sacrifice; there is even nothing more likely than that she will love herself more than him. Several tried to conquer her, but only to one did she give herself forever, however many came afterwards. Those who came afterwards—what were they? Opportunity, accident, nature, place, time, amusement. The first one, he was not your amusement, much less your need like the ones who came later, but the poem itself—the naked poem behind the poems, your love as suffering, your love in the guise of blood, the deepest humiliation of your body, the sacrifice of your conscience, the proudest gift of your soul. You are different to what you were a moment ago, and will never be the same.

"Oh, my uncle!" she cried.

She wept and moaned for a few moments, then she turned away from him and hid her face in the crook of her elbow and lay quite still, apart from intermittent spasms of sobs, as when the sea is dying after a surf. He sat beside her and tried to console her and said beautiful words; the more beautiful the words, the more dulled the conscience. On the way to the ship she leaned against him and held him tightly; her legs moved as if she could not walk unaided.

"Know one thing as proof of my love," he whispered. "On the day you grow tired of seeing me, I shall go away from you forever and ever."

"It won't come to that," she said. "After one day and one night I'll be going away from you, and we shall never meet again."

Instead of slackening her grip on him she tightened it as if she would never let him go, ever, from that moment on; she nestled against him as they walked through a strange town side by side in the bright summer night. She did not see the people who looked at them; they did not exist.

Next night she came to him in his cabin and stayed with him. In the morning she said, "I'm glad I'm going away now. If I stayed with you longer I would find it even harder to leave you."

"May I think about you?" he asked.

"Yes," she said.

"Always?" he asked.

"Not in darkness," she said, "only when the sun shines. Think of me when you're in glorious sunshine."

That same morning the ship cast anchor at a desolate bay just outside a little trading station, and a boat was launched from the shore. In the boat sat a tall, dignified man in a black coat, with a grey moustache, and a silver walking stick. He came aboard for a moment, embraced his little girl, took her suitcase, and helped her down into the boat. She sat down beside him in the stern, serious and taciturn, and the cool morning breeze played on her fair locks. Then the oarsmen took to their oars.

When she had gone, the poet discovered that she had forgotten to take her mirror. It was a very small, round mirror for the pocket or the handbag. It certainly could not have cost more than a few *aurar;* on the other hand, it had mirrored the most beautiful picture in the life of mortal man. All that day, the poet worked on a poem about the mirror.

> *Your mirror I discovered, lovely maid,*
> *The fairest picture mortal man has seen;*
> *O face that haunts my every waking dream,*
> *O precious star of eve, O vernal glade—*
> *Your mirror I discovered, lovely maid.*
>
> *In this your mirror dwells both One and All:*
> *The One I longed for when I was a boy,*
> *The All that brings us comfort, grace and joy—*
> *A hundred thousand million times in all.*
> *In this your mirror dwells both One and All.*
>
> *In this your mirror smiles my sun on me:*
> *Your youthful eyes so deep and clear and kind*
> *Reflect that secret heaven of the mind*
> *Which gives a poet immortality.*
> *In this your mirror smiles my sun on me.*

This mirror you forgot yesterday:
Within it dwells the image of your face.
O lovely maiden, locked in his embrace,
In loving tenderness with him you lay.
This mirror you forgot yesterday.

— 23 —

Ólafur Kárason had always kept to himself and did not interfere in other people's affairs; it sometimes also happened that he was not very familiar with his own affairs. After he came back from the south, he did not even notice the walls of the living room at Little Bervík. For days on end he would disappear, hiding in dells and gullies or wandering about near the glacier. If anyone spoke to him he would give inscrutable replies; people knew he was there but no longer knew where he was. There was a new teacher. The education committee discussed whether Ólafur Kárason would be capable of curing dogs, but Þórður of Horn flatly refused to entrust his dog to him since he had not composed a poem about his mother-in-law; he said the man was not a poet but a useless wretch—the most he was fit for was to instruct beginners in religious education and arithmetic as an assistant teacher. The pastor said that one of the greatest misfortunes that had ever befallen this district had been to send this man south for punishment, because he had become so perverted and depraved in the hands of the authorities that it was obvious he was no longer capable either of teaching Christianity or administering medicine to dogs.

Sometimes the poet got up in the middle of the night and set off over Kaldsheiði towards Kaldsvík. When people began to investigate what he was up to, it turned out that he was posting letters. It was also said that his letters were all to the one person; it was a woman's name, addressed to a parsonage in a far-off district. When autumn came, he sometimes walked a long way in uncertain weather to intercept the post. Once it became known that he had received a letter.

Near the end of October, it was learned that the poet Reimar Vagnsson had taken over the carrying of mails for the winter in another county. When the news reached Ólafur Kárason, he set off from home at once. He found his traveling companion and fellow poet in the shop at Kaldsvík, where he was discussing intricate poetry and practical philosophy with a few men at the counter. Reimar greeted his friend cordially and invited him out into the yard so that they could talk together in peace; they had not met since the year before last when they had traveled together to Aðalfjörður one winter's morning.

"Thank you for untying me from the horse's tail," said the poet.

"Oh, don't mention a trifle like that," said the poet Reimar. "Let's hope one will never be in such a bad way that one can't release a friend from a horse's tail"—and wanted to hear more interesting news.

"Well, there's only one thing to tell about myself, and most people wouldn't think it news," said Ólafur Kárason with that distant smile which came more and more easily to him. "And I don't know what you'll think of it. And yet, as a poet I think you ought to understand it. I have seen beauty."

Then Reimar the poet laughed and said, "You've got me beat there, my lad!"

"And the remarkable thing was," said the Ljósvíkingur, "that on the day I saw beauty, I suddenly discovered immortality."

"The devil you did!" said Reimar the poet, scratched his head and squinted with one eye at his friend.

"Once one has seen beauty, everything else ceases to exist," said the Ljósvíkingur.

"Yes, he who gets burnt knows best how hot the fire is," said Reimar the poet. "Is it a woman?"

"For a long time I thought that beauty was just a dream of the poets. I thought that beauty and human life were two lovers who could never meet. As long as you think that, everything is relatively simple. You can endure any hardship, any dungeon; darkness and cold cannot hurt you; beauty doesn't live on earth. But one midsummer night of white mists, beside running water and under a new moon, then you experience this wonder which doesn't even belong to matter and has no relation to transcience even though it appears in human shape; and all words are dead; you no longer belong to the earth."

For the first time, Reimar the poet looked seriously at his friend with his shallow, opaque eyes; he had ferried this poet, suffering from thirty ailments, on a stretcher over the mountains, and between the country's main towns as a criminal tied to a horse's tail; but now he saw that there was something wrong.

"Listen, my lad, you'll have to get hold of this woman, and sooner rather than later, or else you'll be in a bad way," he said.

Ólafur Kárason put his hand in his pocket and brought out a notebook, and from it a little letter in neat but not very practised handwriting, although she wrote without errors. "Ljósvíkingur," the letter said. "Thank you for the poems you have sent me. I keep them in a safe place. But don't write too often, because Uncle and Auntie have difficulty in understanding it. Forgive me for writing so briefly. I am not very well. The only thing I can tell you is that I think about you too much. You said once that I was unfeeling. That is not true. Please take it back. Bera."

"One has seen them hotter sometimes," said Reimar the poet when he had run his eye over the letter; but right enough, this parsonage was one of the places he would be passing in the coming winter. He was traveling in the county; he had an official post there, probably permanent, and would be coming back here for a brief visit in the spring to fetch his family. Ólafur Kárason asked him to take a letter and some poems for him and be an intermediary and confidant if it was difficult for her to write.

Winter came, and Reimar Vagnsson took up his new duties in a distant district. Ólafur Kárason made a few more trips to Kaldsvík, but he never got any more letters. He became more and more depressed as time passed, more and more taciturn, until he no longer said anything, and stopped getting up, just turned his face to the wall when anyone spoke to him. He broke this habit only at New Year, when the bailiff came to examine him on behalf of the parish council.

"I have a strange suspicion that I base on dreams," said the poet.

"What about?" said the bailiff.

"That Beauty is in danger from bad poets."

"Hardly from any worse poets than you," said the bailiff.

"I am assailed by fears that certain poets have murdered Beauty," said the poet.

"God help a penurious district council to get a young man like this on the parish," said the bailiff. "He could live for thirty or forty years."

These were grave times for the nation.

The poet remained in his bed. Month followed month, and he took care not to betray any sign of life in the presence of witnesses. But late in the evening, although only if no one was in, he ate the food that his wife Jarþrúður had left at the side of his bed. And in the depth of the night, if he felt quite sure that no one was awake, he might light a little lamp beside his bed, and then he would sometimes bring out his notebook and write down a few words with long pauses in between. If he noticed his wife or the child stirring in their sleep, he would put out the light. And so the winter passed.

A week before Easter, Reimar came back to the district again to fetch his family and move to his new post. He made a trip to Little Bervík to have a word with the Ljósvíkingur, and asked everyone else to leave the room so that they could talk in private. His errand was to inform his brother poet that the girl he had called Bera was dead. But when he had broken this news, and was going to tell how it happened, the Ljósvíkingur simply gave a short laugh, as if he were saying, "No, Reimar, you won't manage to make a fool of me this time"—and he would not listen to anything else his brother poet had to say about it.

"Last winter I dreamed that you had murdered her," he said, and smiled apologetically. "But now I am free of that dream again. The versifier doesn't exist who can murder the beauty of the heavens. The beauty of the heavens cannot die. It will reign over me for all eternity."

Reimar the escort took leave of his friend, brother poet and traveling companion, and for the first time was at a loss for words; perhaps he was a little depressed. Every transgression is a game, every grief easy to bear compared with having discovered beauty; it was at once the crime that could never be atoned and the hurt that could never be assuaged, the tear that could never be dried.

—— **24** ——

Though grave-clothes shroud your figure, slender maid,
And silent earth now houses your blue eyes
Where once I glimpsed the beauty of the skies—
O distant star of eve, O vernal glade—

And even though the bloom fades from that lip
That thawed the frozen chains that bound me fast,
And though the hands that freed me are now dust
And death's cold handshake holds them in its grip,

It doesn't harm my song; my memory of thee
Has taken root forever in my mind,
Of tenderness and love and mercy kind,
Just as you were when first you came to me;

Just as you left me, proudly, though you cried,
With tears upon your cheeks that never dried.

—— **25** ——

During Easter Week, the word flew round that the old man in the Ravine farm was failing fast. All the way to the living room at Little Bervík came the echo of the talk of the difficulties that the old woman would now find herself in, left alone with the Invalid one of these days. It was also learned that the Invalid had broken her mirror and could no longer see the glacier.

The weather was calm, with cold nights and days of sunshine.

Late in the afternoon of Easter Saturday the poet got up and asked for his Sunday-best suit.

His wife, Jarþrúður Jónsdóttir, asked Hallgrímur Pétursson reincarnated not to tempt the Lord his God.

"I have heard that the Invalid has broken her mirror," he said. "I promised to give her a mirror."

"It's very late," said the wife. "Let it wait until tomorrow."

"The feast of resurrection has begun," said the poet. "The earth has been given new life."

"It is Jesus Christ who is risen," said the wife.

"No," said the poet. "I am risen."

"At least put a scarf round your neck," said the woman. "And put on two pairs of socks."

But nothing this wife said had any effect on the poet any more; he smiled oddly at her admonitions, and she was a little alarmed and did not dare come too close to him. No, he did not want to wear a hat, either.

He wandered off over the ridges with his drifting gait which made it hard to see which would happen first—that he would fall to the ground in exhaustion, or rise up into the air and fly. Ice-free waters, the cold spring sky was mirrored in the clear pools of the river; honking barnacle geese flew in over the land. He stopped in the ravine, listened to the din of the water, and lifted his face to the exalted calm of the glacier in the gathering dusk. The wind blew in his hair that had not been cut all winter.

The old man had given up the ghost in the middle of the afternoon and the old woman was just finishing laying out his body with the help of a neighbor. The Invalid was crying, and had broken her mirror. The little boy played on the doorstep. The old woman received her visitor serenely, dignified and kindly. She had had sixteen children and had lost them. She worked for them by day and sat up over them by night. And when they smiled at their mother, every cloud vanished from the skies, and the sun, the moon and the stars belonged to this woman. She had become a little hard of hearing, and when the poet mentioned the sky and its beauty she thought he was going to speak disparagingly of the earth, and hastened to interrupt: "If God had been as good to everyone as he has been to me, then earthly life would be beautiful."

And then the poet thought he heard echoing through the house: "And beautiful we thought the earth."

When her children gave up the ghost after difficult death throes, she dressed them in a white shroud and smoothed out every fold with the same care as if she were dressing them for a party. She wept when she stood over their clay, and then went back home to the living. The others she took leave of, fully grown, at the garden gate when they set off into the world. The bones of her daughter Helga had been washed up on a gravel-bank a year after she disappeared; the old woman walked down to the bank herself and collected the bones, and there were other little bones. She sewed a shroud for them all and laid them in a coffin and followed them to the grave and then walked back home to love those who lived. In this house, love reigned. That's how life was eternally greatest: to smile with one's child when it laughed, to comfort it when it cried, to carry it dead to its grave, and to dry one's own tears and smile anew and take everything as it came without asking about the past or the future; to live; to be kind to everyone.

"When I look back over my life," said the old woman, "I feel it has all been one long, sunny morning."

"And the forest fragrance we smelled in our sleep," said the Echo.

"I'm only a poet," said Ólafur Kárason apologetically.

He asked to be allowed to fasten a little mirror to the Invalid's bedpost so that she would see the glacier again and stop crying. "In this mirror dwells One and All," he said. Then he asked to be allowed to lie there for part of the night; but before dawn the next morning he got up, kissed the old woman, and said: "Now I must not tarry any longer, for soon the sun will be up. Good-bye, old woman."

He also kissed the brow of the sleeping Invalid. "When she wakes up she will see the sun rise over the glacier," he said.

The weather was calm, with the moon in the south and a cold, bluish light. He headed straight for the mountain. In the lower reaches there were long steep slopes, farther up they gave way to gentler mossy inclines, then boulder tracts, finally to unbroken snow. The moon's face faded as the light strengthened. Over the ocean, black clouds started gathering. He continued on, on to the glacier, towards the dawn, from ridge to ridge, in deep, new-fallen snow, paying no heed to the storms that might pursue him. As a child he had stood by the seashore at Ljósavík and watched the waves soughing in and out, but now he was heading away from the sea. "Think of me when you are in glorious sunshine." Soon the sun of the day of resurrection will shine on the bright paths where she awaits her poet.

And beauty shall reign alone.

NOTES

p. 6

The *Book of Sermons* by Bishop Jón Vídalín Skálholt (1698–1720) was published in 1718–20; it is one of the classics of Icelandic literature, much admired for its rich language and colorful style. It dominated Icelandic religious life for more than a century.

p. 6

The Felsenburg Stories: translated from a romantic novel by the German writer Johann Gottfried Schnabel (1692–1752) and published in Iceland in 1854. The German title was *Die wunderliche Fata einiger See-Fahrer, absonderlich Alberti Julii, eines geboren Sachsens, auf der Insel Felsenburg.* The story is told in chapters 14–15, below.

p. 6

"Guðmundur Grímsson of Grunnavík" is modelled on a poet named Sighvatur Grímsson Borgfirðingur (1840–1930), a prolific but minor author with whom Magnús Hjaltason Magnússon (the original of Ólafur Kárason) was acquainted.

p. 16

Pastor Hallgrímur Pétursson (1614–84) was the greatest poet of seventeenth-century Iceland, and one of Iceland's greatest religious poets. After a checkered career he was appointed pastor of Saurbær, in Hvalsfjörður, where he wrote his *Passion Hymns* (*Passíusálmar*), a series of fifty meditations on

Christ's passion and resurrection, first published in 1666. They have remained extraordinarily popular to this day. The towering neo-Gothic church in Reykjavík is dedicated to him.

p. 43
A kenning, in its most rudimentary form, is a metaphorical device that uses two nouns in somewhat paradoxical association to suggest a third, like "ship of the desert" for "camel" or "gannet's bath" for "sea." But in classical Icelandic poetry it was a far more sophisticated literary device based on mythological or heroic allusions; thus, since the Nibelung treasure lay at the bottom of the Rhine, guarded by the dragon Fáfnir, a kenning for "gold" could be "Rhine gravel" or "Fáfnir's bed." Kennings frequently have more than two elements, and are in effect brief summaries of the myths on which they are based. Thus, there are several stories which describe how Óðin got hold of the mead of poetic inspiration, and a vast number of kennings for "poetry" could be formed on this allusion.

p. 43
"Ring-bearer" is a simple kenning for "woman."

p. 44
"Fjalar's stream's bird" refers to Óðin: Fjalar was the name of one of the dwarfs who first brewed the mead of poetry, so "Fjalar's stream" means "poetry"; Óðin stole it away in the shape of an eagle, so "poetry-bird" means Óðin.

p. 44
"Hárbarður's mead-horn's liquor" is a kenning for poetry: Hárbarður, meaning Graybeard, was one of the innumerable names given to Óðin; and since Óðin was the god of poetry, the god who brought poetry to mankind in the magic mead he stole from the dwarfs and the giants, the liquor of Óðin's mead-horn would be poetry.

p. 44
This very literal translation of a stanza by pastor Snorri Bgörnsson of Húsafell (1710–1803) contains a remarkable number of kennings for poetry, or poetic inspiration, which he counterpointed throughout with a more homely, sustained metaphor on butter-making.

p. 44
Fjölnir and Rögnir were two other names for Óðin, so "Fjölnir's cream" meant the raw material of poetry, and "Rögnir's bowl" meant the seat of poetry, the mind. Boðn was the name of one of the three vats in which the dwarf Fjalar kept the blood of wisdom from which he brewed the mead of poetry, so "Billing's butter" meant the finished version, the poem. Suttungur was the giant who wrested the poetry-mead from the dwarfs, only to have it stolen from him by Óðin, so "Suttungur's cook" meant the man who makes the finished version, the poet.

p. 51
Brennivín (literally, "burnt wine") is a hard liquor flavoured with angelica root or caraway seeds. It is a kind of aquavit or schnapps, and is familiarly known in Iceland as "Black Death"!

p. 55
Icelandic ballads (*rímur*) were epic narrative poems of heroic or romantic adventure, written in florid and intricate language and complex metrical forms, to be chanted. They took over from the classical Icelandic sagas in the fourteenth century as the most popular literary form in Iceland, and there is a huge corpus of them extant. Sigurður Breiðfjörð (1798–1846) is regarded as one of the most skillful exponents of this unique literary genre.

p. 106
In Icelandic, the primary meaning of the noun *"sál"* is "soul"; but there is another related noun (also *"sál"*), which means "leather bag." It is very much a secondary meaning, and is not found in standard Icelandic-English dictionaries.

p. 134
"Privy Councillor": the Icelandic word coined by Laxness is *estaráð*, used as a purely honorific title which does not refer to any official post. There does not seem to be any specific real-life model for this particular "Privy Councillor"; he represents *any* big businessman, perhaps with some kind of privileged position, who absconds with his money when the going gets rough.

p. 154
Ragnarok, in Nordic mythology, is the Destruction of the Gods.

p. 167
"The Great Verdict" (*Stóridómur*) was a harsh new code of law on moral (particularly sexual) misdemeanors which was imposed on Iceland by the Danish authorities in 1564, after the Lutheran Reformation. The death penalty was introduced for a number of offenses such as incest (including relations between brother- and sister-in-law), and adultery committed three times: men were beheaded, while women were drowned in the Öxará, the river at Þingvellir. These laws remained in force until 1838, although they were rarely enforced after 1800.

p. 176
"The fellow from Skjól" is later (chapter 11, below) identified as Þórarinn Eyjólfsson, who has adopted the pen-name Örn Úlfar. He is a composite portrait drawn from a number of radical, left-wing poets, like Steinn Steinarr (1908–58, the pen name of Aðalsteinn Kristmundsson), who were collectively dubbed *Rauðir pennar* ("Red Pens").

p. 197
The pen name Örn Úlfar is drawn from the words for an eagle (*örn*) and a wolf (*úlfur*), to emphasize his perception of himself as a fierce opponent of capitalism.

p. 206
Norn: the three Norns in Nordic mythology were the equivalent of the Fates of classical mythology.

p. 223
Sir Oliver Joseph Lodge (1851–1940) was an eminent English physicist and pioneer of wireless telegraphy. He also devoted much of his time to psychic research and published several books on the subject.

p. 254
Grímur *loðinkinni* (Hairy-Cheek), from Ramstad in Norway, was the eponymous hero of one of the late medieval Legendary Sagas (*Gríms saga Loðinkinna*). It is a very short tale, and tells how Grímur rescued from enchantment his betrothed (a beautiful princess) who had been transformed into a monstrous troll-woman through the sorcery of her wicked stepmother. One of their descendants, also named Grímur, was an early settler in Iceland, at Grímsnes.

p. 261

This story is an allusion (characteristically embroidered by folklore) to a celebrated murder which led to the last judicial execution in Iceland, in 1830. Natan Ketilsson of Illugastaðir (1798–1828), an unpopular farmer, was murdered, along with his foreman Pétur Jónsson, by two members of his household, Agnes Magnúsdóttir and Friðrik Sigurðsson, on 13 March 1828. The murderers attempted to destroy the evidence by setting fire to the farmhouse, but the corpses of the two victims were not burned; the two murderers were caught, tried and executed at Vatnsdalshólar, in the north of Iceland, on 12 Janaury 1830. The block used at their execution is now in the National Museum of Iceland.

p. 278

Jónas Hallgrímsson (107–45) was Iceland's outstanding lyrical poet of the nineteenth century, and a leader in the awakening of Icelandic nationalist sentiments with his passionate romanticism. As a student in Copenhagen he was one of the editors of the annual *Fjölnir* which agitated for the restoration of the Alþingi (Althing).

p. 332

Bishop Guðmundur Arason of Hólar, nicknamed *góði* (the Good), was a turbulent prelate who was bishop of Hólar, in the north of Iceland, from 1202 to 1237. He developed a reputation as a miracle-worker, and hallowed many wells and springs which bear his name to this day and are thought to have healing properties.

p. 352

Þórður Magnússon of Háttardalur (1829–96) was a Member of Parliament in the 1880s, who later emigrated to Canada.

p. 355

Skarpheðinn Njálsson was the eldest son of Njáll, the eponymous main character in *Njáll's Saga*, the mightiest of the medieval Icelandic Sagas. With his father and brothers, he was burnt to death by a confederacy of enemies in the year 1011.

p. 359

Snorri Sturluson (1179–1241), the great saga historian, wrote *Heimskringla* (History of the Kings of Norway) and *Egill's Saga*. He also wrote the *Prose Edda*, a manual of poetics and Nordic mythology.

p. 373
Grettir Ásmundarson—Grettir the Strong—was the eponymous hero of *Grettir's Saga*, which was written in the fourteenth century. He was immensely strong, and a good poet, but was outlawed for some killings; he survived as an outlaw in the wildlands of Iceland for nearly twenty years.

p. 387
In Nordic mythology, Ýmir was the primeval giant form whose bones, flesh and blood Óðin fashioned the world, using his blood for the sea, flesh for the earth, skull for the sky and brains for the clouds. The name "Ýmir" means "The Roarer," so Örn Úlfar is allowing himself a rare moment of humor by punning on Roarer and Voice.

p. 393
Rix-dollar: an old Scandinavian silver coin (*rigsdaler*).

p. 414
Haraldur *hilditönn* (War-tooth) was a semi-legendary Danish king who lived (if he existed at all) in the seventeenth century. He is said to have fallen at the Battle of Brávellir (c. 800), old and blind, in a war against Sweden; his death was caused by the god Óðin, disguised as his charioteer.

p. 415
Göngu-Hrólfur (Walker-Hrólfur) is better known in Viking history as Rollo (died c. 928), who founded the duchy of Normandy. Icelandic sources say that he was so huge that no horse could carry him—hence his nickname of "Ganger" (Walker). Rollo was granted the lands of Normandy by King Charles the Simple of France in return for defending France against other Viking raiders.

p. 415
Örvar-Oddur (Arrow-Oddur) was a legendary hero with mythical associations who lived for three hundred years. His story was written up in the thirteenth-century *Örvar-Oddur's Saga*. He is said to have been the son of Grímur *loðinkinna* (Hairy-Cheek).

p. 416
Sigurður *Fáfnisbani* (Fáfnir's-Slayer), also known as Sigurður the Volsung, was the legendary hero of the Icelandic *Völsunga Saga* (Saga of the Volsungs). A Germanic hero from the pre-Viking Migration Period, he slew

the dragon Fáfnir who guarded the Rhinegold, and became the lover of the Valkyrie Brynhildur—only to be killed by his brother-in-law Gunnar. The saga was the inspiration of Wagner's epic opera *The Ring of the Nibelungs*.

p. 416

Gunnar of Hlíðarendi was the peerless hero of *Njáll's Saga*.

p. 420

Egill Skalla-Grímsson was the eponymous hero of one of the greatest of the Icelandic Sagas, *Egill's Saga*. Born at Borg in Iceland around 910, he became the outstanding warrior-poet of the Viking Age: a massive, menacing crag of a man who fought as a Viking mercenary for many years.

p. 467

Árni Magnússon (1663–1730) was a brilliant young Icelandic scholar who was appointed Professor of Danish Antiquities at Copenhagen University in 1701. He was sent back to Iceland as a royal commissioner to carry out a land census (1702–12), and used the opportunity to seek out saga manuscripts wherever he went. The manuscripts he collected were sent to Copenhagen University; they have now been returned to Iceland by Denmark.

p. 500

Halldór Snorrason was a loyal follower of King Harald Sigurðsson of Norway—Harald *harðráði* (Hard-Ruler)—and is mentioned in several sagas. He was the son of Snorri *goði*, one of the most prominent Icelandic chieftains in the Saga Age.

p. 502

Guðrún Ósvífrsdóttir is the heroine of *Laxdæla Saga*, the story of the tragic love-triangle between Guðrún and her lover Kjartan Ólafsson and her husband Bolli Þorleiksson.

p. 502

Jómsborg was the name of a fortified military encampment on the Baltic coast, the home of the semi-legendary Jómsvikings in the tenth century. These professional mercenary warriors had a strict code of behavior: membership was limited to men between eighteen and fifty, no women were allowed in the camp, and no one could show fear or dissent. "Jómsborg" has been associated with the town of Wolin, near the mouth of the River Oder in Poland.

ALSO BY HALLDÓR LAXNESS

*"Laxness has a poet's imagination and a poet's gift
for phrase and symbol."*
—The New York Times Book Review

INDEPENDENT PEOPLE

Bjartur of Summerhouses, the protagonist of this magnificent
novel, is an ordinary sheep farmer, but his flinty determination to
achieve independence is genuinely heroic and, at the same time,
terrifying and bleakly comic. Having spent eighteen years in
humiliating servitude, Bjartur wants nothing more than to raise
his flocks unbeholden to any man. But Bjartur's spirited daughter wants to live unbeholden to *him*. What ensues is a battle of
wills that is by turns harsh and touching, elemental in its emotional intensity and intimate in its homely details.

Fiction/Literature/0-679-76792-4

PARADISE RECLAIMED

The quixotic hero of this long-lost classic is Steinar of Hlidar, a
generous but very poor man who lives peacefully on a tiny farm
in nineteenth-century Iceland with his wife and two adoring
young children. But when he impulsively offers his children's
beloved pure-white pony to the visiting King of Denmark, he sets
in motion a chain of disastrous events that leaves his family in
ruins and himself at the other end of the earth, optimistically
building a home for them among the devout polygamists in the
Promised Land of Utah. By the time the broken family is reunit-
ed, Halldór Laxness has spun his trademark blend of compassion
and satire into a spellbinding enchantment.

Fiction/Literature/0-375-72758-2